I0841036

ΛΛΣ

LORDS
OF
MERCY

WE *KEEP*
WHAT'S *OURS*

SAMANTHA RUE
ANGEL LAWSON

THE ROYAL HOUSES OF
FORSYTH
COUNTS
BARONS
COUNTS
TO THE VICTOR
F
DUKES
PRINCES
LORDS
LORDS

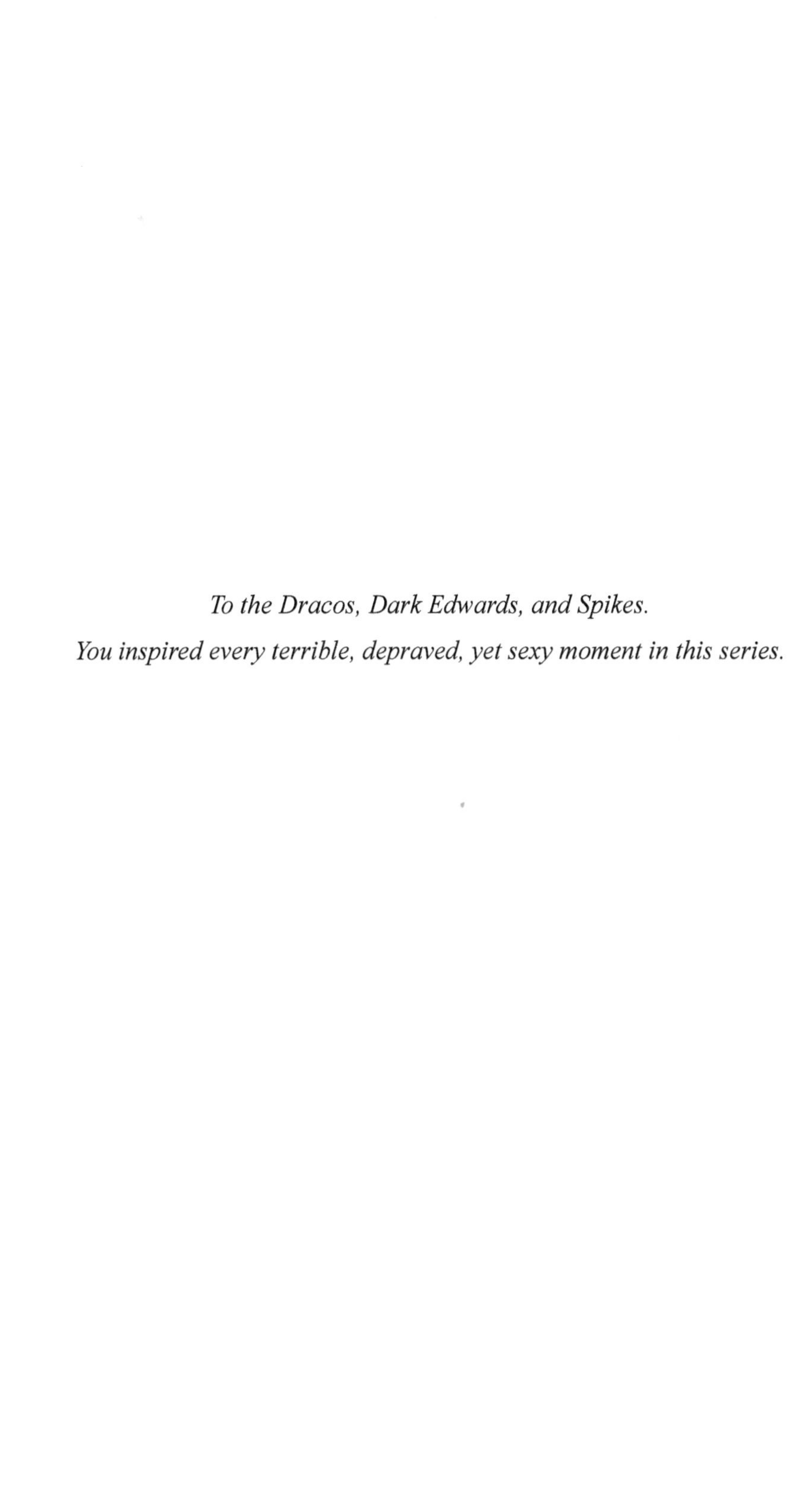

To the Dracos, Dark Edwards, and Spikes.

You inspired every terrible, depraved, yet sexy moment in this series.

1

R E S T L E S S

I DON'T NEED to look at the clock to know it's after midnight. The noises of the old LDZ brownstone keep their own time, from the sound of Ms. Crane's curses echoing down the hallway to the thumping bass of the weekly frat parties. But those sounds have faded. It's Thanksgiving break and most of the frat boys have gone home for the week. Ms. Crane is asleep, so it's just me and my Lords here, filling the dead brick walls with our own signature signs of life. The most telling signal of time is my Lords.

They're restless.

The most present is the shadow crisscrossing beneath my bedroom door, punctuated by the rhythmic creak of the hallway's hardwood floor. It's as symbolic as the chiming grandfather clock down in the library.

My stepbrother is pacing outside my locked door, as he is every night, hoping, wishing, *preying*.

Three weeks ago, we amended our contract. It was a long morning, and I spent most of it stony-faced and refusing to back down from my requests. The Lords spent it pulling at their hair and gnashing their teeth, and slowly— so slowly that I knew I was being taken seriously—accepting the terms that would cement my place here once again.

No more cameras or creeping into rooms uninvited, no more clothing or food demands. No more punishments. The topic of sex was most difficult for me. I'm not so lacking in self-awareness to think I'll never be willing. But the things that happened to me—things they did to me—things I was forced to do…

It has to be on my terms, when I'm ready.

They may have agreed to my demands enough to put pen to paper, but that doesn't stop Killian from pacing outside my door, testing the lock, prodding at my makeshift boundaries to see if tonight's the night I've lowered them. I know more than anyone that if he wanted in, he could snap that lock with nothing but a twist, and I wouldn't be able to do a damn thing about it. To my surprise, he hasn't. Not yet.

Killian's never been big on virtue, but patience, least of all of them. That much is obvious from the way he's itching to get back on the football field despite still being in recovery from the gunshot wound to his gut. Or the way he, Tristian, and Dimitri keep running over vague, vengeful plans to get back at whoever planned the hit.

Ted. Ted planned the hit—whoever he even is.

I roll on my back and stare at the ceiling—or rather, the floor of Tristian's room. I know for certain he isn't up there, because I can hear him, too. The steady rhythm of the basketball down on the court below my window has been beating for an hour. His pattern is as clear as the way his hips drove into me when he fucked me. Seven dribbles that echo off the bricks, then he shoots. Sometimes it's followed by the clean swish of the net or bounce off the backboard, or occasionally… "Motherfucker!" he misses entirely.

I had Tristian go over every inch of my room, unplugging or turning off the sensors. It was an elaborate system, including motion detection and infrared, and it should have stunned me, this knowledge that I've been so painstakingly *observed.* Only, it didn't surprise me at all.

I don't think Dimitri or Killian care that much, but for Tristian, not keeping tabs on me, watching me, is clearly a challenge.

After that night at the Velvet Hideaway, I'm done with being on camera.

The ball bounces outside, and the hallway creaks, but there's one notable absence to the noises of the house.

There's no music.

Dimitri hasn't played the piano, or any of his other instruments, since I humiliated him at the homecoming performance. And although we've promised one another that we're okay about what happened at Daniel's brothel, it's still been a little difficult to look one another in the eye. I don't know what it's like for him, but for me, it's not about shame. It's that Dimitri put himself between me and the world, and I'm not sure how to feel about it.

There was a moment when he was inside of me, protecting me, asking me sweetly to come for him, that I felt something click in my heart. But here, away from all that, I'm not sure if it was real or not. What I do know is that Dimitri sacrificed something to rescue me that night. Something big that weighs on his shoulders. I owe him, but I'm not sure what I owe him for. And I'm not sure he'd tell me if I asked.

I toss again, flipping over to my stomach, my eyes heavy despite the anxiety I feel in the pit of my gut. I haven't gotten a full night's sleep since that night I walked through the door of my own volition. Not because I needed protection. Not because I was being forced to. Not because I felt threatened.

Just because I wanted to.

In a perfect world, that would have made everything easy, but the reality is a lot more complicated. It's as if locking my stepbrother out, and then watching Tristian methodically remove every trace of his ability to watch me, has made me feel impossibly exposed. Anything could happen in this room and they wouldn't know.

Just like every night, I reach for my phone, thumbing it open and going for my most recent contact.

He answers on the second ring, voice quiet, scratchy with disuse. "I think

I'm dying."

I turn on my side and tuck my hand beneath my cheek, fixing my gaze to my dark, empty bathroom. "What is it tonight?"

He sniffs, but the cough that follows belies the haughtiness. "I don't know. Three blunts and a fifth of vodka? Possibly a Xanny, but maybe that was last night." After a beat, he asks, "Wait, what day is it?"

I wince. "Jesus, Dimitri. Why don't you try staying sober for one night?" It's a stupid request. For one, I'm at least partially responsible for everything that's wrong in his life right now. For two, his generally being unable to remember these late night discussions is a big part of why I feel so inclined to have them.

"Why don't you go fuck yourself?" he snipes back, and even though there's no real heat to it, his muttered, "No more rules about that," has resentment just rolling off it.

"Don't feel like it," I lie.

"You're lying." There's a shuffle through the speaker, rustles of fabric and air. "Nothing wrong with needing a nut to get to sleep." Dimitri does a good job of acting like we don't do this every couple of nights. My feigning disinterest. His coaxing me to do what I already want to do. Maybe he really does get so drunk that he forgets, because it always goes the same.

He sighs into the phone, low and gritty in that way that tells me he's just taken himself from his pants. I worry my lip between my teeth as I listen, hand creeping beneath my covers. I can easily envision him in that dimly lit room upstairs, reclined on his bed or his couch. He'd have the phone on speaker, but kept close. Probably already shirtless, the toned muscles in his abdomen flexing as he strokes himself.

"What panties are you wearing?"

My face heats at the question, fingers dipping below the elastic as I roll to my back. I don't need to look to answer, "They're blue."

He hums over the rustles in the background. "The lacy ones with the white trim."

My breath hitches at the first touch, imagining that they're *his* fingers pressing into my clit. "You probably have all my other blue ones up in your room." It's meant to sound admonishing, but the gasp I make when my thighs spread sort of ruin the effect. "And my black ones, too."

"The black ones are best," he says, voice imbued with a hardness that tells me he's stroking himself. Is he already hard? Does he have to coax it to life like he does for me? "I like jacking off with them."

I pause, trying to reorient my mental image of him on that couch. "Really?"

He answers without a trace of embarrassment. "Only if you've already worn them. I like it when you've gotten them all wet."

Warily, I wonder, "And then what?"

"And then I wrap them around my dick," he drawls, voice falling two octaves. "I jack it until I come, and then I shoot my load in the exact spot that's touched your sweet pussy all day."

I breathe a long, stuttered, "Oh." Come to think of it, I'm not sure what else I was expecting. "Are you…right now?"

I can practically hear his teeth raking over his lip piercings. "That get you hot, baby? Knowing I want it so bad that just busting my nut into your damp panties is enough to do it for me?"

I roll it around in my brain, ultimately deciding, "Yes."

"This pair is pink," is his response, and I realize instantly that he's stroking himself with the pair of panties I wore last night. They're not as frilly as some of my others—just simple, comfortable cotton. His breaths are coming harder now, shallower. "Something got you wet yesterday. They were fucking soaked."

I grind my head back into my pillow and buck into my hand, ripe with the knowledge that tomorrow, these blue panties will go missing from my laundry hamper. "Tristian," I quietly confess, sliding my fingers through my wetness. "We were all watching that movie, and I was remembering—"

"That day he fucked you in the entertainment room," Dimitri says, grunting. "Fuck, I still remember the way your pussy looked, stretched around his cock."

It'd been difficult last night, sitting in their presence while some movie played on the screen. I can barely even recall the plot—something with a lot of guns and fast cars—but I vividly remember looking over at Tristian's sprawled legs and wondering what it might be like to climb into his lap again. Like Dimitri, I can perfectly recall what it felt like to have him buried inside me as the world moved on around us.

"He watched it, you know." Dimitri's voice is choppy, and I imagine the way his forearm must look, veins bulging as he strokes himself. Breathlessly, he clarifies, "The video of us, from the pit. I think he might feel bad about it, but I told him—" He makes a low, strained sound. "Told him if there's anyone who should jerk it to that, it's them. They're the only ones who…" His voice trails off, slurring into something indistinct.

My own hand unconsciously syncs to the rhythm I hear in his voice—in the rustle over the speaker. "They're the only ones who have the right."

"Yeah," Dimitri says, his words just as hard as his dick probably is. "Because you're ours. You can make or take away all the rules you want, but it'll always be true."

I always get a little lost when I'm like this. It's why it has to be Dimitri. The booze and the drugs dull his memory of the things I say. It's why it has to be over the phone, neither of us able to physically act on it.

But it comes pouring out of me as I rub my clit, chest hitching with my gasps. "Yeah, I'm yours, I'm yours."

He lets out this deep, tremulous growl. "God, I should come down there and fuck you through the goddamn floor. I should let the others watch. Hell, I should let them get a piece. You've got us so fucking crazy for it…"

It's so hot in here, the fan in the room's corner doing little in the way of cooling my overheated skin. Clumsily, I kick the blankets off, giving me an unobstructed view of my hand disappearing into my panties. Here, in the dark, it could be any hand. It could be Killian's. Tristian's. "Dimitri…"

I seize with the force of my orgasm, thighs clamping hard as I ride my hand. Distantly, I can hear the sounds of Dimitri's grunt, the static-hiss of huffed breaths, but I'm too lost in the pleasure sparking through my brain to care that he's probably painting the crotch of yesterday's panties with his come.

Like it always does, the fall is steep and jarring, slamming back to my body with a heaving chest and a damp brow. I can hear my pulse in my ears like a roaring stampede.

Or maybe that's just Killian pacing outside my door.

As if he's heard my thoughts, Dimitri's rough voice comes through the speaker. "You have no fucking idea what you're doing to us, girl." His words are slurring worse now, heavy with exhaustion. Idly, I wonder what he's doing with my soiled panties. "Maybe you should call one of them next time."

I frown at the bleakness in his voice. "I can't."

There's some shuffling on the other end of line—maybe he's cleaning himself. "Then maybe you should come up here and actually get a full night's rest for once." Dimitri's sigh sounds just as weary as I feel. "You aren't fooling anyone. Maybe you sort of hate us, but you need us just as much as we need you. Own your shit, Story. It doesn't have to be—"

"Three days."

There's a pause, and then, "Is this like a countdown?" He doesn't sound impressed.

I pull my hand from my panties before shucking them off, tossing them in the direction of my hamper. *For you.* "It's more like…a challenge."

"A challenge," he repeats, voice flat.

"Go sober for three days," I swallow, knowing that I'll have to commit to this, "and I'll sleep in your bed."

There's more rustling, and then complete silence. It goes on for so long; I worry the call has dropped. Dimitri breaks it with a low, skeptical, "Sleep."

"Yes," I stress, knowing I have to be careful here. I can't promise something I'm uncertain about my ability to give. "Sleep."

His scoff is loud and full of static. "I can sleep alone just fine."

Then he hangs up.

I glare at my phone's screen, unable to really muster any anger about it. Maybe it's the orgasm, or maybe it's just that I know Dimitri too well. He's hoping I'll sweeten the pot. Even though the four of us are on different terms, they're still who they are. Killian still wants in, Tristian still wants to watch, and Dimitri still wants to manipulate.

I just know how to handle them now.

Part of me wants to open that door and let Killian come in and make me forget everything but the rough heat of his hands. Or go outside and drag Tristian into the hot tub to ease away the tension and stress. Or I could climb the stairs and force Dimitri to play something for me. To play *me*, drawing me out, edging me closer and closer in that way no one else can but him. But my issues with sleeping are the least of our problems. We've all got something else on our mind. Something we've got to get through first.

Thanksgiving.

We've been invited to a formal dinner, and for the first time in years, it looks like I'm going to spend it with family.

My mom, my stepfather, my stepbrother, and his two best friends: My Lords.

One big, happy family.

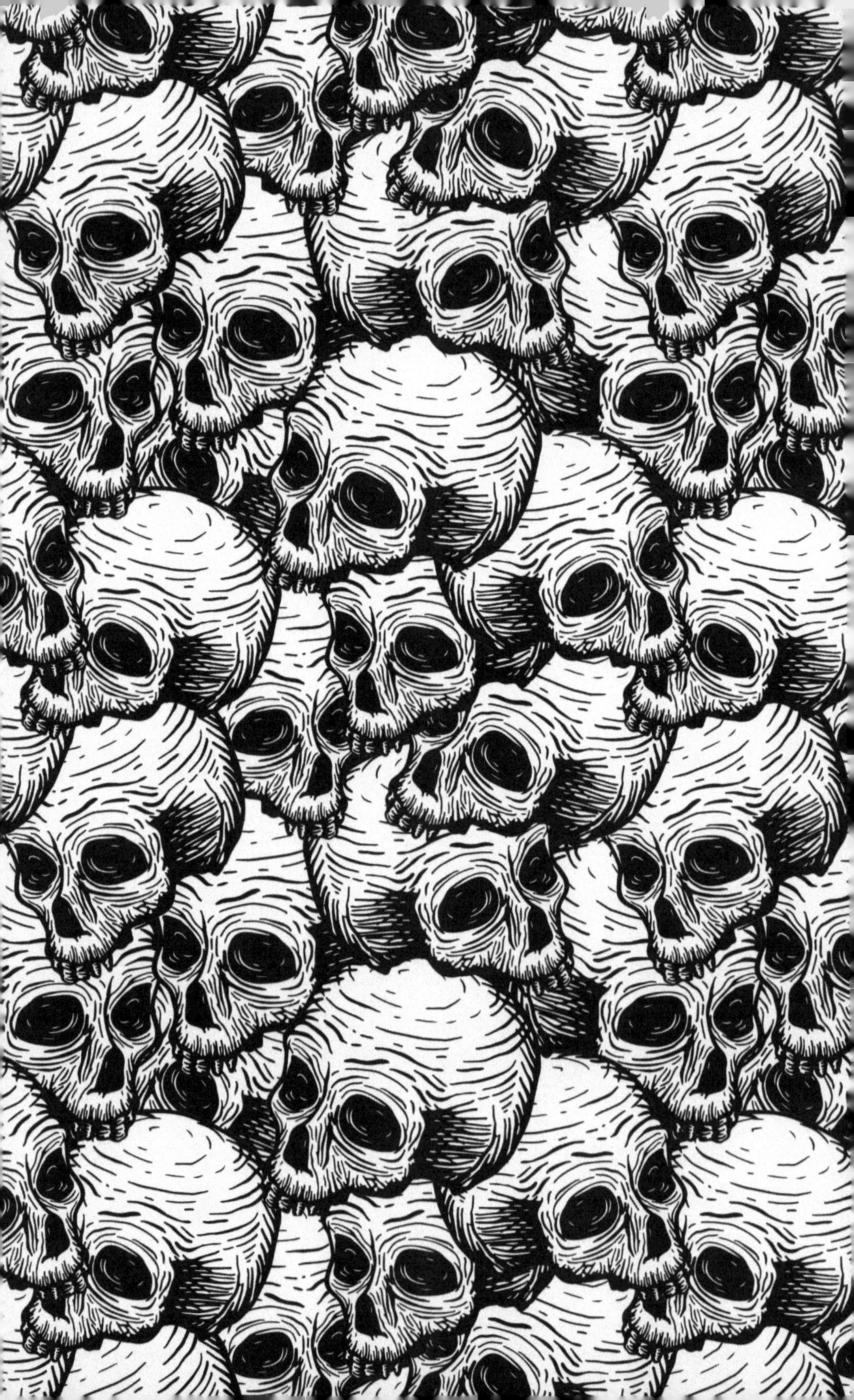

2

TENSION

WHEN I REACH the second floor landing, I'm just hanging up with Izzy, who's having a Thanksgiving dress crisis of proportions that I apparently can't grasp the magnitude of. Since she and Lizzy are going with my dad to spend the holiday with our great-grandmother, I've been spared an invitation. The Mercer matriarch has never thought much of me, but she adores the twins. Who couldn't?

I'm slipping my phone in my pocket when I run into Rath, who appears from out of nowhere. Well, no. Not from out of nowhere. From out of Story's room. Through the wall, I can hear the distant hiss of her showering. I look at the hand he's got shoved in his pocket, and then toward her open door, raising an eyebrow.

"Dude."

He doesn't even attempt to pull off a defensive expression. "So?"

He's practically daring me to say something, which is fair. We're all coping with our Story-imposed sexile in our own ways, and Rath sneaking into her room to abscond with her panties is probably something she'd find most preferable of the three. Hell, Killer stomps around the hall at night, waiting for her to unlock her door, and he's still more subtle than I am. I have absolutely zero room to talk.

So I just sigh, asking, "What color?" He pulls his hand from his pocket just far enough for me to catch a glimpse of blue lace. I give it an appreciative look. "That's a good pair."

It's the same pair she was wearing the day I fingered her in the library.

He clears his throat, cramming them back into his pocket. "I'll be down in a few."

Before he can pass me, I grab his arm, giving him a more critical look. Killer and I have been giving Rath his space. We know everything that went down—his being outed like that at his performance, what happened in the pit— has been hard on him, but Christ. All he ever does now is drink, smoke, and jerk off.

Our boy is on a serious bender.

I ask, "When's the last time you slept?" He's got dark bruises beneath his eyes, already bloodshot, still a bit glazed. His hair is limp. "Or showered? Or ate something with a vitamin in it?"

He sneers, "Don't mother me, Mercer," and yanks his arm from my grip.

Before he can slink off, Killian's door opens, and he steps out, giving us a suspicious look. "What's up?"

Rath says, "Nothing," but I jab a thumb at him, cutting in.

"He's going to jack off into your sister's panties."

Killian gives Rath a long, unreadable look. If I'm expecting support for any kind of intervention, then I'm highly disappointed, because Killer just nods, saying, "Send me a picture," and then walks away.

Rath throws a lazy salute on his way up the stairs.

Rolling my eyes, I briefly consider waiting in the hall for Story to emerge, but decide that there's no reason to. She won't kiss me. Not if we're at home, alone. On campus, sure. We have to keep up appearances for the sake of Royal business, so it's fine there. I get to hem her in against a pillar overlooking the courtyard and lick into her warm mouth. I'm allowed to let my hands wander to her ass, giving it a nice little squeeze. If I kiss down her neck to leave a bruise beneath her ear, then that's just expected. Our weekly parties have some leeway, too. I can pull her into my lap and let her weight press into my hardness. I can take her earlobe between my teeth and stroke her thighs. I can grab her chin and turn her to face me, taking her mouth in a filthy kiss—as long as it's just for show.

But when it's just us?

I can barely get her to brush up against me.

And it's driving me slowly, fucking insane.

I let myself be distracted by the day laid out before me, which is pretty easy. Dinner with the Paynes—aptly named—is bound to be some sort of torture. It'll be our first interaction with Daniel on a social level since Killian shot him. His injury wasn't bad. His son made sure about that. It was a warning, but there's going to be fallout. Something tells me the rings under Rath's eyes may not only be about being cockblocked. He owes Daniel *something* for saving Story in the pit. No one knows what.

I guess we'll find out soon enough.

The sound of banging pots is the sign that Ms. Crane is already awake and working in the kitchen when I get downstairs.

"Did you pack the mashed cauliflower?" I ask, peering into the cooler. "And the Brussel sprouts? I told Posey we'd bring them."

"You mean the stuff that smells like a hooker's twat?" Ms. Crane shoots me a glare as she flings open a window. "They're in there. I don't know why anyone would want to eat something that smells like rotten spunk, but go ahead. Pass it around."

"Because word on the street is Story's mother isn't the best cook," I reply, lifting the cooler. "Thanksgiving for her is probably heavy on the carbs with a side of turkey. If everyone else wants to get a heart attack during dinner, that's their business, but I'm eating this."

"Like anyone else would eat that putrid smelling garbage."

"Sure you don't want to come?" Rath asks her, strolling into the room. He doesn't look much better than when I saw him in the hall, but I can tell he's showered and changed, and the sunglasses he's wearing hide what are sure to be bloodshot eyes.

She snorts. "Unlike some people, I prefer to spend my holidays with people I trust, not a houseful of thugs."

"You *live* in a houseful of thugs," I point out.

"And you're all leaving," she volleys back, giving me a disdainful look. "Best hope you come back in one piece. All of us know better than to think Daniel Payne is going to be hospitable to the likes of you four." The old crone vanishes into the pantry and shuts the door, sealing herself in her tomb.

Rath stares at the closed door for a moment, but then his face scrunches. "Jesus, what is that smell?"

I pull the cooler defensively closer, pointedly ignoring him. "That was quick," I note, nodding toward the stairs. "Usually it takes you forever."

Rath chomps on his piece of gum, giving me a lazy shrug. "It was a functional nut. Clear the tension. Get the blood flowing. You know what this dinner is all about."

Sighing, I pull my jacket off the hook beside the door. "It's an ambush."

"Nah," Rath says. "Ambushes, you don't see coming. This is Daniel trying to measure us up."

"I guess that's what it is for us, too."

We both turn at the sound of her voice, finding our Lady standing in the doorway. She's wearing a knee-length black dress with a scalloped neckline and short lace sleeves. To my eternal fucking torment, she's wearing her hair up off her neck, which is adorned with a string that's been wrapped around it three times and secured in a knot at the base of her throat, the ends dangling toward her cleavage.

I could seriously use one of those hour-long, jack-off sessions right now, but since we don't have time for that, I try to pry my tense jaw apart long enough to greet her. "Story. You look—"

"Like I'm going to a funeral?" She glances down at her dress. Sure, it may be dark and a bit less revealing than I prefer, but it looks good on her.

It'd just look better on my floor.

"You look beautiful," I say, giving her a smile I don't feel the spirit of. This girl is going to kill my dick.

She points to her face. "Even the rings under my eyes?" She sighs, giving her skirt a testing sway. "I heard Ms. Crane before. Maybe she's right. Why are we going to dinner with a man who's proven himself to be a despicable, perverse, immoral human being?"

"Because he's my father," Killian says, strolling into the kitchen, a limp tie ends hanging around his neck. "And although he is all of those things, he's also the most powerful player in South Side." He not so discreetly stops to sweep his eyes over Story. I can't help but notice the matching bags under his eyes. His nighttime roaming is fucking with him. "People are watching. Whoever shot me is watching, and whoever killed Vivienne is watching. We have to present a unified front—it's just part of being a Lord." He reaches up to adjust the tie, grimacing when his elbows lift higher than mid-chest. The pain from the gunshot wound limits his range of motion. "Goddamn it."

"You're right. I know it, but I hate it." She sighs and approaches him. "Here, let me fix that."

Killian's jaw tightens, but he relinquishes the ends of the tie and goes still. Carefully, she wraps and tucks the length of the tie together, making a clean knot. Where she learned to do this, I have no idea, but when she finishes she looks up at him and asks, "Is that good?"

He doesn't even check. "Yes. Thank you."

Facing her, I say, "None of us are excited about today, but it's part of being a Lord. I can promise you one thing, though; you won't be alone in that house for even a second."

We'd agreed on it.

Her eyes dart to Rath's and that same undercurrent of stress that has been flowing between them for weeks flickers to life. "He's right," Rath says. "No one's letting you near Daniel alone, got it?"

She nods. "I've got it. Thank you."

It's been a strange few weeks, but we load up the truck and settle into our seats. Story and Rath sitting awkwardly in the back, Killian and I in the front. The truth ebbs between us.

After everything we've been through, we're determined to come out stronger. We have to.

We're in this together.

"If Detroit doesn't get their defense together, they can kiss this game goodbye," Killian says, frowning at the players in formation on the screen. "Geoff can't cut it as the QB. It was a stupid move to trade Stafford."

"They're rebuilding," Daniel says, lifting his beer with the arm he doesn't have in a sling. If he feels any pain, he doesn't show it. Wouldn't. Weakness and vulnerability aren't acceptable traits for a King. "Every organization has to do it. Trading Stafford was a long game move."

Killian barely hides the curl of his lip. "One I hope the owners don't regret."

"They're building toward the future. You see, son, sometimes you have to make sacrifices now for strength later." This thinly veiled football metaphoring has been going on since we got here and were ushered into the den. Story, meanwhile, has vanished with her mother into the kitchen. I'd started to follow her in, but she shook her head and nodded for me to go with the others. I don't like it, but Posey doesn't offer much of a threat. Killian and his father, however? There could be more bloodshed before pie is served. "That trade for Stafford didn't just get them Geoff. They also got two first round picks in the future. That's thinking ahead." He nods at me. "Tristian, the bottle of Lagavulin

I was saving for today is behind the bar. Care to serve it?"

"I'd be glad to," I say, happy to have something to do with my hands while these two circle one another like wolves. I locate the bottle of scotch and four glasses, opening the freezer to pilfer some ice for mine and Killian's. Daniel and Rath take their scotch neat.

I pour into each glass, but when I get to Rath's, he covers it with his hand and says, "I'm good." Killian looks away from the TV for the first time since we got here and shares my look of surprise. Rath shrugs, not meeting our gazes. "I don't want to fill up on drinks. Just saving room for all of Posey's cooking."

That's the biggest load of bullshit I've ever heard, but I'm not looking too deep into it. Could be he doesn't want to lower his guard here. I can't blame him. Something dark transpired between him and Daniel at the Velvet Hideaway. Rath may be determined to ruin his liver, but he doesn't have to do it today.

"Smart man," Daniel says, taking his glass, "but you did always know how to make the right choice, didn't you, Dimitri?"

Rath's hand balls into a fist by his side, and if I'd had to place bets on who lost it first on Thanksgiving, it wouldn't have been him. He wouldn't have even been second.

Killian senses it too, and says, "Any word on Vivienne?"

Ah, got to hand it to Killer. Like Geoff up there on the screen, he's always playing offense.

His father hums, not deigning to look his son in the eye. "You mean, do I know who carved and mutilated her body with your initials before slitting her throat and letting her bleed out?" He swirls the ice in his glass. "I have my theories."

After a long, weirdly aggressive beat of silence, Killian asks, "Do you care to share? Because it wasn't—"

"I'm well aware it wasn't you," Daniel says, eyes dropping to the gunshot wound in Killian's gut. "You had no problem shooting your old man, but going after an innocent? That's a line you're too weak to cross." Despite the clear insult of the words, his voice is measured and casual. "I know a message when I see it. The hit on you. Taking such...vicious efforts on Vivienne..." He swallows thickly. He won't admit it—can't, really—but Vivian was more than a secretary. She was his confidante, his right hand, and probably also his lover. Although it's hard to know how deep that went—sex doesn't mean much in Daniel's world—going after her was personal. As personal as going after his son. "Cartwright and his little band of heathens comes to mind."

"The Dukes?" Killian repeats, sharing a glance with me. Saul Cartwright's name is already gracing our list of suspects, too, considering he'd been one of Story's sugar daddies back in the day. "You really think they're behind this?"

On the TV, the announcer's voice raises with excitement. We all look up to see Geoff throw a spiral down to the receiver at the other end of the field. Before it gets to him, a player from the other team leaps up and intercepts, snagging the ball out of the air and tucking it into his chest. He carries it twenty yards before Detroit figures out what's going on and tackles him.

"He recently had to pay restitution to the Kings. Hand over assets that are important to him. It was all conducted fairly, but you know how Kings are. We don't like to lose." He swirls the liquid in his glass, eyes pensive. "He's always been a little petty. I can see him lashing out."

"Do we need to look into it?" I ask.

"Not yet," he says, throwing his drink back. "Saul is only one suspect."

"And the others?" KIllian asks.

"I have no doubt it's someone close to me." Daniel looks away from the screen, eyes darting toward the kitchen. "Someone determined to hurt me. Personally. Which is a mistake, because when I find out exactly who killed her," he finally looks his son in the eye, giving him a chilly smirk, "they're going to pay."

STORY

3

DISPLAYS

My mother has always been the master of putting on a show. When she was turning tricks, it was all about being whatever her John wanted. For the parent-teacher conferences, it was all about being a supportive, concerned mother. I'm not sure what show she put on for Daniel, but I admit to being curious. Was it complete subservience? Was it something just awful? I know it was enough to land that fat diamond on her finger, a six-thousand square foot house, and all the security she longed for.

I can't help but think about this as she holds up her glass of wine with one hand, while arranging the centerpiece with the other—all with a serene smile on her face. The scent of roasted turkey fills the air, along with a variety of other delicious-smelling foods. We set the table with expensive china, and the shiny silverware sits on crisp cloth napkins. They're dishes she's probably never cleaned herself. Daniel hires out for that kind of thing. All of this—the cooking, the hosting—it's purely a performance for her. They could have had dinner catered, but my mom wanted to play the part, and in some ways, I understand why.

A flash of an earlier Thanksgiving pops into my head. It's the memory of the two of us eating at a diner out by the highway. The waitress gave me an extra piece of pie when my mom vanished after dinner into the cab of a truck in the parking lot.

This show has all the trappings—everything she could never give me.

"Your hair looks so pretty today," she gushes, fingering a tendril as she passes me. "Did you spend all morning pinning that up? You look so tired."

I glance at my reflection in the large gold-framed mirror over the sideboard. The truth doesn't seem as humble as it's meant to be, which is that I threw it up on the way out of my room to avoid doing anything elaborate. "Yes," I say instead. "It took a little while."

She lifts an eyebrow. "Keep it long while you can. Men like it. It makes you look more youthful." The glance she gives me is pointed. "Much like getting enough sleep."

"I *am* youthful," I reply, following her back to the kitchen. "And I don't care what men think."

"Is that why you told Daniel you didn't want him covering your tuition?" she asks, her harried expression adopting an undercurrent of tension that takes me off guard. The Lords and Daniel are in the living room, standing rigidly around the big screen and acting as if they're talking about football. Killian's game isn't until Saturday, and although he isn't playing because of his injury, he'll travel with the team for the game this weekend. "Is it?" mom repeats, giving a cucumber a pointed chop. "You're too good for our money all of a sudden?"

I work my way through a series of fast blinks, uncertain what to say. Uncertain of what he's told her. Stammering, I lie, "I-I just didn't want to bother him anymore."

"That's what family is for, Story." The way her mouth pinches into an unhappy moue makes her feelings on the matter clear. As far as she's concerned, everything is normal. I should be happy—no, *grateful*—to take my stepfather's money to pay for college and anything else he wants to give me. Even if his plan is to exploit me like every other woman that crosses his path.

"Mom," I start, shifting uncomfortably. It's a risk to bring this out in the open, but it seems like more of a risk not to. "Do you know anything about... er, the Velvet Hideaway?"

The knife hits the counter with a sharp clatter. "Honestly, Story." She levels with me a fiery gaze. "Who do you think you're talking to? Do I know about the Velvet Hideaway?" She scoffs, swiping her hands against her crisp, new apron. "I know everything about the Hideaway. I'm the one who named it!"

My head snaps back in shock. "What?"

She props a hand against the counter, looking deceptively casual. "You're old enough that I don't need to tiptoe around these matters anymore. You know what I used to do."

"Yeah, but..." Staggered, I struggle to regain my footing. "You're not...I mean, not anymore. Right?"

Perhaps it's the wariness in my voice that makes her spine snap straight. "Of course not! Don't be absurd!" She reaches for the knife, eyes focused on its blade as she chops. "I'm a wife now, entirely faithful to my husband. I don't need to do those things anymore. But I also have experience and wisdom. If I were buying property, don't you think I'd ask Daniel for advice? I know you probably don't understand this yet," she says, sliding me a significant look, "but a marriage is a partnership. I took one look at that rotten hovel down on the Avenue and told him in no uncertain terms that he could do better. That he *should* do better—by his girls, and by the clients. I don't know how this may seem to you, but I make my contributions, missy."

My face screws up in distaste. "So you...helped him open that place?"

Her gaze sharpens. "Don't give me that look. I saw an opportunity to better the situation of other women who were struggling. Women whose positions I used to be in. Women who might raise children like you. Don't you dare turn your nose up at that." Beneath the anger, I can see it. The flash of hurt.

It makes my stomach sink. "Mom, I didn't mean—"

With a clipped voice, she cuts me off. "Especially considering it was good enough for you."

My blood turns to ice, pulse stampeding in my ears. It takes me three tries to eke out a response. "What are you talking about?"

She shakes her head. "It's like I said. I know everything about the Hideaway. *Everything.*" She gathers the carrots and distractedly dumps them into the bowl, not meeting my gaze. "I don't want you to think I'm judging you. God knows I'd be a hypocrite. But when Daniel told me you and Dimitri came in, begging for a way to earn fast cash..." She pauses, bracing her palms against the counter, and takes a long breath. "I suppose I'm not blameless. Clearly, I set a terrible example, but Story..." Finally, she looks at me, and all the anger and defensiveness falls away. What's left is just her. My mother. The woman who used to sing me to sleep. The woman who'd brush my hair and call me her little storybook. The woman who'd come into a hotel bathroom bruised and watery-eyed, and plaster on a fake smile, so I didn't get scared. There's a plea in her eyes that makes the lump in my throat swell. "Baby, I don't want that life for you. I've worked too hard, come too far, to watch my daughter walk down the same crooked path. It's not a good life. It's not a *safe* life. Look at Daniel!" She flings a hand toward the living room. "Shot protecting one of his girls. You have a chance to get away from all that, don't you see? Even if it means swallowing a little pride."

How stupid I must have been to believe I'd cried out all my tears that night in the funhouse. They threaten to well up now, and somewhere inside of my chest, something grows. It's too turbulent a thing to be so simple as anger. I think it might be some agonizing howl of rage and violence and grief. Because Daniel told her I wanted it. That I did it for the money. That I'm the whore he always wanted me to be.

And my mom believed it.

"I just thought it was time for me to make my own way." I force the rest over the lump in my throat. "He's done so much for me already."

Her chin tilts. "Did you really do it to make more money for yourself, or was it something else?"

"What do you mean?"

She opens a pot and stirs the contents with a large spoon. "Dimitri doesn't come from the best family, and after his humiliation at the alumni performance, I can imagine his opportunities are drying up."

"This has nothing to do with Dimitri," I grind out, angry that she thinks the man who saved me was responsible for putting me in that position to begin with. "I'm ready to be an adult. I don't want to rely on Daniel."

"Then you really must not understand how marriage, or at least mine, works. We're partners, Story. His money is *my* money, and we help you because we care. You're just as much his child as Killian is mine."

The thought of being Daniel's child makes me recoil. Probably, the thought of being her child would make Killian feel similarly. No wonder my stepbrother and I are both fucked up and drawn to one another like acid-covered magnets.

"And anyway, men like to feel needed," she continues while pulling serving utensils out of the drawer, "especially a powerful man like Daniel. It's important for him to take care of his family. Walking away from his generosity looks unappreciative, Story. And it's not just about him. A prospective husband will notice the slight as well. The right kind of suitor doesn't want a woman who can take care of herself."

"I do appreciate Daniel's…generosity," I bite the word like it's gristle. "But you raised me to be independent, didn't you? To handle things myself?"

She jerks her head toward the living room. "You think Tristian Mercer wants a 'strong, independent woman'?" She laughs, head shaking. "A man like that wants a woman who looks good on his arm and better in his bed. That's the type of man you should pursue. Men who can take care of you, so that you'll never have to—" Her voice clips off, jaw clicking. Smoothing down her apron, she visibly shakes off thoughts of my having to turn tricks. "Independence is a marvelous idea, but why struggle? Tristian would be such a nice match for you. Wasn't he escorting you that night at the alumni performance? He looked interested. You should be encouraging that, not selling yourself. He won't want you if he thinks you're cheap and all used up."

I stare hard at my mother, at the gold earrings and the diamond bracelet, reminding myself of everything she's had to do to earn them, and the truth screams under my skin. I want to tell her why I walked into that pit, under the heat of lights, and cameras, and all those horrible eyes. But here, with my Lords in the other room—with Killian being injured and Dimitri probably packing a loaded gun under his jacket—it seems like a metaphorical H-bomb. This won't be a discussion that ends in pie and ice cream. It'll be a fucking bloodbath.

I swallow it all back and say, "Daniel wanted *you*, didn't he?"

Her lips press into a thin line, and she clearly has more to say, except then we're interrupted.

"Well, isn't this a vision?" I'm not even remotely surprised Tristian has 'suddenly' walked into the room. He was probably listening to every word. "Seeing you two lovely women together." He rests a glass of something amber on the counter, eyes watchful as he assesses me. "Thought I'd come in and see if you needed any help."

"You're too sweet," my mother says, giving me a pointed look. "But you let us girls take care of all this."

"Nonsense," he says, grabbing a pair of oven mitts and sliding them on his hands. "I'm happy to help." He opens the oven and pulls out the turkey. It's so massive that I can see his muscles shifting beneath his sweater as he hefts it. My mother directs him to place it on the counter and he grins. "This looks like something out of a magazine, Posey."

She glows at the praise, but only I can see the traces of grimace in the line around his mouth. He's probably wondering if it's organic, antibiotic-free, GMO whatever.

"How are your parents?" Mom asks. "It surprised me you weren't with them for the holiday."

"They're good. Up in the mountains. I didn't want to give my dear old gran another mouth to feed." His eyes dart to mine. "I prefer to be around Forsyth right now, anyway."

"I bet they miss you. Especially those adorable sisters of yours."

He grins. "I'm sure they do, but they'll be too busy on the slopes to worry about me. They're very adept skiers already."

She walks past Tristian, running her arm over his broad shoulders, and squeezes his bicep. "They're lucky to have such a strong, caring brother." When he grins down, she winks back.

Jesus Christ. Is she trying to make me jealous?

Fuck me.

Is it working?

He gives me a look, eyebrow raised, that tells me he's thinking the same thing.

"It's one," I announce, feeling awkward and hot and annoyed. "Isn't that when you said we'd eat?"

"Oh, yes. Let's get the rest of this on the table." She picks up two casserole dishes, but as soon as her back is turned, Tristian swoops in.

The kiss takes me off guard, although I'm not sure why it would. Tristian takes his opportunities wherever they arise. If we're meant to uphold the image of a Lord and his Lady, then he's more than happy to press me up against the nearest vertical surface and make my head spin.

That's exactly what he's doing now, pressing his mouth to mine in a slow, sensual kiss. He cups my cheek, and it's not filthy like usual—void of all the grabbing and grinding—but it's no less searing.

I knew with the holiday break, we wouldn't be like this for a few days, but I'm only just now realizing how much it'd pained me to give it up. Tristian can kiss me so sweetly when he wants to, gentle and unhurried—like he's giving me something to be savored. Because that's exactly what Tristian thinks he is. It's an unconscious gesture to twist my fingers into his nice dress shirt, tugging him closer, because in many ways, he's right.

Tristian Mercer is absolutely someone worth savoring.

He pulls away, giving me a soft grin, and then turns to take a dish from my speechless, slack-jawed mother. "Allow me."

My face feels overheated, but I recover quickly, stepping forward to take the other dish. "I've got this." The smile I send her feels wan, but she's too busy making her eyebrows disappear up her forehead to notice.

I head into the dining room and place it on the table. Turning, I crash right into Tristian who's inches away. His hand clutches my hip, steadying me, but slowly he withdraws.

"Your mother is very...charming." He clearly wants to use another word. Possibly something that rhymes with 'clutty'.

Sighing, I smooth down a wrinkle my hand had made in his nice shirt. "My mother spent her life manipulating men out of their money." I tilt my head, giving him an assessing glance. "In fact, she strongly implied I should do the same to you."

"Did she?" His fingers twitch by his side. He wants to touch me again, but there's no one around to perform for, so he doesn't. "I guess she knows me better than I thought. I am very malleable when it comes to beautiful women."

He's so close. That kiss was the best we've had in days, and god, the way he smells. There's this lock of blonde hair that's escaped from his careful styling, and this tiny, insignificant, otherwise normal thing suddenly makes him look so mussed and flustered that I find my own fingers twitching.

For a long moment, it's hard to remember what this whole sex moratorium is even about.

"Tris, where do you want this bowl of disappointment?" Dimitri asks, walking into the room. "I tried to toss it, but Posey won't let me."

I look over Tristian's shoulder and see him staring blankly into the bowl we'd brought. If my mom thinks I look tired, then god only knows what she must think of my Lord. He looks pale and haggard, all his usual brashness absent from the drooping line of his shoulders. His voice is just as hoarse and anemic as he appears. When he glances up, Dimitri's dark eyes flicker between us, narrowing.

"I'll take it," I say, side stepping Tristian and grabbing the cauliflower. I find a spot on the table, which is when Killian and Daniel step into the room. And there we all are, standing stiffly, our eyes avoiding one another.

Forget the turkey. The tension is what needs to be cut with a knife.

"Looks delicious," Daniel says, walking directly to the head of the table. Arm clutched to his chest in the sling, he passes my mother, still holding the turkey platter between her hands, and leans down to kiss her on the cheek. "Wonderful job, dear."

"Thank you, Daniel."

She places the dish in front of him and moves to the opposite side of the table. When I shift to sit next to her, a strong hand settles on my shoulder. A chill creeps up my spine when Daniel says, "Story, we haven't had a chance to catch up since you arrived. Why don't you sit down here with me." His words are polite and casual, just like the easy smile on his face.

Resisting the urge to flinch—a futile gesture that will just embarrass me further—I glance across the table at Killian. His jaw is clenched so tightly that it looks painful. I know the rules. For now, we play Daniel's game. He's the King. I sit as instructed and the men follow suit, taking their seats. Beneath the table, I wring my hands, just barely fighting back a disgusted grimace. He's holding the carving knife, and I can't help but stare at the sharp point of it, thinking about Viv and the letters carved into her chest. *KTR*. The same letters that are carved on mine.

The difference is that her throat was slit.

My stomach rolls as he clumsily, one-handed, carves into the turkey. I try to tune it all out. The prickle of awareness of the Lords' eyes on me. The heat from Daniel standing so close. The sight of the blade cutting into the flesh. Maybe Tristian has the right idea with this veganism stuff. My face must be positively green.

Daniel takes his seat, so close that I tuck my limbs in, certain that if I touch him, I really might vomit. There's a stretch of time where we all fill our plates, hands reaching across the table. This has never been a table for saying grace. Back when I was a teenager, I used to amuse myself with the possibility that doing such a thing would cause Killian and his father to collapse in a fit of unholy seizure. Now, I'm just grateful we won't have to do something as absurd as holding hands to pray.

My mom, completely oblivious to the tension, breaks the silence. "Shoot!" she says plucking her napkin from her lap. "I forgot the cranberry sauce."

I frantically sweep the napkin from my own lap, offering, "I'll get it!"

A large hand clamps down on my thigh. "You're our guest, Story. Let your mother give you a nice dinner."

Standing, Mom instantly agrees. "No need for a fuss. I'll just be two shakes."

She's out of the dining room before she can even notice the stiff set of my spine. Daniel's fingers dig in deep, so vicious and painful that it's a physical battle to remain composed, but I do. I refuse to wince. One glance at Killian tells me he'd have this entire table upended if he knew his father's hand was on me. Hurting me. Bruising me. *Marking me.*

The second my mom returns, a ceramic dish in hand, I clatter back in my chair, lurching from my seat. Daniel only gets the barest flash of a moment to let me go, but he does it seamlessly.

"I'll be right back."

"Story?" my mother asks.

"I-I'm fine. I just need to be excused." I give a tight smile. "Go ahead without me. I'll be back in a minute."

My strides are level until I reach the other room, where I draw in a big gulp of air. I keep walking down the hall, putting as much distance between me and Daniel as I can. Reaching for the bathroom doorknob, I push it open, realizing too late that I'm in the wrong room. This isn't the bathroom, it's Daniel's office.

My eyes go instantly to the desk and the chair behind it.

The memory of him drawing me close, pulling me on his lap, feeling the hard bulge in his pants as he ran his hands up my shirt—assessing my *development*. My vision swims, chest jerking with shallow, ineffectual gulps of air. It's just all too close now. The memories. The smell of the bourbon on his breath. Old cigar tobacco. Leather. The cadence of his voice as he husked into my ear about chastity and how nice my nipples were getting, and god.

He'd wanted to sell me.

And in the end, he did.

"Story."

I don't turn when Killian says my name, but I hear the door click shut behind him. I feel his presence behind me. I always feel it. When I'm asleep. When he's pacing the halls. When he watches me. "What would you have done?" I wonder, clutching my sides. "If he'd...given me to you. Like you wanted. Like you thought he would."

There's a shifting sound, two footsteps behind me, and then he speaks, voice quiet and dark. "I would have taken care of you."

"You would have fucked me."

There's no shifting sounds now. Just utter stillness. "Yeah."

"You would have owned me."

Tighter, he repeats. "Yeah."

"You would have—"

"Stop," he interrupts, the word emerging with more weariness than I'm expecting. "Stop making it sound that way. I would have fucked you. Of course I would have fucked you. I was sixteen, and you were—" There's a bitten off sigh, and then, "I would have wanted you to want it, Story. Jesus Christ. I would have wanted you to come to my bed. Stop making me sound like I'm—"

"You?" I ask, turning to glance at him over my shoulder.

His teeth gnash. *"Him."*

I turn back to the desk. To the chair. I told him what happened in this room—he fucking saw it for himself. "I thought I was safe here. Really, truly safe. After all those years of my mom dragging us from seedy hotel to shitty apartment, of sketchy men coming in and out at all hours, I thought this clean, beautiful house and the knight in shining armor who lived here would take care of me."

"You're right," he says. "I should have protected you."

I don't ask why he assumes he'd be the knight in that scenario. It was supposed to be Daniel, only now that I really think about it, that's not right. Maybe it was always supposed to be Killian. "You were so mean." I speak like I'm lost in a memory, and I suppose I am. Running through all those awful barbs and callous stares. Shivering, I remember, "You were so *mean* to me."

"I know." There's some more movement, fabric shifting. I don't need to turn to see his discomfort. The vision of his pinched brow and shuffling feet burns in my imagination. "I'm sorry."

It should make me angry. Apologies are useless now, almost as if they're something to be checked off a long list of tasks I've handed to him. It shouldn't even mean anything.

But I find myself unable to muster anything but some deep, internal sense of sadness. "It doesn't matter now. You might not be your father, but he raised you. He taught you. Aren't we all shaped by our parents? Didn't I turn to selling a part of myself, because it's what I've seen my mother do?" Turning to him, I wonder aloud, "Do we ever break the cycle, Killian?"

Eyebrows pushed together, he asks, "Haven't we already?"

It's not a question I can answer. He let me go, and I'm here because I want to be, not because I need to be. In those ways, perhaps we have. Maybe it's enough, or maybe we're doomed in some unavoidable, intrinsic way.

It's only when his eyes descend that I realize I'm rubbing that spot on my thigh. I can still feel his father's fingers there, pressing into the flesh and muscle, holding me down, but I hastily cover it with my skirt.

Something dark and still passes over Killian's face. "What is that?"

Even though I know it's not meant for me, the quiet, dangerous timbre of his voice makes my lungs clench in alarm. "Nothing." When he steps forward, I step back, like we're two opposing magnetic poles. "Killian, wait."

He stalks forward slowly at first, and then he's storming toward me, uncaring of the way I'm shrinking back, eventually hitting the desk. I round it clumsily, trying to put something between us, but Killian follows so quickly that it's barely the span between two blinks before he's bearing down on me, ripping the fabric of my dress from my fist.

Pressed against Daniel's desk, I go rigid as Killian reveals my pale thigh, and I don't need to look to know his father has left a mark. That's what Payne men do. Instead, I watch the violent emotion swirling in my stepbrother's eyes as he inspects it. He'd be still, if not for the twitch of that muscle in the back of his jaw.

"He did this." It's more of a challenge than a question, the laser heat of his eyes burning into my bruised skin.

"Don't," I plead, voice thin. "It's not worth it, okay? Let's just get through this dinner and go home."

His gaze snaps to mine, eyes blazing. "Twenty minutes."

I blink at him, finding it difficult to think when he's so close, caging me in like this. "To finish dinner? But we'll need to eat dessert, and then—"

"There are a million things I'd do differently if I could," he says, cutting me off. Despite the naked fury in his features, the way he grazes his fingertips over my thigh is feather light. "I would have made a move that night. I would have claimed you, worshipped you." There's no mistaking the hard bulge pressing against the thin material of my dress or the low strain of his voice. It's the one that wakes me from sleep while he's already inside of me. My body aches at the thought. Eyes dark, he continues, "He never would have touched you, because I wouldn't have allowed it. Do you understand what I'm saying?"

I struggle to imagine it.

Before I can, he leans in, brows crouched low. "One by one. Every finger of his that's ever touched you. All we'll need is twenty minutes." His hot lips press against my neck, and I shiver against him. "That's how long it'll take to cut them off."

I know then that I'm not the person I used to be. That girl would be aghast at such a gruesome thought. She'd gasp and thrash and cower away from it. Instead, I turn it over in my head, touching it with my thoughts in the same way Killian is touching me now. Slow and careful, but possessive and indulgent.

Daniel would *scream*.

I shudder out an exhale, responding, "No." Reaching up to hold his shoulders, I worry, "My mom..." He freezes, and from the clench of his jaw, this is an inadequate reason to restrain ourselves.

When I kiss him, it's only half tactical. It's the only way I can think to extinguish the blaze of violence in his eyes, but it's also oddly necessary. I don't know why at first, beyond the heat that settled into my bones for him weeks ago. It's lost in the fog, in the way his tongue feels invading my mouth. This is how Killian kisses—as if he's certain he's not welcome, but he's made a choice to claw his way inside, regardless.

I slide back against the desk, but I frantically bring him with me, parting my thighs for him. All it takes is a hand on his backside, yanking him up against my center, and finally I understand why I need it so badly.

The sound he makes is tight and frustrated when he rears back, hand shooting out to catch my chin. "Story," he says, tension visible in every hard line of his face. "Don't fucking tease me."

I'm already breathless, and there might have been a time that flash of warning in his eyes would scare me off, but I can't remember it. I reach down to pull my skirt up, curling my leg around his calf to bring him closer. "Why would I?" I ask, hooking my fingers into his waistband.

"You think I won't?" It's spoken as a threat, made even more evident by the hardness pressing into me. "I'll fuck you right here, in the same room he used to—"

I can see the moment it clicks for him. This is where his father used to take me—in the chair directly behind him. Pulled into Daniel's lap, my eyes once fixed unseeingly to this very desk as he touched and took.

It's time for me to take it back.

Killian's mouth comes down onto mine in a hard, bruising kiss, but I meet him teeth for teeth, tongue for tongue. He reaches for his belt and there's no denying the hard erection pressing at the cotton of his pants. I reach for him, impatiently unhooking the buckle and lowering the zipper. He groans when I touch him, dipping my hand into his pants and feeling the velvet of his skin. He jerks me forward and goes back under my skirt, yanking my panties to the side.

"Always so fucking wet," he mumbles, rolling his thumb over my clit. There's no other foreplay, no coaxing or coddling, just the shock of him entering me in a single powerful thrust. It's all I can do to bite down on the cry I want to make, but he doesn't give me time to adjust, tangling one hand into the hair at the base of my skull as the other takes a greedy handful of my ass.

"You were always going to be mine," he grunts, holding me painfully close as he punches his hips into mine. Beside us, something clatters to the floor, but neither of us pay it any attention. "I knew you were mine then, the same way I know you're mine now."

I gasp against his lips, fingernails scrabbling for purchase against his shoulders. "Oh my god!" All those nights staying up on the phone with Dimitri—all those afternoons on campus, pressed against Tristian as he kissed me senseless—couldn't have prepared me for how good it feels to finally have one of them inside me again.

Killian is hard and thick, and he fucks me in these short, brutal bursts of power that would have me sliding up the desk if it weren't for his arms, crushing me up against the expanse of his flexing muscles, forcing me to take it. "Unlock your door tonight," is his gnashed demand, pounding into the cradle of my thighs. "Let me fucking *in*."

My fingers curl around the edge of the desk, holding on for dear life. Killian is not a man used to being denied and those restless nights outside of my room surge through him in hard, fast, thrusts. His arm winds around my back, pulling me close to him, holding me steady as he fucks into me over and over. I'm surrounded by his scent, his heat, his breath and want. The past falls away, and everything is consumed in this moment. Me. Him. Us.

There's no room for anyone else. No other history. Just what was always supposed to be.

Story and Killian.

"Killian," I breathe into his mouth, clamping my teeth on the soft flesh of his lower lip. "Don't stop, don't stop—please—oh, god—" Shuddering waves roll down my spine, and my walls clench around him just as tightly as my thighs. I whimper from the force, and he swallows my cries with his kiss, keeping me quiet—keeping me to himself.

The rock of his hips grows impatient, erratic, thrumming into me with wild abandon. It feels so good, so deep, that it borders on pain, but I hold on to him and don't let go, because as long as we're like this, there's nothing else out there. No perverts, no hit men, no murderers, no dangerous thugs. There's no complicated past, or painful reminders of what was—what could have been. There's just his body and my body, and how it feels when we're like this. Wild—feral—primal. And within that moment of mindlessness, a thought comes to me, unbidden, but so true that it settles into the very marrow of my being.

Killian and I were made for this.

We were made to fuck.

To be together.

"Let me in," he grunts, burying his head into my shoulder as he drives into me. His fingertips dig into my soft flesh, making his own bruises into the marks his father had made. His voice is all hard viciousness, but there's something buried below it. A plea that stretches with desperation. "Let me in, let me in, let me—fuck." He goes rigid, and then I feel it: his dick pumping me full of his hot come. He lets out a growl that tapers off into a long, pained groan. "Goddamn, little sister. You're trying to fucking kill me."

It's only when he pulls back, face red and pinched, that I realize. "Oh my god, I didn't—are you okay?" He can barely handle a necktie with his gut wound, and here I am making him fuck me.

His fingers, still clamped around the junction where my leg meets my hip, massage into the tendon there. When he speaks, he pitches his voice so low that I have to strain to understand it. "You know he's going to see this, don't you?"

I hold his gaze, surprised to see the dread swimming within it. He's worried I'm going to freak out or blame him. But the truth is, I've become so conditioned to being watched that it's just second nature to assume anymore—and especially in this house. In the back of my mind, I wonder where exactly the camera is, but the brief flick of his eyes to the bookshelf to our left is proof enough.

Tilting my head, I answer, "Of course."

He looks almost as shocked as he does relieved. "You want him to," he realizes, eyes searching my face.

I bite on my lip, still thrumming even as I feel Killian softening inside of me. "Does that bother you?" It'd be fair if it did. I won't let Killian into my room—not yet—but I'll use him to make his father angry. To show Daniel that I don't belong to him. To take back whatever sense of self I'd lost here, trapped in this room as a naïve, powerless little girl.

Killian's answer comes in the form of a slow, malicious smile, easing his hips back and leaving me empty. Only I'm not really empty. He reminds me of this when he straightens the crotch of my panties and then presses his palm into my center, whispering into my ear, "Sit in my cum through the rest of dinner and we'll call it even."

I shiver at the low tenor of his voice—at the flash of dark satisfaction in his eye when I nod—and help him back into his pants. I should be uncomfortable and humiliated when I head back to the dining room, but the sticky warmth between my legs provides a comfort—security.

Like a lion marking its territory, Killian claimed me.

And everyone in the room, including his father, will know it.

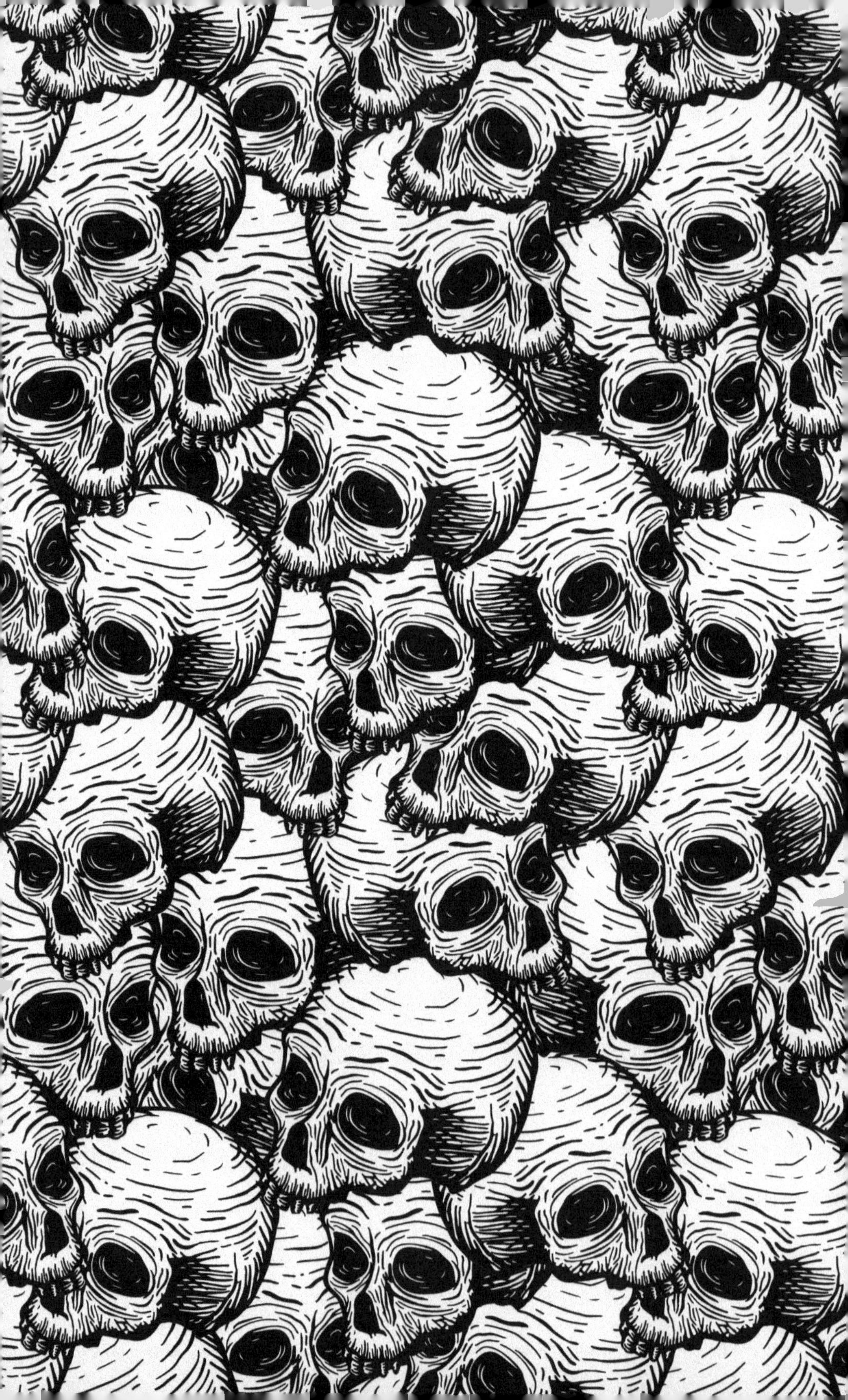

4

PARANOIA

"STILL LOCKED OUT, huh?" Tristian asks, snorting. I ignore him and cross the room, heading straight to the bar. Both the pain in my gut and having to deal with my father all afternoon make me want to down the entire bottle, but I pull out three shot glasses instead.

Story went straight to her room when we got home, locking the door behind her. Whatever transpired between us in Daniel's office obviously doesn't apply here. I knew it was a long shot, anyway.

At least I got laid, which is more than I can say for these two pitiful fuckers.

"So? She told us it would be on her terms." I pinch the glasses in my fingers, carrying them back to the sitting area. Rath sprawls next to Tristian on the couch, looking limp and listless. I hand them each a shot and ease into the armchair, wincing. Okay, so I may have overdone it with Story on the desk. Not that I regret it. She was so fucking hot, spreading her legs for me, fingers shaking with impatience as she drew my dick out and pulled me close. The thing about fucking Story when she's asleep is that it's total control. I can make her mine in any way I want. But the thing about fucking Story when she's awake is that it's comprised of a short, frantic series of electric surprises. When she's awake, I can only make her mine in any way *she* wants. And that?

It might just be the better of the two.

Although my opinion on the matter might be a little muddled by the fact she wants to be mine at all. Still, a nice dinner, good scotch, and some truly fucking fantastic revenge sex means that I haven't felt this relaxed in weeks.

So why can't I stop thinking about that goddamn locked door?

"Is that what happened during dinner?" Rath asks, staring at the liquor for a long moment before placing it on the table. "Her terms?"

"That?" I swallow back the burning liquid. "That was therapy."

Rath raises a skeptical eyebrow. "I don't think people usually give therapy with their dicks."

"Did you see Daniel's face when you walked back in? I thought he was going to break a tooth, he was grinding his teeth so hard." Tristian laughs and swipes Rath's shot off the table. "You fucked Story during Thanksgiving dinner." He holds up the glass in a toast. "You have balls, my friend. Huge fucking brass balls."

"Was it that obvious?" I ask, glancing between them. It's not that I really care. My dad's probably already watching the video, and a part of me wonders if it could possibly look as scorching hot as it felt. A bigger part of me knows it couldn't. There's a reason I didn't rip the straps of that dress off. We might have wanted him to know what we did, but the rest of that was ours and ours alone.

"I don't think her mom noticed," Rath says, rolling his eyes. "She was too busy flirting with Tris."

Tristian disagrees, "I was trying to distract her from the fact her stepson was defiling her sweet daughter in the other room. You're welcome, by the way."

I shake my head, unsure why I need to explain, but feeling like I should. "We're not the only ones she needed to gain some control back from. My dad's been pulling those strings since before I ever knew there were any. That room—that office—something happened there. Sure, we fucked, but it wasn't about me. It was a message."

Rath smiles wryly. "You're saying she used you."

"Like a cheap piece of meat," Tristian adds, eyes dancing with mirth. "I respect that."

I don't refrain from rolling my eyes, pouring myself another shot. "What do you think about what my dad said? About Cartwright being involved in this? The Dukes?"

Tristian sighs, suddenly looking tired. "Man, who knows. The frats around here have our own drama, but the Kings? They take it to another level. I didn't think murder would be a part of it, but it wouldn't exactly shock me. We all know how Kings are made."

Rath's eyes narrow. "There's no real motive, though. Dukes and Lords aren't exactly cuddle buddies, but we give each other our space, which is more than I can say for other houses." Disregarding the glass I slide his way. He leans back, face pensive. "If anyone should want to take Daniel out, it's you. You're the heir."

"Yeah, well, I don't want it." It's the truth, but I also know it's futile. Football—getting out of here—all of that is a long shot. South Side has its tentacles in me, and they're latched on deep and painful.

"No, but think about it," Rath goes on, and I'm surprised to see some life spark back in his eyes. "You have the clearest, most obvious motive. Daniel fucks with your Lady. His boot-licking foot soldier tries to kill you. Plus, those initials? This isn't about Daniel. It's about you." Head snapping back in realization, he adds, "It's about us. All four of us. Someone wanted Daniel to think we were responsible. But why? To get us all pissed at each other? What's the end game there?"

"We're going to have to figure out who's behind all this," is my answer. "I don't like not knowing who's got a gun pointed at my fucking temple."

"Speaking of which, we shouldn't be talking about this without Story," Tristian says, pointing to the ceiling. "We promised."

"I have no intention of making any moves without her."

There's a knock on the library door and we look over, startled to see Martin in the doorway. He's dressed casually, in a sweater and khaki pants. A manila envelope is in his hand.

"What are you doing here so late?" I ask, putting my glass down. "It's Thanksgiving. Don't they give you the day off?"

The Lords employ Martin and he provides legal counsel for the frat—primarily us. But all said, we have nothing to do with his job. Even my father, the King, is only loosely involved. Martin's firm has been representing LDZ since long before any of us were involved. It's a testament to Forsyth's foothold in this town that a tradition like this isn't even thought about twice. He's just here to serve us as needed.

"I took a few hours," he says. "I didn't expect you to be back so soon."

"Yeah, we booked it after pie," Rath says, resting a hand on his stomach. "Sitting through another hour of father-son-step-Lady tension isn't anyone's idea of a good time."

"Well," he says, walking in the room. "I wanted to drop off Marcus' discharge paperwork. He'll be fine."

I blink at the envelope, remembering. The three of us have been a little busy with more pressing matters, but LDZ is chugging along. Some of the more senior guys organized a prank against the Counts last week, ambushing the rival frat members' poker game. Marcus had been caught speeding away from the scene of the crime and graciously took the fall.

"You got him off?" I ask, only giving the contents of the envelope a cursory glance.

"Of course I did," is Martin's response. He doesn't even sound arrogant about it, just matter-of-fact. Tapping his temple, he sagely says, "A good lawyer knows the law. But a great lawyer knows the judge."

Tristian and Rath share a low, appreciative chuckle, but it makes my eyes tighten in suspicion. "You know a lot of people, don't you?" I shift to stand, wincing at the tug and pull in my side. The alcohol and pills aren't enough to cut through all the pain. I lift the hem of my untucked shirt, revealing the healed bullet wound. Martin's expression is neutral, carefully contained to nothing but a quizzical slant of his eyebrows. "Do you know who did this to me?" I ask.

His gaze flicks down to the wound and back up to my face. "There's been chatter, sir. Gossip and such."

Tristian leans forward at this. "What are people saying?"

Martin nods at my gut. "Well, I don't put much stock into scuttlebutt, but Lord Killian was shot, and no one's seen Nick Hoplite since. There's been varying speculation as to how those two situations might be connected."

I take a guess. "They think I killed him."

Martin doesn't even bat an eye. "That's the gist."

Lowering my shirt, I offer, "I didn't."

That one belongs to Story.

He shrugs. "Might as well let them think you did. I don't think I've ever seen the frat this well organized to retaliate against the other houses. Have you seen the board? Those boys are out for blood."

"Wait," Rath says, a divot appearing between his eyebrows. "They think the other frats are involved?"

Martin's eyes flash in surprise. "Aren't they?"

Tristian and I have a short, concise discussion with our eyes, but I'm the one who decides, "You're right, Martin. Let them think whatever." We've been slacking when it comes to The Game, so it can only benefit us to have the frat fired up. Plus, it's not like the truth is so far divorced from the gossip. I didn't kill Ugly Nick, but I would have, given half the chance, and whoever put the hit out on me was the same person who killed Viv. Even my father suspects another house. No skin off my back. "I don't know what you hear or how much you're privy to, but if you hear anymore gossip about who put this hit out on me, I want to know. Immediately."

"Yes, sir."

Nodding, I wave him away. He takes one slow step back and then saunters off. A moment later the front door opens and closes with a click. I lumber back to my seat, lowering myself slowly.

"Was it just me, or did he seem really composed?" I ask, lifting the bottle of whiskey.

"Stick-up-his-ass Martin? He's always really composed," Rath says. "Why?"

"More composed than usual," I elaborate.

Tristian looks over at me. "You're paranoid."

"Fuck yeah, I'm paranoid." I tip the bottle to my mouth and take a huge gulp. "Martin has access to the house, the cameras, our computers. Did you ever think about that?"

Rath sighs and stands, grabbing the bottle from my hand. "Paranoia's going to get you killed. It'll get Story hurt. We're Lords. We're logical. Calculated. Controlled." He carries the bottle over to the bar, snatches up the cap and puts it away. "We're going to find the motherfucker that did this and take him down. But until we know, we do this the right way."

"Is this what sobriety does to you?" Tristian asks. "Because I think I like it more when you're the house substance dumpster."

"Fuck you." Rath heads to the door, giving him the finger. "I'm going to bed."

"Same." Tristian follows, stopping to look back at me. "You really need a good night's sleep, Killer."

"I know." We stare at one another for a long moment, before he shakes his head and vanishes down the hall. He's right. I need to sleep. Even if I'm not playing this weekend, I have to travel with the team, but that doesn't quell the urge that sends me to the second floor. To test the door. To pace the hall.

I'm not just out here hoping she'll let me in.

I'm out here making sure no one else gets in.

It's on my third pass up and down the hall that I glance into my room and see something on the foot of my bed. I leave my post and cross the room, curiosity getting the best of me. It doesn't take long to recognize the items—or know who put them there. It's all of my superstitions lined up neat and straight: the socks, the guitar wire, the baseball card and gum.

The ribbon.

I think back to the night she took them from me, my memory still hazy around the edges. Story got me good that night. Fucked me good, too. That's what I remember the most. She could have done *anything* to me, and she did. She tied me up, stole my things, and got me to reveal my secrets. But she also climbed on top of me, sheathing her body over my cock and rode me hard. Little sister isn't just here for the revenge. I know that now. She wants more. She wants us.

I'm here to make sure that no one takes her away from us ever again.

5

R O T T E N

FUCKING SHOOT ME.

I take a long, hard look around me, foot crunching on a burger wrapper. It's the day after Thanksgiving. Killian is gone and I'm still sober, which are the only two reasons I decide to clean up my room. For an anal retentive freak, Killer has this thing where he's happy to ignore my mess right up to the point that I intend to do something about it, which is when he turns into a drill instructor. He has a harder time watching someone clean a mess than make one and I'm not in the mood for that shit, so I wait until he's halfway to Houston to pick through the debris on my floor.

I'm a slob, but I admit that it's particularly bad, even for me. The task is slow going, mostly because I'd rather be taking a swan dive off a cliff than gathering up all my empties, old food, and dirty clothes.

The nausea doesn't make it any better. I haven't had a drink in almost two days, and I also haven't taken any pills or smoked any weed. My stomach has an opinion about cold turkey, and it sounds a lot like me dry heaving over my toilet all day. Our Lady is going to find out real quick that sobriety doesn't suit me.

I make a pile for trash, and then a pile for shit that needs to be taken downstairs, and then I pause for a cigarette, which I smoke while leaning halfway out my window.

Two hours later, I run into Story on the second floor landing.

I'm cradling three bottles of liquor in my arms. The vodka is half empty, but the whiskey is almost full, and the third is just an embarrassingly almost-empty bottle of cheap malt liquor.

Oh yeah, you can take the boy out of South Side…

She pauses, eyes falling on the bottles, and then does this…thing. It's a little too annoyed to be called a frown, but it reeks of disapproval and hurt, and it pisses me right the fuck off.

Before I can explain, she turns on her heel and bounds down the stairs, ponytail swaying behind her.

"Fuck you, too," I mutter.

She didn't call me last night. It was probably the first night in weeks we haven't spoken over the tinny connection, one or both of us usually shoving our hand down our pants and coming apart as the other breathes all hard like a stalker creep into the speaker. I'm smart enough to see those calls for what they are. We walk around here all day tense and restless, orbiting each other in liminal spaces, and a nice orgasm is the closest thing we have to a catharsis. I wasn't awake long enough this morning to dwell on my disappointment, exhausted and queasy with the craving for an oblivion I won't let myself give in to.

It's not that she automatically thinks the worst of me. I'm pretty sure I've earned that. It's that she's hitching some kind of expectation onto me, like I should stay sober for three days because I care about and want her enough. Like the thought of her getting a full night's sleep beside me in bed is easily worth the hassle.

Mostly, I'm annoyed because she's probably right.

Since my luck is demonstrably dog shit, she's nowhere to be seen when I heave it all into the kitchen and start pouring it down the sink, watching angrily as the liquid disappears down the drain. It's a waste of perfectly good liquor that Tristian or Killer could easily enjoy, but suddenly the sight of the bottles makes me want to hurl.

"Don't you dare."

I look over my shoulder to see Ms. Crane walking out of the pantry. "You want them?"

She doesn't even look at the bottles. "The only thing I want is to not be cleaning up whatever rancid sludge is currently occupying the bottom of your stomach. If you throw up, then you can find the bucket and mop yourself. Got better things to do." The 'better thing' would appear to be the unlit cigarette she's got pinched between her fingers.

I turn back to the sink, dragging a wrist over my brow. "Don't sweat it. There's nothing left to come up."

There's a long beat of silence, and then she lets out this loud, long-suffering sigh. "Finish that up and follow me."

I STARE DOWN at the Formica tabletop, stomach rolling once again. Even the sight of the crackers and ginger ale makes me want to blow chunks, but Ms. Crane just pushes them closer.

"Doesn't look it now, but it'll settle it," she assures, looking annoyed that she needs to. Her rooms are tidy and dimly lit, and I keep looking around, surprised to be invited in here. Ms. Crane isn't exactly the mothering type, but she has her rare moments. Unfortunately, I seem to have fallen prey to one of them. "You think you're the first soggy drunk I've had to nurse back to the land of the living?"

"I'm not drunk."

She flaps a hand until I warily crunch on the corner of a cracker. "I've seen worse. Once had a girl so strung out on dope that she looked possessed by a goddamn demon. Took a week to get her back to something coherent."

I gnaw on the cracker, wondering, "Yeah? And where is she now?"

Ms. Crane nods at the ginger ale. "She's running the Velvet Hideaway, evidently."

"Augustine?" I can't tell if my grimace results from the cracker hitting my stomach or the mention of Daniel's shiny new madam. "I didn't know she used to be a junkie."

"Some of my girls did," she responds, her eyes faraway. "Pimps like that, you know. Get a girl hooked on dope, and you've got yourself a nice little pet. You can pay them with it, punish them with it, keep them on a short leash with it."

"Your old man used to do that to his girls?" Usually, I wouldn't ask her about Mr. Crane, but usually I also wouldn't be in her private rooms. The questions never do anything but put her in a shitty mood, which I guess is understandable. When you stab your husband to death, you probably want to just forget he ever existed. But their old setup was a thing of legend, and even though Mr. Crane owned the operation, Ms. Crane was the icon behind it.

She doesn't look put off by the question, giving me a slight nod. "Oh, yes. No leash was beneath him. Can't even tell you how many beatings I took standing between him and whatever sorry new piece of stock he'd dragged in there."

Well, fuck.

Now *I'm* in a shitty mood.

It doesn't get any better when she adds, "She'd be good for you."

"Who?" I ask, even though I already know.

"My Auggy." She takes a slow, contemplative sip from her mug of coffee. "Tough girl. Disciplined. Hard worker. Someone you could trust. It's the only reason I could leave them all behind. I know my girls will be in good hands with her." Tipping her chin down, she tacks on a smug, "And she's had her eye on you since the first time you walked into my whorehouse, pierced little fuckface and all." She gives me a long, unimpressed glance. "Don't really see the draw, myself. But can't deny that the girl is smitten."

"I don't want Auggy." I say this in no uncertain terms. I could have had her years ago—I'm not a fucking idiot here. She may be charming and disciplined, but she's never been subtle. I've done my best not to be a complete dick about it, but the truth is, it got old quick.

"Of course you don't. Because you've got shit for brains." She sniffs, examining the rim of her mug. "At least she's not being hunted by some psycho who wants to axe murder any man who jams his prick into her cunt."

I snort. "Probably because no one has that many axes."

Her eyes flash, and on anyone else, it'd look like anger. "Look here, you rat-faced degenerate. There's nothing wrong with choosing what's safe. Sometimes that means working for Daniel Payne. Sometimes it means settling for someone who's stupid enough to care for you."

I give her a series of fast, surprised blinks. "I'm sorry, is this whole thing actually a cleverly-disguised expression of concern?"

She completely ignores this. "And what's it matter to you that my Auggy's got experience? That girl has skills that would bring you to your goddamn knees. Could suck a watermelon through a straw. And god knows Pollyanna up there isn't in any hurry to wrap those scrawny thighs around you."

Fucking *yikes.*

Ms. Crane has been out of the business for so long that it's easy to forget her girls were always more than products to her. I've never been able to tell if she sees them as daughters or as works of art she's crafted with her own two hands.

Either way, she's obviously insulted.

Gently, I begin, "Delores…" I can count the amount of times I've used Ms. Crane's first name on one hand, but it seems necessary here. She just basically tried to give me her best girl. Possibly that's a show of affection I'm not even prepared to calculate. "There's nothing wrong with Auggy. It's not even that she hustles, it's just—" I pause, realizing the words I want to say are going to sound stupid.

I can't imagine myself playing music for her.

I can't imagine watching her from across the room, or tucking her against me while we sleep, or pulling her into a bath and rubbing the tension from her shoulders as we smoke a blunt. I can't imagine fucking her and being overtaken by the urge to look into her eyes as I do it, worried that it'll be too exposed, but unable to give a shit. I can't imagine her ever being mine, and I can't imagine ever being hers.

Not like with Story.

Ms. Crane wouldn't get it. She's set her girls up with men before. Nice men who'd take care of them, treat them right, get them away from whoring—away from South Side. This offer is the highest compliment she could probably ever give me, because that's what relationships are to people like her; arrangements that are made because they're convenient and sensible. It's why Auggy wants me so much, because maybe she really is like a daughter to Ms. Crane, but she's also that piece of art that's been shaped by her worn, rough hands.

Carefully, I explain, "There's no spark there. If I let it happen, that's exactly what I'd be doing. Settling." I bitterly wonder, "Don't I do enough of that?"

Her mouth wrinkles up with a purse as she stares me down. I'm not sure what she sees on my face, but whatever it is makes that ember in her gaze disappear. "Yeah, you've got it real hard in your mansion, with your fancy schooling and rich friends." There's a curl in her lip when she slides her gaze toward the door, and I think at first it's meant for me. But then she says, "Living here has made us soft, rotten little shits, hasn't it?"

I bite another cracker. "Probably."

"How long you suppose it's been," she asks, eyes dark, "since you slept with your shoes on?"

I spare her a low chuckle. It's an old South Side meme by now, but no less accurate. People in the neighborhoods we come from sleep with their shoes on so they can bolt at a moment's notice. "Not since moving in here," I confess. But in a way, I was eased into it. Back when I slept over at Tristian's or Killer's houses, it felt wrong to go to sleep without my shoes, but more wrong to picture the looks they'd give me if I tried. After so long, it wasn't so difficult to conceptualize the line between safety and home, and the exact moment I was crossing over it. "You?"

She gives me a perplexed look. "I never stopped."

I'd suspected as much, but it still makes a heavy, disappointed weight settle in my gut. "Killer's right, you know. It might not be safe for you here, so if you need to leave—"

"I couldn't give two fucks about 'safe'," she sneers, pitching forward. "Wasn't a day in my life I ever was. I might be old and tired, but I'm not stupid. The second I walk out that door, I've got a bounty on my head. A dozen or more paranoid old men just waiting in the rafters for the chance to take my head off with one clean shot. You think I'm here because it scares me, boy?" She fixes me with a long, challenging stare. "I'm not scared to die. I made peace with my maker before you were even a stain on your mama's tattered bed sheets. Death is coming for me just as sure as it is you. All that matters now is what I'm dying for."

"Well, you sure as fuck didn't come here to die for us," I argue.

There's a suspended moment of silence as her gaze wanders to the distance, a pensive frown creasing her face. "I came here because I was sick of training South Side pussy for scum like Daniel Payne. Me and my girls worked hard building an empire we never had a chance of running. Knock one of them down, another pops up in his place." She flicks her hand in a sharp, frustrated gesture. "I can't keep stabbing men to death."

I snort. "Not with that attitude." It's the first time it occurs to me that maybe she didn't just kill her husband because he was a major league piece of shit. Maybe she thought she'd inherit it all, do it her own way.

And then Daniel had to swoop in and save her from prison.

That doesn't come cheap.

She continues, "Now we have some psycho running around killing women who work for Daniel. I'd rather fuck myself with a chainsaw than work for the likes of him again, but you listen to me, boy." She shakes a finger at me. "If something happens to Auggy, or any of my other girls, I'm going to be using those shoes I'm sleeping in to run my crusty old ass back to them, and none of you three are going to stop me. You hear?"

Ah, so this isn't just about me setting my sights on safer pussy.

She wants someone with Auggy. Someone who'll watch out for her, protect her, shelter her. It's such a fucking joke, because I've been stoned and drunk out of my mind for the past six weeks. Something heavy and alarming churns in my stomach at the realization that anything could have happened and I wouldn't have been in the position to stop it. Killer and Tristian were there to pick up my slack, but I wasn't protecting a goddamn thing. I was a weak link. A perforation.

Suddenly, I don't feel worthy of whatever approval was hidden within Ms. Crane's offer. I push my hair from my eyes, promising, "We'll try to keep a closer eye on the Hideaway. But whoever this guy is, I don't think he's interested in them. I think he just wants to piss us off." Looking up at her, I add, "So my showing an interest in Auggy will just make it worse for her."

She doesn't exactly seem relieved, but some of the tension fades from the lines in her face. "You don't care about that. You'd just rather be gunning for the pussy upstairs." Sniffing, she leans back into her seat. "Can't say I'm surprised. We don't got it in us to go for the simple stuff. She might be a lot of things, but easy isn't one of them."

"She fucking drives me crazy," I burst, thinking of those empty bottles of liquor. "She can't sleep, but she refuses to sleep with someone else, even though she's walking around here all day like a goddamn zombie. So now we have to…what, exactly? Fuck if I know. Prove ourselves or wait for her to come to her senses. It's fucking stupid. The whole point of having a Lady is that you don't have to play these games, but here I am, dancing like a goddamn monkey." I shove my fingers through my hair, too agitated to care about the bemused look Ms. Crane is giving me. "And you know what else? I'm the one who should be pissed at her. You heard what she did to me. Am I making her jump through hoops about it? Fuck no."

"I tried to tell you," she says, tapping her pack of cigarettes. "There's only so much a woman will take before she strikes back."

I don't need to notice the dark gleam in her eye to know she's talking about herself as much as she is about Story. "So what do I do?" I ask, realizing that Ms. Crane has, like, perspective here. "How do I wear her down?"

Snatching my empty ginger ale can away, she stands to walk it over to the garbage can, pitching it in. "She played your games for weeks, you sadistic fuckwit. You can't handle a little monkey dancing? Then maybe you *should* give Auggy a call. God, men are the biggest pussies. Everything we put up with from you, and you're bellyaching about a little—" She pauses, narrowing her eyes at me. "What does she want you to do?"

"Stay sober for three days."

On her way past, she lobs a sharp smack to the back of my head. "Get the fuck out of my kitchen."

I clutch my head, scowling. "I'm being serious!"

The glare she levels at me isn't anything but serious. "You want to know how to 'wear her down'? Here's the secret, you flaccid sack of meat. You don't. If you really cared about that girl, you'd try building her up for once. You think this is a game to her because that's how you and your rich pals work. She's not playing a game. She's trying to find one fucking crumb of something genuine from a bunch of boys who make it their business to be anything but." When she scoffs, looking away to mutter, "Eat my goddamn crackers and shut your mouth," I know she's letting it drop.

Mostly.

For the next ten minutes, I let her berate me for being soft. For not being 'South Side' enough. For being too big of an asshole to women. For being a pussy. For claiming that I don't want to settle, but then bitching about having to work for what I want. For living with the likes of a Mercer and a Payne, and accepting their scraps like a stray dog. I take it like a man, because I know it's something I need to hear. I don't belong in their world any more than they've ever belonged in mine. But what Ms. Crane doesn't understand about us is that we don't need to. We'll make our own world.

And I'm going to make damn sure Story is a part of it.

Even if it kills me.

6

PROSPECTS

"Nine dollars an hour?"

The barista shifts his green visor, nodding. He doesn't stop working while he talks to me. It's the Sunday lunch hour at the local coffee joint, and if this is what it's like during a holiday weekend, then what the *hell* is it going to be like when all the students are on campus? As if reading my mind, he adds, "It's more than minimum wage." He doesn't sound pleased about it, either. "I can give you twenty hours a week."

I wince at both the number of hours and the wage. The guys are being cool about me finding a job, even suggesting this place, but I doubt they want me spending too many hours away from them. Being a Lady is an obligation I agreed to—it covers my room and board. Even if I could spare the time between classes and frat duties, making less than $180 a week after taxes isn't even close to being enough to pay my tuition. I need to face the facts here. No entry-level job is going to be.

How are people supposed to lead straight, moral, legal lives when this is the alternative?

My stomach sinks.

"The application is online," he says, moving to the next customer. "I plan on filling the position by the end of the week."

I give him a wan smile, saying, "Thanks," but I already know I'm not going to apply. Turning, I freeze at the sight of Tristian and Dimitri occupying a table in the corner near the window. I was expecting them to just drop me off and go do their own thing, but instead, they're huddled close around Tristian's opened laptop.

When I approach, I realize why.

Killian is on the screen.

Narrowing my eyes, I take a moment to process my irritation, but slowly let the tension slip from my shoulders. They're closer than ever now when we're away from home. Killian has spent less time in the weight room recovering from his injury and more time scanning the area for potential threats. And sometimes I think my wanting to go out is the only thing that's pulled Dimitri from his dark, smoky bedroom these past few weeks.

"How did it go?" Tristian asks, standing up and pulling the chair between them out for me. I notice a plastic takeaway container, but don't blink at it. I've gotten used to Tristian bringing his own food wherever we go.

"Not great." I eye my brother's image on the monitor. From the looks of the background, he's in a brightly lit hotel room, the bed already tidy behind him. Idly, I wonder if he woke up and made it himself, or if he just never went to sleep at all. "There are jobs around, but the pay and hours are shitty." I slump against the back of the chair. "The only way I'm going to afford tuition is if I go work at the Velvet Hideaway."

"Don't even joke about that." Killian's tone is hard, even over the tinny speaker. It takes a moment for some of that stony anger to bleed from his features, but Dimitri's sharp gaze is still burning into me at the words. "There's another solution to this. You're just refusing to take it."

"You're right. I am refusing to take it." I hold my stepbrother's eye. This is the first real conversation we've had since Thanksgiving, and after worrying for two days whether or not the sex in the office was going to complicate things between us again, I'm relieved to find it still comes easy to insist, "You're not paying for my education. It's no different from taking the money from Daniel."

"It's not Daniel's money, it's Lords' money," Tristian says, pushing his food toward me. He's not ordering for me anymore, but whenever he gets the opportunity, he 'shares' his meals with me. Reluctantly, I pick up a slice of avocado and pop it in my mouth. "It's at our discretion to use. We'll just have a few less house parties."

I shake my head. "No. I want to do this on my own." There's no way Daniel hasn't had some hand in making the frat's money.

Dimitri's eyes track something across the shop, but I'm so distracted by the rare sight of them, clear and alert, that I almost miss his mutter. "Fuck. What the hell does this joker want?"

I follow his gaze and watch a guy coming our way. An instinctive wave of rage and nausea rolls over me, but I don't know why at first. I just know that face—those cheekbones—and the lip curled into a smirk. Unthinkingly, like an instinct, I lean into Dimitri's side.

There's a moment of tense, silent stillness, and then Dimitri is draping his arm over my shoulders and tucking me close.

His long fingers toy with my hair. "It's okay, baby," he says quietly. "Even though it looks like Nick, it's not. That's Simon, his brother."

The instant he says it, it all clicks. Why looking at him invokes memories of that day at the Hideaway. The way it suddenly feels like there are too many eyes in here. The instinct to hide behind Dimitri. At first glance, this man looks nothing like Nick. He's darker-skinned and cleaner-cut, possibly older. But the closer I look, the more obvious it is. Their eyes are exactly the same. The structure of their faces. Even the way he holds himself is just like Nick, broad shoulders a perfect line, chin lifting as he surveys the three of us.

His hooded sweatshirt is emblazoned with Greek letters. DKS.

"Pretty Nick's brother is a *Duke*?" I ask, stunned.

"Simon? No," Killian answers, snorting. "He's just a regular frat boy." I look at Simon again and feel like disagreeing. He may just be a frat boy now, but there's an edge to him. An authority. It's familiar because I live with it every day. This guy has aspirations.

"What do you want, Sy?" Tristian asks before he reaches the table.

"Why do you think I want something?" he asks, strolling up. He even sounds like Nick, his voice a perfect deadpan. "I can't just come by and say hello? Inquire about Killian's health? Nick says he took a pretty bad hit." I realize instantly that this Simon fellow couldn't care less about Killian. It's the air of superiority he holds himself with, but also the boredom in his stare, like it's a second away from wandering to something more interesting.

Killian answers from the speaker, "It's healing," and the guy—Simon—doesn't flinch at the realization he's on the other side of the screen.

Smoothly, he adds, "Well, good job standing up to your dick of a father. I've been trying to get my wayward little brother away from him since high school. Maybe seeing his idol taken down a notch will make him see sense." His eyes dart over to me. "But dealing with family is always a bitch, right?" Being under the weight of his stare is unnerving—far too intense a thing—but it doesn't last long. He lives up to his brother's descriptor: Pretty. But unlike Nick, Simon works for his prettiness. His jaw line is perfectly stubbled. It's not the look of someone who's a few days behind a shave. It's the look of someone who intentionally keeps it that length—immaculately, maybe even compulsively. I bet he's the same way with the tidily trimmed sides of his hair, even though the curl in the longer, top part is clearly natural. Biracial, would be my guess. It makes me wonder about him and Nick. Which parent do they share?

"Spit out whatever you came over here to say, Sy," Dimitri says, arm tightening, "or leave."

Simon watches us for a moment, face giving nothing away. "We need to know if you're in for the wrestling match." Again, his eyes wander over to me. "The deadline was yesterday, but since our houses are...*amicable*, we wanted to give you notice, considering you've been occupied."

"Wrestling match?" I whisper to Dimitri.

He shakes his head dismissively. "Nah, LDZ isn't doing the match this year."

"Is that so?" Simon stares me down, unbothered by the way it makes me tense. "Because there are a lot of rumors going around about your Lady. Bets are already in her favor."

"Bets?" I say, looking between Tristian and Dimitri. "Why do I feel like I'm missing something important? What does a wrestling match have to do with me?" There should really be a frat event handbook or day planner or something. I'm getting tired of being blindsided.

"It's just a dumb Royal tradition," Tristian says, giving me a look. "A bunch of chicks get into a ring and wrestle for a shitty tiara. They call it Screw Year's Eve, but still try to brand it as some silly charity thing. Nothing you'd want to do, trust me." When I don't look convinced, he adds, "Like everything else at Forsyth, even holidays are marked and branded. The Dukes get New Year's Eve. The Princes, naturally, claim Valentine's Day."

Killian scoffs. "Naturally," and then Simon arches a brow, echoing, "*Naturally.*"

"The Counts throw a big ass barbeque on the Fourth of July," Tristian continues.

Dimitri jumps in, "The Barons claimed Halloween."

"Obviously," Killian says with a hint of annoyance.

"What about us?" I ask.

"Oh," Tristian's face lights up. "We get the big one: Christmas."

It's a lot to absorb, and that's probably Tristian's point—distraction. I get us back on topic.

"Is this something I'm supposed to do? One of the Lady's duties?" The three of them don't respond, so I look at Simon. "Are the other Royal women participating?"

Simon is far more stoic than his brother, glancing at the others before answering. It occurs to me that he's seeking permission. "Of course they are. The gate goes toward the winning frat's charity, and Screw Year's Eve brings in a huge crowd." His mouth curls up into a dark, lopsided grin. "Don't tell the Duchess, but all things considered, the Countess is the one to beat. Word on the street is you've got beef."

"You mean Sutton," I clarify.

"The one and lonely."

Leaning forward out of Dimitri's embrace, my interest is piqued. "And I'd have to...wrestle her."

Simon stares at me. "That's the plan."

"Violently."

Simon's smile grows, but it's Killian who answers. "Story, there isn't any reas—"

Reaching over, I slam the laptop shut. "And you say there'll be gambling? How much will the winning wrestler get?"

Simon shrugs. "Last year it got up to fifty Gs."

"Story," Dimitri says, pitching forward to tuck me back against him. "We're not going to make you do this."

"Make me wrestle Sutton in front of all the house royalty?" I stare at him bug-eyed. "Hell, I'd do that for free."

Simon gestures to me with his cup of coffee. "See? Your girl's got the spirit."

"She's not a girl," Tristian snaps. "She's our Lady."

I cut him a glare. "You're right. And this is one of my responsibilities. Just because we've changed some parameters of my contract doesn't mean I don't want to help when I'm supposed to. Especially with the charity work." And especially when it means pounding my fist into the Cuntess' face. I still owe her one for kidnapping me and offering me up on a platter to that rapist, Perez. I nod to Simon. "Sign me up."

He gives me one of those raised chin nods, saying, "Smart Lady," before sauntering away.

Neither of them look happy.

"You shouldn't have done that," Tristian says. "I'll talk to one of the Dukes and get them to take your name off the list."

"Why?" Hotly, I insist, "It's for a good cause, and it'll earn me money. I want to do it!"

Tristian growls, "Well, we don't fucking want you to."

There was a time that tone in Tristian's voice—low, full of threat—would cow me. Now it just makes my hackles rise. "Why the hell not?"

It's Dimitri who answers, and I realize now how still and rigid he's become. "Jesus, don't you get it? Watching you traipsing around like that in front of all those fuckers?"

"Like what? Dressed up in some slutty costume or something?" I roll my eyes. "I'm not stupid, Dimitri. If it's not exploitive, it wouldn't be the Royals' brand."

"It's not just wrestling," Tristian says. "It's Jell-O wrestling."

"Slicked up, string-bikini, tits out, hot pants, bullshit wrestling," Dimitri adds, flopping back in his seat with a glower. "No one watches it for the wrestling, Story. It's just your run-of-the-mill spank bank fodder."

"And you're not going to be a part of it." Tristian shoots me a pointed look and opens the laptop, his tone brooking no argument.

My instinct is to argue anyway, but I'm coming at this all wrong. They don't want to share me, and frankly, I don't want to be shared. But this is *it*. This is the thing I need to get ahead—not just financially, but in this whole sick, twisted world of Forsyth. I reach out to touch Tristian's arm, just letting my hand rest there, and he freezes. Calmly, I ask him, "Do you think I can beat Sutton? Be honest."

He flicks his gaze from my hand to my eyes, lips parting. "Do I think you could beat Sutton?" Tristian finally concedes, "Well, obviously, but—"

"Then let me do it," I plead, knowing full well what I'm doing with my eyes. "Let me get my revenge on that skank, and you can make sure the winner's pot is nice and fat."

"No." Dimitri's voice rings with finality, and while it'd be easy to sway Tristian with a little affection and eyelash batting, Dimitri isn't so easily manipulated. He rubs the bridge of his nose, eyes clenched shut. "You're not doing it. That's final."

Crossing my arms, I level him with a look. "How many times do I need to remind you that I'm not your poodle?"

He goes still, sliding his dark, stormy gaze to mine. I know before his lips even part that I'm not going to like what he says next. It's in the razor-sharp gleam of his stare. "I don't know, Story. How many times am I going to have to step between you and a room full of sweaty, horny assholes?"

It hits just like he wants it to, a twist in my gut, a blade slicing into my skin, a grip around my lungs. I try not to let it show, but I'm not like them. My armor is new and feeble, and I see my reaction reflected in the twitch of his throat.

"Rath," Tristian says, voice full of warning.

"Fuck this," he mutters, lurching from his seat. "My head hurts. I'll be waiting in the truck."

I watch blankly as he leaves the shop, and it doesn't matter how much I refuse to feel guilty for what happened that day at the Velvet Hideaway. It still churns hot in my stomach.

LATER THAT NIGHT, the two of us are in the den running through a list of suspects, and coffee is the only thing keeping me lucid. It isn't until my fifth cup that Tristian's eye twitches. He watched me down the first four without blinking an eye. But this, it seems, finally makes him crack.

"What is that?" he asks, trying to seem barely interested. "Your fourth cup?"

I take a sip of the coffee. "Fifth."

"Hm." He taps at some keys on the laptop, not raising his gaze. "It's pretty late in the day for that much caffeine." The words come out dripping with disapproval, but he tacks on a hasty, "It would be for *me*, at least."

I stare at him as I take a slower sip. "It doesn't bother me."

"Hm," he says again, and then, "Hmm."

Hum all you want.

"So who is this guy?" I ask, pointing to a name on the spreadsheet. Dimitri should be here with us, but he'd begged off as soon as we arrived home, citing a migraine, and disappeared into his room again. It's probably a good thing my thoughts are thick and muddied with exhaustion, else I'd be fixating on what he's doing up there. Probably getting drunk or high. Running into him yesterday with all that liquor made it clear he hasn't been bothered about my offer.

Idly, I wonder if he'd answer my call tonight.

"Lionel Lucia," Tristian reads, looking almost as tired as I feel. "He's another King, fronting the Counts." Saul Cartwright from the Dukes is below him, and then two others, presumably the Kings of the Barons and Princes. "The Kings make our house disputes look petty in comparison. Imagine a shit head like Perez with all the resources of one of these guys at his disposal. We're talking CEOs of Fortune 500 companies, state government, brokerage firms that can manipulate any commodity…"

I shiver at the thought. Perez had been behind my kidnapping—he'd planned on raping me. "So these guys are pretty bad, huh?"

Tristian tilts his head, forehead creased in thought. "Bad? Who's to say? Life will get a lot easier for you when you realize there's no such thing as good and bad. The world isn't black and white, Story."

Steaming hot take there from Tristian Mercer.

"Whatever," I sigh, leaning in close to get a better look. His arm comes around me, loose but solid, and I swallow hard. "They're like, enemies, though, right?"

"Kind of," he answers, thumbing at my hip in a thoughtless motion. "Old beefs carry over, so sometimes there are alliances. Other times, it's kill or be killed. The Lords have always been at odds with the Counts, though." He taps the screen. "Lionel Lucia makes Perez look like a harmless infant, but the problem is, he's never quiet about it. Lucia's the kind of guy who'd brag. This cloak and dagger shtick isn't his style." He raises an eyebrow. "It's really more Daniel's."

"Someone really wants us to think this is Daniel."

He agrees, "And someone really wants Daniel to think we're striking back." He blows out a hard breath, clicking around the cells. "But none of these are jumping out at me. Maybe we're looking at this all wrong."

"Wrong, how?" I ask.

"We're assuming this is someone tied to Daniel, but what if it's someone tied to you?" He turns to look at me, his blue eyes boring into mine. "Or someone tied to your mom, even. An old boyfriend? A pervy john?"

I grimace, thinking back. "Before Daniel, I don't really remember my mom dating anyone. She had some repeat clients, but—"

"Okay," he interrupts, fingers poised over the keys. "What do you remember?"

It's admittedly not much. My mom always tried to keep me out of that part of her life, even when she was forced to cart me around with her. There were quiet men, loud men, mean men, sometimes even kind men. "Most of her clients were one-offs, but there were a few bread-and-butter types—men that mom could always count on for a dependable cash flow." It feels weird to talk about so casually, like I'm bringing some dark, dirty secret into an unbearably bright light.

Tristian doesn't even blink at the words, however. "Anyone in particular? This person would need to be wealthy, have connections."

I snort. "She didn't really attract that kind of clientele. Daniel was the flashiest guy she ever landed, I guarantee you."

This just piques his interest more. "Someone cheap like that…she'd probably have a pimp, right?"

I wince at the word—*cheap*—but he's not wrong. "Once, I think, when I was really young. I don't remember anything about him. I just know it left an impression. She was willing to take the drop in exposure if it meant being…uh, freelance." He does me the courtesy of not laughing at the term.

"Well, if you remember something, write it down." I watch as he makes a column for 'Posey' and then one for 'Story'. "How about your old sugar daddies? The chances of some rich, old perv latching onto you is the most obvious option."

"Like Cartwright?" I ask, still remembering that brief encounter with him in the athletic department. He'd played dumb, like he didn't recognize me, but I don't trust any of these men.

"He's still a possibility, but he'd need a mole on the inside." Tristian rubs his fingers over his mouth as he looks over the spreadsheet. "That's what this column is for." He nods at the screen, musing, "These are people who could be accomplices."

Some of the names on the list surprise me. "Martin? Really?"

Tristian cuts me a look. "Would you trust a lawyer?"

Wrapping my arms around my middle, I admit, "I'm not sure I'd trust anyone at this point."

"Exactly."

"Wait," I say, zeroing in on another name. "Augustine? The girl who works at the Hideaway?"

"The girl who *runs* the Hideaway," he corrects. "She probably has more connections than eighty percent of this list. Plus, there's all that drama with Rath."

My eyes jerk up. "What drama with Rath?"

Tristian waves a hand. "Augustine's been chasing his dick since high school. Girl's got it bad, but he keeps letting her down easy." Shaking his head, he adds, "A torch like that's probably exploitable."

I take in this information, remembering snippets of our interactions.

Tell Rath there's always an open invitation…

For some reason, the first thing that comes to mind is, "She's really pretty." I can't imagine Rath turning down someone like Augustine. She's not just 'pretty'. She moves, speaks, and breathes like sex personified. She's someone I could never be, and suddenly I'm struck by something sharp and hot, stinging like razor blades in my chest. It's something urgent and I don't really understand it at first.

Not until Tristian touches my chin, turning my gaze to his. Gently, he says, "Not as pretty as you," and I realize that's what it is. Not jealousy. Just this burning certainty that if push came to shove, I couldn't measure up. It's the same way I feel whenever I see that tattoo on Killian's arm. Tristian's thumb sweeps against my chin as he searches my eyes. "Go talk to him, sweetheart."

I bite my lip, considering. "I don't think he'd want me to."

"Because of what he said earlier?" The problem here is that Dimitri was partly right. I keep digging myself into these…*situations*. I stand by the fact the wrestling thing is a good idea, but at some point, maybe I do have to consider this becoming a pattern. Tristian's mouth tightens. "Don't let that get to you. He's just a cranky shit on account of being sober for three days straight."

Everything screeches to a standstill. "What?"

"You haven't noticed?" Tristian's eyes follow his fingers as they reach for my hair, sweeping it over my shoulder. "He's been clean as a fucking whistle since Thanksgiving morning. Between you and me, sometimes it's all I can do to not force something down his throat. Rath and detox go together like gasoline fumes and a Zippo. Don't take it too personally."

I blink at him, trying to reorient myself. "Are you…sure? Because I saw him yesterday coming down the stairs with a lot of booze."

Tristian rolls his eyes, running a fingertip over my exposed neck. "Come on, you know Rath. Anything worth doing is worth doing in the most dramatic way possible. Apparently, you can't sober up for a few days without pouring all of someone else's liquor down the sink. That bottle of whiskey was fifteen years old, by the way. Although," he adds, eyes narrowing, "it will be nice to open the liquor cabinet and find it not-empty for once."

"Three days," I realize. "He's been sober for three days."

Tristian arches an eyebrow. "He can, on occasion, do that."

There's a flash of surprise in his eyes when I lean forward to kiss him, but it's quickly hidden by the way they darken, falling shut as he cups my neck. I know he wants more—all of them do, all the time—and it's made obvious by the way he chases me when I pull away, rising to my feet.

I tap my thigh, feeling fidgety. "Thank you." He doesn't ask what for, just stares up at me with this glazed, dumbfounded expression. "I think…I'm going to go talk to him."

Tristian blinks. "Okay."

I nod back. "Okay."

But the entire way up the stairs, I just feel anxious and guilty. I don't feel much better about it when I'm standing in front of his door, rapping my knuckles against the wood. For a moment, I hear nothing, and I worry he'll just ignore it. But then there's a small, quiet series of thumps.

The door swings open and he's standing there, shirtless and disheveled, eyes heavy with sleep. "What?"

It's not said unkindly, but it still makes me shrink into myself a bit. "You were sleeping?"

He rakes his fingers through his hair, visibly trying to rouse himself. Behind him, the room is shrouded in darkness. "Headache," he rasps, scrubbing a hand down his face. "Sometimes sleeping helps."

My chest twists even further, remembering what he told me that day in his bathtub. Darkness and weed is what he'd usually use to alleviate his headaches.

But he's sober.

For me.

"Did it work?" I ask, wincing.

"Not really."

A long beat passes between us, neither of us wanting to admit to what we really want. Really *need*. But the truth is that I'm the reason he feels like shit. He did this for me, and the fact he hasn't shoved it in my face tells me it's about something more than getting me back in his bed.

If Dimitri Rathbone can give up his crutch for me, well, then it's time I give something up for him, and right now that something is my stubborn pride.

"Maybe I can help," I suggest.

His eyes hold mine for another lingering moment. "Yeah, maybe you can." He pushes the door wider and steps aside.

As I step over the threshold, it's not lost on me that Dimitri has given me the choice. He made me decide, just like I demanded.

I think it's time for me to show him how much I appreciate that.

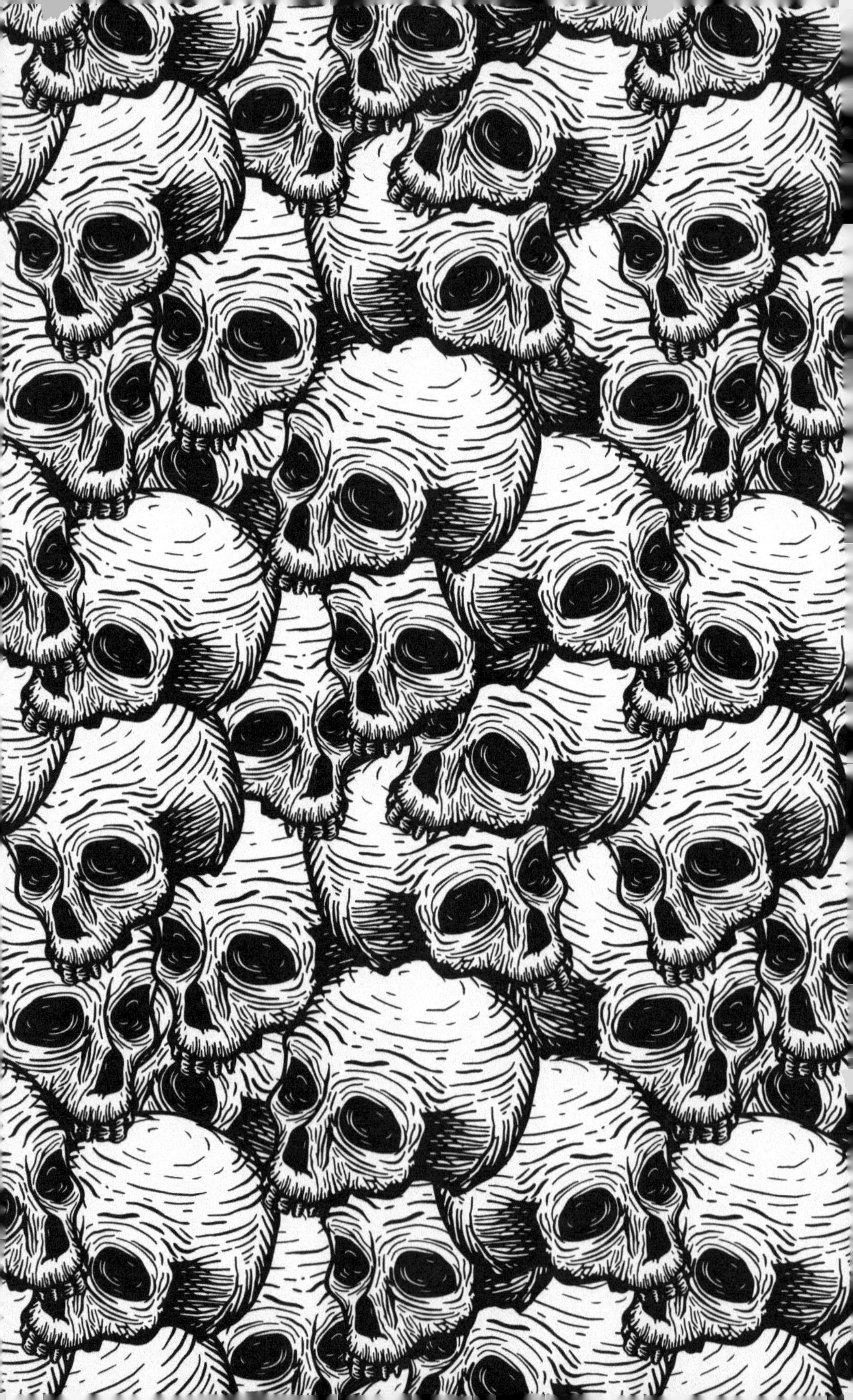

7

GRIM SYMPHONY

I WATCH AS she takes in the room, reaching up to card my fingers through my messy hair. I still feel groggy, thoughts like sludge, but I can tell she's surprised. I'd cleaned everything within an inch of its life—Killer would be so proud, and he can *never fucking know*—only partially because it was such a sty. Mostly, it just kept my hands and mind occupied.

"Wow," she breathes, eyes taking in the space. "You've been busy."

"You don't need to sound so shocked," I say, walking past her to the bed. There's this way shit goes kind of sideways when I'm close to her. No one else has ever made me feel like that—annoyed and tender, all at the same time. As I pass, I reach out to graze her hip, just a little greeting so she'll know what this is.

No hard feelings, girl.

Surprise registers, once again, in the flash of her eyes, and she's not alone. Holding grudges is sort of my thing, but with her? I'm so non-stick, she could fry an egg on me.

"You should have told me." When I turn to her, she's got her head tilted, scrutinizing me. "I didn't realize you'd—I mean, I knew you'd cut back, at the very least, but you've been sober for days now."

I give a loose shrug. "I'm not really the bragging type."

Her eyes narrow. "Yes, you are."

Another shrug. "Yeah, I am."

She shifts her weight and crosses her arms, but aborts the gesture, letting her arms hang awkwardly at her sides. "You really don't want me to wrestle?"

"Would it matter?" I might not be holding a grudge, but the thought of it still makes my blood simmer. It's not all about the wrestling. Most of it's about the memory of the pit and all those fucking perverts taking a piece of what's mine. *Ours.* "If I asked you not to do it, would you change your mind?"

"Honestly?" she asks, giving me a hapless look. "I don't know."

Well, that's a surprise. She's well within her rights—legal and otherwise—to do what she wants now. I gave her a 'final answer' because old habits die hard, but I'm not stupid. It doesn't actually mean anything anymore.

Only it's possible it does.

But she's gazing up at me with those wide, guileless eyes, and I see it for what it is: a sort of plea. She's begging me not to make her find out, because there's fear there, too. She doesn't want to face the fact she might care, might cave, and doesn't want to give me that power.

I approach her, documenting the subtle changes in her expression. Her eyes flick down to my chest, lower, and then ping back up. When I reach for her wrist, she lets me take it and doesn't move away when I lean in close, grazing our cheeks together. "Only if I can be there with you."

I'm not sure if it's the low murmur or my breath hitting her ear, but she shivers. "Of course you'll be there with me. If you want to."

Humming, I skate my fingertips up her arm, reveling in this newly earned ability to touch. "And you're here to…what, exactly? Show your appreciation? Make good on your offer?"

Her throat clicks with a swallow. "I keep my word."

"I bet you do." Her jaw is soft and warm beneath my lips, but I don't kiss the skin. I just rest my mouth there, speaking against it. "What was the deal, again? That you'd sleep in my bed?"

Her jaw twitches beneath my lips when she answers. "Yes."

"And where am I sleeping in this arrangement?" My fingers reach the strap of her tank top and I inch one beneath it, sliding it up and down. Up and down.

Her chest contracts and expands. "Beside me."

"And what are we wearing in this—"

In a move more swift and assured than I think she's capable of, she twists her head and pushes her mouth against mine. Always surprising me, this one. Her mouth is warm and aggressive, brow furled in an expression that looks all frustrated and surly. She's never been good at taking the initiative—at taking what she wants—but she's fumbling her way for it, anyway. She puts her hand on my chest and it feels cold, or maybe my skin is just overheated, but I wind the strap of her tank top around two fingers and use it to yank her closer, plunging my tongue into her wet mouth.

She makes a breathless noise and tips her face to me, letting me take charge of the kiss. No, *requesting* that I take charge of the kiss. It's the only reason I pull back.

"Aren't you tired?" I give her an out because I suspect this isn't really about showing 'appreciation'. I just wonder if she can do it. Can she fuck someone without it being repayment, or reward, or obligation, or the threat of something worse looming over her head? The way she's looking at me, that flash of hunger beneath the small, timid gestures…can she make it about want, about desire, about *us* and nothing else? Because make no mistake about it, the next time I fuck this girl, it's going to be because she's fucking *aching* for it. No terms. No manipulations. No forced situations. Just us.

From the way her mouth purses, she thinks I'm being a tease. "Am I tired? Right now?" Her hand slides down my chest, over my abs, hooking into the waist of my jeans. My stomach caves at the tickle of her knuckles as she fiddles with the fly, popping it open. "Not particularly."

I stand still and just watch as she fumbles with her instincts, throat bobbing with a gulp as she grabs my waistband and gently hitches it down. She pauses in fits and starts, like she's expecting me to protest.

I arch an eyebrow, willing to see where this leads.

Her lip gets caught between her teeth as she casts those big eyes down, gaze tracking each slowly exposed inch of skin. She stutters to a stop when my cock appears, springing free. I've been hard since before she even knocked on my door. My dreams have been full of the promise of the panties I'd absconded with this morning and everything I planned to do with them later.

It's looking like that might not be necessary.

But it's not until she drops to her knees, her palm curling around my shaft, that I begin to actually let myself hope. I've never been the optimistic type. I figured the best I could count on tonight might be something that couldn't be referred to as cuddling by anyone who wanted to keep all their digits, but let's face it, totally fucking would be.

I hook a finger under her chin, forcing her eyes to mine. For a long moment, I just look, searching for a clue. When all I find are her dark, steady eyes, I quietly ask, "You want my cock, baby?" She answers by pitching forward and running her tongue over the swollen head, never breaking our stare. My jaw clenches at the feeling, and it'd be easy to feed her my cock, to tell myself she's on her knees because she's hungry for it, but it's not enough. "Tell me."

"Dimitri." She speaks with her lips right against the head of my dick. "I've wanted it for weeks." Her fingers blaze a trail down my thigh, and then she sinks her mouth onto me. It's so fucking toe-curling that I let out a long hiss, watching myself disappear between her lips. She goes and goes, and she doesn't stop, pushing me deep into the back of her throat and resting there.

It takes me so long to gain any semblance of equilibrium that by the time I do, her face is red. "Goddamn, girl." I wind my fingers into her hair, easing her back. "Hey, hey, I'm not Tristian."

She pulls back with a loud gasp, and her eyes, holy shit. They're all watery and wide, and it's true that choking girls on his dick is more Tristian's thing than mine. But with the way her eyes shine up at me?

Jesus fucking Christ.

Fine.

I see the appeal.

She takes me shallower, watching me as I watch her back, lips and tongue sliding up and down my dick. I know she's good at this. Even though I can see Tristian's deft hand in the bald fucking ambition of that deep throating, I'm the one who taught her how to suck cock—guided her, molded her, right here in this very room. I talked her into getting on her knees for me. Let the others watch from the camera in the corner as she fumbled, unskilled and uncertain. Made her ask for it, just like she did now, so I could maximize my point gain. And then I watched as she steadily grew more assured, learned the ways a man wanted to be sucked and touched and handled.

It was the first time I really felt like she was mine.

I pull her off my cock, so laser-focused that I don't even give myself time to admire the thread of spit leading from the head to her red lips. Instead, I haul her up and crash my mouth to hers, swallowing her soft, surprised sound, because this isn't a show. The camera is long gone. The only people here are the two of us, and I don't need *skilled* or *assured*.

I slide one hand under her hair and the other over her tit, squeezing, feeling out the pebble of her nipple. "Gonna let me fuck you?" I ask, finally tearing that strap over her shoulder. It's a frantic, barely-restrained movement that completely belies my words, because I'm already yanking half of her top below her chest and giving her breast a massage that's too rough, too impatient.

She's a stark contrast to it, her mouth gentle as it skitters over my jaw, lips finding a spot on my neck. "Maybe you'll let me fuck *you*."

I freeze, unaware that my dick could even get any harder. What the fuck?

"Can I?" she whispers, giving me this tiny little shove toward the bed. "Like you said, back when you told me your plans. You said—"

"I know what I said." I remember it like it was yesterday, Story between my legs as I edged her senseless, whispering dirty little things into her ear.

"I would have let you be on top…I was going to show you how to ride me, nice and slow. Let you set the pace."

I step back, kicking off my jeans as I go, and she watches with dazed eyes, hand still held halfway aloft, a moment suspended in time. I lie back on the bed, bared for her. Cock hard. Hands tucked behind my head. Waiting.

It takes her a second to get with the program, but when she does, there's no hesitation. She works her tank top off, tossing it aside, giving me a nice view of her perfect tits. I watch, enraptured as she shimmies her pants down her legs, panties and all. It makes me think of those early days, back in high school—days when she'd be shy about wearing something too tight, nights where she'd pull a cardigan around her middle, hiding all her womanly curves from our predatory eyes. Story's not that same shy teenage girl, though. Since living here, she's become unabashed about showing her body to the three of us. Baths, showers, hasty shirt exchanges—punishments—she rolls with it, uncaring, almost mechanical in her nudity.

When we were first rolling around the idea of making her our Lady, I used to have all these fantasies about what a future would be like with her in it. Living with us, catering to our every whim, our perfect, pale, irritated doll. She could do homework naked, a leg slung over the arm of a chair as she lounged back. Make phone calls topless. Eat dinner at the table, stark-ass nude. Come to bed naked, wake up naked, take a shower naked. She could just never put anything on, existing for us in a constant state of bare-bare-bare. It was a juvenile thought, some vestige of a tired, teenage daydream, but it still had some shine.

Now, I'm not sure if any of us have a future at all.

If we don't, we might as well enjoy the present.

I stay perfectly still as she knees herself up on the bed, slowly—fucking agonizingly slowly—crawling over me. Her tits look nice from this vantage and I enjoy the view, biting down a flinch as her long hair tickles over my thighs, hips, sides.

It must be a tease, the way she manages to not touch me in any significant way as she does this. I lick my lips and wait for her to engage, touch, anything—she could do *anything*, what will *she do*—and it's embarrassing how long I take to understand what this fizzy, frenetic thing inside my chest is.

Excitement.

She sits back, holding my gaze as she rests her center right on the hard, throbbing length of me. I can feel her wetness and heat without even having to thrust against her. That's one of the best parts of Story, that her body will always let me know what it's thinking.

Like how her cheeks have gone pink, or the quaver in her voice when she says, "It's weird being in here without music."

Unable to stand it anymore, I let my eyes descend, taking in the sight of her body mounting me. "Then I guess you need to make some." That's how it's been, my putting the phone on speaker at night, letting the sounds of her rushed breaths and small, tortured cries fill the space with our own melody. It'll be good to hear it without all the static between us, to watch as she makes it, to be the one to drag it out of her.

Usually I try to avoid looking at her scars. They always come with a rush of conflicting thoughts and one can't possibly reconcile with the other—guilty thrill, somber possessiveness. They're both hideous and breathtaking. But tonight, I let myself look. I let myself notice how the 'R' carved into her chest is a little thicker, deeper, than the 'K' and the 'T'. I let myself remember the way I'd felt that night, because nothing less would be fair. I told her once I couldn't bring myself to regret it, but it's not that simple.

Under her gaze, I prop myself up, ducking my head to press a kiss to the puckered skin. I can barely feel my initial beneath my lips, but if I close my eyes and focus, the raised skin is unmistakable. I turn my head, mouthing over her supple tit, and sightlessly find her nipple. She makes a soft noise as I wet it with my tongue, her hips rocking down into me, fingers tangling in my hair and pulling me close.

"Demanding," I mutter, finally taking her nipple into my mouth, but we both know I like it. I can feel the rush of wetness sliding over my twitching cock, seeking, waiting.

That first moment of pressure and hot-slick-tight as she sinks onto me makes me fall back, and I give in to the instinct to relish it. To watch her lips part. To see her eyelids grow heavy. To feel that sweet pussy finally taking me in, making me a part of her. To anchor her as she braces her hands on my chest, arms pushing her tits together as she rocks down, and I'm filled with one singular thought.

Thank fucking god I'm sober for this.

She exhales this little, "oh," when our bodies meet, my cock buried deep. For such a small sound, it's saying so much—that she's surprised at how good it feels, that she's overwhelmed with it, that she wants to take more.

I slide my palms up her thighs, my gaze raking over her body as my hips flex into her. "That feel good, baby?"

She nods, mouth still agape at the stretch. It's been a few days since she and Killian…and even longer before that. She's so tight that it makes my teeth clench with the urge to lift her, to feel that friction sliding up and down.

But I wait.

I wait for her to inhale and roll her hips, my body going rigid as she tests the connection, seats herself the way she likes. I wait and I let my hands roam, sliding up her ribs to cup her tits in my hands, but I can't keep them still. I grab her waist and reach around to squeeze her ass, her thighs, palm rubbing into the flat of her stomach like maybe I could feel the bulge from my cock, but even though my hands are restless and indecisive, my eyes watch her face. She looks fierce and soft, rocking into me as her fingertips curl against my chest.

My balls clench. "Goddamn, you're sexy."

Her hips stutter, but don't stop. The flush on her cheeks bleeds down, tinting her chest a vivid pink. "As sexy as Augustine?" she asks, voice small.

I'm so filled with the sensations of her, the scent of her hair, the heat of her eyes, that it takes me a long moment to process the words. When I do, I go still. "What?"

"Augustine," she repeats, and it's possible she tries to hide the shy, sad thing in her eyes, but she's not exactly successful. "Do you think—I mean, can I be as sexy as her?"

I lie there for a minute stumped, and not because I don't know the answer. I just have no fucking clue where this is coming from. "What does Augustine have to do with anything?"

"Nothing." She says it too quick, too flippant. "I just wondered."

Yeah, bullshit.

"Did Tristian tell you something?" It's not exactly a secret that Auggy's had her eye on me, but no one else around here would bring it up to Story.

She drags her lip through her teeth, her hips doing this little, unconscious roll that momentarily blanks my thoughts. "Nothing that isn't already obvious."

I stare at her, too stunned to form words, because this can't be jealousy.

Can it?

I know it's true when she averts her eyes, using that moment to lift and fall, whiting out all my sense with the drag of her pussy over my cock. Shooting out my hands, I grab her hips and still her, fighting back a shudder at the restraint it takes.

"Look at me," I demand, but when all I get is a quick flick of her eyes, I lever myself up, sliding a hand behind her neck. I pull her face to mine, forcing her to watch me say, "Auggy's sexy. She could probably get a man off with the tip of her pinky, and you wanna know why? Because she's a whore." At the furrow in her brow, I stress, "There's nothing wrong with that. It's just the way it is. I respect her hustle. But, baby…none of that's real." I brush her hair back from her cheek, letting my fingers linger against the soft skin below her jaw. "She couldn't hold a fucking candle to you."

Story watches me, eyes pinging back and forth between mine. "I've done…

things, for money," she whispers. Her mouth pulls into a self-deprecating slant. "And I wasn't even good at them."

I snort. "You were good at them because you *weren't* good at them." I don't need to see her brow knit to know how confusing that statement is. "You're real," I explain, pressing a kiss to her jaw. "Sometimes you're so real, it fucking hurts to look at you."

Blinking, she asks, "Why?"

"Because you make me…" My voice trails off, partly because I can feel her clenching around my dick, but partly because I don't think I can put it into words. "You make me wish I could be different. Do more. Be less. It's hard to explain." Laughing darkly, I add, "You called me empty once, but I have no fucking clue how. I feel so full of this shit that its gotta be bleeding from my ears."

She reaches up to touch my mouth, fingertips resting lightly on my lips. Frowning, she breathes, "I don't think you're empty."

"No?" I ask, raising an eyebrow. "What's all this about, anyway?" My fingers slide down her collarbone, trailing along her sternum. I graze my fingertips over the scar, tracing the letter I'd carved there. "You already know you're mine. Everyone does."

She chooses that moment to rock against me, her hips undulating in a short, lazy rhythm. "I am yours," she replies, winding her arms around my neck. "But you're not mine."

"What?" I'm already guiding her hips, distracted with the push and pull. "What are you talking about?"

"All of you," she clarifies, eyes falling closed as she rocks into me. "There's nothing tying you to me. Not really. You could—" Her lips part on a gasp when I push her down, grinding her against me. "Killian has that *girl* tattooed on his arm, and you have an actual *professional* after you. Any of you could go to someone else. There's nothing to stop you. Even the contract is just…" She doesn't finish, her pussy clenching around me.

"That's what this is about," I realize, breathing hard into the space between us. "You don't think I'm yours?" I want to tell her she's crazy, but I doubt it'd be taken very well. "You're the only girl any of us have fucked in months, and most of that was basically spent celibate and fucking miserable."

"Exactly." Her chest hitches, forehead screwing up in pleasure as she rides me. "Someone like Augustine wouldn't—you wouldn't ever be celibate or miserable—oh, god, Dimitri…" The last part results from me flopping back, planting my feet, and driving my dick into her hard.

"Look at me, baby." I wait for her to meet my stare before asking, "Do you want me to be yours?"

She rolls her hips when I push them, only to pull them back. "I-I don't—"

"Don't fucking lie to me." Sharper, I add, "Don't lie to yourself. Do you want me?"

There's a beat where I think she's not listening because her eyes are so glazed with the way I'm pushing my dick into her. But then she nods, voice quiet and ragged. "Yes."

The problem with this whole arrangement is that it's always been hard to know. She came back—she wanted to stay here, to be ours—but it was tied up in revenge and vengeance. Now that we're past that, there's a distinction to be made between being wanted and wanting.

It isn't until something barbed and tense unwinds in my chest that I realize how bleak I'd felt about it all. The things we've done to her… there's no taking them back. There's no changing them or turning them into something that isn't ugly. I figured they were much like those scars carved into her chest—a permanent mark of something mangled.

I shove my hand beneath my pillow, not having to fumble to find what I'm looking for. I've slept with it for weeks now, tucked beneath my head as I laid here, night after night in the silence and fog of too much liquor. I pull it out now, the blade glinting in the low light of the lamp, and Story freezes, thighs clenching.

Before she can react, I grab her wrist, pressing the knife into her palm.

She looks at it, still perfectly frozen. "What…?"

"Then do it," I demand, curling her fingers around the handle. "Right here."

Her eyes grow wide when I guide the tip of the blade to my chest—to the exact same place my initial is carved into hers. "Dimitri, I—I can't just—"

"Yes, you can." I let her hand go and clutch at her knees, bracing myself. "I did it to you, didn't I?"

There's a long pause where she just stares in bafflement at the blade against my skin. "You want me to cut you."

The answer comes out easily. "Yes."

"You want me to cut my initial into your skin."

Again, "Yes."

Her eyes jerk up to mine. "But it'll hurt."

I smirk. "Oh, baby girl. You say that like it'll put me off."

That makes her eyebrows climb a little higher, but she seems to disregard it. "The scar will be there forever."

I hold her gaze, willing her to see the gravity in mine. "That's the idea."

She lets out this short, disbelieving laugh. "You don't even know me."

I narrow my eyes, searching her face. "I know you want to do it, but you're scared. I know when you brush your hair, you look sad, like you're missing someone, or feeling nostalgic. I know you test Slytherin on every quiz you've ever taken, but swear up and down you're Gryffindor. I know you didn't like sweets half as much before you moved in with Tristian, and I know you can't get a full night's sleep because it freaks you out that none of us can watch over you. I know that, despite that, you'd rather hold your ground because you're god-awful stubborn." Running my thumbs over the dimples in her knees, I list, "You make bad decisions when people threaten you. You hate ska, but somehow like Sublime. You're curious about your dad, but figure the reality will never measure up to the dream, so you don't try to find him. You miss being places where no one knew you. You always sleep with a fan on, which is why Killer put one in his room, even though he despises the thought of dust blowing around. I know you noticed it, but pretended not to." Raising an eyebrow at her expression, I add, "I know that blush on your face right now has nothing to do with you sitting on my dick."

Her throat jumps with a swallow, eyes moving anxiously from the blade to my face, as if she's expecting me to reveal this whole thing is a prank. When I don't, she breathes, "You're serious."

"As a heart attack." Raking my lip through my teeth, I gently urge, "Come on, baby. Make me yours."

The shudder that goes through her body might be subtle, except I can feel it all around me. It's nearly as electrifying as the way the blade feels, finally piercing into my skin. She sucks in a short inhale at the bubble of blood, big eyes pinging to mine. "Are you…?"

"Keep going," I insist, staying still. "Make it deep." Wetting her lips, she returns her gaze to my chest, pressing the blade in deeper. "That's it," I breathe, going limp beneath the surge of endorphins. It makes my cock jump and I know she feels it—can tell by the way her lashes flutter—but she doesn't stop. Not even when the blood pools in the valley between my muscles.

Her breath is coming quick and shallow, and I don't need to see the tremor in her wrist to know she's afraid. Afraid of hurting me, perhaps, but more likely, afraid of what it means to have me.

To *really* have me.

The 'S' might be bigger than my 'R', but when she pulls back, ashen and slack-faced, I look at it and can't tell. There's too much blood to see the edges.

I lift a hand and run my fingers through it, smearing the blood across my skin.

Yours.

But instead of inspecting it, I reach up to slash a long line of scarlet across her parted lips. For a moment, she looks stunned, transfixed and frozen as I prod my bloody fingertips between her teeth, forcing her to taste me. I know she's lost when she lets me, a slave to this trance, just like I am. Slowly, I lean up, holding her gaze as I fuck my fingers into her mouth, pressing against her tongue, making her just as open and gruesome as we both know we should be.

And then I lick her.

Over her lips, around my fingers. Her tongue meets mine somewhere in the middle, sharing the taste as it rubs against my tongue in a grisly offering.

I grab the knife before rearing up and flipping her over. She lets out a startled yelp, but it's over just as fast as it begun, and then I'm gazing down at her, pressing our bloody chests together as I kiss the shocked noise from her mouth. The taste is sharp and bitter, a metallic edge that doesn't go away.

The way I look at her might be tender, but the first punch of my hips into hers is anything but. Her body jerks with the movement and she clings to me, brows collapsing in rapture. But she doesn't close her eyes. That's how I know she feels this too. This wild intensity running between us, the thrill of wanting and having.

Give me a masked man in a dark alley any day, because this?

This is terrifying.

"Don't stop." She lets out a whimper, fingernails digging into my shoulder blades as I pummel into her, and it'd be easy to pull it back, to give away less of myself, too close my eyes and hide the fact I want her so badly it fucking hurts.

But Ms. Crane was right. People like us can't do 'easy'.

So I grab her by the chin and make her see it—all of it. "There's never going to be anyone else for us. Do you understand that?"

She looks just as scared as I feel, breath bursting from her blood-stained lips with every body-jolting thrust. "You can't know that."

"Yes, I fucking can." I steal the kiss—there's no other word for it—forcing my tongue inside, making her take me as I fuck her. It's not how I wanted it to be. It's nothing like that soft, sleepy morning fuck I'd promised her all those weeks ago. What's happening here is all desperation and sharp edges, a grunt being pulled from my throat as my hips drive mindlessly into her body.

Somehow, it feels fated to be this way, though. Fast and rough and bloody.

It's how I know it's real.

She comes with a cry tearing from her chest and it makes me crazed, both hands reaching up to grab the headboard so I can get closer, dig deeper, batter her even harder. It's senseless, this notion that if I can just get enough of myself inside her, she'll never be able to exorcise it.

I realize she's made her way out of this maze of deranged lust when I see she's gone limp and passive. A strand of her hair has gotten caught on her lip and it billows away from her mouth as she pants into the space between us, eyes fixed sightlessly on mine. For once, I don't drag it out, the days and weeks of not being inside of her testing my limits in a different kind of way. Teeth clenched, I hiss, spine going stiff as I pump her full of my come. Maybe it's not the sweet morning sex I'd envisioned, but an energy shudders between us, and when she reaches up to sweep my hair back, it expands and ebbs, the crescendo of a grim symphony.

And then, its bittersweet coda.

She kisses me back just as sweetly as this was supposed to be, bringing me down from the brink with her sticky lips and soothing fingers. I think it's like that for a while, but my brain's too slow to notice, because all it cares about is not breaking this connection. My cock's going soft, but I keep surging against her cunt, keeping it burrowed inside.

We take a long time to catch our breath. Probably because we won't get another, our kisses turning slow and languid, but no less fervent. It isn't until Story turns her head to the side, gasping, leaving me to nip at her jaw, that I let myself roll away.

"Fuck me, that was worth the wait," I mutter, staring up at my ceiling. Normally, I'd reach for a cigarette or a bottle. Instead, I reach for her, ready for that very first post-sex cuddle.

Thwarting me, she bolts upright. "Oh my god! It looks like a massacre! Are you okay?!"

"I just had the best nut of my life," I tell her, stretching my arms above my head. "I'm fucking aces."

She assesses the bed, pulling the (formerly) white sheet to her breasts and using it to wipe away the smear of blood on her mouth. "Tristian is going to have a coronary if he finds out we did that!"

I snort. "Tristian? Ms. Crane will tan my hide if she sees this." I give the sheet a firm tug, ripping it out of her hands. I'm not ready for her to cover up. "I'm burning these. No one will ever know." Again, I reach for her, but she winces, catching herself before she falls into my side.

"We need to clean that. And us. And our mouths. Oh, god."

Catching her, I roll us so she's on her back, pinning her to the bed. "This isn't exactly the post-orgasmic glow I was hoping for. How are you squirming around like this? I was throwing you my very best in dicking downs, girl. You should be halfway comatose."

She pauses, tongue peeking out to wet her lips. "Sorry." She doesn't look sorry, though. She just looks bright-eyed and a little too wired. "It's not you. I just had, like, ten gallons of coffee tonight."

"You must have if that didn't fuck it out of you." Sighing, I roll away, heaving myself off the bed. "Fine. We'll clean up, then sleep."

But even after we've had a hasty wiping down and toothbrushing session, I'm still watching her fine ass zip around the room, stripping the bed, gnawing on a fingernail as she inspects the cut she'd made, jiggling her knee as she perches on the mattress and rubs ointment over the wound. I can tell she's grossed out by it from the way her forehead puckers, but the shine in her eyes as she flicks her gaze up to me fucking beams with satisfaction.

It's almost enough to chill her out.

Ten minutes later, we're laying in the dark, me wrapped around her, nose buried into her hair. I wasn't lying before. That was an epic fuck—easily the best I've ever had. It's still zinging through my veins, filling my head with sounds and melodies. But here, with her, it's quiet.

Except for the rustle of sheets as she fidgets.

"You're still not tired?"

"Not really." She shrugs and looks back at me, giving me an apologetic smile. When she whispers, "It's so quiet," it's such a perfect mirror to my own thoughts that I press a laugh into her neck. If things were different, I'd get out a blunt and blow her as many shotguns as she needed to finally settle down. I've already won both the challenge and the prize. There's nothing stopping me.

But maybe I can cool it for a little while longer.

She squirms again, rolling to her back and looking across the room. "Maybe if you," her voice is quiet, timid, "played something for me?"

I follow her gaze to the piano, and my fingers twitch instinctively. It happens every time I look at or walk by it. Groaning, I push my hair back. "Fuck, Story."

"Please?" She leans into me, her bare chest drawing my gaze to the scar, the letters that mark her as ours. "I miss hearing you play. It always gives me good dreams."

I look at her, waiting for that ball of dread to rise in my stomach at the thought of pressing the keys. But whatever transpired at the performance between us was over. She hurt me. I hurt her. She made music for me. She made music *on* me.

Relenting, I lift her chin. "For you," I kiss her mouth before climbing from the bed, "anything."

8

H E R   L O R D

THE TEAM GETS back late, so the house is already dark and quiet when I climb the stairs to my room. It's been a shitty away game trip, a worthless stretch of time that included twiddling my thumbs and spending too long stewing in my own thoughts. My skin feels stretched too tight, and even though I spent most of the trip itching to get back, the second I reach the familiar hallway, something heavy settles in the base of my spine like a burden.

The first thing I do is check Story's doorknob. To my shock, it's actually unlocked, although it may not have mattered. I've been pissed for twenty-four-hours, filled with visions of me giving this fucking doorknob a nice snap, violating the locked-door rule once and for all. Now maybe I don't have to.

I resent the way my chest goes light finding this, as if she's gifted me something precious and shiny: admittance. I don't have time to dwell on the things I'm going to do once I'm inside, because the feeling doesn't last long.

Her bed is empty.

I know from the tracker she's home, but it's not great at pinpointing her location inside the house. I toss my bag in my room and head to the third floor, listening carefully for signs of life. What I get is the sound of voices floating from Tristian's room. I tap the door with my sore knuckles, but don't give him a chance to respond before pushing it open. He's lying back on the bed, shirtless. His lower body is covered by a sheet, a laptop resting on his thighs, and it doesn't matter that he closes it the instant he spots me. The sounds of the video he's watching are unmistakable. I may have watched it a couple times myself, closed up in my room, hand flying over my dick as I watched Rath pounding into Story. Unlike Tristian, I watch it muted. The sounds of the pit make my dick soft.

He lifts his chin in greeting, seeming unbothered by the interruption. "You're back."

"Yeah. It was a long trip." I rub the back of my neck and wince at the pain in my fist.

If he notices, he doesn't mention it, but adds, "Especially when you're side-lined." I've only got one question, and he already knows what it is. "She's in his room. Went in a few hours ago. I'm pretty sure they made up." He gives me a long look. "Loudly. And acrobatically, if the mattress squeaks are to be believed."

Ah, so that explains the video. I guess now Tristian is the only one who hasn't fucked Story since the new rules. All of our balls are aching, but she's really iced him out by turning off all the cameras. Still, I'm surprised. "Really?"

"They weren't exactly subtle about it." He shrugs, but I can tell from the tightness around his mouth—not to mention the bulge beneath his sheets—that he's rankled. "It could have been a psycho rage-fuck, you know how they are, but…" he pauses for dramatic effect, "afterward, he was playing the piano."

Huh. That is news. "Well, good. His incessant moping was fucking with the vibe of the whole house. He needed to get back in the saddle."

Tristian smirks. "If by 'saddle' you mean 'pussy', then consider the mission accomplished."

I ignore that and leave him to his porn. Crossing the hall, I pause outside the room, pressing my ear to Rath's door. I made a deal with Story that I wouldn't violate a locked door or enter her room without invitation, but make no mistake about it, that shit does *not* apply to Rath's. No sounds come from the other side of the door, and I carefully turn the knob.

From the threshold, I'm shocked to find the room spotless, cleaned to levels I haven't seen since we moved in. Everything is tidy. Records on the shelves, instruments on their racks, the usual piles of sheet music sorted and organized. And for once, the room doesn't smell like a corpse is rotting under a pile of dirty clothes and blunt roaches. At first, I wonder if it's Story's doing, but this is something that would have taken at least a whole day, possibly two. I'd consider that maybe Ms. Crane did it. Only Rath isn't lying dead in a shallow grave out back, so I assume not.

As surprised as I am to see the tidiness of the room, that's not what draws me deeper inside. It's the two of them in the bed.

Story is naked, her bare ass facing the door. A flash of heat—the anger I've been carrying since she shut me out of the conversation with Simon—surges. One minute, I was there and involved, the next, the screen was black. I thought about it on the bus, in the locker room, and on the ride home. That kind of shit doesn't play. I'm a Lord. *Her* Lord, despite what these new rules say.

Isn't shutting me out of her room enough?

For a long moment, I imagine what it'd be like to drag her ass-first to the edge of the bed and drive my dick into her, a long, hard, rough punishment for her defiance. But she's not alone. She's nestled into Rath, thigh thrown over his, hand resting loosely against his stomach. He has her tucked firmly into his side, fingers knitted into her hair as they sleep.

I stand over them for a long time, feeling not just the old urges coursing through me, but new ones, too. Seeing her with Rath like this, all sweet and comfortable…

She did that with me, once.

Well, technically twice.

I remember that first time; her curling up against me, all warm, naked skin and soft curves. I remember wondering if it was something I wanted—

something I even liked. It wasn't until later, tired and wounded on a cold cabin floor, that I admitted to myself it was. There's something about her, so small and vulnerable and trusting, that makes me wish I were in that bed. I thought I was over jealousy when it came to him and Tristian, but it swells within me now. There was a time—so fucking brief that I barely had the chance to enjoy it—when I could come home to her in *my* bed, all naked and pliant.

I take a reluctant step forward, but Rath's hand appears, sliding out from beneath the pillow. A sharp, familiar blade glints in the dim light.

So do his narrow, alert eyes.

I hold up my hands, whispering, "It's me."

He blinks, chest caving with a long, silent exhale. "Dude," he mutters. We stare at one another for a long beat, and as he wakes, he recognizes it for what it is—recognizes me for what I am. Story's in his bed, naked and sleeping. It might be his room, but this is my territory, and he knows it.

He slowly extricates himself from Story's sleeping body, pushing the pillow against her so she doesn't miss his heat. He fusses with her like that for a minute, but then stands there, naked, staring down at her like he's pondering if maybe he should do something else. Like he's unsure if he should leave. Like he doesn't want to.

Seeming to shake it off, he stalks toward the bathroom.

The light is so dim that I barely see it, but I grab his arm and hold him back, inspecting the center of his chest. The wound there is fresh, the 'S' raised and red and still bleeding a little beneath the sheen of ointment coated on top.

"Did you do that?"

It's her initial, carved into his chest, just like our initials are carved into hers.

"No," he answers, glancing over his shoulder at her still form. "She did."

I look at his face, searching for…something. Embarrassment? Defiance? But there's nothing like that. He stares baldly back, eyes void of that dull, frenetic hopelessness that's been driving him around like a zombie for weeks now. "Payback?" I ask, honestly curious. Is this what it takes to get her like this? An eye for an eye? Because goddamn, I've only got the two, and that's not going to be enough.

But Rath just gives me this look, mouth tipped into a loose, crooked, and decidedly post-coital grin. "Not even."

. Well, that's fucking baffling. "Then why?"

He reaches up to rub the skin above it, a thoughtless gesture. "Territorial pissing. Same reason we like seeing it on her." He watches me take this in, rolling his eyes at my shocked expression. "I don't know why you think she's so different from us. You ever wonder why this whole thing works? Fuck, man, the four of us basically made each other. My advice? Tell her about that tattoo on your arm sometime." He goes to walk away, but pauses, doubling back. "Or if you want some really freaky sex, you could let her think it's some other girl's face for a while. When it comes to you, she never can see what's right in front of her."

He disappears into the bathroom, leaving me to process that. A moment later, I hear the shower turn on. Now that Story and I are alone, I fight the urge to climb into bed with her, to replace Rath's warmth with my own. There are two reasons I don't, one being that, even though this might be Rath's room, it's still breaking the spirit of our agreement. The second is a lot more complicated, but it involves me not being able to trust myself.

I slink away and lounge back on the couch instead, considering that I could sleep here. Rath wouldn't mind. Chances are they'll get up to some morning sex, and that could be fun to watch. It's more action than Tristian's sorry ass is getting, anyway.

I haven't considered what to do when she wakes, which is inconvenient, because she does. Rath is still in the shower when she suddenly stirs, likely feeling his empty side of the bed. I don't move, glued to my spot, watching as she sits up, hair messy. At first, her expression is serene. She's obviously been well-fucked. But when she sees the empty bed, it morphs to a deep, troubled frown. She spends so long considering Rath's absence that I almost give myself away to reassure her.

Idly, I wonder how they did it. Did he bend her over? Did he curl into her from behind, mid-cuddle? Did he climb over her, between her legs? Did he eat her pussy first, make her come before sliding his dick inside? Was it slow and intense, or was it like Tristian said: a psycho rage-fuck?

She stretches her arms over her head, giving me a perfect view of her tits. She doesn't see me, barely even looks my way before bending to snag a black hoodie off the floor. With a glance to the bathroom, she shrugs her arms into each sleeve, zipping it as she stands. I wait for her to notice me, to sense me as she so often has, to catch me in the dark doing the one thing she's forbidden me to do.

It never happens.

Her eyes go to the bathroom door, but she doesn't follow him inside like I expect her to. Instead, she crosses the room, padding barefoot across the clean hardwoods and stopping in front of the closet door. A moment later, warm yellow light spills from inside. My suspicions pique. The last time she went into *my* closet, she roofied me, fucked with my stuff, strapped me to the bed, and then fucked me. Sure, that was *before*. Before our agreements. Before we let her go. Before she chose to return, under her own terms and conditions.

But Rath made a point before.

Sometimes it feels like I barely know her at all.

Impatient and curious, I leave my hiding place and occupy the closet door. She's down on her knees, poking through a cardboard box on the floor. It's the Dimitri Rathbone equivalent to a reinforced steel vault. Boy keeps everything in there.

Or he did, when he had something to keep.

I cross my arms over my chest and lean against the doorjamb. "It's not there."

She jumps a mile, yelp caught in the back of her throat as she whirls around.

She shudders a long exhale when she sees me, eyes dropping closed in relief. "Jesus Christ, big brother. Wear a fucking bell around your neck." She wraps her arms around her body, looking small in his sweater. "How long have you been in here?"

"Long enough to see the tag you left on Rath's chest."

"That's between us," she says, her voice still shaky from the surprise. That's bullshit anyway. What happened in the funhouse was between the three of us. We all carved her up. Why is this any different? She looks me up and down, adding, "Just like anything else that happens in this room."

Oh yeah, she's pissed.

Join the club.

Her comment is pointed and I choose to deflect, glancing down at the open box on the floor. "Find what you needed?"

"I was just looking for his weed. He had a headache earlier, so I was going to—" I raise an eyebrow, and she looks back down, frowning as it dawns on her. "Where's his piano money?"

There's no way she doesn't know. "Where do you think?"

She stands a foot away from me, in that oversized hoodie, bare underneath, with that innocent, sexy look on her face that drives me fucking wild. "I didn't take it if that's what you think. I know I'm desperate and broke but—"

"Of course you didn't." I cut her off, scoffing. "But that doesn't mean he didn't spend it on you."

She cocks her head, forehead wrinkling. "What do you mean?"

Guess I'm going to have to spell it out for her. "Why do you think Daniel let you fuck Rath down in the pit instead of Pretty Nick? My dad speaks two languages, little sister: English and money."

"I—" Her eyes, filling with dread, dart back to the box. "You don't mean…"

I jerk my chin in a nod. "Rath bought you."

"No." Her shoulders deflate, and I'm surprised at the way her expression crumbles.

The memory of yesterday callously makes me want to rub it in. "Daddy didn't throw you a familiar bone because he cares for you. Rath saved you. Not just by showing up, but by sacrificing everything. Do you have any idea how long he'd been saving that for? Honestly, since before I even knew him."

She looks up at me, eyes wide and wet. "I didn't know."

I manage a dry little laugh. "I'm sure you didn't. Else you would've been in here bouncing on his dick a lot sooner than tonight."

Her expression does this clean wipe from dismal horror to hard outrage. She scowls at me, the spark of kinetic energy that flows between us jolting back to life. "Why are you acting like such a jerk?"

"Oh, I'm not acting."

"What, you're like… mad at me?" When I do nothing but stare blankly in response, her head jolts back in disbelief. "What can you possibly be mad about? I haven't even seen you all weekend!" I realize too late she's looking me over. Even sensing how angry I am, she doesn't hesitate to grab my wrist and pull my hand away from my body, her cool fingers running over my scraped, bruised knuckles. Her face loses some of those harsh lines when she asks, "What happened here?"

I shrug, twisting my hand loose. "I punched a wall."

"Seriously?" She shakes her head, peering up at me with big, puzzled eyes. "Why the hell would you do that? It's almost like you don't want to get back on the field."

I step into the closet, closing the gap between us. I know she finally understands about this red-hot thing boiling under my skin, because she flinches as I bear down on her. She has no choice but to go backwards, tripping on a pair of boots and then stumbling over the box on the floor. Just before she crashes into the wall, I grab her and hold her upright, yanking our faces together.

"I punched the wall, little sister, because the other option was breaking my goddamn laptop." She blinks in confusion and it rubs me raw, this evidence that she'd done it so unthinkingly. My teeth clench around the explanation. "You shut me out of that conversation the other day—just closed the computer like my voice didn't even fucking matter."

"I-uh-what?"

"About the wrestling match," I bark, holding her like a rag doll in my hands. Narrowing my eyes, I lean in so close our noses nearly touch. "Do you know how many times, how many fucking discussions, I've put a stop to because you weren't there for them? Do you have any fucking idea what it's taken to sit here on my hands like a coward because I know you couldn't stand the thought of being cut out? Do you?!" She gapes at me, body slack beneath my hands. "The three of us could have had this guy—whoever the fuck he is—down on his knees, execution style, weeks ago." There's a flash of something in her eyes, and it's too mild to be called fear, but too strong to be mere wariness. "You're the only reason we're playing this slow. Because you asked us to. Because anything less would put you at risk. You're the only thing keeping Tristian from burning this whole fucking place to the ground. You're the only thing stopping Rath from tearing a warpath through South Side. You're the one thing," I hold up a finger, thrusting it right in her face, "standing between me and my dad. But you want to go off, making decisions that affect all of us? I don't think so."

She gives me a series of rapid blinks. "I didn't think it was that important."

"Everything you do is important," I growl, shaking her. "This stalker of yours? You'd better believe he watched that night in the pit. He knows when you leave the house, when you get to campus—hell, he probably knows you just fucked Rath." A gnawing disdain grows within my chest. I don't like this guy knowing more about her than I do. It makes me wild, crazed, turning my voice into a deadly hiss. "You can lock me out of your room, you can turn off the cameras, you can flaunt your pussy in here with Rath. That's all fine and fucking dandy. But you will not shut me out of decisions that involve you showing your tits and ass to the entire Royal system." I fume right into her face, mouth pulling into a sneer. "If you're that hell-bent on being a whore like your mother, then I'll go find an ATM right now. Maybe then, you'll actually—"

I see the strike in her eyes long before it's made flesh. It's a spark of fury—the twitch of the vein in her temple—and then, astonishingly, her palm cracking hard against my face.

For a long moment, everything goes white.

"How dare you," she seethes, face boiling red. "You use your body every day to get ahead, be it out on the field, or over in South Side, muscling your way around, showing off your tattoos, trying to look so big and tough. But you—all *three* of you—look down your noses the second a woman tries to do it." Shaking her head, she gives a low, humorless laugh. "God, you're all *unbearable hypocrites.*"

I'm rigidly still, the roar in my head too much to contain. I try anyway, desperately struggling to shove it all down, to breathe, to keep my fingers from crushing the bones in her arms—from wrapping around her pale, slender neck. This is the second time she's struck me. The first time, I worked off my anger jumping in the ring down at the Duke's gym.

This time, I uncurl my fingers, one by one, rusty knuckles protesting against it. It's in opposition to every ingrained instinct, but I let her go, dropping her to her feet with a bitten out warning. "Keep testing me like this, Story. One of these times I'm going to decide this agreement of ours is a failure."

I leave her before I do anything else—before I react to the defiant fire in her eyes, the one that's daring me to make good on my promise. Maybe Rath is right about that, too. Story is more like us than I want to admit, which doesn't bode well for her.

No one hurts us more than we hurt ourselves.

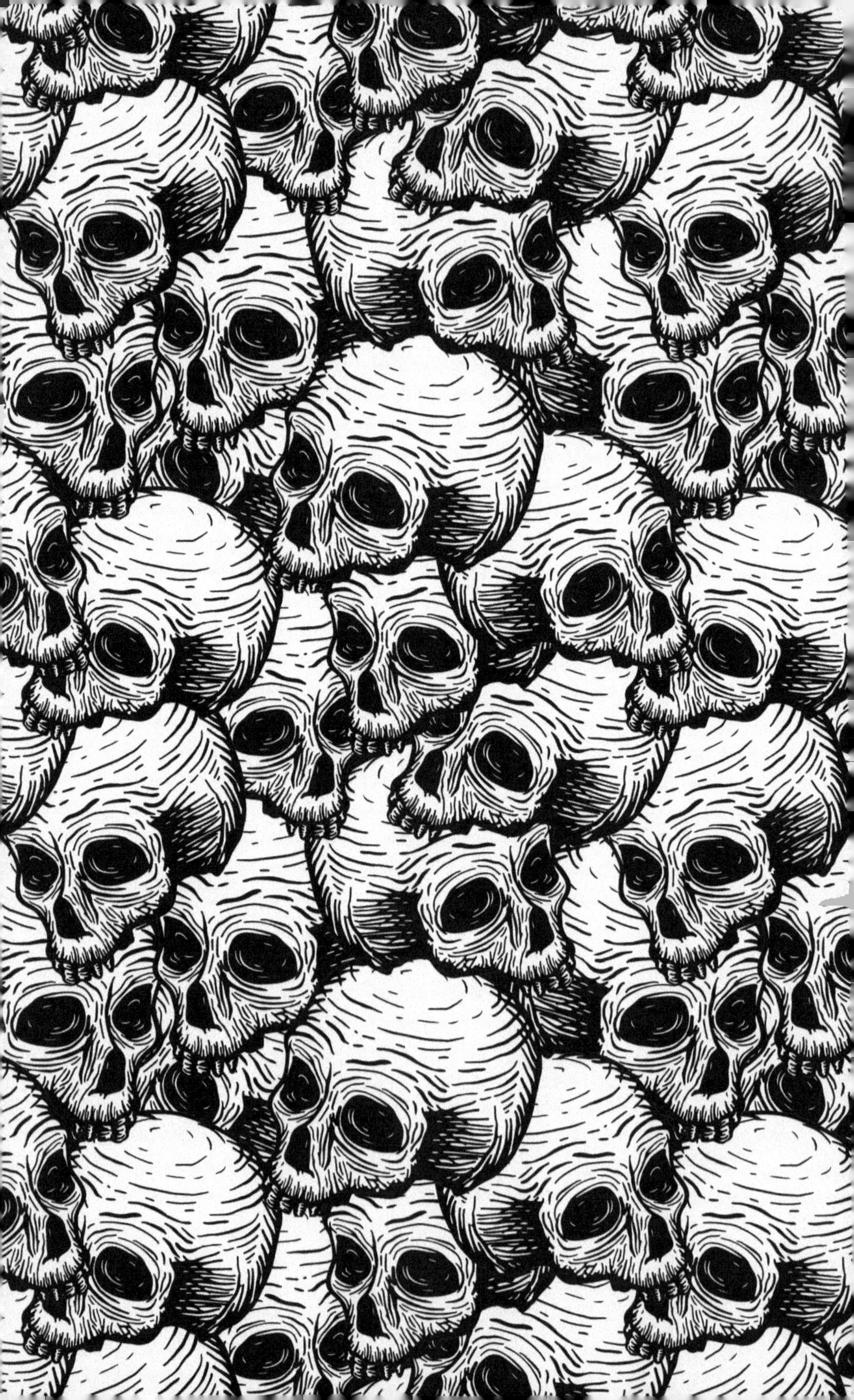

9

REFEREE

I WATCH AS Story builds herself up, dabbing her mouth with the napkin before jabbing her fork into her mashed potatoes. Cutting her eyes to Killian, she asks, "Can you please pass the salt?"

Ah, there it is.

The words are perfectly polite, but the tone is all low and cutting, as if he's been holding the salt hostage just to inconvenience us all.

Killian doesn't even look up from his plate when he reaches toward the salt, and in one quick snap of his wrist, flicks it down the table. She flings a hand out to catch it, mouth pressing into a tight, angry line as she glowers at him.

"*Thanks*," she drawls, giving the salt a violent shake over her potatoes.

Rath and I share a long-suffering look.

Jesus, dinners in their old house must have been straight up theater.

It's been like this now for three days. I figured with us heading back to classes and everything, it'd settle down. We're busy and overbooked, and have way too much to worry about to indulge all this petty, bullshit squabbling, but here we are, watching Killian shoot daggers at her with his eyes the second she looks away.

The way Killian tells it, Story had disrespected him, left him to stew in it, and then slapped him in the face when he confronted her. The way Story tells it, she was just minding her own business when Killian stormed in and went into full caveman mode. They both had the marks to prove it—Killian's red cheek, Story's bruised upper arms, and most of all, the tension that's been sparking between them since.

Rath hasn't been helping. "You know, this is the first time I've really felt like I was living with siblings."

Story's head snaps up. "We are *not* siblings!"

Desperate to go one meal without their bickering, I try, "I saw the new Princess today."

Rath hums, sounding only halfway interested as he scrolls down his phone. "She hot?"

"Naturally." Not that it would have mattered. The Princes struck out with that one girl—Autumn, I think her name was—so they forfeited the chance to cherry-pick. "Some Phi Nu guys in my stats class were taking bets on how long it'd take to put a baby in her. I'm in five Gs deep for it happening before the new year."

Rath sends me a smirk. "Ballsy, considering they don't have any."

"It's the desperation," I explain, casually sliding my salad toward Story. She looks into the bowl, nose wrinkling, but stabs her fork into a tomato. "I saw one of the new Princes nailing her in the parking lot, bent right over in his back seat. This batch has initiative."

Rath snorts. "Gotta respect a work ethic."

I point my fork at him. "Especially when that work ethic involves pussy."

"Do you really have to talk about this now? We're eating." Story roots around the salad distractedly, but then pauses, glancing up at me with a frown. "Wait. Did you, like… watch?"

I hold her stare. "Of course I watched. He was railing her right there, for all to see. I'm only human." When her frown deepens, I reach over to caress her cheek, tucking her hair behind an ear. "It's just like watching porn, sweetheart. It means nothing." The words are true, but even I know they're kind of bullshit. Truthfully, the Prince and his Princess weren't super compelling, it's just that this is the longest I've gone without pussy since Gen. It was the pathetic equivalent of an Oliver Twist character, standing out in the snow, gazing longingly into a window as the family inside enjoys a warm, hearty meal.

Jesus Christ, my dick is starving.

She looks like she wants to argue, but before she can, Killian finally speaks.

"So we can't even *watch* other people fucking now?" His bitter gaze fixes on her, jaw twitching.

Her expression snaps into a scowl faster than I can parse it. "We can all watch you go fuck *yourself.*"

Rath stands, rubbing his temple. "Okay, I'm out. Your sibling drama is giving me a goddamn migraine."

"We're *not* siblings!"

That might have been really convincing, except for the way it's said by both of them, in the most pitch perfect unison that even my twin sisters couldn't hope to be so in sync.

An hour later, Rath is upstairs on the piano, I'm in the library typing out a paper for psych class, and Killer and Story are *still* going at it. I can hear them downstairs and it's seriously fucking with my concentration. It gets to a point where I just can't take it anymore. Slamming my laptop shut, I storm out of the library and down the stairs, following their voices into the den.

"It's the only Ticonderoga in the house! I need it for my homework!"

"It's mine."

I try to figure out what the hell they're talking about, but when I see the yellow stick in Killian's hand, it all clicks. "You're fighting over a pencil?" I ask, unable to hide my bewilderment and annoyance. "A fucking fifteen cent pencil?"

Story throws her hands up. "It's the best kind of pencil, and I specifically bought it at the bookstore today."

"Prove it," Killian sneers, holding it up in a taunting manner. "Prove that you bought this pencil, and maybe I'll give it back to you."

Story's hand balls up into a fist, and Killian holds the pencil like a weapon. Since our names being featured in a headline about a grisly pencil stabbing doesn't strike me as beneficial, I march up, snagging the pencil out of the air.

"Hey!" they both shout. Apparently pissed I didn't let the Forsyth Pencil Massacre take place in our living room.

I snap the pencil in two and toss a piece at each of them. Killian instinctively catches his. Story's bounces off her chest and falls to the ground. I glare at my best friend. "What the fuck is this about, and don't you dare tell me it's about a pencil. Lizzy and Izzy act more mature than this." When he just keeps seething, throwing me a dark look, I shake my head. "We can't afford this right now. If you've got something to say to her, spit it out!"

"The agreement," he grinds out, fists clenching, "was that we follow her 'parameters' and she'd keep belonging to us. That means I still have a say!"

"Jesus titty-fucking Christ," I mutter, squeezing the bridge of my nose. Suddenly, I can relate to Rath's migraine issues. "It's not that hard to please a woman, Killer. Did you even think to butter her up a bit? To ask for something nicely? No, because you're too busy nursing a grudge for something she had no way of knowing would upset you *this* much."

I can see him really revving up now, that vein in his neck bulging. "After everything we've done to keep her included, she just decides *unilaterally* to—"

Cutting him off, I wearily snark, "Yes, you had some good points to make about the day at the coffee shop—which Rath and I have heard, at length, *daily*—and I'm sure you delivered them to her in a calm, rational, reasonable way." Narrowing my eyes, I add, "I saw the bruises. You ever wonder *why* she keeps shutting you out? Newsflash, Einstein: It's because you're a controlling asshole. And this is coming from *me*!" I say it like the whole damn world has gone crazy, and it's possible it has. Story's quiet snort takes me by surprise, but even though my lips twitch against my will, I don't find it funny. This whole thing is twisted. "I mean, goddamn, Killer, maybe she just wants to be sure *when* she lets you in, she can still have space for herself. Do you think she feels like she has space when you're pacing outside her fucking door every night? Shit, sometimes I want to shut the laptop on you, too."

His eyes harden, head shaking vehemently. "She knew exactly what shutting that laptop would do."

I throw my hands up, palms out. "I'm sorry. Are we still pretending this is about the laptop and not the fact the two of you are psychotically horny for one another?"

"What?!" Story sputters, head snapping back. "You're delusional!"

I give her a long look. "Oh, please. This vicious cycle has been spinning since the day you stepped in here. Maybe sooner." Like I'm speaking to a small child, I explain, "You pushing him to the brink of breaking is the biggest flirt in the Story Austin handbook. You do this shit *constantly*. Look at the two of you!" I gesture between them. To the tension. The sparks. The fury and the pure sex in the way they glare at each other. "You're practically begging him to throw you up against a wall and fuck your brains out. You *like* it! It's just not working this time, because you both know he can't control himself. Not now. Not when he's losing it this badly."

Slowly, she shakes her head. "What are you even talking about?"

"I'm talking about the answer to all of this," I say, thrusting a finger at Killer. "He's been off the field for over a month. A *month*, Story. You know what he does when he's pissed off and losing it like this?" I can see her working it out, outraged disbelief dawning in her features. "He either takes it to the field or he fucks it out of his system. Given he's still benched from the gunshot wound, plus the parameters of the contract *you* set, he can't do either of those things, now, can he?" Before that fuming argument in her eyes can manifest itself, I stop her. "*Don't.* You're obviously the horniest person in this house."

"I am not!" she hotly insists, shoulders snapping back. "You're completely out of your mind if you think I want this jerk anywhere—"

I approach her, casually shoving my hand down the front of her pants. Her words cut off with a strangled yelp, but even though she tries to lurch away, she doesn't get far. I curl an arm around her waist and jam my hand between her legs, raising an eyebrow. "Not horny, huh? Because your pussy is *drenched*." She's close enough now that I can see the blush rising on her cheeks. Part of it might be embarrassment, and some may be indignation, but the rest is all about the way my fingers feel sliding through her folds. I let myself indulge a bit, leaning in to whisper against her ear. "Want Killer to fuck you, sweetheart?"

"N-no," she stutters, clearly struggling to keep the resentment in her voice.

It wouldn't be this hard to convince her if she really did. She's stubborn, but she's also reckless. This is why I think to ask, "Why not? You want him. I know you do." There's a pause as she breathes, and I use it to stroke her, spreading her wetness over her clit.

"He'd be…" Her hand curls into my shirt, voice pitched to a rough whisper. "He'll be mean."

Humming, I glance over my shoulder to witness the look on Killian's face. All the tightness in his jaw has disappeared, replaced with a slack, dazed expression. God. He really is clueless. "Are you afraid he'll be too rough?"

At her small, timid nod, Killian's jaw clicks shut. "I'll be rough?!" he exclaims, jabbing a finger into his chest. "*Me*? You're the one who hit me! And the other night with Rath, you were—"

"Shut up," I bark. Turning to Story, I touch her chin, forcing her gaze to mine. "What if I don't let him? Hm?" I brush my lips over her warm cheek, asking, "What if I was here to make sure you're safe?"

The thing about Killer is that he never learned the right way to be with a woman. A long string of hookers, pre-game bimbos, and unconscious girls has completely stunted this guy. He doesn't like having to work for it—having to consider someone else. For her, I'm betting he'd try, but he wouldn't know where to start.

I know the suggestion probably irks him, so the utter silence coming from behind me is a testament to how badly he must want it. "You know I wouldn't let him hurt you," I say, pressing my thumb into her swollen clit. Her fingers tighten in my shirt. "Not unless you like it. You do, don't you? Sometimes you like it."

Her throat bobs with a hard swallow, eyes falling closed. "Sometimes," she breathes. "A little."

"Okay." That, we can work with. Still, when I take my hand out of her pants, she sort of... tips over, chasing it. I steady her, turning us around to Killian.

He looks unimpressed. "What, you're going to be our sex referee?"

"You're too good for it?" Calmly, I lay out the options. "Because you could stay here and fuck this out of your systems like adults, or you can go back to bickering all the time and jacking your dick in an empty bed. Your call."

Killer was never going to turn this down, and he doesn't bother making noises about it now. He just looks away, inhaling hard. "Fine," he grinds out, nostrils flaring.

Oh yeah, I'm sure this is such a burden. Killian Payne is a giver.

I slide behind Story, leaning down to say, "Go kiss him."

She stiffens beneath the hands I'm resting on her shoulders, moving jerkily when I give her a nudge. She approaches him stiffly, looking anywhere but at his face. He's not much better, flexing his fists and pulling himself to his full height. Always trying to intimidate. There's a second where she stops in front of him but no one makes a move, and I'm rolling my eyes because I can be a sex referee, but if they need help *kissing*, then I might as well just fuck her myself.

I know it's bad when Killer makes the first move, puffing this sharp, irritated breath before ducking down to smash their mouths together. He raises a hand and fists the back of her hair, yanking her head back.

I step in, tugging his wrist away. "Easy, easy. You don't have to hold her down. She's a sure thing, brother."

So he abandons her hair just to grasp at her ass, yanking her up against his body. From this vantage, I can see the way he's kissing her. It's so aggressive and imposing that I can't even catch a peek of tongue. He's just absolutely *dominating* her mouth. Because of this proximity, I can see the exact moment he pulls back, nipping hard at her lip.

She hisses, jolting away. "Ow! He bit me!"

Killian licks the sharp point of his canine tooth, eyes dark and hard. "Oops."

I shove his shoulder. "Unnecessary roughness, dickwad. I think that deserves a penalty."

"So help me god," Killian says, rolling his eyes heavenward, "if you keep on with the referee stuff, I'm going to strangle you with the cord of a whistle."

Ignoring him, I push my hands under Story's shirt, working it off. She lifts her arms, letting me slide it away, and when I undo the clasp on her bra, Killian's mouth loses some of that arrogant slant. His eyes drop, taking in her soft, bare tits. I'm the one to touch them, though. I stand behind her and cover them with my palms, feeling the pebble of her nipples as I massage.

She looks enticing like this, standing out here in the open. I let Killer watch as I squeeze her tits, feeling my cock harden at the way we must look. "You're going to come with me over here." I guide her to the couch, pulling her down in my lap, the pressure of her ass against my cock making me twitch. "And you," I say to Killian, "are going to lick her twat until she's nonverbal."

He watches with this dumb expression on his face as I carefully slide Story's pants down her legs, exposing her fully. I know Killer and Rath think I must be going crazy, not having gotten any in so long. They're right, of course, but I was honest before. Story is a sure thing. I know she is.

She's still shaving her pussy.

It's nowhere in the new contract. She's free to keep her pussy any way she likes it, but she's kept it the way *we* like it. Yeah, I'm going to get mine. I can be patient.

Probably.

"What are you waiting for?" I ask him, pulling her hair to the side and pressing a kiss into the soft spot below her ear. I watch as he takes her in, the naked swath of soft, supple flesh waiting in my lap. I don't know if Story gets as much out of being watched as I do, but I know when she's hamming it up, and when she tilts her head, the writhe of her hips pulling a quiet grunt from my throat, I know her eyes are on her brother. Teasing.

Brows crouched low, he stalks over, not looking happy about it. He can't lie to me, though. I can see the tent in his jeans and the dark glint in his eyes.

Still, Story takes a little warming up.

She has her knees pressed together, and even though she's leaning against my chest, she still feels a little too rigid. I run my palms over her tits, trying to get her to relax, or barring that, horny enough to stop caring. She releases a slow breath and tips her head back on my shoulder, apparently committed to not watching his approach.

"Come on," I whisper, walking my fingers down her flat belly. "Spread your legs for Killer, sweetheart."

"If he bites me," she says, clenching up.

I shush her, parting her thighs. "He wouldn't dare," I assure, giving her earlobe a friendly nip. "I'd cut his balls off, and he knows it."

The look Killer gives me says he'd like to see me try, but he drops to his knees, anyway. I pull her legs apart, undaunted by the stiffening of her tendons and muscles, and hook her calves around my own. I don't need to wonder what she looks like. I see it reflected in Killian's reaction, his eyes dropping to her pussy, mouth parting at the sight of her, all spread and ready.

His fingers press divots into the soft skin of her thigh when he ducks in, licking a hard path up her pussy with the flat of his tongue. Story jolts at the contact but instantly melts, closing her eyes.

"Oh," is shuddered out on her exhale.

"No, no, no," I say, smoothing her hair back from her forehead. "I want you to look. You've got him on his knees, between your legs. Watch him eat your pussy." I've always wondered if it's the same for girls, the surge of power a guy feels when he's getting his cock sucked. So I observe the knit in her brow when she opens her eyes, watching Killian's mouth work between her legs. It's probably not the same—she can't exactly choke him on it—but it still makes her lips fall apart, hips bucking up.

Killer doesn't give a lot of head.

He's never said as much. It's just that I can tell by what he's doing—the lack of technique—that I'm working with a novice. No shocker or anything. The word 'generous' does not come to mind when I think of Killian and sex, and it doesn't apply now. He's tonguing her with no rhyme or reason, dipping low to prod at her entrance. If anything, he seems like he's just impatient to get to the good stuff.

To be fair, Story doesn't exactly look put out about it. Her chest rises and falls with these short, hitched breaths, and her hands might be clamped around my forearms, but her hips keep wriggling, trying to direct the pressure where she most needs it. She's clearly used to futilely asking for things he refuses to give. Killian ignores the obvious cues, digging his fingertips deeper into her flesh as he holds her still.

Wincing, I reach down and take him by the hair, directing him higher. "You have to learn to listen, Killer. She's telling you where to go."

He gives me an irate glare, which is hilarious given that he doesn't miss a beat, tongue flicking at her clit. Story's fingers tighten around my arms, back arching as her lip gets caught between her teeth.

"You like that, sweetheart?" When she nods, I glance my knuckles over her nipple, saying, "Don't tell me. Tell him." If Killer needs to learn to listen, then maybe Story needs to learn to talk. Smoke signals have better communication than these two.

Exhaling shakily, she finally opens her eyes, dropping her gaze to him. He's staring back at her, eyes still sharp with animosity. But then, in this soft, hushed voice, she says, "Oh, god, that feels good," and just like that, all the sharpness in his stare melts away.

He closes his lips over her at the praise—oh, yeah, he's really getting into it now—but it isn't until I watch his fingers ease up on her thighs, skating up to feel her tits, that I relax. Story's feet hook around my calves, using leverage to lift her hips into the things he's doing with his mouth. When he pulls away to prod her clit with the pointed tip of his tongue, I reach down with both hands, spreading her lips apart for him, wide and obscene. He makes a gruff noise and cups the backs of her thighs, really getting in there.

See?

Teamwork makes the dream work.

Story whimpers deep in her throat as Killer assaults her clit with his tongue, thighs flexing rhythmically like she just can't help it. I watch her face, the way her brows furrow as she loses herself, mouth hanging open on deep, gulping breaths.

"I bet you taste good," I whisper against her ear. "She getting nice and wet for you, Killer? How sweet is that pussy?" He rumbles in response, making her thighs tremble. I pry one of her hands from my arm and guide it to his head, making her touch him.

Grabbing blindly, she knits her fingers into his hair, toes curling. "Killian." It's said in this long, soft whine that makes his gaze bolt right up, and I know instantly what's going through his head.

Killer lurches up, all stunned and frantic as he claws at his fly.

But I stop him. "Keep going."

He freezes, nostrils flaring wide as he gestures to her pussy. "But she's—"

"Still verbal," I note, nodding toward her spread cunt. "Job's not finished."

He snaps his mouth shut, glowering mutely as he gets back to his knees. Story's forehead is already damp with sweat when I ease her head back to my shoulder, soothing her.

"You want to come, sweetheart?"

"Yes," she gasps, Killian getting back to work. She puts her hand back in his hair, directing him lower, and then higher, and then lower. Seems she enjoys a little of everything, teeth digging into her bottom lip as she lets loose a strangled cry. At some point, Killian grows more determined than impatient, a challenge to be conquered, and he really starts throwing his back into it, lifting her up to fuck her with his tongue before rising to blast her clit. I keep her spread and ready for each return, not daring to bring her off myself.

Eventually, she really does go nonverbal.

She trembles, head thrown back as she bucks, panting, and I know she's close when she finally pries her eyes open to look down at him.

Story is so pretty when she comes.

First, her eyes get all wide like she can't believe what's happening, even though we've been building toward it for ten minutes. Then, when the first shudder hits her, she lets out this series of nonsensical fricatives, pouring from her throat like she can't help it. She gives this delicate little quiver, and I can just imagine what it'd feel like clenching around my dick.

The second the muscles in her thighs go lax, head collapsing back, Killian is tearing off his shirt. He runs it over the mess she's made on his face, but it's done hastily, an afterthought to the way he's shoving his jeans down his thighs, hard cock springing free.

I can tell from the crazed, almost violent sharpness in his eyes that he wants nothing more than to pummel right into her.

But the second he curls close, looming over us like a horny, sex-crazed giant, I swat his hand away from his cock. "Start slow," I explain at his outraged expression, shamelessly grabbing his dick and guiding it to her entrance. "She's probably still sensitive. Jesus, dude, look at her. You'd be fucking her like a rag doll."

"*And?*" he replies, and okay. Yeah. I doubt that's really a turnoff, but he grits his teeth and lets me line him up, bracing his hands on the couch beside our heads. Waiting until I give him a nod, he gives his hips a little pointed jab.

I don't need to feel or see his cock slotting into her to know she's taking him in. She arches her back, pushing her tits out, and I let Killer get a little deeper, cognizant of the knot of twitching muscle at the back of his jaw.

"Fuck," he grits out, digging his fingers into the upholstery. "Fuck, she's tight."

"Yeah?" My dick gives an eager twitch, and I watch her eyes grow more alert with every slow, agonizing inch he sinks into her. She shifts around, hands hooking around his biceps, and it makes her ass grind into my dick. Hard as fucking nails here.

Killer's cock is just as thick as the rest of him, and from the whine in her throat and the strain around his eyes, I'm betting it's a nice stretch. Gently, I shush her. "You're taking his cock so good, sweetheart. Almost there. Then he's going to give you a second, okay?"

When he finally bottoms out, Killian twists his head to wipe the sweat from his brow, but his lips catch the fingers she has clamped around the muscle. For a moment, he just rests there, feeling her against his lips, eyes sliding closed.

When she wiggles her hips, making these restless, hitched breaths, I speak. "Come on, Killer, show our Lady how good you can be." Giving him a pointed look, I add, "Show her you can be with her without making it hurt."

He drags his hips back before fucking into her, nice and slow. Killian's good at exercising every muscle except restraint, and I see him grappling with it now, hunger rippling through him with every flex of his hips. Story's still boneless and breathless, but she's present in the moment, watching him with her lip trapped between her teeth.

Faintly, she says, "I can take… more."

This time, when Killian kisses her, he holds back, lets her tongue meet his in the middle, giving me a peek of it all, a slick tangle of pink joining their mouths. Damn, they look good together. Her thighs cradle his powerful hips like they were made for it, the dark ink of his tattoos a stark contrast to her porcelain skin. The cords of his muscles shift with every thrust, dwarfing her slender, delicate arms. They're hard and soft, leather and satin, and I can't help but move with their rhythm, indulging in the friction against my cock.

God, if Killer only realized how lucky he was.

But when she breaks away to gulp in a breath, wrenching her head to the side, her eyes zero in on something and she jerks her gaze away, back stiffening.

The tattoo on his arm.

Rath mentioned she wasn't aware it was a tattoo of *her*. Apparently, she'd asked about it, in a roundabout sort of way, but Killer's too much of a pussy to own up to it.

That's only one of the many and varied things I'm burning to spell out. It's then, as they're lost in the zenith of their kiss and the rock of their bodies, that I put my lips to Story's ear. "Do you have any idea how much this guy loves you?"

That's the thick of it, anyway.

Killian rests his forehead against hers, but his face is set into a deep, sharp frown. "Don't." He won't even open his eyes to catch her slow blinking reaction.

I go on, "He can't help it. It makes him crazy. You know Killer can't do anything by halves—least of all *want you*."

"Shut the fuck up," he growls, snapping his hips hard into Story. It pushes her back against me like a punch.

For the sake of her small, startled cry, I change tacks. "You didn't mean to upset him, did you?"

She's still staring at Killer, expression lost, when she breathes, "No."

"And you're sorry, aren't you?" Unable to help myself, I curl my palm around the inside of her thigh, trapped between them as he pistons his hips, feeling how the two of them meet. "You know he just wants to protect you. Make sure you're safe?"

Nodding, she reaches up to touch his rough, stubbled jaw. "I know." Killian shudders against the tenderness of the gesture, and Story quietly confesses, "I wasn't thinking."

"And Killer," I continue, easing my fingers up toward her clit. "You overreacted. You know you did." He makes a curt, gruff sound as I press my fingers into her clit. "Tell her."

His reply is as mindless as the way he's fucking into her, eyes glued to her mouth. "I did."

"There, see?" There's plenty more to be said, but it's going to take a lot more than one supervised fuck to cover Killer's massive, throbbing abandonment issues. "Now fuck like you mean it. You've been walking around here wanting each other for god only knows how long. Doesn't it feel good?"

Story responds by grabbing Killian by the hair and hauling him into a long, breathless kiss. Killian reaches down to roughly palm at her tit, grunting as his rhythm ratchets up. Finally, I just let myself enjoy the sight of them. The way she feels against me. The pulse of them fucking right into my body—against the hand that's still working Story's swollen clit. My balls ache with how badly I want to be him, but it's almost good enough to just watch. To see the way he loses control in a different sense. The gentle way he looks at her between obscene, rough kisses. The swell of her slender throat as she struggles to control her cries. I don't think I really understood them until right now, witnessing the turbulence of their affection for one another. It's a fine-edged blade that's too used to cutting.

Killian is proof that it's possible to want someone too much. "Look at me," he demands, voice growing as ragged and deep as the pointed punches of his hips. Story blinks her eyes open, and he slams hard into the cradle of her thighs. "This is mine."

I wonder if she knows he's not even talking about her pussy. He's talking about the current that flows between them, always hot enough to burn. The way he can't look at her sometimes. The sight of her like this, barely coherent but so fucking rapt. He's talking about that sweet, vulnerable thing in her eyes as she gazes up at him, and the way she touches his cheek when she realizes she can't shut him out.

Not from this.

"Show me, big brother."

And then I watch as he unlocks his own door, letting her watch him come apart. It all makes a sad sort of sense then. Killer's never wanted her to see how much he feels. It's no wonder he prefers fucking her when she's sleeping, because this?

There's no hiding the raw, halfway wounded sound he makes as he comes. I can barely make out the curse he spits into her red, abused mouth, because it's just as gnarled as his breaths. Story writhes between us, making a sound that's all at once satisfied and frustrated, and I can take a guess why.

"Is he filling you up, sweetheart?" I press the question into her temple so I can feel her restless nod. "Don't worry, I'll make sure you get what you need." It takes Killian a long moment to peel himself away, red-faced and huffing as he captures her mouth, drawing out the vestiges of that connection that's still got him gooey-eyed and uncomfortably soft.

When he finally does, it's possible he collapses on the couch beside us, but I'm too busy burying two fingers in her cunt to notice. "Fuck, I can feel him in there. So wet. You want to see?"

She looks absolutely wrecked, pupils blown wide, flushed, chest heaving.

When she nods, I doubt she even knows what she's agreeing to. But when I slip my fingers out of her pussy, pressing them to her lips, she takes them in, tasting what she and Killian are like together. It's one of the best things about Story—how nasty she's willing to get. She probably doesn't even mean to bat her eyelashes at me, watching me with glazed, heavy eyes as I feed her the mingled taste of their obsessions for one another.

I have to know.

Grabbing her chin, I wrench her face to mine, licking into the crease of her lips. They're sweet and bitter, her slick tongue pushing the taste into my mouth. Whatever threads of control I've had are rapidly breaking, and the whine she makes into my mouth isn't helping.

Her answer when I ask, "You need some more?" demolishes it entirely.

"Please," she whimpers, guiding my hand back to her center.

It's only then that I notice Killian really has collapsed beside us, and only because I'm lifting her, turning to pour her into his lap this time. It feels right, arranging her there against his chest, pushing her knees to straddle him, watching as he just...takes her, folding her into him.

Frantically, I unbutton my pants and shove them down, getting my aching dick out. She looks tired and strung out as she rests her cheek on his shoulder, but when I grab her hips, hiking her ass up, she's quick to comply, weak legs struggling to get her knees underneath her.

The noise she makes when I thrust into her is a gasp of surprise, followed by a mewl of approval.

"Hold her," I tell Killian, who lazily pushes his fingers into her hair and cradles her against his body. I fuck her, hips pounding hard into her ass. It's just as tight as Killian said. Only her pussy is fucking sloppy wet now, filled with his come. She reaches back to touch me, her fingertips skating over my thigh as I hammer into her. This isn't like it was with Killian. I don't need to be taught when to be gentle and accommodating. I fuck her hard and fast, yanking her hips into mine with every thrust, and all she can do is hang on to Killer and ride it out, burying her sharp cries into his neck. When I glance at the mirror over the drink cart, I see a man possessed, still clothed, strung tight and ready to snap.

"Damn, Tris," Killian mutters, watching as he idly strokes his fingertips through her hair. "Look like you're about to detonate. Should jack off more."

I huff, already so close I can feel my balls start to tingle. "Get her off," I grind out. "*Now.*"

Killian reaches between them to do just that, and whatever he's doing with her clit is making her clench up around me, a rhythmic pulse that just drives me faster and harder.

"Don't stop," she's saying, abandoning Killian's arm to clutch at the back of the couch.

It takes everything in me to wait until she finally seizes, shoulders jerking with a delicate shudder as she comes apart around me. When she does, Killer speaks, his words hazy and indistinct, obscured by the rush of blood in my ears.

"Come on, Tris. Make her yours."

I let go, slamming hard into her pussy. For a white-hot second, that's all I can think about—adding my release to Killian's inside her, cock pumping her full, making her pussy mine.

Making it ours.

"How's that feel, little sister?" Killian is saying, holding her by the hips. "Having us both inside? Knowing you're ours?"

"Full," she answers, panting. "Feel so full."

She drops her head to Killian's shoulder and his eyes meet mine. The moment is uniquely intimate—the two of us claiming her, filling her up, making her fall apart. We've always been brothers, we've always shared, but it's never been like this, and at the same time the warmth spreading across my chest tells me it was always going to lead to this.

I pull out and drop to the seat next to them, muscles burning in the best of ways. Fuck, but it's been a long time since I indulged in a nice, hard fuck. Bonelessly, I take off my shirt, fully intending to clean Story up with it.

But Killian is already pushing the come back up her thighs.

He gathers it up, burying it back into her pussy with two fat fingers, and then brings them back to his mouth to lick them clean. My dick gives a feeble, satisfied twitch at the sight. She hums as he does it, curling into his lap, but reaches out to flop a hand on my chest, giving it a badly coordinated stroke.

My head lolls over, finally satiated, and I realize Killian's staring at me. "What?"

"That whole sex referee thing was a joke, but you're actually pretty good at it."

"Well," I reason, watching him casually finger-fuck our come back into his sister. "I know a thing or two about watching people fuck."

Rath and Killer don't really get my thing for watching and being watched, but that's the only time humanity makes sense to me. I'm not talking about fake, over-acted porn, either. I'm talking about two people moving together, so open with it they barely notice anything else. It's why a glance in the mirror, mid-fuck, makes my balls draw up.

Profoundly, I mutter, "I fuck, therefore I am."

Story snorts.

Knowing my exhaustion probably shines through in my smirk, I lift her hand to my mouth and kiss her knuckles. "Just promise me that the next time you decide to go pistols at dawn over a pencil, you'll just fuck it out instead."

Killian lifts his fist, and I bump it with my own. These two will probably never stop fighting—they are siblings, after all—but at least now I know the best way to get them to shut the fuck up is a good, old-fashioned dicking down.

STORY

1 0

WATCHED

THE PAIN BEGINS sometimes during the night; a dull, pulsating throb, deep in my lower belly rousing me more than once. It's joined by a sharp ache in my lower back and followed by what feels like my uterus trying to strangle itself. By the time the sun comes up, shining harsh and too bright through my curtains, I'm a tired and tragic specimen of a woman.

When Tristian knocks, I'm still in a fetal position.

"Ms. Crane says if you don't get downstairs for breakfast, she's going to come serve it on your floor with a side of—" Tristian stops in the doorway, blue eyes blinking at my form beneath the blankets. He lifts a hand to gesture at my general state. "You're not dressed. Are we doing the whole rebellion thing again? Because I thought we'd moved past that." When I don't answer, peering miserably up at him, his eyes narrow. "Oh, Christ. You're sick, aren't you? I knew you shouldn't have eaten the meat in that lasagna last night."

"It's not food poisoning." I bring my knees to my chest and hug them. "And the only thing rebelling is my uterus. You can tell Ms. Crane it hurts worse than she could. She'd appreciate the gravity of that."

"Wait, you mean…" His forehead scrunches as he pulls out his phone, frowning down at the screen after a few taps. "No, you can't be on your period.

It's not for three more days."

"Tristian." I stare at him, already knowing the answer, but needing to ask. "You track my cycle?"

He gives me this long-suffering look, like this is the stupidest question ever asked. "Of course I track your cycle. It's an excellent indicator of how efficiently your body is working. You know, you women have it good. If one of our bodily functions got out of whack because we were too stressed, or didn't eat enough, or had some kind of imbalance, we'd have a much easier time monitoring our health."

"Yeah," I grind out, teeth clenching against the next wave of pain. "I feel really lucky right now."

To his credit, he does grimace. "I just mean this isn't a good sign. You're usually so regular. Are you too stressed? Is it Killian? Or school? Or maybe your diet is fubar. Your body is trying to tell you something."

"I think it's telling me I'm not pregnant," I argue, feeling suddenly annoyed. "I got the birth control implant, okay? Spotting and cramps are common at the beginning." Or so said the gynecologist at the student center. The Lords had me on the pill, but part of the new terms of my contract is that I get to choose what I put into my body—and that isn't limited to food and dicks. "But after a while, my period could disappear altogether." This, plus the fact I don't need to take a daily pill, had been big draws.

Tristian looks horrified. "When the hell did you do that?"

"Before Thanksgiving holiday," I explain, pulling my blanket up to my chin. "It was a simple procedure. I was in and out before lunch ended."

He reaches up to tug at his hair, eyes tight. "What brand is it? Did you research it? Because hormonal changes can be—I mean, shit. Why didn't you tell me? I would have gone with you, helped you read up on the side-effects, told you what to choose."

The smile I give him is sharp and sarcastic. "Gee, Tris, I was going to, but you know… I figured you've put enough implants in me."

His mouth pulls up into a cool grin. "I'm going to let the attitude slide on account of your womanly troubles."

"And on account of me being right."

He ignores this, sighing as he looks me over. "So what are we going to do with you?"

"I'm fine," I insist, my wince belying the words. "I just need a few hours for the cramps to go away. Maybe I can meet you at school a little later, or—"

Turning on his heel, he says, "I'll be back," and sweeps out of the room. A moment later, Dimitri appears in my doorway, taking a bite out of a bagel.

"What's he doing?" His dark eyes take me in, jaw pausing mid-chew. "What are you doing?"

"I'm not feeling great," I explain, shivering. It's getting deeper into winter, which is evidently when the brownstone shows its age. Drafty windows and a subpar boiler have pushed me to add more blankets to my bed. "Is it okay if I have the morning off?"

His mouth forms a line. I know I don't technically have to ask him for permission because we worked that out in the new contract. And even if I did, Dimitri's never been the type to control my comings and goings. But I've come to realize I've developed some habits while living here. Survival instincts, I'm sure.

"I dunno." He rests his hand on the doorjamb, taking another bite of the bagel. "What's wrong?"

"Girl stuff."

The look of confusion doesn't go away, jaw working as he chews.

"Female stuff." I wave my hand around my uterus. "You know…"

Comprehension dawns on his face. "Oh, shit. That." He stares at me for a long, pensive moment, like he's trying to work out what that looks like, and god, part of me really wants to know what he's thinking, but the other part doesn't. Dimitri has a taste for blood, and I have no idea how deep that runs. He swallows, straightening. "Do you, uh," and then cringes, "need anything?"

Did he just offer to assist me with my period? This is all just too weird.

I blink. "No. I think I've got it under control."

"I got a guy who'll sell me Percs for dead cheap," he offers. "Or I can go get Ms. Crane." He leans back to peer down the hallway. "Although, I doubt she'd make you feel better."

I laugh, and then wince as another cramp attacks. "Please do not bring her up here. She'd probably just tell me I'm a wimp, and that real fucktoys don't get their periods."

He raises an eyebrow, but before he can respond, Tristian appears behind him, giving his shoulder a shove. "I've got this, Rath. Get the fuck out of the way. You're making things worse."

"I'm just standing here."

"In the way." After pushing his way past Dimitri, Tristian enters the room with a large serving tray. From this vantage, I can see there's a mug, a teapot, an assortment of snacks, a bottle of pain reliever, and a large glass of water. It isn't until he carefully places it on my nightstand that I see the heating pad tucked beneath his arm.

"From my reading," he begins, bending to plug the pad into the outlet, "although you're probably craving something salty, you should stay away from sodium because of the bloating." Without any fanfare, he tugs my blanket down and starts tucking the warming pad against my stomach. "But I also know that cravings are your body telling you what you need, and since our bodies are temples—"

Dimitri snorts. "Ancient and crumbling?"

Tristian pointedly ignores him. "—I have a few snacks here to take off the edge. Sweet, savory. Crunchy, chewy. Got you covered."

"Er…thank you?" I look behind him, past Dimitri, noticing Killian has stepped into the doorway. Great.

"What's going on?" he asks.

"Your sister's on the rag," Dimitri says, gesturing to me with his half-eaten bagel, "and Tristian's doing his most nauseating impression of a Prince."

"Ah." There's no mistaking the hint of amusement on my stepbrother's face. "Gotcha."

"Ignore them," Tristian says, immediately pouring a cup of tea. "The tea is hot, so don't burn yourself. The health food store had a variety of teas for this time of the month, but I settled on the one with the best antioxidants. Make sure you drink the water, though, because it'll help flush out the toxins, which, from my understanding, is what causes most of the bloating. I've also added a protein bar, a banana and a cup of berries." He fusses with the heating pad, looking unbothered when I swat his hands away. "This should help soothe the cramping. If it gets too hot, you can adjust the temperature." He tilts his head, scrutinizing me. "Do you find your cramps settle more in the stomach or lower back?"

"Jesus Christ, Tristian," Killian grumbles, "She's been having her period since she was fourteen. I'm sure she's got this under control."

All eyes in the room swing to him.

"Fourteen?" Dimitri repeats. "That's awfully specific."

"We shared a bathroom," Killian says defensively. "You've seen her. She's a slob like you. Left her shit all over the place."

Tristian visibly shakes off that information. "Story is our Lady, and my job as her Lord is to see to her health and needs. Just because you monsters don't appreciate her superior reproductive functions doesn't mean I'm going to ignore it." He turns back to me, stroking his hand tenderly over my hair. It's really starting to creep me out. "You take the day to yourself, sweetheart. Text or call me if you need anything. I told Ms. Crane not to be such a major league bitch today, but it turns out she's spending the morning at the doctor. Lucky you." He frowns, forehead creasing. "I'll need to clean up the broken plate she threw at me before we head out."

It's weird and overbearing and a little scary, and I must be a hormonal cesspit, because all I feel is strangely touched.

I look at him in bafflement. "That's… uh, really nice of you, Tristian."

When he leans down to kiss me, he keeps it light and chaste—sweeter than the chocolates he's left for me.

And then he ruins it by saying, "I know." Not catching my eye roll, he adds, "And I downloaded some movies for you. Rom-Coms, tearjerkers, whatever helps you feel better."

"This is pathetic," Dimitri groans, throwing his head back. "Chick flicks aren't going to make her cramps go away, moron."

Tristian throws him a dirty look. "She might need an emotional hormone purge."

"There's only one thing she needs," Dimitri argues, licking the cream cheese from his finger. "I can have you that Percocet in thirty minutes flat. Say the word, baby girl."

"No, but thank you," I say, meaning it. After all the manipulation and revenge, it's nice to just have someone want to take care of me.

Tristian hesitates and then bends, kissing me on my forehead. "Take it easy, okay?"

"I will."

The guys leave the room, Killian giving me one last look before he shuts the door.

For a long time, I doze, the heat from the pad lulling me into a comforting stupor. Every time the cramps twist me up, I roll over, readjusting the heating pad until I repeat the cycle. The sounds of morning traffic contrast with the stillness of the house, making it appear as though I'm ensconced in a bubble. It's easy to close my eyes and disappear inside it, if only in small snatches of time.

It's been a long time since I felt this normal.

The next time I stir, I resolve to sit up and down the glass of water. The berries and banana are eaten more for the benefit of not taking the pain reliever on an empty stomach than any real sense of hunger, but the more I eat, the more

I feel like I can actually get out of bed.

There's a few minutes in the bathroom spent staring at the empty stretch of wall where my mirror used to be. Killian and I don't talk about the night I cut my wrist, but sometimes—over dinner, in his truck, every time I hand him a drink—I'll catch him looking at my wrist cuff, as if he's imagining the thin scar that's hiding beneath it.

He's never mentioned having my mirror replaced.

After a long, hot shower, I twist my hair into a loose braid and decide to take my dishes downstairs.

That's when I find the box.

It's small and sturdy, wrapped in a shiny gold bow, and sitting on the floor right outside my door. I pause before stepping on it, backing up to consider the gift. God only knows what Tristian's left me now. Organic, hand-woven tampons?

Oh, no.

Did he find out about *menstrual cups*?

I bend to pick it up, knowing whatever's inside is going to be embarrassing, and—let's face it—probably hilariously off-mark. I haven't watched a rom-com since I was thirteen. Not drawing it out, I hastily untie the ribbon and open the box.

It takes me a moment to parse the contents—something beige and red, laying on a bed of fine, white satin. It isn't until I see it rolling on the floor that I realize I've flung it away, mostly because my heart's in my throat, pulse thundering so loud. *So loud.*

The hallway tilts a little.

Slamming my door, I throw myself back so fast that I fall, landing hard against the corner of my bed. It's odd how moments can move both fast and slow. It feels like it takes me hours to find my phone, hand flapping out wildly, blindly, without consideration to the teapot I send crashing to the floor. But it's as if the phone is suddenly in my hands, time rushing and pausing in these tiny, confusing stretches.

I keep my wide, panicked eyes fixed to the door as I thumb up the first contact.

Lady: *cone hime*

Lady: *come hum*

Lady: *COME HOME*

My thumbs are as spastic as my breaths, ears straining to hear any disturbance within the stillness of the house. But it's just like it had been before, when I'd been lying in bed. Empty. Silent.

Deceiving.

My phone lights up before the tone rings out and I frantically swipe to answer it, knowing who it is. "Someone's here," I rush out, and even though I try to keep my voice low, it still emerges in a high, panicked screech.

Killian doesn't ask who. "Where are you?" he asks, sounding almost as clipped and tense as I feel.

"In my bedroom." But after saying it, I bolt to the bathroom, locking the door behind me.

"Did you see him?"

"No," I answer, knowing he means Ted. Frantic, I add, "But I saw the severed finger he left outside my bedroom door, and it's pretty convincing!"

Killian spits a low curse, a flurry of sounds penetrating the static. "I'm pulling out now."

"Tristian and Dimitri—"

Killian interrupts, "It'd take too long to get them. I'm crossing the lot." I try to inhale, wondering how insane it'd be to climb out my bedroom window. I look around for something, anything, that might help me defend myself, but all I come up with is a curling iron. As if reading my thoughts, he asks, "You know where my piece is, right?"

"Across the hall, under your bed," I lament, wishing I'd tried harder to demand a gun. After what happened with Ugly Nick, the thought of holding one in my hands again made my chest tight and heavy, something dreadful roiling away at my insides.

"It's loaded, so if you can just get to it, then—turn a little slower, you piece of shit!" The last part is shouted, followed by the ear-piercing sound of his horn.

"Okay," I say, taking a deep breath. "I can run for it, right?" I ask this uncertainly, peeking out of the bathroom before I creep across to my door. "Stay on the line, okay?"

"You, too," he grinds out, clearly indulging in a little road rage as the horn blares again. "I'm about five minutes out."

I try not to think about what's on the other side of the door, out in the hallway, waiting for me. It's only a few steps from my door to Killian's room. A straight shot. I can do this.

Every muscle in my body is strung as tight as Dimitri's piano wires as I turn the knob, easing the door open. My heart batters in my chest as I peer out the crack, sprung and ready to retreat. But all I see is an empty hallway. The sound of distant traffic mingles with the grandfather clock ticking at the end of the hallway, my thin, shallow breaths joining them. But even straining my ears, I hear nothing else.

I swing the door open and dart across the hall.

There could be someone in Killian's room, poised and ready to catch me, but I don't think about that. I dive for the floor, reaching for the box I know holds his gun.

"I got it," I rush out, thrusting the barrel toward the hall. "I've got the gun."

"Good," he responds, the word sounding assured and very deliberate. "Now here's what I want you to do. You listening?"

"Yes," I reply, panting. My hand trembles, but the gun is solid in my hand, easing some of the rushed panic. I can shoot a gun. I've done it before. I've taken a life, bullet after bullet buried into a man who would have killed us first. Sometimes I still see his face, nightmares filled with the sight of the hole in his cheek and his dim, lifeless eyes staring through me.

"Go and close my door. Lock it." He waits until I obey to go on. "Put the phone on speaker and set it somewhere. I want you to check the bathroom. Make sure it's clear."

"Okay," I answer, tightening both hands around the gun, just the way he taught me, as I inch toward Killian's en suite. "I'm going in now." My voice is shaky, but he doesn't draw attention to it. After flicking on the light and checking the shower, I announce, "It's clear."

"Now, the closet."

I repeat these tasks, making sure every nook and cranny of Killian's bedroom is empty of anyone but me. After, he demands, "Go to the corner—the one by the window—and wait there for me. Back to the wall, got it?"

"Yes."

"I'm almost there." After a stretch of silence, he adds, "Don't stop talking."

"Okay. Yes." It feels like that's all I've said. Yes. Okay. Yes. Okay.

He seems to understand. "Tell me about what happened."

As I wait, I relay to him the details of the box. Of almost stepping on it. The golden bow. How I thought Tristian had left me something. I tell him about opening it and realizing what was inside. A slender finger, chopped clean at the knuckle and nestled in a bed of satin.

By the time I'm done, he's pulling up to the house.

"I'm coming through the door," he says, sounding rushed.

"Be careful!" I try to keep my shout to a whisper, but the thought of Killian walking into an ambush makes my lungs constrict. "He could be out there."

"I'm coming straight to you," he says, disregarding my worry. "Don't freak out, I'm running up the stairs." I can hear him, his footfalls quick and heavy and drawing near, and I dart across the room to meet him at the door.

The first thing he does when I let him in is take the gun from my hands and tuck it into the back of his jeans.

The second thing he does is haul me into his chest.

I breathe in the clean, masculine scent of him, amazed at the way my chest loosens. I wonder when that happened. When did I stop seeing Killian as a necessary evil, and start seeing him as someone I felt safe with? Was it the cabin? Was it afterward, the night at the Velvet Hideaway when he shot his own father to protect me? Or was it right now, right here, his concise, collected orders to protect *myself*?

Either way, I feel it—this tight, panicked prey-instinct unwinding at the pressure of his powerful arms around me.

He pushes his nose into my hair, inhaling. "You're okay."

"Yes." *Yes. Okay.* "I mean, I'm…I'm fine." Now that he's here, arms folded around me, my cheeks heat. There's a severed finger out there in the hallway, but I can't shake the feeling I'm overreacting.

When he pulls away, he cups my face, searching my eyes. "You want to wait here while I check the rest of the house, or—"

I shake my head. "I'll come with you."

His mouth forms a grim line. "Why don't we start upstairs, work our way down, get an extra gun, huh?" He gives me this little chuck on the chin that should feel patronizing, but instead just makes my mouth twitch.

"Lead the way."

I follow him for the next hour as he painstakingly clears each room of the massive house. I watch the muscles beneath his shirt flex and coil at each corner we round, every door he pushes open. It's different from how he is on the field, as if he's slipped on another skin. This one is precise and deadly, a stark contrast to the raw, uncontrolled fury of Killer Payne, star quarterback.

In the end, it's almost a disappointment to find nothing.

"He had to have had a key," Killian says when we reach the den. He dumps the box with the finger on the table and glares at it. "We locked this place up like Fort Knox before we left."

Shivering at the sight of the 'gift', I ask, "Cameras?" Tristian had sworn they were all disabled, but a part of me doubts that's the case.

So when Killian looks me in the eye and says, "Zero," I admit to being surprised.

"Oh." I balk at the remorse I feel for making the demand, resentful that—in this house, certainly—security and privacy run in counterpoint.

Just then, I'm hit by a wave of cramps, and Killian must notice the grimace on my face, because he jerks his head to the couch and says, "Sit. Tristian and Rath will be back in a few." He crosses the room, fiddling with something over by the fireplace, and returns with a glass of amber liquid. "Loosen your nerves a little," he says at my skeptical expression, setting the gun on the table.

The whiskey burns going down, and for a second, I miss being upstairs, in bed, feeling so normal in my little fake bubble. But this isn't so bad, Killian sinking onto the sofa beside me. He's warm and solid, and lets me lean against all that strength, his shoulder firm beneath my temple.

I don't even realize I'm falling asleep.

"It's old." Dimitri's voice is distant and quiet.

So is Tristian's. "There aren't even any wrinkles."

"No, I mean, it's old. As in 'not fresh'." There's a beat of silence, and then Dimitri adds, "Probably refrigerated. It doesn't have that much decomposition."

Tristian suddenly hisses, "Don't touch it! That's disgusting."

"It's just a finger."

"It's a dead, decomposing finger," Tristian argues.

"With a red painted nail." Dimitri's reply is pointed. "Are you guys thinking what I'm thinking?"

"If you're thinking that's Vivenne's pinky?" Killian answers, voice a strong rumble beneath my ear. "Then yeah."

"She's been dead for weeks," Tristian responds, voice dripping with disgust.

Dimitri says, "Read the note again."

I try to swim through the barrier of slumber. A note? I didn't even realize there'd been a note, too panicked and freaked out to bother looking.

Tristian recites, "*Dear Sweet Cherry. It's been a long while since we last spoke. Digital correspondence is so lacking in intimacy, don't you think? I thought it better to write to you personally, like the old days, but you're so hard to reach. Those barbarians you live with actually believe they can keep me from you. Quite silly of them. Consider this gift a small example of what happens to whores with inadequate security. Be seeing you soon. Forever and faithfully yours. Ted.*"

My eyes open, taking in the expanse of Killian's chest. At some point, he'd pulled me down to lay on the couch, and now I'm wedged between it and him, my leg thrown over his knees, nestled up into his body's warmth.

His fist is massaging a slow, firm rhythm into the pit of my lower back. "We need to lock our shit down. No more guests, not even LDZ. Not until we find this motherfucker."

"Agreed," Tristian says, folding the note and placing the lid over the box. It's then that he notices I'm awake, peering blearily up at him. There's a softness in his eyes that I'm always surprised to find there. "You need a less exciting life, sweetheart."

"I *really* agree."

"I was in a lecture." Tristian comes close enough to stroke his knuckles down my cheek. "You good?"

Nodding, I exhale at the way Killian is massaging that spot in my back. "I'm good."

Dimitri clears his throat, plucking the box up. "I'll go find somewhere to put this. We should keep it on ice for a bit, just in case." He looks between the other two. "Beer freezer?"

Tristian looks *horrified*. "Gross! I don't want that thing mingling with my beer."

Dimitri arches an eyebrow. "Would you rather have it 'mingling' with your food? Because the 'severed appendage freezer' is in our *other* house."

"Fine," he grumbles, giving the box a disdainful look. "Just put the box with the finger in something airtight. Like a Ziplock." He pauses, face screwing up. "It's always the weirdest shit around here, I swear to god."

"I know the feeling," I say, shivering. Guns and intruders. Attempted murder and actual murder. Rotting fingers and threatening notes. It doesn't feel as though things are getting any better. That's why I force myself to say what's been on my mind ever since Killian rushed home. "I think we need to turn the cameras back on."

Tristian's eyebrows shoot up his forehead. "Is that so?"

"*Not* all of them," I clarify, even though the enthusiasm in his voice makes my lips twitch. "Just the ones in public areas. Don't you think so?"

"It's a good idea," Killian says, abandoning my lower back to rub some warmth into my arm. "Foyer, hallways, front and back door. Get the one in the garden, too."

Dimitri goes to stash the finger while Tristian heads upstairs to handle the security from his laptop. Even after we're alone, neither of us moves. It's just so comfortable here, Killian's body is warm and safe—another thought I never expected to have.

It's weird. There's no anger, no manipulation. Just two people comforting one another. It can only be one of two things: either Killian genuinely cares about me, or he's just as freaked out about everything that happened here as I am.

Either way, I owe him this.

"Thank you," I say, looking into his eyes when he turns his head to face me. "For getting here so fast, and talking me through it. I just—"

The kiss is broadcasted in a million ways. He hooks a finger under my chin, lifting it. He tips his face down and pauses for a millisecond, eyes heavy. I meet him there in the middle, ready to feel his tongue against mine, but unprepared for the gentle way he strokes our mouths together. I'm used to his hard, angry kisses. Kisses that are meant to claim and conquer. Kisses that leave me weak-kneed and breathless and vaguely embarrassed.

This kiss is slow and luscious and achingly tender.

"Little sister," he says, lips brushing against mine, "we protect what's ours."

THERE'S NOT MUCH time to dwell on what happened over the next few days.

Life, I've noticed, with these three, is a rollercoaster of peaks and valleys. They have one foot in and out of two worlds. There's the first world, where intruders break into your house and leave decomposing fingers, and then the other, comprising football games, exams, and the daily monotony of college life.

More and more, I wonder how I'm a part of either.

As December crawls on, time unwilling to pause for the sake of catching our breaths, my Lords grow increasingly restless about it all. I can see it over dinner, snarky comments and arrogant smirks replaced with somber discussions about Kings and their crimes, brothels and informants, frats and their legacies. Despite the tension, they play nice, and with each of their lingering glances they think I don't see, I suspect it's because they want to keep me calm. I don't hate them for it. In fact, I might just love them for it.

Such an odd notion.

Love.

It wasn't very long ago the idea of anyone loving these three—let alone me—would have been outright laughable. These men aren't made to be loved. They're made to be hard and cruel, and avoided at all costs. Only now I've seen their softness. It's there when Killian looks at me at night, just before we go to bed. He wants to ask to be let inside, but he doesn't. I'm not stupid. He still paces the hallway, waiting. But he tries to hide it now.

The same softness is there when Dimitri sits beside me on the way to school, mouthing sweet, dirty words into my neck as he covertly composes a melody on my thigh. It's there in the evenings, if I ask, because he'll take me up to his room and play it for me on the piano, his dark gaze just as heavy with meaning as the music he plays. It says, *Stay.*

And Tristian.

Well, in some ways, he's the easiest of all.

I curse when I see the laundry basket pushed into the corner of my bedroom. I'm wrapped in a towel, wet from the shower. I'd gone through all my clean underwear the day before and forgot to take the hamper down, so naturally Ms. Crane is going to kill me.

"Shit," I mutter, rummaging through one of the drawers in the dresser. I'd worn them all. Even the basic cotton ones I arrived with got used during my period.

I pick up my phone and shoot off a text.

Lady: *I need something.*

Tristian's response is immediate.

Lord T: Anything, sweetheart. I'm at your service.

I bite down on my lip to restrain my smile. The thing is, sometimes I think it's completely genuine, as if I could ask him to walk in here on all fours and lick my toes. It's an odd feeling, wondering if I should take advantage, test the bounds of it.

Lady: *You wouldn't happen to have bought me any bras or panties that you didn't give me?*

Lord T: Did Rath finally take them all?

Lady: *Mine are all in the hamper. Dirty. Including the ones Dimitri returned when he cleaned his room. This week has been kind of crazy and I for—*

The sudden knock interrupts my typing. I secure the towel with one hand and reluctantly pull the door open with the other. Tristian is standing on the other side, posture loose and casual as his blue eyes sweep up and down my body.

He holds up a pink bag with familiar lettering on the side. His favorite lingerie shop. "I bought this before the new rules were made. I'd been saving it. For something special"

"Really." *Unlikely.* I take it from him, anyway, just grateful to be saved. "Thank you."

He props a hand against the jamb, gaze fixed to the top of my towel. "Need any help getting it on? I'm a master with a bra clasp."

When he reaches out to finger the edge of the terrycloth, I bat his wrist away, giving him a sweet smile. "I'm sure you are, Tris, but I think I've got it."

He lets out a deep sigh. "Very well. But I'll be in my room if you get in a bind."

"I'll remember that."

I let him step away before closing the door, refusing to fall prey to the wild flip in my belly at his heated stare. I haven't forgotten that day in the living room. I'd never admit it to him—I can barely admit it to myself—but in some ways, he was right. Those long, lonely nights spent on the phone with Dimitri as we brought ourselves off. Thanksgiving in Daniel's office, Killian's hips punching into me. My going to Dimitri's room that night, ready to give in.

I might just be the horniest person in this house.

A moment later, I have the new set laid out on the bed. It's beautiful. The fabric is a pale blue—almost silver—with delicate lace and a tiny bow in the center. The back crisscrosses in a layer of intricate straps. The panties aren't what I'm used to finding in my drawer, especially from him. Those are mostly thongs that are barely worth wearing other than covering my pussy for the tiny skirts they like me to wear. These are far from being the trashy underthings I'm used to suffering through.

This is the kind of lingerie a classy woman would wear.

The kind expected of a woman a Mercer would date.

Wondering what Tristian might have been saving this for, I dry off completely and put the bra and panties on, glancing at myself in the mirror. I'm stunned at how good the color looks against my complexion and how it feels almost painted on—like a second layer of skin. Somehow, Tristian knows every part of my body.

My phone buzzes on the bed, and blushing irrationally, I reach for it.

Lord T: How does it fit?

Lady: Perfectly.

Lord T: You sure you don't need me to come check?

Lady: You wish.

Lord T: Sweetheart, you have no idea.

I stare down at my phone, the last message from Tristian left hanging, because yes, in some ways Tristian is the easiest.

But in others, he's the most difficult.

It'd be so easy to fall into him. To let him steer me, control me. He's not like Killian. Even if it's at times misguided, Tristian only wants to take care of me. But there's something about the way he's always in control that makes me feel I'm teetering on the edge of a cliff. One false move and I'll fall. The way he guided me and Killian the other night, drawing us from the edge of hot, rageful anger to the darkest, sexiest seduction...

That's powerful.

He's not physically imposing like Killian, or broody and dangerous like Dimitri, but he's insanely confident, ridiculously rich, and absolutely in control, even when he's holding a match in his fingertips, seconds from lighting a fire. It doesn't matter that I've been under his heel before. That I've seen what he's like when he crosses over the boundaries of sense. That I know what it feels like to be on my knees for him—because of him—*forced* by him. Tristian Mercer still seems almost too good to be true.

He makes me want to stop worrying about all that so I can just take and have, and that may be the scariest thing of all.

I just need to hold on to my own control here—at least a little. I look over at the skull on my dresser. It's covered in rhinestones and glitters in the light. It's also equipped with a camera tucked in the eye socket. Even after turning all the cameras back on, there are no open feeds in my room.

Not unless I enable it.

I feel a knot unwinding in the back of my neck as I pick up the skull. It's a testament to how twisted this thing between us has become that turning off the cameras and locking Killian out hasn't been an easy decision to endure. I don't think I've allowed myself to admit what Dimitri had been trying to get me to face all those long nights on the phone. I might have secured my privacy and exercised my control.

But I miss them.

Navigating that with Dimitri has been simple, and Killian might be harder—more turbulent and unpredictable—but it's still a certain kind of familiar. The other day in the living room, I realized that I miss the weight of Tristian eyes. The sense that he's watching. The knowledge—no, the anticipation—that any one of them could walk through my door and touch me. I miss the way Tristian's hands make me feel, because he's not rough like Killian, or cunning like Dimitri. He's unexpected, pushing me to explore my limits over and over again.

I flip on the camera and settle it back on the dresser, pointed at the bed. Then, reaching for my phone, I take a picture of the skull with my camera and type: **He's watching. Are you?**

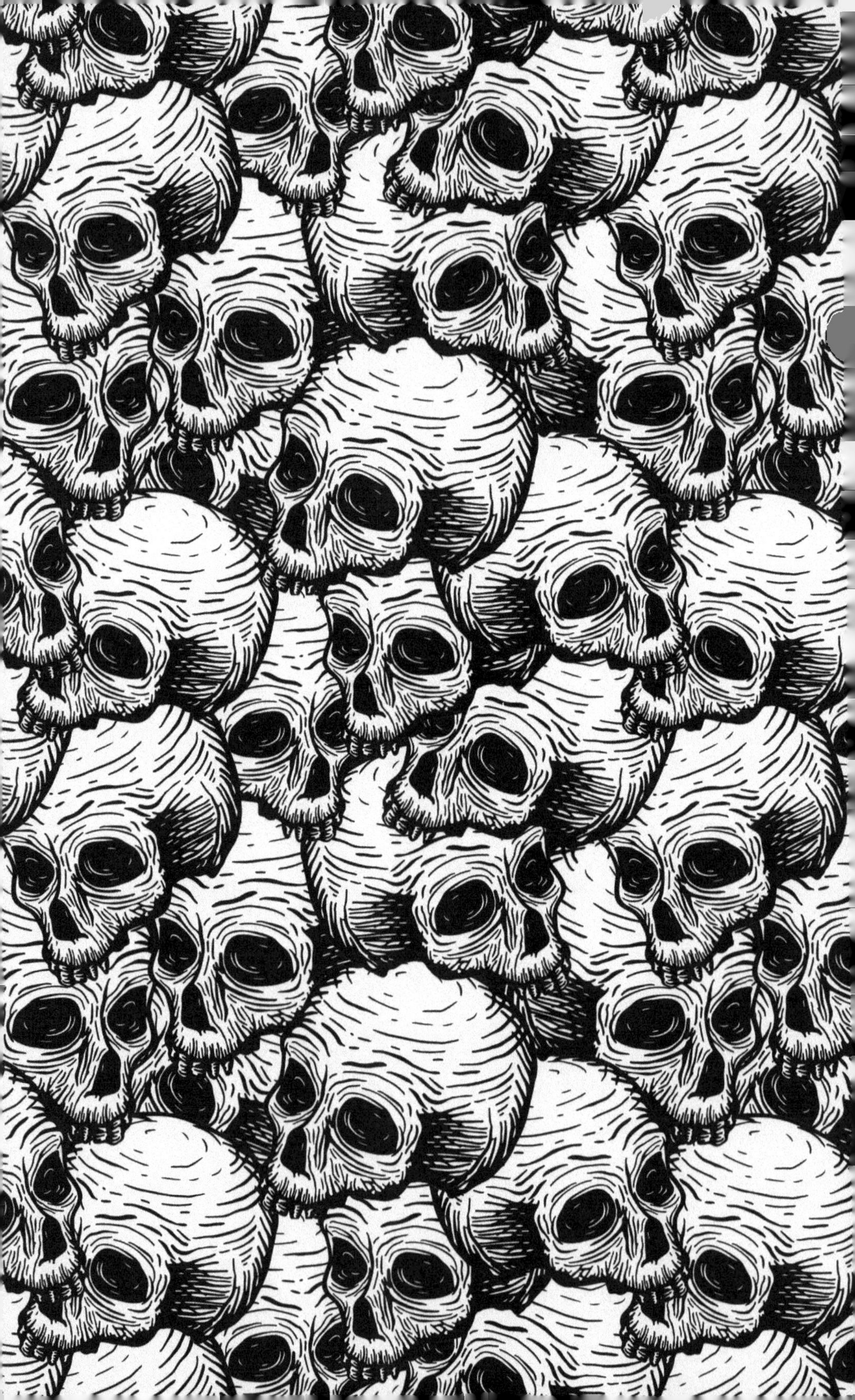

11

FINGERED

I STARE AT the text for a long moment, remembering three days ago, when I showed her how to enable the camera in the picture, before my body shifts into action. It's not just the laptop that I open, or my fingers stroking across the keyboard to get the video to load. It's my cock, hard and full, just knowing my girl is downstairs in that lingerie.

Unless she's fucking with me.

God, please don't let her be fucking with me.

The circle icon on the screen spins as the stream loads, but the video quickly blinks to life. The image is clear—I sprung for 4k, two-way audio for this one—and Story suddenly fills the screen.

"Fuck *me*," I mutter to myself, my erection throbbing. I knew the set would look hot on her—she's gorgeous, after all—but damn, she looks like an absolute vixen. The cups of the bra push her tits up into a nice, supple cleavage, and I can fully appreciate why Killer enjoys fucking them so much. I can just imagine the head of my dick pushing through those things, knowing what's hiding beneath. The scars are partially hidden between them, but I can still catch a peek of raised, discolored skin. I wonder if the sight of my initial carved into her flesh will ever stop making my blood simmer.

Doubt it.

She walks back to the camera and reaches to the back of the skull, giving me a nice view of the panties. Scratchy feedback comes through my speakers, and then her soft, tentative voice. "Can you hear me?"

My lips quirk, voice emerging a couple octaves too low. "Loud and clear, sweetheart."

"Well," she moves back in front of the camera, giving me a flash of her ass, "what do you think?"

"I think you're the most beautiful thing I've ever seen." I sit back in the desk chair, wincing at my painful erection. "I also think if Rath steals those panties, I'm going to commit arson on the piano."

I can hear him in there right now, pounding away at the keys. Ever since the night Story disappeared into his bedroom, the sounds of their fucking loud and obvious, he's been a raging musical lunatic, playing into all hours of the night. It doesn't bother me anymore, but he's clearly recaptured his muse.

She laughs, shyly tucking her hair behind her ear. "I'll try to hide them."

Reasonably, I offer, "You can come up here and hide them on my face."

God, but she's fucking sexy like this, looking like a dish, but still so coy and uncertain as she ducks her head to hide a grin. "I don't know if I ever thanked you for taking care of me during my period. And for…" Her eyes slide away, a rosy blush spreading over her cheeks. "… before, with Killian."

"Trust me." I reach down to give my dick a squeeze. "The pleasure was all mine."

She sits on the edge of her bed, and I can practically see her gathering up some courage. I don't know what for, at first. But then her thighs fall open, giving me a view of the smooth expanse of skin, leading to the lacy fabric between her legs. My eyebrows climb my forehead as she intentionally runs her fingertips along her inner thigh.

"I was just thinking how…" Her head tips to the side, showing me the long column of her neck. "… you've really kept to my boundaries lately." Her teeth rake over her lip as those fingers on her thigh slowly climb. "That's not easy for you, is it?"

"You have no fucking idea." My jaw flexes as I watch, realizing what this is. "But I keep my promises."

"I kept my promise, too," she says, moving her other hand to play with the strap of the bra, a slender finger tracing the lace detailing. "Even though I don't have to anymore, I haven't touched myself. Not without permission."

Muttering a curse, I reach under the waistband of my shorts and take my cock in my hand, giving it a slow stroke. "No? Why did you do that?" God knows the rest of us have been beating our dicks like they owe us money.

"I don't know," she answers, her fingers making tiny circles on that pale patch of inner thigh. "I just don't think I could bring myself to do it. Not if one of you isn't a part of it. It wouldn't be as… good? I think I just want to save it." She says it with this little pensive crease between her eyebrows, like maybe she's learning something about herself. "I want to save it for you."

My head falls back, a groan rumbling in my throat. Jesus, this girl. I try to contain myself, keeping my voice low and controlled. "Do you want to touch yourself now, sweetheart?"

She nods, biting down on her lip. "I do, but only if you're okay with it."

Okay, now she's toying with me. I know it. She knows it. But I don't give a fuck. I don't give a fuck that she knows my weaknesses, or that there was a time in high school she did this sort of thing semi-professionally. It still feels like mine. For me, and me alone. It's sexy and sweet, and this woman might be the most dangerous fire I've ever played with, but fuck it.

All I want is to get burned.

Slouching back—getting comfortable—I reply, "You have my permission," and pull my cock out of my shorts. It bobs dramatically, and I run my thumb over the precum accumulated at the top. "Just take it slow and make sure you're in range of the camera. I want to see *everything.*"

"Like this?" she asks, tugging down the straps of the bra and letting her tits free. Her fingers roll her nipple, tugging it into a sharp peak, while her other hand slides between her legs, pulling the panties aside to give me a view of her sweet, wet cunt. She blinks guilelessly at the camera. "Is this good?"

Yeah, she knows exactly what she's doing.

"Just like that, sweetheart." I mimic her movements, rolling and tugging my balls in my palm. "You're such a good girl, aren't you?"

She leans back on the bed, legs hanging over the edge, and lets her thighs fall further apart. "Only for you." The pads of her fingers make a quick rubbing motion against her clit and she moans from the friction. My breathing matches the rise and fall of her chest, but I notice when her eyes dart to the side. It takes me a moment, but I realize she's looking at the door.

Ah, big brother is on the prowl.

"Is he out there?" I ask, cock surging at the thought of her touching herself for me while he's so close.

"Always," she breathes, fingers keeping their slow, circular rhythm.

Fisting my cock, I wonder, "Are you going to ever let him back in?"

She gives me a slow blink, but doesn't stop her movements. "I-I don't know."

"You fucked him," I point out, eyes fixed on the image of her pussy. "Twice. Why the freeze on this?"

"Because letting him in here…" She leans back again, breath hitching. "I'm just not ready."

It's fair. I know what he does to her at night. I had the two of them pegged that day in the living room, realizing that Killian still has a lot to learn. He knows how to own her, but he doesn't know how to let her move and breathe and be. I might be a control freak, but I'd be lying if I said a part of me didn't get off on seeing her like this. Not knowing what she's going to do. Having to work for it. The slow march of time wearing at my patience, and the willpower to hold on to it.

It's a certain kind of foreplay.

I watch as she poises an index finger at her entrance, ready to enter herself, and I find my body going tense at the thought. Unthinkingly, I command, "Stop."

"What?" she asks, staring owlishly at the camera. Her cheeks are red, eyes all glassy and dazed, halfway to losing any sense. "Did I do something wrong?"

"No, no," I assure, giving my cock a slow stroke. "I have a request."

She runs her finger up and down her slit, slow and pointed. "Oh. Okay."

Clearing my throat, I start, "I know the agreement is that we can't tell you who or what to fuck, but…" Well, there's not much to add to that. It is the agreement. Nevertheless, I take a chance. "Don't finger yourself. I don't want anyone inside you but us." A strange feeling builds in my chest at hearing the words come to life. "That pussy's so precious, sweetheart. And it's ours, isn't it?"

Her lips part, eyes shining back at me through the camera. "Y-yes. It's yours."

All the tension in my spine melts away. "That's right. And when your pussy clenches around something, it should be one of our cocks. Don't you think?"

I don't have the right to ask. I gave that up—willingly. But Story nods, lip trapped between her teeth. "I understand," she says, voice shaky.

I swallow back a groan and twist my palm around the head of my cock. "That's my good girl. You don't need it anyway. You can come just like this, can't you?"

She writhes at the praise, eyes never leaving the camera as she circles her clit, nodding. "Can you?"

My laugh is ragged and quiet. "Oh, sweetheart, I could absolutely come just from watching you play with your clit like this. But I do have my cock out."

I know what she's going to ask before the words even exit her mouth. I can see it in the spark alighting her eyes, the way her thighs clench around her hand. When she breathes, "Show me?" I'm scrambling for my phone, opening the camera and pointing it right at my dick.

Now, as a rule, I take a lot of time with my dick pics. Lighting, angle, and grooming are all very important to the integrity of the piece. Philistines like Rath would just snap a shot in any old position with no care as to composition and form. But a good dick pic takes time and heavy consideration. It's not something I snap on a whim after a workout. I carve out a good hour, really give the girls something worth opening and sharing around.

Right now?

I couldn't fucking care less.

I lift my dick in my hand and hit the shutter, hastily sending it off in a text. A moment later, she's grabbing for her own phone, thumbing the text open.

She breathes out this quiet, slow little, "Oh," that has my lips tugging up into a smirk.

I continue stroking my cock. "Like what you see?"

She looks away from the screen, eyes heavy as she works her clit. "Does it feel good?"

"Not as good as you," I confess, matching the rhythm of her slowly rocking hips. Words spill from my lips like an avalanche. "Fuck, you were so wet and perfect the other day. Haven't had a fuck that good in so long. Should have gotten Rath in there. We would have pumped you so full of our come..."

Shit, that really gets her going, head falling back as her fingers grind into her clit, mouth opened on choppy breaths. "H-how… how would you…"

"We could take you just like before. Back to back," I answer as my fist bobs up and down, voice gruff. "Or…"

The muscles in her thighs flex as she rocks into the motion of her hand. "Or?"

"Well," I offer, vividly imagining it, "three of us. Three holes…"

Her head shoots up, stare wild and heavy as that blush crawls down to her chest. "You mean…?"

"I'd fuck that pretty, wet pussy." My hand speeds up on my dick as I watch her shudder. "Rath could take you from behind, give that tight little asshole of yours a proper breaking in. Killer could take your mouth, fuck your face." She looks both stunned and electrified, which is exactly how I know she's moments from coming. "You'd like that, wouldn't you, sweetheart? Taking all of us at the same time? I bet you could handle it. All three of us making love to our sweet, nasty little slut…"

She lets out a soft, almost pained cry when she comes, thighs trapping her hand between her legs as she quivers so prettily. Mine is messy, practically an afterthought considering where my mind is, lost in the images of everything I'm describing to her.

By the time I come back into myself, she's out of frame, the image showing nothing but her empty bed.

I stare at it for a long moment, my fist and stomach covered in my spunk, before exhaling jaggedly. It's not until I'm in bed, showered and clean, flicking off the light by the bed, that realize how bone-tired I am. It's the first night I haven't spent down on the basketball court, or jogging the darkened streets of Forsyth, looking for any healthy way to blow off steam. It's either been that, or me jerking off to the video of her and Rath down in the pit, and I've about worn that clip raw.

What I needed was to see my girl biting down on her bottom lip. To tell her all these dirty things I've had rolling around in my mind. To breathe life into them. To plant their seeds into her brain. To know they can make her come like that, watching as the orgasm rippled through her. That's what finally settles me.

As my eyes adjust to the light, I notice the screen is still up on my laptop—and that the camera is still filming in night vision mode. Story is in her own bed, covers pulled up to her chest, with one pale leg jutting out.

She didn't block me out.

I lay on my side, staring at her sleeping form, trying to figure out what kind of hold Story Austin has on me. I know it's more than her physical looks. It's her fight—the way she pushes back—the roiling emotions under the surface. Maybe it was the way she begged Rath to fuck her with the knife handle that night in the funhouse. Maybe it was the day in the computer lab when she got on her knees for me. Fuck, maybe it was even before all that. Maybe it was that night, years ago, in Killian's laundry room, when she looked up at me with those eyes.

She's innocent, yet dirty and depraved, and strong enough to take it. It ignites something in me that no one—not Genevieve or any other female—has sparked before. She makes me want to make her feel good. She makes me want to give her everything. I don't want to burn her down.

I want to burn with her, high and bright.

"No." My father's voice is clear and brooks no argument.

"It's only one year," I reason, wiping my face. My morning workout had been hard, pushing me to the brink. I usually try to keep it chill, but I knew this godforsaken call was coming. "I have too much to do. I can't drop everything for a dumb Christmas party."

"Dumb?" Fuck. I know that low, dangerous tone. "The annual Mercer Christmas party is dumb now?"

"I didn't mean it like that." I can't exactly tell him the truth, which is that we're dealing with some psycho murderer who wants our balls on a platter, and the exposure of the annual Mercer Christmas extravaganza would be idiotic. "I just mean that it's a bad time."

"Oh, I'm so sorry." My father's voice drips with sarcasm. "I know how incredibly difficult it must be to be the heir to the Mercer fortune."

"Dad," I start, but he interrupts.

"No, no, no. I completely understand. Just like I completely understood when you blew us off for Thanksgiving. Your mother and I have only been planning this event since March." Christ. Real guilt tripper, my old man. "Do you think I'm stupid?"

Well, that's a whiplash moment. "Stupid? Where did I imply—"

"This is about Daniel Payne," he says, voice hard. "And I think you need to remember whose son you are. You're going to be here on the 24th at seven sharp. You're going to wear the tux your mother's had painstakingly tailored for you. You're going to smile and shake hands and be so goddamn charming that people are still talking about you at the next one. You're going to be the immaculate representation of the family you actually bear the name of. Is that understood?"

My father doesn't make threats. Never has, doesn't need to. It's unspoken, but plainly obvious what denying his request will mean.

Silently fuming, I bite out, "Yes, sir. Seven sharp."

"Attaboy," he says, hanging up.

I toss my phone on the weight bench, pushing my sweat-dampened hair back. Rath doesn't know how easy he has it. His dad is some absent sperm donor he's never met, and his mom couldn't care less what he does. Killian and I have to exist with the knowledge that some asshole holds the keys to our future, and they're constantly being dangled over our heads, just out of reach.

Except Killer's actually grown enough balls to fight back.

I think about this as I shower and change for classes, dreading that fucking party. It's always a huge spectacle, the Mercer Christmas party. It's more of a ball than a party, full of champagne and pretense, and usually I'd be all over it. But this year, I have more important things to worry about. Like keeping Izzy and Lizzy safe from this psycho. Like watching over Story. Like finding out who the hell this guy even is. I don't have time for photo-ops and speeches and waltzes.

I'm just heading down to find Killian—he'll feel my pain—when he finds me.

"Got a meeting in ten."

I pause on the second floor landing, inspecting the hardness that's fallen over my friend's features. "Meeting? We have classes in—"

Fists clenching, he explains, "It's the only time he'll see us."

Ah. So Killer really can feel my pain.

Crossing my arms, I ask, "You told your dad about Viv's finger." He gives a jerking nod. "And he wants to talk it over? Compare notes?"

"That's the plan," he says, the vein in his temple jumping. "Now or never."

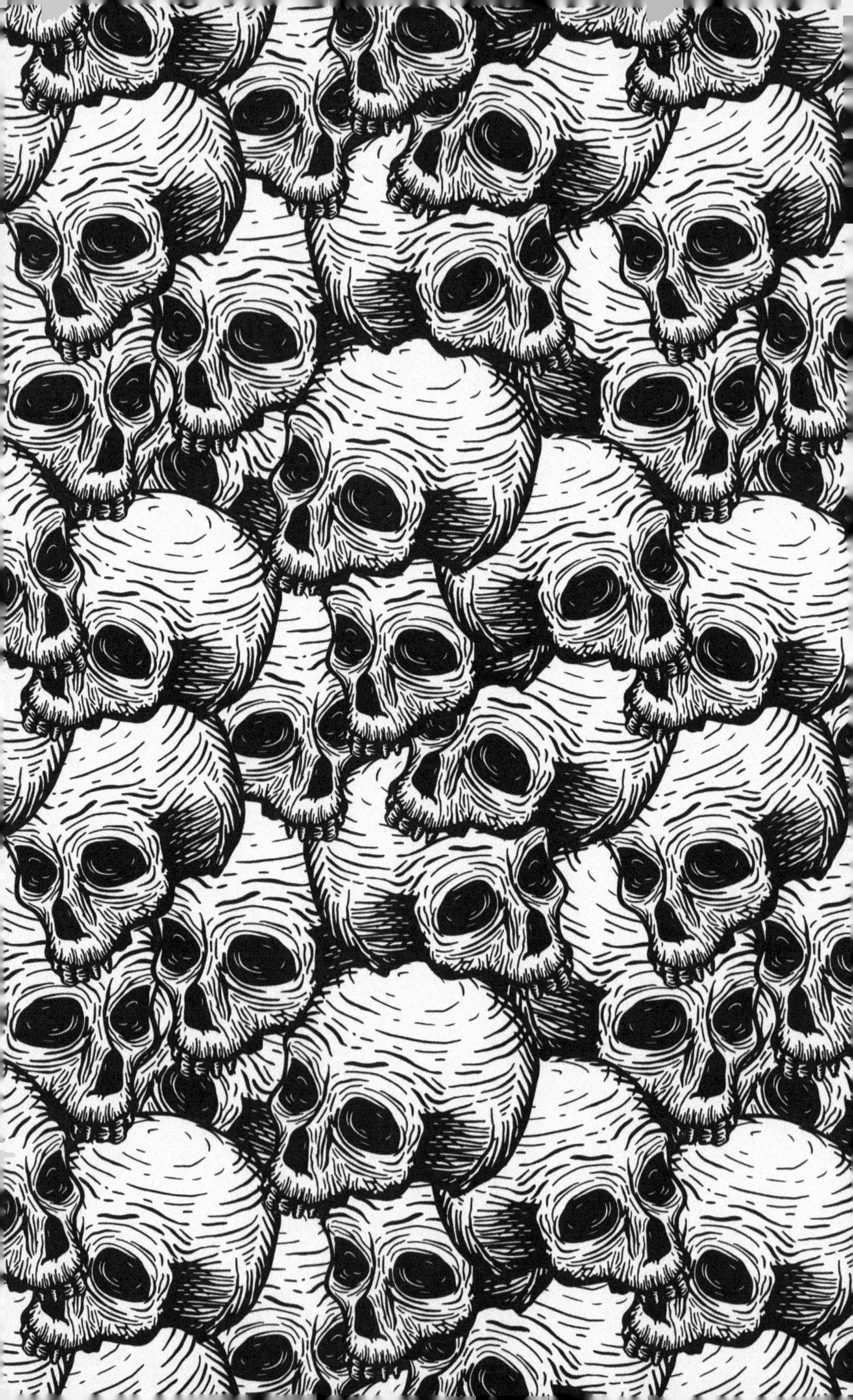

1 2

BIRDS OF A FEATHER

IF IT WEREN'T for all the tension, I'd probably fall asleep in the elevator leading to Daniel's office. I was up all night writing a new piece, parts of which the music director heard yesterday morning. She told me to go home and flesh it out, because it's worth more than half a shit, so that's what I did. Until four in the morning. I'd planned on sleeping it off until Killian pounded on my door, telling me Daniel wanted to see us; now.

It's not just the lack of energy that I'm fighting. It's dread. The weight of the debt I owe Daniel presses hard on my shoulders. I don't regret going in the pit for Story—hell no—but I'd made a deal with the devil. Avoidance has worked for me so far, but I feel like my time is running out. I can only lie low for so long.

Luckily, these two have enough energy radiating off them to fuel a fucking passenger jet. Killian's easy to understand. This is the first time he's seen his dad since that clusterfuck of a Thanksgiving. But who even knows what's got Tristian strung so tight.

I don't have to wonder for long.

Halfway up, he reaches out and pounds the elevators stop button, turning to us with a sour look on his face. "I have to go to my family's Christmas party."

Killian and I both stare at him blankly, but it's me who drawls, "Yeah…"

"And water's wet." Killian gives him a deadpan look. "When we were twelve, you had scarlet fever, and you still had to go to that Christmas party."

I add, "When we were fourteen, you got into that accident with your cousin, what's-his-name."

"Carson," Tristian offers.

"Yeah, and you broke your collarbone, and your parents didn't care. You still had to go to that fucking party." I roll my eyes. "Point being, this isn't exactly news."

"It's a bad time," Tristian says, head shaking. "I tried to tell him, but he just…" His hand balls into a fist, jaw clenching. "I want to take Story. As my date."

Killian looks him up and down, scoffing. "You're not taking my sister to your glorified rich-people mating dance."

"Yes, I am," he coolly argues, looking unfazed. "Because Rath took her to his performance, and you've got that dinner on your birthday coming up—yes, *that* one."

Killian scowls. "I'm not going to that."

"Sure you are. It's for the team, which you're still a part of." Shrugging casually, he reasons, "And you'll want her to be your date. So that means I get one."

My eyes ping back and forth, watching the standoff.

It's saying a lot about how shitty this meeting with Daniel is going to be that Killian caves, teeth clenched. "Fine. But you're responsible if anything happens."

Tristian presses the button on the elevator, jolting it back to life. "I'll take care of it."

When the elevator doors open, we all step out in tandem, but then we just… pause.

Vivienne's desk is empty.

The lobby is silent, completely void of her clacking nails and soft voice, and I think the same thing is probably going through all our thoughts. It's no wonder Daniel hasn't filled the vacancy yet. It didn't matter that she was sucking his cock on the reg. Viv was genuinely good people. She always did right by us, made sure we were looked after, treated us with a respect I'm not entirely sure we deserved. She was a professional, through and through, but she was also thoughtful about it. That's not something you see much of in this world—in South Side's world—in Daniel's world.

And she died with our initials carved into her chest.

It's some sick fucking game going on here, and I'm over it. I want to find this fucker and bury a blade into his throat. *Slowly.*

Killian takes a hard breath. "Let's get this over with."

I enter Daniel's office behind Killian and Tristian, the box hanging loosely from my hand. The man in question is standing behind his desk, arms crossed over his chest, and he doesn't look happy to see us. Oh, definitely not. This is not a civil Thanksgiving dinner within earshot of his pretty little trophy wife.

This is business.

"Show me."

I shoulder past the other two to toss the box. It lands on the desk with a loud clatter, still half-frozen. Despite that, when he snatches it up, it opens easily for him. He stares at the contents for a long time—long enough for me to get bored and start scanning the room. Things are messier than usual, the desk covered in papers. There's a gun lying to his right, which might seem sloppy to anyone else, but all of us know better. Daniel's always been good at posturing, making sure people see what he wants them to, and nothing more. His monitors are all dark, and from the wrinkles in his shirt, he's been here a while. Possibly all night.

"Well," he begins, closing the box and setting it carefully aside. "This doesn't look good for you, now, does it?"

Killian's eyes narrow. "Don't bullshit. You're smart enough to know this wasn't us, and we're smart enough to realize it. We need to find out who's doing this."

Daniel gives a loose shrug. "My people are clean as a whistle."

Tristian snorts derisively. "No one who works for you is clean."

"And what does that say about you?" Daniel asks, swinging his gaze to Tristian.

"It says that I'm here to protect the Mercers' interest in South Side," he replies, voice sharp in an icy, deliberate way. "Maybe you've forgotten why my father put me here, but I haven't."

Daniel scoffs. "When's the last time you even—"

Tristian's back snaps straight. "Your stake in Mercer holdings is dwindling, but you still have a firm grip in the commodities. You take a bigger cut of the illegal import fees than you have any right to; you've managed to distract the feds with a pointless runaround on migrant workers near the docks; and your brand new whorehouse was barely breaking even until a few weeks ago." It's been a while since I've seen Tristian like this—cold and cutting—but he's in fine form now, shooting Killian's father a menacing grin. "Don't be fooled by the fact Killian is a brother to me. I have another father, and I report everything I see directly to him. Always have, always will."

Daniel has nothing to say to that. There are only a few people in this town more powerful than him, and Tristian's dad is one of them. Instead, he changes tacks. "If you saw everything and weren't so busy thinking with your dicks, you could see what's right in front of you. You're not nearly as smart as you think."

My eyes narrow. "The fuck is that supposed to mean?"

"Someone is trying to split apart our *happy* family." Daniel says the words like they're sharp as knives. "This person has ties to us both, grudges against all of us, and access to everything." He waits a beat, looking between us. "Unbelievable. You really are stunted little idiots, aren't you?"

"I'm tired," Killian says, voice clipped, but even. "I'm tired and I'm busy, and I don't have time for your bullshit, dad. Spit it the fuck out."

Daniel does exactly that. "It's the *girl*."

Killian responds instantly. "Not possible."

"No? Where was she when this little package was delivered?" he asks, flinging the box down the desk. "Where was she the night Vivienne was killed? Not in your house."

"And how can you possibly know that?" I dryly wonder.

But pretense is dropping like flies around here. I know it is, because Daniel easily answers, "I checked your camera feed. And don't give me those looks. It's never been a secret that I have access to the Lords' property. It's not my fault you all assumed I wouldn't bother."

If that's true, then there's no telling the things he's seen. The things he's heard. The things he knows.

"That just swings it all back around to you," Tristian points out, twirling a finger.

Daniel gives him a long, incredulous look. "Oh, her pussy must really be something. She's actually got the three of you fooled, doesn't she?" Casually, he retrieves a folder from his desk, flinging it open. "Distribution of sexual images of a minor." He holds up a paper, text messages, photos of Story when she was younger stapled to the side. *Sweet Cherry*. "Grand theft auto." He holds up another paper, a grainy image of Story attached. "Breaking and entering. Grand larceny. Destruction of property. Felony identity theft..." He flips through them, page after page. These must have happened when she was in Colorado. "This one is my favorite," he says, holding up a bland-looking autopsy photo of Ugly Nick's corpse. "Murder."

"It's not Story," Killian snaps. "And the longer you focus on her, the more at risk you're making all of us. Here are the facts." He stalks forward to press his hands flat on the desk, pitching forward with a dark expression. "Someone got to Ugly Nick behind your back. Someone killed Vivienne. Look in your ranks: your suppliers, your contractors, your lawyers, one of your whores, someone. This is your mistake, bleeding over into our life!"

Daniel absorbs this with a visibly diminishing self-control. Mirroring his son's pose, he leans forward, fixing Killian with a narrow stare. "You're right, son. This is my mistake, bleeding over. The truth is, I should have taken care of that little slut the first time you snuck into her bedroom."

Killian's hand is only a couple feet away from that gun on Daniel's desk. All it would take is half a lunge to grab it—not that he'd need to. He's also got one tucked into the waist of his jeans.

Tristian and I are poised to pull him back, because while the thought of Killian shooting his dad again does hold some appeal, we have enough bullshit to worry about it.

To our shock, we don't need to.

Killian just *laughs*.

It's a malicious, humorless sound, making his shoulder blades bounce. "You just can't handle that you lost her, can you?" Glancing at us over his shoulder, he nods. "You lost your ripe little 'asset' to three men who are younger and better than you, and then you watched us slowly defile her. How did that feel, dad?" Mouth tugging up into a spiteful smirk, he wonders, "Did you watch me take her virginity? Did you watch me fuck her those nights in my bed?" He tilts his head, as if he's genuinely curious. "Did you watch me fuck her on your desk at home? Did you see how much she *wanted* it? Because that's really got to sting."

For a long, tense stretch of time, Daniel grinds his teeth. Oh, his face is all cool and composed, but he's got this muscle in his jaw that keeps writhing around. No one knows how to push his buttons better than his own creation: Killer Payne.

"I still remember the day you were born," Daniel says, feigning a wistfulness that none of us buy. "You were a week late. Did you know that? Your mother kept waiting and waiting. I walked in on her crying once, because she was so sick of being burdened with you in her tiny belly." It's a low, almost pathological blow, and Killian takes it exactly like I expect him to, flinching backward. It makes his father's eyes spark in satisfaction. "You came out of her, all bloody and wailing, as if we owed you something. My god, and you were such an enormous baby. Far bigger than you should have been. Her body never was the same, you know. You swelled her up, and then ripped right through her, a gruesome little savage from your first breath."

Tristian is the first to see the twitch, to lunge forward and pull Killian away before the fist he's throwing out can meet his father's jaw.

"And you two," he says, eyes flicking from Tristian over to me. "You're not even my flesh and I've given you opportunity and support. I've allowed you privileges that even my most loyal soldiers don't get."

Anger rushes through me and I blurt, "Like letting me buy your stepdaughter?"

Tristian's mouth opens slightly, like he's just figured it out. Killian...the way he keeps his eyes steady on his father, implies that he already knew. How? Who knows? He's his father's son.

"Yes, Dimitri," Daniel says slowly, "Negotiation is a privilege, one I allowed you because of our personal relationship."

"You're a sick bastard."

Daniel laughs, and it's the exact same sound his son had made moments ago. Empty, joyless. "In honor of the sacrifices that were made to bring Killian into this world, I think I'll give you until your birthday." Ignoring Killian's thrashing jerk out of Tristian's grip, Daniel straightens, sniffing. "You have until then to bring me a more convincing suspect. Else, I will handle her, and none of you will stop me."

"I'm done with you, and so is she," Killian sneers, straightening out his shirt. "We'll find this asshole ourselves."

He leaves the box with his father, and storms out of the office and into the empty lobby with the oppressive silence. Tristian and I are right on his heels, but before we cross the threshold, Daniel's voice rings out.

"Rath can stay." He looks perfectly composed when I turn to arch an eyebrow at him. "Since you brought it up, we may as well attend to our matters."

Fuck my fucking big mouth.

So much for lying low.

I turn back to Tristian, who must see the dread in my eyes.

"No," he says, flicking his eyes to Daniel. "Fuck this guy, Rath. Blow it off."

Lowering my voice, I explain, "I have...debts."

"I have money," he reasons, but I just shake my head.

"We both know he wouldn't take it."

Tristian searches my eyes and then mutters a curse. "You've got your gun?" When I tug up my shirt, his eyes dart down to catch its gleam behind my waistband. He jabs a finger into my chest. "You fucking call us if anything goes sideways. I mean it. Don't let him send you into something you can't handle alone. Killer might be done with him, but he'll still have your back."

I close the door on the daggers he's glaring at Daniel behind us. "Killer's right, you know." When I turn to face him, Daniel is sitting in his chair, looking carefully distracted. Such an obvious tactic, acting like none of this matters to him. "Story isn't violent unless she's pushed into a corner, and even then, it's more about protecting someone else. She's all about the emotional punch. If she wanted to hurt you, it wouldn't be by taking out an innocent."

I say all this because, in a way, I get it. From where he's sitting, it doesn't look good for her. But he didn't see that gut-wrenching look on her face when she found out about Vivienne. He didn't spend night after night on the phone with her, listening to her pour out her nightmares about Ugly Nick in that alley, dead and bleeding. He didn't hold her afterward in that cabin, didn't feel the sobs against his chest—sobs she tried so hard to hide. He doesn't know her.

Not like we do.

"You're going down to the Avenue," he begins, sorting the papers on the desk. "I have a bit of property I need moved. Nicholas will meet you there."

"Is this really worth it?" I ask, more pissed about it than curious. "Is losing your own son worth winning?"

Daniel finally looks at me then, and he doesn't need to answer. I can see it crystal clear in his eyes that he's washed his hands of the business of caring.

Still, he answers.

"That boy was lost to me the second she stepped foot in your house."

HE COMES OUT of the shadows the minute I get to the corner. Pretty Nick slinks out of the alley, looking both in and out of place. He's comfortable down here on the Avenue, with the hustlers and whores, the muscles in his body loose and easy. But his face? Well, I'm not particularly into dudes, but everyone knows this kid lives up to his name. The ink tattooed down his temple doesn't diminish his good looks. There's a reason Daniel chose him to defile Story that night in the pit.

"Hey, man," he says, sticking his fist out. I look at it for a beat, taking the gesture for what it is. No hard feelings. The thought of what this guy was going to do to my Lady down in the pit makes me want to peel the tattoos off his skin with the knife tucked inside my boot.

But it wouldn't be fair.

He's caught up in Daniel's bullshit as much as I am. Hell, Nick probably has his own debts he has to pay off down in the pit. In our world, enemies have to be chosen with care. Checks and balances. Add up the columns, see if it's worth it. Making an enemy of Nick wouldn't be. He and the Dukes are so low on the list of people who have pissed us off, it's hard to even give a fuck. Frankly, until we figure out who the fuck Ted is and stop him, all the frat stuff— The Game, the partying—seems trivial in comparison.

I reach out and bump his fist with my own, indulging him in an old-school, over-involved South Side shake that neither Tristian nor Killian have ever bothered to master. Nick's good people at the end of the day, even if he's been slumming it beneath Daniel's heel a bit too long. Like Killian, Nick is a Forsyth legacy. *Duke* legacy, to be exact. A born and bred Bruin, through and through. But unlike Killian, he's abdicated it. Left all the glory to his big brother, Sy, so he can play in the sewage with the rest of us.

Nick quirks me this easy little grin like he knows.

I might be a Lord, but down here, he and I are birds of a feather.

"So," I start, shoving my hands into my pockets and following him down the sidewalk. "Any idea what this job is about?"

"Just transporting some stuff," he says, casually. *Too* casually. Drugs? Guns? Whores? Whatever it is, it can't be good. I interfered with Daniel's little sex show, and I'm not dumb enough to think he's let it go. Sure, he took the money I offered him to be the one to have sex with Story in the pit, but it wasn't the money that did it. He likes money, but he loves control more, and by taking every cent I had, he put me right where he wants me. Desperate. Broke. Indebted. The nervous twitch in my gut tells me wherever Nick is taking us isn't going to be pleasant.

After a moment of silence, Nick rolls his shoulders. "I hear your Lady is going to be in the Screw Year's Eve wrestling match," he says, jerking his head for me to follow him up a set of stairs. I notice we're at a shitty hourly hotel. Garbage is piled up by the front door and a guy with acne scars on the sides of his face makes a '*want some?*' gesture at me. I give him a hard look and glance away. Whatever he's selling, it's a hard pass.

"She wanted to do it," I reply, following him into the sour-smelling lobby. The lights cast a sickly, jaundiced glow on the older man sitting behind the counter. "She's really into the charity stuff for the South Side kids."

"A little do-gooder, eh? The fuck's she doing shacked up with the lot of you?" He says it off-hand, clearly meant to be a joke. Only it isn't a joke, and we both know it.

"We're her Lords, and she's our Lady," is my answer. "That's just how it's done."

He cuts me a brief look at this, like I've just said something unintentionally profound. "Hey, Earl," he calls to the old man. Earl nods but doesn't look up from the newspaper he's reading. Seems Nick has been here before. He starts up the steps and looks back at me. "Well, for what it's worth, I put all my money on her."

"Oh, yeah?" I follow him up the narrow staircase with worn, ragged carpet. "Why'd you do that? Isn't the Duchess, like...Duke-trained?"

Nick gives a quiet, rumbling laugh. "The Duchess is fine, but the Lady is tougher. Any other female would have broken down in the pit, including some who work upstairs." He raises his eyebrow. "Not your Lady. She does what it takes. I bet she plays dirty, doesn't she? When it's really on the line?" When all he gets from me is a blank stare, he shrugs. "Plus, I hear she's got beef with the Countess. Who doesn't want to see that conniving bitch get hers?"

He climbs three flights of stairs at a slight jog, barely out of breath when he steps into the hallway. He may have eschewed the Dukes, but it's common knowledge he still fights. Daniel doesn't keep him around just for his good looks.

I follow him down the dimly lit hallway, noting the peeling wallpaper and faint odor of urine. I swear to Christ, if Daniel sent me here to pick up a dead body, I'm going to go back and shoot him myself. Nick stops at a door and pulls out a flat brass key.

When he slides it in and turns the lock, I brace myself for what's inside, holding my breath in anticipation of the stench of decay and bodily fluids. My lucky day, there's no dead body on the bed.

But there is *somebody*.

A girl, about Story's age, is curled up on the bed, staring at the flickering TV. She's got blonde hair that looks like it's seen better showerheads, and legs for days. Attractive, for sure.

But the look she sends us is ugly.

"I thought we all agreed he'd stop sending you," she sneers. The expression is so severe that one could almost forget that split second of dull melancholy on her face before she realized we'd entered.

"Chill, little bird." Nick shoves his hand into his pocket and emerges with a crinkly wrapper. "I brought you a treat and everything."

She doesn't stop glaring, but beneath the thick tension of disdain in her features, a subtle, surprised longing appears. "Hand it over then," she says, voice sharp.

"Not until we're done." Nick stuffs the candy back into his pocket, cutting his eyes to me. "Trying to impart a bit of positive reinforcement. You understand. Pets need structure."

"What the fuck is this?" I ask, uneasily. A quick scan of the room reveals a small box mounted in the corner near the ceiling. No mistaking what that is. Fists curling, I grind out, "If he thinks I'm doing another show—"

A frozen hardness comes over Nick's face. "Not a fucking chance. I told you. We're here to transport." Eyes narrowing, he clarifies, "More accurately, *I'm* here to transport. You're here to make it awkward because Daniel thinks I won't do anything to her if there's someone else around. For the record, he's wrong." Nick swings his gaze back to the girl, smiling darkly. "It's just that I have impeccable self-control."

"Control *this*, dirtbag." She flicks him the middle finger, scowling. "And if you're going to feed me, then you better not have brought shitty tacos for dinner again. I'm pretty sure I found a rat aorta wrapped in the meat."

"Good afternoon to you too," Nick says, greeting her glare with a smirk. "It's time to flap your wings."

Her body stiffens slightly, barely noticeable, but I caught it. "Now?" Her tone is carefully indifferent, but there's apprehension under it. Considering Daniel's history with Story, I don't have to think too long about what kind of shit he's pulling with this girl.

"Now, little bird." Nick gives the wrapper another crinkle. "Your new digs are all ready for you."

"Great," she drawls, turning off the TV with the remote and tossing it on the bed.

Unsure of what I'm doing here, I take in the girl as she slides off the bed. Despite the cold, she's in a black T-shirt and a pair of cut-off jean shorts, showing off the tattoo that snakes up from her calf to her thigh. Her feet are bare, but a pair of flip-flops is on the floor by the dresser.

Nick bends to pluck them up, tossing them to her. "Someone lost shoe privileges," he says to me, grabbing her bag off the mustard yellow chair. "Sweet little Lavinia here is a kicker." He crams a toiletry bag on top and tosses a jacket to her. "It's cold. Put that on."

"Lavinia," I repeat, the name ringing the bell. "As in Lavinia Lucia? As in Lionel Lucia's daughter?" I take a step back, going rigid. "What the fuck's going down here? Because Daniel is bad enough. Pissing off two Kings isn't the kind of fire I like playing with." Lionel Lucia is King to the Counts, a federal circuit judge, and not someone I want to be on the bad side of.

"The less you know, the better." Nick throws the bag and I catch it. "But you don't need to worry about Lionel Lucia. Let's just say every part of the Royalty is down with what's happening here. Got it?" I very seriously do *not* fucking have it, but when Nick says, "Let's roll out," I clutch the bag in one fist and feel for my pistol with the other, poised for the worst. She dawdles by the bed so he grabs her by the bicep, yanking her out into the hallway. Huffing, he grits out, "Why do you make me drag you around?" It's said in a low voice, close to her ear, like he doesn't intend for me to hear it. "Is this how you flirt? Because if you like it rough, you don't need to try so hard, little bird."

I follow, shutting the door and keeping close on their heels. The girl keeps trying to put distance between her and Nick, but he's got a nice grip on her and keeps tugging her back.

"Keep close," he tells me. "We'll go out the back door. The van's parked in the alley."

It all seems like a simple plan.

We get Lavinia into the back seat, and I must be crazy—I must be seriously fucked in the head—because it's like this instinct takes over. The Daniel instinct. The psych department at Forsyth could probably spend years dissecting it. This thing buried deep in my hindbrain that puts me into soldier mode. It's what drives me to duck inside and yank the seatbelt over her lap.

One second I'm strapping her in, and the next, I'm flying away, dropping to my ass and clutching my shoulder. "Ow, fuck!"

Nick gives a lazy laugh. "Told you she was a kicker."

I grab the gun without thinking, lurching to my feet. Because that's the thing about Daniel mode. It doesn't make allowances for 'sweet little kickers'. "You fucking bitch," I spit.

But Nick is shoving me back, face rearranged into a stiff, emotionless mask. "Put that fucking thing away, Rathbone. If you hurt her—"

I rub my collar bone, teeth gnashing. "I don't give a fuck about Daniel's property."

"She's not Daniel's property," he says, voice a low hiss. "She's the Kings' property. That makes her untouchable until they say otherwise." Nick's gaze flicks down to the gun, eyes flashing as he places himself between me and the girl, hand resting on his own piece. "And trust me when I say they're not the ones you should worry about." He's standing there all big and hulking, like he'd be glad to let the Bruin loose—the bear with all its claws—and it hits me.

Rolling my eyes, I tuck the gun back into my pants. Fuck. He's into this girl. "So it's like that."

Eyes narrowed, he says, "Yeah, it's like that," and turns to shut her door. Before he can, a glob of spit smacks him in the face, rolling slowly down his cheek as he freezes. Nick blinks at her scowling face, barely flinching as he pulls the collar of his shirt up, wiping it away. For a long moment, there's utter silence.

And then the crinkle of a candy wrapper.

He tosses the candy into her lap before slamming the door, turning to me with a ragged smile. "Ain't love grand?"

It's not my place to question fucked up relationships, but as I get into the passenger seat, glancing over my shoulder at the girl curled up in the back, I do know one thing.

Whatever's going on with Lavinia Lucia is a fucking disaster.

And I don't want any part of it.

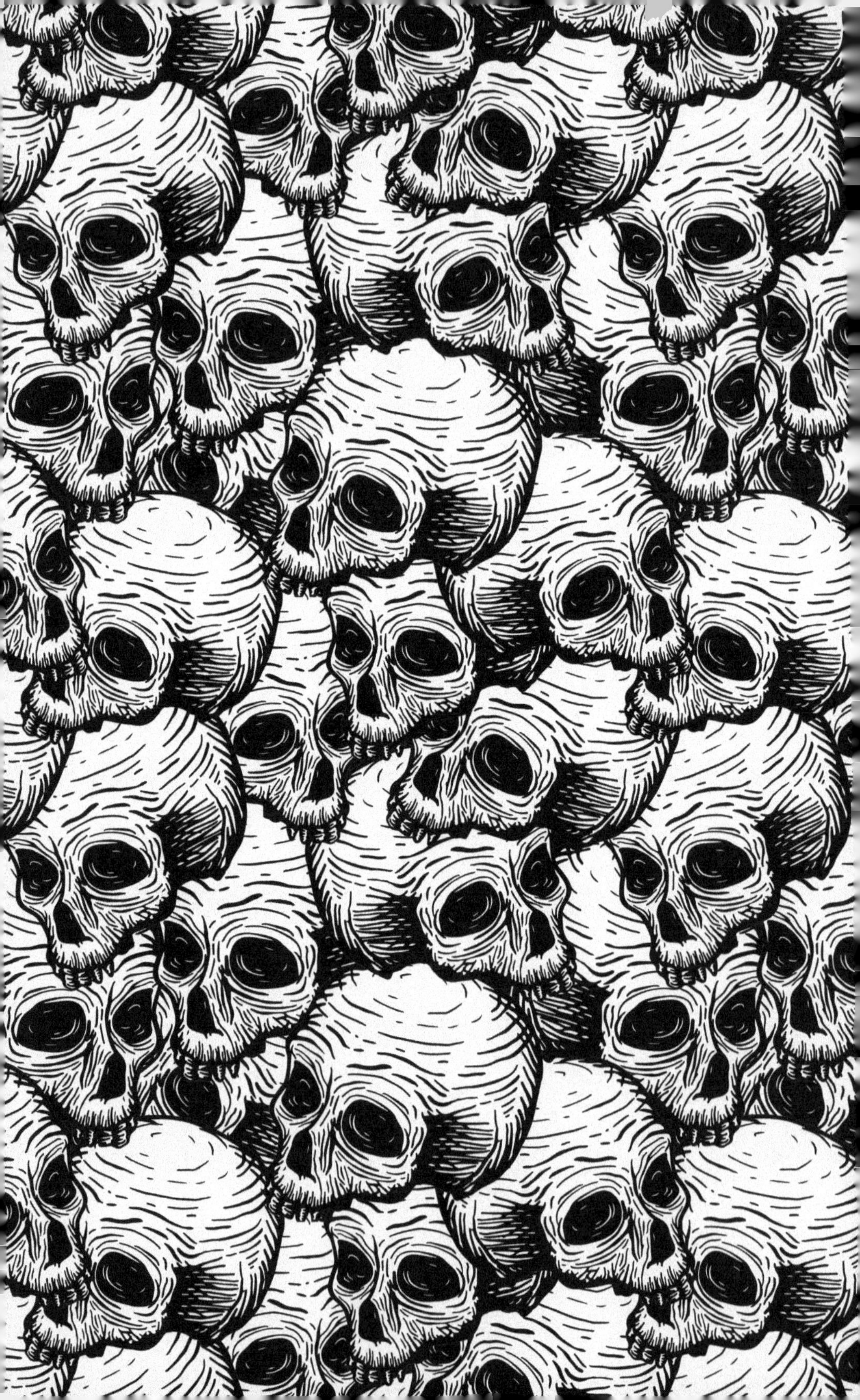

13

SHADOWS

"How did he ask?" Mom asks, voice pitched high and excited. "I want all the details. Don't leave anything out!"

My face heats, even though the chill makes me shiver. The temperature dropped fifteen degrees once the calendar rolled into December, and now I'm bracing myself against the wind. I hate the cold weather, but I've always had a fondness for the Christmas season. I don't know if it's the music, or the pretty lights, or the fact everyone always seems a little less hostile, but it's my favorite time of the year.

"He sat down," I begin, but she instantly interrupts.

"Where were you?"

Rolling my eyes, I start from the beginning. "We met in the student union for lunch." Just like always. Tristian doesn't tell me what to eat anymore, but he still makes sure I have access to his own personal choices. Sometimes I'll take them, enjoying the pleased kiss he'll press to my neck when I do. Sometimes I'll eat my greasy slice of fifty-cent pizza and do a little shoulder dance as he grimaces and grumbles disapprovingly. "He sat down and ate some of his disgusting soup, and then he asked if you and I had any plans for Christmas."

"Which we don't." I can practically hear her pout.

"Which we don't," I parrot, remembering the relief on his face. "Then he asked me if I'd escort him to his family's Christmas party."

"Escort him!" she gushes. "How fancy!"

I let her go on about this for a while as I dodge around a couple holding hands and scan the shops. I'm on a hunt for something to get the guys for Christmas, and it's not going well. What do you get the guys who have everything? Not a severed finger, that much I know.

Ignoring that I'm too broke to bother with much, it's just nice to walk around like a normal person for once. The side streets of Forsyth are decorated to the nines, decked out with candy canes and reindeer, string lights and garland that accentuates as daylight wanes. It's odd how it makes me nostalgic for something I never had. When I was a kid, our Christmas tree was a foot tall and made out of pipe cleaners.

Still, it's a big deal that the guys let me run these errands without them. It's rare that I'm left unsupervised, considering how tense they've been since the break-in. Hell, considering how tense I've been since the break-in, I rarely find it in me to protest anymore. But I've been dealing with one version or another of Ted for a long time now. I'm not letting that asshole ruin Christmas. Not this one. Not when I've finally found a home—however fraught living within it may be—and something that's messy and painful, but confusingly close to being called a family.

I've got gifts to buy and a party to shop for, so ho-freaking-ho.

Santa's coming to town, stalker or not.

Of course, these are easy thoughts to have when I still have their tracker beneath my skin.

"Story, are you listening to me?"

"Yes, Mom." I side-step a Salvation Army Santa. "I'm listening."

Nothing, not even my mother's voice on the other side of the phone, or the fact I've been out shopping for the perfect outfit to wear to the Mercer holiday party, can kill my buzz.

"I just want to reiterate that nails and eyebrows are a must. Good grooming is a signal to the wealthy. They can spot neglect a mile away. Oh!" At this, she lowers her voice. "And please tell me you've already been waxed? Men like the Mercers are going to expect a certain…ah, shall we say, smoothness, to their beaver friends."

"*Aw,* mom, *gross*!" My face might be screwed up in distaste, but let's face it. She's not wrong. "I have an appointment with a salon, but this is not a big deal. Tristian and I aren't dating."

I keep telling her that because I don't know how to tell her that I'm sort-of, in the most convoluted way possible, dating all three of them. I mean, isn't that what we're doing? Hell if I know. I've never been anyone's girlfriend before.

"If he invited you to that party, it means something. They plan this event all year. I hear there are paparazzi!" Her voice turns a little bitter. "Even your father and I don't get an invitation. It's incredibly exclusive."

I wince, guessing that a crime boss and former prostitute don't pass the Mercer muster. As much as I want to argue with my mom, she's probably right. An invite like this from Tristian is a declaration. I'm just not sure what he's declaring, or who he's declaring it to.

"Then I'm honored to be invited," is what I say aloud.

"My goodness, and there's the *dance.*" She sounds like someone who just struck oil, the words emerging fast and frantic. "Every year, the Mercer men take their escorts out onto the dancefloor at midnight sharp. It's all anyone talks about the week after. Such a lavish tradition, don't you think? Oh, I bet he's going to take you! Do you know how to waltz?" She laughs, high and giddy. "What am I talking about? I don't even know how to waltz!"

I blink, trying to process her words as fast as she says them. "I don't know how to waltz, but if it's, like…this big thing, I doubt I'll be involved."

Mom makes a *pssh* sound, and I can just imagine her flapping a hand. "He's taking you to the party, so he has to take you out on the dancefloor. If he doesn't,

I'll give that man the what-for."

I smirk. "Whatever you say, mom."

"And are you positive you're okay about Christmas Day?" she asks.

"It's fine," I say, trying not to sound like it's too fine. Because it is. Fine. '*Fine*!' even. God, it's the best news I've gotten all year. Apparently, after they sent me to boarding school and Killian entered college, the Paynes stopped celebrating Christmas as a nuclear family unit. Halle-freaking-lujah. "You two have fun on the cruise."

She sighs, the static buzzing through the phone's speaker. "It's just your first year home, and we missed out so much—"

"No, mom. It's really okay. This semester has been hard. Adjusting to college and all? Honestly, I'm just looking forward to a break before the next one starts." I don't mention that the guys have some kind of annual Christmas party that sounds way more fun than playing dodge-the-creepy-stepdad all day. "You guys deserve a break, too. I know Daniel's still upset about Vivienne."

"You're right," she relents. It's all a good show. I know for certain my mother already has her bikinis packed and ready to go. "He really does deserve something nice, don't you think? He works so hard. Lately, there are nights where he doesn't come home at all. Just sleeps right there in his office, too bogged down with work to make the drive back home. He's such a good provider."

I roll my eyes, but when they refocus, I stop abruptly. "Shit." The street ahead is blocked by a thick crowd waiting to enter Forsyth's single toy store. I step into the road to cut around them, but at the obnoxious blare of a horn, hop back to the sidewalk.

"What's wrong?" she asks, sounding worried.

"Oh, it's nothing." I look around, noting the small park that cuts through to the street where the other shops are located. "I just—I need to go, okay? It's really busy out here and I don't want to miss my appointment."

"Fine, but I want all the details on this party, okay? Don't make me hear about it second hand."

Smiling, I tell her, "I promise."

Right before I hang up, she orders, "And you'd better learn that waltz! Look it up online!"

I tuck the phone into my pocket, searching for a break in the traffic to cross the street. When I find one, I jog across the asphalt and into the park. From the outside, it looks like a straight shot to the shops on the other side, but once I'm toward the middle, I realize the path veers around a big fountain. I check my watch, hoping none of the places are closing soon.

My phone buzzes in my pocket. Instantly, I know it's one of the guys. Any deviation from my approved path was bound to set them on edge. I slide my thumb across the screen, lips twitching at the thought of one of them—or maybe even all of them—sitting around the GPS and gnawing their fingernails down. The bright light of the screen casts a glare into my eyes, but not enough that I can't see the words.

That color blue looks good on you, Sweet Cherry.

I freeze, hand gripping my coat. My blue coat. I spin around, scanning the area, but the park is quiet and still, only the slow gurgle of the fountain and distant traffic filling the space.

My phone buzzes again.

But I prefer the lace you wore in the pit. Is that what you're wearing underneath?

I take a faltering step forward, then two more at a faster clip, eyes pinging back and forth from my phone to the path ahead.

Or did Rath keep those in his top drawer with all the other trophies he's stolen from you?

Fear races up my spine, and I see a shadow move on the other side of the fountain. Or at least, I think it was a shadow. I blink, heart racing in my chest, and then stumble the other direction, zipping off the path entirely. A horn blares in the distance, beyond the wooded area I've stumbled into, but I'm not far from the road. If I keep going, I'll be out of the park.

I'm far from the fountain when the phone buzzes again.

I shouldn't look, but I do.

Did you like the way the knife felt in your hands when you cut him? I know I enjoyed carving those letters into Vivienne's flesh. You already have my initial cut into you, but I look forward to giving you another. Wouldn't you like that, Sweet Cherry?

He knows all about us. Not just where we live and how to find us, but who we are. Where we are. What we do together. Why we do it. "Who are you?" I ask aloud, more to myself than anyone else. The snap of a twig propels me forward, and I ignore the phone when it buzzes again. I can't tell if there's someone in the park or if Ted is just fucking with me, but I'm not hanging around to find out. Through the brush and bramble, I see the glow of lights ahead, and when I feel the sidewalk under my feet, I don't stop rushing toward the nearest open store. I push open the door and step into the bright fluorescent light of a tiny convenience store.

My phone vibrates again with the unread message. I duck into an aisle, and despite my instinct to pretend it doesn't exist, I check the message.

I'm closer than you think, but far enough that you'll never catch me.

My hand shakes as I stare at the message, panic rushing over me. What was I thinking coming out like this? That it felt nice to act normal? That it'd be worth being the mouse in the cat's game if it meant I could walk down the street and look at some lights? Stupid. So incredibly stupid.

I fumble for the map on my phone, dropping a pin in my location and sending it to the group text. I add the text:

Lady: I need a ride.

"Lady?"

Tears obstruct my vision and I swat them away, so frustrated that I can't even do something as simple as Christmas shopping without him ruining it. Frustrated that it's working. That I'm trembling. That I'm shaking.

Frustrated and just.

So.

Fucking.

Angry.

A hand lands on my shoulder. "Er… Story?"

"Don't touch me!" I jump back, screeching the words. The first thing I see is that I'm standing in front of a row of feminine products, boxes of pads and tampons laid out neatly before me. The second thing I see is Autumn, the Princess—the *former* Princess—throwing her hands up.

She clutches a box of tampons in one of them. "It's just me."

Pressing my hand to my chest, I try to breathe. "Oh, shit. Autumn." I don't trust any of the Royal bitches, but Autumn isn't a killer. She's spent the last three months trying to get knocked up, and the tampon box, plus the bags under her eyes, implies she's got bigger issues than stalking a rival.

"You look—" she starts, but swallows it. "Are you okay?"

"I'm fine." I sniff, refusing to show any weakness in front of this girl. I nod at the box of tampons. "Are you?"

Her eyes drop, lips smashed into a flat, tense smile. "Well, I'm not pregnant. I'm sure everyone's heard." I don't have to respond. The Royals are like gossipy church ladies. She and I both know it. I don't expect her to continue. For some reason, she does. "They kicked me out." The shrug she gives is loose and casual, but the wetness of her eyes belies the gesture. "And the Princes already replaced me. Can you believe that? Like… how do they even know it's my uterus that doesn't work? Maybe it's their shitty sperm."

Doubtful.

I purse my lips to stop the word from emerging. The Princes probably picked their strongest and most fertile to continue their crazy-ass tradition. "I mean, did you really want to be tied to those guys for the rest of your life, anyway? Who wants to be some rich kids' glorified incubator?"

"Glorified incubator?" Autumn's face crumples into twisted horror. "Being the Princess is an honor. You still don't get it, do you?" When all she gets in response is my dull stare, she explains, "I would have been taken care of for life. My child would have been the equivalent of royalty. We would have been set, Lady. Do you know how many mothers out there would love to be in that position? To give their child the best life possible? To give them legacy and pride and a place in this world?"

It's an uncomfortable parallel to my mother, which is the only reason I say, "I think a child should be allowed to choose their own place in the world. That just sounds like a lot of expectations a baby never asked for."

All the wistfulness, the sorrow and pain, flickers right from her eyes. It's replaced with something stony and cold, and I know before she even opens her mouth that she means to cut. "What would you know about it?" she sneers, snatching a box of panty liners from the shelf. "All your Lords want to do is to possess. Land, territory," she looks me up and down, scoffing at my beat up sneakers, "low-rent pussy with trashy trimmings. The complete lack of future those three thugs would give to you isn't even worth the price of admission. At least my Princes wanted something more from me than a few minutes on my back." Raising an eyebrow, she makes her final blow. "Better a glorified incubator than a cheap whore."

It must be the adrenaline still pumping through me—the click of a switch that's turned her from innocuous to foe—that drives what I do next. I thrust both hands out, smacking hard into her shoulders. The shove sends her knocking into the shelf at her back, an expression of stunned disbelief frozen on her slack face. "Look here, Autumn." I step toward her, flicking her chest. "I'm not going to even justify explaining to you what goes on between me and my Lords, but there's one thing I know for sure. They wouldn't toss *me* out on the street like a used piece of trash. *Ever.*" I can see the hit land and slice right through her façade, her mouth snapping shut. Pleased, I go on, "Do you want to know why? It's because I'm their Lady. Where the four of us come from, that means something more than using each other to get a little ahead in this world." Her teeth are clenching now, jaw locked as her eyes flash in anger. "And here's something else to think about while you're shoving that cotton up your twat. The new Princess? She's prettier than you, Autumn. They can't keep their hands off her. I'm sure there'll be an announcement soon. Did you know there was a betting pool? Everyone knew you couldn't pull this off. My Lords cashed in big." I give her a sharp, nasty smile. "Maybe I'll have them use it to buy their whore a new pair of shoes."

Autumn's face turns red, tears filling her eyes. She looks like I slapped her, which isn't far off from the truth. The second her lips wobble apart to speak, the silence is broken by the shrill jangle of the bell on the shop door.

Dimitri's voice calls out, carrying over the aisles, "Story? Where are you?"

"I'm here," I say, sauntering back. I'd started to the front of the store, but Dimitri finds me first, popping into sight at the end of the aisle. I exhale in relief to see his face, my muscles struggling to unwind as he strolls toward me. It gets a little easier when he immediately drags me into his chest, eyebrows furrowed.

"Something happen?" he asks, lips brushing my forehead.

I shake my head, but then say, "Later, okay?" He searches my eyes, but doesn't push it, letting me burrow into his warmth. "You were quick." The brownstone is at least twenty minutes away and I've barely been here for five.

"Yeah, I was…"

I look up at the pause, taking in his dark eyes and tousled hair. He's wearing the leather jacket he'd given to me once, weeks ago, in a dark parking lot on what felt like the edge of the universe. "You stayed close, didn't you? Because you were paranoid."

Now, he frames my face in his palms, lip piercings shifting with his slow smile. "You caught me." Right there, in front of Autumn and all the tampons she'll be needing, Dimitri leans down to press a soft, lingering kiss to my lips. Against them, he asks, "Ready to go home?"

And I answer.

"Yes."

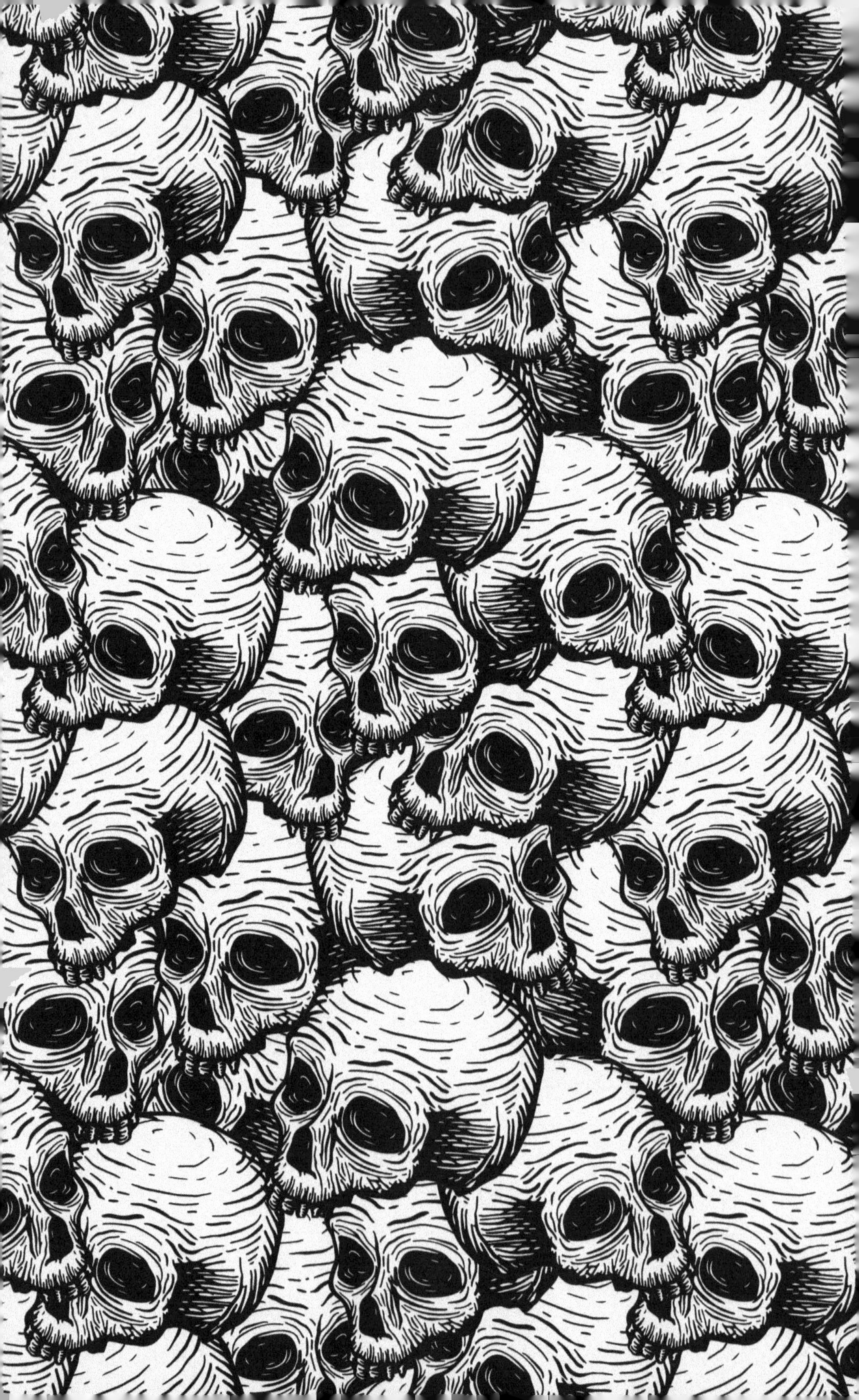

14

SET-UP

Killian's arms cross over his chest as he watches me down the shot, forearm muscles bulging. Unlike Rath, Killer's good at taking care of his body. Honing it. Making it efficient and useful. I used to envy his frame and how his muscles could get so big. Few people are aware of it, but I was a tad scrawny when I first began having growth spurts. I filled in, of course, after many mornings spent going through a trainer-designed body resistance routine. But I've long come to terms with the fact I can never be that. Hulking. Looming. Making people twitchy with my mere physical presence. There was a time in our teens when I tried to bench whatever Killer was benching at the time, and it damn near killed me. Gave up on that shit real quick.

"Tristian," he starts, and from the sound of his voice, he's got a lot to say about what's going down tonight. I watch him start and stop, visibly piecing together all his grievances with this. In the end, all he says is, "What are you doing?"

"Pre-gaming." I swallow the spicy liquid, catching his gaze in the mirror over the bar. He's in a t-shirt and sweats, but I'm in a three-thousand dollar tuxedo, handpicked by the biggest Karen in town, my mother. I'd much rather be him for the night. "The Mercer Christmas party is a subtle form of torture.

It's best if I'm loosened up before I go."

"And you've decided to drag Story into it?"

I place the glass on the bar and run my fingers through my hair—arranging it into the perfect mix of messy and styled. "She can handle it."

"And your parents?"

He knows the answer to that. We all do. Although my mother played nice at the football game when they first met, that was just societal niceties. It's the same way she pretends to accept Posey. It's surface deep, artificial. At the game, Killian is the star, and it's worth pretending the Paynes are acceptable company. But outside of that, their status drops. Significantly. The truth is that our blood and money are bluer than a priest's balls. There are expectations and Story Austin doesn't meet the criteria.

"They'll survive," I reply, not exactly believing it, but there's a reason I'm bringing Story home with me. I'm making a point. One they'll have to accept. When all he does is glare back at me, I try, "Jesus, Killer. I thought if anyone could understand the need to blow your life up a little, it'd be you."

"She's not a bomb, she's our Lady." He walks around the back of the bar and fixes me with a firm stare. "Don't send her into your twisted family bullshit just to prove a point."

I take in his narrowed eyes, the way that tendon in his neck is starting to pulse, and arch an eyebrow. "So only you're allowed to do that?"

His brows crouch low. "Fuck you."

"This would be so much easier if we could just have our Christmas party." Rath pulls the earbuds out one at a time and looks up from his phone. "You could make whatever grand gesture you have planned there without sullying your perfect son status."

"You think I'd declare my intentions for Story at the Lord's Christmas party?"

It's like these people don't even know me.

Usually, the LDZ party is held on Christmas Eve and consumes a two-block radius around the brownstone. Since the Lords are South Side royalty, the two worlds often collide, making it wild enough that people are still talking about it come St. Patty's Day. I barely even remember last year's party, aside from absolutely demolishing the Barons in Jingle Bell Pong and Killian nailing a petite little brunette on the pool table downstairs. She had bells on her pigtails that jingled every time he thrusted inside. The year before that featured a casualty count; nine citations for indecent exposure, four cases of alcohol poisoning, three contributions to the delinquency of minors, two assaults with deadly weapons, and a partridge in a pear tree. The Lords' Christmas bash is infamous enough to draw half the presence of the local police force.

But not this year.

Ted has forced us to lock the doors and shut ourselves up. We still have big things planned, but it'll be smaller. Just the four of us. I refuse to let Ted take Christmas from us, too. The bastard has ruined enough this year.

"I think you're a glutton for punishment," Rath says, re-plugging his ears and going back to his phone. We may have downsized the party, but he's still going to make a kick-ass playlist.

"This isn't just about making a statement to them," I tell Killer, straightening my bowtie. "She needs to know what she is." Giving him a pointed look, I stress, "To us, and to me."

I know he understands when he drops his arms, losing that bullying posture of his. "Christ, Tris." He runs his fingers through his hair, for once looking at a loss. "If that's what you want, can't you just buy her fucking flowers or something?"

I bring my hand down on his shoulder, giving him a little shake. "Brother, you give me so little credit."

We're interrupted by the click-clack of heels approaching down the hall. I swallow the last bit of my drink just as Story enters the den, sweeping through the arched doorway like something out of a movie. A ball of fire burns in my chest and I know it's not the whiskey. "Goddamn," I mutter under my breath, abandoning the glass.

Rath's eyes lazily go to the door, then he straightens. "Fuck me," he mutters.

Even Killian is stunned, face going slack as he takes her in. It's not often we get to see our Lady dressed like this, which is probably a good thing. We'd get absolutely nothing accomplished.

"What?" she says, looking down at her gown. It's made out of a clingy green satin that sticks to her bodice like a second skin. It accentuates every slender curve of her womanly figure, and it doesn't matter that the neck isn't low enough to show her cleavage. Killer and I both know what's under there. Panic ignites in her eyes. "Is this wrong? I went to the boutique you suggested. The woman that helped me said it would be appropriate for a fancy party. Is it too much? Too little?" When we continue staring, her shoulders fall. "Give me something here, guys."

"Oh, I can think of a couple things we want to give you." I cross the room, pretending I'm not calculating how to get this dress off of her. Will the tight skirt push over her hips? Is there a zipper? God, please tell me she's not wearing a bra. "We're just speechless on account of the awe."

Killian clears his throat behind me. "Yeah, little sister. You clean up… sufficiently."

She shoots him a glare, because Killian always lives in that vague spot in and around 'asshole', but I know he means it.

She's *stunning*.

Before I approach her, I veer off toward the armchair in the corner, reaching behind it to retrieve the very thing I'd gone out earlier to buy. Paper crinkling in my hand, I extend the bouquet to her. "For my escort." I shoot Killian a sly smirk over my shoulder.

She blinks at the flowers, her impeccable red lips spreading into a shocked grin. "Oh my god, these are gorgeous, Tristian!" She's visibly flustered as she gathers the bouquet into her arms, cheeks flushing. There are fifty of them, which took some time to find, given the season. After fingering a couple of the petals, she finally meets my gaze, eyes curious. "Why do you always get me daisies?" After a beat, she rushes to add, "Not that I don't love daisies."

"Don't you remember?" I point to the doorway. "The first day you came here, you were wearing a little sundress, and it—"

"—had daisies on it," she finishes, head snapping back in shock. "You remembered that?"

Oh, I remember everything. I remember her letting the straps fall down her shoulders, putting her full tits on display for us. I remember thinking how badly I wanted to bend her over and stuff her full of my cock. I remember noting the way she looked among the backdrop of the dark brownstone, soft and sweet, like a warm ray of sunshine.

Like the daisies on her dress.

"How could I forget?" I say, reaching out to run my knuckle along her jaw.

"Shoot me," Killian mutters.

"Don't mind him." I slip into my jacket, giving her a roguish grin. "Some men know how to treat a Lady." But before I can tuck her hand in my arm, she jumps back.

"I need to put these in a vase! I'll just be one second." And with that, the click-clack of heels races into the kitchen. I wait obediently, hands clasped behind my back, until she comes clicking back, a vase clutched to her chest. Killian and I watch mutely as she fusses with it, arranging the flowers just-so.

She sets it on the mantle, up among the mounted buck and skulls, and sends us a sunny smile. "Brightens the place up, don't you think?"

Nodding, I pretend I wasn't just staring at her ass. "Absolutely."

Dimitri stands to approach her then, trying to steal her attention away from the flowers. "Baby, look at me." She does, turning to him with a quizzical expression. He answers by touching her chin, boring into her with his eyes. "Rich people—people who are Mercer-rich—they're dicks."

"Hey!" I glower at him, but it's half-hearted. "I resemble that remark."

Dimitri ignores me. "They're stuck-up snobs, and if someone treats you like shit, you're completely free to tell them what they can do with their opinion. Understood?"

Story gives him a slow nod. "I understand."

"Good." With that, he leans down to press a kiss to her lips, and I roll my eyes as it goes on. And on. And on.

I check my watch. "Lift your leg and piss on her already. The car's waiting out front."

He finally lets her go, leaving her glassy-eyed and dazed, eyelashes flicking as she blinks it away. "Good luck," he says, turning her toward me.

And then Killian brings his hand down on her ass, giving it a nice, loud smack.

She stumbles, voice full out of outrage when she squeals, "Asshole!"

Killian gives her an expressionless wink.

I press my hand into the small of her back, ushering her out of the den. "Don't wait up for us!"

In the foyer, she asks, "When's the last time you brought a date to one of these things? My mom made it sound like it was a big deal." She frowns contemplatively. "I have no idea what I'm expected to do."

Helping her into her jacket, I pointedly ignore her question. "You're expected to look stunning and listen to me complain about the hors d'oeuvres. The first one, you've already got in the bag." I turn her around, stroking a finger down her exposed neck. "Seriously, Story, you look amazing. If my mother wouldn't hunt me down like a dog in the street for being any later than I already am," I lean in to brush my lips against the shell of her ear, "I'd fuck that dress straight off you right now."

She throws me an exasperated glance, but it's quickly overtaken by an anxious look. "Tristian, I'm serious. Are you sure this is a good idea? I barely know how to act like a normal woman."

"Sweetheart." I cup her cheek, thumb stroking over the soft skin. "You're not a normal woman." She's the woman who shot a man to protect us. She's the woman who took the brunt of my darkness at a time when I couldn't find the light, and then she was the woman who forgave me for it. She was the woman who walked through this door and shone so brightly that I haven't been able to see anything else since. In a moment of unutterable weakness, I quietly confess, "A normal woman wouldn't make me feel this way."

She stares back at me, lips parting as if she's hypnotized. "What way?"

I try to answer. I genuinely do. It's just the words get caught somewhere in my chest, wound tightly around a fear I can scarcely put a name to. Clearing my throat, I open the door to the chill and the darkness, knowing that she'll light the way.

"Right now, you're making me feel late," I say, rushing her out of the house.

"Wow," SHE SAYS, peering owlishly out the window as we approach. "This place is amazing! Do your parents rent it out every year, or do they change venues?" When I don't answer, she turns to me, taking in my even stare. "Wait." She whips around to get another look at the manor, jaw dropping. "No way. This isn't your house."

The sheer terror on her face as we step out of the car is the only thing that stops me from boasting, which is absolutely something I'm used to doing. It's not a house. It's a sprawling property, complete with the mansion and all its trappings. Mercer Manor makes the garish enormity of The Velvet Hideaway look microscopic in comparison.

"Story," I begin, but she shakes her head.

"I'm not sure I can do this."

"Hey, no," I say, sliding my arm around her waist, "I know this party must be intimidating, but you've already met my mother at the game earlier this year. And Dad is a sucker for a beautiful woman, so you've already got him on board." I kiss her on the forehead. "Plus, the girls will be there, and they'll be so excited to see you."

The mention of the twins makes some of that hard panic in her eyes soften. "It's just… I'm sure your parents have heard the gossip and rumors about me from high school. And your dad, at the very least, has a mortifyingly good idea of what goes on between the Lords and their Lady." She twists the cuff on her wrist. "I don't want to draw any attention."

She's not wrong. My parents have heard the gossip. Hell, my mother has her entire bridge club on speed dial for just this reason, and my father definitely knows the role of a Lady. Intimately. And that doesn't even go into their thoughts about her mother or the shady side of Daniel's business.

"They'll behave." Because that's what they do. "You're my guest. You're my date."

She grabs my arm, stopping me. "You've never brought a proper date to this party before, have you?"

That's a minefield, right there. If I tell her truth—that twice in high school, I'd brought my ex, Gen, as a date—then it'd be giving her the wrong idea. Our parents were friends, and it was less of an invitation than a solid expectation. But Genevieve is dead to me, as is that memory.

Likewise, if I tell her she's right—that I've never brought a proper, intentional, declarations-to-made-about date—then it's going to make her even more nervous. That's a lose-lose situation.

So I deflect, nudging her up the enormous, red-carpeted front steps. "If it gets to be too much, just let me know. There are plenty of hiding spots in the house. You know," I snake my arm around her waist, "hidden passageways and secret pantries."

She glances up at the house with this look on her face, like it's looming over her. "Seriously?"

Shrugging, I confirm, "What's the point of having a house like this if there aren't various hidey-holes to fuck your hand-picked staff in?"

The look she gives me is incredulous, and a touch bothered at the possibility

I'm telling the truth. Which I am. Completely. It's too late to ask any more questions, though, because the front door opens and a figure fills the entrance. "Master Tristian." The man nods. "Pleasure to see you, sir."

His face is stone, absent of any emotion, but I grin widely. "Benedict! How are you?"

"Very well, sir."

"Benedict, this is my Lady, Story Austin. Story, this is Benedict. He's been with our family since before I was born."

"Nice to meet you," she says, demurely holding out her hand.

Old Benny disregards it, assessing her with a cold eye. That gossip Story worried about? It starts with the servants. He turns his gaze to me. "Your mother is in the ballroom. She'll be thrilled to know you've arrived." His eyebrow lifts. "With a *guest*. And through the front door even."

The word 'guest' is accentuated, but I ignore the old man. He's almost as cantankerous as Ms. Crane. I usher Story past him and help her out of her coat. "I may have a history of sneaking tail into the house. But I promise you'll only ever enter this house through the front door." I give her ass a nice, firm squeeze. "I, on the other hand, am definitely down for a little backdoor action."

"Tristian!" Her cheeks burn a delicious shade of red as she glances at Benedict to see if he heard. The servant stares straight ahead, seemingly unaware.

"Don't worry. He's paid to ignore us." I toss her coat at him and then mine.

"Well, don't pull that in front of your mother." She shoos my hand away from her backside. "Jesus."

"God, I love it when you're all flustered and red-faced." I wind her fingers in mine. "Come on, my mom hired this new chef that specializes in vegan farm-to-table cuisine and I've been dying to see if she lives up to the hype."

Story takes in the elaborate decorations, and I take in her reaction, eyes alight at all the garland and baubles. I keep her close as we pass the grand staircase, down the marble-floored corridor that's lined with Christmas trees.

"I guess blue and silver is the theme this year," I note as she slows to inspect the trees. "Much better than the red plaid from last year. We looked like a fucking lumberjack convention."

Story gently fingers an ornament, wide-eyed and hushed. "There must be like twenty trees! And they're all decorated so… so…"

"Professionally?" I bite back a laugh at her childlike wonder. "Yeah, mother hires interior designers to put these up. Then she hires tailors, and stylists, and caterers—all to make sure everything flawlessly matches the theme." We pass an elderly couple I don't remember the name of, but luckily, a manly nod at the husband suffices. "Sometimes I think she wanted twins because it gave her more opportunities to color-coordinate."

She seems to shake off some of the awe. "I suppose the girls were rather matching the last time I saw them."

Snorting, I correct. "No, she gave up on that years ago. I meant me and my twin."

Her head snaps up. "You have a twin?!"

Now I really do have to laugh. She sounds both horrified and intrigued at the prospect of me having a clone. "I did, for a hot second. Twins run in the family. He was stillborn, though."

"Oh." Her face falls. "God, Tristian, I'm so sorry. That's terrible."

I give an easy shrug. There are times I wonder if things would be different if my father had a spare heir apparent. Maybe it'd be less pressure. Maybe he'd have a favorite and the other could just do whatever he wanted. Maybe I'm carrying the expectations of two sons in the disappointment of only having one. But this is all I've ever known. It's hard to miss something you never had. "I was only an infant. It's not a big deal to me." Before she can voice the question I'm used to hearing, I groan. "Please don't ask if I feel like half of myself is missing. I hate that woo-woo twin bullshit. The whole name thing is bad enough without people reading into it."

"The name thing?" she asks, head cocked.

Wearily, I explain, "I was supposed to be named Tristan, and he was supposed to be named Christian." I flop out a hand. "Ergo, Tristian. And if you want my opinion on the stupidity of coordinated twin names, we'll be here all night."

She squeezes my arm, sending me a soft grin. "Then I won't ask."

The ballroom is filled with people my parents know, from family, to friends, to business partners, social acquaintances and anyone my mother thinks will improve her and my father's position on the social ladder. It's so crowded and loud that our arrival doesn't make much of a ripple. I pull Story into my side and whisper little details in her ear. "That group of men? They're in my father's social club. Combined, they're worth about a hundred billion."

"Dollars?" she squeaks.

I nod, pointing to another man. "That's Robert Wilson, president of Wilson Tech."

"The guy building a rocket ship that looks like a dick?"

"That's him." I grin and tilt my head at the redhead standing nearby. "The woman with him is his third wife, Lacey. She was the Baroness when I was a freshman."

Lacey gives me a small smile as we pass, and Story twists to get a better glance. "You're messing with me."

I give her a sober look. "Not in the slightest."

"Tristian!" My name lifts over the party noises in a high-pitched squeal. A moment later, Izzy and Lizzy are pushing insistently between a woman in a beaded dress and a man in a gray suit. "You're here!"

"Told you I was coming," I say, dropping Story's hand to reach for Lizzy. I pick her up and give her a big hug, then do the same for Izzy. The two of them then bombard Story, grabbing her by the waist and hugging her tight.

"He didn't tell us you were coming," Lizzy says, giving me the stink eye.

"It was a surprise," I insist, patting her on the head. "I was just telling Story that the woo-woo twin stuff is fake."

Lizzy looks at Story, nodding. "When Izzy hurt her ankle, I didn't feel anything but annoyed. Because she complains a lot."

"Hey!" Izzy says, giving her sister a playful shove. "You'd complain too if you had to walk around with a crutch for two weeks."

Story laughs. "When was this?"

"Last year." Izzy tugs at the collar of her frilly blue dress.

As nice as it is to see Story and the girls get along, I know that wherever they are, my mother will be sure to follow. Having the girls wasn't easy. She went through hell to get pregnant a second time, which turned her into a bit of an overbearing parent.

Sure enough, a moment later she's found us.

"Tristian, darling," she says with a smile, swooping in. I lean in to kiss her cheek, pausing at the tense, aggressively cheerful comment she whispers into my ear. "Tell me you didn't bring your frat house sex toy to our Christmas party?"

The comment doesn't come as a surprise. No, I'd been waiting for it, but it still raises my defenses. I plaster on a matching smile and say, "Mother, you remember Story, Killian's stepsister?"

"Of course, yes." She instantly looks down at the twins, apparently unwilling to give Story more face time than that. "I think it's time for you two to head upstairs."

"But—"

"You know the rules," my mother says, face stern. "You can be here for an hour. After that, it's just adults. It's already half past ten, which means you've swindled me enough."

Izzy opens her mouth to protest again, but I drop down to their eye level. "You really want to hang out down here with a bunch of boring adults?" Lizzy nods. She's no fool. "Look, I'll have Benedict send you up a surprise. It'll be worth it."

Izzy eyes me skeptically. "A good surprise? Not your gross, healthy stuff?"

Story snorts next to me, earning an alarmed look from my mother. She bends, cupping her hand beside her mouth to fake-whisper, "Don't worry. I'll make sure it's the good stuff."

Lizzy's face lights up. "Thanks, Story!" They both give her another hug before conceding the night to the stuffy old people.

As they disappear upstairs, my mother says, "They seem to have taken to you, Miss Payne."

Story's gaze snaps up at the name. "Oh! My last name is Austin, actually. And they're such sweet girls."

Mother pats me on the cheek. "Just like their brother."

"Oh, yes, he's the sweetest," Story says, but I see the dark flicker run through her eyes. It's brief, but I know how to read it. I've been anything but sweet to this girl. I forced her to deep throat my cock. I defiled her in public. I held her down while Rath fucked her with a knife. I carved my initial in her chest. "I'm a lucky girl."

I've tried making it up to her. I turned off the cameras. I've kept my hands to myself when we're in public. I doted on her during her period, not even making a fuss out of all the processed carbs she ate. I even agreed she should do the wrestling match. I know better than anyone the urge to make your own way and get out from under the thumb of expected constraints. But even though we've made some progress, I don't know how to prove to her that I'm in. That I'm really, truly, fully, *all-in.*

Except maybe to bring her here.

I wind my arm around her waist, pulling her close. "I know what you're thinking, mother, but I've been brushing up on my waltzing skills, and I'm about eighty percent sure I won't fall flat on my face out there."

I can't remember my mother ever being speechless before. She is, as a rule, unable to keep her mouth shut at any given moment. But right now, she's staring at me and nothing is coming out. It's not that she doesn't try. Her lips keep parting, chest swelling with an inhale, but then it just floats out of her nostrils like a phantom.

Story is stiff against my side, and the only reason I look away from my mother's alarmed expression is to give her a reassuring smile.

"Don't worry, sweetheart, I know how to lead."

"The Carters!" my mother suddenly bursts, gaze fixed somewhere over my shoulder. I'm immediately suspicious of the relief in her eyes, which is smart of me. She's gathered herself back up into the proper hostess, beaming as she adds, "I didn't think Holden would be able to attend, considering how sick he's been. But there they are, see?" She waves, gesturing to me to follow her gaze.

Stupidly, I do.

All the color drains from my face.

Genevieve is across the room, dressed in scarlet and black, and she's staring straight at me. Smiling, she raises her hand to give me a little wave.

My arm falls away from Story as I grab my mother's wrist, hissing, "What the fuck is she doing here?"

"Tristian!" she scolds, shaking free. "Watch your language! The Carters are our oldest friends, and they're going through a dreadful time right now."

My jaw locks as I fight to contain the rage thrashing within my chest. "That doesn't answer my question."

My mother gives me a weary look. "Gen is their daughter, and the invitation was to the family. You can put two and two together."

Oh, I sure as hell can.

This is a set-up.

Story looks almost as blindsided as I feel, whipping around to glance at the object of my eternal bitterness. I could achieve immortality, stand on the edge of the world a million years from now, watching the heat death of the universe, and it'd still be in the back of my thoughts.

That bitch.

"I didn't know." I bite the words out, said more to Story than my own conniving mother, but that's who answers.

"Well, you might have," my mother says, giving me a pointed look, "if you were more involved in the family's affairs and less distracted with your other..." She presses her lips into a flat smile, cutting her eyes at Story. "… activities."

I mirror her barbed smile. "You're being so fucking rude, I don't even know where to start." Her smile falls, but before she can chide me, I demand, "Don't organize an ambush and expect me to watch my fucking language." I turn to Story, grazing my fingertips over the cuff on her wrist. "Sweetheart," I say, in a voice as calm as possible. "Will you go to the kitchen and make sure they send up something extra sugary for the twins?" I stare across the room. "I need to talk to my mother for a moment."

"We can leave," she says quietly. "I know—"

I cut my eyes at her. "Now, Story."

She recoils, and I know why. There are few things that can bring out this icy sharpness in me, and one of them is standing across the room. I can't explain to her why Gen has this hold over me. From Story's vantage, it probably looks wrong, because hating someone—true, chaotic, red-hot hatred—means you still feel something for them. It means they can cut you, because you'd let them. It means they live rent-free inside your head, taking up space and driving you crazy.

That's not the reality.

Probably unsure what to do about my darkness when it's not directed at her, Story gives me a slow nod. I jerk my chin in the kitchen's direction and she takes a hesitant step forward, giving me one last worried look before she slips through the crowd.

"Let's go say hello," Mother says, ignoring my obvious rage. "Doesn't she look radiant?"

"Stop," I tell her. "Go get father. We need to talk."

She pauses, giving me a long look. "Tristian, we're in the middle of a party. We can't just walk off."

"We can do it in private, or we can do it right here." My voice is low, dangerous, full of threat. "Which do you prefer?"

She holds my eye for a long moment until understanding takes hold. Defiance isn't my thing. Mostly because they let me do what I want. But things are changing. Rapidly. I'm not a little kid staying out late, drinking until I puke, and having threesomes with debutantes. I'm part of something bigger, and the stakes are higher. The little box they thought I'd grow up to live in will no longer hold me.

"I'll get your father and meet you in the library."

Good. That gives me time to get a drink.

She grabs my lapel, her perfectly manicured nails digging into the fabric. "But don't think just because I'm giving you an opportunity to speak that it means I'm backing down on this," she says quietly. "I've put up with a lot of your nonsense over the years, but coming in here and declaring your intentions with that," her face twists, "*trash*, isn't in the cards."

She walks off, leaving me in the middle of the room, lines having been drawn. I came here tonight to make a point. To blow my life up a little, burn it down and see what survives in the midst of the ashes. Genevieve being here doesn't change a thing.

If anything, it just makes the fire burn hotter.

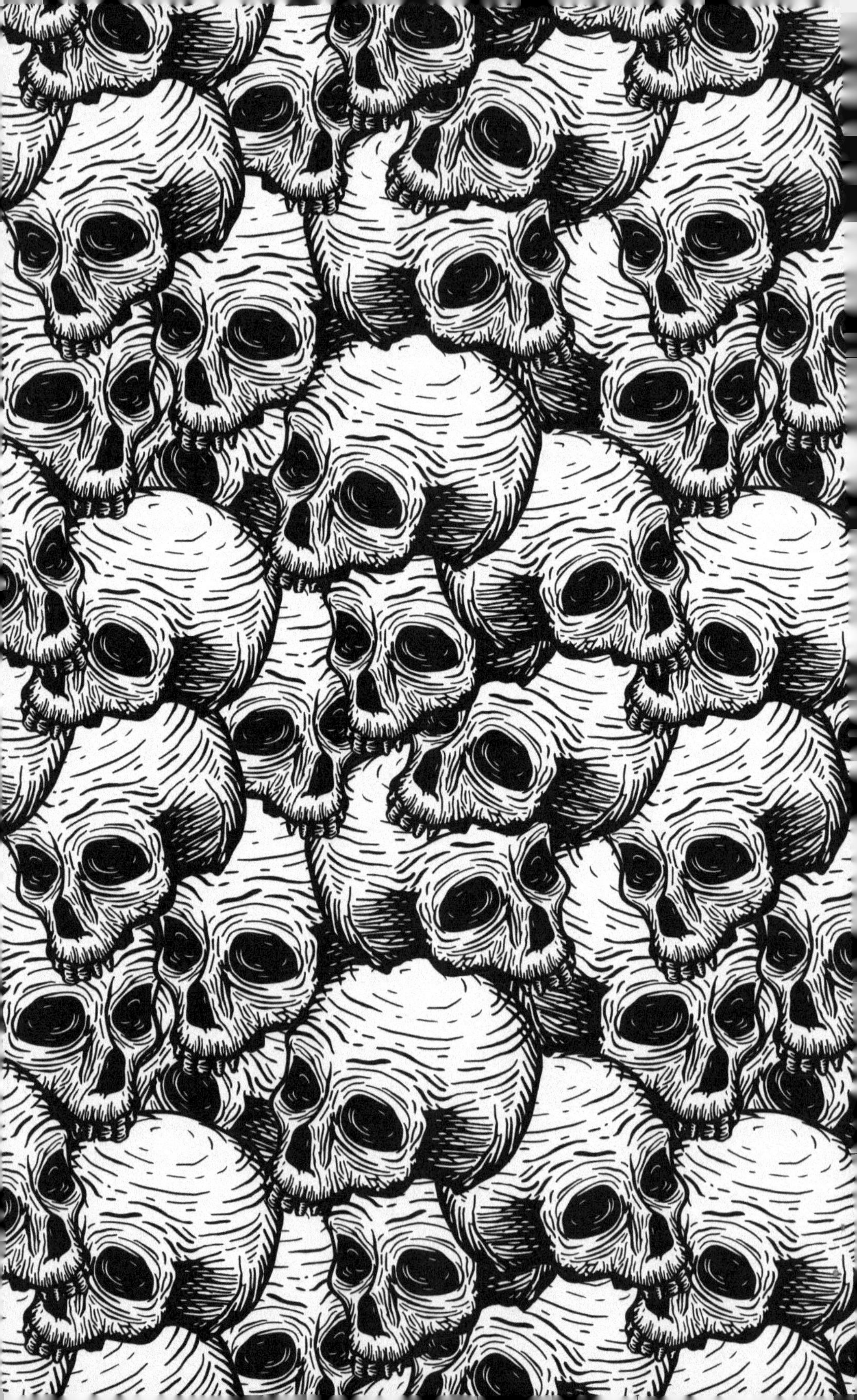

STORY

1 5

INSANITY & DEVOTION

I don't know what it is about Genevieve Carter that turns Tristian from a charming, handsome suitor to a callous, chilling man, but that's what she does. I try not to be hurt by the abrupt way he dismissed me, or by how he reacted to his ex-girlfriend being at the party, but Tristian's hang-ups when it comes to her make something inside me bristle and boil. She cheated on him, humiliated him, and slashed at his unwavering narcissism. And she still gets to him, even after all this time. Gen was the catalyst to him assaulting me that night in the laundry room. No matter what else changes in our life, Gen and that night—those ten minutes of complete cruelty and debasement—still stand between us.

I knew coming here was a bad idea. Everything about this party is above me. The successful people, the magnificent estate, the glitz and glam, the dresses and decoration... hell, the cost of catering alone could probably cover a semester's tuition at Forsyth. Even Daniel's lifestyle is a fraction of the Mercers', and I'm not technically even a Payne. I'm the daughter of a sex worker who's currently in a contract to serve three men. No wonder Tristian sent me to the kitchen with the staff. That's the kind of place I belong.

The least I can do is make good on Tristian's promise to the girls. If anyone deserves something sweet, it's those two. But I don't make it to the kitchen. Instead, I grab the arm of a waiter and tell him exactly what I need. "Chocolate. Cookies. Ice cream. Sweets. Whatever you've got. Please have Benedict send it up to the twins' room."

His eyes sweep over me, but I must look authoritative enough, because he nods. "Yes, ma'am."

Now that I've accomplished that, I do the exact thing I shouldn't.

I go looking for Tristian.

Whatever is happening with his parents and Genevieve, it involves me, and I'm not about to get blindsided. I spot the top of his blond hair as he turns down a hallway. Due to the congestion in the room, and a woman stopping me to ask where I got my shoes, by the time I break free from the party and head down the hall, I barely see the dark wood door swing shut—not quite latching.

There's no mistaking as I approach the door that I've found Tristian and his parents. His father's voice carries into the hall.

"The simple fact that I understand what it's like to be a Lord is why I've allowed this to go so far. The parties and excess—including exploits with the Lady—are part of this phase of your life, one I encourage, but bringing her *here*—"

"Her mother is a hooker, Tristian!" his mother cuts in, voice belligerent.

To his credit, Tristian argues, "She *used* to be a hooker, mother. And let's be honest. It's not the hooking part you have an issue with. Half the women in that ballroom are using sex to get ahead. You're just looking down on Posey because she didn't charge enough."

There's a brief pause, and then his mother's hiss. "I've had to put on a good face because of your father's business with Daniel Payne, but there's no way in hell I'm allowing you to trot that girl out on that dance floor at midnight."

"But you think Genevieve is a good choice?" Tristian says in a low snarl. "The bitch who humiliated me in front of the whole—"

His mother scoffs. "That was years ago, Tristian! You were both kids. She made a mistake, but even she realizes that it's time to grow up, make amends, and get back to the business of building a stable future with a good partner. An *appropriate* partner."

"She's not a broodmare and I'm not your goddamn stud." I flinch at the sharpness in his voice. "None of this is your business."

"That's exactly what it is," his dad's voice rings out. "It's *business*. You have an obligation, and it's not to South Side or Daniel Payne. You're not a thug, Tristian. You're a Mercer, and you've tarnished your reputation enough. You're certainly not going to ruin it further by making some kind of declaration about your house girl." His father lets out a scornful laugh. "Everyone knows Royal women are good for two things, and both of them are located between their legs."

Tristian snaps, "Watch what you're saying," and his father barrels right over him.

"I've allowed this spoiled, petulant, entitled behavior to go on too long. Christ, son, you were held at gunpoint!"

"And that bastard is dead," Tristian argues. "*Because* of Story."

"We can't allow these kind of people around the twins," his mother says, tone softer now, as if she's begging him to understand. "You know I'm right. You've had your father stepping up security around them for weeks. You're killing yourself driving over here every two days, texting them all the time. Something has you scared, and you can't tell me she isn't a part of it."

This is all news to me. Tristian is scared for the twins? He's been over here that much?

"I have it under control." The words sound ground out through gnashed teeth, and they make my stomach sink. Because she's right. I can hear it in his voice—can just imagine the steely shadow crossing over his face as he says the words.

He *is* scared for them.

I'd been fine until that point. I know what Tristian and I have. I know it runs deep, but I'm fully aware that it's unconventional and impossible to maintain. It's dark and dirty and sexy and depraved, and could never be explained to the likes of his *mother*. I light the match, and he sets the fire. He tells me to bend, and I let him push me until I'm about to break.

But there are some things he just can't control, and the complete nightmare known as my life is one of them.

With my heart in my throat, I step away from the door, not even knowing where to go. It takes me a long moment of wandering to find the corridor we'd entered the ballroom through. On either side of me, the Christmas trees twinkle and shine, but it doesn't penetrate—not like it had when we first arrived and I'd swelled with wonder and joy at the sight of it all. Now the blue and silver looks too cold, the lights too bright, the branches looming and greedy. I feel suddenly exposed, as if one glance could reveal me, an imposter in a pretty gown and shiny shoes.

By the time I find a bathroom to duck into, my feet hurt.

It's a well-lit space that's almost as big as my room at home. An enormous mirror sits above two decorative basins, and there's a pile of elaborately embroidered hand towels stacked by each. It's immaculately tiled—perhaps more marble—and the light fixture has crystals hanging from it. I focus on these details to slow my breathing, reaching into my small clutch to retrieve my phone.

He answers on the fourth ring.

"What happened." It's not a question. Killian's just a hopeless pessimist in that way.

"He threatened them, didn't he?" My lungs still feel constricted, but I push through an exhale, and it shudders out of me. "The twins. Ted threatened them." There's a long stretch of silence before Killian answers.

"Kind of."

I blink away a sudden surge of tears, voice cracking when I say, "I shouldn't be here."

"Do you want to be there?" he asks. "Take away Ted and all the snobbery. Do you want to schmooze with Tris and do all that dumb ballroom dancing bullshit, 'kissing under the mistletoe' garbage?"

Easily, I answer, "Yes."

"Then fuck him." I can practically hear Killian's dismissive shrug. "Seriously, fuck Ted and the horse he rode in on. If you want something, then you fucking take it."

Sniffling, I add, "His parents hate me. They think I'm trash that's going to tarnish his name."

"Then fuck them, too."

"Killian..." I groan, leaning against the counter. "They invited his ex to be his real date."

This, at least, gets a rise out of him. "Ex-fucking-scuse me?"

"You should have seen the look on his mother's face when he talked about dancing with me later. And his dad said..." I trail off, cringing at the memory of his words.

Killian's voice is ominously low. "What did his dad say?"

I roll my eyes at my sensitivity. "He said the only thing I'm good for is located between my legs."

"And he's completely right."

I freeze, phone pressed to my ear as I turn.

Genevieve stands in the open doorway, skinny and lithe in her beaded dress. She's holding a flute of champagne, and I must have been completely caught up in my discussion with Killian to have missed the sound of the door opening.

"I'm going to call you back," I tell Killian, ignoring his protest as I hang up, sliding the phone back into my purse. "Gen." All those old feelings of inferiority come rushing back. Not just about Tristian, but of being that awkward girl in high school. Gen was the queen bee and I was never anything but the peasant class, barely worth even acknowledging. "I didn't know you were coming tonight."

"I'm sure Tristian didn't either." She stalks forward in that feline sort of way, steady and confident in her six-inch-heels. "I know you've been caught up in your Royal games, but Tristian is more than a Lord. You realize that, right?" She blinks at me with her big blue eyes. "He's not the spoiled spawn of a crime boss, or some dirty street-urchin from South Side. He's a Mercer. And Mercers have their own rules and traditions." She reaches out to finger the leather cuff on my wrist, seeming unbothered when I yank my hand away. "Girls like you don't stick around. At least not in public, and not for long." She's not saying anything I haven't thought of myself, but I hate the way she's looking at me, somehow both smug and sympathetic. "I'm not trying to be mean. I just think it wouldn't be fair to you to sugarcoat it."

"Tristian is different," I say, knowing how weak that sounds, because even I don't believe it. Not that I'd give her that satisfaction of admitting that. She doesn't understand what we've been through. The bullets and bloodshed. Fire and ash. Jesus, I have this man's initial is carved into my chest. "Whether his parents accept it or not, he's a part of something bigger."

She laughs, teeth white and straight. "Nothing is bigger than the Mercers. Truth is, you're just a convenient pussy for him to dump his come into." Head tilting, she gives me a long, narrow-eyed look. "I have been wondering, though. Does he still fuck like a robot? More interested in how he looks than how it feels?" She drops close, whispering in my ear, "He looks anywhere but at you when he comes, doesn't he?"

My hand snaps up and clenches around her throat, my sharp nails pressing into her flesh.

"Ah!" she gasps, hands flying up. "Let go—"

"Not until you understand something, bitch." Sneering, I slam her back into the wall, barely hearing her champagne flute shattering on the tile. "Just because you don't know what to do with a man like Tristian Mercer doesn't mean I don't." My fingers squeeze tighter and I enjoy it—the pained pinch of her brow, the bitter heat in her eyes. The rage takes me over, because the thing is, I'm remembering.

I'm remembering the chilling, lost look in his eyes that day at school when I got on my knees for him in the study room. He didn't look anywhere else. Not once. I saw every bit of agonizing desperation in his eyes.

"I want to see your complete devotion. Show me."

I'm remembering his gentle kisses afterward. The way his lips look when he calls me sweetheart. How it feels when he tells me I'm his good girl. The sight of his face collapsing when I take him into my mouth. The weight of his eyes, always on me. The pressure of his arms around my waist when we're on campus and I let him make a show of claiming me. All these memories come to me in a tidal wave—touches, glances, his fingers stroking a lock of my hair away from my face—and nothing about it seems anything less than painfully human.

I know exactly what Tristian wants.

"I want to be very clear, Gen. The reason it felt like you were fucking a robot when you were with him? It's because *you* were flawed. Tristian couldn't look at you because you were a fake, uncommitted cunt." I'm the one to smile then, making sure to show all my teeth. "But what we have isn't just about the sex—which, I can assure you, is fucking transcendent." I give her a hard shove against the wall. We're so close I can feel her heart race in her chest. "He would kill for me, Genevieve. Put a bullet in a body. Set a building on fire. Do whatever it takes to keep me safe." Narrowing my eyes, I wonder, "Do you have a man in your life who would do that for you?"

I stare at her, waiting for an answer, and she finally shakes her head, croaking out a short, "No."

"Well, I have three," I snarl, releasing her with one last push against her windpipe. "You can think about that when you're sleeping tonight, all alone in your bed. Because maybe he can't be mine," I slam my palm onto the wall beside her head, nose-to-nose with her, "but Tristian will never be yours. I will make fucking sure of it. I'll show the Mercers which of us is the real trash. I'll slander you. I'll get you kicked out of Forsyth. I'll have you exiled from this whole goddamn town if I have to. And Gen?" She coughs dramatically, rubbing her throat. There's only one more thing I need her to know. "I'm not a fickle little bitch like you. I keep my promises."

It isn't until I step back that I see the figure standing in the doorway. I fight back a recoil at the realization we're being watched, though I don't know why I'm surprised.

Watching is what Tristian does, after all.

I'm not sure what I'm expecting. Perhaps a scolding, or maybe his cheering me on, or getting in a few of his own digs. He deserves that much, after all. But what I get is far more confusing.

He's staring at me, face set into a motionless and unreadable mask. "Get the fuck out of my house." I worry at first he's talking to me, because his stare doesn't waver when he chews out the words. But then he does look away—a simple flick of his eyes to her—and his nostrils twitch, flaring. "*Now.*" It's a quiet, but undoubtedly deadly command.

"You psychos deserve each other," she growls, pushing past me and then pushing past him. She scurries down the hall, her high heels clicking like an automatic weapon.

He doesn't speak until the sound has completely disappeared. "You heard my parents before."

I look away, but all I get is the reflection of my face. Red cheeks. Wild eyes. Lips that are pressed into a tense line. "They're wrong about Gen," I tell him, working up the courage to look into his eyes again. "But they're not wrong about me."

He watches me, the sounds of the party echoing down the corridors, not shattering the tense stillness between us. "You asked me before how you made me feel," he starts, finally moving. Tristian stalks forward, slow and deliberate, until he's right in front of me. "Do you still want to know?"

I swallow, reaching to grip the counter at my back. "Yes," I quietly confess.

His blue eyes bore into mine, and try as I might, I can't find the softness there. "You make me feel so fucking irritated," he says, bearing down on me. "You won't let me take care of you, even though you don't take care of yourself. You don't ask for help. You're stubborn and impulsive. It makes me want to lock you inside your goddamn room and never let you out." The words are blunt, without inflection or warmth. But when I look away, he reaches up to grab my chin, forcing me to look at him as he goes on. "You make me feel powerless, because I can't order you around anymore. I have to wait and just, fucking," his fists his free hand into my dress, right against my thigh, "*hope* that you do the right thing. That you come home at night. That you call us if something happens. That I won't wake up tomorrow and find your bedroom empty, all your shit gone." After a pause, he tacks on, "Or worse."

I try, "Tristian," but the words get locked in my throat when he yanks my dress up, the muscle in the back of his jaw ticking.

"You make me feel helpless. I spend the better part of every day worrying about you, and I'm not like the others. They would have let you go before. But me?" There's a spark of dread in his eyes that I'm alarmed to see. "I would have followed you. I would have been your next Ted, only I would have been worse. Do you know why?" He answers his own question as he slides my skirt over my hips, bunching it around my waist. "Because I know you want me back. I would have tracked you every fucking hour. It's insanity. I don't like it."

When he fumbles for his belt, I do nothing but stand there, a deer caught in headlights, a bug trapped beneath a microscope. Because he makes me feel the same way.

This is insanity.

And I want it.

I want it even though I'm terrified of it. Of the way he's watching me with those shuttered eyes. Of how much he looks like that man who forced me to my knees in the laundry room, years ago, and of how much he *doesn't* look like him. I'm terrified of his dad being right about this being all I'm good for, and

I'm terrified for him.

"You make me feel all of that," he says, reaching into his pants. "But mostly?" He grabs my hips and pushes me onto the counter, unstoppable as he forces himself between my thighs. "Mostly you make me feel like I don't care. About any of it. Being irritated and worried and so fucking crazy about the thought of you leaving..." He reaches between us, grabbing the crotch of my panties, and I flinch, eyes flying toward the door.

It's wide open.

"People will see." The words are rushed and panicked, and it doesn't matter, because Killian's words are still ringing in my ears.

"If you want something, then you fucking take it."

I spread my thighs for him.

"Let them see," is what he says, lining himself up and shoving his cock inside me.

My jaw drops on a gasp, fingers clawing at his shoulders, but I don't speak. The words I need are locked tight in my chest, pinned under the weight of his heavy, intent stare as he fills me.

"If you think I can't be yours," the slow drag of his cock pulls a whine from the back of my throat, "then sweetheart, you haven't been paying attention." He braces one hand on the mirror behind us, and winds the other into the back of my hair as he fucks into me.

The punches of his hips are short, calculated, his eyes never leaving mine. It's almost too much to hold his stare, because I see inside of it exactly what I'd realized before. What Tristian wants, above all else. It's the thing that makes him mean. It's what drives him. It's the very thing Gen could never give him. It's the reason the sight of her still bristles at his insides, and it's probably not even because he loved her. It's because he feels foolish for having believed her.

Tristian Mercer just wants someone who wants him.

Not for his money or his status, or his good looks or charming smile, or for his future or his past. He wants someone who's seen him stripped bare of it all and still finds what's left worthwhile.

I touch his jaw, my fingertips caressing the tense muscle there, and it's true that I remember his softness and warmth and sweet touches. But likewise, I remember his hardness, coldness, and cruelty. Like Killian and Dimitri, he's not just one thing. Nothing that felt so good could ever be that simple.

I stroke his cheek as he fucks me, forehead braced against my own, and the words tumble free in a flutter of sharp, shared breaths. "I think I might love you."

He freezes there, just like that—pressed so close that I can feel the flex and surge of his muscles as he struggles to still them. So close that I can see his lips part and his eyes close. Close enough that it only takes the tiniest tilt of my head to fuse our lips together.

It's all different then.

I wind my legs around his waist just as he invades my mouth, tongue plundering deep and forceful. He reaches down to grab my hips, hitching me closer to the edge of the counter, and then he digs his way inside. It's so deep—I'm so full of him—that I don't want to let him go. My calves burn with the strain of squeezing him closer, and even when he grunts into my mouth, slamming into me, over and over, I wonder if it could even be called 'fucking'.

Maybe there are people walking down that hallway, but neither of us would hear them over the sound of our hard breaths. It's frantic and uncoordinated, and it's how I know that, whatever it is I'm feeling—love, devotion, want— Tristian feels it, too.

Because we must look so ugly.

There's no showmanship here. No flair or pretense. Tristian digs his fingers into my hips, baring his teeth as he hammers against my tense thighs, and it's completely primal.

It's just like he said before.

Insanity.

He never once looks into the mirror behind me.

"Don't you dare," he's grinding out, cheeks flushed with the way he's driving into me. "If you're thinking of leaving, don't you *fucking* dare."

And I'm chanting, "I won't, I won't," because maybe that's what I *should* do. I should leave them behind and take all this rot with me. I should make sure they're all safe. The Lords, my mother, the twins, Ms. Crane. These pieces of the world that assume the awkward shape of a family... I should protect them. All of them deserve so much better than my bullshit.

But in the end, I'm selfish enough to take Killian's advice.

"If you want something, then you fucking take it."

Maybe that means I'm a bad person.

Or maybe it means I've finally found something worth fighting for.

That's what I'm thinking of when my body shudders out its orgasm. Hands, arms, legs, ankles—everything clutching him closer to me as I quake, teeth clenched around a choked wail. He makes a raw, animalistic sound in response, crushed so close that I think for a moment he might just crawl right up on this counter and fuck me through it.

In the end, it's a hard drive of his hips that marks its end. He grunts into the air we're sharing between our mouths, slamming me back as his body stiffens. There's a moment of crushed stillness, and then I feel him inside, pulsating, hot and slick as he slowly fills me.

His exhale takes all his tension with it, leaving him limp and sated against me.

He's still breathing hard into my neck, even minutes after. I run my fingers through his hair idly, enjoying the closeness. His breath is damp and warm, and his cock has gone soft inside me. Anyone could walk past and see. I'm messy and a touch sore, and *I don't want him to move*.

When he does, I feel the loss like a physical ache.

His forehead glistens with sweat as he eases back, lifting my dress high enough to watch his spent cock slip free. It's embarrassing, the way I writhe, chasing it, wanting it back, but he's stroking my cheek and saying, "Shhh."

All of the warmth and softness I'd been missing earlier is here now, present in the way he kisses the corner of my mouth, my cheek, my temple. It's as if he pumped all that fire out of his veins and left it inside my body to warm me from within. When I close my eyes, he presses a kiss to each eyelid, feather light and so sweet. It helps me to see those cold, masked moments from before for what they are: a privilege to see. If I were anyone else, he would have smoothed over it, put on a smile, and faked his charm. But he wants me to see—to know that he's not always going to be the gentle, handsome man who pampers and coddles me. Sometimes he's the harsh, cold jerk who has to let the veil drop.

He wants to know it won't drive me away.

"You're perfect," he says, reaching between us to feel where he's leaking out of me. He brushes his lips over my jaw, whispering, "God, you're so fucking perfect," and uses two fingers to push his cum back inside. "And you're mine."

I bite down on a moan at the drag of his fingers, in and out, achingly slow. "But your parents," I argue, immediately latching onto the kiss he plants onto my lips.

"I don't care," he says, heavy-lidded eyes boring into mine. "They can't stop me. No one can, except you." *And you won't*. He doesn't say it, but I see it in the curve of his smirk as he lazily fingers me.

"Your sisters." His smile falls, hand stilling between my thighs. I don't protest when he pulls away. "I can't let them get hurt over this. They're just sweet, innocent kids."

"Story, look at me." His face is stone again as he pulls several tissues from the box on the counter and wipes my thighs. He tosses them and hastily runs his hands beneath the water. "Do you really think I'd ever let anything happen to them?"

"Let?" I ask, feeling tired. "Of course not."

When I look down to lower my dress, he jerks my chin up, mouth pressed into an unhappy line. "You think this guy is better than me? Than us?"

Immediately, I answer, "No."

"Then have faith." The riddle in his eyes unfolds, allowing me a peek at the resolve underneath.

Faith.

That's never been something that comes easy to me, and by the plea in his eyes, he knows it. Despite this, I give him a slow nod, working hard to gather up my resolve. "I trust you."

His expression shifts then, the intensity of the moment twisting so fast that I can barely keep up. "Then come on." Tristian briskly dries his hands before holding out a palm. When I place my hand in his, he eases me off the counter and carefully straightens my dress, smoothes down my hair. "Follow me. There's only a few minutes."

* * *

Tristian's fingertips tickle the small of my back when he leans down to whisper against my ear. "At midnight—in two minutes—all the Mercer men will take their women out onto that dance floor. See that guy over there? He's my uncle." He points to two others. "His oldest son is married, and his youngest is engaged." A pause. "My parents, of course." He nods to our right. "Three more cousins over there."

"Are you sure you want to do this?" My eyes ping around the crowd, wide and panicked.

"Showing my family and all the other blowhards in this room that you're mine?" He plants a sweet kiss on my neck. "Sweetheart, there's nothing I want more."

My insecurity is more about me than him. He laid himself bare in that bathroom and I believe him. But the scrutiny of the men and women in the room—well, I've had the attention of people before. Dozens of men when I was in the pit. An entire frat when Killian forced me to suck him off in the LDZ basement. Moments that have left me shaken and changed to the very foundation of my marrow.

And somehow, neither of those were as intimidating as this moment.

The song ends and Tristian's fingers link with mine, just as a clock chimes somewhere deep in the house, starting its ascent to twelve. The couples he'd pointed out to me step onto the dance floor, one by one, each settling into position. I watch the women and their excited grins, backs straight with perfect posture, and try to imagine myself looking like that. Like I belong. Like this isn't a moment I'm just recklessly stealing.

No one here knows my heart is threatening to escape from my chest as Tristian smoothly walks me into the center of the room. I try my best not to look at the others, unable to see the scorn on his parents' face. I've been claimed before, with knives and trackers and bruises and marks. But never gently, proudly, *formally*.

Tristian Mercer has elevated me. The second one of his hands settles on my hip and the other grasps mine, I'm no longer Story Austin, daughter of a sex worker, Lady to the LDZ Lords. I'm Story Austin, Tristian's partner.

"Take a breath," he says quietly, eyes twinkling with a light I've never seen before. "Push your shoulders back." He's loving this, I realize. He's basking in the publicness of it. The declaration. I shouldn't be surprised. This is a man who's been taught his whole life the importance of image. That something isn't yours until you've flaunted it about and seen the envy reflected back at you.

I suck in a deep breath and straighten my spine, shoulders back, eyes locked with his. I see a flash of movement over his shoulder and glance up at the balcony. Izzy and Lizzy beam from between two enormous plants, spying. They both wave when they spot me, and I can't help my smile. "At least not everyone in your family is against this," I say, nodding discreetly.

He turns his head, following my gaze, and grins. "You sent them piles of sugar. You're their favorite."

"I doubt that," I say, smoothing down his lapel. "They worship you."

"Not as much as I worship you." The final chime of the clock rings and the music starts. His grip tightens, and he says, "Just follow my lead."

My first steps are tentative, but soon he has me sweeping along, caught in the rhythm of music and his arms. I ignore everyone else, all the music and dark looks, the threats outside of this house and the drama that awaits, and simply revel that, for now, and forever, Tristian Mercer is mine just as much as I am his.

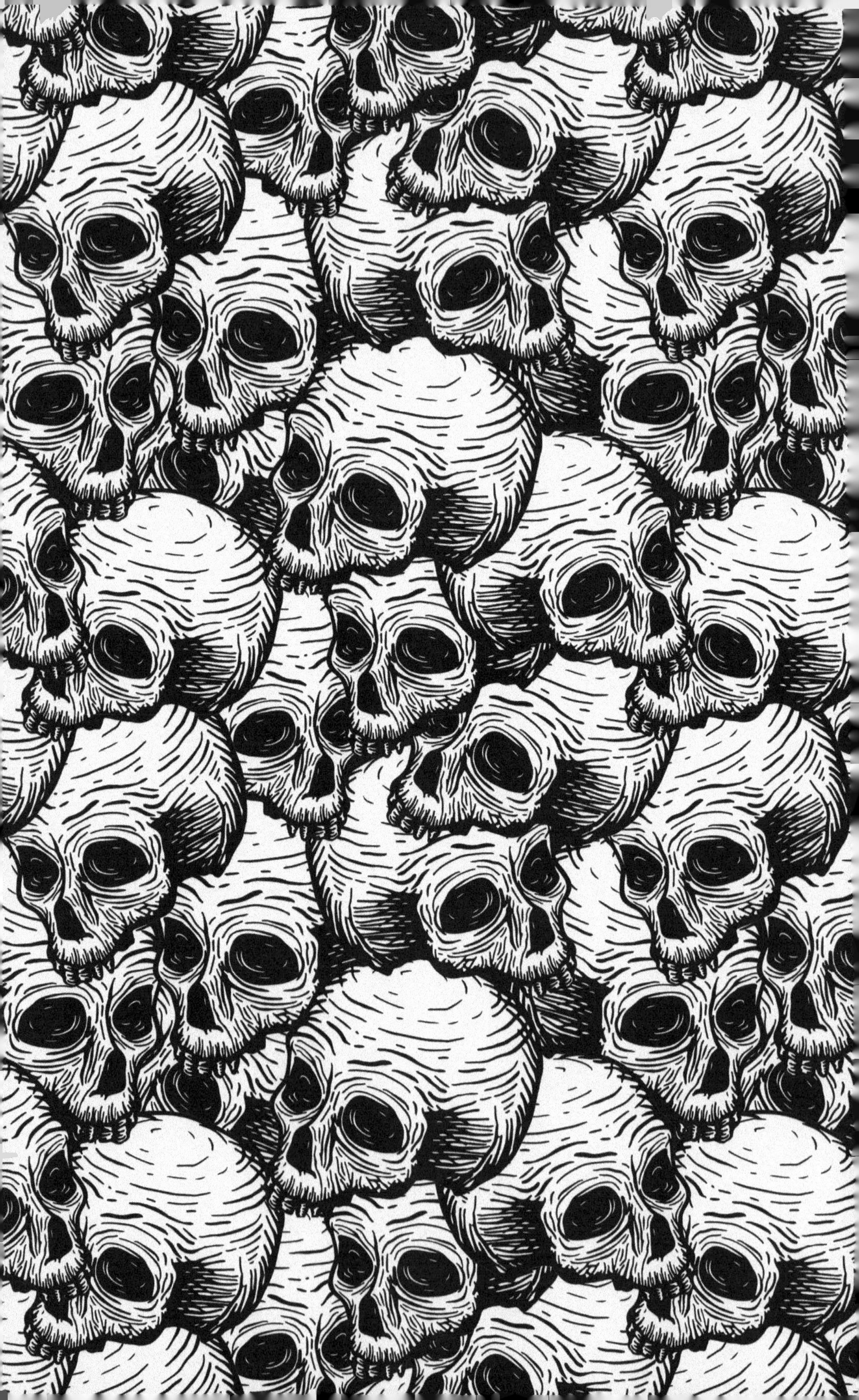

16

BED HOPPING

In the dream, it's cold.

I'm not sure when it happened. First, I was dancing, sweeping along the marble floors in elegant twirls, wrapped in Tristian's arms, and the next, I'm awash with it. It's not cold like it was last night on the way home, the chill of the winter air invading my bones. It's a refreshing sort of cold, soothing my overheated skin with intermittent flutters of warmth and softness. I curl into it, because even though I'm not sure why, I know this is a good cold. Good, like blue eyes. Familiar. Comforting. Safe.

The intermittent warmth moves up my body, from my hip to my breast, lingering there for a moment, soft and wet around my nipple, and then up to my collarbone. My neck. My ear.

Tristian's whisper barely penetrates my comfortable fog. "If your brother could see you right now, he'd cream himself." There's a deep, low chuckle, but the mention of Killian hits me like a contact grenade.

It explodes in my chest, a longing so internal and fierce that my belly clenches with the need for it. For him. I need Killian's hands on me. I need his mouth on my sleeping lips, coaxing them open for his tongue. God, how long has it been since I heard his hushed voice in my ear, telling me how hard

I make him? When was the last time he pulled my knees apart and took me all for himself? Was it only mere months ago that he was on top of me as I slept, rocking so sweetly between my thighs?

I've known I missed it, but right now, it's worse than ever, because Tristian is here instead, and I love him. I love Tristian. But he's not Killian, and the enticing pitch of his whisper doesn't fill the space. It just makes the absence more noticeable, as if he's showing me that something is missing.

Mindlessly, I sigh. "Killian..."

There's a quick intake of breath, and then Tristian's gentle rumble. "You miss him, sweetheart?" There's a rustle near my head, and then the tickle of something in my hair. "You miss Killer waking you up with his cock, don't you?"

"Mmmm," I hum, turning my head as if I could find his lips with mine. I don't, and it doesn't make sense.

It doesn't make sense that Killian's not here.

"Shhh," Tristian says, and then the warmth is against my forehead. A kiss to soothe my frown. "You know you can have him whenever you want. Don't worry."

The voice drags me closer to the surface and I stretch my toes, fighting against the weight of sleep to follow it. When I blink my eyes open, I realize Tristian's dragged the blanket down, revealing the naked expanse of our bodies. He's propped up on an elbow as he gazes down at me, temple resting on his fist. His other hand is holding his phone. It isn't until he lowers it that I realize he's been recording me.

"Urgh," I grumble, trying to cover myself up. "No videos."

He gives me a rueful grin, catching my hand in his own, knitting our fingers together. "Sorry. I couldn't think of anything to get Killer this year. He's so hard to buy for."

"You're all hard to buy for." I rub my eyes, still feeling the heaviness of exhaustion.

"Want me to delete it?" he asks, thumb sweeping against the back of my hand. "I will. You can watch me."

I take a long second to think about it—about Killian seeing me like that, so needy and desperate for him. On one hand, it might be a horrible tease. On the other...

Well.

It might be a horrible tease.

I give a slight shake of my head.

"Ruthless." Tristian smirks at me. "That's my girl." His expression darkens, even as his eyes take in my naked body. "He's going to need something to get him through the next few months."

"What?" I stretch, flexing my calves. "Why?"

"That choice I made last night? The one where I picked you?" He runs his finger over the scars in my chest, gently tracing the letters. "I wasn't just picking you. I was choosing them. Us. *This*." He makes a vague but expansive gesture. "Your big brother is going to have to do something similar, and that means leaving some things behind."

"He's going to leave Daniel?" As soon as I say it I know that's wrong. "No. He's going to quit football." It settles in my gut with a hard certainty, and suddenly, I don't know how I hadn't seen this coming all along.

"Getting shot, the shit going on at the Hideaway, all the threats with you..." He sighs, head shaking. "Things are out of control. He can feel it. We all can, and it's his job to step up. That's what Killer does, you know." Tristian raises his eyes to mine, searching. "When things get hard, he makes the calls no one else has the guts to."

"So he's giving up his dreams." A wave of sadness crests over me. Dimitri's already lost his dreams because of me. Now Killian? I meant it last night when I vowed to stay, but I'm not some starry-eyed little girl anymore. I know what I am to the people closest to me. An albatross.

The smile Tristian gives me is small and bittersweet. "No, sweetheart, he's claiming his destiny. That NFL life was just a fun distraction and we all know it. It's why he's trying not to go to that banquet in a few weeks. You know he's usually the type to rip the band-aid off, but not here. The banquet is honoring student-athletes as a precursor to the draft season. He's got that shit in the bag, but once he accepts it and is forced to tell the coach he's quitting the team, it all becomes reality."

"I guess...it's just always been part of his identity." Images of Killian back in high school, wearing his jersey in the halls, his sweaty clothes in our shared bathroom hamper, the trophies and wins. He's right, this is going to be as hard on him as it was for Tristian to take me on that dance floor in front of his family. As much as Dimitri giving all his money to Daniel to pay for me in the pit.

I'll never understand why the price of this—of *us*—is so high.

"He'll survive," he says, tipping my chin with his finger. "It's what we do."

The room's darker than it should be and the cold is rapidly becoming something of the bad variety. I remember us getting home late—after midnight. After the dance. After the *Christmas party*. I remember coming up the stairs with him and letting Tristian take my dress off. I remember taking off his clothes, mapping out his toned muscles with my curious fingertips. None of them have ever let me do that before—just explore—but Tristian laced his fingers behind his head and laid there while I... *discovered* him, the arrogant arch of his brow doing nothing to dampen my enjoyment of it. His body is immaculate. A temple, he'd called it. Afterward, I remember his lips on the back of my neck as he curled around me. But nothing else.

"What time is it?" I croak.

Tristian curls his fingers, skating his knuckles over the curve of my breast. "Six."

"In the morning?" I'm not sure what face I make, but it must be one for the ages, because Tristian actually full-out laughs, shoulders shaking.

"Yes, six in the morning." He grabs my thigh in a gesture that's probably thoughtless, but makes my spine tingle with how proprietary it is. "I kind of have plans for the next hour, so I thought you might like to go back to your room. I don't want to keep you awake with my talking."

I press my leg into him, enjoying the way he's massaging my thigh. "Talking?"

"Video call with the twins, so we can open presents together." He gestures with a nod to his chair in the corner.

"Oh." There are two very badly wrapped presents sitting in the middle of it, covered in bows and ribbons and glittering stickers. I smile. "Awww."

He nods. "Yeah, they went a bit hog-wild on the trimmings."

Suddenly, it hits me, and I rub a hand down my face. "God, you should have stayed the night over there with them instead of carting me all the way back here."

"Not a chance in hell." He tips down to kiss me, and even though he hovers there, pinching my bottom lip between his, he doesn't deepen it. He pulls back to look at me with those blue eyes, and it might be the first time I've ever seen him like this: sleep-mussed and soft, a pillow crease still branded into his cheek. "This is the best Christmas I've ever had."

I'm not sure how the same man who has the power to turn my blood to ice can also melt my insides so effectively, but that's what he's done. I'm sure there's more to say. I can see it in his eyes as they search my face, the litany of things he wants to give to me. It hasn't escaped my notice that he hasn't said it back.

"I think I might love you."

But I didn't say it hoping he would. The moment was more a gift to myself than one to him.

"It might be mine, too," I say, pouting. "Except the part where you're kicking me out of your bed. And before the sun's even risen, at that."

He frowns. "I'm not kicking you out. I just know you're tired. We only went to sleep a few hours ago."

"I know," I assure him, turning into his body. "I'll go. Just let me work up to it. My bed's going to be all cold." I whimper at the thought of sliding between the chilly sheets.

"Hmm." He cups the back of my head in his palm, giving my hair a stroke. "I'm sure we can find somewhere warm for you to cuddle up for a few hours. Come on."

With that, he rips the blanket away, making me yelp at the sudden rush of frigid air. I cover my breasts uselessly, fixing him with a glower. "You know, a girl could feel a little cast aside here!"

He hops up from the bed, just as naked as I am, but looking a lot less shivery about it. "Please, you know every man in this house lives and breathes for the possibility you'll come to his bed." Bending down, he snatches his dress shirt up from where I'd dropped it hours ago and holds it open for me. "Up you go."

Groaning, I climb out of bed, but even when he helps me thread my arms through his crisp, white shirt, it does little to ease my chattering teeth. He doesn't make me stand around waiting, though. Without even bothering to pull on some boxers, he threads our fingers together and drags me right out of his room and into the much colder hallway. The wood floor is like ice on my feet, so I tiptoe behind him, not even bothering to pay much attention to where he's taking me.

Tristian pushes open the door opposite of his and leads me into Dimitri's room. This room is just as dark as Tristian's, but there's music playing through the speakers—something fast and punky. It's still tidy, with a clear pathway to the piano and bed. Tristian pulls a face at it, but tugs me toward the bed and the dark lump in the middle of it.

"Rath." Tristian waits, but when he doesn't get a response, he cups a hand over his junk and lifts his leg to push the lump with his foot. "Wake up, you degenerate."

There's a flinch from beneath the blankets, and then a flurry of motion that ends in Dimitri bolting upright, large knife clutched in his fist.

Tristian flings out an arm to push me back. "Easy, dude, chill. It's just us."

"What?" Dimitri asks, blinking an alarmed, but sleep-heavy gaze over the room. "What happened? What's wrong?"

"Nothing," Tristian assures, keeping his voice low and calm. "Just need a warm body to park our Lady beside, brother. That's all."

Dimitri's eyes finally fall on me. The tension drops from his body like a bag of bricks, and he flops back down, stuffing the knife back under his pillow. "Fuck, about gave me a goddamn heart attack." He disappears beneath the blanket once again.

Only this time, a hand emerges.

He curls his palm in a 'gimme' gesture, and Tristian pushes me forward, watching as I grab the outstretched hand. Dimitri yanks me into the bed hard enough that I basically tumble into it, but just as quickly as I hit the mattress, he's swallowing me up in his nest of blankets, dragging me into his warm, bare chest.

He makes a soft, pleased sound after arranging me to his liking. "Fuck yeah."

It's so incredibly warm, the blankets blocking out anything but his heat and steady breaths. Every muscle in my body melts as I nestle into him, dragging in a lungful of his spicy scent.

I hum, my eyes growing heavier. "Merry Christmas to me."

From outside the blankets, Tristian's distant, muffled voice says, "I can buy you three hours. After that, I make no promises." And then a click of the door closing.

Promises about what? I mean to ask, but I'm dragged so quickly under the warmth of Dimitri's embrace, impossibly intoxicating, that all I can do is give in to it.

IT'S ODD HOW sleeping is so different with each of them.

Sleeping beside Killian means the constant promise of danger and thrill. The entire time is spent with this morsel of anticipation growing inside my mind, impatient for that first soft touch. It's not a surface thing, either. It's subconscious, as if he's burrowed into my brain and planted his seeds there. If I know he's coming—hell, sometimes even when I don't—it's all I dream about. The wait. The hope. The exhilaration.

When I sleep beside Tristian, I dream of being weightless, gliding across an expanse of zero gravity. I never have to worry when I'm sleeping with him. My brain just shuts itself off, as if it knows I'm being cared for, looked after, in the presence of a danger to anyone but myself. When I'm with him, everything feels okay.

But Dimitri?

Sleeping with him is like a drug. It's the very first temptation I ever gave into in this house. The warmth and comfort, the sleepy pull of our bodies as we curl up like soft animals, the gentle way I wake when I'm with him...it's addictive. There are mornings where I wake up alone and ache with how much I'd rather be here, in Dimitri's bed, burrowed into the cradle of his body. There's nothing sharp or painful here. No barbs or thorns. No hurts worth paying mind to. Just the two of us, gradually emerging from slumber.

I know he's awake when I feel his cock twitching against the thigh I have thrown over his hips. I've nestled my cheek into the crook of his neck, and I'm laying on his arm—which must be numb—but he's using it to clutch me to his side, so maybe not.

When I open my eyes, the first thing I see is the healing wound on his chest. The 'S' I carved there is scabbed over, but all the redness around the edges has dissipated. The second thing I notice is that he's on his phone, casually scrolling through a playlist. I watch like that for a while, not giving away that I'm awake, and it feels like a little thrill, stealthily observing him. He's unnaturally still, his chest rising and falling evenly, but his thumb is erratic, swiping through songs at light speed. One of the best things about Dimitri is how unpretentious he is about the music he likes. He'll add Bach to the same playlist that boasts obscure internet trap hop, Motown, Scandinavian death metal, and a remix of an eighties cereal jingle. There's no rhyme or reason to his choices except for one that's entirely internal.

Idly, I wonder if this is what it feels like for Tristian, getting a glimpse at someone's behavior when their defenses are down.

Speak of my devil. His name pops up on the screen with an incoming voice call.

Dimitri swiftly declines it and then pulls up their text window. I watch as he sends off a series of emojis:

Sleeping face, book, middle finger.

A moment later, Tristian sends his own:

Knife, syringe, gun.

Dimitri responds:

Yawn, eggplant, 'ok hand'.

Tristian responds with a single emoji—pinching hand—and it makes Dimitri's chest hitch with a silent laugh.

"If I'm reading this right," he barely startles at the realization I'm awake, "you fell asleep with a book, so Tristian should leave you alone. Then he threatens you with assorted violence. And now you're going to jerk off until you go back to sleep again."

His voice is deep and still rough with sleep, rumbling beneath my ear. "You've decoded our secret language." Dimitri's hand moves over my ribs, making me squirm. It's even warmer and more comfortable here than I remember it being when I first tumbled in beside him. My ankle is tangled up between his, and he gives it a slow rub with the heel of his foot. "The knife is Killer," he quietly adds, turning to press his nose into my hair. "You're the book."

"Oh." I bite my lip, looking at the screen. "What's Tristian?"

Dimitri brings up the emoji library and clicks on an elaborate cupcake.

"Drives him crazy," he explains.

I bury a smile, and the yawn that accompanies into it, into his neck. "I can only imagine."

He sets the phone aside and rolls into me, pressing a series of lazy kisses to my jaw. "I think Killer's getting impatient. He says he doesn't have all day, but between you and me, I think he just wants to do presents."

I hum, turning my head to give his wandering lips access to my neck. "There are presents?"

"Of course there are presents." His hand finds the crease of Tristian's dress shirt and dips beneath it, invading the spot of skin right below my breast. "Tristian and I always get him the same thing. Credit with his favorite ink man. He and Tristian always get me credit at the overpriced instrument shithole in North Side. And I always get Tristian drugs."

That brings me up short. "Tristian doesn't do drugs. Not, like, real drugs."

Dimitri lifts his head to look at me, eyes sweeping down as he pulls my shirt back. "Sure, he does." His fingertip circles my nipple, watching it stiffen to a point. "Once a year, Christmas day, he'll let me get him fucked up without asking where I got it and what it's cut with." Gently—almost tenderly—he cups my breast in his hand. "It's the one day he actually lets go. He even eats junk."

I snort, skating my fingertips over his wrist. "No way."

Dimitri gives me a lopsided smirk. "Just wait, you'll see. Tomorrow he'll act like a little bitch about it. Probably do some kind of detox cleanse or whatever the fuck. But today, I get to pump that fucker with absolute garbage. It's amazing, you'll love it."

I wish I'd known that. "I couldn't find anything to get the three of you," I confess.

But he just shrugs. "We figured." So casually that I'm not even expecting it, he bends down to take my nipple between his lips. Just like that, I'm a mess of white-hot want. The cool metal of his lip rings against my skin does little to soothe it. "Don't worry, we didn't get you anything ridiculous. Sometimes they don't understand, you know?" His dark eyes rise to mine. "That money makes people like us twitchy."

I'm sure there's a point to be made, but it's hard to focus on it when he's hovering over my breast like this, pensive and unhurried. I thread my fingers through his hair and arch against his mouth, eliciting a ragged laugh.

He brushes his lips against my nipple, saying, "The thing I got you was free, though."

"It was?"

He cuts his eyes to the bedside table, nodding. "Top drawer. Check it out."

When I reach over to open it, he moves his mouth to the center of my chest, kissing the scars as I rummage through. I raise an eyebrow, holding up a box of condoms. "Did you keep the receipt?" Because there might have been a time I wanted them, but I can't even remember it. Now the thought of them being inside me without leaving a trace of themselves behind is actively off-putting.

"Those are old," he says, grabbing the box and flinging it across the room. "The paper, on top."

I find it, pulling it from the drawer and giving it a long look over. It's a paper on Soviet dystopias, written by D. Rathbone, and features a simple rubric, written in red cursive:

Analysis - B, Grammar - D, Evidence - A.

In a big circle below it is the letter 'C'.

I bolt upright, ignoring his groan of protest. "Oh my god, you got this on your own?"

He flops back, looking put out as I cover my chest with the paper. "Not really. I'm kind of seeing someone—for extra help."

"A tutor?" For some reason, the thought of him sitting with someone else—another *girl*—and working through his reading issues makes my chest ignite in a hot, possessive fury.

He doesn't make me suffer long, reaching out to twirl a lock of my hair around his finger. "The music director set me up with this guy. A literacy coach." The corners of his eyes tighten at the admission. "I had to give up my studio space on Tuesdays and Thursdays to work with him, but it's free, and he's not a dick about it."

"Holy shit. A real literacy coach?" I say, gaping at him. Not just some tutor, or some student who'd bend at his every whim. An actual professional who understands his limitations, but also understands his potential.

I tackle him with a kiss that's too full of my own smile to reach the proper ambition.

As much as I don't mind helping Dimitri, I know that actually asking someone for help, with zero strings attached, is huge. Revealing his vulnerabilities to me was easier because he had the power. I've never been prouder of this man.

"If I'd known you'd be this excited about a 'C' maybe I would have tried harder a while back." His hands slip to my hips and I rock against him. Building warmth rises between us but before my lips can meet his again, a loud banging on the door jolts us apart.

He picks up his phone and checks the time. "He said three hours. On the dot."

I expect him to ignore it, but he doesn't. A different sort of energy sparks through him. "Come on," he says, rolling me off. "Let's go see what Santa brought us."

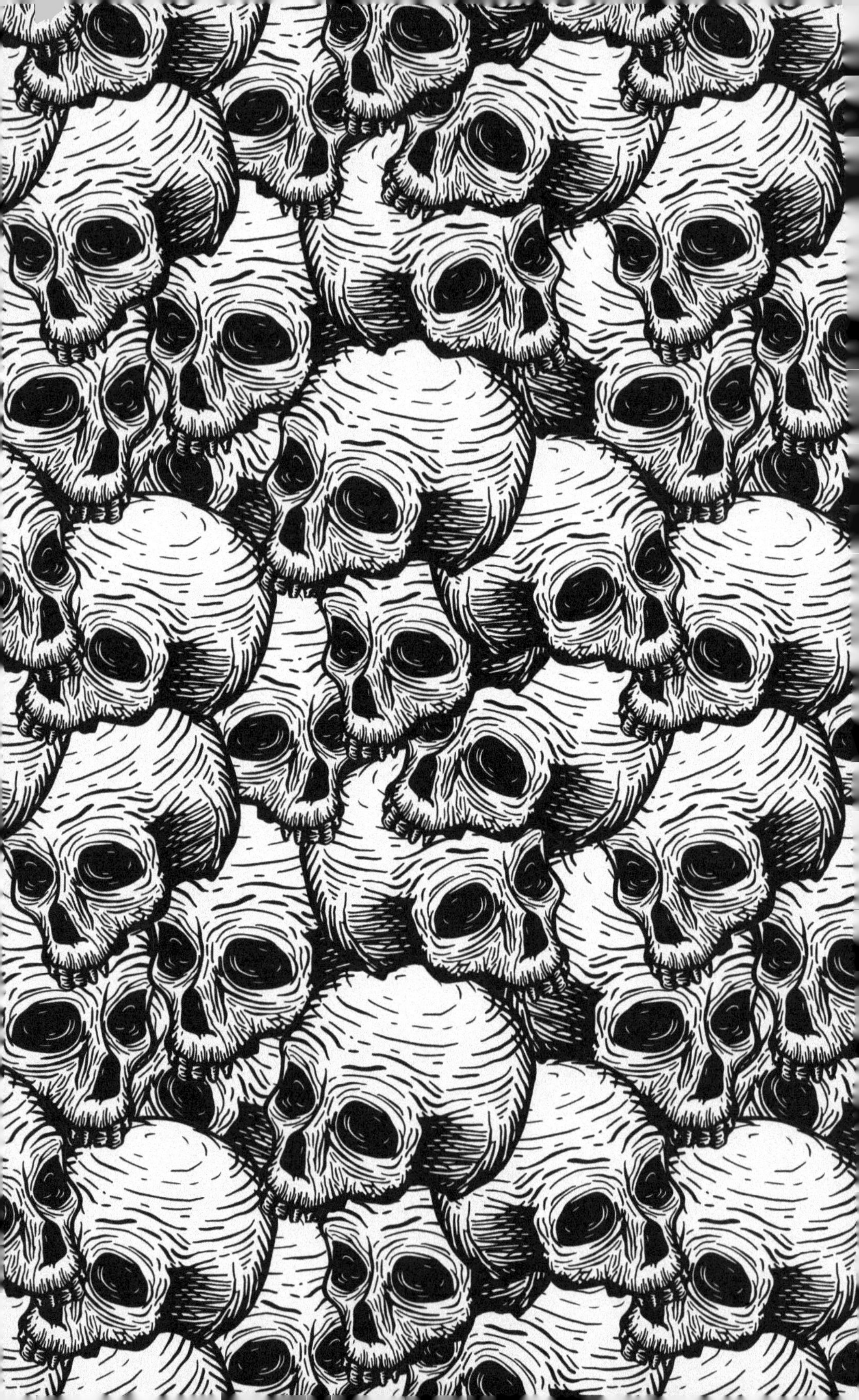

17

SNOW ROLLING

I watch as Story sighs my name; the camera moving from her supple tits to her sleeping face. Her lips are slightly parted, cheeks flushed a soft pink. Once again, I reach down to adjust my boner, listening to Tristian ask her if she misses waking up to my cock.

The hallway feels too hot, even though it's December and drafty, and if I had a little less respect for myself, I'd just whip my dick out right here and get off like an animal. But I don't. In the time it takes Story and Rath to wake the fuck up, I've replayed the video Tristian sent me a time or two. Or five.

Or… twenty eight.

I wait until precisely nine to pound on the door, tired of pacing out here with that video playing on a loop, both on my phone and inside my head. It's getting real fucking old. She wants it. She wants me in her bed. She *wants* to wake up to me. That little frown on her face while Tristian was whispering in her ear was pure disappointment.

So what the hell does a guy have to do?

Rath's the one to yank the door open, looking surly and tense. From the tent in his boxers, I can guess why. "You're the worst goddamn cockblock, you know that?"

I look over his shoulder just in time to catch a flash of Story's bare chest as she closes her shirt. My dick throbs. "You can't hole up in here all fucking day. Let's get on with it."

With that, I leave them, fully intending to march my horny ass back up there in ten minutes if they don't show. I look for Ms. Crane next, but she's a lot easier. I find her in the garden, back hunched against the cold as she aggressively puffs at a cigarette. This isn't generally an unusual state to find her in. For being such a curmudgeonly bitch, she follows the rules about not smoking in the house.

It's just that, this morning, she's wearing a red and green reindeer sweater—I'm pretty sure there are bells on it—and an elf hat.

She peers one beady eye up at me when I stop, speechless at the sight in front of me. "What are you looking at?" she sneers in her rough voice.

"Funny." I stare at her. "I had the same question."

She flicks the ashes from her cigarette. "You're looking at an old woman getting her morning nicotine fix. Christ, you're sharp as a marble."

"I just mean, you're looking so," I waver, wondering if the lashing I'm sure to get is worth it, "festive."

Her left eye twitches. "'Tis the fucking season, is it not?"

"Yeah, but—"

She points two fingers at me, the cigarette wobbling between them. "The last forty years, Christmas has meant jack shit to me but a houseful of cranky, bipedal erections. If I want to wear shitty sweaters and bake cookies, then that's what I'm going to do, and the whole lot of you are going to keep your goddamn mouths shut about it."

I hold up my hands. "By all means."

Cookies?

Jesus wept.

I catch Tristian in the kitchen before he can make the same mistake. "I think

Ms. Crane is into the whole Christmas spirit thing. Don't mention it to her."

He pulls a face. "Seriously?"

Ms. Crane will be content for the day once she sees what we left her. A bottle of Scotch, a box of French chocolates, a fat blunt, and a new copy of Paul Newman's Butch Cassidy and the Sundance Kid with extra scenes. She'll be drunk, fed, horny over Paul, and out of our hair for the night.

"You got her gift?" Tristian asks.

"Wrapped and ready."

Buying a girl a gift—any girl—isn't something I've ever done before. My motto has always been 'no expectations-no strings' and frankly, getting a taste of the Killer D is gift enough in my opinion. But shit isn't the same with Story. Nothing is the same. Everything has shifted between us.

At nine thirty, Story and Rath finally appear, dressed but trudging down the stairs, like they'd rather be in bed. She's pulled her hair up, some of her makeup from last night still visible around the edges of her eyes. I only caught a brief glimpse of her and Tristian coming home from his parent's party, but it was enough to see his hair was tousled, eyes glazed over as he watched her glide toward the stairs. I don't know if he was drunk, stoned, or high on pussy. The blissed-out expression on Story's face when she walked past the den has me placing odds on pussy.

Ms. Crane insisted we have a tree, and sometime during the craziness of the last week she put one up, gaudily, with those strings of tinsel that get all over the place. There are no big gifts or stockings filled with treats. We're three adult men living in a frat house. This year is an exception only because Story is here. Her gift is the only one I actually care about. Story takes a seat between Tristian and Rath on the couch and looks at the package on the coffee table curiously.

"You didn't have to get me anything," she says, shifting uncomfortably between them.

Rath throws an arm over the back of the couch, insisting, "Just open it."

Although this was mostly my idea, Tristian tells her, "It's from all of us."

He still throws me a skeptical look. Even Rath is worrying his lip ring against his tongue as he watches her pick it up, peeling away the wrapping paper.

I completely expect the flash of stunned disbelief in her eyes when she lifts the lid on the box. "No way." Her wide eyes jump to mine, cheeks spread into a grin that looks automatic. "This is mine? Really mine?!"

There's a strange bloom of warmth in my chest. I have to stop myself from reaching up to rub at it. "You have to learn how to take care of it," I warn, not expecting her to lurch up from the sofa and fly toward me.

She squeals, and even though I've stiffened instinctually at the sudden explosion of movement, I catch her in my arms, lost for a moment in the soft, feminine scent of her hair.

"Thank you." She presses a quick, thoughtless kiss to my neck before zipping away, and I'm not prepared.

It feels like my lungs have collapsed.

I clear my throat, watching her test the weight of the pistol in her grip. "It's a smaller caliber, but—"

"It's so pretty!" she gushes, the light catching on the silver as she closely inspects it.

My boys and I share a perplexed look. We've heard guns referred to as a lot of things, but 'pretty' is a first. I'd chosen it carefully, because Story isn't the type of girl who'd say so, but I can tell guns have made her a little twitchy since she shot Ugly Nick. This one is smaller than the one she used that night. Lighter. Easy to conceal. I arch my eyebrow smugly at Tristian.

Told you so.

Fucker wanted to get her jewelry.

I can tell when she catches sight of the engraving on the barrel because she squints, reading it aloud. "Lady's choice…" When her gaze lifts to mine, a current passes between us—a memory.

"What was it I gave you?"

"A choice, big brother."

I tear my eyes away, squirming under the weight of it. I'm not a good person, not a good brother, and god knows I'm absolute shit at being something more. But sometimes, when she looks at me like that, all soft and assured, it makes me think I could try.

"Okay," Tristian says, tapping his fingers against his knee. "Now that everyone is *armed...*"

"Marcus texted me last night," Rath says, sprawling out. "He says the snow hill is ready, and he got the machine to pump out extra." Marcus is an excellent linebacker. He's also a mechanical engineering student and handy as fuck to have around.

"We're really going to go sledding?" Story asks, still holding her new gun. She looks excited about it, and Rath and Tristian share a grin.

"Oh, this isn't just sledding, baby." Rath reaches out to grab her hips, tugging her closer, "It's *snow rolling.*"

She tilts her head. "What's that?"

Five hours later, we're all standing in the kitchen getting geared up to go to the hill, and Tristian is giving Rath a rundown of terms and conditions. "Make sure I'm hydrated," he says, eyes narrowed at the Molly in Rath's palm. "But not too hydrated. And don't let me grind my teeth so much. My dentist is already on my nuts for brushing too hard."

Rath rolls his eyes, but nods along. Same shit, different year. "I know how to handle you when you're rolling, Tris. Just take it."

Begrudgingly, Tristian sticks out his tongue, and Rath drops the tablet on the tip of it.

"I don't know why you bother acting like you're so above this." I pull on my jacket before grabbing Story's off the hook and passing it to her. "We all know you look forward to this dumb shit every year. In an hour, you'll be creaming your pants over how much you love the texture of air or whatever."

Story cranes her neck to watch as Tristian takes it into his mouth. "What does it feel like?"

Rath gives her a quick, surprised glance. "You've never done ex?" When she shakes her head, he explains, "It makes you feel good. You know, like... euphoric."

Tristian adds, "You want to touch everything."

"You want to *fuck* everything," I offer.

"You get hot." Tristian holds up his hoodie—no coat for him—before tugging it over his head. "And thirsty, and like you just want to bite the fuck out of something."

"Everything just feels amazing." Rath's crucial mistake is that he shows her the baggy, which must have at least a dozen still in it.

I wince, already knowing what's coming.

Her eyes sparkle as she stares at the bag. "I want some."

I'd long ago brought up the difference between rolling on Molly during our epic Christmas rager versus being stuck at home with no one but each other and her. No girl is prepared for that amount of clinging horniness. Because of that, we'd all agreed it'd just be Tristian today. The two of us could keep him in line.

But Rath is giving me this dark, impish little smirk. "What do you think, big brother? I have enough to keep everyone rolling until after sundown."

Biting back a curse, I look at our Lady. "You'd better be fucking sure." The last thing I want is her coming down and getting all pissy about whatever happens out there. Rolling or not, if she starts rubbing up against me, I'm not holding back.

She gives a quick nod, raising her chin. "I'm sure."

Rath looks at Tristian before reaching into the bag. He approaches me first, placing a tablet on my tongue, but when he gets to Story, he plucks one from the bag and places it on his own, giving his tongue a wiggle.

She raises an eyebrow, straining up on her toes, and in a move that I sincerely fucking hope is setting the mood for things to come, closes her lips around his tongue, cheeks hollowing when she sucks.

I watch a shiver run through Rath as she pulls back, giving him a peek of the tablet between her teeth.

This is either going to end really fucking bad or really fucking good.

"HERE WE GO," I mutter, watching Rath zip down the hill. "He's going to wipe out."

"No. I'm sure he'll—" Story stops, her hands covering her cheeks as we both watch the impending crash. Rath's sled hits a small bump built into the structure and he goes flying, arms and legs flailing as he rockets into the air. "Oh, no!"

He tucks and rolls, coming to a sliding stop at the bottom.

I give a slow, loud clap. "Graceful as fuck, Rathbone!"

The only movement from the dark shape of him sprawled on the ground is the emergence of two arms, raised to flip me off.

It's a shame this is being wasted on the three of us. Mount Marcus, named after our frat brother, is the best sledding hill yet. I can just imagine fifty wasted frat boys tripping over themselves to break a bone on this fucker.

"Here," I offer Story the sled. "Your turn."

"I'm okay," she says, flashing a small grin. "You go again."

Her snow hat is askew, and I can tell the Molly is hitting her because she's gnawing on her hoodie string like it's a bone. Although her expression is cute and innocent, her pupils are blown wide, two deep pools of black peering up at me.

I've been three times and the guys have each gone four.

"What gives, little sister? Don't trust Marcus' handiwork?" I nudge her with my elbow, but the Molly must be hitting me too, because she stumbles with the force of it. I shoot my hand out to catch her, yanking her into my side. "Oops."

She gives me an uneasy laugh. "Oh, I trust his skills," she promises, but looks down at the bottom, where Tristian is helping Rath off the ground. "I'm just not super into, um, my own. Right now. Specifically." She's gnawing on that string and staring wide-eyed at the expanse of white slope, and Ah.

I look at her dubiously. "Is it hitting you too hard?" Well, she is a tiny thing compared to the three of us. Maybe Rath should have started her off with half a tablet. Fuck.

"No, it's not that." Her arms cross and the pom-pom on the top of her hat bobs. "I just don't think I'd like how it feels."

It isn't until her eyelashes flutter that I realize I'm fondling her hair. I consider stopping, but decide it feels really good against my fingers. Like spun sugar or gold or something. "Sounds like you're scared."

Which is surprising and funny. This woman has shot a man, faced down my father, avoided a stalker for years, and exacted revenge on the three of us. Yet she's scared of a fake, snow-covered hill.

She lifts a shoulder. "So what if I am?"

I drop the sled on the top of the shoot and position my legs around each side. Just before I sit, I reach out and grab her, pulling her against my chest and dragging her down.

"Killian!" she shouts, fighting against me. "Let me go!"

I struggle to settle her thrashing little body between my legs. "Stop fighting," I growl, cinching my arm around her waist. "If you'll just chill out for a second," I say, blowing a strand of hair out of my mouth. "I'm not going to let anything happen to you."

She finally stills, but her spine is rigid, shoulders all stiff.

"Lean into me." I nudge her toward me, and she relents, tipping her back against my chest. "What are you afraid of?"

"I don't like the way my stomach feels when I go down big hills," she admits, fingers curling around my knees. "You know, that crazy swoop you get?"

"I've been in the car with you." I clench my teeth at the way she's rubbing the denim over my knees, all mindless like she doesn't even realize she's basically feeling them up. "You drive like a fucking maniac."

"That's different." I feel her ease a little, sinking into my chest. "I drive the car, it doesn't drive me. I trust myself."

I get a little lost in the way she feels against me, like I could get us both naked right now and not even need to nut. Just feeling her body against mine would probably be the most amazing fucking thing I've ever felt.

And then her words register. "So you don't trust me." Fuck, I'm not expecting the sting of that, but even I have to admit, "That's fair."

She looks back at me, her dilated eyes giving me a blink. "Is it? We've both done some shitty things to each other, but we've also had one another's backs." Frowning, she looks down at the slope, giving my knees another idle petting. "I suppose we've moved past that, haven't we?"

The cut of her jaw is too tight, muscles and tendons flexing, and I touch her chin mostly to ease the pressure there. To remind her that she doesn't need to clench up. To get those eyes back on mine, so I can say, "I think we have."

I brush my lips over hers, tasting the hot cocoa she drank earlier, but she instantly deepens it, opening her mouth to my eager tongue. The rush of heat that spreads through my limbs makes me rumble, deep in my chest, because I've changed my mind. The slick warmth of her tongue against mine has to be the most amazing thing I've ever felt. I could easily succumb to it, let myself fall into how good it is, just being inside her mouth.

But I pull back, jaw going tight at the restraint I need to do so. "Take this ride with me, little sister. I'll keep you safe."

Her eyes flutter open, and she might be high right now, but I know some of that glassiness in her gaze is on account of me. "Promise?" The question is loaded—more about than just a simple sleigh ride. It's about life and everything hurtling our way.

And it's easy to answer.

"I promise."

She faces forward and squirms her ass against me, making my cock swell. *Rubbing up against me.*

But despite my earlier thoughts about not holding back, I just can't bring myself to ruin the moment by pushing anything. Her arms loop around mine, holding on tight, and it does something to me, having her in my arms. It's the same way I felt those few times she curled against me to sleep. Like this is something I need to protect. Something I need to be careful with.

I rock back and forth, gaining enough momentum to push off, sending us down the chute and onto the ice covered hill. She lets out a shocked little screech, but it's followed by a sudden peal of laughter. Down at the bottom, the guys cheer us on, and I feel the tickle in my belly—the one she talked about—that swoop that feels loose and out of control.

It's not the ride or the drugs that make me feel it.

It's the girl.

THIS HAS BEEN seven solid hours of agony.

The Molly's good—Rath knows his product better than most—which means that we spend all afternoon looking for excuses to get Story into our laps. Sledding was the easy bait.

She acts like a cat, rubbing herself on the three of us. She seeks skin; pressing her icy hands against our faces and slipping up shirts. It's the tiniest of touches, but everything is heightened and by the time it's dark and we're all sitting around Tristian's ambitious bonfire, I've had a boner for hours.

I'm actually grateful we're coming down. Or, at least the three of us are.

Story is still stroking the back of Rath's hand. "You were right," she whispers, staring wonderingly at his skin. "Everything feels amazing." She shivers and he wraps his arm around her, pulling her close. We've been out here for a few hours and the chill has settled in.

"I can't believe you're still rolling." Rath looks at her the same way she's looking at his hand. "Your metabolism is fucking insane."

"Remember freshman year?" Tristian pokes at the fire with a stick, stoking the flames. He always gets this devious glint in his eye around an open flame, like the little imp inside his head is dying to come out and play. "That pledge who got so high they had to tie him down? Handsy little fucker."

I laugh, replaying the memory. "I wonder if he was actually gay, or if the drugs were just that good."

"In all fairness," Tristian says, "the hot tub was a sausage fest that year. When it comes to pussy, options are never good for a pledge."

Story looks around and then turns back to us, a smile tugging at the corners of her mouth. "The hot tub! Would that feel good, too?"

"Oh," Rath says, already standing and pulling her with him. "Let's find out."

Tristian bends over the box of fire supplies, still muttering about the fire. "If I add some lint and rearrange the kindling—"

"Tris!" I bark. His eyes snap up, and I point toward the house. "Hot tub, dude. Priorities."

His eyebrows shoot up as he watches Story and Rath jog over to the tub. She stops by the edge and unzips her hoodie, and he springs into action, closing the box. "Oh, right. Good call."

In the blue light coming from the tub, I see Story shivering in a t-shirt and panties, dipping a toe in the steamy water. While she eases in, cautiously dipping beneath the surface, Rath punches the button on the panel, starting up the gurgling jets.

We all take our beers with us as we approach, Rath undressing first to step into the hot tub in his boxers. Tristian peels off his clothes as he walks over, carefully laying his outfit on a nearby chair. He gets down to his boxer briefs and drops them, too.

"These cost two hundred dollars," he says, holding them up. "All natural and organic fibers cultivated in Peru. I'm not subjecting them to all that chlorine." He jumps in next, looking pleased when the splash makes her shriek.

I strip down, shucking off my pants. The cold air slaps my ass and I do a full body shiver. All three of them look over, and I shrug. "Commando today."

I don't hesitate to get in the water, the blistering heat warming my toes. The hot tub is big, being made for a frat and all. We've had more than one party out here, plenty of big guys and their tail of choice packed in ten, fifteen deep.

The water sloshes as I sink under, but my eyes zero in on Story's tits. Jesus. She's sitting across from me, between Rath and Tristian, still in the white shirt, but it's pasted on like a second skin, nipples dark and round beneath the clinging cotton. I feel the blood rush to my cock. From the way Tristian and Rath are staring at them, I'm guessing they know the feeling. But she's too distracted with feeling the surface of the water to notice.

"Crackly," she murmurs, swirling her fingers around.

"No offense, Tris," Rath says, resting his arms on the edge of the tub. "But this is way better than your shitty fire." He dips his chin toward the glow in the distance, the flames already beginning to die.

"A good fire requires constant attention. You have to feed it, stoke it." He grins over at Story, watching as her eyes track the paths her hands are making just below the surface. "Kind of like this Lady of ours."

She flicks him a quick, absent-minded glance. "Did you just compare me to a fire?"

"It's a compliment." He kisses her neck, sucking on the skin below her ear. "Trust me."

That at least gets her attention away from the water. She gasps, tilting her head to give his mouth more space. "What else do you do during these parties? Besides the sledding and bonfires and hot tub things?"

I tip back my beer, thinking of our previous bashes. "There's Jingle Bell Pong. Which...is basically beer pong, only with bells instead of ping-pong balls." Come to think of it, "It's not really a good substitution."

Tristian gestures to me with the neck of his own beer bottle. "There's also the thot patrol."

"Plus, Candy Cocks," Rath throws in. "And too many drinking games to remember."

"What's a thot patrol?" she asks, even though the look on her face says she's not sure she wants to know.

"It's where the Lords gather up the hottest bitches to pair off with the highest-scoring LDZs." Tristian's fingertips skate down her neck, dipping just beneath her collarbone. "Have to keep the soldiers incentivized, yeah?"

Her forehead wrinkles. "So they, like, go off to have sex with them?"

"Uh..." Rath looks to me for guidance, but ultimately agrees, "Sure, yeah. They go off." When she narrows her eyes, he buckles. "Well, sometimes."

Shrugging, I see no point in sugarcoating it. "Other times, they just take them right there in the basement where everyone can see."

Tristian explains, "When the parties get that wild, private fuck spots are a hot commodity."

She purses her lips. "Hmm." It's a much milder reaction than I'm expecting, which is why I'm caught off guard when she asks, "What's 'Candy Cocks'?"

I choke on my mouthful of beer, coughing, but Tristian sends her a smirk.

"That's a game for the Lady." His eyes dance as he watches her, beer halfway to his lips. "The Lords and five lucky LDZ brothers all drop trou, hide behind a screen, and then the Lady has to try to guess which cocks are her Lords'." It's a gentle description, since most games of Candy Cocks end in the Lady giving a generous amount of head.

Surprising me again, Story just buries a laugh into her palm. "Are you serious?"

"Absolutely," Tristian answers.

There's a beat of pensive silence, and then her jaw drops. "You were going to make me do that?!"

"*Make*?" Rath's eyebrows climb his forehead.

Quietly, I explain, "No one's ever had to make a Lady play Candy Cocks before."

This was always an issue, I suppose. Story didn't choose to become our Lady—not really. She was here for protection, maybe some revenge, but it was never something she wanted. I doubt she'll ever be able to understand that some girls do, and it's not always just because of the status and benefits. Candy Cocks, the house rules, the rivalries, the crazy, uninhibited sex...

It's supposed to be a good time for all.

Sure, there are Royal women who get dogged on. God only knows what kind of sick shit the Counts get up to behind closed doors, and the Dukes, well... they brand their goddamn house mark into their Duchesses. The Lords have rules—*strict* rules—for their Lady, and I'm not deluded enough to think it's an easy position to fill. Some have cracked, others have probably persevered past their own limits. But even though we might all be sadistic fucks to a certain degree, no one who isn't at least a little bit into it would audition. No one's that crazy.

The silence that falls over us is awkward, slicing right through the easy fun of the day.

Weirdly, Story's the first to shake it off.

She tips her head back, eyes closing. "Just so we're clear, I would have crushed it."

My eyes follow the rise and fall of her chest, the steam not thick enough to hide the flush of her cheeks. "Is that so?"

"Yep." She lazily cuts her arms through the water. "I could totally pick your dicks out of a lineup. Any day, any time."

Tristian shoots me and Rath an amused look. "You really think so?"

She lifts her head, nodding. "Oh, yeah. They're so distinctive."

I'm the one to ask, "Distinctive?" A dick's a dick, if you ask me, and I've been in a lot of locker rooms.

"Oh, definitely," she says, eyes so wide and guileless that butter couldn't melt. "For instance, Tristian is—" She pauses, and then suddenly leaps through the water at me. "Here, I'll show you."

I let her guide me between the others, and when she makes a lifting gesture, looking frustrated when we all just stare at her, I'm the first to get the hint. "Well, we already know mine's the biggest," I say, standing.

Tristian catches on, whipping his head around to laugh in my face. "In what fucking universe?"

The air is like icy razors against my skin when I prop myself on the edge of the tub, and from Tristian's hissed inhale as he follows suit, I'm guessing he feels the same. Rath's the last to get with the program, but when he does, he rolls his eyes.

"Aren't we a little old for a dick measuring contest?" He reaches beneath the water, shoulders shifting as he pulls off his boxers. "Pretty sure I won this Junior year of high school."

When we're all lined up on the edge of the tub, Story rubs her cheeks and just...looks. Her eyes ping from one dick to another, taking them in. Despite the cold, Tristian and Rath, like me, are already approaching full staff.

"Yes, see?" She bobs up between Tristian's knees, sliding her palms up his thighs. "Tristian's is always so nice and trimmed. He really takes care of it, you can tell." We all watch, transfixed as she reaches up to run a fingertip down its length. "You can tell he's proud of it. He always smells so good, even down there." She gives his cock a long, considering look. And then she nods, like she's come to some very grave decision. "I like it."

He reaches down to tuck a palm behind her neck, and I'd know that flash of darkness in his eyes anywhere. "Show me, sweetheart." He wraps his other fist around the base, nudging her close. "Show me how much you like my dick."

She barely has to be encouraged. One second, she's inspecting it wistfully, and the next, she's swallowing it down.

Tristian puffs out a cloud of warmth into the chilled air, letting his dick go only to press a palm to the back of her head. He pushes her down—forces her—

until I can see her shoulders contract with the struggle to breathe.

"Tris—" I start, but he just fists his fingers into her hair.

"Nah, she can take it." After a moment, he tugs her back, dick twitching between her lips at the wetness in her eyes. His voice is gravelly, but somehow still soft when he asks, "You like taking my cock like that, don't you? Tell them, so they know."

She nods, gazing up at him. "I like feeling you in the back of my throat." Her voice is rough, but she doesn't clear it. She ducks in to plant a long, sucking kiss to the head before backing away. Tristian tries to drag her back, but she's already swimming to Rath, eyes taking in his cock next. "Dimitri's feels the best inside, because it's got this wicked curve right here." She runs her lips over the shaft, voice hushed against the skin. "And he knows just how to use it. He's always so precise and teasing." She tilts her head, pressing her pensive face against his thigh. "It hits all the right places. I'd know this one anywhere."

Rath watches her with parted lips, his wet hair hanging in his eyes as he flexes his hips. Story takes the tip between her lips, and looks up, holding his gaze as she sinks down.

"Fuck," Rath sighs, shoulders going slack. He touches the part of her cheek that hollows with a suck, but it's weirdly tender—a brush of his knuckles against the flushed skin. "Your mouth's so fucking good, baby."

She hums and it looks indulgent, the way she slowly slides away, a thin string of spit following her retreat.

I fist myself, stroking my dick through the ache of want that's got it pulsating so hard and ready when she finally appears between my legs.

"And you," she whispers, raking her lip through her teeth as she watches my hand squeeze the shaft. "It's so thick that sometimes it hurts, and I think..." She glances up at me, quick and reluctant. "I think I kind of like that part of it. But the best part, by far?" My body stiffens as she leans in. The warmth of her breath against the tip is enough to make my toes curl, but then she drags the slick point of her tongue over it, eyes sliding closed. "You taste the best."

"Yeah?" My voice feels like it's dropped three octaves as I run the head of my cock over her tongue. "You like my cum, little sister?"

She answers by taking me into her mouth—just the tip—and humming. I catch a peek of her tongue as it swirls around, like she's trying to catch the taste. I lean back, groaning at the heat of her mouth, and rest on my palms to watch. Rath and Tristian are ramping up, too, their dicks in their hands.

Fuck.

How long have I wanted this, craving the sight of her head in my lap? How many nights, mornings, afternoons have I spent with my fist around my cock, imagining what it'd be like to have her sucking me like this? All those nights back home, sneaking into her bedroom and running my cock over her mouth, don't compare. That day down in the basement, making her suck me as punishment as the whole frat watched…

I wish I could just fucking erase it.

This is what her first real, coherent taste of me should have been. Her slick lips gliding down my shaft, hands so soft and insistent as they touch me. I'm fucking drowning in the heat and suction, and I know when my dick starts surging with precum, because she chases it greedily as she takes the flavor onto her tongue.

Tris slides over, cupping a palm against the back of her head. "Come on, sweetheart. Show your big brother how deep you can take it." He pushes her down, but I can feel that he doesn't need to, that she's driving it into the back of her throat under her own will, fingertips pressing divots into my thighs.

Suddenly, the air feels too thick, too hot. I'm gulping it down and shaking with the effort it takes not to just...grab her face and fuck the *absolute shit* out of it. How the hell do Tristian and Rath handle this? How do they keep from fucking it up and losing it?

Tristian looks at me, saying, "Do it," and I laugh. It's a ragged, broken sound, because these three people know me too well. "Fuck her throat, Killer," he insists, and behind his words, a moan emerges around the head of my cock.

She drags herself off my cock, sucking in a series of wet, deep breaths, before staring up at me. "I can take it."

Her jaw is loose beneath my thumbs when I cradle her skull, guiding her back onto my cock. The Molly must still be pumping through my veins a little bit, because when I buck forward, cock hitting the back of her throat, something thunder-like erupts in my chest. I wrap her hair around my fist and thrust, bringing her down as I drive forward. For a short moment, it's mindless, animalistic, brutal as I pummel her throat, because that's the reality. I can't control myself. I never could—not when it comes to her. But at the same time, I know.

I know my brothers will stop me if I go too far.

It's what allows me to really let go, to hold her head in my wide palms and growl as I fuck into her mouth. She's making these sloppy sounds, deep in her throat, almost identical to the water slapping against the walls of the tub.

Tristian is the one to ease me off, thumbing a tear track from her cheek when I free her. "That's my girl." His encouragement propels her to suck and lick my head, sending shivers down my spine. Tristian strokes his cock slowly, not in any rush as he looks up at Rath, "Come over here and touch her tits. Keep her warm."

Rath stands, water sloshing around the edges of the tub, but when he moves behind her, the first thing he does is start peeling that white shirt up her body. He tugs her away from me, shushing her when she makes a plaintive noise. "Just real quick, baby." True to his word, he gets the shirt over her head and lets her go at my cock again.

He mouths at her shoulder as he palms her tits, and Tristian and I watch him, groaning at the way his hands look over them, squeezing. It's one of those things I wasn't expecting, the way the two of them look with her. It's just like that day she held onto me as Tristian fucked her.

She moans, releasing me to gasp, "Oh, that feels good. Hot and cold. Cold and hot." Spinning, she faces Rath and kisses him, winding her arms around his neck. I have to admit it. They look good together. Right. Like they fit in some incomprehensible way. My eyes drop to her ass when his hands do, her silk panties clinging to her like a second skin. Her kisses trail down his neck to his chest, down his belly and back to his erection, bobbing just above water. "Dimitri's all about the process, dragging it out as long as possible." She laves her tongue over the tip. "But he doesn't waste a single second. It's all so good. *So good.*" There's this expression on her face as she says it, almost pleadingly, as if she's begging someone to understand why she can't stop herself from taking Rath into her mouth.

Dimitri must hear it, because he makes a low, gritty sound and gathers her hair back, saying, "You can have this dick anytime you want, baby."

The urge I've been suppressing all night washes over me, and I just can't stop myself from dropping back into the water. My hands fit perfectly around her hips. I've always liked that about her, the way she looks so small up against me, like I could toss her around or swallow her up in my arms. I press my cock against her ass, nestling it between those sweet cheeks of hers, and I wish I could go back in time to the crazed motherfucker I used to be, just so I can tell him we get it.

She lifts away from Rath, turning to examine me through heavy, wet lashes. "Jealous, big brother?"

I don't get out an answer before her hand thrusts out, gripping my cock. The smooth touch of her fingertips sends sparks flickering under my skin, and I know it's the lingering effects of the drug, but it feels electric, like every nerve ending is connected to the searing point of her touch.

"I sure as fuck am," Tristian admits, sliding off the edge.

Her gentle laugh as she turns to face him makes my lungs constrict. "Tristian Mercer demands attention. I'm shocked."

He doesn't bother disagreeing, the spoiled little fucker. He just sighs when she touches him, her hand dipping lower to fondle his balls. Her lips look red and swollen as they sink down onto him. If I'm looking for any cues that this isn't actually something she wants to do, then I'm failing to find them. She moans when Rath reaches out to touch her, arching into the press of his palm on her neck.

Rath pushes her down, insistent but easy, like he's curious to see just how deep she can drive herself onto Tristian's cock.

The answer to that is, apparently, really fucking deep.

Rath's voice is low, full of awe. "Goddamn, girl." He strokes his own dick as he watches her nearly bottom out, lips stretched wide around the root of Tristian's cock. "Am I gonna get some of that next?"

She pulls off Tristian, and without missing a beat, spins to take Rath into her mouth. She doesn't perform as much for him, and it takes me a second to realize why. She knows what Rath likes. How many evenings has she spent up in his room doing this, learning what makes his shoulders hitch like that, finding out what elicits that rumble from his chest?

I try to be patient. I swear to fucking god; I do. But she's basically making love to Rath's dick with her mouth, and I need it. For myself. Luckily for me, all it takes is a touch on her shoulder and she's whirling around, sinking her lips onto me. She lets me thrust into her mouth, but I don't fuck myself into the back of her throat like last time. I don't need it. I just need the way she looks up at me with those dazed eyes, so eager and trusting. It'd be enough to make anyone bust.

And then Tristian scoots close, caressing her cheek.

She takes us like that for a long while, deep throating Tristian until Rath gets impatient. Lavishing Rath's dick with affection until I can't take it anymore. Savoring my cock until Tristian nudges her. It's quiet and over-warm, the three of us standing in some fucked-up, erotic triangle, thigh-deep in the bubbling hot tub, as we breathe too loud, eager for our own turn.

Rath licks over his lip ring as he watches her bob up and down on his dick. "Apparently, ex makes our girl a multi-tasker."

And good at it, too, because it's only moments later that she's stroking me closer to a different kind of ecstasy. This one is so much more pure, natural enough that I feel it settle into my bones. It's not just the drugs, it's her. *It's all of us:* the breath, the heartbeat, the aching balls. It's Tristian's gentle words of praise. It's Rath's quiet, dirty promises. It's my soft grunts as I fuck myself against her slick tongue. It's her little, barely suppressed whines as she enjoys us.

I'm not a musician like Rath, but I know a symphony when I hear it.

This is new territory for the three of us. Sure, we've been blown by the same girl before, but never like this. Never with her being passed from one to the other. Never with me watching that dark, possessive glint flash in Rath's eyes, or the flicker of something tender and satisfied in Tristian's as he makes her choke on it. If I'm being honest, I wouldn't think one girl would be enough for a trio of sick, horny bastards like us, but here she is. Fucking killing it.

She's wrong about one thing. I'm not jealous. Maybe there was a time watching her so hungry for them might have rattled around in my chest, but it's long ago settled into its place there, wound tight around whatever sad, corrupted organ could be called a heart.

Story nudges us all closer, until we're shoulder to shoulder, hip to hip, and our cocks are all in her face. She licks and sucks, running her tongue over each. I glide my hand up and down my shaft, keeping up the pace whenever her focus is on the others.

Finally, her mouth closes around me and I cradle her face in my hands, tipping her gaze to mine. "You ready for my cum, little sister?"

I don't know if it's my words, her anticipation, or the way I'm rubbing the pads of my thumbs against her cheeks, but she slows, staring up at me with eyes that are so open and full of longing that it makes my stomach clench. It's what triggers the tightness building at the base of my spine.

She takes it just like that, opening wide, my cock jerking against her bottom lip. I make this shuddering gasp of a grunt that I might think to feel embarrassed about later. Right now, I come too hard to care, shooting right onto the pink of her swollen tongue.

She doesn't swallow it.

The second I'm done wringing my orgasm from the tip of my dick, she's turning to pull Tristian's cock into her mouth. "Holy fuck," he breathes, hips rearing back, only to plow back between her lips. "God, I love how fucking sloppy you get." My cum is leaking from the corners of her mouth, and I know he's close when he starts muttering broken, obscene things. "Such a perfect little slut for us. You'll take it all, won't you?"

Rath reaches down to touch her chin, running his fingertip through the trail of come, and then he prods it back into the corner of her mouth, slotting his finger right up against Tristian's dick. Her lips stretch to accommodate it, and she hums like she's grateful for the help.

If I hadn't already come, I'd do it again just watching them keep my cum inside her. Lurching forward, hips frozen mid-beat, Tristian releases with a long, agonized-sounding groan. Tears burn at the corner of Story's eyes, but she takes it. She takes all of him—everything he has to give—dick shooting into the back of her throat.

"Don't swallow," he directs her, panting. "Not until Rath finishes."

She nods, jaw tense, and that's when I swoop in, grabbing her from behind. I settle her between my legs, back against my stomach, to cradle her as Rath takes position. Slowly, he strokes up and down his cock, eyes tracking the path my hands make to her tits. I massage them in my palms, pluck at her nipples, and she tilts her head back, waiting.

Rath dips forward to run his cock over her lips. "Can you take it?" he asks.

She nods, unable to speak.

Like always, Rath takes his sweet time, jerking his cock slow and steady against the crease of her lips. Every now and then, Tristian or I will push our cum back into her mouth, or Rath will nudge it back inside with the swollen tip of his cock, and fuck.

My cock gives a feeble twitch at the sight of it.

When he finally starts tensing up, shoulder bobbing in short, quick jolts, he shoots out a hand to steady himself, landing on my thigh. He raggedly whispers, "It's coming, baby. Open up for me," and she does, back arching to catch the first thick rope that erupts from his dick. It dribbles over her lips, but Tristian and I are there to catch it, feeding it back to her.

Tristian waits until Rath backs off to rest his fingertips against her throat. "You can swallow now, sweetheart. Take your time. Get every last drop."

She chokes it down, and when I put my sticky fingers to her lips, she sucks them clean, not wasting a single fucking drop. Part of me wonders if we—if *I*—trained her to like cum this much. But I know there are some things you just can't force on people. She enjoys it too much to be anything other than genuine.

"Do you still like the way I taste the best?" I ask in her ear, dipping my fingers between her legs.

"Yes." She pants and squirms against me, confessing, "But I also like it when you're all together. It's all mixed up, but I can still taste each of you. And it's… it's mine. Right?" Her eyes fall closed when I find her clit, and she opens for me so easily, spreading her thighs wide. "No other girl has ever…?"

"No one," Rath promises, still breathless when he ducks down to lick into her slick, abused mouth.

"Good." She licks out to catch his tongue, bucking against my fingers. "Then it's special. All mine."

My gut twitches and I hoist her out of the water, keeping her warm against my chest. I use my hands to keep her thighs spread wide, and I don't need to tell my boys what to do. They're already stalking forward, eyes fixed to her pussy.

"Now?" she asks, as Tristian and Rath approach. Rath shimmies off her panties, losing them in the water. She doesn't fight, but I hold her anyway, back against my chest. That push-pull turns her on, just as much as Tristian's tongue swiping over her clit, and Rath's finger teasing her pussy. She tenses against my chest, breath caught, already horny from sucking us off.

"Ho, ho, ho," I say, while running my thumbs over her nipples. The boys are in the giving mood. Holiday spirit and all that shit. We finish off the night like this, warm in the tub, bringing our Lady to the tip of the sharpest edge, then toppling her over, allowing her the freedom of riding out the pure ecstasy of the four of us together, safe in this bubble. When the orgasm finally hits, I lick her lips and whisper, "Merry Christmas, Little Sister, from all of us."

18

SCREW YEAR'S EVE

"WAIT," I SAY, frowning out the window. We're no longer near campus, but in a different part of town altogether. It's not quite South Side, but it's still somehow… well, similar. "Do the Dukes live down here?"

"They may as well," Tristian mutters from the front passenger seat. "Filthy street-urchins."

"You know that old clock tower at the back of campus?" Dimitri asks, lolling his head against the seat to look at me. We're in the backseat, his legs sprawled wide enough to press against mine. Thinking, I recall the tower that looms over the older section of Forsyth. The buildings back there are ancient—maybe even historical—and gorgeous-looking, if a bit rundown. I figured most of it was abandoned or, at the very least, on the cusp of a very extensive renovation. In his smooth, deep voice, Dimitri explains, "The Dukes live there, and this is their territory. They say from the belfry, you can see all the way to Widow's Rock."

"Figures the Dukes, of all houses, would get the best view." Tristian turns to give me a sardonic look. "Completely lost on them."

I think they all know how nervous I feel about what I'm about to do, but they're doing me the favor of not coddling me about it. Christmas day was a nice distraction. Fun, to say the least, even though I spent most of the next day feeling unnecessarily embarrassed about what happened in the hot tub.

Even now, I catch sight of Killian's eyes in the rearview mirror and feel my cheeks heat.

It'd be easy to blame it on the drugs, and I suppose a part of my behavior that night could be owed to how high I was. But it was only the part where I actually acted on something I wanted, without fear or shame or pressure. At first, I was worried there'd be no going back, as if I'd enter my bedroom the next night and find them all on the bed, waiting for me, ready to pick up where we left off.

The week between Christmas and New Year's was busy. Killian took me to the range to try out my new weapon, spending an inordinate amount of time making sure I knew how to use it. It was impossible to know if he just used the opportunity to give himself an excuse to get close to me physically; hands on my hips, cheek close to mine. Tristian dragged me to the gym to prep for the wrestling match, including private lessons with a trainer. After wearing me out, we'd go back home, and he'd massage my aching muscles, forcing me to relax. Dimitri's bed was a warm comfort at night. We'd listen to music, smoke a joint, and sleep late. The barriers I'd built are rapidly eroding. I'm defenseless to their touch, their kisses and demands. I was tired of fighting, so I didn't. But now I have to face what comes next. In truth, there's something disturbingly familiar about jumping into a ring to make money. At least this time, I'll get to keep it.

Assuming I win.

Killian goes on, "The Dukes occupy the West End. The Counts, the North Side. Princes, the East End. All of the territories push against one another. The Kings, and therefore us, are always in some kind of bullshit squabble." Killian turns the truck down a dark road. The buildings on both sides are industrial with high metal walls. "The Dukes do their business down here in the warehouse district. And this," he slows the truck, pointing out the front window, "is their gym."

It doesn't look like much, but I do see the sign over the door; DUKES UP. In a lame attempt at forgotten festivity, Christmas lights are draped over the doorway, and a sad-looking, weather-beaten wreath hangs on the door. People walk down the street, guys and girls slipping in through the door, and again, I remember why I'm here, igniting another wave of nerves in my stomach. Dimitri takes my hand and pulls it to his mouth, lip rings cool against my skin when he kisses my knuckles.

"You don't really have to do this," he assures, dark eyes holding mine. "We can find another way. People like us always do."

Nodding, I reply, "I know."

People like us. The people who are used to having nothing. We get by because there's no other option. Others might throw their hands up in the air, but people like us don't have that luxury. We find a way.

What I don't tell him is that it's not the fight that's got me all twisted up inside. It's the possibility of letting them down. Of embarrassing them. Of showing all these people that the Lords chose a Lady who can't handle her own. I don't care about whatever pissing contest these frats get into, but even if my Lords seem to have abandoned this stupid game to become Kings, it means something to them to be the best, the strongest, the ones at the top, and it's not just about their egos. In their world, a loss is a target on your back, just begging for someone to come by and hit the bull's eye. Like it or not, I'm a part of that now. That means I'm either a credit or a liability. A strength or a weakness.

But in the end, I'm not here to gain our frat fighting cred. I'm here to beat the Countess' ass and earn a fistful of money doing it, and that's what matters. "I'm good." Pushing my shoulders back, I open the door, steel filling my voice. "Let's do this."

Tristian is already there, extending a hand to help me down from the seat. I take it and lean on him, jumping to the pavement, and when he takes my bag, slinging it over his shoulder, he sends me a little wink.

"We've got you."

They flank me the same way they do on campus, but this time, I feel less like an ornament and more like a prize they're protecting. I've already proven myself. I killed Ugly Nick. I saved Killian from certain death. I negotiated directly with Daniel. I've spent the last three years running from a psychotic stalker, and I'm still standing.

No, I'm no longer an ornament. I'm one of them, and tonight, everyone else is going to know it, too.

THE INTERIOR OF the gym is decked out in more lights. It's flashy and brash, smoke thick in my nostrils and burning my eyes, and loud music blares through the cavernous room, echoing off the eaves. It's hard to look at the ring in the middle of it and not see the pit, but I try. A banner above it greets us, boasting, "Tenth Annual Screw Year's Eve!" Beside the dramatic lettering, an illustration of a sneering woman is riding a bear, brandishing a trophy high above her head as her breasts bulge from her bikini top.

Pure class.

We start through the crowd, and it's not so bad at first. Everyone's so occupied with drinking their beers and watching the ring that they don't even notice us walking in.

Until they do.

One by one, heads turn to look, guys nudging whoever they're with to get their attention, girls pointing and whispering. Tristian casually drapes his arm over my shoulder, tugging me close enough to plant a smacking kiss on my head.

"These people aren't shit, sweetheart."

Unlike the pit, I don't avoid their stares, my gaze passing over them. "I know."

But my mask of indifference gets hard to keep up. Killian leads us through, clearing a path through the boisterous crowd. People fall away, out of fear of his size or intimidation. Either. Both. But it doesn't block out the gossip being whispered as we pass. There are comments about Killer shooting his dad. About their Lady being an actual whore. About the real fight that's sure to come between the King and a Lord.

We're getting close to the center when some asshole calls out, "Yo, the Lady's about to give us another show!"

"Don't react," Tristian whispers.

But the guy doesn't stop there. "You gonna take them all this time? Three dicks, one cunt!"

I'm not sure anyone besides the three of them notice me freezing. It barely lasts a second before Tristian nudges me back into motion, but it takes my breath away, the comment stabbing right into the vulnerable part of me that's still shy about what happened on Christmas.

When I hear the skirmish behind me, feet quick on the hard floor, I realize they know it. I don't need the glance over my shoulder to know that Dimitri is back there, taking out some of his own vengeance, but I still do it, a quick flick of my eyes. It's fast enough to catch the punch he lands on the guy's face, the fleshy sound of bone hitting bone making me wince.

At least he's not brandishing his knife.

Killian breaks through to the front, stopping by the edge of the ring, and then he turns to me, expression so impassive that one might think this is just another day.

"You need to sign in," Killian says, pointing to the table set up by the ring.

I glance over his shoulder and see that the normally flat stage has been modified with a large inflatable pool. Inside is what must be hundreds of pounds of red and green Jell-O. My nose wrinkles at the thought of stepping into it. The cloud of cherry-lime smell is practically visible.

"We're all in luck." The DKS guy from before—Simon, Pretty Nick's brother—is sitting behind the table, a metal box opened in front of him. His eyes are fixed to the stack of money his fingers are deftly carding through, counting, but he's speaking to my stepbrother. "This match just got a whole lot easier. The bracket's always a bit fucked when there's five."

Tristian watches him, jerking his chin. "What, someone drop out?" My stomach sinks at the possibility Sutton won't be here.

But it's unnecessary. "Yes." Simon finally looks up from the money, giving the stack a tap on the table. "As of three hours ago, the Princess took her tiara out of the ring."

Tristian lets out a loud, harsh laugh. "No shit?" It takes me a moment to catch on. It's when his blue eyes meet mine, mouth smirking, that it hits me. "Looks like I'm winning all kinds of bets tonight, sweetheart."

Still, I ask, "She's pregnant? *Already?"*

Simon shrugs, jotting something down on the paper before shoving it into the box. "Can't risk the health of the demon spawn. That means you're fighting the Baroness first. Whoever wins that match will square up against whoever wins the match between the Duchess and the Countess." He points to the left side of the ring, where a giant chalkboard has been set up with our four positions.

I give Killian a frustrated look, not expecting this. "I came here to beat the Countess," I tell Simon, letting Tristian's arm fall from my shoulders. "So you're saying if one of us loses, I can't?"

Simon leans back in his chair. "You're talking to a future Duke, Lady." His eyes rake down my body in a way that makes Killian step closer. "We don't need some sleazy, Royalty-organized charity event to gift someone with a gold-star ass-whooping. But, hey. If you do?" He raises an eyebrow, face stony. "Then my advice is to not lose." Before I can argue, he slides a notebook across the table, slapping a pen in the middle. "The rules are so basic, even a girl can handle them. First to tap out loses. No weapons, no hits below the belt, eyes are off limits. Other than that, you can consider this no holds barred. So if you're going to get all precious about a few bruises and a little blood, then there's the door. Don't waste our time."

Killian bites out a sharp, "Watch it, Sy."

Simon doesn't miss a beat, pointing to the sheet next to the book. "The rounds last one minute each, three rounds total. The leader is determined by crowd approval, so if you want to win, you better put on a show." The guy looks up at me with a cold expression. "But that should be no problem for you, right?"

"I said," Killian slams his hand down on the table, "*watch* it."

"She's a big girl, isn't she?" Simon holds my stare, and a few months ago I might have withered at the hardness within it. Not now, though. "For some reason, my idiot brother has put down a lot of capital on you winning this."

"Then he can send me a fruit basket when I do," I reply, shooting him a saccharine grin. These people might be vipers, but I've got fangs of my own.

Simon looks away, head shaking. "We don't mind a little dirty play, Lady, but don't forget what this is: A charity match. Try to keep your tits inside your bikini. We host fights, not pornos."

My eye twitches, but when Killian shoves in front of me, I grab his arm, dragging him back. "That's rich, coming from a member of the house who chose the sleazy costumes for their sleazy event."

He gives me a mean smile back. "Wasn't my decision." As one last parting blow, he adds, "Oh, and don't forget. You have to stay on your knees. Or your back." He glances around, catching sight of the other Royal women. "Probably just another Tuesday for one of you."

I feel the rage in Killian, seconds from boiling over, but I tug him away from the table, Tristian glowering at Simon over his shoulder.

"Ignore that shit for brains," he says, bringing a hand down on Killian's shoulder. "You know how he gets about women."

The tendon in Killian's neck is already bulging, and I'd know that simmering darkness in his eyes anywhere. If I'm not careful, he's going to lose it. "I don't care if he's got issues with pulling tail. I'm not going to let him talk to her like that."

I watch Dimitri make his way over, flexing his fist as he inspects his red knuckles. "You're not getting into another fight tonight. They might throw us out." I glance back at Sy, who looks just as scathing as he signs the Baroness in. "He's probably just trying to rile us all up so we put on a good show."

Killian's nostrils flare. "He's going to lose his teeth." Everyone thinks Killian is so difficult to handle, like he's always one second away from detonating. In a way, they're right.

But they don't know him like I do.

I touch his chest and strain up on my toes, pressing a soft kiss to the tense line of his jaw. "Well, wait until after I've got the money, okay?"

He looks down at me, and it's like magic. First, there's a slow exhale, his hand coming out to hold my hip. Then he shifts his shoulders and the tendon in his neck disappears. I know when his eyes fix to my mouth, face losing a tightness that I hate to see there, that I've pulled him back from the brink.

"If anyone fucks with you, you tell us. I mean it, Story."

I run my hand down his side. "I will, big brother. Don't worry."

The mild, lopsided smirk he gives me when I call him 'big brother' sparks a fire in my lower belly. If he keeps smiling at me like that, I'm going to end up keeping my door unlocked at night.

"Come on," he says, nodding upstairs. "Let's get up on the balcony to watch for a minute, then you can go change."

I have a beer with the guys while we're up there, my eyes taking in the scene below. The Countess ducks into the ring, followed by the Duchess— Bianca. They each give the crowd big smiles, but it's clear Bianca is having more fun with it, flexing her muscles elaborately, hamming it up for her Dukes, who are watching against the ropes, cheering her on. The Counts are on the other side, standing silently as they watch their Countess wave to the room.

Tristian stands behind me, arm around my chest as he narrates. "See how the Countess left her hair down? That's exploitable."

Dimitri leans on the railing at my side, tipping a red cup to his lips. "Rookie move. Girls are always all over the place when they fight—totally fucking undisciplined—so here's what you do. Grab a handful of hair and—"

"Guys," I bark, giving them each a glare. "I went to an all girls' school for a year. I know how to win a fight against the campus bitch."

Dimitri holds his hands up. "Excuse me, Lady Thrown Down. Was just saying, the Countess is going to fight dirty, so be prepared."

This is made evident halfway through. The first round is all exaggerated grimaces in the Jell-O and lighthearted grappling. Bianca howls with laughter for most of it, big and toothy as Sutton grabs for her, feigning growls for the crowd.

But somewhere in the second round, things change. I'm not sure if it's a solid hold Bianca gets Sutton into, or if the Countess has just been biding her time, but suddenly, her elbow comes up, catching Bianca hard in the nose. Bianca's hands fly up to her face and Sutton tackles her, getting Bianca flat onto her stomach and smashing her face into the Jell-O. Bianca fights back hard, the vibe of the crowd shifting from fun chants to mean barbed shouts. It turns toxic on a dime, and the Dukes are red-faced as they yell across the ring at the Counts, who are smirking as they watch.

It's unnecessarily brutal. The Duchess never recovers from the initial blow, blood streaming down her chin as she sneers and bucks and takes swipe after swipe. She gets in a few hits, but the Countess shakes each one off, striking out like the viper her house medallion bears.

"Fuck," Dimitri mutters. "The Dukes are about to go after them." He nods to the Counts, where Perez is crouched down, coaching Sutton in a series of shouted orders.

"Take that bitch down!" he's barking, face contorted as if he's the one in the ring.

But Bianca is already reaching out to slam her palm against the Jell-O, tapping out.

Tristian hisses as the Dukes all fly into the ring, pulling their Duchess out of the pool. "They're not going to take that well."

Stepping away, I grab my bag from the floor. I'm not interested in the frat fallout. I've seen what I need to. "Maybe when I win," I say, grabbing Dimitri's hand, "the Dukes can send me a fruit basket, too."

The guys decided before we arrived that one of them would always be with me. I choose Dimitri to escort me to the empty locker room, because that's what I need. His quiet darkness. The demon eyes. That thrumming, vicious energy that he never has to externalize.

I unpack my bikini, feeling him so close that it prickles on the back of my neck. "You don't need to guard me," I say, efficiently stripping off my clothes. "It's not like everyone out there isn't going to see me like this."

"Don't remind me," he replies, eyes sweeping over me as I pull the tiny bottoms over my hips. "I'm just here to make sure these bitches don't pull a Tonya Harding on you."

I raise an eyebrow. "Tonya Harding?"

"You know..." His tongue peeks out to prod his bottom lip, eyes glued to my bare chest. "Took out her opponent before the Olympics or whatever? Nancy Kerrigan." He makes a bat-swinging motion. "Got her thug of a husband to hit her leg with a pipe."

I stuff my tits in the triangles, and work on getting the strings tied tight. I know there's going to be a nip-slip out there, but I'm determined to try my best to keep it minimal, not the least to stick it to Simon for suggesting I wouldn't. "And you think someone wants to sabotage me. Before the charity wrestling match."

"You saw how it was out there. There's a lot of money on the line, but it's also about The Game points. The Royal woman's frat gets a lot of points if she wins." He walks behind me and brushes his fingers over the back of my neck. Goosebumps rise across my skin, and he takes the string away from me. "These assholes have no boundaries. I'm just here to make sure they don't cross them."

Using his nimble fingers, Dimitri loops the tie behind my neck. My breasts lift as he tightens the string, and I feel his warm breath. Humming, he says, "That should hold," before dragging his fingers down my shoulders. He bends to put my clothes into the bag, but pauses, pulling out a bottle of baby oil.

"They said I should grease up," I explain, gathering my hair up into a high bun. "To, you know, make it more slippery."

He gives me a devious look from beneath his lashes, straightening. "I can help with that," he says, popping the cap and pouring a liberal amount into his palm. He sets the bottle on the bench and rubs his hands together. Standing behind me, he starts at my shoulders, palms gentle as they spread the slippery oil onto my skin. His fingers dip over my shoulders and onto my chest, gliding over the tops of my breasts, until he unapologetically slides them under my top. His hips press into my backside, but even though his hardness is obscenely obvious, he doesn't act on his desire. He just continues to oil up my body, hands gliding down my belly, rubbing below my navel. He crouches, hands curling around my thighs. The touch is firm but unhurried, an almost reverent glide between my legs, covering every inch of exposed skin.

I fight down a shiver as I remember him being in the same place on Christmas night, his head between my thighs as he brought me to an orgasm that had me quivering in Killian's arms.

When he finishes, he stands, spinning me around. Dimitri holds my gaze with his dark eyes, fingertips skating across my lower back as he watches me, and my stomach swoops at the heaviness in his eyes.

I swallow, letting him pull me close, chest to chest. "What?"

He answers by tucking his fingers beneath my bikini bottoms, dragging them along the crease between my ass cheeks. Voice low and close, he asks, "You know what this stuff is really good for?"

When I do nothing but blink back at him, he curls closer, hand dipping low, and even knowing where this is going, I can't find it in myself to protest.

I don't even flinch when the tip of his finger finds my puckered hole. My heart bangs a wild rhythm in my chest, but I hold his eyes, not backing down. Channeling the girl I was in that hot tub only a few nights ago, I reply, "I don't know. Are you going to show me?"

His jaw twitches, and when his finger pushes past the resistance, it's slick and easy, making my jaw go slack at the deliciousness of the burn. I curl my hands into his leather jacket, barely recognizing the sound that emerges from my throat.

He pecks a slow, teasing kiss at my lips. "You like it, baby?" I nod frantically, forgetting about the wrestling match, tuition, Sutton—anything but the drag of his finger sinking into me. He licks into my mouth, and his tongue is so warm, as slick as the finger he's fucking into my ass. "Soon," he breathes, knuckle curling inside of me, "I'm going to bury myself in this tight little hole and listen to you beg for more." He kisses down to my jaw, my throat nosing into the space below my ear. "We've been arguing about it for days. Who should be the one to take it?" His voice is a low, hot whisper. "I won."

"You guys talk about me like this?" I wonder, feeling breathless. "Fight over me?"

"We talk about you all the time. You're our Lady." He continues kissing down my neck. "Usually it's cordial, but sometimes, like with the big stuff, your virginity, or... this," he curves his finger slightly, applying more pressure inside, "we have to fall back on the system—the points—to declare the winner."

"Please." I barely know what I'm asking for, but I know I want it. Whatever it is. Fingers. The cock I feel hard and eager against my belly. I'll take anything. I'll take any of them. All of them.

The thought alone has me gasping, knees shaking.

Suddenly, he pulls away, eyes flashing at the sound of my agonized whimper. "Sorry, baby. Now it's your turn to win. If you want it, that is."

"You," I pant, squeezing my slicked-up thighs together, "are *such* a jerk."

Smirking, he extends a hand toward the door. "After you, my Lady."

TRISTIAN IS THE first to grab the back of my head, hauling me up against the ropes to take my mouth in a short, but no less scorching, kiss. He pulls away to say, "Good luck," and Dimitri is next, planting a hard kiss onto my lips.

"Eye on the prize, baby girl." He gives me a dark, devilish grin before reaching down to give my ass a light slap.

Instead of a kiss, Killian takes my hand, looking around with a weirdly hunted expression as he tucks something into my palm. "*Don't* lose it." Confused, I uncurl my hand to find a tattered, faded ribbon. I immediately recognize it as one of the crazy, superstitious game day trinkets I'd stolen, and then later, given back to him. "Trust me," he plucks it from my palm, "this is better than a kiss." I hold still as he ties it around my bare wrist—the one without the cuff. "I've never lost a game with this. Not once."

"What is it?" I ask, turning it on my wrist. Obviously, it's a ribbon, but it must have some significance.

He looks up at me, brows knitted together. "You don't remember?"

I frown, but before I can pay much mind to it, a Delta Kappa Sigma guy announces my match.

I'm not sure if it's the escalation of the atmosphere or the fact everyone's had time to ply themselves with the beer they're paying seven dollars a cup for, but the crowd seems louder than it had the previous match. I stare at the Baroness, who's kneeling in the Jell-O across from me, and offer her only this: "No hard feelings." It's a lie. The only feelings I have for the lot of them— Bianca excluded—are of the hard variety. I call up the memory of that day in the courtyard, when the three of them looked me in the eye, laughed with me, and treated me like the friends I was so excited to finally have. I remember the way it felt, so happy to have people who understood. Who I thought understood.

I remember what it felt like to be betrayed.

The match against Marigold is admittedly a bit of a blur. All that runs through my head is the knowledge that she's standing between me and beating Sutton's ass. The way I go after her is borderline mechanical. It's a vicious instinct, just like the sharpness that was present in the locker room with Dimitri. I don't need to showboat it, it just happens, her skin beneath my hands as I wrestle her into the stick gelatin.

She gnashes out a word now and then. "Fuck," and, "Bitch," and, "Let go, whore!" but I hardly hear them. I'm so focused on taking her down.

In the end, I don't even know what makes her tap out. Maybe it's my forearm against her windpipe, or the way my knee is jamming into her pelvis. Possibly, she's just not built for this. The fight, the struggle, the pain of the blows. Not everyone is.

Either way, her palm comes down, smacking hard against the floor. The next thing I know, Killian is dragging me away. Hell, it barely registers that it's over, my arms and legs flailing as I'm rudely lifted out of the pool.

"Save it," he says, grunting with the struggle to hold me when I try to lunge for her again. "Come on, little sister. You won, you got her."

He drags me to the others, holding me up when I slip in the gelatin. Tristian shoves a water bottle in my hand and starts wiping off my face. Dimitri just laughs, bragging, "You wiped the fucking floor with her! Look," he points over my shoulder, "she's crying."

The first match was just a warm-up, and I don't let myself decompress one damn bit. I slick back my hair, retying it as Sutton takes Marigold's place. Eyeing her across the pool, I'm fueled by the obnoxious smirk on her face. I've felt adrenaline before; back in the illicitness of my sugar baby days, driving the get-away car, setting that fire with Tristian. But this is different. Raw, full-on vengeance.

"That's the bitch I want to make cry," I tell the guys.

Dimitri takes the water bottle out of my hand and replaces it with a shot of something amber. "Here, baby. Drink that and go ruin her fucking face."

I expect Tristian to argue before the liquor hits my lips—likely some bullshit about dehydration—but he doesn't say a word. Killian stands in front of me and adjusts the triangles of my bikini, saying low, "Sutton twisted her left knee freshman year at the intramural softball match. She should have had surgery, but she brushed it off."

"She's also probably high as a fucking kite," Dimitri says, taking the empty shot glass from me. "The only girls who go for Perez are the ones with bad habits, feel me?"

Tristian adds, "From what I saw earlier, probably coke."

I give them a long look. "How the hell do you know all of this?"

"Honestly?" Eyes narrowing, Killian brushes his fingers over a bruise I can already feel developing on my jaw. "Dad."

"Yeah." Dimitri kneads his fingers into my shoulders, like he's trying to get me to loosen up. I don't. "The first thing Daniel taught us was how to assess an enemy for vulnerabilities."

"Any weakness," Tristian points out. "The Royal women have always been a weak spot. For all of us. That's why they kidnapped you in the first place."

Rath's voice drops, hands skating down my arms. "And why Daniel put you in the pit."

But Killian's the one who drops the biggest bomb. "It's the reason Royal women exist, Story. Everyone thinks the Kings gave us Ladies and Duchesses and Princesses as a privilege. They think you're just toys to be played with because we're entitled enough to find it fun. But if you want to know the truth?" He levels me with a long, intense stare. "Put three horny fuckers in a house with a nice piece of tail, and they grow...attachments." His mouth tightens, but he doesn't look away. "You're here to be our weak spot, little sister. And it worked."

I glance between the three of them, trying to process that confession in the middle of all this chaos. It was never about us—the women, the house girls, the *tail.* Of course, it was always about the heirs to Forsyth. It was about giving them something to lose. A soft, vulnerable underbelly. The more I think about it, the more it fits.

I straighten my bikini strap and roll my shoulders, and there might be alcohol pumping in my veins, but there's also something else. It's too complicated to be called anger, but it burns just as hot. "You're not seeing the whole picture, big brother. Love doesn't just give you something to lose. It makes you stronger because it gives you something to fight for. Something worth more than some stupid game. Can you think of anything scarier?" The bell rings, cutting through the noise of the gym, and I glance back at the ring, grinning. "Hold that thought. I have to go ruin this bitch's whole goddamn year."

I leave them behind me, blank-faced and in varying degrees of stupor. It isn't until I lift my foot to climb into the pool that I hear Tristian's voice.

"Fuck me. She's right, isn't she?"

I don't hear anything else, not over the yells of the crowd, but even if I could, I can't concentrate on anything but Sutton stepping into the cool gelatin across from me. The energy of the crowd amplifies just with us getting in position. Everyone's here, and it's not just the Royalty. Right behind my Lords, stands the whole of LDZ's frat, cheering me on with loud whoops, beers held high. Truthfully, I used to hate them all. For seeing me that night in the basement. For acting like it was fun. For not doing a thing to stop it. For being a part of this whole twisted system and vying for their own places within it.

Now, I shamefully find their cheers putting steel into my spine, because these forty guys would kneel at my feet if I told them to.

One day, I just fucking might.

But the Counts' Kappa Omegas are here, too, and pushing up to the front, the Dukes' Deltas look angry and severe. I know there's money on this fight— big money—and everyone wants a share. Fuck them. That cash and the title is mine.

A man's voice blasts through the speakers, echoing off the metal ceiling.

"It's time for the final event! Who will win the Throw Down Crown and become our New Year Queen? The Conniving Countess or the Shady Lady? The Lady can take care of herself, but we all know the Countess bites!

The noise of the crowd swells as Sutton and I wade toward one another, gliding through the smooth gelatin.

"Sweet little innocent Story," Sutton coos when we're a few feet apart, "Guess your Lords decided to let you out of the whorehouse to come out and play?"

Just like Dimitri said, her eyes are dilated, wide and bloodshot at the edges. I look down, noting that she favors her right leg. "At least I don't have to be drugged up just to get through the day. Can't say I blame you, living with those three pieces of crap."

"Me?" She bends, bracing herself on two knees, and I do the same. Her eyes flick down to my tits. "My Counts haven't carved me up like a fat turkey. I wonder if they're going to give you some new letters tonight? I can think of five." Her lips curve into a snarling grin. "L-O-S-E-R." Laughing, she points to my cleavage. "I guess they can tack it on to the 'R' you've already got. You could be a crossword by the time you graduate."

That taunt hits home, because she doesn't know what I did to earn these letters, no more than she knows that the guys have scars of their own inflicted by me. The second the bell dings, I lunge forward, using all of my force to slam into her. We crash to the ground, grunting, and her fingernails dig painfully into my shoulders. Baring my teeth, I grapple her, rolling around, fighting for dominance. It takes a laughably short amount of time to get on top of her, but it means freeing her arm. When I do, she strikes out and clamps her fingers on my nipple, pinching hard.

They'd warned me she'd fight dirty.

"Owwww! Motherfucker!" I shout, but when I fail to bat her hand away, I decide fuck it, and slap down hard across her boob. She yelps, letting me go instinctively, defensively covering her chest. The crowd absolutely loses it.

Yeah, nothing better than two women tit slapping each other to victory. "You fucking cunt."

She reaches her claw fingers out again, but I'm ready for it, this time. I snatch her wrist into a tight, bruising grip, and when she struggles to get free, I grab the other one, tightening my fingers like a vise. I pin them beside her head, and then I dig the heel of my foot into her knee.

She tries to hide her wince of pain, but I see it.

I lower my face to hers to snarl, "I should have let my Lords defile you the way you'd planned on letting Perez take me. You think he's bad? It's nothing like having the three of them on your bad side. You wouldn't walk for a week." I bring her hand up to her temple and force her head to the side. "But there's no goddamn way I'd let them near your skanky, diseased-riddled pussy. So I'm going to have to finish this here."

She tries to buck me off, but there's this little thing where I've been held down before. I know just how frustrating and futile it is to find no purchase with my feet, my elbows, my weight.

I increase the pressure on her knee and she yelps, jaw gaping wide with a pained cry. I release her hand to grab a fistful of Jell-O, and then I shove it into her mouth, jerking around as she thrashes. There was a time I would have been wary of something like this. What if she chokes? What if it goes too far? Am I a killer?

I know the answer to that now.

If I need to be.

She gags, coughing up gelatin as she lashes out with her free hand, but I don't stop, cramming more and more of it in her mouth, into her nose and eyes. Her hand strikes out blindly, catching me hard on my mouth, but even though it stings like a bitch, I forge on, ruthless, until she's flapping around like a fish. "They blindfolded and gagged me," I growl, smashing another handful into her face. Distantly, it registers that I'm tasting blood. "How do you like it, *Cuntess?* How does it feel?"

The sad thing is, I get it. I understand why the Kings brought women into the Royal fold. It might have even been a good idea, giving spoiled little jerks like this something to love and protect. Teaching them that there's something more important than ego and power. But people like Sutton and Perez have corrupted it too much to be anything but perverse. Royal women should be stronger than these bitches. We should look at each other and see an ally. We should form something worth a damn, because no one else in this place could ever understand what it's like. Not like we do. Instead, it's just another game.

God, I am *so fucking sick* of games.

No one needs to pull me off. I kneel up, digging my knee into her stomach, and watch breathlessly as she fights for air, unable to rear up far enough to spit it out.

"One! Two! Three!" the crowd chants. The Dukes' Delta Kappas are against the ring, pounding into the floor with every second. "Four! Five! Six!" LDZ is behind my Lords, and all of them are heaving their fists into the air. "Seven! Eight! Nine!"

"Get up!" Perez shouts from across the ring, face mangled with a sneer. "You're going to let this trash take you down?!"

When the crowd rings out with a booming, "Ten!" the bell dings, and then everyone is jumping and screaming, and here's the hard truth.

I look down at her sputtering that Jell-O out of her throat, and mostly, I just feel pity for her. For whatever her Counts are going to do as punishment. For the next sad Royal girl who falls under their spell. I feel pity for all of them, because when the Counts walk away, leaving her there, I know I'm right. Love makes you stronger.

And they're the weaker ones for not feeling it.

1 9

SHARING

S TORY IS SITTING in the backseat of the truck with Rath, the remaining body glitter sparkling in the passing lights. The queen's crown sits askew on her head, and she is fucking *glowing*. "I can't believe I won this," she gushes for the tenth time, spreading the cash out like a fan. "Oh my god, guys. This is fifty-grand! Look at it!"

For the third time, I gently point out, "That's not fifty grand, sweetheart."

For the third time, Killian agrees, "It's *maybe* two grand."

For the third time, Rath lifts his shoulder in a shrug. "For someone without money, they might as well be the same thing."

The money she's holding is her official cut for just participating. Merch sales, mostly. People pre-order the FU Screw Year's Eve shirts a week in advance, even if they have no plans to attend. Never underestimate the marketing power of a good pun. But the check for the rest is sitting in my pocket—have to keep it protected—and she's beaming, as she should be, so fucking proud of the win. It makes me wonder if she's ever had one before. A big win. An important win, with a crowd cheering you on and your team having your back. Because that's what this was.

She's always been our Lady, but tonight was the first time she actually wielded it, owned it, used it, and goddamn, it looked good on her. The sight of her up on that stage, the whole of LDZ gathered around her as Killer hoisted her onto his shoulders, is still branded into my memory. She's not the only one who's proud. Our girl kicked the Cuntess' ass, and it was glorious to watch.

"You were amazing," I say, turning to face them from the front seat. I take a swig from one of the champagne bottles Rath nicked from the after-party and hand it back to her. "I thought for a minute someone was going to have to do CPR on that bitch if you kept cramming Jell-O down her throat."

"I thought about it," she says, taking a swallow from the bottle. It's a sloppy swig that leaks out the corner of her mouth, bringing up the memory of Christmas evening. She'd been fantastic tonight, tits and ass barely covered, rolling around like a girl possessed. Fuck, like a *Lady* possessed. "But then I remembered tonight is about charity, not murdering bitches." She gives me a toothy grin. "The most important charity being mine."

"That's our girl." Rath slides an arm around her waist, dragging her close. Although she showered off in the gym locker room, the thick scent of cherry Jell-O still clings to her, filling the cab of the truck. Rath drags his tongue down her neck and nips at her collarbone, like he's tasting it. He hums out a low, "Sweet cherry..."

She looks up at him, and I know what's coming seconds before she covers his mouth with hers. I'm used to watching their teasing backseat antics by now, but it's usually Rath driving it, flirting with the skin of her inner thighs or coaxing her into quiet, wet-sounding make out sessions. This time, she's the aggressor, surging forward to push her tongue between his pierced lips.

"You taste good, too," she purrs, tucking her hand beneath his faded black shirt. "Taste good, smell good, *look* good..."

Damn, she must really be amped up, burning from her win. I'm not sure I've ever seen her like this—ever—and when she climbs into Rath's lap, I think both of our brains shatter. We share a stunned look over her shoulder, but his focus is short-lived, stolen away by her mouth on his neck.

She rocks down against him, saying, "I still have more prizes to collect."

"Fuck yeah, you do." Rath's eyes are like magnets to her mouth. "You gonna let them watch?"

She nips at his bottom lip, right between the piercings. "Just watch?"

I don't know what this prize is, but consider my attention piqued.

In my periphery, I see Killian glance in the rearview and do a comical double-take. "Hey," he barks, whipping his head around. "No orgasms in my back seat. Upholstery is a bitch to clean."

Rath makes an agreeable sound, reaching down to get two big handfuls of her ass, hitching her up against him. The roll of her hips is very deliberate. Rhythmic. Undulating. Jesus, I didn't even know she could move like that. It's pure sex, the way she's grinding against him, and I know it's gotta feel good, but there's some part of it that just...*feels* like she's putting on a show.

Rath sprawls out, legs spread so he can buck up into the movement of her hips. Her ass is facing me, and her shirt rises up, exposing the smooth skin along her lower back. The top of her thong peeks out of her pants, and it's just. Like. Give me a break here. I'm only one man.

I reach over the distance to run a fingertip down that delicious peek of spine, plucking at the thong until it drags against her ass. She arches her back in response, which pushes her tits right into Rath's face. He reacts immediately, cupping them in his hands, rolling his thumbs over her nipples.

My cock throbs in my pants and I say, "That's it, sweetheart. You won big. Celebrate a little."

"We *should* celebrate," she says, taking a break from her *obvious fucking humping* to take a big swallow of champagne. She tilts the bottle toward Rath's lips, and the alcohol spills out, dribbling out of his mouth. "It's New Year's Eve. I've got the Throw Down Crown and fifty Gs. We have champagne." She plucks a bill out of her waistband and waves it in Rath's face. "I'll give you this if you let me see your cock."

Killian snorts a laugh. "Save your money, little sister. He'll give you his cock for free.”

“It’s true,” Rath agrees, smirking up at her. “My dick’s a non-profit, baby. Just call me UNISEF.”

There’s a beat of laughter, muffled against his neck, and then they’re kissing again. It gets heavy quick. Rath’s hands are all over the place—sweeping up her shirt, curled around her neck, tangled in her hair, stroking up her thighs. It looks like he’s down to fuck her right here, just like this, because soon they’re plucking at each other’s flies, arms all wedged between their writhing bodies.

Unthinkingly, I reach down to pop the button on my own jeans.

And then the truck comes to a hard, abrupt stop.

Before we can all get pissed about it, Killian says, “Let’s get inside,” in this deep, strained voice. He’s been watching them, too. I can tell from the grimace on his face when he slides out of his seat, reaching down to adjust himself. She doesn’t know it yet, but after what happened with her on Christmas, we talked about it happening again. It was so goddamn good, but also a bit disorganized on account of it being *super fucking unexpected*. We’re not getting caught unprepared for something like that again. Next time, everyone knows their role. I’m pretty sure we’ve all jacked off thinking about it. It’s rare we get Story like this, all hot and squirming with need. It needs to be capitalized on. Now.

“Baby, baby,” Rath is saying against her mouth, “we’re home.” He reaches for the door just as I hop out, jogging around the truck to watch Killian wrench their door open. The two of them are already glistening with sweat, and whatever she’s doing with her hips must work for her, because it’s like she doesn’t even realize we’re here. She keeps kissing him and rocking against his lap, and it takes him turning away to tear their mouths apart.

Rath gives Killian a glazed, helpless look.

Killian answers by reaching inside, winding an arm around her waist and wrenching her back. “Just a second,” he says at her plaintive cry, and it’s a good thing he’s basically spent all night peeling her away from people, because the way he throws her over his shoulder is quick and efficient.

"Hey!" she shouts, kicking out as her expression transforms to outrage. "I was busy."

"You can get busy in the house," Killian says, clamping his arm down on her swinging legs.

Rath gets out of the truck, adjusting his jeans, trying to get his hard on under control. Luckily, it's late and a holiday, so there's no one around to see that all three of us are bulging in the crotch.

"Put me down!" she shouts, making a dog bark down the block. "I can walk!"

Another plus to no one being around. I don't even want to think what this looks like.

"Jesus, she's fired up," Rath says, looking a little rattled as his eyes scan the street.

"A little help," Killian says, struggling to get in the door. Story is still fighting against him, kicking and squirming in his arms. She's not going anywhere, Killian's strong as an ox, but the new lock system I had installed scans off our phones, and it can be a little fussy. Not missing a beat, I whip out my phone and put in the code. There's a moment of unified distraction, because Killian gets fed up with the thrashing and decides to take care of it the only way he knows how.

He reaches up and crams his fingers below the crotch of her shorts.

Story freezes, her breaths loud in the silence of the porch, and Rath and I both watch as Killer's fingers shift beneath the fabric. "Oh," she moans, squirming.

Rath asks, "Is she...?" and Killer's jaw goes tight.

"She's fucking soaked," he says, kicking at the door. "Come on, get this thing open."

As soon as the door unlatches, Rath swings it wide, allowing Killer to carry her over the threshold. She grunts and whines, but it's a lot less ambitious now that big brother's probably got two fingers buried into her cunt.

I think we'd all prefer her in a bed, but the stairs might as well be the third stretch of a triathlon for how unattainable climbing them seems. Killian leads us to the den instead, dumping her without ceremony onto the couch. She bounces with a small, pained sound, but her fists are clenched into his shirt, so she drags him down with her.

"You're a fucking asshole, you know that?" she says, eyes narrowed, cheeks flushed.

He glares back, pinning her down. "Well, you never fucking listen."

"You never fucking ask nicely!" She thrashes out, but he catches her wrist, and I can see the flash of excitement in her eyes when he forces her into submission.

"You don't want me to be nice!" he growls, seeing it, too.

"Yeah, they're definitely horny," I sigh, grabbing two more bottles of champagne out of the refrigerator behind the bar. Rath is sitting on the chair closest to the couch watching the two of them. "This is foreplay for these two."

I look over just in time to see Story's hand get loose and rear back. Killian stops the hit, snatching her wrist right out of the air. He lowers his face until it's an inch above hers. "Why are you always such a cunt? Can't you ever act like a normal girl?"

"Normal?" She squirms beneath him, her cheeks getting redder. "The last thing you want is normal, big brother. If you did, you wouldn't be here on top of me. You'd be with that girl you have tattooed on your arm."

A tense pause falls over the room.

Rath and I share a look, and he's obviously as surprised as I am that she still doesn't know. I'm half committed to telling her myself. It might be a violation of our bro code, but letting her think he's got some random slut inked into his skin has to be a violation of something else.

Killer makes the decision for me. He grabs her beneath her tense jaw, fingertips digging into her cheeks, and snarls, "I *am* with the girl tattooed on my arm." The shifting muscles underneath his shirt are the only warning she gets. He crashes his mouth into hers, so fast that I can't even tell whether she understands the confession.

She fights back, but it's weak, her hips rising off the couch to meet his. Killian makes a rough sound and presses back, surging into the cradle of her thighs. They grind against one another for a long stretch of time, and neither Rath nor I stop them. They're good to watch like this, always pushing and shoving, pulling and grasping.

Without tearing my eyes away, I nudge Rath's foot with my own. "What was the prize?"

Rath tips his head to the side, observing them through dark lashes. "Anal."

I sputter on my mouthful of champagne. "Seriously?"

Secretly, I found the prospect of working up to that daunting and annoying. She obviously likes it when we play with her ass, but girls are always so irritatingly coy about shit like that. I should have known she'd be different.

Still, this one goes to Rath, fair and square.

It's the only reason I interrupt the impassioned dry humping currently happening on our couch. "Come on, Killer." I give his shoulder a tap, noticing how deep Story's got her nails embedded in the skin of his neck. "Get her naked, brother."

Killian's good at taking instruction—I know that from the last time we fucked her together—but it's still a relief to see him reach between their bodies and start unbuttoning her shorts. He makes quick work of it, jostling her entire body as he yanks them over her thighs, panties and all. That's why it has to be Killian. Rath would drag it out, and this is not the fucking time.

He goes for her shirt next, pulling it up her torso and over her head, but the second it clears her ears, he's already bending to mouth at her nipple, gathering the weight of her tit in a palm to give it a hard suck. She keens, bucking up into him.

I think I like it like this. Her skin all naked and bare as he looms above her, completely clothed. There's a roughness to it that I bet she can feel. The denim of his jeans against her soft thighs. The texture of his hoodie against her flat belly.

Licking my lips, I reach down to squeeze my cock, ordering, "Flip over. Get under her."

He lifts her effortlessly, and Rath and I watch appreciatively. Killer has this habit of tossing her around like a doll, but it's hard to protest when it ends with her settling on top of him, looking flushed and flustered, a little divot appearing between her eyebrows as she rucks up his sweater.

"Off," she demands, clawing the fabric away, even as he tugs it over his head. Her eyes go to the tattoo and linger there for a dozen heartbeats, her chest heaving as she inspects it. I don't know how she never realized it was her face. The dark hair, the sad eyes—it's got everything but her name emblazoned beneath it.

I try to get things back on track. "Get his dick out."

She licks her lips, holding his gaze as she thumbs his fly, pushing up on her knees to shove them down. Killer's cock catches on the elastic of his boxers, and then flops hard against his hip when she frees it with a swift yank.

"Easy," he snaps, reaching down to protect his balls. "Goddamn, fucking impatient, crazy-ass—" His words cut off when she lunges down to kiss him. It's a pointed kiss, full of teeth, and the second her bare pussy drags against his cock, the grunt in Killer's throat dissipates. He palms at her thighs like he's memorizing the softness of the skin there, and fuck. The way they look. I could get off just at the sight of this alone. That slow, visible transition from annoyed to enraptured. The way his inked hands look, curling just below her hips. The quiet, gentle sound she makes when she rocks against his dick.

Rath bends to reach into the bag he'd brought in from the truck. "Hold this," he says, throwing me something.

I snatch it out of the air, realizing it's a bottle of baby oil. Right. Preparation prevents poor performance. Dragging in an inhale, I whisper to Rath, "Do you think she could take it?" I give him a significant look. "Both of you?"

He tugs his shirt over his head, eyes glued to her writhing body as he approaches. "Guess we'll find out." He starts off with nothing but the sweep of his palm down her spine, but it's enough to make her arch up, chasing it.

He's already got his pants unzipped, cock in his hand as he slowly makes a path down her back, which is why it's easy for her to turn her head and zero in on it. Rath's other hand is on his cock, his long fingers stroking up and down, toying with the tip. He doesn't need her mouth right now.

But when she leans in to mouth at the head, he doesn't exactly say no.

I know all about his edging kink. This fucker can draw it out all night, waiting his turn, holding out until it probably halfway kills him. Christmas night aside, Rath isn't usually a joiner. When he plays music, it's just him and the piano, and it's the same when he fucks—just him and Story holed up in his shitty room, doing god knows what.

But not tonight.

If he wants her, then he has to share her.

20

HAVING

I watch Killer stroke her thighs, and I get it.

I've never really felt the need to indulge in a girl before. Usually it's suck, fuck, goodbye, and good luck. Story's got this skin, though. It's all creamy and silky. It's the kind of skin you want to feel up against yours, put your mouth to and make a mark in. So good that I'm still skating my fingertips over her spine as she tongues my cock. Her head game is solid. It's just that I'm imagining this back beneath me when I push into her. I thumb a spot on her shoulder, thinking to myself, *here.*

I'm going to sink my teeth into this patch of skin when I come.

I abandon the thought to sweep a lock of hair away from her cheek. "Who do you want inside you first? Me or Killer?"

She's grinding on Killer's shaft, the tip of his dick shiny with her slick, but at my question, she pauses, peering up at me with dazed eyes. "But I thought... weren't you going to... uh, you know..."

I lift her chin. "Fuck your pretty little asshole?"

Killian's head snaps up. "You're going to *what?*"

"Don't worry, baby girl." The corner of my mouth quirks at the flush that comes over her cheeks, and I can't help but touch it, stroking my fingers over the warm skin. "There's room down there for both of us, you know."

Comprehension dawns over her features, her mouth forming a sweet little 'o' as it hits her. "I-I can't... that's not..." She wets her lips, eyes wide. "What if it's too much?"

I shrug, tapping her lips with the head of my cock. "Then we'll trade off."

Killian stares at me, biting out a low, "Oh, fuck me."

She processes this in fits and starts as she mouths at my dick—as she slides against Killer's cock—as her eyes wander to the sight of Tristian undressing behind me. "Yeah," she finally decides. It's almost exactly like when we arrived at the gym. She pushes her shoulders back and nods, features hardening with resolve. "But you first, okay?" she says, eyes shining up at me. "I want my prize."

Killian's head flops back to the arm of the couch, fingers digging into her hips. "If I have to sit through him fucking your ass open, then you're gonna have to cool it with the bump and grind." The muscle in the back of his jaw ticks when she squirms. "Unless you want me to bust my nut right fucking here."

Story freezes, tongue peeking out to swipe at her lips as she looks at him. "I understand."

She's such a sexy little trooper, too, not even flinching when Tristian kneels onto the couch behind her, the bottle of baby oil clutched in his hand. "All you have to do is relax, sweetheart. We'll take care of everything."

The emotion that runs over me as I watch him lift her hips isn't jealousy, but it's still possessive and electric. The need to stake my claim and bury myself into her thrums hot in my blood. She's theirs—ours—and although I'm willing to wait until I can devour her at my own pace, it's fucking agony to watch Tristian in my place. He was the first to take her mouth. Killer was the first to take her cherry. This one is *mine*.

"Chill, Rath." He gives me a quick glance before tipping the bottle, sending a stream of oil right down her crack. "I just want to make sure the two of you don't tear her up. Let's do it right."

My teeth clench, but I stand there and watch as he pushes his fingers down her crease, gathering the slickness. Leaning in to get a better look, I reach out to palm her ass cheek, spreading her wide enough that I can see her sweet, puckered hole pulsating at the first touch of his fingertip. I know from fingering her earlier just how tight that passage is. I squeeze the base of my dick as Tristian pushes inside.

"Oh!" Story's gasp is almost too quiet to hear.

Killian hears it, though. "Is he in there, little sister?" He surges up to nip at her jaw as his hand wanders between them. I watch it appear from beneath her, Killian's fingers seeking out Tristian's. When he finds it buried all the way to the knuckle, Killian groans. "*Fuck.*" He rears up to pluck a wet, sucking kiss at her gasping mouth. "One day, that's gonna be me. I'm going to fuck your ass with this fat dick. What do you think about that?" He punctuates this by grabbing his dick and running the head up and down her slit.

She looks like she wants to answer—and from the furl of her brow, I'm guessing it's going to be something catty and sharp—but then Tristian pushes a second finger in, and the only sound that emerges from her mouth is a high keen.

Tristian's watching her ass in much the same way I am—heavy-lidded, mouth parted, transfixed by the sight of his fingers sinking inside. "She's so fucking tight, Rath. You're going to blow in three seconds flat."

I shove my fist into his shoulder. "Fuck off. No one can hold their nut like I can." Bending, I cradle the back of her head and guide it to mine, ripping her away from Killian's kiss. She seamlessly latches onto my own tongue, letting me feel her silent little grunts as she's stretched. There's a wrinkle in her brow that I'm not sure I like, and it makes me ask, "You good, baby?" I've fucked a couple girls up the ass before, and they always complained about it hurting, wanting me to get it over with quick. That's not my style. I want to be buried in that ass for hours. I want it to remember me for days.

She nods against my mouth, hips pushing back into Tristian. "I want... I can take more. *More*."

It feels like someone just punched me right in the solar plexus. "Fucking *A*," I breathe, awed that I somehow managed to stumble into something this lucky. It's not just that she's so eager to have her ass stuffed, either. It's that she's a pretty girl who knows me, understands me, and can handle all the messed up bullshit that comes along with it. A bitch who can bite back. A muse who can inspire a symphony with nothing more than a sleepy morning sigh and the serpentine curl of her naked body. A runaway who always returns. A woman who can face us down while getting on her knees for us.

An actual fucking Queen.

I kiss her hard and deep, muttering thoughtless, embarrassing nonsense in between plunges of my tongue. Shit like, "You're so goddamn gorgeous," and, "I'm going to fuck you so good, baby," and, "Want to make you bleed."

The last one is said with the thinnest thread of restraint, and I kind of can't stand that Tristian and Killer hear it, because it's not the way it sounds. They wouldn't get it.

But Story does.

"Yeah," she gasps, fingers threading through my hair. "Just like that. Please."

Tristian makes a small, disapproving noise. This is why I fuck her in my room. "You want him to fuck you," Tristian says, making way for my fingers when I reach back to feel the stretch around his own. "That's what you want, isn't it, sweetheart?"

Her eyes meet mine just as I sink a finger in alongside Tristian's. "Yes."

"Tell us exactly what you want," Tristian softly demands. "You are, after all, our Queen."

My gaze bolts up to his, and I realize he's feeling it, too. That Story Austin is more than just a Lady. There's only one person who could be here right now, taking all of us, in every way imaginable, because maybe we made her, shaped her to suit our own twisted fantasies, fucked her up too much for someone normal and nice. But she's molded us just as much.

The four of us have absolutely *ruined* each other for anyone else.

Her eyes flash at the word—*Queen*—and I realize she loves the title just as much as we love bestowing it on her. It's not like she hasn't earned it. She's sacrificed everything for the position. "Remember that night?" She turns to glance at Tristian over her shoulder, her fiery eyes following our arms and wrists, disappearing behind her. "The camera in my room. When I touched myself for you?"

Tristian has a lot of room to talk about two pump chumps. He looks like he's about to explode. "Of course, I remember."

She wets her lips, nodding. "You said...you told me not to...finger myself. You didn't want anything inside me but you. The *three* of you." Killian spits a low curse, drawing her attention. It's why, when she speaks, she's staring into his eyes, hips rocking back onto our fingers. "That's what I want. I don't want you coming anywhere else but inside me."

All three of us freeze, and I can't speak for the others, but I take a second to get past the shock of her making such a dirty fucking request to actually parse the contents. A few months ago, this girl couldn't even look us in the eye as we took our pleasure. Now she's asking to be our cum dumpster?

Killer's chest caves with a low, tortured laugh. "Trust me, that's the last fucking thing you want."

"Baby, if you took every load we made, you'd never get a break," I agree, thrusting my finger deeper. "You'd have jizz coming out your eyeballs."

Tristian's fingers move again. "You're seriously underestimating how much we jerk off. But, hey, hey," he's quick to add, sensing the same thing I am. The clench of her ass. The way she's closing up. "Maybe we can try saving it up for you, hm?" He curves over her back to press a kiss to her shoulder, his free hand wrapping around the delicate column of her throat. "*Try*," he stresses. "That means you'll have to be a little more..." Tristian seems at a loss for how to finish that sentence.

But I'm not. "Available."

Killian tips up to mouth at her nipple. "Willing."

"It's like Rath said." Tristian muffles his laugh into her shoulder. "You'd never get a fucking break."

Her jaw falls open, but her eyes slide closed. "O-okay."

Killer and I share a dark look.

Okay.

O-fucking-kay.

"Rath." Tristian leans back, dipping his head to watch as his fingers slip free. "I think she's ready for you."

My finger's still knuckle-deep, so I give it a couple of testing thrusts. Part of me is annoyed Tristian doesn't trust me to do this myself. I'd be patient, teasing, methodical as I got her loose and slick for my cock. A bigger part of me knows Tristian would be more careful, though. This is her first time, after all. She deserves the care he's taken just as much as she deserves the tender look in Killer's eyes when he shifts her hips, getting her in position for me. She deserves for someone to soothe away that nervous spark filling her eyes, which is why Tristian reaches up to give her shoulders a slow massage.

"You've got this, sweetheart."

Suddenly, the thought of doing this with her upstairs, all alone, seems completely fucking unappealing.

Tristian gives her shoulder one last kiss before climbing off the couch. I take his place, accepting the bottle of oil when he tosses it to me. "I know I don't need to tell you to take it slow," he says, watching as I get my dick nice and slick. "Just go easy."

He gives me a look, and I hear what he's not saying.

Make it good.

Make her like it.

Don't ruin it for her.

Don't ruin it for the rest of us.

"Yeah," I reply, tossing the bottle somewhere on the floor. "Consider me sex refereed, Tris."

Story wriggles her hips impatiently, and from this vantage, I can see the sweat beginning to bead up on her lower back. I rake my teeth over my lip as I take in the view: Story straddling Killer's hips, his legs spread wide enough to accommodate the knee I've got digging into the couch cushion, the curve of her spine as she bows her back, putting everything on display for me.

"Shit," I mutter, grabbing each ass cheek and spreading her wide open. My dick falls right into the crease and I follow, thrusting against the warm, oiled skin. I could easily get off just like this, fucking her ass crack like some horny fresher.

"Dimitri?" One of her dark eyes peers at me over her shoulder and I clear my throat, trying to stay focused.

"I've got you," I say, using one hand to grab my dick while the other guides her hip. I can feel Tristian's presence beside me, and I know his eyes are glued to the head of my cock, pressing up against her hole. "Ready, baby?"

"Yes."

"Look at me," Killian says, cradling the back of her skull.

I push, gentle at first, and then harder, forcing the head of my cock past the resistance. Her sharp, loud gasp is like static in my ears over the hammer of my pulse, and I grunt, "Ah, *fuck...*" Her ass is so goddamn *hot*, I'm regretting all that talk about being able to make this slow, because the only thing I want to do is slam right into her. I gnash my teeth, using my free hand to sweep up her back.

Killian's whispering things to her as he holds her close, but only snatches float back to me. "...gonna make you so full...bet you're so tight, little sister... don't close your eyes, let me see..."

Gulping in a breath, I grit out, "Can't stop," and push another thick inch of my dick into her ass.

Her hand flies back, grabbing blindly until it finds my thigh. "Oh god, Dimitri..."

Killian's arms lock around her middle, but he doesn't fight when I get a fistful of her hair, tugging her up to pant a series of sharp breaths against her temple. It makes her hips rock down, sinking another inch into her.

"Goddamn, her ass is so tight." Through the dampness of her skin and the oil on my hands, I try to get a grip good enough on her to thrust in deeper. "Almost there," I say when she makes a small, strained sound, hands clawing at my forearms. "Just a little more."

Tristian's crouched beside her, hand shoved between her and Killian, rubbing at her clit. "You're taking it so good, sweetheart. He looks like he's barely holding on. You can take the rest, can't you?"

The hair tangled in my fist tugs with her nod. "I can take it, I can take it."

I clench my fingers against her scalp and hook my other hand over her shoulder, giving one last, hard shove. I bottom out with a grunt, fully sheathed inside her.

Through the rush of *hot-tight-slick*, I distantly note that Tristian is whispering. "That's our good girl. Look at you, taking it all. How does it feel, sweetheart?"

Her back expands with a tight inhale. "It burns, but...it also...*god*, I can feel it twitching."

Oh, it's twitching alright—angry, impatient, mindless twitches, because it's taking every ounce of restraint I have not to start pounding into her. I use the moment to drag her up against my chest, wrenching her head to the side for a long, sloppy kiss. Killer follows, sucking a bruise into her neck as Tristian leans in to lick a wet loop around her nipple.

Her face is so red that, this close, I can see the fan of broken capillaries on the apple of her cheek. "Does it... feel good?" She whispers the question right against my mouth, and beneath the strain and breathlessness, I can hear something I don't like.

"Open your eyes," I demand, holding her chin steady so she can't look away. "You always feel good, baby. Always." I lick at the tip of her tongue and she licks back, because she's so perfect that she understands it's giving Tristian and Killer a nice little show. Despite that, I get so distracted with it that I completely miss Tristian pushing to his feet.

Suddenly, his dick is inches from our faces.

Getting the hint, I give her tongue one last parting suck before using my grip on her chin to turn her attention to the hard cock currently leaking in front of us.

"That's it," Tristian says, feeding her the tip of his cock. "Just relax for a minute. Let yourself get nice and loose for him."

It'd be absolute torture, kneeling here motionless as her ass strangles my dick, except that it's weirdly not. I nose into the damp nape of her neck, pulling in the scent of cherries and sweat and *her,* and she suckles on Tristian's dick and Killian's kisses as she waits. By the time she finally gives her hips an experimental roll, I don't even feel like I might die if I don't start slamming into her like a goddamn psycho.

As I ease my hips back, dragging my cock away, Killian asks, "Do you know how long we've talked about doing this?" If she hears his question, we wouldn't know it, not from the loud whine she makes as I thrust back inside. He answers anyway. "So long that we didn't even know what you looked like underneath all those cute little dresses you used to wear."

Fuck, I'd almost forgotten about those evenings in high school, holed up in the basement getting drunk and stoned, talking about what it'd be like to stuff her full of our cocks. It didn't even mean anything back then—not like it does now. It was just dumb, ridiculous teenage fantasies shared between buddies. I know things have changed between us, because back then, Killer would struggle to play along, silently seething at the thought of sharing his new shiny toy, even though it was nothing but talk back then. Tristian had Gen, and I had zero interest in pissing off the heir to South Side.

Now, he reaches behind her and grabs her ass, spreading her open for me as I fuck into her. "How does it feel, Rath?"

Puffing hard breaths into her cheek, I answer, "Like I'm fucking a goddamn vise grip." It's not entirely true. I can feel her loosening up with every hitched gasp she makes, rocking back into me.

To Killian's credit, Tristian's the one to ask, "You ready for Killer, sweetheart?"

She plants her palms on Killer's chest—one covering each tattoo—and shudders. "I'm ready."

21

KEEPING

I DESERVE A medal for being this patient.

There's an ache in my balls that's spent the last ten minutes fanning out, settling around my back molars from all the teeth grinding. Story already looks absolutely wrecked, her pupils blown as Rath fucks into her. Everywhere I touch her—hands gliding over her hips, cupping her tits, skating up to cradle her cheek—is searing hot, and *fuck*, I can't wait to get my dick inside her. I want to fill her up, pussy and ass, claiming every inch of her body for the Lords.

It's feral and territorial, zinging through my blood like a sickness. That's how I feel. Sick to the very marrow of my being. And the only cure is the way I'm rubbing my cock between the lips of her drenched pussy.

"Slow down," I growl, letting my foot drop off the couch to give me leverage. "I need to get inside you."

I know when she braces her knees that she's ready for me, but Rath is just as lost as I want to be. He's huffing against her cheek, knocking her body forward with a pointed thrust. Story spreads her hands out, palms digging into my chest. I steady her hips and watch her mouth part, wide eyes gaping down at me.

"Oh, god, he's so deep," she gasps, teeth sinking into her lip.

Tristian, ever watchful, lays his hand on Rath's shoulder and says, "Slow down, brother. Let him get in there."

Their movements abate just enough for me to nudge around with the head of my cock, but I don't push inside. Not until her eyes finally settle on mine, dazed and heavy. I watch every twitch of muscle in her face as I plant my heels, finally driving my dick up into her. The angle is difficult, but when it comes to her, I'm used to making do, stealing whatever I can grab and savoring it like a drug. I clutch her hips, dragging her closer as I slowly impale her on my cock.

Her jaw gapes open in a long burst of panted breaths, and I don't say anything when her nails dig into my shoulders. "Killian," she gasps, face screwing up. "I don't—I don't know if I can take—"

"Yes, you can," I grit out, meeting Rath's eyes over her shoulder. I can tell from the strained look on his face he's feeling me in there, her body crowding us together, clutching onto us as we make her full.

Tristian's hand is curled around the base of her neck, and he leans in to whisper dark, dirty encouragements into her ear. "Just breathe, sweetheart. He's almost all the way in. I know Killer's thick, but you were made for this. You were made to take them."

She nods frantically, her nails stinging as they embed into my flesh. "Just... just let me..." She wriggles her little hips around, adjusting and rocking, until—

"Oh, *motherfuck*." I still her, grunting as she bottoms out, and I barely have time to enjoy that overwhelmed look on her face before Tristian is ducking in to kiss her.

"So good," he pants against her mouth, shoulder jerking as he fists himself. "So fucking good for us."

She gulps in huge, fast breaths, her chest swelling and caving with each one. "I can't believe I'm...it's so *much*."

"You look perfect," Tristian says, and from the brush of his wrist against my thigh, I assume he's giving Rath a tap. "They're going to fuck you now, sweetheart. Ease down." He pushes at her back and her elbows buckle, but when she collapses against my chest, I catch her, winding my arms around her back. Tristian pets her hair. "You don't need to do a thing. Just let them do the work."

With that, Tristian gives me and Rath the signal, nodding.

Rath's the first to move, pulling his hips back and then surging forward. I hiss, because I feel it. Every fucking inch of his cock as it retreats and digs back, dragging against me through the wet wall of her pussy. She buries a soft noise into my throat, and I tighten my arms around her as I move my hips, only getting a couple inches of my cock out before driving it back into her.

Now, it's Rath's turn to hiss, our eyes meeting over her shoulder.

It takes a minute for us to fall into rhythm. His thrust, then mine. His, then mine. I know when he looks at me, he's letting me set the pace, probably too lost in the tightness of her ass to trust himself with it. So I make it slow at first, indulging myself in her little cries against my neck as Rath and I take our turns fucking into her.

"What's it like?" Tristian asks, and the low, guttural sound of his voice makes me look over, getting an eyeful of his fist sliding up and down on his cock.

"Better," I pant, jerking her body down as my hips snap up. "Better than I expected."

It's quiet after that, nothing but our harsh breaths and Story's strained cries as she holds on and takes it. And fuck, that's exactly what she does. She takes it when the pace ratchets up, Rath following as my thrusts grow deeper, more pointed. His pupils are so dilated, they look black as they move from me to her ass, over and over, like he's thinking, 'If you could see this, you'd blow your load'.

And he's probably right.

I think we're all shocked when Story begins making those sounds.

They're tense, sharp sounds, her hand slapping around until it finds something to claw into the crown of my hair. We're shocked because we know those sounds. We've heard them against our ears as we fucked her, pushed into the air as we ate her pussy, buried into a pillow as we slammed into her from behind.

I give Rath a warning look.

Don't you change a fucking thing.

Tristian edges closer to be a little more explicit about it. "Jesus Christ, she's close."

Rath looks like he's barely clinging to sense, the line of his jaw so tense that he speaks through his teeth. "You gonna come on our dicks, baby?"

She answers with a writhe of her hips, grinding down as I bottom out. "Don't stop, don't—"

"Come for us, little sister," I say against her temple. "Let go. We've got you." My muscles coil as I hang on, feeling the rush of wetness, the swell of Rath's dick in her ass, Tristian's loud breaths as he watches, enraptured.

Story comes with a *scream*.

Her body wracks with a shudder that makes me clamp down tight, crushing her to my chest as Rath and I finish her off with hard, punishing thrusts. Tristian leans down to soothe her through it, even though his voice is strained and his words are getting so fucking filthy.

"... can't wait to come down your throat as you take their loads. Then you'll really be ours, won't you? We're going to pump you so full of our cum..."

Everything's a little more complicated once she's gone limp, so open and wet that it's impossible to hold ourselves back. Rath curls over her back and shoves her into me with the punch of his hips. I answer back by bucking hard, slamming her up into him. It's a conversation, a game of push and shove that Tristian only wishes he could be a part of.

Which is why it's no surprise when he inches forward and nudges her shoulder. "Look at me, sweetheart."

She opens her bleary eyes, lashes wet, but when she catches sight of

Tristian's dick, bobbing stiffly over my shoulder, she doesn't miss a beat. Prying her fingers from the cushion, she levers herself up and reaches for him.

"That's it," he says, guiding her head. "Kiss it."

She does, but it's more tongue than lips, sloppy and tired, but no less enthusiastic. Tristian is the one to push it into her mouth, pulling her onto him until I can hear her struggling breaths. I take the chance to palm at her heavy tits, Rath and I not slowing as we watch Tristian fuck her throat.

It hits me that this is it.

It took us a long time to get here—years—but the pieces we set into motion all those years ago have finally come together. Rath's heavy breathing and Tristian's soft encouragements are mixed with the soft hums coming from Story's throat. We're all inside her, fucking her, using her and claiming her, and it's just like Tristian said before. Making her *ours*. It flows between us in an energy we could probably never explain to someone else. Through the wet sounds and ragged grunts, we're all connected. Unified. For some reason that isn't apparent to me yet, I get the feeling that there's no going back. None of us could be whole again without the other three. This is matrimony disguised as dirty, hardcore fucking.

I'm the first to lose it, my toes curling as I watch her throat swell with Tristian's cock. It's more my awareness of it all than the act itself, although the way Rath's dick is shifting against mine certainly doesn't fucking help matters.

I come with a soft, plaintive grunt that I'll deny until I die, which is why I miss Tristian's hand shooting out, clutching onto the arm of the couch as he follows. Rath doesn't pause as he feels me pumping my cum into her, but he does crush her against me. His dick snugged up to mine through the barrier between us.

That's when I see Story. The wildfire in her eyes. Her tongue swiping out to catch Tristian's cum, dripping down her chin. Unthinkingly, I surge forward and kiss her, my tongue pushing it deep in her mouth, because I haven't forgotten her request.

"I don't want you coming anywhere else but inside me."

Tristian's hand presses against my neck, urging me closer. But there is no closer. I'm in her mouth, in her pussy, her tits rocking against my chest as Rath fucks her. I feel every one of his thrusts, and when our eyes meet over Story's head, I know he's close. His jaw tightens and his teeth bear down on his bottom lip. He's teetering on the edge, but he wants to make sure we're done. People don't know that about Rath—that he's never content taking something until he knows everyone else has gotten theirs.

"Your turn." I clutch Story against me, using my remaining strength to hold her for him. "Fill her up."

Rath looks relieved and crazed as he rears back on his knees, getting a good hold on her hips as he punches into her. I stare at the 'S' carved in his chest, and a strange swell of emotion catches me. This woman trusts us enough to defile her in any way we want. To love her in the only way we know how. Hard, angry, and intense.

Tristian drops to his knees. "You're beautiful, sweetheart. Your face, your pussy, your ass. Rath's almost there. Can you take it?"

She nods, an agonized furl creasing into her brow. "Yes."

"I know you can." Tristian kisses her, running his hand up and down her back, until Rath's hips abruptly stop, his spine going rigid. I hold on to her, readying her for that final slam into her ass. It comes with Rath curling over her back, mouth pressed to her shoulder as he comes. I must feel him the same way he felt me, the pulsation of his cock against mine as he shoots deep into her ass. It isn't until the muscles in his neck tighten that I realize Rath's not mouthing her shoulder.

He's sinking his teeth into the flesh.

It's punctuated with Story's sharp gasp, her head snapping up, eyes slammed closed. But it's all so quiet compared to the hard, feral sound Rath makes around the chunk on shoulder he's got in his mouth. They both look like they're drowning in rapture.

When he finally pulls back, breathless and sweating, his teeth are tinged pink.

Tristian leans down to press a kiss to the wound. "Sweetheart, are you okay?"

She nods, wordlessly shuddering as the two of us carefully pull out. For a second, I worry she's not. That we went too far. That the weary curve of her shoulders means she's realizing this is something she never wants to do again, even though I already know the three of us will want it.

But then she collapses against my chest, nestling her nose into the side of my neck, and the sound she releases can only be described as a purr.

Tonight, Story not just claimed the crown, she claimed all three of us at once.

Proving once and for all that she's our Lady.

Our Queen.

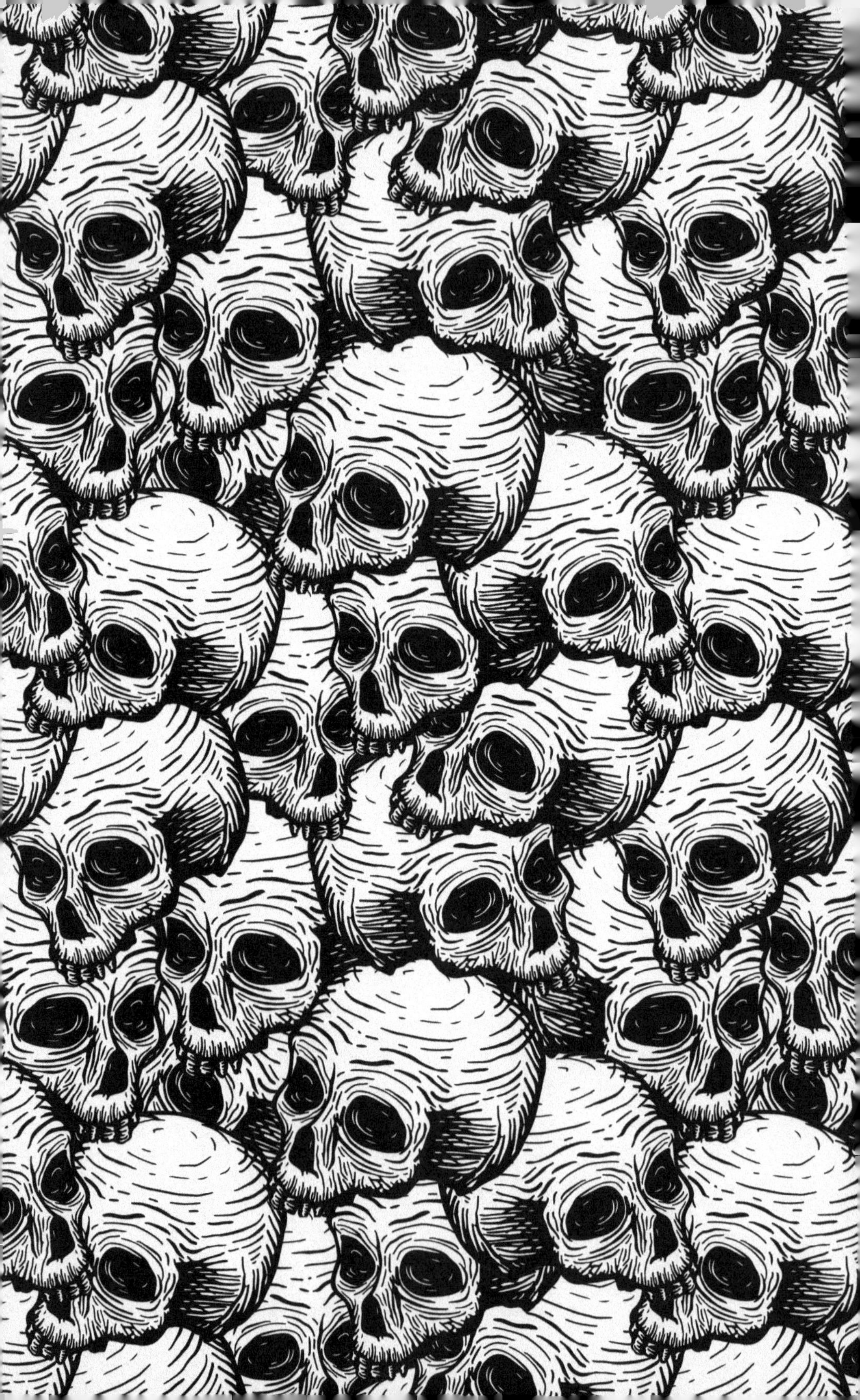

2 2

A S S E T S

THE DREAM IS warm and weightless.

I can feel a throb somewhere between my legs, but it's distant, thrumming in the background of my awareness. Beyond it is the frozen sense of time. I don't know where I am, but I know I'm safe here. Comfortable. Protected. Something inside me has been wound tight, and I know it has, because now it's gone. I'm free of the worry, the razor-sharp thoughts, the hyper-aware tick of my brain wiped away by the whooshing rhythm in my ears.

Dimitri's breaths.

I'm resting on his chest, I realize, groggy eyes blinking open. The first thing I see is the 'S' carved in the center of it, and then hands. So many of them. Tristian's, reaching over Dimitri to touch me. Killian's resting on my arm as he curls around me from behind.

I spend a long moment soaking it in, knowing they're still sleeping. Killian's skin is hot against my back, and I feel his hardness slotted up against the source of my ache. One shift of my thighs makes it clear I'm going to be feeling that for a couple of days.

Dimitri's head is turned, puffing shallow, even breaths into the crown of my head as he sleeps, and there's no blanket to cover him. Every inch of his body is on full display.

As is Tristian's.

He's almost too much to look at, in sleep. Tristian's hair is messy, but in just the right way. His eyes shift behind his lids, as if he's dreaming, too, and I spend a long time wondering what of. My knee is wedged between Dimitri's, slotting his thigh right up against my center.

I catalogue all these things—the skin and the infinitesimal movements that make up their sleep—before even remembering where we are.

That awareness comes rudely.

And loudly.

"*Lucifer's hairy scrotum.*" There's a sharp crack that makes me flinch, and then Ms. Crane's shrill voice. "Get the hell out of the den, you goddamn sickos!"

I feel Killian startle awake, and then watch Tristian bolt upright, but I'm too busy trying to futilely cover myself to catch their expressions. I remember now, last night, Killian unfolding the mattress from the sleeper sofa near the fireplace. It'd been so warm and cozy and—

Well, truthfully, I could barely get my legs to work enough to carry me to the bathroom, let alone up a flight of stairs.

So we'd finished the bottle of champagne and curled up here, in front of the fire.

Ms. Crane's irate glare passes over the four of us. "A dozen fucking bedrooms in this place, and here you are with your ball sacks hanging out! Twenty-dollar tricks have more couth than this. Get up, get up!"

Dimitri, who's slept through the whole ruckus, barely stirs when the pair of jeans she lobs smacks him right in the chin.

I snatch them up to cover my breasts, mortified. "I'm so sorry, Ms. Crane! We didn't mean to fall asleep."

Killian flops back down onto the flimsy mattress, scrubbing his fingers through his hair. "Oh, I absolutely meant to fall asleep."

Tristian props himself up on his elbows, looking unbothered by his general state of nudity. "I could have stayed up a couple more hours, if I'm being honest."

Dimitri's rough, sleep-thick voice rings out, even though he hasn't bothered to open his eyes. "Chill the fuck out, mommy dearest. You're harshing my afterglow."

"Mommy dearest?!" Ms. Crane's eyes narrow into slits. "If I were your mother, I'd poison your breakfast to spare myself the embarrassment!"

Tristian smiles serenely. "If you were my mother, I'd eat it."

She bends to pick up a sweater off the floor, pitching it across the distance. "You have ten minutes to cover your asses and clean up your mess. I don't get paid enough to see your limp dicks at six in the fucking morning."

"First of all," Killian argues, "you definitely get paid enough to see that."

Tristian follows, "Second of all, there's not a limp dick in this room." He punctuates this by shooting me a quick, unapologetic wink.

Dimitri mutters, "Well, there is now," and reaches down to cover himself, finally opening his eyes. In a loud, droll voice, he assures, "We'll take care of it, Delores."

"You'd fucking better."

I wait until she's left the room to bury my face in my hands. "Oh, my god. I can never look her in the eye again."

Someone's hand—Dimitri's, going by the precision of his fingertips— comes up to rub gently against my back. "Come on, that woman's probably seen more orgies than the Kings combined. Don't sweat it, baby."

Despite that frankly disturbing assurance, I still jump off the mattress, wincing at the ache between my legs, and begin plucking clothes from the floor. The guys are predictably a lot less urgent about it. Each time I glance back, I catch someone falling asleep again.

"Get up!" I hiss, tugging Dimitri's faded black shirt over my head. When that doesn't work, Tristian tucking his hands behind his head and flexing his thighs, I stand there with my hands on my hips, watching them.

They really are a sight like this. Three strapping, naked, gorgeous men, all sprawled out before me like something an erotic Renaissance painter dreamed up. Killian's ink is on full display, and in places I don't often see. He's laying on his side, his back to me, and I take a second to appreciate the tattoos before my eyes wander to Dimitri. He's the personification of indulgence, stretched out laconically. His hair has gotten longer over the winter and it's flopped forward to one side, covering one of his closed eyes. It's impossible to not look down at his cock and remember where it's been, what he's done with it. My attention wanders to Tristian next, but his attention is fixed on me. He's not even tired. He was probably awake an hour ago.

"The last one of you to get up," I tell them, eyebrow raised, "isn't invited to my shower." With that, I turn on my heel, sweeping out of the room.

When I hear the sudden, frantic flurry of movement behind me, my lips curve into a smirk.

But before I even reach the door, my phone goes off, making me freeze. A tight ball of anxiety forms in the back of my throat. It's a holiday. Seven in the morning. I just had a public appearance, followed by something interesting and sexually new to me.

If Ted were going to make contact, this is when he'd do it.

It's the only reason I pad over to my discarded pair of shorts, bending down to fish my phone from the pocket. From my periphery, I see the guys all watching, waiting.

When I see the name on the screen, I release a hard breath, shoulders deflating. "It's my mom," I tell the guys, answering.

"Storybook!" my mother greets, sounding bright eyed and annoyingly bushy tailed. "I was afraid it'd be too early for you to answer. Did you have a fun New Year's Eve?"

I look over at my men in various states of undress, Dimitri hopping into what I'm pretty sure are Killian's boxers. "Uh. Yeah, I definitely had a good time."

"I know you're in college now, so I won't ask what antics you got up to." In the background, I hear movement, shuffling, the jingle of keys. "I hated the thought of waking you, but I wanted to catch this New Year's sale downtown. I just need you to ask your brother a quick question for me."

I wince at the word. "Killian?" His head snaps up at the sound of his name, gaze locking to mine.

Mom explains, "It's just that Daniel hasn't told me a thing. I need to know how formal this banquet is. Is it a black-tie affair, or something more casual? I'm heading out now—the doors open at eight sharp—and I thought it'd be a good opportunity to buy something nice."

I don't suppress my eye roll. Undoubtedly, my mother already owns an extensive wardrobe. I cover the speaker and lift my chin at Killian. "Mom wants to know the dress code for the banquet."

"Nothing," is his answer, eyebrows crouched low. "I already told him I wasn't going"

"Well, she thinks *they* are."

The room falls silent as Dimitri and Tristian both wait for his response. Killian's gaze holds mine, jaw going sharp and tense, and I almost wish I could turn the clock back nine hours. It's taken a single minute for it to all come flooding back. South Side. Ted. Football. Injuries. And that's only the stuff I know about.

"Story?" Mom asks. "Are you still there?"

I sigh, looking away from Killian's tense face. "Put away your fur, Mom. Killian's skipping the banquet."

"Skipping?" She gives a sharp, incredulous scoff. "That's ridiculous. He's the guest of honor!"

"He already told Daniel he's not going," I explain, finding my panties wedged beneath a cushion. "I guess he forgot to tell you. Sorry."

I can sense the disappointment on the other side of the phone. My mother would probably love nothing more than to get dressed up and ride the coat-tails of her successful stepson. She may be the last one to figure out those days are rapidly ending.

Her sigh is long and forlorn, as if she's expecting him to change his mind in the time it takes to empty her lungs. "Well, I guess I won't bother with a new dress."

A pang of sympathy runs through me. She didn't get invited to the Mercer party, and now she's not going to the banquet. The opportunity to attend formal social functions seems to be dwindling for the Payne household.

Primly, I reason, "You know what? You should buy one anyway. Go find something fancy and pretty. That way, if something comes up last minute, you have a solid choice."

This seems to perk her up. "Maybe you could come out with me! The campus is on the way."

"Oh, gosh, Mom. I'd love to go shopping with you this morning." I pull a face that makes Tristian bury a laugh into his fist. "It's just that I'm... well. Super hungover?"

"Oh, Story." She probably tries to sound disapproving, but she misses the mark. "I'll send you a recipe for the perfect hangover remedy. Hydrate and get some sleep."

"I will. Bye!" Before she can go on, I hang up, giving Killian a pleading look. "Are you sure you won't at least consider—"

"I think you promised us a shower," he says, giving me a look that says to drop it. "Even Rath got up."

I relent, partially because I know it's pointless to argue with Killian about this.

But also I just really, really want that shower.

THE FIRST DAY back at school is easier than I'm expecting.

Part of that is being unburdened with the worry of how I'm going to pay for it. Part of it is the three men always meeting me around campus, and the way we fit so much more seamlessly now than we have before.

Part of it is that I keep passing LDZ guys and getting the true Royal treatment.

When we run into two of them at the end of the day, I hear a loud hoot, and then, "Wrestling Queen!" Grant Patel curls his arm, flexing his bicep.

Jordan Hashford holds the door for me as we exit the student center, sweeping out an arm in a low bow. "My Lady."

Fighting down my smile, I give both of them a thumbs up. "Thanks, guys!"

"Well, aren't you a celebrity?" Tristian says, narrowing his eyes at Jordan as we pass. It takes me a second to realize why: Holding doors for me is usually his thing.

"Stop," I say, even though my cheeks heat. "They're just having fun."

What I don't say is that *I'm* having fun. Things are far too tense and dangerous to let it go to my head, but it's been a nice fantasy, walking around campus and being greeted like someone who's important. I'm no fool. I know it's flimsy and fleeting, built with something that barely resembles respect.

"Let our girl enjoy the fame." Dimitri pulls me a little closer to his side. "Those other Royal bitches are constantly getting the campus glory. It's our time."

"They're just excited it put LDZ in the lead." Killian glares at another passing group of guys over his shoulder. "But if those Beta Rho fuckers don't stop looking at your ass, I'm going to stab their eyes out."

I touch his lower back, fingertips idly pressing into the skin above his waistband. His jealousy streak seems worse lately, but I know my stepbrother now. A few soft touches can settle him, if I place them just right.

We're almost to the truck, chatting about a party the Barons are throwing over the weekend, when Killian freezes. I almost run into his back, but Dimitri stops me, pulling me up short.

"No fucking way," Killian says, voice low and tight. "No fucking way he's here right now."

It isn't until he begins marching forward that I see it: a man leaning casually against his truck, arms crossed, face tipped up toward the afternoon sun.

Nick.

When Killian reaches him, he takes a fistful of his shirt and jerks him upright, hissing, "What the fuck are you doing here?"

Nick's eyes flick down to Killian's hand, but he looks distinctly unimpressed. "Obviously, I came to see you and yours."

"Here?!" Killian's narrow eyes ping around the parking lot. "You can't be here, motherfucker. You stick out like a sore thumb!" He flicks the tattoo inked into Nick's temple, but Nick shrugs him off.

"Where else am I supposed to catch you?" His eyes find Dimitri, and then Tristian. "You never reply to texts during class. No one ever answers at your house, and you stopped coming to South Side when you buried a bullet into your old man. Turns out, hiding under a rock like a giant pussy kind of makes it hard to conduct business."

Killian plants his fist into Nick's shoulder, knocking him back into his truck's door. "No one here needs your commentary on shit you know nothing about." They stare at each other down in that way guys always do—the one that looks like they're about to kiss. The thought would make me laugh if seeing Nick here, in this world—our world—didn't make my stomach churn nervously.

Nick's the first to break their staring contest, abandoning Killian's glower to look at Dimitri. He thrusts his chin up. "It's your business I'm here about, anyway. Got a minute, or what?"

Dimitri steps forward, but I grab his arm. "What kind of business?"

Nick barely spares me a glance. "South Side business. None of yours."

"Fuck that." Tristian shakes his head. "Any business you have with him, you've got with all of us."

"This doesn't concern either of you." His blue eyes flick to each of the Lords before stopping on me. "And it definitely doesn't concern your piece of ass. So why don't you just—" Nick's words cut off when Killian's hand shoots out, clamping hard around his throat.

"If you like having a tongue," he sneers, knuckles going white, "then you want to watch how you're speaking to us." He leans in closer, voice turning deadly. "And if you like having something between your legs, then you really want to watch how you're talking to *her*."

My big brother has been quick-tempered all week. I'm not sure if it's because of his birthday—the banquet—coming up and the fact he's officially quitting football to dedicate his life to South Side, or something else, but it's like he's dialed up every impatient and threatening part of his personality to eleven.

I begrudgingly decide to intervene. "Killian, stop."

Nick reaches up to pry Killian's fingers from his throat. "You don't scare me, baby Payne. But relax, alright? I didn't mean anything by it."

Mouth pressed into an annoyed slant, Dimitri says, "Just tell me what the fuck, Bruin."

But now Nick's the one looking shifty, glancing around the lot. "Not here. You got room for one more in there, or what?" He nods to the truck and Killian makes a sour face at the suggestion. Nick gives him a cold smirk. "What's wrong? Afraid the smell of South Side will rub off on the leather?"

"Just get in," Killian growls, wrenching the back door open. Dimitri climbs in after Nick, but when I go to follow, Killian grabs my elbow, nudging me toward the front. "Up here. With me."

Christ, it's like having a guard dog.

I settle in the front with him while Dimitri and Tristian bracket Nick in the back. It's comical, the three of them crammed back there, elbows fighting for dominance. The first thing I see when I glance back is Nick's knee, jutting out of a hole in his jeans. For the first time, I wonder who he is. Where does he live? What does he do for Daniel? Why is it his brother, Simon, is all clean cut and on the road to academic excellence and Duke's royalty, and Nick is a thug?

He doesn't start talking until Killian has steered us off campus, the hum of the engine the only noise in the cab. "Word came down last night, Rath. Got another job." He makes a rolling motion with his hand. "Well, an extension of the last."

"No." I look back to see Dimitri shake his head. "My debt to Daniel is paid. I'm done."

"Wait." I turn in my seat, looking between them. "What's he talking about? What job? What debt?" From the tight set of Killian's jaw and Tristian's cold gaze, they at least have an inkling of what's behind this visit.

Dimitri gives me a shuttered look. "Baby, it's just some old shit. Nothing to worry about."

Raising my eyebrows, I say, "There's no such thing as 'old shit' when it comes to Daniel. You know that."

Nick's unsettling gaze stares me down. "At least your Lady's more than tits and fists. You should listen to her."

"That's it," Killian says, hand slamming down on the turn signal.

"Dude, chill," Tristian says before he can pull over. "Tell us what the job is so we can drop your ass off on the nearest street corner." *...where you belong.* He doesn't say it, but I see it in the curl of his sneer.

Nick turns his head, meeting Dimitri's gaze. "Daniel's merchandise needs moving again. As you know, it's a two-man job." There's a crack in his armor when he looks away, something worn and weary falling over his eyes. "Jesus, sometimes I think it's a three-man job."

My stomach fills with dread as I look at Dimitri. "What kind of merchandise? He doesn't have you running drugs or something, does he? Because you can tell him no. You *should* tell him no."

Dimitri gives me a long, blank stare. "It's not drugs," he says, but no other information is forthcoming.

I look at Tristian, who's avoiding my gaze, and then Killian, whose attention is pointedly fixed on the road ahead. The only one who'll actually look me in the eye is Nick, who lets out this ominous little laugh.

"Man, you guys haven't told her shit, have you?"

Killian snaps, "She's none of your goddamn business."

But I am, and Nick makes this clear when he jerks his chin at me. "I was supposed to fuck you that night in the pit, but Romeo over here couldn't handle it, so he paid Daddy Payne a fat stack to take my place." Sniffing arrogantly, Nick lifts a shoulder. "But you know Daniel. Money's never enough for him. He wanted something else."

I glance at Dimitri, my stomach sinking. "What did he want?"

"Officially? A favor. *Unofficially?*" Nick barely reacts to the elbow Dimitri jabs into his ribs. "Leverage, probably. He's had all of you by the balls, in one way or another, for as long as I've known him." He glances at Dimitri, and if I had to decipher the expression on his face, I'd say he looks resentfully impressed. "Except for your boy here. That's a plus to being born and bred in South Side, I guess. Everyone already expects the worst of you."

That can't be true. The whole reason I agreed to the show in the pit in the first place was to protect myself and him.

But Dimitri doesn't know that.

A tight ball of anxiety winds in my chest as I stare at him. "What did you do?"

The expression on my face must say enough, because he looks away, setting his jaw. "Daniel has another... *asset.*" He runs his fingers through his hair. It's a sharp frustrated gesture, made all the more apparent by the flat line of his mouth. "When he couldn't pin you down back in high school, the Kings found a 'Plan B'. He was keeping her out in Ms. Crane's old Avenue slums, but the Barons needed—"

"Asset." My voice feels flimsy and indistinct, but I know he hears me. He won't even meet my gaze. "You mean another girl. A *prisoner.*" The tension in the cab of the truck is so thick that it stalls out in my lungs.

No one says *anything.*

Killian parks the truck, but I don't even think to wonder where he's taken us. Not until I wrench the door open to a large, empty parking lot in the warehouse district.

Dimitri exits the truck next, reaching for me. "Story," he begins, but I flinch away.

"And you're moving her around like *merchandise*? You know what that is, right?" My eyes must be an inferno when Dimitri finally looks at me. "That's human trafficking. You're a fucking trafficker, Rath!"

His head snaps back at the use of his nickname. "Don't fucking judge me, *Sweet Cherry.*" There's a sharpness to his sneer that anyone else would call cruel. But I know him well enough to hear the stung, wounded thing within it. "I had no idea what I was getting into when he told me to do it, and I didn't have a choice." He throws his arms out wide. "Debts get paid! The fuck do you want me to do?!"

"What does *he* want you to do?! He won't stop. You know he won't! Which means you're involved with trafficking some poor girl for whatever Daniel has planned for her, and he has proof of it!" I press my fists into my stomach, a wave of nausea rolling over me. "I can't believe you'd do something like this."

"Story," Killian says, meeting us around the front of the truck, "This isn't just some random chick we're talking about. It's Lavinia Lucia. Do you know who she is?"

"Lucia." I blandly repeat the name, a memory sparking in mind.

Killian nods. "The King of the Counts, Lionel Lucia. She's his daughter."

I gawk at him. "That makes it worse! He'll come after us!"

"You don't understand," Tristian says, slamming his door. "He knows. He's involved. *All* those fuckers are involved. There are some parts of this game you have to play, regardless of who gets hurt."

"Really?" My face screws up in disbelief. "That's all women are to you? Collateral damage in your bullshit game? Is that all I was when he put me in the pit?"

"Don't be dense," Killian snaps, fisting his keys until his knuckles turn white. He thrusts a finger at Dimitri. "Rath fought for you! I put a fucking bullet in my father for you! We take care of our own."

"And this girl? Lavinia?" My horrified gaze passes between them. "Who takes care of her?"

"I do." Nick slams the truck door, stalking forward with a hard expression.

"You?" I bark an incredulous laugh. "The guy who was going to fuck an unwilling girl in front of a hundred strangers, just because his boss gave him the order? Yeah, you're a prize. She must feel so reassured."

Dimitri shakes his head. "Story, she's not our problem. And in case you missed it, we have plenty of our own."

"Correction," Nick says, shooting Dimitri a look. "She's *your* problem. At least until we get her moved into the Hideaway."

Disgust roils in my gut so sharply that I stagger back, voice cracking. "The Hideaway? They're imprisoning her in Daniel's *whorehouse*?"

I always knew he wanted me for something nefarious and perverse, but seeing it so tangibly laid out in front of me is like a slap to my face. That's what he wanted me to be. A little doll to lock away, ready to be used and exploited.

The steel veneer over Dimitri's expression crumbles at whatever he sees in my eyes. "Baby, come on."

I let him drag me into his chest because I'm weak. I breathe in the scent of him, cool against his leather jacket, and am selfish enough to let it soothe away the jagged edge of betrayal. "She's there because I'm not," I whisper, begging him to understand. If I hadn't run—if I'd let Daniel take me, have me—then maybe this girl would be living a nice, normal life. Maybe I've set something into motion. Something terrible. Something *unconscionable*.

"She's there because her father made the choice." He touches the back of my head, pressing me close. "This isn't on you."

But it is. I feel it in my bones. "We could get her out, couldn't we?"

Killian is the one who answers, voice sounding closer than I expect. "If it were just my dad, then maybe we could. But, Story..."

"It's the Kings," Tristian says, and I know when I feel a flutter against my neck, it's his fingers, sweeping my hair back. "All of them, combined. They're too big."

Of course, they're right. Daniel and Saul Cartwright are the only Kings I've met, but even facing down the two of them at once seems a daunting task. All five Kings, with their combined power and influence? It isn't just David and Goliath. It's David and MechaGoliath.

Grabbing onto Dimitri's jacket, I beg, "Please don't do this."

His chest swells with a stilted inhale. "Who would you rather be there? Me or some other asshole? You know I'm not out to hurt this chick." He rubs my back, ducking down to speak close to my ear. "I can't say the same for anyone else Daniel would send. Guys like Ugly Nick are a dime a dozen."

He has a point. It's just difficult to acknowledge it. "Then promise me after this, you won't deal with him anymore. Any of you."

Killian sighs. "It's not that easy."

"Because he's your dad?" I turn my head to peer at him above Dimitri's arm wound around my neck. "That hasn't mattered in a long time."

"It's not that." He huffs, shifting his weight from foot to foot. "Look, he gave me a deadline, okay? To figure out who contracted Ugly Nick and killed Vivienne. That day we went to see him, he told us..." He holds my gaze, finishing reluctantly, "Story, he thinks it's you. All of it. Ted, that guy back in Colorado, the threats, Viv..."

"What?!" I tear myself away from Dimitri, lava sparking in my blood. "He thinks I've been stalking myself for the last three years?"

"It's just convenient for him," is what Tristian says, looking almost as angry as I feel at the accusation. "If you're the person behind this, then it solves all his problems."

"That's convenient for us," Dimitri says, shooting him a brash look. "We need to face it. Shit looks bad from where he's sitting." To me, he carefully adds, "Think about it, baby. You're the only one who's ever talked to this guy. He waits until you're alone to make contact. You were gone when Viv was murdered. You were the only one home when you found that finger in the hallway." When my jaw drops, he lifts a hand, stopping me. "I know it's not you. I'm just saying, it seems like this guy is hoping we'll think it is."

"It doesn't matter," Killian cuts in. "My dad thinks it's her, so he's not looking for the real motherfucker. It's up to us."

Suddenly, my body feels too heavy to carry. Unthinkingly, I drop to perch on the concrete parking bumper behind me, dragging my palms down my face. "When's this deadline?"

Killian gives me a wary look. "Saturday." Right. His birthday. Probably another reason he doesn't want to go to that banquet. He insists, "I'm not worried about it. If he comes for you—"

"If?" Nick interjects, looking bored. "There's no 'if' here, Payne. Your father is pissed. He's out for blood." He gestures at me. "*Her* blood. He would've made her pay it off on her back if you three hadn't pissed all over her, but that ship has sailed."

Killian locks his jaw. "Bruin, I swear to Christ—"

Nick doesn't back down, even though Killian looks like he may actually break his spine. He steps forward and says in a low voice, "You need to listen to me. It doesn't matter if you prove who really did it. It doesn't matter if you find a smoking-fucking-gun. The dirt he's got on your Lady will bury her six feet under." He looks at me, a hint of pity in his eyes. "I've seen the file he has on you. So have your boys here. It's so thick, it's bulletproof."

"Then we don't actually need to bring him a suspect," Dimitri says. "We just need to get all the dirt he has on her, and destroy it. Buy us some time."

Nick barks a sharp laugh. "Not a chance. It's in his highly fortified office building. Locked in the secret compartment in his desk. There's so many locks and security measures between you and it, you're better off finding a mole."

Killian's eyes flick to the other Lords. Something I can't interpret passes between them.

Nick takes the lull as a chance to leave, turning away from the truck. "Rathbone, meet me at ten. You know the place. Lady, stay safe." He spins on his heel and walks off like he doesn't feel the fire of three dragons breathing down his neck.

"Well." Tristian speaks first. "I guess we know what we have to do."

"Get the dirt." Dimitri shrugs like such a suggestion is easy.

"Nick is right." Killian rubs his temple. "There's no breaking into that office, guys. Trust me on that."

"That's the beauty of it," Tristian says, clapping Killian on the shoulder. "Maybe we won't technically need to."

His grin is full of a malevolence that sends a shiver down my spine. I don't know what it's about, but I know whatever it is, I'm either going to hate it or love it.

I HAVE THIS bad habit.

I never seem to leave anywhere with my hands clean. The trail of incriminating bullshit I leave in my wake…

It's not intentional, but Nick was right. It's enough to bury me. I'm surprised it's taken him this long to gather it all up into a weapon jammed beneath my chin. It's the only reason I don't object to the plan they come up with—even though it's completely insane—and I'm betting they realize it. It's what I'm thinking about later that night, sitting on the front stoop. Because I'm waiting.

Waiting is all I ever do these days.

The door opens behind me, but I don't need to turn to see who it is.

It's almost ten.

"Colder than a witch's tit out here," Dimitri mutters, shrugging on his leather jacket. There's a crinkle and a '*shnick*', and then the glow of the flame as he lights the cigarette hanging from his lips. "You should go inside. Tris or Killer can warm you up." When I don't answer, he exhales a plume of smoke, his dark eyes fixed to me. In the shadow of night, he looks like a wraith, nothing but a sharp slice of distant headlights to make out the curve of his jaw. "Or you can go upstairs. Sleep in my bed."

I tighten my arms around my middle. "Do they hurt her?"

The question makes him pause—only for a split second. "I don't think so. Supposedly, that's why I'm the one on the job. No one's supposed to touch her. Kings' orders." He makes a small scoffing sound, reaching up to rub his chest. "Honestly, she's a bit of a bruiser. Kicked the shit out of me." Quieter, he adds, "I think they're saving her for something. It's like she's just..." The ember on his cigarette makes a zig and a zag with the flick of his wrist. "...being kept. For now."

"I know." Finally, I look up, meeting his gaze. "I know exactly what they're keeping her for."

It's always the same thing. It's not even surprising or original. It's the reason Daniel was so interested in me in the first place. It's the reason his son, raised on his own bullshit ideals, was so obsessed with it. It's the reason Daniel isn't interested in me anymore, since I'm unable to be an 'asset' to him.

"It's because she's a virgin."

In a way, that's good. It buys us time. Daniel is far too busy right now to capitalize on it, and even though I have no idea what the other Kings want from her, I'm betting Daniel's endeavor comes first. That means she's safe.

For now.

Sighing, Rath bends down to peck me on the lips, fingertips cold on my cheek. "Don't wait up for me."

"Thank you," I blurt, grabbing his jacket before he can move away. "I don't think I ever said that, but...thank you. For what you did for me in the pit. For giving Daniel all that money. For protecting me."

He crouches, eyes searching my face, and then reaches out to tuck my hair behind an ear. "You don't need to thank me for that. It wasn't exactly a choice."

I nod, understanding. It wasn't exactly a choice to agree to it, either. "Still." I tip forward to kiss him again—this time slow, full of a weight that we don't have nearly enough time to get into.

He must sense it, too, because he pulls away with a sigh, thumbing my jaw. "Chin up, baby girl. It'll all work out. You'll see."

"Be careful," I say, trying on a smile that feels just as fake as it is.

He answers, "Be in my bed when I get home." I watch him walk away—the shape of his body, the lazy rhythm of his gait—and decide to take his advice.

I find Killian in his bedroom, curled over his desk as he jabs the keyboard. Killian always types like he's engaged in a battle to the death with his laptop. It used to drive me crazy in high school, because I could hear his aggressive fingertip-punches through the wall like a semi-automatic going off.

Without looking up, he asks, "He leave?"

Nodding, I lean against the doorjamb, tugging the ends of my sleeves over my fists. "You know it's a King, don't you?" I wait until Killian looks up, a confused crease pinched in his brow to clarify, "Ted."

Killian leans back in his chair, holding my stare. "The possibility had occurred to me."

I enter the room, dawdling in front of his dresser. "It all makes sense now that I know what Daniel wanted me for. Or, at least, who he wanted me for." I turn to him, smiling unhappily. "That just makes everything a lot harder, doesn't it?"

He gives me a slow nod. "Maybe."

If it is a King, Saul Cartwright or one of the others, that means evidence will be hard to come by, and even if we somehow find any, Daniel will either not believe us, or look the other way.

"I should be the one to go tomorrow," I decide, thinking of the plan they'd worked up earlier. "It should be me."

His brows crouch low, a dangerous expression crossing his face. "How the fuck do you figure?"

"You're closest to the Kings because of your dad. We need to protect you from suspicion." Shrugging, I fiddle with the change on his dresser, arranging it into a flower. "But no one knows about us. I mean, your dad, obviously. But other than him?" I glance at him through the mirror. "No one knows we're..." I struggle to find a word that fits, settling lamely for, "together."

He frowns. "What are you talking about?"

"Dimitri and Tristian," I explain, turning. "They take me places. They treat me like their girlfriend. Everyone's seen us together. Kissing. Touching. But you aren't like that. I mean..." I look away, irritated that this isn't coming out right. "When we're at home, you are. But you're not public about it. I'm just saying, if I do something, almost no one would suspect that you're connected."

I immediately regret saying it, because it digs at something raw and tender inside my chest to catalogue all the touches he hasn't made. The good luck kiss he never gave me before the Screw Year's Eve match. The way he looks at me at parties, over the press of the crowd, never pulling me close. It isn't a big deal. It's not like I need another leg lifted to piss on me.

"Well, I can't just..." There's a long beat of silence before Killian speaks again. When he does, the words are awkward—quiet, like a secret. "Story. People think you're my sister."

My eyes jerk up to his. "People think I'm a whore." It comes out more sharply than I'm intending, but I don't regret it. "That doesn't stop me from walking with the three of you. I'm not so cowardly that I let what people think stand between me and something I want." I watch the words hit his eyes, tightening at the corners. It makes my stomach sink, because the last thing I want tonight is another fight.

"You're right," he says, surprising me. When he reaches out, tucking his finger into the belt loop on my jeans, I let him tug me closer. "I'm a coward."

"I didn't mean—"

"Yes, you did." He pulls me into his lap, straddling him, hands firm on my hips. It's rare anymore that we're this close—not like this. Alone. Not fighting. From here, I can see the freckle on his temple. The sweep of his eyelashes. The texture above the dark circles settled beneath his eyes. "Rath thinks he's dumb because of all his bullshit reading problems, but you want to know the truth? He's the smartest person I know." He tucks his thumbs beneath my shirt, hitching me closer. "It's not book smarts. It's the useful smart. You know he only needs to listen to a song three times before he can play it?" Killian shakes his head. "Rath will always be good at what he does. And Tristian..." His eyes drop to my chest, finger hooking in the neck of my shirt. He tugs it down just enough to expose the 'T' carved there. "He'll always be a big deal around here, because he's a Mercer." One of his eyebrows arches. "And because he's a fucking psycho."

I breathe a laugh, winding my arms around his neck. "Just a little."

He palms the small of my back, continuing, "Having him at your side will open doors for you, whether you want them or not. But I'm not worth tying around your neck. Not like that. Not anymore."

I watch that dull glimmer pass through his eyes—this thing he feels is truth—and lean in to speak against his lips. "Bullshit."

The kiss is the strangest thing.

It's slow and sweet, completely void of the sting I'm used to with Killian. Even when he grabs a thick handful of my ass and drags me up over the bulge in his lap, it's without the usual hostility. That doesn't make it any less gut wrenching, a sharp, white heat settling between my legs as I rock against him.

He grabs me by the back of the head, breaking away to mouth at a patch of skin below my jaw. Gruffly, he whispers, "I've been saving it," and then bucks up into me, swallowing my gasp with quick lips and an invasive tongue. "Come to bed with me and I'll give it to you," he says, chasing my mouth when I rear back.

"I can't." Despite the protest, I lift his shirt over his head, exposing the hard expanse of his tattooed chest. It's habit now to let my gaze skip over the face on his arm. "I told Dimitri I'd sleep in his bed tonight."

A dark, frustrated look passes over his face. "Then I'll come with you. He won't care."

"I can't," I repeat, reaching for the zipper on his pants. I dip my hand inside and grasp his cock, and even though I'm kissing him, I'm still saying it. "I can't, I can't. Give it to me now. Please?"

The edge of his jaw is tight beneath my lips when I descend, indulging in the coarseness of his stubble.

"You want it?" he asks, hot and heavy in my palm. "Tell me."

I wait until my mouth moves toward his ear, making sure he hears me clearly. "I want you to come inside me, big brother."

He makes a soft, rough sound before wrenching us both upright. The flurry of movement disorients me until I feel the hard edge of the dresser digging into my backside. Killian rucks up my shirt, lifts my arms, and then rips it over my head. There's a brief moment where his mouth is on me, tongue flicking my pebbled nipple, before he's spinning me around.

It all happens so fast then. I watch his reflection in the mirror as he shoves down his pants, taking out his cock, and then I'm doing the same thing. I claw at the button to my jeans, but he's the one to drag them down my hips, hands so eager that my body jostles with the force. He plants a hand into the middle of my back and pushes me down, and then he's shifting his feet, lining himself up, and shoving his dick into me.

I cry out, sounding more shocked than I should be. He feels hot and so hard, thick and right. He doesn't take it slow. Maybe I could have had that, if I'd let him sleep beside me. Maybe he would have waited until I was quiet and still, and then he might have peppered me with kisses and made love to me. Maybe he would have been sweet and tender and quiet.

The alternative isn't exactly a disappointment.

He digs his fingertips into my hip bones and fucks me. There's no other term for the way he slams into me, over and over, face frozen into a stony, urgent frown. I grab the dresser and hang on, bouncing back into him with every thrust. The force and rhythm might be punishing, but it doesn't feel like punishment at all.

It just feels like desperation.

The dresser cracks against the wall—*bang, bang, bang*—but it's not even the loudest thing in the room. That'd be me and the sharp, strained squawks clawing their way from my chest. Killian responds to them with low, ragged grunts. It's a language only we can speak.

It doesn't last long.

My orgasm arrives with an abruptness that staggers me. I slap my hand onto the nearest surface for leverage—the cold, smooth glass of the mirror—and grind back into the wild punches of his hips, shuddering out his name as it takes me.

His thrusts get harder, more pointed, and then he's stumbling into me with a final slam into my body. The best part of this is that I can feel it. His cock swelling inside me. The way it pulses as it pumps me full of him, hot and so unbelievably slick. Killian curls over my back, growling with his surge against me, muscles all coiled tight as he crushes us together, seizing through the vestiges of it.

After that, it's breathless panting and the sweep of his palm over my breast.

Maybe it could have been tender and sweet.

But this was exactly what I needed.

"Story."

I look up when he says my name, meeting his eyes through the reflection in the mirror. Ten minutes ago, I wanted to sting him. I wanted to tell him how incredibly fucked it was that he gets off on me being his stepsister, but then has the gall to be embarrassed by it in public. I wanted to tell him the real reason

I can't sleep beside him anymore. I wanted to tell him that I refuse to be some secret midnight fuck he can hide away.

Now, I just want to make sure his cum stays inside me.

"I was wondering," he says, giving me a meaningful look, "Do you still have that green dress?"

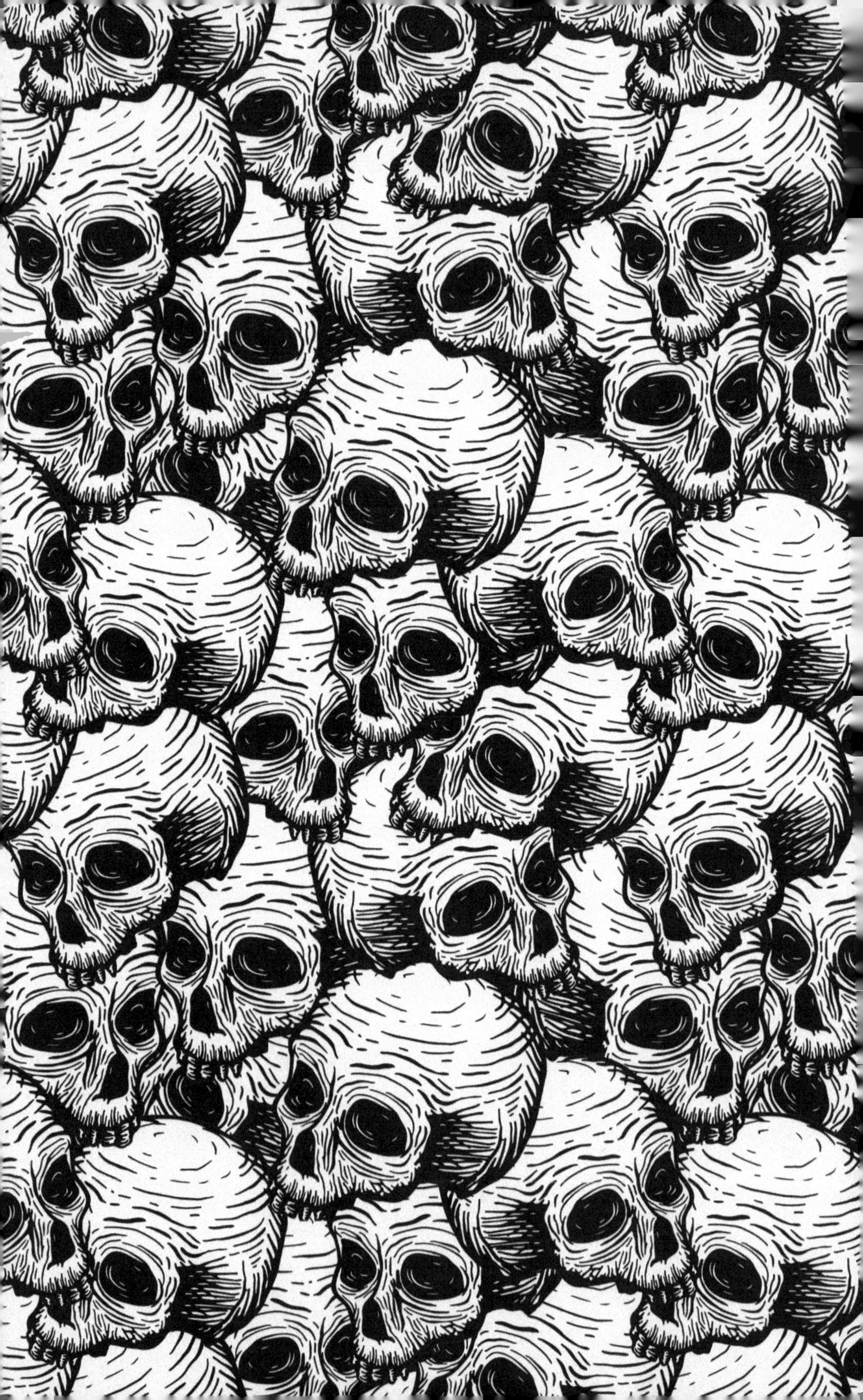

DIMITRI
RATHBONE

2 3

LOGISTICS

THE HOUSE IS dark when I get home, tired and cold and limping. This Lavinia chick sucks, and not in the wet and sloppy way we all know and love. Saying she's a kicker is the understatement of the goddamn century. My shin is going to be throbbing for days.

I climb the stairs, wincing with each hobbled step but too impatient for what's waiting for me to take it slow. I know she's there the second I open my door, sensing her in some indistinct, primal way. Sure enough, she's nestled beneath my covers, her dark hair fanned out over the pillows.

I kick off my shoes, dropping my keys, wallet, and pistol on the dresser before crossing the room to her. I'm not like Killer. Although I'm sure it's nice, I don't get off on the thought of her unconscious and pliant. This is why I climb right on top of her, still fully dressed, and cover her mouth with mine.

If she's asleep, then it's not a very deep one. She responds instantly, spreading her legs for me to settle between, hands fisting into my jacket.

"You smell cold," she murmurs, dragging me closer.

"Yeah?" I pull the blanket back, shoving it down between us. "You can warm me up."

When her eyes blink open, soft and heavy, I can tell there's a question forming in her mind. But since the thought of talking about Nick and Lavinia would definitely make my dick soft, I distract her by plunging my tongue into her mouth.

She's wearing nothing but a tank top and panties, so much warm, bare, soft skin laid out beneath me. I don't even bother undressing. I get my hand between us and shove it down the front of her panties, swallowing down her moan when I find her clit.

The second I bury two fingers into her, I pause, pulling back. "Which one?" I ask. She's slick. Someone got to her first.

She blinks up at me, chest swelling and caving with heavy breaths, but it isn't until I raise an eyebrow, giving my fingers a pointed thrust, that comprehension sparks in her eyes. "Killian."

I give a low chuckle, pressing a kiss to her heated cheek. "Was wondering who'd crack first. Tristian owes me a tenner."

She rolls her eyes, saying, "Stop betting with him," but all it takes is me ripping those panties off and settling my face between her legs to shut her up. I eat her pussy slowly, taking the time to painstakingly lick the remnants of Killer from her well-fucked hole as she bucks and gasps. There's a subtle, metallic edge to the taste of her, like he nailed her fast and a little too hard, but if it hurts, then she doesn't seem to mind. Story spreads her legs for me—thighs outstretched like she's welcoming a good friend inside—and pulls my hair so hard that I forget about the throb in my shin.

I wait until I have her right at the edge, muscles taut, thighs quivering, to pull my cock from my jeans. Before she even has a chance to miss the warmth of my mouth, I'm entering her, bottoming out with one smooth thrust.

She stares up at me with those wide, gorgeous eyes, mouth agape. "Don't tease me," she begs, shoving at my jacket. "Not tonight."

I fuck her as she undresses me in fits and starts, getting my jacket halfway off before winding her legs around my hips. It's good—it draws it out, without it being my fault. She goes to peel my shirt off, but we won't stop kissing long enough for her to get it over my head. Her heels drag against my jeans, pushing them down my thighs, but even that's half-assed, her attention diverted by the rock of my hips into her. I take it easy. Killian probably fucked her within an inch of her life, which is hot to think about, but that's not what she needs.

She needs me to kiss down her neck and tug down the strap of her top, baring her tits to me. She needs the way I hook her thighs over my arms, bending her in half as I fuck into her. She needs slow and gentle, and the dirty things I whisper into her ear. Our hips rise and fall, until hers take on a frenetic rhythm of their own, muscles quivering and clenching around me. She cries out, biting down on her bottom lip, squirming with release. I don't slow, picking up my pace, cock full from the feel of her orgasm.

"Were you gonna keep his cum in you all night, baby?" I ask, watching her tits bounce as my hips fall into hers.

She clutches me to her, hand fisted in the back of my hair. "Yes."

I nip at her jaw, panting, "Guess I'll need to replace it."

When I do, crushing her into the mattress as I come, it feels like a bolt of lightning that's been gaining energy for days. In some ways, it has. I don't know the first thing about having a girlfriend. Not the kind I'd find waiting in my bed when I got home at night, and certainly not the kind I tuck against my side afterward, sweaty and breathless and so fucking indulgent. Her thigh is soft beneath my fingers when I drag it up, across my spent erection. I think I like that, feeling her drenched pussy against my hip as she snuggles closer. It's the nasty kind of thing Tristian or Killian might object to, despite loving the thought of their cum leaking out of her. I don't have an issue with it. Stain my sheets, girl.

It takes her upwards of three minutes to finally speak the question I'd seen in her eyes before. For that, I feel reluctantly impressed with my skills. "How'd it go?"

My arm is wedged beneath her shoulders, and I use it to curl her closer, enjoying her tits against my ribs and the hot wash of breath against my neck.

"Went fine. Got her settled in."

Story's fingers worry at the hair below my navel, plucking and stroking in a way that makes my stomach cave. "Did he... put her in the pit?"

"What?" It takes me a second, too come-brained to realize she's asking about the living arrangements. I snort a laugh. "No, she has this whole, like, suite. Real boujee shit. She's comfortable, trust me."

She stiffens. "Yes, I'm sure she's a very comfortable *sex trafficking victim*, Dimitri."

Her saying my name still grabs at my spine, pulling every fiber of my attention to the way it rolls off her lips. I thought it'd wear off after so long, but it hasn't, and I have to take a moment to face it down, look it in the eye, and stroke my thumb over her flushed cheek.

Fuck, I'd do anything for this girl.

"I haven't told the guys yet," I begin, and even though I can keep my voice quiet, I can't keep it light. "We're going to make a deal with Nick."

I watch from my periphery as she frowns. "A deal with Nick? Are you sure that's wise?"

"Not even a little." My fingers trail from her shoulder to her back, tracing her spine, and she gives a small, delicate shiver. "But he'll help us tomorrow night, if we can find him a way into the Hideaway somewhere down the line."

She looks up me, cheek dragging along my shoulder. "Why does Nick want into the Hideaway?"

The thing about Story is that she can be dirty. I saw the sort of things Daniel has on her. Hard things. Dark things. Story Austin has seen some shit, and she's contributed to plenty of it. I understand about survival. Fuck, no one here understands that better than me. But even though she'd probably have trouble admitting it, she attracts the necessity of survival a whole hell of a lot.

But sometimes, she'll look at me—a lot like she is right now—and there's nothing there but pure, unadulterated naiveté. I can't speak for the others, but it's those moments that make her so hard to walk away from, because she can be dirty, but goddamn. She can also be *so clean*. A patch of light in a pitch black room.

It's not as easy as having a dark side, because not everyone can be as tidy as Tristian. Story is made up of bits and pieces—black, gray, white, red—and sometimes you just have to get close enough to find their edges.

I'm looking at one right now.

"I think..." I choose my words carefully, thoughtfully. "I think he's got a thing for Lavinia."

It's kind of bullshit. I've seen him with her twice, and 'a thing' is just as understated as calling that bitch a kicker. Nicholas Bruin isn't the kind of guy who develops 'things' for girls. He probably has an effigy of her crammed beneath his bed, and I bet he pulls it out at night and fucks its eye socket. The only pretty thing about Nick is his face. I doubt he's acted on it yet, because the Kings would geld him, but the fact of the matter is, Daniel made Nick her jailor, and that's not something you give a guy who has two settings: *'Off'* and *'demented infatuation'*. At least Lavinia seems aware enough to sense it, her eyes always tracking him suspiciously.

But Story doesn't need to know that, and from the spark of excitement in her eyes, I'm smart to leave it out. "He's going to break her out."

"Maybe," I stress, not wanting to get her hopes up. "Nick is good at throwing fists and being hired muscle, but he's about as subtle as a sledgehammer." I roll my eyes. "You know, in case the face tattoos haven't made that obvious."

"I have access to the office building," he said an hour ago. *"He makes me lock it up every night. He trusts me there. But he doesn't trust anyone with his whorehouse."* He gave me a meaningful look. *"No one but baby Payne."*

Fuck, Killer is going to bitch me the hell out.

"But he wants to try, and we can help," she says, draping herself over my chest, and there's a lightness to her eyes that I don't have it in me to extinguish.

"Sure." I don't know how true it is, but as I run my fingers through her silky hair, I know I'll try to make it as true as possible. "But we need to get through tomorrow first. Put some time between us and a solid plan. Avoid suspicion. One fucked up psycho at a time."

I wince, expecting to see that light in her eyes extinguished anyway at the mention of Ted.

Instead, it just sparks brighter. "Killian asked me to the banquet tomorrow. As his date."

My head snaps back in shock. "Seriously?"

She nods, her chin digging into my sternum. "That'll help, won't it? It's a solid alibi?"

"Well...yeah." We'd already had a plan for him, but it was shaky, at best. "I just thought he'd cut off his own dick before showing up to that thing."

Killer has this way about him. When he commits himself to something, he goes one-hundred-percent. It's part of what made him so good at The Game. He has discipline in spades. But the second he makes a choice to drop it? That's it. It's done. He doesn't want to waste one more iota of energy on it.

Story must sense my skepticism, because she sighs, turning to lay her cheek on my chest. "I think he's wanting to make a statement." Quieter, she clarifies, "About me."

Ah.

"You're his date," I say, understanding. Twirling a lock of her hair around my finger, I muse, "He must have it pretty bad."

Don't we all.

"Do you think it's dumb?" she asks, rubbing our thighs together. "Since we're...you know. Step-siblings."

I scoff. "Baby, this is Forsyth. By the time you find your table, there'll be a much juicier scandal than some guy banging his stepsister. Have you noticed that Nick is white as fuck?"

She meets my gaze again, frowning. "Yes?"

I raise an eyebrow. "Sy isn't."

"So?" She shrugs, making her nipples drag against my chest. "I assume they're half-brothers."

I tilt my hand in a so-so gesture. "Technically, but it's mostly because their mom has two husbands." Her face goes slack, making me laugh. "Like I said, this is Forsyth. Does it really surprise you that a system like this—" I gesture vaguely to the house at large. "—attracts and breeds the unconventional? Trust me, you and Killer will be nothing."

She looks floored at first, and then fascinated, but before she can pull me too deep into the subject, I cup her cheek.

"Tomorrow's going to be a bitch of a day, baby girl. Let's get some sleep."

She curls into me, her warm breath fanning across my chest. She feels safe here, which is more than I could ask for. It's a shitty world outside these walls and she's barely scratched the surface. I'll protect her as long as I can, the only way I know how; by taking out anyone that threatens to harm her.

"Where'd you find this place?" I ask, eying the dark building as Tristian puts our rental car in park. It's a shitty sedan, and we found out pretty early on that the heat doesn't work, so our breaths billow clouds into the chilled air, making the deserted alley seem even more sinister. We're tucked away behind an old strip mall far away from the Avenue, but still in South Side proper, which makes me twitchy. I scan around, looking for cameras, which is when I realize Tristian's attention is fixed on his phone. "Hey," I hiss, snapping my fingers. "Are you even listening to me?"

Tristian drags his eyes from the phone, finally looking at the drawing I've made of Daniel's office. It's a crude diagram I scrawled on the drive over with nothing but an old marker someone had abandoned in the glove compartment, and an abundance of imagination. Pure fucking art here.

A list of supplies is jotted down the side.

"I'm listening." Still, he looks back down at the phone.

"Dude, what's distracting you?" I yank the phone out of his hand, impatient and annoyed. In no universe should Pretty Nick Bruin be a better crime accomplice than my boy, but compared to last night, Tristian is looking slack as hell. I lower my gaze to the screen, trying to keep my face impassive at what I see there. "She'd better fucking know you're doing this."

On the screen, Story is crossing her room, zipping from her closet to her bed, and she's wearing nothing but a bra and panties. She's obviously getting dressed for the banquet, and from the flushed sheen on her face, is harried about it. Her hair is pinned up in wide rollers, and when she bends over to reach for something in the nightstand, I can almost see where the string of that thong is going.

"We have an agreement." Tristian snatches the phone from my hand, a defensive crease forming between his brows. "She turns on the camera when she feels like it. I get an automated alert."

"Fucking sloppy," I mutter. She can't possibly expect Tristian to remain focused when she's flouncing around her bedroom looking all cute and sexy and flustered. "Now's not the time."

Tristian rolls his eyes, but they return right to the screen. "Well, you hogged her all night. Always keeping her all closed up in your room."

"You could have come in," I point out, unable to help myself from watching Story carefully step into her green dress.

"Could I?" He gives me a skeptical look.

"Well, yeah." I reach up to scratch my jaw, nails rasping over a day's worth of stubble. "I don't keep her in there because I'm a controlling douchebag, you know. She just really likes sleeping in my room." After a beat, I muse, "She'd probably like it more if you and Killer were in it. You know, if the two of you could get over it not being a sterile icebox."

Tristian's eyebrows hike up. "I'll consider that an open invitation, then."

"Okay." I stare at him. "Good?"

We share an uncertain look, but it's Tristian who calls it out for what it is.

"Sharing a chick is kind of weird."

"But," I add, head tilting as I watch her methodically remove the rollers from her hair, "also strangely not weird?"

"Yeah, that about sums it up," he agrees, frowning. "Just, like, fucking *logistics*, man."

I give a series of fast blinks, trying to remain focused. "Okay, that's enough," I say, swiping the phone back and shutting it down. "We can't afford to make any mistakes tonight. Work now, logistics later."

He won't admit it, but he knows I'm right, which is why he stuffs his phone in his pocket and visibly writhes into his second skin. Like me, he's already wearing the uniform. Black jeans, black shirts, black gloves, and black ski masks pushed up to our foreheads—for now.

"My dad bought this shithole a few years back," he says, jerking his chin at the strip of empty shops. "He mostly uses it for storage—something off the books."

We leave our rental car parked, but still running, as Tristian leads me to the back door of the end-cap shop. If memory serves, this used to be a trashy hookah joint. Before my time, though.

It's dark inside, but Tristian immediately finds a switch illuminating a squat store room. The air smells like stale tobacco, rat poison, and diesel fuel. My nose wrinkles as he crosses to the far wall, rifling through a deep shelf I recognize the contents of.

"Jesus," I mutter, getting a good look at the stockpile of weird pyro shit. "How long have you been hoarding all this stuff?"

"You mean my fire-starter kit?" I try to hand him the list, but he ignores it, deftly plucking things from the shelves. "Since that night with Perez's truck. Daniel wasn't pleased I used his materials, so I said fuck it. Started collecting my own."

"What are those for?" I ask, nodding to a pile of weird fabric-looking scraps.

"Fabric softener strips." He picks up a container next. "I've also got smokeless gunpowder, newspaper, a bag of dryer lint, and three types of accelerant. Just depends on conditions."

"Is all this shit really necessary?" I ask, glancing at the list he'd made me write on the way over. "How hard can it be to set a fire? Douse it in gasoline and light the match."

Tristian turns to me with a disbelieving look. "We have approximately thirty minutes to send a four-story *brick* office building up in flames. That means rigging an ignition point in a vulnerable location, analyzing the air flow, and hoping like hell it can catch the asbestos-riddled, 1960s-era, toxic insulation before someone can call the dispatchers." Without breaking my gaze, he pushes a canister into my chest, ranting, "I don't question how you play Mozart, do I? No. Because when it comes to music, you know your shit. But when it comes to fires?" He shoves a box of scrap fabric at me next, flashing a wicked grin. "Brother, this is my symphony."

I sigh, "Fair enough," and let him load me up like a pack mule.

Just then, my burner phone rings.

Cursing, I balance the box of fabric and a jug of something wet and pungent to pull it from my pocket. I instantly recognize the number, answering it with a low, "What's wrong?"

"Nothing," Killian says, muttering under his breath. "About to leave for this fucking bullshit award ceremony." There's a loud, hard huff, and then, "Are you guys set?"

I flap my hand at Tristian's worried expression. "Tris checked us into his dad's penthouse suite at the Maddox towers. I ordered room service, and the girls Auggy sent us from the Hideaway are already shit-faced. I doubt they've even realized we left." The lack of reply tells me Killian is either impressed or thinks this is a terrible idea, and it's not that I don't appreciate the reluctance, it's just that... "It's time to end this Killer. I'm fucking sick of waiting around and doing fuck-all, and you know you are, too. It's not us. It's not what we do."

There's a brief pause, and then, "I know."

Tonight is Killer Payne's last hurrah as Forsyth University's celebrity athlete. It's also the night we burn our bridge with his father. This isn't just a move we're making. These are the moves that are going to make us.

"Just try to have a nice night," I tell him, following Tristian out of the building and to the car. "Show her a good time. She was excited about this, you know." I think of her on that stream on Tristian's phone, all harried and rushed—can still hear her voice from last night, soft and so reluctantly hopeful. "I know it's a shit night for you, but channel your inner Prince for a bit. Hold the doors for her. Get her drunk. Eat her pussy in the parking lot. You know." I shrug. "Romance."

"Romance," he repeats in a numb, flat voice.

Tristian gets close enough to say into the phone, "Don't fight with her."

I wrestle the phone back. "Happy birthday, man. We've got this under control. See you on the other side." I hang up and shoot Tristian a look. "Fucking logistics." This dance Killer and Story have been doing is making shit a lot more complicated than it really needs to be.

"Maybe this will be good." He shakes his head, opening the trunk. "I can't referee everything."

We're silent as we pack away all the supplies, our focus slowly redirecting to the matter at hand. Killian can romance our Lady—maybe make some goddamn headway with her—and we'll take care of the hard stuff.

Before the night is over, we'll be one step closer to dismantling a King.

WE WATCH FROM the car as Nick exits the office across the street.

It's late enough that the office *looks* deserted. There are no cars around, and almost zero traffic. South Side has a way of getting empty at night, everyone either huddling up in their homes or congregating to the more exciting places.

The seedy motels. The busy back alleys. The smoky gambling dens. Whatever dark corners the vampires around here are dealing dope out of.

Daniel's office isn't one of them.

We watch, coiled to strike, as Nick raises his arm to scratch at his shoulder.

The signal.

My knee jiggles restlessly as I watch him walk away, hands shoved deep into his pockets, looking as casual as can be. One of the perks of living around here is that people just aren't noticed. Poor people are invisible people. It works in our favor.

"Got it," Tristian says, holding up the device to prove the cameras are off. Daniel's security system isn't as high tech as the stuff the Mercers have at their disposal. "We've got ten minutes."

I set the alarm on my watch and I can't help but think it doesn't seem like enough time. Tristian is wired, though, amped up on adrenaline as we hop out of the car, lower our ski masks, and grab the supplies. I have a moment of panic when we reach the door that Nick fucked up and it'll be locked, or that when we open it, Daniel and his goons will be inside. But it goes off smoothly. The first floor is empty and eerily quiet.

"Spread this around," Tristian says, handing me the gunpowder. "Get it under the curtains and on the floor. This shit is synthetic and will go up quick."

I do as I'm told, while Tristian stashes wads of lint and accelerant-soaked fabric into various spots. Under couches, in a desk drawer, inside a lampshade, in the ceiling tiles. He's methodical and humming, his whole body vibrating. When I'm out of gunpowder, I walk over to where he's building a small bonfire, filled with combustible material, and tell him, "Three minutes."

"Perfect." He digs in his pocket and pulls out a box of matches. I admit it. I'm fucking mesmerized when he removes a single match and strikes it on the outside of the box. The match catches and sizzles, the scent of sulfur filling the air. Tristian flicks it toward the bonfire. It ignites quickly and a slow, dangerous smile spreads across his face as the fire flickers its reflection in his eyes.

With the bright gleam sparking in his gaze he looks like a fucking fiend. I'd never say it to his face, but I thought that scene with Story at his parents' party was a mistake. Tristian has the kind of wealth and privilege that South Side kids like me have dreamed of our entire lives. Secretly, I've been rubbed a bit raw at his willingness to risk losing it all. It's not that Story isn't worth it, because she is. It's that he can never really understand the magnitude. It's not even his fault.

But looking at him now, I come to this realization.

The life the Mercers want for Tristian isn't *him*. He'd blow his goddamn brains out. Tristian was born for a life of menace, the danger of the flame, the heat of the blaze, the tenacity of the ember. Probably the thought of leaving all this behind for crisp suits and glass walls is as unbearable to him as slinking back down into a South Side gutter is to me.

The heat builds and I grab his arm. "Come on, dude. Time's up."

At the door, he takes one last look, whistling appreciatively. "Fuck, man, she's a beauty. My finest work yet."

I glance back at the fire. He's not wrong. The licking flames, the way it zips from one spot to the next, up the curtain and across the ceiling… "I see it."

"What?"

"The symphony," I answer. It's a living thing, riled and writhing, reaching its spindly fingers toward the ceiling.

We step out into the cool, quiet night, the door shutting behind us. The first window shatters by the time we reach the car. The flames are on the second floor when we're pulling out of the parking lot. Sirens echo through South Side as I shift the car into third and hit the highway, but we'll be long gone by the time they arrive.

Two fiends vanishing in the night.

# STORY

ALIBI

WHEN I SLIP into my coat and turn around, I'm hit with a tidal wave of déjà vu.

"Oh," I breathe, gaping at the bouquet of flowers.

My stepbrother is holding it in front of him stiffly, but pulled to the side a bit, as if he's holding a weapon. When I just stare at them, too taken aback to form a proper reaction, he says, "You like flowers." It's not a question. In fact, it sounds more like a heated accusation.

"I-I-I do," I say, reaching out to take them. They're daisies, which isn't a surprise. What is surprising are the dark chrysanthemums scattered within the bouquet. They're absolutely gorgeous. An exercise in contrasts. Light and dark. Cheery and muted. I try to imagine him at the flower shop in town, picking them out. Did he ask for someone's advice? Or did he choose them himself?

For a second, I half expect him to yank them away and storm out of the den. Instead, he waits for me to grab them before jerking his hand away. He uses it to straighten out his tie. "We should leave soon."

I'm so busy smelling the flowers, reaching out to stroke the spiky mum petals, that I don't hear him. "I should—"

"Put them in a vase," he interrupts, extending a hand toward the mantle.

"I remember."

There's already a vase waiting there—the same one I'd used for the daisies Tristian had given me. They died long ago, before being strung up in my bedroom, pressed and currently drying. It'll be nice, I think as I arrange the flowers in the vase, to have some life back in here again.

Killian waits patiently as I fuss with it, turning the vase just-so, and once again I'm struck with the feeling I've done all this before. Only that's not quite right. There's a nervousness here that wasn't present the night I escorted Tristian to his family's Christmas party. I can hear it in the way Killian is shifting restlessly behind me, buttoning and unbuttoning his blazer, only to button it once more. I can see it in my hand's tremble when I go to pick up my clutch purse. I can see it in the lurch of his eyes when I turn around, rising from my ass to the flowers on the mantle.

Assuming what some of the nervousness is about, I pull the ribbon from my purse—the one he'd tied around my wrist on New Year's Eve—and offer it to him. "For good luck."

He stares down at it, but when he reaches out, he just uses his fingers to close my fist. "I wasn't lending it to you. I was giving it back." I tilt my head in confusion, and he releases a slow breath. "You wore that ribbon in your hair, the first time you came to one of my games."

"Really?" I blink, trying to place it in my memory. "Tied around my ponytail," I suddenly remember. It used to be a far more vivid shade of cobalt blue; our high school's spirit color. "I thought you didn't want me there," I admit, giving a confused laugh. "You were so grumpy all night."

His mouth twists into a rueful line. "I was pissed because I won," he confesses, still holding my fist in his hand. He looks down at it, as if lost in the memory. "I remember thinking I won because you were there, and it made me..." He shifts his shoulders uncomfortably. "I mean, people can leave. I didn't like the thought of giving you that much power."

The conclusion is automatic, pieces clicking into place. "So you took my ribbon. Something you had control over keeping."

He shrugs. "It's the same with the others. The scrap of wire is one of Rath's old guitar strings. Tristian offered me a piece of gum on game day, freshman year. The baseball card was something Ms. Crane gave me when I was little." He slides his eyes to mine, voice wry, "She said football was for little pussy barbarians, and that real men learn to hit balls with sticks."

I give a little laugh, imagining the words were probably more colorful. Unflinchingly, I take the ribbon from my palm and grab his wrist, looping it around. "Well, thank you for returning it, but I like being your good luck charm." He stands still as I tie it, pulling the sleeve of his blazer down to cover it.

He buries that hand in his pocket, less like he's hiding the ribbon and more like he's protecting it. "Ready?" he gruffly asks.

"As I'll ever be." I shoot him a shy smile when I touch the crook of his arm, feeling how we fit together like this. Formal. Proper. Lovers more than step-siblings. His amber eyes drop down to my hand, a crease forming between his brows. Before I can think to doubt the gesture, he reaches up to place his hand over mine, tucking it further into the space between his bicep and body.

Meeting my eyes, he says, "You look... really nice."

It's not like its anything special. I'm wearing my hair down tonight, but he's seen me in this dress. These shoes. This makeup. Still, try as I might, I can't detect a trace of mockery or insincerity in his words.

"So do you," is my response, and this time, when I smile, the hard lines of his face soften—ever so slightly.

It's nothing like it was with Tristian.

But it feels just as right.

THE BANQUET IS one of those fish or chicken events held in the ballroom of a hotel not far from campus. It's not just football—every sport is represented, and they're segregated by tables. When we take ours, I'm startled by Killian lunging ahead of me, pulling out my chair. I give him a quick blink, but recover quickly, taking my seat with a nervous grin.

Around us, the small gymnasts and cheerleaders pick at their plates. The basketball team towers in the corner. The rowing club is up front, sounding like the rowdiest of the bunch. Mixed in are tables filled with coaches and their wives, and an assortment of administrators, press, and important people. Our table is crowded with broad-shouldered football players and their dates.

Marcus is one of them. "May I say that you look stunning tonight, Lady?"

"You may," I answer giving him an exaggerated nod. Marcus is on our list of suspects, but truthfully, I don't see it. I just don't get a creepy vibe from him, and these days, I consider myself a bit of an expert.

"That dress does great things for your shoulders," he adds, dipping his head appreciatively. From the three empty glasses in front of him, plus the way he somehow misses Killian's glare, Marcus is way ahead of us on the booze. "I'm sure everyone thinks so."

"Not if they know what's good for them." Killian keeps glaring, but the words lack their usual bite. Come to think of it, since the sex last night, he seems to have lost a lot of that temper.

I can't stop myself from poking the beast. Just a little. I bat my eyelashes at Marcus. "Are shoulders what you find most attractive in a woman?"

Marcus gives a scoff that's just this side of sloppy. "No offense, Lady, but the only part of a woman I find attractive is her brother." My eyebrows shoot up, but when I swing my gaze to Killian, he's rolling his eyes.

"He's gay, Story."

My jaw goes slack. "Ohhh." This is news to me. Massive, unexpected, spreadsheet-changing news.

"Don't worry." Marcus leans back in his chair, eyes roaming the room. "Killer here isn't my type. Way too uptight."

Killian drapes his arm over the back of my chair, face blank. "I'm everyone's type. Now shut the fuck up."

I soak that news in, but the more I think about it, the more it makes sense. No wonder Killian trusted Marcus with me most, out of all the LDZ guys.

Over the next hour, Killian sits stiffly next to me as President Whittmore hands out awards. Marcus gets one for the highest GPA in the football program, and when he stumbles on the steps up to the stage, a spattering of obnoxious applause erupts from various tables. LDZ, I eventually realize, is scattered throughout the athletic programs. Marcus brings the award back to the table and lets the other players 'ooh' and 'ahh' over its cut glass and etched words.

But it's a trinket compared to what Saul Cartwright hauls up to the podium.

I've spent the last hour staring at the back of his balding head, but the moment he breathes into the microphone, my body goes rigid.

"I'm sure you all know by now," he begins, voice sending a slimy shiver down my spine, "that Forsyth's football department has had an excellent year. And that's what I want to talk about right now. Excellence." The more he talks, the more wound my muscles get.

I watch from my periphery as Killian slides his arm from the back of my chair, hand disappearing beneath the table.

A second later, I feel it on my thigh, thumb sweeping soothingly against the satin of my dress.

"Our player of the season is someone who excels," Cartwright is saying, "both on and off the field. Tonight, it's an honor to personally present this award to star quarterback and all-around Forsyth royalty, Killian Payne."

A rush of chants swells from the same smattering of people who'd laughed at Marcus before. LDZ is shouting, "Killer Payne! Killer Payne!" and I barely get to give his hand a squeeze before he's rising from his seat, buttoning his blazer, and stalking up to the stage.

There's a moment when Killian approaches the podium, reaching out to shake Cartwright's outstretched hand, that I notice the tightness in his jaw. The belligerence in his eyes. The way Cartwright's eyes narrow in response.

If I had to guess, Killian is crushing that man's hand.

He doesn't even look at the award he's handed, setting it heavily onto the wood of the podium before looking out over the room. Now I'm tense for an entirely different reason, wishing I could be beside him. Wishing I could tell him he doesn't have to do this. Wishing I could see the softness in his eyes I'd put there earlier, with nothing but a smile and a tentative touch.

Now, his face is hard as stone.

But he's looking right at me.

"When I was young," he begins, bending his neck to speak into the microphone, "people used to tell my father I had a problem. They'd complain about me being too aggressive. Too angry. Too physical." There's a pause, but he holds my shocked gaze, adding, "Among other things."

"Too sexy!" one of the LDZ guys in the back shouts.

Killian pays no attention to it, addressing the room in a somber voice. "But out on the field, there's no such thing. You can be angry. You can tackle some guy from thirty yards out and absolutely crush him, and afterward, he'll shake your hand. Your coach will tell you 'good job.' The student body will start calling you by a cool nickname. Your parents will hang your jerseys and brag about you to their friends." There's a murmur of agreement from our table in particular, but it doesn't last long. "I think I'll always appreciate this game the most for giving me that. For allowing me to point my anger at something that weighs two-fifty and is wearing armor. For showing me I have power that's all my own. And I'd like to thank someone else," he says, dropping his gaze to the award, "for helping me realize I don't need it anymore."

A grim hush falls over the room, and even though I see Marcus' gaze flick to me, everyone else's is plastered on Killian and the tense line of his mouth.

"This week, I'll be formally withdrawing from the Forsyth athletic program—" He pauses at the swell of protest from the crowd, but quickly recovers. "—to pursue a different path, both at this school and in my life." He lifts the award, rushing out a hasty thanks, and then steps away, brows set low as he lumbers back to the table.

I'm stunned. Not because he quit the team, or even that he announced it. It's the realization that football meant so much more to him than just some dumb game that gave him the glory to escape his father's plans for his future. It's the knowledge that this is an even bigger sacrifice than I thought it was.

When he takes his seat, flashing me a glance, he shakes his head. "Don't."

It's only one word, spoken quiet and soft, but it makes my heart twist. There isn't a trace of bitterness in it. This is a man who came to terms with the decision before I even realized he was making it.

Instead, I reach beneath the table and cover his hand with mine, hoping it's a distraction from the football players casting him deep, betrayed frowns. "You didn't have to do that tonight," I say, leaning in close.

He answers with a shrug, picking up his glass of champagne. "We're here to build an alibi. Everyone will remember me being here now." He flips his hand, pressing our palms together, and squeezes. "And you, too."

When I think about it like that, it's genius.

"How long do we need to stay?"

The words I whisper into Killian's ear might feel rude, except I can tell he's just as anxious as I am. President Whittmore has been slow to wrap this up, talking for twenty minutes about the outstanding achievements of the school's athletes, a clear attempt to drum up boosters and donations from alumni. I've tried my hardest to relax and not think about what Dimitri and Tristian have been doing all night—Killian's speech had certainly been a distraction—but now my neck is itchy and tense, and my palm feels clammy against his.

"I'm waiting for their text," Killian says, releasing my hand to rest his arm on the back of my chair. He keeps his voice a hushed whisper, leaning in to breathe it against the shell of my ear. "They're fine. You know that, right? In and out. Nothing they can't handle."

I turn my head, so close to catching his lips with my own. "You act like they're professional cat burglars or something."

"They may as well be," he says, eyes searching mine. If there was any ambiguity about what we are to one another, it will be wiped clean when he dips down, brushing his mouth against mine. "Rath's been picking locks since he was seven. His brother Alessio taught him. And Tristian? You know what a nosy bastard he is. He started breaking into the Vice Principal's office in middle school, reviewing security tapes, changing grades on the servers." He tucks his fingers under the back of my dress. "That doesn't even get into the fires. He was into all that shit before he even met me."

He's playing it cool, but I know he's worried. His knee keeps bouncing under the table and he's checked his phone a million times. I've had to keep our clasped hands on his knee for the past half hour just to keep the silverware from bouncing off the surface. "I'd feel better if I was driving the getaway car."

"Well, I feel better having you by my side."

Changing the subject, I give his thigh a subtle rub. "You deserve that award you hid under the table."

"Probably." He shrugs, looking away from my mouth. "It's just going to make my retirement that much more complicated. Marcus looks like I just stabbed his puppy."

It's not as bad as all that, but he keeps shooting Killian these small, sullen looks. It's a big deal, and one day, when we've both gained some distance from that tension sitting in his spine whenever he sees the award, I want to ask him about it. Football, his anger, how he knows he doesn't need it anymore, and if I'm the person who's helped him realize it. But for now, there's a big picture, because South Side is calling.

Literally.

Our phones vibrate at the same time, but I don't bother pulling mine out, watching as he thumbs the text open.

Rath: *237*

"What does that mean?" I ask, shifting nervously.

But the relief is clear in Killian's eyes as he tucks the phone back into his pocket. "It's the city penal code for 'mayhem'. If you recall, Nick's got it tattooed down his temple because he's got all the class of a vandalized bathroom stall." He meets my gaze, fingertips skating down my shoulder. "It means it's done."

I'd like to say all the tension drains from my body, but I'm not as stupid as all that. This is just the beginning.

"Let's get the fuck out of here." He bends and grabs the award before standing up. I follow, offering Marcus and the others a small parting smile, trying to play it just as cool and charming as Tristian might. But I'm so eager to get out of here that it's a struggle not to sprint toward the exit.

Whittmore's voice follows us out the ballroom door, only silencing when we're in the lobby. That's short-lived, though. A group of reporters right outside the front spots us. A chorus of 'Mr. Payne!' and 'Killer!' accosts us.

"Mr. Payne! Can you tell us why you're quitting the team? What are your plans for senior year? Is there a chance you might return to the field next year?"

Killian grimaces as the shouts continue, turning to shield me from the commotion. "Let me deal with this. Can you grab the coats?" He cups my cheek, ducking down to press a kiss to the corner of my mouth. A burst of bright camera flashes makes me flinch. "I'll just be a second."

"O-okay." We split apart, but I look back, watching him pull himself to his full height as the first reporter asks his question. I've seen some of these guys doing press before, and they're all terrible at it. I've always wondered why they need to bother. They're good at what they do on the field. Isn't that enough?

But not Killian.

He holds eye contact, and when he answers, he projects his voice, lifting his chin in a way that would look arrogant on someone else. He has presence, exudes an authority and competence that I know Forsyth's athletic department is going to sorely miss. Football or not, watching him standing there, commanding the attention of the people before him, I know that's where he's meant to be. Leading.

I finally turn away and approach the coat check, unzipping my purse for the ticket. Unfortunately, there's no one behind the little desk. I'm peering impatiently into the closet when I hear, "The President *is* a bit dry, isn't he?"

My stomach drops at the voice.

Saul Cartwright. "I don't blame you for making a break for it. Pretty little thing like you, on a night like this? You should be out painting the town."

I wasn't surprised he was the one to present Killian's award. He's the Athletic Director, after all. But now that I know Ted is likely one of the Kings—and Saul being more likely than the rest—my heart rate jacks up to eleven.

I turn reluctantly, forcing myself to meet his gaze. "I'm in a hurry, so if you'll excuse me..."

His eyes fall to my chest, ignoring my brush off. "You look lovely tonight, Story."

I try not to let him see the way my muscles stiffen at the way he's looking at me. "Don't let Killian hear you say that. Not if you want to keep your fingers."

"Ah, yes." He glances back at his star player, so surrounded by the reporters that he doesn't even notice us. "I've heard he's become quite protective of you. The other Lords, as well. A spirited bunch, aren't they?" The smug tilt to his mouth deepens. "Not as hardy as my Dukes, but passable, I guess."

Impatient to leave, I circle around the desk and step into the closet, scanning it for our jackets. It's jammed packed, though. I can't tell one black coat from the other, but one thing is painfully noticeable.

Saul's presence behind me in the doorway.

When I turn, dread pooling in my stomach, I see him standing with his hands in his pockets, deceptively casual-looking. *Fucking stupid*, letting myself get cornered. So anxious to get back to my Lords that I disregarded everything they've taught me.

Saul's eyes flash with satisfaction. "You know, I caught your little show in the pit. That sure is some pussy you've got." From a distance, no one would know he was talking about something so crass, and so brashly. "I was... well, disappointed. You were always so pure back in the day. Those little rainbow panties..." He wets his lips, for the first time acknowledging that he remembers me from my sugar baby days. In all our interactions, Cartwright has never openly admitted it—not that he needs to. He was one of my more memorable customers, a pale, perverted face on the other side of my computer screen, plying me with filthy compliments. But I've learned that he's way more than just some old guy paying for underage pussy. He's even more than the director of athletics at this school. He's a King—the leader of the Dukes, and one-fifth of the upper echelon that keeps the Royal machine chugging along.

I clutch my purse to my stomach, willing the champagne from earlier to remain down as I frantically search for an exit. "I don't know what you're talking about."

He dips his head, looking at me through his lashes. "Oh, Sweet Cherry. Give me more credit than that. I was a loyal follower." He props his hand on the doorframe, looking completely comfortable to block my way. "If you want to know the truth, at first, I was just watching to case the goods. See whether Payne was shirking his duties. But there you were, sweetheart. The real deal." The endearment makes my chest throb. Only one person calls me sweetheart. "I was the first one to sign off on you, you know. This new girl we've got lined up..." He pulls a face, flicking his wrist. "She doesn't really do it for me. Not as cute as you are. Not as...innocent. Bustier. She's got that slutty look about her." His eyes slide down my body and he adjusts his belt, hiking it up against the early stages of a paunch. "Some men like that, I suppose. I hear she's a fighter. You're more gentle. Our sweet little cherry."

There's no doubt that the girl he's talking about is Lavinia.

But if he thinks I'll cry, then he doesn't know me at all.

It's what makes me lash out, jaw locking. "Now that you mention it, I do remember you. I remember having to force myself not to vomit up my dinner at the sight of you, jacking off like a sweaty, hairy lump of meat." I approach him, calculating how fast I can duck beneath his arm and call out for Killian. "I remember your ugly dick and your uglier face. I never forget sick, pathetic, disgusting old men."

His arm thrusts out faster than I'm expecting, palm slamming into my chest. It knocks me back into the closet, and then he's kicking the door shut, bearing down on me with a snarl. "You want to see ugly, little girl? I never forget, either." His nostrils flare, a wild look taking over his eyes. "Four long years. That's how long I've waited to get what was owed to me." He reaches down, jerkily unbuckling his belt. "This wasn't exactly what I had in mind, but it'll do, don't you think?"

"You're crazy." My heart pounds in my chest, but the flurry of thought rushing through my head is too chaotic to slow. Am I right? Is this flustered, angry man towering above me, Ted? Was it Saul all along? Is this the bastard who stalked me, sent me pictures, killed my friend? Did he send Ugly Nick after Killian? Carve those initials into Vivienne after slitting her throat? "You're fucking insane," I realize, everything coming together.

"That's what happens when some little bitch makes your balls blue for four years." The sound of his zipper—the jangle of his belt buckle slapping against his thigh—is shockingly loud in the oppressive silence of the closet, but there's no space in here. No room to move away. No way past him to the door. He's close, so close. Frozen, I keep my eyes on his face and clutch my purse against my stomach like a pathetic shield, but he just tucks his pants below his balls, exposing his half hard cock to me. "I know you let them defile your mouth and pussy, but what about your ass? I bet you haven't let them fuck you there yet. You were always such a tease."

My instinct is to fight back, but he's a tall man and I'm in these fucking heels, and even in the best of circumstances, I'm no athlete. I need to use my brain. I need to buy some time. I need some goddamn space.

I don't get any.

What I get are his rough hands suddenly grabbing at my shoulders, trying to spin me around. A wave of fury swells in my chest—that rush of red-hot instinct to fight for survival—and that's exactly what I do.

I fight.

I kick out, thrash around, open my mouth and belt out a scream. He's a solid wall against me, but I strike out anyway. Fists. Elbows. Knees. He grunts in his effort to contain me, face contorting with rage.

He reaches back before swinging. His enormous palm contacts with my cheek and the slap rocks me. My head snaps to the side. Pain explodes up my cheek, throughout my skull, and I have to be still then, bringing my arms up to cover my head.

It gives him the opening he needs to twist me around, his hand clamping hard onto the back of my neck. As I blink away the stars in my vision, he's shoving my face down into the shelf of coats and rucking up my dress.

"Like I was saying," he growls, fingers aggressive as they dig into my hips. He doesn't even sound winded. "I don't mind a little fighting. You think I'm ugly now? You should have seen me in my day, *Lady*." He sneers the title, and I fumble for my purse, thinking that I just need a few seconds. A minute at most. "I was the hot shit around here. You would have been on your hands and knees for my dick back then."

I stop fighting, forcing my limbs to go limp as I catch my breath. The crack in my voice is only half-faked as I whimper, "Okay, okay, I'll let you—"

"*Let* me?" He barks a laugh, ripping my thong to the side.

"Just don't leave a mark," I plead, planting my feet wide. "They'll punish me if they know. And if Killian gets through that door, he'll kill us both."

There's a brief pause, and then his derisive snort. "I knew you'd cave. You're nothing but a dirty whore, just like your mother." There's a sickening sound—him spitting a wad of saliva into the palm of his hand. Sick dread fills my belly as I know he's prepping himself, the wet sound of him slicing up his stubby cock filling the surrounding air. "You know I found her first? Fucked her after the bowl game, almost six years ago. Her phone rang and this picture of a sweet little girl's face came up. *Your* face. I knew right then you were meant to be our new pet." He leans into me, breath hot against my neck. "All the other Kings are married, but Daniel...well, he had himself a bit of a domestic vacancy. So I had to give the two of you up to him." My hands shake and I take the chance to dip my fingers in the open zipper of my purse. "It wasn't really a surprise when you showed up on the Daddy sites. Like mother, like daughter." His fingers graze over the bare swell of my backside and nausea mixes with my rage. "He was supposed to get you ready for us, but then you left, and look what you became? Just another predictable whore. Four years, Sweet Cherry. I've thought about this for *four years*, and if you think I'm not going to make it hurt, you're very, very wrong."

My fingers brush against the cool metal just as the spit-slick head of his cock slides between my ass cheeks.

I whirl around, pressing the barrel of the gun against his cock. It's a fast move that sends him off balance, but the bald shock in his eyes, the way he freezes, tells me he can feel the cold steel.

"Touch me again," I sneer, flicking off the safety, "and I'll blow your goddamn dick off."

Both of his hands dart into the air and he takes a step back. It really takes the steel out of the stern look he gives me. "If you know what's good for you, you'll put that gun away."

I keep it aimed at his pelvis, extending my arms just the way Killian taught me. "Oh, really? Why's that?"

His dick is still hanging out, hard and pointed right at me. "Daniel has all the dirt he needs to ruin your life. Adding in the assault of a respected school administrator?" He begins lowering his hands, tsking. "No one will believe it's self-defense. I'm a cornerstone of Forsyth's community, and what are you?

Like I said. Just another whore."

White hot rage pulses through me, a burning hatred that's been growing and growing for years, winding itself around my lungs like a sickness. It's a combination of exhaustion and pain, adrenaline and hurt. Everything he said... it all makes sense. *'You were always so pure,' 'I never forget,' 'just another whore,' 'four years, Sweet Cherry.'*

That's why I know.

I finally have him in front of me.

Ted.

I cock the hammer, letting the telltale click fill the room. "You've terrorized me for years. You've abused me, you've stalked me, you followed me halfway across the country to fuck with my head, to terrify me, to ruin my fucking life!" His eyes never leave the barrel, but I see the crease appear on his forehead.

Behind him, the door suddenly bursts open, swinging so violently that it bangs against the wall and recoils back.

Killian stops it with his foot.

There's a moment of awareness as Cartwright turns.

Killian shifts his gaze between my red face, the gun, and Cartwright's dick.

When I speak, it's a message. Not just to Cartwright or Killian. To myself. "You won't control me anymore, Ted. This is done."

Killian reacts with stunning immediacy, lifting the ten pound crystal award and bashing it into Cartwright's jaw. The crack of his bone crumbling rings sickeningly in my ears, but despite my flinch, I don't lower the gun. It's trained on him like a guided missile, jerking to the left when he rears up to tackle Killian, then to the right when Killian dodges, tackling Cartwright instead.

He takes him to the ground and straddles him, teeth bared as he pulls a fist back and buries it into Cartwright's cheek. What happens next can only be described as a brutal assault. Punch after punch, Killian red-faced and huffing as his fist rears back only to return, knuckles meeting bone and teeth. The lurching shift of his muscles, the grunts that tear from his chest with each hammering hit, the harsh lines of his face, the lava-bright brilliance of his eyes...

It's raw, animalistic power, and I'm struck with a thought that takes my breath away.

Killian has never been more gorgeous.

Blood sprays from Cartwright's mouth, sending droplets all over Killian's white shirt, and the explosion of *hate-hurt-mine-beautiful* in my chest gains a new companion. Fear.

Killian has murder in his eyes.

This isn't how we beat Ted. Not here, with witnesses, in the middle of a plan to take down Daniel. This is sloppy and impulsive, and it's up to me to salvage it. To approach the feral animal in front of me. To bring him back.

In the end, it only takes two words.

I drag in a shaky inhale, my voice a quiet, jagged whisper. "Big brother..."

Killian swings his fist, but pulls it back a hair's breadth away from making contact. It trembles, the tattoos over his knuckles almost unreadable through the blood and swelling. I'm worried at first it won't be enough, but he surprises me, opening his fist and pushing his hair back. There's a silent moment, Killian breathless and stiff, before he bends to spit in Cartwright's mangled face.

"That's for Vivienne, you motherfucker."

He lumbers to his feet, but wobbles, body solid and almost too much to support when I rush to him. It doesn't take long for him to find his footing, though, turning to me with a dark, tense expression. Wordlessly, he reaches up to brush his fingertips over my cheek. "He put his fucking hands on you."

The touch is gentle, but still smarts, making me gasp. "I'm fine," I say, grabbing his wrist.

Killian's knuckles are already turning purple.

He says, "Put the gun away now, little sister," and it's only then that I realize I still have it pointed at the unconscious mess of blood and bone on the floor. "Safety first," he quietly coaches, placing his hand over the barrel.

He's always two steps ahead. That's what makes him different. A leader. A

Lord. A future King.

Somewhere in South Side, a building is burning.

But here with Killian, it feels like the heat of the flames could never touch me.

2 5

E T C H E D

THE SECOND WE get through the door, Story's grabbing my elbow and hauling me through the dining room. "Come on," she says, but it's completely unnecessary.

I follow her like my body is magnetized.

We're both still amped up from the thing with Saul, and when we reach the kitchen, she dumps her purse on the counter; the gun clunking loudly against the granite.

Story takes my hand, inspecting it with a frown. "Does it hurt?"

I stare at her unblinkingly, flexing my fist as I catalogue the crease in her forehead. "No."

She doesn't look convinced, turning on the tap and guiding my knuckles beneath the stream of cool water. "At least it doesn't look like you'll need stitches," she muses.

It's the first time I really look at my knuckles, swollen and purpling. One is split, but it's superficial. I've had worse injuries out on the basketball court with Tris and Rath.

I don't tell her this.

I let her handle my hand—so gentle, feather-light touches, cradling my palm in hers—and watch mutely as she fusses over it. Through the fuzzy fog of *soft-warm-sweet*, I mutter, "There's some ice packs in the freezer."

Her head snaps up. "Oh! Yes, for the swelling."

"For your swelling," I correct, eying the welt on her cheek.

But before she can answer, my phone goes off with another text. I fumble it out of my right pocket with my left hand, clumsily thumbing the message.

Rath: *gn.*

She edges in close to read it, brows pulling together. "What does that mean?"

"Good night. It's another code," I explain, watching her mouth. "They're lying low for the night. Could be there are too many cops out, or they're worried about being followed back here." Her eyes spark with alarm, but I soothe it away by thumbing her chin, inspecting the welt more closely. "Don't worry. If it were something really sketchy, he would have sent a different code." Or *no code at all*, I don't say.

This seems to assuage her fear a little. "lie low? Where?"

"We talked about it last night," I assure her. "Everyone agreed that the Mercers' cabin was a good place."

She nods, grabbing a towel from the drawer and wrapping it over my knuckles. "They'll be fine then."

I realize she's saying it more to convince herself than me, but I still answer. "They're smart."

I let her fuss over me for a few minutes, even though my hand isn't that bad. If the others were here, they'd laugh at me. They'd tell me I was hamming it up to get more of those soft touches, to draw out the concerned hiss that escapes her lips when she presses the ice pack to my hand, so careful that it's barely touching it. They'd say I was being a little bitch about it.

They'd be so jealous.

After she's satisfied there's nothing left to do for my gruesome, truly tragic injury, we climb the steps together, her two ahead of me. I stare at the holes in her stockings, the tear up the back that reveals her pale skin. Her shoes hang loose in her fingertips. Her shoulders might have eased with the text and my ensuing promises, but I know she's going to be worried until she sees them walk through the door.

It's been a hell of a night.

When we get to our bedroom doors, she pauses, falling back against hers. "Do you really think that's the end of it?" The curve of her shoulders looks heavy and as tired as her eyes. "That we unmasked Ted, and all of this is over?"

I take a second to answer, because there's a nudge in my gut to be wary about it. These men, these *Kings*, are slippery as fuck. She has no idea. I don't know if there's any stopping them until they're dead. I left Cartwright a bloody mess, but he was still breathing. That means retaliation. It means a grudge that probably won't disappear until another Duke takes his crown. It means *bullshit*.

And I'd do it again in a heartbeat.

"It fits." I lower the ice pack and sweep my eyes down her body. She got dressed up so pretty for me tonight, and there was a moment there before leaving, where Rath's words seemed true. She looked so excited. Sighing, I mirror her pose, propping my shoulders up against my bedroom door. "I'm sorry it ended like that. I wanted us to have a good time tonight, not get caught up in an attempted murder."

Her bounce of laughter is more genuine than I'd expect. "I don't know. It seemed pretty on-brand for us, don't you think? Dress up, get an award, fight to the death." Her smile falters, eyes dropping. "It's probably the gods telling us something."

"Yeah, like don't fuck your sister."

She blinks at the harshness of it—the truth. We can joke all we want, but the two of us together? Nothing good has ever come of it. Even when I try. Even when I go out of my way. No matter what I do, no matter how much we sugarcoat it, we'll never be anything to one another but toxic.

Which is exactly why I say, "Good night, Story."

Her eyes flick up to mine, and if I were a more selfish person, I'd see the flash of disappointment in her eyes as proof that I'm wrong. "Night," she says, reaching back to curl her fingers around the knob of that fucking door.

I watch it close behind her, clicking softly in the silence of the hallway.

But I can't make myself move.

I've memorized the door in front of me, night after night, mapping out every grain of wood, knowing that she's behind it, if I could only get through. I know it's not right, this sick obsession I have, but I can't shake it, because it's not just about the sex. It's not even about needing to watch over her.

It's that look she had in her eyes tonight after I gave her those flowers. That shy, pleased, surprised thing that made her shine. It's that she wants me back, and for once, she's not afraid to show it. It's about her and tonight, and even if it's toxic and fucked up, it's about making sure she knows.

What she means to me.

I lurch forward, banging my bruised fist on the wood.

The door opens a moment later, the hinges whining softly. She's still in the dress, but the torn stockings are gone. Her hair hangs loose over her shoulders, and she looks at me with this startled, expectant expression.

But when I open my mouth, nothing comes out.

Her forehead creases. "Killian?"

"Tonight turned out wrong," I burst, impatient to get the words out. "Not just the shit with Cartwright, but... it didn't go like I planned."

Her expressions smoothes, blanking out. "I know you didn't want to go. But we needed an alibi while the guys broke into Daniel's office, and—"

I shift my weight, huffing. "No. It's not that I didn't want to go. It's just that my life is a fucking mess, with quitting football and my dad being so—"

"Jesus, Killian, look at me." She spreads her arms out, but they instantly fall, hanging limply at her sides. "I know a thing or two about messy lives."

"That's fair," I sigh, reaching up to push my hair back. "But when we decided to go, I thought it could be my chance to... well, you know," I stumble over my words, which is something I'm not used to. I either have something to say or I don't. Taking a breath, I try to calm the kinetic squirm happening in my chest. "I wanted it to be something special. I wanted to show up with you on my arm looking sexy and hot, and—like you were *mine*."

Her eyes search mine, frown deepening. "It *was* special. You won that award, and I might not totally get the football thing, but I'm... proud of you for—"

"Fuck! Story! Just listen!" I fist at my hair, knuckles stinging with the force. "I invited you because you're my girl, and I want...I *need* the whole goddamn world to know. I just…" My exhale sputters out, and I hate it. I hate this fucking ineffectual blathering. "I don't know how to do all the romance stuff Rath and Tris do. I can't take you to balls, or write you a song, or bring you tea and tampons when you're on your rag." She raises her eyebrow and I glare back. "Christ, you know what I mean. I forced you on your knees. I took your virginity. I shoved a tracker in your neck. I marked my initial in your chest. I gave you a fucking gun for Christmas." Put like that—yeah. I really am hopeless. I shake my head, muttering, "A gun. Jesus Christ."

Her head snaps back, outrage flashing in her eyes. "Hey! That gun came in pretty handy tonight. I love my gun."

"That's not the point." I reach out and brace myself on the door frame, chest feeling so tight that I have to force myself not to grind my fist into it. "All of those things might tell the world—tell me—that I own you, but that's not what this is about. I think I want everyone to...no." I start over. "I want you to understand how I feel."

Her shoulders straighten and she stares right at me—seeing me. Listening.

I grip the collar of my shirt and pull it apart, buttons tearing at the fabric, revealing my chest. My heart pounds, blood pumping to my ears, but I ignore both it and the puzzled look on her face as I reach into my pants pocket and clasp the smooth wood in my fingers.

I pull it out and flick open the blade. The glint of silver metal shines between us.

Comprehension washes over her features. "Killian," she says softly, using the voice she saves for calming me down. I like that voice. I like the soothing touch that follows, and I like knowing that it's only for me. But this isn't my temper showing here. She doesn't need to calm me down. I know exactly what I'm doing.

"I'm not going to hurt you," I say, disliking the cagey look in her eyes. "But I need you to understand."

I look down at my chest and find a spot in the center. It's easy to pierce the skin. I might not get off on it like Rath does, but pain doesn't bother me. I have no issues pressing the tip of the blade into my flesh, carving the top curve of the 'S'. Blood beads up, then dribbles sluggishly down my chest, but the trail is halted by Story's fingertips.

"You don't have to do that!" she rushes out, trying to catch my wrist. "I get it Killian. I understand."

"Do you?" I ask, not stilling as the knife slices through my skin.

Her hand drops, and when she looks at me, she doesn't look shocked, or even freaked out. She looks exasperated. "You love me."

She says it so plainly, so matter of fact, as if she didn't just put voice to the sick, black thing roiling inside of me.

"I love you," I repeat softly. It's not a question, but whispered devotion. It gives me what I need to finish the letter, swooping the final stinging curve, because maybe she doesn't need it, but I do. "Do you have any idea how much?" Blood spills faster that she can catch it and she grabs the hem of my shirt, pressing against the flesh with a hitched breath. I barely feel the sting. "So much that it's paralyzing. Sometimes I watch you, and I can't blink. Can't swallow. Can't breathe. I'm too busy wondering what it'd be like."

Her eyes fly up to mine, wide and stunned. "What it'd be like?"

"If you loved me back." Yanking down the sleeve of my shirt to expose my arm, I confess, "I got this tattoo not long after you left. I was so drunk that my guy wouldn't do it until I sobered up, because he said—" I pause when she touches it, blood-sticky fingers leaving a smear over the tattoo's lips. Shuddering an exhale, I go on, "He said it was a curse. That you never get your girl's name or face tattooed on you, because it'll doom you. But even when I got sober, I didn't care. I made him stay until he finished it, outline to shading. When he did, he looked at me and he said, 'Five hours. That's how long it took to doom you.' And you know what I said?" I laugh at the memory, but it's a humorless, broken thing. "I told him it actually took about ten months." I say the next words because it feels like it'd be agony not to. "I love you, Story Austin. And just so we're clear, *not* like a sister."

She looks into my eyes, her own shining with a wetness that I didn't mean to put there. "Do we have to be doomed?" she asks, voice cracking. "Or can you just stop being a fucking bummer for five minutes and kiss me?"

I catch her by the back of the neck and pull her mouth to mine in a hard, unforgiving kiss. It's teeth and harsh breaths and my blood is staining her pretty dress. But if all we're destined to be is calamity, then we'll make it the best fucking disaster this world has ever seen.

I barely realize she's dragging me into her room, her palm curled unrelentingly around my neck, but at some point, it penetrates.

She kicks out blindly, shutting the door behind us.

"You sure?" I ask, not daring to open my eyes.

She speaks against my lips, voice a mere whisper of breath. "I kept you out because everything we had was in here, buried so deep in darkness and shame. You barely touched me in public, unless you were putting me or someone else in their place." When I open my eyes, she's looking up at me, eyes wide and guileless. "I just...needed to know we could be something more than that. That you could want something more from this than how messed up it was."

I hold her face in my hands, fervently insisting, "You are so much more than that." I feel the pain of loving her in the burning cuts on my chest, but that's not what it is. It isn't surface-level. It's so deep that sometimes I think it's etched into my bones. "So much fucking more."

I grab her, lifting her off the ground. No sneaking. No darkness. Just me and my woman, together.

"The blood," she says, even though she steals a slow, wet kiss from my mouth. "It's going to get everywhere."

"Fuck it." I march on, unapologetic, as I carry her over to the bed, unzipping her dress as I go. The green satin falls away like shedding a skin, and when I lay her down, I take a second to catch my breath, knowing that she might be exposed, but no one here is more naked than me.

I look at her for a long time, drinking in every inch of her, from the crown of her head to the tips of turquoise-painted toes, and all of it is perfect. The freckle on her stomach, the scars on her chest, the discolored patch of skin near her elbow. But the best part of her, by far, is that she's awake for what happens next.

Shrugging out of my shirt—ripping off my tie—I bend, kissing down her heaving chest. I detour at her nipples, licking out to catch the pebbles on my tongue, but stay on task, dropping lower as her heavy eyes track my descent. I map her ribs with my lips, nip my teeth into the patch of skin beside her bellybutton, drag my nose along the swell of her pelvic bone. Hooking my fingers in her panties, I tug them off, so eager to spread her thighs that I miss her body going rigid.

"Shit," she says, pushing up on her elbows. "The camera. It's still on from earlier."

I glance back at the skull, imagining Tristian's eyes glued to his phone, cock in his hand. I let out a low snort. "Eh, he did a good job tonight. Let him watch."

Let him see that I can love you.

She acts all shy at first, covering her face as she laughs, but when she pulls her hands away, she sends the camera this cheeky little wave.

I turn back to the legs spread before me, zeroing in on her cunt. Aside from wanting to shove my cock into one, I've never really paid much mind to other girls' pussies. But Story's is so erotically fucking inviting, it's basically commanding a warm tongue to lap between her folds.

A good soldier follows orders.

Her thighs fall wider at the first touch of my mouth, but I still force them further apart, straining the tendons beneath my thumbs. Her body shudders beneath me when I catch her clit in a long, sensuous kiss, tongue painting loops around the swollen bud.

I'm expecting her fingers to wind in my hair, but I'm not expecting the softness of her touch—the way she strokes her fingertips against my scalp. I'm expecting the buck of her hips when I move lower, dipping my tongue into her tight hole, but I'm not expecting the drawn out mewl she makes. I'm expecting her to chase my mouth with every rise and dip of my tongue, her body telling me what she wants, what she needs.

I'm not expecting her to come undone so fast.

She comes with a body-wracking tremor, mouth opened in a silent cry as I flatten my tongue to her clit, letting her ride against me.

When I rise on my knees, swiping my wrist over my mouth, she's still trembling, and all I know to do is drop down beside her, dragging her into my chest. I don't ask if I can stay, and she doesn't tell me to leave—even though she knows I would.

She just murmurs three little words against my neck. They're words I've been aching to hear since the first night I saw her. Words that leave me feeling hollowed out and filled back up. Words that carve themselves into my skin just as deeply as her initial in my chest.

"Sleep with me."

I clutch her to me, nosing into her hair, because I don't need the brush of her hand against the front of my pants to understand what she's asking.

What she's giving.

"Always."

DESPITE THE FACT I've been waiting for this for months, long mornings spent in the shower with my hand flying over my dick as I imagined it, I somehow fall asleep, too.

I wake up with her hair in my mouth and my dick rock hard.

In the soft glow of the streetlamp through the window, I can perfectly make out her silhouette. The bare curve of her shoulder. The elegant line of her bare thigh. The curl of her fingers against my red, scabbing chest. Her tits are mashed up into my side as she sleeps, breaths steady through parted lips against my throat.

I reach up slowly, brushing my knuckles along the swell of her breast. When she doesn't move, I carefully—*so fucking carefully*—roll her to her back. She makes a sleepy, plaintive sound, curling back into my warmth. I shush her by hovering close and pausing, waiting for her to fall back into the deep sleep that makes that unhappy divot in her forehead disappear.

When it does, I dip in to whisper against her lips. "I love you."

It feels perverse to speak the words aloud—more perverse than my fingers sliding between her legs.

She's still slick, and when I extend my tongue, painting a wet strip across the crease of her mouth, I imagine she can still taste herself on it. Her thigh shifts, opening for me, and my dick throbs. She looks like an angel when I let myself take her in, and it's almost exactly what I said before. Paralyzing. In no universe should I have dominion over something so painfully sweet.

But that's exactly what I have.

Breathing hard, I fumble for my pants, unbuttoning them and shoving everything down my thighs. My cock springs free, hard and angry, bouncing against her hip. I have to force myself to slow down, to be quiet and placid, to not wake her up by slamming between her thighs like an animal.

Delicately, I knee in between her open thighs, balancing myself so the bed won't rock her awake. My cock brushes over her inner thigh, light enough to be a tickle, and it makes her twitch away, opening up wider for me. I spend a long moment slowing my breaths, because even though it's winter and her fan is running in the corner, sweat is still springing up on my neck.

Before I can even get inside her, my hand directing the base of my dick to her folds, pre-cum is already leaking out of the tip, threatening to drip onto the bed below us. But she doesn't want it there. She wants it inside her—nowhere else.

So I hastily burrow the head of my cock into her hole.

Her fingers twitch against the sheets, as if they're grasping for something. Unthinkingly, I reach for them, lacing our fingers together as I remain suspended, barely inside of her. I wait a long moment for her to fall back into slumber, and then give my hips a nudge, sinking in deeper.

I wasn't lying before, about her being more to me than some risky, illicit, midnight fuck. That doesn't mean the thrill isn't there, though. The fact that Tristian and Rath could be watching just makes it that much more heady, the way I screw my hips down into hers. I play it like a game—dig and wait, dig and wait—wondering how long I'll be able to do this without waking her. It makes my blood zing, electrified by the slack line of her mouth and her eyes moving beneath her eyelids.

When I finally bottom out, I curl over her, lifting our linked hands to her chest, nestled between us like a precious, secret thing. I don't know what it means to make love to someone, but if this isn't it, then I'll never be capable of it, because it hurts. It hurts to keep it slow as I rock my hips into hers, but the thought of disturbing it all hurts even more.

I kiss her lips just the way she'd touched my sore knuckles earlier—feather-light, gentle. The only time she stirs is when I try to force my tongue inside, so I don't. Not until I push the weight of my pelvis into hers, pressing against her clit and making her jaw go slack. It's all so easy then, licking into her mouth, tongue pushing between her teeth to seek the softness within. She's so wet and tight around me, and everything is so fucking perfect and soft and sweet that I doubt I can last much longer, already feeling my balls draw tight.

I know when her tongue moves against mine that she's waking, slowly rousing herself from the fog of sleep to curl her fingers, squeezing our linked hands. It's not like it used to be. There's no swoop of disappointment at the realization, no nagging voice in the back of my head telling me I've lost the game, no stab of insecurity that she's felt something too substantial, too tender.

There's no fear.

There's just me, moving inside her as she sleepily kisses me back, pushing a moan from her throat. I know then that I can finally pull my hips back and fuck her, and even if I keep it light and slow, her body still rocks with the force of it.

The shift from sleep to wakefulness gives me the best of both worlds, making my dick impossibly harder. Her legs coil around my waist, her fingers bend and clench, holding tight. The breathy moans, the precipice of her orgasm, heats my skin and *Jesus*, she takes it, the relentless pounding, the hungry kisses, everything I throw at her. She takes it all.

"Come for me, little sister," I demand. I'm so fucking close, and I want her to go first. I want to see her face when it happens.

I feel it first; the muscles tightening around my cock, then her jaw slacks, nose wrinkling. Her eyes flutter open and hold mine. "I love you," she says, gripping me behind the neck and pulling me forward. Her nails dig into the back of my neck and she shatters around me, stealing my breath with a kiss.

For the first time, I experience the whole of the moment. Not just the physical but the emotional. The words she says, the sensation of her pussy quivering around me, grip my heart as much as my balls, and I come, *claim*, my cock pulsing as it spills inside of her. She swallows the embarrassing, overwhelmed sound I make as I pump her full, crushing her into the mattress.

Sweaty and spent, I press my forehead to hers, my cock still sheathed in her warmth. Her ribbon's still tied around my wrist, as secure and solid as the cuff wrapped around hers, and it's easy now to speak the words.

They're no longer impossible to hold on to.

"I love you, too."

RATH IS THE first one through the door the next morning.

I run into him just as I'm coming down the stairs, dressed in the boxers and t-shirt I'd snatched from my dresser before coming down. I'm fully intending to grab coffee and something with more carbs than protein to haul back up to Story's bedroom. It's only eight. There's still an opportunity for a third round.

But then Rath comes through the door, messy-haired and manic-looking. "Good, you're up." He shrugs out of his jacket, hair flopping into his eyes as he looks down to stomp the dirt from his shoes. "It was fucking art, bro. Wish you could have been there to see it." When he glances up to flash me an impish grin, his gaze catches on my bruised knuckles—on the spot of blood staining the center of my crisp white teet—and he freezes, dread slacking his features. "Aw, shit. What happened?"

Scab opened a bit.

"Later," I mutter, passing him to enter the dining room. Story told me everything that happened with Saul on the drive home last night, but it's still too jumbled in my head to put into a coherent narrative.

Ms. Crane already has a few things sitting out. I go for the coffee first while Rath snatches up two slices of bacon and instantly pinches them between his teeth. Tristian walks in from the kitchen—he must have been parking in the garage—and comes right for me, slapping my shoulder hard enough to make my coffee slosh over the rim of my mug.

"Hey!" I growl, but he's all grins.

"Let me start by saying thank you," he says, dropping into his usual seat. "For allowing me to watch that outstanding display of game last night. You let her come first and didn't even ask her to suck your dick afterward. You've grown, man, and I'm proud."

There's a part of me that wants to punch the smug grin off his face, but he's right. I did my woman right last night and then she did me right later on. We work like that.

"You're such a fuckin' weirdo," Rath says, taking his own seat at the table. He has circles beneath his eyes, like he didn't get much sleep. I don't know if it was from watching us all night, nerves from the job, or the cabin just being kind of shitty.

They wait until I take my seat at the head of the table to start briefing me.

"Like I was saying," Rath extends a hand to Tristian. "Art."

Tristian smirks. "Flames took that fucker so fast, it was already a lost cause by the time the dispatchers called it in."

They spend a while going over the details as I sip my coffee, flexing my sore fist. Tristian and Rath both keep looking at it, waiting for my explanation, but before I can give it, Ms. Crane walks in with a plate of toast. She plops it in the center of the table and asks, "Where's the fucktoy?"

"She's still asleep, so keep it down." Rath scowls, although it doesn't stop him from snagging a slice of the toast. "And don't call her that."

"She doesn't mind me calling her that." She starts filling the three empty mugs with coffee, even the one for Story. "My police scanner was going off all night. Shit went down in South Side. Arson, four alarm." Her eyebrow raises at Tristian. "You have anything to do with that?"

He lifts his mug of black coffee and takes a slow sip. "You need to mind your own business."

She slams down the pot. "This is a delicate ecosystem, you little cunt-weasels. Any aberration, any ripple of unrest, and the whole house of turds starts to crumble. Do you get that?" She points at the ceiling. "You brought a deviation into this house. She was supposed to be disposable, but look at you three. So determined to keep her that you're happy to burn this place to the ground. Don't," she snaps, thrusting an accusing finger at Tristian, "deny it. I'd know that fucking address anywhere."

"What do you care?" I ask, leaning back in my seat. "You're miserable here. If Daniel has less control, then things could ease up on all of us. Especially you. He needs to understand that he doesn't have us under his thumb. We're not just pawns in his game. We're players in our own."

"You think you have all this figured out, don't you?" she sneers, snatching up a towel. "Boys playing at being men. There's going to be hell to pay for what these two did last night. And there's going to be even more for what you did." She jabs her finger at me. "Trouble in South Side wasn't the only thing on my scanner. The police are looking for a suspect in an assault at the hotel your little jack-off awards ceremony was hosting last night." She pulls in a breath, nostrils flared. "Now, I'm all for courting trouble, especially when it comes to fuck-stains like your daddy, but the three of you are doing more than courting trouble. You're fucking it raw and bloody."

"You've had enough time on your back. You should be used to it," Tristian mutters.

There's a beat of silence, and even knowing Ms. Crane and her temper, I don't think any of us expect what comes next.

She hauls her hand back and brings it cracking against his face.

The sound of the slap is loud and jarring, but even Tristian is too stunned to do more than gape at her wordlessly.

"What the hell is going on?" Story says, walking into the room. She's wearing my shirt from last night, a dark smear of blood dried around the buttons, and her phone is clutched in her hand.

Tristian rubs his jaw. "It's nothing. I had it coming. I was being a—"

Rath springs from his chair, asking, "What's wrong?" because he catches it a second before Tristian and I do.

She's deathly pale, her eyes wide and full of a panic that has me rising out of my chair, too. "My mom just called me," is her reply. But even though her lips part, breaths jerking from her mouth, nothing else emerges.

"Story?" I ask her, seeing the tremble in her hand. "What's going on?"

"It's your dad." She lifts the phone, staring at it like it's an unfamiliar object. Her eyes rise to mine, but not before her chest hitches with a sharp, panicked breath. "Daniel's dead."

2 6

MAYHEM

THE AIR IS thick, and it's not just tension and my mother's grief. It's a numbness that I can't penetrate. A panic I can't sweat out. A dread I can't shove down.

Did we just kill someone?

Again?

My mom still hasn't taken the tissue I'm holding out to her, but it takes me too long to drop it, opting to rub at her back instead. We're sitting on her sleek, designer couch. Her shoulders hitch with strained breaths beneath my palm, and even though her eyes are downcast, I can tell they're empty.

"The remains were found among the debris early this morning," the detective is saying. He has bright, shrewd eyes and a hard mouth bearing very few laugh lines.

"Oh, my god," she gasps, covering her face. "This can't be happening."

But it is. Last night, a fire broke out in South Side, burning a building to the ground. Within the debris, the remains of a man were discovered. In Daniel's office. He was wearing a ring—with a skull.

"The fire investigators say the building was old and filled with the kind of material that burns quickly." The man frowns, his bushy eyebrows looking like two aging caterpillars. He's sitting on the armchair across from my mother.

For the last ten minutes, his focus has vacillated between the notepad in his hand and my mother's cleavage. "Someone in a neighboring building called it in around eleven. The fire trucks were there in five minutes, but old buildings like this, ma'am..." He gives her a pitying look. "It went up like kindling. Took less than an hour for it to burn to the ground."

My mom pulls her hands from her misty eyes, head shaking. "I thought he was just working late. He'd been doing that a lot lately. Staying at the office. He was so upset when Vivienne was killed. He just couldn't sleep."

My mother weeps next to me, soft cries that don't quite smear her makeup, because even now—maybe even especially now—presentation matters to her. I suppose I understand. I hold her hand as we sit on this couch—this fucking ridiculous, expensive, sterile couch—in her formal living room. *Daniel's living room*? No. Not anymore. He's dead.

Daniel is dead.

Killed in a fire.

I try to keep my thoughts here, in this room, because I can't think about what's happening back at the brownstone. The guys must be at a total loss. Killian would have been present for this, but since he's the closest next of kin who could stomach the idea of it, he's identifying what's left of the body.

"I understand this is hard to think about," the detective says, adopting a low, sonorous tone that he probably thinks is comforting. "But sometimes the people closest to the victim hold the key. It's well known that Mr. Payne had his share of enemies. Is there anyone in particular you think we should look at?"

My mother sniffs and looks over at Martin, who's been standing nearby, silent and still for the last hour. His back is straight, and from the pained, anxious expression on his face, this isn't his usual flavor of lawyering. The firm sent him over to oversee the questioning, but I'm guessing this is the first non-frat job he's been given, because he's been as stiff and bland as cardboard since he followed me through the door. He nods at my mother, giving approval for the question.

I watch her visibly gather herself, adjusting her shoulders into an elegant line. "Daniel had a difficult job. People didn't want to see progress in South Side. They prefer to keep things as they are: run-down and derelict. They resented him for his compassion toward the downtrodden." She finally takes the tissue from my hand, dabbing beneath her nose. "Drug addicts, sex workers, migrants. The sort of people South Side exploits. He believed everyone was part of the community—no matter your circumstances."

It's a physical struggle not to roll my eyes at the makeshift eulogy.

Since she's rambling and not answering the detective's question, I carefully prod her. "Mom, did Daniel piss anyone off in particular lately? Anyone noteworthy?"

Besides me, that is.

Daniel must have more enemies. He *must*. Otherwise, all four of us are screwed, because I'm not sure how to handle this. Do I misdirect the detective? If so, then how?

She pauses, her red eyes shifting to Martin, and then to the detective. "There is one person he kept getting into very...hostile disagreements with."

"Who is that?" The detective gently asks.

She dabs her nose with the tissue, giving Martin a long look. His expression back is stony, but she answers anyway. "His son, Killian."

I jolt back. "You think Killian killed his father?"

She sighs and crushes the tissue in her palm, shooting me a pointed look. "Don't pretend you haven't seen the tension between the two of them. Their relationship has always been difficult, but lately, things have escalated. Ever since you returned."

"It's not Killian." I insist, looking to Martin for some backup.

He just offers me a puzzled shrug.

The detective takes out a small writing pad. "Why do you think it's your stepson, Mrs. Payne?"

"Why?" She laughs a bit hysterically. "He shot him two months ago!"

I'm stunned speechless for the second time today, not realizing she knew. What was it she'd told me at Thanksgiving?

"Shot protecting one of his girls…"

The detective's eyebrows wiggle at that revelation. But I'm not letting my mother drag Killian down. Not when she's so far off base. Even if the body is Daniel's—even if the fire we planned killed him—Killian had no part in it. It wasn't his idea; it wasn't his execution, and it wasn't his intention.

"That was an accident," I lie, giving the man a beseeching look. "They were civil after all that, ask around. And in any case, it doesn't matter. I know it wasn't Killian. We were at the Forsyth athletic banquet all night."

The detective straightens. "Other people can corroborate this?"

I nod frantically. "Dozens, maybe even hundreds. There were photographers. We sat at the main table, Killian won an award, he made a speech…" I trail off, thinking about the scene in the coat room. It's a part of the alibi, but not one that'll shed Killian in the best light. "I'm sure plenty of people can confirm we were there until after eleven."

"What?" she says, swinging her head to stare at me. "You both said he wasn't attending that banquet." I'm not sure what her accusing tone is meant for; our not inviting her, or her being skeptical that we really went.

"He changed his mind at the last minute." To the detective, I explain, "He wanted to announce his withdrawal from the team. It was an incredibly difficult thing to do, and I'm sure he didn't want his parents there for it." I say the last part sharply, so she'll understand. But she just keeps gawking at me with that pale, betrayed expression. I narrow my eyes at her. "Do you want to blame Tristian next?"

Her eyes widen, palm flying to her chest. "A Mercer? Goodness no. A young man with that type of upbringing would never do such a thing. But Dimitri?" She nods at the detective, sniffling. "You should check him out. I can definitely see him doing something like this."

Jesus. My *mother*. You'd think she'd figure it out by now that the rich guys are the worst. She grew up waiting for that knight in shining armor, telling me stories about them, wanting my life to be a page out of a storybook, just like the name she gave me.

Which is why this will fucking destroy her.

"Mr. Rathbone and Mr. Mercer already have alibis," the detective says, looking almost disappointed as he closes his notepad. "They spent the night at the Maddox hotel. Camera footage has them arriving at nine and leaving at seven the following morning."

"You checked them already?" I ask, bafflement mingling with disgust. "Why?"

The detective looks unbothered by my tone. "Both Mr. Mercer and Mr. Rathbone have prior run-ins with the police, most on behalf of Mr. Payne himself. They were part of his inner circle of, er...colorful associates." He looks at me, assuring, "It was nothing personal. We checked everyone in that group first."

"Are you sure?" my mother asks, fanning herself. She's breathing fast and her eyes are welling up again. "This is too much. It's *too much*."

I interrupt. "Sir, could you give us a moment? My mom's barely had time to digest all this."

"Of course, ma'am." He stands, but even though he dusts off his knees and says, "We don't need to do this now," I see his eyes taking in the house, scanning, documenting, observing.

"Come on, Mom," I say, resting my hand on her shoulder. "You should rest. Let me take care of you for a while, okay?"

She nods and offers the detective a brief, watery glance, muttering, "Thank you."

"Call me," he says, handing her a card. "Any time."

I ignore the implication in Detective Eyebrows' tone and walk her to her room as Martin escorts him out. I'd love to think this guy isn't a dirt bag, but my mother and I have been surrounded by them our entire lives. It's why she told the man who came to deliver the news of her husband's horrible death 'thank you'. It's why I understand her neurotically straight posture and efforts not to smear her makeup. Sometimes, appearances are all we have. The mask we pull over our faces to hide the ugly sadness beneath. My mother taught me plenty, but few lessons so important as this:

We are whatever people see.

If they see a whore, they'll treat her like a product to be consumed. If they see a sweet, virginal princess, they'll do whatever they can to mar her purity. If they see a woman who's upstanding, wealthy, straight-backed and put together, they'll shake her hand and hold her door.

We pass Daniel's office on the way to their master suite, but I keep my eyes forward, refusing to look inside and remember. A strangeness settles over me as we approach her bedroom. After all this time, the threats and the drama, it's hard to believe that he's really gone. That he'll no longer have power over me and the guys, and with the fire, the slate will wipe clean. Whatever dirt he had on me is gone.

I step into their bedroom for the first time since high school, idly noting the muted decor. It makes it easier to ignore that he slept here, woke here, *fucked here*, on that very mattress, with the woman I'm leading to it.

I prepare myself for the breakdown. The sobs and the cries. Tearing at the bed sheets. The futile question of 'why'. I prepare myself to console my mother, because it doesn't matter that I hated her husband. She loved him, whatever that might have looked like between them. I think of losing one of mine—Killian, Dimitri, Tristian—and it makes me hurt *so badly* that I have to turn away from it, refusing to put myself in these shoes a second before I'm forced to.

She leans back on the pillows, her wet eyes staring sightlessly across the room. "He has appointments," she suddenly says, forehead crinkling. "I'll need to cancel them. And there will be a funeral. Won't there?"

I'm frozen as she looks at me, so lost. "I don't think you need to worry about that just now."

"And the house," she goes on, as if she's not hearing me. "Will I have to move out? Will I have to close our accounts and give everything to—" Her mouth clamps shut, a hardness coming over her eyes. "I suppose it's all his now."

"That's not true," I say, bending my leg beneath me as I perch on the bed beside her. I don't need to ask who she's talking about. "You're his wife, that must mean...something. Legally. Financially." I want to tell her Daniel wouldn't have left her in the position to be destitute, but at this point, I wouldn't put anything past him. "And even if it doesn't, Killian wouldn't ever just toss you out in the cold."

"How do you know?" she asks, turning her agonized eyes on me. "You know your brother. He's so spiteful and mean. He's always hated me."

I shift uncomfortably, unable to disagree without lying. "You don't need to worry about this now," I repeat. There's a throw blanket at the foot of the bed, and I drag it over her, tucking her in the same way she once tucked me in.

"There's so much to do," she mutters, clutching the blanket to her chest. "I don't know how I'm going to manage."

"We'll figure something out," I stress, taking her hand in mine. It seems wrong somehow to borrow the words of a man she thinks so little of, but I do, remembering Dimitri assuring me with them on New Year's Eve. "People like us always find a way."

This makes something in her eyes finally spark. "You're all I have now." The grin she gives me is watery and limp, but when she squeezes my hand, her grip is strong. "My little storybook. My perfect fairytale."

The sobs come then.

Deep, body-wracking, ugly sobs.

I hold her, and try so hard to rearrange things in my head. I pet her hair and pretend that I'm not responsible for her grief and hurt. I pull the mask over my face and become the fairytale she needs.

Because the one she married into is gone.

I'VE BARELY WALKED into the den when Tristian stands and asks, "How's Posey?"

"Knocked out on sleeping pills. For now, at least." I drop my bag onto the chair, surveying the men around me. I hide my surprise that Killian is back so soon. For some reason, I'd had it in my mind that they'd... keep him. Hold him. Detain? Isn't that what they call it?

The atmosphere in the room is heavy and oppressively quiet, and for a long stretch of time, no one says anything.

Slowly, Tristian sits back down.

Killian's sitting in his leather armchair with his head resting all the way back. His right hand is balancing a glass of something amber on his knee, finger tapping the glass. "What did the detective say?" He doesn't look at me when he speaks, eyes fixed on the glowing embers in the fireplace.

My stomach cramps with hot, churning acid. "He was asking Mom questions. Looking for enemies. Suspects."

Killian nods, eyes reflecting the flames in the fireplace. "And?"

I tuck my hair back from my face, huffing. "She thought you did it." His eyebrows twitch, but aside from that, he gives no reaction. "And when you had an alibi, she brought up Dimitri."

"Typical," Dimitri mutters. "It's always the poor guy." He's hunched over the console table behind the couch Tristian is currently occupying, fingertip tapping the trackpad of a laptop. Where Killian and Tristian are both nursing glasses of the amber liquid, Dimitri has opted for the entire bottle. He hasn't even glanced at me since I arrived, eyes pinched with focus at whatever's on the screen. Even when he brings the bottle to his mouth for a long swig, he doesn't look away.

Tristian sees the question in my eyes. "I was able to get access to the coroner's files, but they haven't updated the initial report yet." He jabs a thumb to the space behind him, in Dimitri's direction. "This one's been refreshing the page for two hours."

Standing awkwardly in the middle of the den, I say the one question that's been bouncing around inside my mind all day. "Is it really him?"

Killian lifts the glass on his knees, speaking against the rim. "It's him."

Even though I know no one could possibly be as certain as Killian, I still wait for something more concrete. Something to make this real. Something that will drag me out of this dream-like trance.

Tristian senses this, offering, "Some of his face was still...partially identifiable. Plus, there was a tattoo on his calf." There's a sickening lurch in my gut at the thought of whatever Killian saw. 'Partially identifiable' will forever be etched in my memory as the most disturbing thing I've heard today.

"There was a metal pin," Killian adds, tipping his glass back. "In his shoulder, where I shot him."

"And dental records," Tristian adds, resting his elbows on his knees. His fists hang between them, and I don't need to notice the dejected curve of his shoulders to know what this is doing to him. The hollowness of his blue eyes is quite enough. "There's no doubt Daniel's dead."

I'm not sure I have it in me to put voice to the second question that's been throbbing inside me since I got the call. Not when it hangs above us like a storm cloud, present in everyone's eyes.

Did we kill him?

The last question is something so cold and unfeeling that I'll probably take it to the grave with me.

Do we care?

Before I can gather the courage to ask anything at all, Dimitri makes an alarmed sound, spine snapping straight. "It's up."

Tristian's head jerks up and he twists, looking over his shoulder. His eyes bore into the back of the laptop as if he could see through it. "What does it say?"

"It says..." Dimitri's forehead scrunches. "Something about... uh, frackt... *fractures* of the cal... calvuh? Fuck!" His fists come down hard on the keys. "I'm too fucking stupid to read this shit!"

Tristian surges to his feet, but I get to Dimitri first, laying a palm on his tense back. "You are not," I whisper, because this isn't Killian and one of his rages. I don't think I've ever seen Dimitri like this, drawn taut as a piano wire, flinching away from my touch.

I don't like it.

He slaps a hand out, snagging the bottle of whiskey in a smoothly violent gesture. "You read it," he tells Tristian, whirling away from the laptop and crossing the room, as if he's trying to create a physical distance.

Tristian takes his place, tipping the screen up, eyes narrowing. He gives a quiet scoff as his eyes scan it. "Dude, you're not stupid. I can't read this shit, either. It's fancy medical jargon."

"See?" I try, stepping between Dimitri and the fireplace. "It's going to be okay."

He curls and uncurls his fist, not meeting my eyes. "I don't have a problem with being a murderer. I don't even have a problem with murdering Daniel, because I'm sorry, Killer, but your dad was fucking garbage, and we all know he had it coming." His black eyes glint in the glow of the fireplace, jaw just as taut as his shoulders. "But not like this. Not fucking sloppy, accidental *bullshit.*" He punctuates the last word by angrily throwing the bottle into the fireplace.

A hot burst of fire explodes outward, the heat licking at my calves, and I yelp, almost tripping in my haste to hurl myself away from it.

In an instant, Killian is between us, slamming Dimitri into the wall beside the fireplace. "Watch what the fuck you're doing!" he booms, and it's as if his eyes absorbed the flames.

But Dimitri isn't paying attention to him. For the first time since I got home, he's looking at me, his face pale with shock. Mine probably is, too, but he's also seeing the scared, wounded thing in my eyes. I can tell because his face falls.

"Baby, I didn't mean to—"

Killian's lips pull back in a snarl, cutting him off. "Making it into a habit now?"

"Guys," Tristian says, but they talk over him.

"Oh, fuck you." That spark of stunned guilt in Dimitri's eyes is wiped away in an instant, face shuttering. "Like you have any fucking place to lecture me on hurting her—"

"Guys." Tristian repeats, approaching them.

Killian shoves a finger into Dimitri's chest. "Don't you fucking bring that up like shit hasn't changed—"

Tristian snaps, "Guys!" and yanks Killian back, placing himself between them. "Shut the fuck up and listen to me!" He waits until Killian backs off to let out an annoyed huff, looking between them. "None of this matters, because Daniel *didn't die in the fire*."

"What are you talking about?" Dimitri asks, rubbing the shoulder Killian had planted the heel of his palm into.

"Gunshot wound to the back of the head," Tristian explains, twisting to take in Killian's stunned expression. "Execution style."

My mouth works around a series of aborted replies, because that doesn't make sense. Does it make sense? What finally emerges is, "He was dead before the fire even started?"

Killian goes back to his chair, dropping heavily into it. "What the fuck."

Shoulders dropping, Dimitri parrots him perfectly. "What the *fuck*?"

"Someone shot him," Tristian says, like he's hammering it in, eyes bright and full of fire. "Probably just after everyone went home for the day."

"Who?" I ask, the word barely forming.

"No clue. Around lunch time, the security footage went blank. Someone else turned it off. Probably whoever went in and out set the alarm. It looks like an inside job." Tristian leans back on the console table, and even though there's an irritated tightness in his eyes, there's also a relieved looseness to his posture.

This is a man who just dodged a massive bullet. "It reminds me of when that finger was left here. Too easy. No footprints."

My stomach flutters.

"Well, we know it wasn't Saul," Killian says. "But other than that, it's open season."

"Could be Lionel Lucia." Tristian glances at Dimitri, jerking his chin. "Maybe he found out about you interfering with his daughter. Assumed it was a Lord thing."

"He doesn't give a shit about that girl," Dimitri says, eyes fixed to my legs. "Execution style, in his own office? This feels personal."

"No. You know what it feels like? Really fucking convenient." Killian shakes his head, looking between Dimitri and Tristian. "This was someone who knew we were going to set that fire, thereby destroying a crime scene, and making whoever set it look like the real murderer."

The wheels turn behind Tristian's eyes. "Only five people knew we were torching that building."

Killian gives him a meaningful nod. "And we know it wasn't any of us."

"Oh, that motherfucker," Dimitri breathes, teeth clenching.

"Wait." I hold my hands up, trying to find my balance. "Are you saying Pretty Nick killed Daniel?"

Dimitri gives a sharp, bitter grin, his metal piercings catching the glow of the fire. "It's fucking perfect. He makes a deal with us to get the Kings' little pet, kills Daniel, gives us the signal, and watches us walk right into his goddamn spider web." He's the next to collapse, falling onto the couch with a sour expression. "And I fucking fell for it."

Tristian says, "Hold up," making a timeout gesture with his hands. "Nick's whole thing is mayhem, right? Two-thirty-seven. What's the criminal definition of mayhem?" He's looking at Killian expectantly, but I'm the first to answer.

"Destruction? Mischief?"

"No." Killian sinks back in his chair, eyes clouding over. "The criminal definition is very specific. It means disabling someone by…"

"Amputation." Dimitri stares between them, eyes darkening. "Like an arm or a leg or—"

My jaw drops. "A *finger*."

"Son of a bitch." Killian shoots to his feet and begins pacing, muscles rippling with every flex of his fists. "If this Ted fucker got to Ugly Nick, there's no reason he couldn't have gotten to *Pretty* Nick."

Dimitri looks just as pissed, but there's a rueful undercurrent in his words. "He really fucking sold it. The way he acted around that girl? It was like a dog watching a pork chop. I really thought he just wanted her that bad. Bad enough to turn on Daniel."

Killian stops his pacing, turning to him. "No. None of this is on us. You understand? All of you." He looks directly at me, stressing, "This isn't on us."

Nostrils flaring, Dimitri reaches behind him, pulling a pistol from his pants. "I'm going to fucking kill him." It doesn't matter that he remains sitting, dark eyes fixed to the barrel of the gun. The way he says it—low, calm, deadly— gives me no doubt he means it.

But Killian shakes his head. "We're too hot right now, Rath. We can't afford to get caught in a retaliation when we've got detectives breathing down our fucking necks."

"Maybe," I suggest, watching Rath begrudgingly tuck the gun back into his waistband, "we should just let them take care of each other."

Tristian snaps his fingers, pointing at me. "Send them to Nick as a suspect."

"If they aren't already sniffing him down," Killian says.

"The detective said," I remember, "they're checking his inner circle first. They checked Tristian and Dimitri. What are the chances Nick has an alibi more solid than ours?"

"Not fucking likely." Tristian scoffs, blue eyes glinting. "Nick doesn't exactly have an overabundance of brain cells. He's all brawn and fists."

Dimitri adds, "And does this Ted jackoff strike you as the type to give a shit about his lackies getting caught?"

Killian reaches up to pinch the bridge of his nose. He looks exhausted and spread too thin, and I have no idea how to help, but I'm pretty sure it involves touching him. Before I can, he mutters, "I need to think," and promptly stalks out of the room.

I blink in his wake.

Tristian says to me, "It's been a long day."

He doesn't even know the whole of it. Not what we went through last night. The fight, quitting the team, carving up his chest. We were physically and emotionally drained *before* we found out his father was murdered.

"Let me go talk to him."

Dimitri catches me as I pass, hand curling around my knee. "Wait." He looks up at me, and even though his brow is eerily still, his mouth moves in a complicated, hesitant maneuver. "About before. I didn't mean to—"

"I know."

"Sorry." His eyes fall closed when my fingers push into his hair, stroking it back from his forehead. "I'm a shit," he says, hooking his hands around my thighs and pulling me between his knees.

"Yeah." I give his hair a gentle tug. "But you're my shit."

The corner of his mouth tips up, and I bend down to press my lips to it, not missing the gentleness of his touch as his palm sweeps down to my calf. He puts his hand over the patch of skin the flame might have touched, if not for my jeans. "I'm fine," I assure, giving him one last kiss before pulling away. His fingertips drag against me like he wants to haul me back. But from the look in his eyes, we both know Killian needs me more.

I take the same direction, walking toward the kitchen, and find the back door ajar. He's in the backyard, slapping a basketball against the concrete pad. I watch silently as he lifts his arms, taking a shot and sinking it.

"Hey," I say, not feeling reluctant as I approach him.

He glances over, eyes still shuttered. "Hi."

I toe at a stain on the pavement, wishing I knew what to say. "Crazy stuff, huh?"

He retrieves the loose ball and dribbles it a few times, taking another shot. He misses this time. It spins around the hoop and falls off.

Killian watches the ball bounce and roll toward us, ultimately coming to a stop right at his feet. He stares at it for a long moment, brows pushed together. "God, I really fucking hated him."

I bend down to get the ball, passing it to him. "I know."

He takes it without looking, eyes fixed on the trees in the distance. "I hated him, but he wasn't just a King to me. He was a god. Untouchable, indestructible." His lips press into a hard, grim line. "Immortal." He holds the ball between his two palms, squeezing it together. "But you know what I saw laying on that table this morning? Meat. Flesh and bone, just like the rest of us. He looked so..." His face contorts, and I want nothing more than to plug my ears, because I know whatever's coming next will haunt me. "He looked so fucking *mortal*. His eyes were gray and his skin was all—"

I don't mean to make a sound. I might not want to be haunted by it, but I can't stand the thought of Killian shouldering it all himself. Despite the ugliness of it, I want to take some of the weight. I want to fold it up and tuck it away where we won't find it.

But he pauses, eyes flicking to me. "Sorry."

I shake my head. "I can't imagine what it must have been like to see...that."

He looks away, jaw clenching. "You want to know what it felt like?" His bruised knuckles strain as he digs his fingertips into the rubber. "It felt like... nothing. He was laying there in this disgusting pile of charred pieces, and I didn't feel anything at all." Sightlessly, he bounces the ball. "My dad was dead to me a long time ago, Story."

I wince at the idea of Daniel's body. "But still—"

"Did you know he met my mom in high school?" He bounces the ball again, harder this time, eyes tight at the corners.

I've had so many shocks today that this one barely penetrates. "They were together that long?"

"If you can call it that," he says, scoffing. "He came here to FU, became a Lord." There's a weight to the ensuing silence, and then it hits me.

"He had a girlfriend while he... uh, had a Lady?" It's not like it's a surprise. Daniel never struck me as the faithful type. But still, the thought of any one of my guys doing that...it makes my insides squirm around.

"Yep." His face twists with more disgust at this than it had describing his father's burnt corpse. "He spent a year fucking his Lady, then graduated, married my mom, and had me."

Warily, I ask, "What happened to her? Your mom." Killian's never talked about her before, and I'm used to the topic making his eyes ignite in a fury I've never comprehended.

Now, he just locks his jaw and slams the ball against the ground. "She didn't like what my dad was doing even before he started to buy up South Side. It wasn't clean work." He slides his eyes to mine. "He ran a lot of drugs with the Counts. Guns with the Dukes. Hooked up with Tristian's dad. He mowed over this town like a goddamn bulldozer. But you know what got to her?" He stares at me, punching the ball into the pavement with every dribble. "Finding out how he won."

Frowning, I ask, "How he won what?"

"The Game," Killian clarifies, pointing his gaze into the distance. "Kingdoms are passed through blood, Story. To win The Game—not just the silly frat stuff, but to *really* win it, kingdom and all—you have to be born into it, or you have to take it."

Slowly, I repeat, "Through blood."

"It's not as easy as killing the King," he goes on, a dreariness filling his eyes. "If that were the case, the Kingdom would have been up for grabs as of last night. You have to kill the whole line. You have to kill the father and his sons."

"What?" I step in front of him to catch his eyes. "Killian, that's crazy."

He gives a slow, emotionless nod. "I know. It's why they all go ape-shit about having heirs. It's why the Princes kick out babies like a conveyor belt. It's why my dad gave me my first gun at the ripe age of ten, and it's why he wouldn't let my mom take me when she left. He needed me." He gives the ball another slam against the ground, stressing, "He needed me to carry on the name, not because he wanted me." He shakes his head and the dribbling finally stops, ball clutched between his palms. "Everything changes now. I thought I would have to fight him tooth and nail to take his spot by force, but now…it's just mine."

Is this what's bothering him? Taking over as King? "I've seen you, Killian. Not just on the field, but in front of the cameras. Behind a gun." I make a strained, frustrated sound. "This whole Kingdom thing is dangerous and barbaric, and I'm not going to lie to you. I think it's insane. But you were born for this."

He doesn't look convinced. If anything, he just looks annoyed. "I was supposed to win it, not inherit it, like those other rich pussies. There are so many shifting rules to this fucking game." He snorts, tucking the ball under his arm. "Why do you think we have Martin?"

I arch an eyebrow. "To cover your muscular and very attractive asses?"

That earns a ghost of a smile. "Well, yeah, there's that. But also to make sure tradition is upheld and everything is done right. Technically, Rath or Tris could challenge me. I'm the end of the Payne bloodline."

"They could?" The idea is chilling. If they turned on one another… well, there's already enough bloodshed in South Side.

"Yes. But they'd have to kill me and they wouldn't. That's why my dad was so hell-bent on us being friends. Having a Mercer in your corner is always an advantage, obviously, but it wasn't just about that. He wanted us to love each other, like brothers." He sighs, shoulders shifting uncomfortably. "And the funny thing is that it worked. Still, it won't be a smooth transition. The other Kings will have something to say about it. It's going to take time to build influence, get access to my father's resources. Plus, the law's gonna be nosing around—even if we do have alibis. "

"Martin is working on it with Mom," I assure, taking the chance to reach out and touch his shoulder. "It'll be fine."

I don't know what to expect next, but it's not the shudder down his spine, and it's certainly not him hurling the ball, arm jerking as it catapults it down the court. The ball slams into the backboard and ricochets, the sound of hollow rubber echoing as it bounces away.

"Why?" he says, shoving the heels of his hands into his eyes. "Why did he have to be such a dick?"

The weight of his words rock me. Daniel was the closest thing to a father I've ever known, but it was never real. "I don't know."

"Everything was a game to him." He looks up, eyes ringed in red. "His businesses. My mother. Even Ms. Crane." I step toward him and slide my arms around his waist, ignoring the tightly coiled tension in his muscles. I lay my cheek on his chest, hearing the rumble of his voice. "He fucking destroyed her, you know that? He took everything from her, just because he could. He liked to break people. He fucking loved it. Lived for it." The tension in his body doesn't go away, but his palm on the back of my head is as gentle as his voice. "He wanted to break you so fucking bad."

I tighten my arms around him, eyes falling closed. "Well, he didn't."

"But I did. Didn't I?" His hand runs up my back and I feel the tremble in his fingertips. "Is that what I am? Just another fucked up Payne mowing people over?"

I look up at him, my voice as strong as the grip I have wound around him. "No." It's true that they tried, but they also fought for me. Bled for me. Championed me. I was put through the gauntlet and came out stronger. Very carefully, I tell him, "It's okay to both hate him and be sad that he's gone."

"I'm not sad he's gone." But despite his words, there's grief in his eyes.

I take a guess. "Then it's okay to be sad that his *potential* is gone. The potential to wake up one day and be better. But Killian..." I let him go to take his face in my hands, making sure he hears what I'm saying. "The potential isn't gone. He left it with you. Maybe I was wrong before. Maybe you weren't born for this. Maybe you were born to do it better." When he rolls his eyes, I angrily jerk him back. "You know what my mom told that detective? She told him Daniel cared about South Side. That he had compassion for the downtrodden. You and I both know that's bullshit. I'm sure she does, too. But it doesn't have to be. Not for you."

He makes a soft, derisive sound. "What do I know about the downtrodden?"

"Probably nothing," I concede, lifting a shoulder in a loose shrug. "But Dimitri does. Ms. Crane does. I do. That's the difference between you and him, Killian." I strain up on my toes to press a kiss to his cheek. "You're not alone."

He drops his head to my shoulder and clings to me like a lifeline. I fight my own tears. Not because I'm sad for losing Daniel, but because I know that Killian's right. Everything changes now.

If Killian is about to become King, what does that make me?

STORY

2 7

QUEEN

"Do you want to stop for something to eat?" Marcus asks, driving away from campus. Cars are pulling in, cars are pulling out. The sidewalks are full of co-eds and administration, going for drinks, going for dinner, going home. The sun is slumbering its way toward the horizon, painting the sky with warm, amber hues.

So strange that the world keeps on turning, even when it's been knocked off its axis.

"No, I'm fine," I answer, watching life happen as we pass by. "I'm ready to get home. It's been a long day."

What it's been is a long week. I've known dead people before, but yesterday was my first funeral. It took Killian and my mother—separately; myself acting as an in-between—two days to plan it. I'd like to say it was sparsely attended and exceedingly dull; the exact kind of sending off Daniel deserved. In reality, it was a tense, crowded affair, full of important people and too many accolades. My stomach is still sour at the memory of all those people—business leaders, politicians, anyone who's anyone—speaking of Daniel as if he were god's gift to humanity.

Through it all, I sat between Killian and my mother, both my hands wound with theirs, trying to be their strength despite all my weaknesses. My mom's tiny, agonizingly controlled sobs still ring in my ear, but the sound that burrowed its way inside my chest was Killian's pointed silence. He stared directly ahead the whole time, still as stone, even as people bent to give him condolences. There was a moment I almost considered telling him to try to act sad, but in the end, I didn't.

Let people see Daniel's real legacy: A son so apathetic about his death that he seemed more annoyed at the obligation than anything.

Sometimes, people would give our linked hands a lingering glance, and I'd occupy myself by putting them into categories. The old society ladies would smile sadly at the sight, because they saw a brother and a sister, unified in their grief. Other people's eyebrows would twitch, because they saw us for what we were.

If Killian noticed or cared, he didn't show it. At one point even resting his arm against the pew behind my shoulders. Seeing as how he spent the rest of the day with the lawyers and the estate people, it was the last stretch of time I got to really exist beside him.

In other words, I'm anxious to get home. Ready for a touch that isn't full of unnecessary pity. Ready to climb into someone's lap and feel their arms around me, anchoring me down to this new reality. Ready to feel *life* instead of death.

If only Marcus, my escort to and from campus, would stop dawdling.

From the driver's seat, he gives me a couple of quick glances. "Pizza? Sushi? Oh, how about that new salad place? You like salads, don't you?"

My nose wrinkles, but I don't tell him the truth, which is that the reason he sees me eating so many salads is owed to Tristian; a man handsome enough that Marcus himself would probably understand. "I'm alright."

"Hm." His fingers tap on the steering wheel as he turns right, toward the strip of eateries north of campus. This path will tack another five minutes on our drive. Marcus acts as though he doesn't see my glare. "What about coffee, then? Coffee and pastries?"

I side-eye him, wondering if there's a specific reason he doesn't want to take me straight back to the house. The look he gives me in return is suspiciously innocent. "Seriously. I'm good. Someone ordered pizza at the study session. I had a piece." Flippantly, I add, "Don't tell Tristian."

He holds up his fingers. "Scout's honor, Lady."

I can't imagine the scouts approve of the Lords and their activities, but it's hard to be annoyed with Marcus. "You were told to keep me away from the house," I guess, knowing from the flash of alarm in his eyes that I've hit the nail on the head. He's a good guy, and I know he's just following orders. Unfortunately for him, I'm not great at following them. "Take me home, Marcus. I'll deal with the fallout."

For a moment, he seems to weigh who's the bigger threat, me or the guys, but he ultimately sighs and mutters a string of curses under his breath. Ten minutes later, he pulls right up to the front door of the brownstone, and then cuts the engine. He starts for his seatbelt, but I stop him, holding up my hand. "I can walk the twenty feet to the house by myself."

He looks at the front door, and then at me. "I don't know, Story. If the guys find out I didn't take you all the way home, there will be hell to pay."

"No, there won't," I say, opening the door. "Because I will kick every single one of their asses if they do." I lean over and kiss him on the cheek. "Thank you for driving me home and being such a good bodyguard."

"No problem, Lady," he smiles, blushing a little. "Wave to me when you get inside."

I promise him that I will and hitch my backpack over my shoulder on the way up the front steps. I'd had a study session after class, but the guys had some kind of important meeting they couldn't miss. Hence, the bodyguard. In a way, I'm grateful for the time away. We've spent so long shut up in this house that the walls felt closer and closer by the day. Despite that, I enter the house with a sigh of relief.

This is home.

"Guys?" I call, dropping my bag in the foyer. "I'm home."

I strain my ears, listening for footsteps, but all I hear is the distant hum of muffled voices, floating down the hall toward the parlor. I toe off my shoes before following the sounds, approaching the end of the main hallway.

When I hear Killian's voice, something inside of me unwinds. "And signing these papers? That makes it official?"

Peering inside, the first person I see is Martin, standing quietly by the edge of the desk. He's not the one who responds.

"Signing those papers transfers your father's estate to you. It has nothing to do with you becoming a King. *That contract* is signed in blood—which has already been spilled. You're his blood, Killian. You know how this works. That passes his kingdom down to you."

That voice is familiar, but unexpected. I sneak closer, angling myself for a more expansive view of the room. Killian is standing behind the desk, and Mr. Mercer—Tristian's dad—is sitting across from him. But it's not just him. There are four other men, along with Dimitri and Tristian. There's a crackle of tension in the air that immediately sets my teeth on edge, and it takes me a second to understand why. None of these strange men are standing stiffly. There's not a hostile expression among them. Hell, three of them are nursing glasses of whiskey, looking as comfortable in this room as they might in their own home.

That's what it is.

They're too comfortable.

"Someone must fill the role of running South Side, Mr. Payne," one of the men says. "You've positioned yourself to take over by becoming a Lord. Is that not what you want?"

Martin clears his throat and says, "What the Mayor is trying to say—"

"I know what the fuck he's saying," Killian growls, resting his weight against the fists he has pressed into the desk. "I just don't like you all coming in here and telling me what my role is. I don't need your approval. I've earned this title, and if my father hadn't been tragically murdered, then I would have taken it from him directly." My stepbrother speaks in even, clear tones. "Everything in South Side belongs to me. The properties, the Hideaway, the police, the hard-working, the junkies and whores. What I do with those things is up to me."

"There's the minor matter of Mrs. Payne," Martin says, mouth pinching tightly. "She was his wife, which means—"

"Nothing," another man says. I don't recognize him, but he has a strong, distinctive face. I've only heard one word come out of his mouth, but I already hate him. He flicks his hand dismissively. "Widows gunk up the works, son. Shove some pills down her throat, make it look nice and clean, and rid yourself of the headache." To the mayor and Mr. Mercer, he says, "It's not like she mothered his children. Wasn't she Avenue trash?" The man lets out a scoffing laugh. "If you think widows gunk up the works, then let me tell you about whores."

My jaw drops in outrage, but a swift, cutting reply makes me freeze.

"If you want to leave this house with a beating heart," Dimitri's sprawled in a chair, looking for all the world like he has a million bigger cares than this particular discussion, "you'll watch how you talk about whores under our roof." His dark eyes rise from the knife he's cleaning his nail beds with, leveling the man with a long, deadly look.

Even experiencing it secondhand, I shiver.

Beside him, Tristian shifts forward menacingly. "That whore is our Lady's mother, Lionel. She's under our protection from this day forward. You can go ahead and spread the word on that." Leaning back in his seat, he casually adds, "And she's quite nice, actually."

Dimitri lowers his eyes again, muttering, "To you."

"Posey will get half of his liquid estate, and more, if she needs it." Killian looks at Lionel, voice dropping to a low, cold tone. "And just so we're clear, Lucia. That's the last time you call me 'son'. I'm fully aware of how you treat your spawn. Can't say I care for it."

My backpack slides off my shoulder, thumping softly against the wall. I jump back out of sight, holding my breath, but the silence in the room is a clear enough signal that they've noticed me. A moment later, Dimitri appears in the doorway, eyes darting down the hall.

They land on me and immediately soften. "Baby," he says, looking cagily over his shoulder, into the room. "You're not supposed to be here yet."

I jab my thumb in the foyer's direction. "My study group let out early, so I strong-armed Marcus into bringing me home."

Dimitri snorts. "Fucking pushover."

"Rath..." A shadow moves behind him, and Killian fills the doorway, nudging him aside. "I've got this."

Dimitri gives him a nod and slinks back through the door, pushing it partially closed behind him

"Sorry," I tell Killian, mouth twisting as he reaches out to touch my hip. "I didn't mean to interrupt."

Killian gives me an odd look, ushering me a few feet down the hall. "This is your home. You don't need to be sorry." Even though the words sound genuine enough, I see a certain strain in his eyes when he glances back toward the parlor. "I didn't want to do this here, but since Daniel's office is nothing more than a charred ember and we had to meet on my territory, this was all I had."

I tug at the hem of his shirt, searching his eyes. "Is there a reason you didn't invite me? I thought we made an agreement to—"

Killian cuts me off. "That was before Daniel died. Before..."

Comprehension washes over me. "Before you became a King."

He nods, pushing his fingers through his hair. "Things are different now. How I operate and present myself...it's important. Those pricks in there are nothing but posturing and ego. It's a part of the game I have to play."

It's a part of the game I told him he was born to play. Regardless, an insecurity scrapes its way through my chest. "You don't want your fucktoy around."

His reaction is so fast that I feel his hands before I see them, framing my face in a hard grip. "Never think that." There's an angry furl to his brow that I know isn't meant for me, but still makes my stomach clench nervously. "Everything I do is to protect what's mine—foremost, *you*."

There's a ferocity to his words. An unmistakable intent. This isn't about keeping me out of things. It's about keeping me safe.

"This is new," he continues, eyes pinging back forth between mine, "and I need to get a feel of things before I make my moves." He tips forward to press our foreheads together, all that hardness draining from his eyes. "But one thing is for certain, you are part of this. Part of me. Part of us. Just give me time to find my footing here. Give me time to make sure I can protect you."

I let out an airy laugh, hooking my hands over his powerful forearms. "Patience isn't my virtue."

"We're LDZ royalty, little sister." His mouth tilts up into a smirk. "We can't afford virtue. I'll settle for some trust."

Well, geez.

When he says it like that...

"Okay," I sigh, fingertips dragging against his arm as my grip falls away. "Go back to your meeting. You can tell me about it later, can't you?"

"Of course," is his answer, followed by the brush of his thumb against my bottom lip. He stares at it there for a long moment, but doesn't dip down for the kiss I'm waiting for with bated breath. It might have something to do with the question forming in his eyes.

"What?" I ask.

"Do you still love me?" The rest of the question is unspoken, but I hear it anyway. *Like this.* As a man that deals with these people. As a King.

I push to the tip of my toes, erasing the distance between us. "Yes."

The kiss is short, but it takes my breath away. In all this time, I never would have thought I'd get Killian like this. Tender and slow and so sweet that it lingers into an ache.

Satisfied, he slips back into the room, leaving me in the hallway. I feel lost for a moment, all of my men inside while I stand out here, waiting to be invited. I want to think that I'm necessary—part of what's happening behind that door—

but the hard truth is that I'm not. The Lords have been setting up these chess pieces long before I even thought to see the checkerboard beneath my feet.

I hear something behind me and realize Ms. Crane is in the kitchen. Because apparently I'm a glutton for punishment and insist on doing all the wrong things today, I enter the kitchen.

When she turns, making eye contact, she asks, "They kick you out of their little circle jerk?"

"No." I say, a little too defensively. "Things are complicated."

"You got that right," she mutters, walking over and opening the cabinet over the stove. She pushes up on her toes and grabs an ornate bottle of something I suspect is alcoholic. "Shit's gonna get worse before it gets better. That's always the way, little fucktoy."

"Do you know who those men are?" I ask, looking over my shoulder. "I don't recognize all of them."

"You see one asshole, you've seen them all," she answers, casting a glare toward the hall. "You can tell by their shoes. You know the difference between good and evil, don't you?" She gives me a meaningful look. "Fashion sense."

Snorting, I suppose, "Tristian *is* a snappy dresser."

She raises the bottle in a salute. "Exactly."

Perching on a stool at the island, my shoulders slump. "Why is he in there talking to those monsters, anyway? He doesn't need their approval."

"He's not looking for approval. He's just lookin'." She snags two glasses out of a different cabinet and sets them on the island in front of me. "All of this is theatrics. No King can rule without allies, can he?" She tips the bottle, filling the two glasses. The writing on the label is Japanese, but one word stands out in English: Sake. "I'm cultured," she says, seeing my expression. "You should see me fuck in a kimono."

I take the glass, giving it a dubious sniff. "Thanks for that nightmare."

"You're welcome."

Together, we toss the shots back; me shuddering delicately at the potency, while Ms. Crane swallows unflinchingly.

"I guess this is what the King's fucktoy does." The thought comes to me abruptly as I'm inspecting the bottom of my empty shot glass. "I guess it's what my mom did."

Ms. Crane barks a harsh, raspy laugh. "Don't let that thundercunt fool you. She had her hands in more stews than you realize."

Nodding, I note, "The Velvet Hideaway," and rest my temple on my fist, spinning the glass. "But that was before, and this is...now. What's a queen without her King?"

Ms. Crane pours us another shot. "A lot more powerful, historically speaking." She taps her glass against mine and throws it back.

"Do you miss it?" I wonder, not missing the sneer on her mouth when she speaks of my mother. "Your girls, the business?"

"My girls," she answers, sliding onto the stool beside me. There's an uncharacteristic, soft sentimentality in her eyes, and it startles me to see it. It's gone before I have a chance to dig into it. "But the business is business. Dicks come in hard and go out soft. Nothing there to miss." She fills my shot glass and nudges it toward my hand. "Do you miss it?"

I give her a puzzled look. "Miss what?"

She nods towards the hallway. "Not being shackled to three insufferable jackasses."

I pick up the glass, testing the weight in my hand. "I can't remember a time I wasn't shackled to one insufferable jackass or another," I confess, thinking of being a child. Probably even then, some asshole had sway over my mother and quality of life. "But these three...they're different."

"I know they are." She nods, eyes fixed to the far wall, as if lost in a memory. "My husband ran girls for Daniel sometimes, but he never did like him much. Used to tell me Daniel Payne would take his slice of South Side's pie over his dead body." She raises her glass in a casual toast. "But he'd come in a lot, you know. Daniel. It wasn't always for business." Her eyes slide to mine, brow arching. "A lot of men prefer 'em young and dumb, but he always liked the most desperate girls best. The ones who'd do anything for a bag of dope. The girls with three kids and no boundaries. Then one day, he dumped this little shithead in my office. Asked me to look after him for a spell. *Angry...*" Her face contorts, head shaking. "Such an angry little shit, that Killian. I didn't think someone so young could be so pissed off at the world. But there he was, barely eight years old, trying to punch a hole in my wall because his daddy was off nailing some dope-sick, lost cause." There's a tiredness in her eyes that's probably older than I am. "I thought to myself, 'well, here's one more'. One more boy who's going to grow up and throw his hurt around, because no one ever taught him otherwise." She meets my gaze, dipping her chin. "So I taught him otherwise."

I wince, just imagining Killian as a tiny ball of fury. "What did you do?"

She shrugs. "Well, first, I slapped the absolute piss out of him."

My jaw drops. "Ms. Crane!"

She flaps a hand dismissively. "Eh, you would have slapped him, too. Should have seen the look on his face when I did it. He was stunned stupid." She lets out a little snicker, looking way too pleased at the memory. "But then I sat his spoiled ass down and asked him what the fuss was all about. And you know what he did?"

Wryly, I guess, "Talked back like a little jerk?"

But Ms. Crane shakes her head, frowning into her empty glass. "He cried." My chest clenches at the words, but just as much as the way they're spoken—gentle and hushed, as if it's not something she ever wants to ridicule him for. "Oh, he tried really hard to be a man about it. His little lip was quivering. He tried so hard to hold it in. I put my arms around him and he couldn't hold on to it anymore. I don't think he'd been hugged in a long time." She pours us each another shot, ignoring the shine of wetness in my eyes. "After that, he came every few days. He'd sit in my office and do his homework. He never was much of a talker, but he'd listen to me blather on about this and that. If he wasn't being such a little fuckhead, I'd bring him cookies and milk." She lets out a raspy laugh. "A few years later, he started bringing this other little shithead with him. Skin and bones, that one. He was angry, too, but it was a different kind of angry. Real quiet. The kind that makes you wonder if maybe he's not quite right."

"Dimitri," I realize, imagining what they were like as boys.

Ms. Crane tells me, "Mean little fucker. Almost told Killian not to bring him around anymore. But then they came one day, and the night before, my old man had gone on a tear. Left me black and blue something awful. Wasn't anything new to me, but Rath—Dimitri—took one look at me, got real quiet in that way he does, and you know what he said?" She laughs at the memory, downing her shot. "He offered to shoot him." Her fingers come together in a sharp snap. "Just like that, real adult-like."

I smile, thinking of a little Dimitri offering to murder someone. "When did you meet Tristian?"

"Oh, I met that shit-for-brains later on down the line, right after I shanked my old man." She flashes me a dark smirk, winking. "Still working on breaking that one."

My eyebrows shoot up my forehead. "That's why you're so hard on him?"

She scoffs. "I'm hard on him because he deserves it. When the day comes he doesn't, I won't be."

"He's right," I say, head shaking. "You really are diabolical."

The wicked delight drains from her smile, flattening her smile into a hard line. "It's hard to make a mark on this world—you know that as well as I do. But those little shits were the hill I planned to die on. I swore to myself twelve years ago, crouched down on that grimy motel carpet, that I wouldn't let him become another monster." She jabs the tip of her forefinger into the counter. "Not this one. Not this boy. Not if I could help it."

I cover her hand with mine, feeling the rough, papery texture of her skin. "You're a good woman, Ms. Crane."

She shifts uncomfortably, eyes sliding away. "Yeah, yeah. Don't let it get around. I'll deny it." She waits until my hand falls away to go on. "Anyway, that's your job now. I've done what I can do. To save him." She levels me with a long, significant look. "To save the girl he ends up falling for."

I put all this together, and the big picture is a rich tapestry bearing more than an obligation. "You love him," I realize, keeping my voice low.

"If you want the truth?" She tips her head close, eyes glassy with the liquor, and quietly confesses, "I love them all. Even that steaming tower of blond excrement."

I give her a sad, understanding smile. "So do I."

"Good." She straightens, capping the bottle of sake. "That's what it'll take."

I'M IN KILLIAN'S room when the men leave, watching their departure from the window. They file down the front steps in their dark suits and expensive haircuts. Killian's among them, shaking their hands as they descend the steps. These are the men behind the machinations steering Forsyth, and now Killian is a part of their circle of thorns. Ms. Crane is right. He's going to need someone who loves him just as much as they've once hated him. He's going to need someone that strong. Someone who doesn't flinch away from the hard reality of what he is. Someone who, even if he's down, can rise up and carry on.

"It's weird for us, too." I turn and see Tristian leaning against the doorjamb, his blond hair glinting in the light of the lamp.

I smile feebly. "You also get kicked out?"

He shrugs, looking around the tidy space. "They were learning the secret handshake and fitting ring sizes." It's a joke, but there's a truth hidden in the lackadaisical tone that he's missed the mark at hiding. There's a reason Killian and Daniel were the only ones with the LDZ skull rings.

Kingdoms are passed through blood.

He gives me a dry, weary grin. "We've always been equals. I mean, we always fought to best one another, but it's always been evenly matched."

"And now he's the King."

"That, he is." He pushes off and approaches me, plucking the drawstring from my hoodie off my chest. "Are you mad he didn't let you in the meeting?"

"Not mad," I insist, watching him wind the string around his forefinger. "More like...hurt. Excluded."

He kisses the tip of my nose, and then my cheeks, working his lips to my mouth. "He's worried about you. We all are. If anything happened to you—"

"Nothing is going to happen," I say, trying not to melt under his touch. "I appreciate the concern, but Daniel is gone. Ted is through. Killian has a top position."

"A top position," Tristan agrees, taking my bottom lip between his own. "A position that other people are going to want, and a Lady he'd kill for. That makes you a target."

"Sounds like a Tuesday," I sigh, running my fingers through his soft hair. "I don't want to worry right now, Tristian. I'm so goddamn tired of worrying. Can't I just enjoy this for once?"

"Enjoy what?" Dimitri asks, stopping at the door. He pauses to take us in, eyebrow rising as Tristian's kisses trail down my jaw. "Oh, we're enjoying that." He leans back, checking the hall before entering, but Tristian spins us so I can't see Dimitri's approach.

I can feel it, though, hard and eager against my backside as Dimitri's mouth finds my shoulder. "You want something, baby?" The words are quiet and enticing, but beneath them, I can still find that ring of threat I'd heard in the parlor before. This one isn't malicious—he's just drawing me out, making me ask for it. But the memory of his coolly violent promise still rattles against my spine like lava. The hands that are tucking themselves beneath my shirt, sweeping up my ribs...

These are hands that could kill people.

Maybe they're hands that have already killed people.

I've never asked.

And it wouldn't change a fucking thing if I had.

"I want you." My response is very clear, even though it's spoken through a ragged sigh. "Both of you. All of you."

Tristian rumbles, wedging his hands between me and Dimitri to take two big handfuls of my ass. "You want us inside you, sweetheart? Like last time?"

I barely complete a nod before he's spinning me around. Dimitri catches me against his chest, hands grabbing my jaw to take my mouth in a searing kiss. His fingers move to unzip the hoodie and I feel Tristian push it off my shoulders in an impressively coordinated series of movements. He lifts my hair off my neck next, kissing the warm skin back there.

Shoving my fingers up Dimitri's shirt, I push it over his head to reveal his lean, cut torso. I love the sharpness of his muscles. The efficient wiriness of him. There's strength here, my palms descending to his hard abs, but it's tightly contained. I can't help but duck down, pressing a kiss to my mark on this chest. When I slide back up, Tristian's fingers replace my mouth, tracing the 'S' in Dimitri's chest.

"Couldn't help but notice Killer has one of these now, too." Tristian speaks into my cheek, curled around me as he inspects Dimitri's scar. If I didn't know better, I'd say I detect a hint of jealousy in his voice. The dark and possessive flicker in Dimitri's eyes makes it clear he hears it, too.

"Your body is your temple," I tell him, turning to kiss the curve of his jaw. "I wouldn't expect you to deface it."

"Hm." His eyes tighten, but just as quickly as the topic was raised, it's forgotten by the warmth of his palms sliding up my ribs, catching my shirt as it ascends. Dimitri makes a hungry sound when the hem clears my breasts, tipping down to mouth at my nipple. Into my ear, Tristian says, "I can't wait to bury my dick into you."

Tossing my shirt aside, his hand dips down the back of my leggings and yanks at my thong. I feel the sharp sting against my ass. I know what he wants and how he wants it. I also know what it feels like to give it to them, to feel two of my Lords inside me at the same time, and I'm ready to feel it again.

So damn ready.

The clink of Dimitri's belt buckle draws my attention back to him, but I'm already pushing him back into the bed, soaking in the surprised flash in his eyes when he lands on the mattress, hard and off-kilter. "Oh, really?" he says, smirking, but then I'm grabbing his jeans and yanking them down his thighs.

I grin. "*Really.*" My mouth waters as I take in the curve of his cock. Suddenly, I want nothing more than to taste him, to suck him until he's gasping and begging for release. I push my ass against Tristian's crotch, feeling the hardness in his pants, and he pulls me against him, flattening his hand across my belly.

"Look how hard he gets for you," Tristian says, breath hot in my ear as Dimitri strokes his cock. "I bet he misses jacking off into all your pretty little panties since you asked us to save it for you."

Dimitri looks up at me through thick, dark lashes, fingers fanning up my ribs, below my breasts. "Nah. The real thing is better." His thumbs roll over my nipples, rising them to peaks, then licks and sucks them until I'm curled over his head, panting.

"Jesus, your ass," Tristian says, pushing down my leggings. His fingers are cool against my overheated skin, squeezing my cheeks and then spreading them. "I'm still pissed Rath got to you first."

Dimitri smirks around my nipple. "Sorry, brother. Fair is fair."

"But that just means he loosened you up for me." I hear his zipper lower as I kick my clothes away, but he doesn't come closer. "I won't have to fuss around so much to get you warmed up."

Tristian, god help me, knows exactly what he's doing. All this talk, the jokes, the teasing, the mind games. He's just trying to rile me up, and I'm irritated that it's working. My pussy is drenched and aching.

"You know what's not fair?" I say, snapping upright. "You two being pussy-teases all the time. It's been a really stressful week and sometimes a girl just wants to get her brains fucked out by two of the men she loves."

"Uh." Tristian goes still behind me, trying to process what I just said.

I don't wait for him to figure it out, climbing right into Dimitri's lap. He startles, eyes glued to the tits in his face. "Should we wait for Killer?"

"No," I answer, reaching between us to guide his cock where I want it. "He can find me after both of you have fucked me into unconsciousness." Without waiting for a response, I sink down.

"Shit," Dimitri spits, hands clasping my hips. "Goddamn, girl. Give a guy some warning." The words may chastise, but they're spoken in a low, reverent tone as he pushes me down, impaling me on his cock.

"God, that feels so good." I gulp in a few overwhelmed breaths before forcing his chin up, making him look at me. "*You* feel so good."

Dimitri has this way of looking at me that makes it feel as though the whole world is falling away, darkening at the corners until my awareness is teetering on the point of his pupils. If I had the privilege of whimsy, I might call his stare enchanting, even though it wouldn't fit. It's too demanding and wicked, a chasm I'd fear falling into if I hadn't already surveyed the depths and made a home of them. It's why I can't hold it against Auggy, the fact that she wants him. I remember the bitterness in her voice that night Dimitri had come for me in the pit, and she was right to feel it, because being under the heavy weight of that dark stare is even better than she could imagine.

As if hearing my thoughts, he takes my hand, pressing it to the scar on his chest. "Remember?" he asks, pressing his palm against the scars on mine. Nodding, I rock against him, hearing what's left unsaid.

But these are the days of Kings and corpses.

We can't afford to leave things unsaid.

"I love you." I speak the words against his lips, barely touching, and watch as his eyes slide closed.

"I love you, too." It's a tickle against my mouth, metal against skin, breath colliding with breath, and when I wind my fingers into his hair, I have this notion that I'm lucky to have him inside me. In more ways than one.

I could be luckier, though.

I glance back at Tristian, who's just standing there with his dick in his hand. Literally. "You going to put that in me sometime this year?"

"Just enjoying the show." A slow, crooked grin spreads across his face. "But if you insist..."

Dimitri grabs my hips and rocks me against him, falling back onto the bed as I seat myself, preparing. I feel the soft touch of Tristian's hands as they run down my back, pushing me down onto Dimitri's chest, and then his fingertips dragging down my ass, spreading my cheeks. The shock of his mouth thrusts me forward and Dimitri grunts in response. For all his talk about not warming me up, he does it anyway, getting me good and slippery with his tongue. Dimitri teases me through it, tongue tracing the seam of my mouth, teeth nipping at my jaw, hands palming my breasts.

I get so lost in it—so impatient to feel Dimitri moving inside of me—that I almost miss the sudden absence of Tristian's mouth, the head of his cock brushing against me. I look back over my shoulder just in time to see a glob of spit fall from his lips to the head of his rigid cock, jutting against my backside. It must make its mark, because he instantly presses it into me, eyes meeting mine as he forces it inside.

My body seizes up, still not used to the strange invasion, but Dimitri forces his fingers into the fist I'm making in the covers, threading our fingers together. "Relax, baby. Let him in." I suck in a breath, watching as Tristian's fingertips dig divots into my hips. His eyelids flutter as he sinks another thick inch into my ass. "You see that?" Dimitri asks, breath hot in my ear. "He's thinking about how tight you are. I bet he's thinking that he's not gonna last. That's how I felt. I felt like you were going to take it all out of me."

When I'm panting, bucking forward on Dimitri, I feel that pressure, the good kind that stretches and pulls and fills me up inside, and I take it because I already know I can. I gasp into Dimitri's neck and let him whisper dirty things into my ear as Tristian painstakingly fills me, bottoming out with a tight, strangled noise.

"That's our girl," Tristian says, rubbing soothing circles into my lower back with his thumbs. "Is that good?" He reaches around me and grabs my breast, lifting it toward Dimitri's mouth. Dimitri complies, enveloping me with his tongue, and I rock against him, pulling Tristian forward with me. It draws him deeper and I cry out at the intensity. "That's right, sweetheart, you set the pace."

I wasn't lying before about needing it hard, frenetic. For days, I've felt like a livewire, all this energy and emotion thrashing around inside my chest, begging to be expended. It's just like Dimitri said before. I want to feel them take it all out of me. I want to feel them stretch me, fill me, pound away with their lithe, strong bodies. I fall on top of Dimitri and he grabs my hips, fingers interlacing with Trisitan's. I buck and bounce, telling them how I need it.

They don't make me wait.

The two of them take control swiftly, hips surging, slamming into me. With every pound of Tristian's cock into my body, Dimitri thrusts in tandem, swallowing my cries with his serpentine tongue and wicked eyes. I feel them everywhere, underneath, above, inside. There's no place where they begin and I end. It's just one mass of sweaty, hungry lovemaking, and I don't want it to end.

But while Dimitri sets the fuse with every punch of his hips, Tristian is igniting it with the deep drag of his cock.

The live wire in my chest erupts.

The shockwaves of the orgasm ripple through me, taking me to that transcendent place where it's so intense, there's nothing I can do but ride it out and let it carry me away. Possessed. It's like being possessed, taken out of my own body to make room for what they're doing to me.

"That's it." Dimitri's voice is tight with strain as he coaxes me through the whine that tears from my throat. "Jesus, I can feel you, baby. I can feel you coming around us." He puts his lips to mine, breathless words colliding with my cries. "You're so fucking beautiful..."

I'm held up by the two of them, hands on my hips, cocks thrusting into me, even when I collapse. They work in tandem and I close my eyes, just listening, feeling. Tristian whispers my name, attaching it to every punch, until he comes with a strangled grunt, heaving into me, spilling thick and hot in my ass. I can feel every pulse, slick and so deep, and I imagine myself—the soft, inside parts—clutching it greedily, calling it my own.

"Goddamn, baby," Dimitri says, voice deep and guttural. "Goddamn, god*damn*." He seizes beneath me with a hard thrust, crushing our hips together painfully. His head lifts off the bed, neck straining as his cock jerks, pumping me so full of him that I swear I can taste it on the back of my tongue. "God-fucking-damn." He crumples onto the bed, chest heaving, and for a long moment, the three of us are made human again. Tristian curled over my back, panting into the space between my shoulder blades.

"He needs us," I tell them later, after we've cleaned ourselves up, lazy and uncoordinated, attracted like magnets into the center of Killian's ridiculously large bed.

Dimitri's on his side, running his fingertips across my lower belly. "Every King needs his court," he agrees, watching my stomach twitch at the tickle of his touch.

"And a Queen," Tristian says, taking my hand and brushing his lips over my knuckles.

I spread my thighs, making room for the fingers Dimitri uses to push his cum back inside me. "Get some sleep, baby," he tells me, those black eyes finding mine. "We'll make sure he finds you."

I lie between them, basking in the sensation of being thoroughly fucked and safe in our King's bed, waiting for him to return and make us complete.

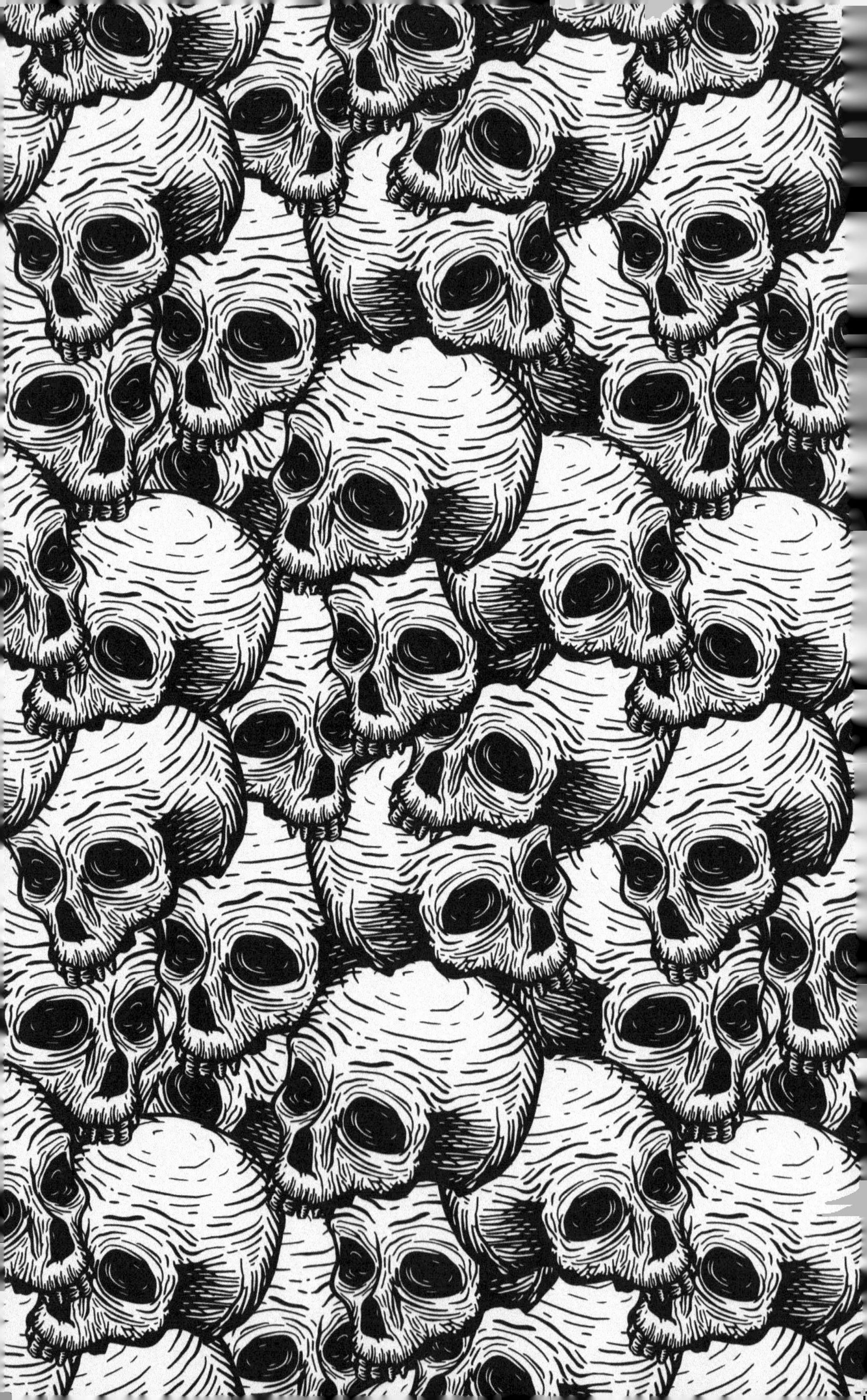

28

DEATH IS COMING

STORY BARELY STIRS when I roll her into Tristian, waiting until she's curled into his chest, thigh slung over his hips, to creep out of bed. I spend a second watching them, memorizing the way they fit together, Tristian making a snuffling sound into her hair as his palm finds the swell of her ass cheek.

I swear I see him flex a pec.

Blame it on the South Side childhood, but I've never been a deep sleeper. This is unlike Killian, who's spent years sleeping on busses or planes, wherever he could get the chance. Tristian exercises and masturbates his way to exhaustion every day, so he's always been pretty good at passing out the moment his head hits the pillow. This all came in handy when we moved in here together, because there was no way I'd find myself living in the same room with a piano as sweet as the one upstairs and not play it all hours of the night. That's how I get to sleep; music or a fat blunt to chill me out. I require a certain level of peace to relax, and those are the only two things that help me achieve it. Until Story came along, that is. Baby girl knows how to soothe a guy into sleep.

Usually, anyway.

Tonight, I'm fucked out but mentally restless. My mind keeps going over the funeral and that meeting in the parlor earlier. All the things there are to do. Daniel had a lot of shit going on, and now Killer has to decide what he wants to do with it all. It's going to mean rounding up the foot soldiers. The dealers. The working girls. Showing them all there's a new boss and hoping no one gets mouthy about it, because there's also this:

Examples will need to be made.

It's not pretty, but it's how shit's done. Tristian isn't going to like it, because he's used to being a fat wallet and a pretty face. He's the guy we trot out when we need a sweet-talker. He maneuvers with his mind and all that shiny Mercer influence. But Killer's going to need to cultivate some fear.

He finds me just as I'm finishing rolling up the blunt.

I pause, eyes flicking up to watch him enter his bedroom, but it takes him a second to notice me because his eyes are glued to the bed—to Story's naked, unconscious body, draped over Tristian like some kind of erotic blanket. He takes her in with a tick in his jaw and a hand reaching down to squeeze his crotch.

Then he sees me, eyes skittering past the window and jerking back.

I stare at him, frozen, the blunt halfway to my mouth. "Don't be a dick," I whisper. Killer has this really hardass rule about smoking in the house, and he won't even relax it for poor old Ms. Crane, who hauls her rattling bones out to the garden every morning. "It's cold as fuck out there," I reason, gesturing to my boxers. The rest of my clothes are stuffed somewhere below his bed, probably. "We left you a present and everything."

He glances back over to Story's sleeping form, and the way she's got her thigh hiked up on Tristian's belly has her legs spread nice and wide for him. His chest expands, contracts, and then he walks toward the window, muscles jumping as he heaves it open a couple inches. "Me first," he says, brows crouched all low and ornery, like he didn't just walk into the living manifestation of his goddamn wet dream.

Rolling my eyes, I hand him the blunt and the lighter.

This is the good part about Killian being off the team. No drug tests. No coach looking over his shoulders. No trainers or teammates. Just the two of us, hunched on either side of his cracked window, puffing a blunt. For a moment, it's just like old times.

He catches my gaze when he passes it back, throat jumping with a restrained cough. "We'll go find Nick tomorrow?" he asks, voice all business, even though his eyes keep wandering back to the bed.

Nodding, I assure, "We'll track him down." Lionel Lucia came to us with intel as to Pretty Bitch's whereabouts. Hiding out in some gambling den on the Avenue. It's like he's not even trying. When I watch him nod, eyes tracing the milky curve of her thigh, I fight back a laugh. "Jesus, just go. Can't fuck her from all the way over here."

But he takes one more long drag off the blunt before handing it back and approaching the bed. He undresses more slowly than I'm expecting, drawing it out as he observes them. Can't say I blame him. Tristian and Story look hot as fuck, like something straight out of a porno. I bet she's still slippery wet with our cum.

His cock's already jutting hard when he shoves his pants down, and when he climbs into bed, it's a sophisticated operation. Slow and careful. Barely even jostles them as he settles in behind her, hand stroking over his cock. Killer isn't exactly the most expressive guy. I know his dad dying shook the foundations of something I can't possibly understand. I don't know if it's grief or uncertainty about the future, but there's been a weight in his eyes that I haven't missed.

As soon as he hovers above her, it melts away.

It makes me wonder how many times he's done this. How familiar is this to him that it's as solid a constant as coming home?

Slowly, he reaches out to touch her, palm resting lightly on the swell of her ass. The ember of my blunt glows bright when I take in a long drag, watching Story's shoulders shake with a shiver.

"Shhh," I hear him whisper, "go back to sleep, little sister."

She murmurs and sighs, nestling all up into Tristian's warmth.

It feels dirty to watch, the way he spreads her, fingers disappearing as he explores what we've left inside her. He only spares me a brief look before slotting himself up against her back, cock in hand. He moves swiftly, with expertise, pushing his cock between her legs without waking her. His muscles tense under the restraint of doing it like this; slow and careful. Killian's body is a work of art, both literally, with the tattoos inking his skin, and figuratively, from the intensity of his training and honed physique. He's the picture of brawn, muscles bulging and flexing, but he doesn't use it. Not here.

He enters her with a gentleness I didn't know he possessed. I take a drag on the joint and stare at the place where their bodies connect, her pussy glistening in the pale light as she takes him in. He pauses there for a beat, lips resting against her shoulder, and I feel the nudge of arousal press at my balls. Goddamn, this girl is going to kill us. I'd warned her about demanding that all of our spunk go inside her. There aren't enough hours in her day.

Fuck, there aren't enough hours in *our* day.

Holding the joint between my lips, I push my hand under the waistband of my shorts, idly indulging in the slow rhythm Killer starts fucking her with.

The thud downstairs stops me before it can get too ambitious.

I pause, listening, trying to hear over the subtle squeak in Killian's mattress. Beyond that are his shallow breaths and the chilled wind blowing in through the crack in the window. But there's something else. A muffled, distant voice that must belong to Ms. Crane.

The fuck is she doing up this late?

I sigh, remove my hand, and take a final drag before stubbing out the joint. It isn't until I straighten, stretching my back, that I realize Tristian's awake. His eyelids are just barely lifted, gaze fixed on Story's tits, all smashed up into his chest. Killer's basically fucking her on top of him, but Tristian is… Tristian.

His response is to palm at the thigh she has hitched over his hips and spread her wider.

Killian's too engrossed in fucking her to notice me crossing the room, but Tristian and I make eye contact and his forehead creases in question. I shake my head and flap a hand—*enjoy your show*—and head out into the hall to check.

It's not like Ms. Crane to be up and about this late. Once her clock is punched, she locks herself up in that room downstairs like she's sealing a tomb. But it's not like me to be spending my night in Killer's room, so what the fuck do I know?

Well, I know it's cold as fuck, for one. The temperature of the hallway is roughly arctic and makes my balls want to climb up inside me, and the staircase isn't much better. I huff warmth into my fists as I scamper down, too stoned to question any of this.

I'm not too stoned to freeze at the lumpy shape of a body at the foot of the stairs.

Since I am stoned, it takes me a second to parse the reality of what's in front of me. She's laying there, lifeless in the shadows, a dark pool of blood blooming from beneath her head.

"Ms. Crane!" My muscles kick into gear so fast that I'm landing on my knees before I really understand what I'm seeing. "Shit!" My hands flutter uselessly over her, because I'm struck with the uncertainty of moving her. If she fell down the stairs, her neck could be broken or something. "Hey," I say, reluctantly shaking her. "Wake up, you fucking Life Alert cautionary tale."

I touch her cheek, and it's still warm, but I don't exhale until I hear her low, annoyed moan.

"Oh, Jesus ass-licking Christ." Breathless, heart still trying to jump out of my fucking chest, I look around the hall, toward the foyer, trying to remember where I left my phone. "I'm going to call you an ambulance or something. Just—" My voice sticks in my throat, because this isn't Daniel. He deserved it. The only thing Ms. Crane has ever done is survived—helped her girls to survive—and I still hear her voice in my head from the talk we had that day.

"Death is coming for me just as sure as it is you. All that matters now is

what I'm dying for."

"Well, you aren't fucking dying for this," I growl, climbing unsteadily to my feet.

I'm halfway up off my knees when I see the movement in my periphery. I could be stone cold sober, and I still wouldn't have time to react. That's what I tell myself when the blow comes, a blunt smash right into my temple, sending me crumpling to the floor.

The last thing I see before my vision blanks out is Ms. Crane's feet, shoes laced tidily.

2 9

ELECTRICITY

THE LOOK RATH gives me as he leaves the room is indiscernible, but I don't stop to question it. I'm too distracted by the fact Killian is basically fucking Story right on top of me. Her cheek is pressed into my shoulder, these little breaths punching from her parted lips with each of his deliberately slow thrusts. Killer lifts his knee, slotting it right up against mine so he can get a deeper angle, and it doesn't even matter that his nuts are dragging over my thigh.

This is hot as *fuck*.

He mouths at her shoulder, and I know it's an awkward angle. The only thing stopping Killian from crushing her into me is the forearm that's holding him up. But he makes it work, the muscles in his ass shifting as he pushes into her, dragging back and surging forward in gentle, precise movements that I wouldn't have thought him capable of. He barely jostles me with it, and he doesn't even look impatient. This is, I realize, something he wants to savor.

For a long time, Story sleeps through it. She'll sigh or twitch, toes tickling the hair on my calf, but she doesn't rouse. I think about playing asleep, but decide I can't muster the motivation for pretense. Killer knows I'm awake, will sometimes raise his heavy, sex-darkened gaze to mine, like he's inviting me to react to a secret he's been keeping. But I don't. I watch because it's all starting to make sense.

This is how Killer makes love to her.

I know it's a fucked up thought to have, but a part of me envies him. Not for the King thing—it was never a title he wanted to wield alone, anyway—but because he doesn't have to deal with his father's disapproval anymore. He doesn't have him looking over his shoulder. Doesn't have a legacy dangled over his head and the weight of the obligation that comes with it. I don't want my dad to die. I want him to trust me to do what's right for my name. Unfortunately, he made it clear a few hours ago that he still doesn't think much of Story. Of Rath. Of South Side's new King, and my place at his side.

Success to a man like my father means marrying a woman from an influential family and contributing to the Mercer empire, and *only* the Mercer empire. He disapproves because he's realizing that Killian becoming King is the first step to the three of us—the *four* of us—building our own.

I lift my hand, sweeping a lock of hair away from the apple of her cheek as he rocks into her body. "Sweetheart," I whisper, and Killian doesn't stop me. He could. It wouldn't take anything but a quick glare. Instead, his forehead drops to her shoulder as he digs his dick inside her, letting me rouse her from slumber. "You want to watch your big brother make love to you?"

She wakes slowly—so sweetly that I wish I could freeze the moment in time, that split second of *sleepy-happy-horny* on her face as she stirs. "Killian," she mutters, eyelashes fluttering. It's not a question. She probably knew he was inside of her the second he entered.

Killer reacts by thrusting deep, crushing her hips into me. I bend my knee just enough to press my thigh against her clit, and she responds with this tiny, feline-like writhe, curling her hand around my shoulder for leverage. Killer's restraint is almost more powerful than his full-on strength, and Story remains limp and docile under the brunt of it, eyes glazed from lust just as much as sleep.

He looms over me to duck in for a kiss, licking into the seam of her mouth.

He fucks her like that for a while—long enough that my cock fills again, throbbing at the thought of taking her right after. She's riding my thigh as he rides her, gasping as their movements grow pointed and a little less controlled. When she comes, mouth opened in a silent cry, I can't really be held responsible for the suggestion I'm about to make.

"We could go all night," I whisper, hand wandering to my stiff cock. "We could chain-fuck you like this. One after the other. Pumping you so full of our cum that you won't even be able to hold it all."

Killian makes a rough, eager sound, pulling back to slam into her. I know he's coming when she claws at my shoulder, pushing her ass back into him like she's desperate to take his load as deep as it can possibly go.

I watch appreciatively, smirking. "Hail to the King."

I know it's love when Killian doesn't even blink at the mess we've all made of his sheets. He collapses onto us, chest heaving, toes flexing out of their curl.

"Shower," he pants out, giving her cheek one last kiss.

I wasn't lying about us going all night, but something like that is going to require sustenance. Proper hydration. Possibly towels. Killian's two steps ahead of me, climbing out of bed to lumber his way toward the bathroom. Moments later, I hear the shower sputter to life.

Story rolls over and stretches her arm to the side, as if she's searching for something. She frowns at the empty spaces on either side of us. "Where's Dimitri?"

"He left a few minutes ago."

She gives the vacancy a series of slow, drowsy blinks. "Why?"

"Probably just got the munchies after smoking." I trail my hand down her leg, feeling the sticky jizz on her inner thigh. "Okay, up we go."

She makes a protesting sound as I pull her from the bed, her knees still wobbly. I catch her, tucking her beneath my arm to lead her toward the bathroom. "Killer can clean you up. I'll go hunt down our wayward pothead and see about some clean sheets. That sound good?"

She looks up at me, mouth pulled into a loose pout. "And something to eat?"

I freeze, thinking, '*oh, fuck*'. I don't think she's ever asked me for something before—not like this. My chest clenches and I swallow through the sudden assault of hot, possessive want swelling in my chest. She has no idea that I'd probably go out there and try to lasso the goddamn moon if she asked me to with those big eyes and plaintive voice. "You bet," is what I say, thumbing her chin.

Killian's just ducking his head beneath the spray when I open the glass door to his shower. Yet again, I get a look at the cut on his chest. It's all scabbed over and irritated, probably full of bacteria and god only knows what else, and the funny thing is, it doesn't even look good. It's a fucking horrid version of a 'S', all blocky and jagged.

So why does it make my jaw tight to know he and Rath have one and I don't?

Whatever.

Some of us have game without the risk of tetanus.

"Easy," I tell her, helping her over the lip, but Killian instantly enveloped her in his arms, dragging her beneath the water. "I'm going to go find Rath and something to eat. Want something?"

"Something carby." She tips her head back, eyes sliding closed as Killian guides her head beneath the spray. "Maybe the pasta from last night?"

"Whatever you want." I close them up in the steam, padding out into the bedroom to find my boxer briefs. Walking out into the hall, I'm thinking maybe I'll return in time to get in on some of that shower action. Lather her up. Clean my cum out of her ass and then replace it as Killer feeds her his cock.

I only get to the bottom of the staircase, lost in this fog of erotic possibilities, before I hear it.

The click of cocked gun snaps me to attention.

Freezing, I take in a litany of sudden details. The thick scent of cologne.

The buzz in the air. The eerie silence of the darkness, and what I'm just now realizing, is a cold, sticky substance beneath my feet.

Mostly, I notice the gun pressing against my head, just behind my ear. "Move, scream, say a word," a low voice warns, "and I blow your brains out. Then, I go for her." The nose of the gun presses harder. "Got it?"

Stiffly, I give a single, slow nod, but inwardly I'm wondering whose blood I walked into. I slide my eyes to the side, trying to get a look at the intruder, but he's nothing but a dark, tall shadow. "I have money," I say, raising my palms. "Just name your price."

He shoves the barrel of the gun into my skull. "Arms back. *Now*." Through the hardness of the demand, I hear a hint of something strained and annoyed, and I'm pretty sure I know why.

Slowly, I do as I'm told, putting my hands behind my back. I wait until he lowers the gun to grab my wrists. Something plastic and hard—a zip tie— looping around them, before making my move.

I spin and slam my elbow into his chin before tackling him to the ground. We land with a crash, in a tangled whirl of flailing fists and gnashed teeth.

"Then, I go for her."

She's with Killer.

I'd like to see this piece of shit try.

It's why I know he won't shoot me. It'd alert them, and he's banking on the element of surprise, and he needs it. It makes it easier to wrestle him, slamming his head against the floor. No doubt Rath got his own shots in, all the more obvious from the strangled sound the intruder makes when I plant my knee into his side. But there's blood on the floor, and Rath isn't fucking *here*. I get the upper hand quickly and then go for the gun, lunging at his wrist.

I'm actually feeling really good about it.

Right up until a second set of arms clamps around my neck, jerking me back. Maybe it's not smart, but all I can see is the night in that alley, getting choked out by Ugly Nick as he raised a gun and shot my brother in the gut.

I kick out, catching the first guy's temple with my heel, and then rear back slamming my head into the other guy's face, only—

Only the responding yelp doesn't belong to a man at all.

Come to think of it, her grip on my neck isn't exactly insurmountable either. It's laughably simple to pry her forearm away—to clamp my fingers around her delicate wrist and *snap*.

"Ah!" Her scream is stifled into a low, pained growl, but the second I turn on her, fist snatching a thick fistful of her hair, a wild shock of heat explodes up my torso. I lose control of my grip, my muscles, my thoughts, and I tumble back, head slamming into the banister as I crash to the floor.

Vision cloudy, I look up at the woman, trying to blink away the stars. "I don't know who you are, bitch," I push up onto my palms, swaying, "but you're fucking with the wrong people."

Footsteps echo across the marble, and I turn to watch the second hooded intruder stiffly approach me. I struggle to scramble to my feet, trying to get leverage, to calculate my odds, to figure out a move.

But I can't get my body to work right. Whatever that bitch shoved into my side has knocked me all off kilter. Nerves shot.

Electricity. That's the source of the heat in my side.

I've been tased or something.

Motherfucker.

The shiny tips of the guy's shoes gleam as he stops, looming above me. "I've got him," he says, voice muffled by the mask. "Go do what you need to."

It's the gun that I see in her hands as he grabs my arms and drags me down the hall, not even attempting to get me on my feet. "No!" I shout. "Killer! They're—" but a gloved hand slaps over my mouth, replaced a second later by the glove itself.

30

HOPELESS

I'VE ALWAYS HAD a nebulous concept of what a family is. My mom was family. When I think of her, I think of Sunday mornings in the garden, getting muddy until she yelled at me. She wasn't an angel or anything. She almost always smelled like one sort of alcohol or another. She never wanted to go places with me. She cooked and cleaned, but she always let everyone know how unhappy she was about it. But she'd play games with me. She'd tell me I was handsome and strong and smart, and when she smiled at me, it felt like a ray of sunshine. For a short time, she was the only thing in life that didn't seem unbearably bleak.

My dad was family. Maybe the hardest pill to swallow is that he wasn't the devil. He loved me, in whatever twisted, fucked up way he was capable of, more than anyone else in this world. It was a burden to be that—the one thing he held close and worth caring for—but I coveted it almost as much as I resented it, because I figured I'd never be that to anyone else.

My blood family was never much, but it was all I had.

Until it wasn't.

One day, there was Ms. Crane. She was the first person I met who was as pissed off as I was, the first one to really understand and confront the crazy napalm filling my chest all the time. And then Rath appeared, and just... never went away. He was the first kid to look me in the eye and say he wasn't impressed. That's scary as fuck for a ten-year-old who didn't have anything to offer the world except two fists and a legacy to follow, but Rath? He stuck to me. That's the only word for it. Tristian came along soon after, with his quick wit and icy grins, and he wasn't like Rath. I had nothing to give Tristian. He already had it all. The name, the money, the legacy. But while our dads were deciding they liked the idea of us growing connections—for business, for our family's interests—we were setting shit on fire and making our own decisions.

And now there's *her*.

We're perfectly still as the water beats down on us, foreheads pressed together. I've already forgotten why. I think after she washed her hair, I meant to kiss her, but ever since that night she let me into her room, I need to stop, and just... warm myself in front of this new reality.

Against all odds, and on account of nothing that I can see, Story Austin loves me back.

If I had a morsel of optimism inside me, I might even say I was happy.

"Brr," she says, giving this little shiver I can feel down to my marrow.

With a start, I realize the water is going cold. Shooting the showerhead a useless glare, I reach out to turn it off, swiping the wetness from my hair. I'm surprised Tristian and Rath didn't come in to join us. They could have—I wouldn't have minded sharing, packing us all up in here like sardines as we pressed against Story's wet, naked body.

Fuck, how am I already getting hard again?

I grab two towels from the rack, watching idly as Story wrings the water from her hair, accepting a towel with a grateful smile.

"I like it when you're like this," she says, shooting me a quick glance.

I wrap the towel around my waist. "When I'm like what?"

She seems to think pretty hard about the answer as she dries herself. "Nice," she answers, ducking her head to hide the bloom of pink on her cheeks. "Sweet.

Not a jerk."

There's a pang in my chest at her words, knowing that I've caused hurt. I'm not stupid or anything. I know I'm a hard person to care for, let alone love. Chances are, I'm going to blow it at some point. Maybe that's why it has to be this way—the four of us. Because when that crazy napalm knocks me off course, Tristian will be there to guide me back. Rath will be there to sneeringly inform me that I'm not hot shit. Ms. Crane will be there to slap me upside the head and demand more of me.

And maybe then, Story will stay.

"Hey," I say, taking the towel from her hands, tucking it around her chest. "I'll keep being like this, so long as you keep being like *that*."

She peers up at me, head tilting curiously. "Like what?"

Bending down, I rumble into her ear, "Mine."

She gives a soft, silent laugh, palms warm as they land on my chest. "Okay." She accepts my kiss while battling a smile. "Can I be yours while I'm wearing underwear?"

I let out my best put-upon sigh as she slips away. "Can I take them off later?"

She raises an eyebrow, stopping at the bathroom door to say, "If Dimitri doesn't get to them first."

Story laughs, leaving my room and crossing the hall to her bedroom, the light from the open door casting a glow into the hall. I get dressed with little ambition, figuring it's going to all come off soon, anyway, slipping into a hooded sweatshirt and sweats. I imagine warming her against me when we climb into bed again. That's when I hear her door snick closed across the hall.

I look over my shoulder, through my doorway, a sourness settling on the back of my tongue at the sight of her closed door. I'm not sure what propels me to it. An old, lingering hurt, perhaps. A scab I can't help but pick at. But it's more likely that, when I reach out, touching the knob, it's more of a test. I just can't tell who it's for; her or me?

Both of us fail.

Locked.

My hand balls into a tight fist, but I rap it softly against the door, listening carefully for a response. When all I hear is the grandfather clock down the hall, I swallow down the growl building in my throat. "Come on. Seriously?" I give the knob another try, irritation flaring through me when it doesn't budge. "Story? We're doing this shit again?"

I grab either side of the door frame, propping myself up there, because I just don't get it. She loves me. She's said it. She's shown it. But this *fucking door* still feels like a rejection. Locking me out is the single worst thing she can do to me. Actions speak louder than words and all that shit.

"Fuck it," I mutter, knowing I'm probably overreacting. Maybe the lock slipped. Maybe she just needs a minute to compose herself after hours of getting fucked repeatedly by three horny guys. Space, I think. She just needs a little space. She needs to feel in control for a few. That's what Tristian would say.

Of course, then he'd go check the camera after saying it.

All of these thoughts buzz through my head, and I find myself staring daggers into the door, fighting the urge to force it open. But then what? She spends the rest of the night, week, *month* pissed off and avoidant?

Not worth it.

That's why I step away—because I'm growing. As a person. Possibly.

The stair behind me creaks, and I turn. "*Finally.* Story's in there—"

The sucker punch comes from out of nowhere, snapping my head to the side. I stagger back, falling into the wall so hard that it feels like my bones rattle. It's not enough to knock me out, but it's enough to steal my footing and knock me off balance for the second hit. This one is a hot jolt of electricity that detonates through my chest and neck. That growl I'd swallowed back earlier tears its way up my windpipe. The pained yell explodes through my clenched teeth before my vocal cords seize, muscles cramping. It's like being struck by a NFL linebacker who's harnessed lightning. I fall to the floor in a breathless, rigid heap, not even getting a look at the attacker.

But I still feel him. Hear him.

First, his footsteps, heavy and solid against the hardwood floor. Then his hands grabbing my wrists and yanking them high. I hear his low, soft grunt as he plants his feet and begins dragging me down the hall. The muscle in my right shoulder pinches and twinges—and old injury from varsity—as it takes all my weight, sliding me in wrenched tugs down the hall.

I try to get my jaw to work around a warning for Story, to get my ankles to move my feet, to flex my arms, to propel this motherfucker forward—*anything.* But it's all I can do to suck in these small, ragged breaths, because my pulse is jerky and my vision is a blur of black and red, and my muscles just *won't fucking work.* It's even worse than when Ray strapped me down to that bed after being shot, a powerlessness that's wound so tightly around a precise hurt.

And that's before we reach the stairs.

This piece of shit, whoever he is, rests for a moment at the landing. I can hear his hard breaths, my wrists loose in his grip, which is when my body begins slowly coming to life. My fingers twitch and I can almost get my knee to bend, and I'm feeling pretty good about it, because this guy's almost out of stamina, and I'm going to *break his fucking neck.*

And then, in one quick, brutal motion, he gives my wrists a violent yank that heaves me right down the stairs.

I tumble down like a sack of bricks, feeling every skull-rattling step as I roll. I smack face-first into one of them, get my arm caught awkwardly beneath me on another, and end up landing at the bottom in a tangle of bruised limbs and furious breaths.

His heavy footfalls come down the stairs as I'm struggling to get my feet beneath me, slipping in something wet and infuriatingly inconvenient. I can't even manage much more than some ineffectual bucking when he grabs my wrists again, spinning to drag me down another hall. It takes a few for me to realize we're going to the parlor, and going by his strained breaths, it's a super fucking necessary location. Otherwise, he wouldn't be going through the trouble of hauling my heavy ass all this way. That's information that I keep close as he finally drags me into the room. I'm just not sure it's useful—especially when he maneuvers me to my stomach, wrenching my arms behind my back to secure my wrists.

Whoever he is, he's not that big. He grunts as he lifts me to a sitting position against the wall. I stare into his eyes as he arranges my limp limbs, trying to suss out who's behind the mask, but all I see is blank darkness. Nick would be my first suspect, but this guy's physique is all wrong. Too narrow and compact. Plus, Nick wouldn't hide his face like this.

So if not him, then who the *fuck*?

When he moves, I get a broad, if darkened view of the parlor, and it takes a dozen blinks for me to make out the shape of the person sitting across from me, head bowed.

Ms. Crane.

Her arms are bound behind her, too, blood caked down the side of her face, and she looks lifeless. Drained. Meat and fragile bones. When the man passes, she lifts her head just enough to glare at him, and the tight ball of grief in my chest falls away, because she's alive. And she looks almost as pissed off as I feel.

It takes me a minute to get past that swell of relief, but when I do, I realize she's not alone. Rath is right beside her. His eye is almost swollen shut, and there's a smear of blood up his left arm, but he's conscious, looking exactly as he did when he left earlier. Shirtless, pantsless, and most notably, stormy-eyed as his gaze bores into mine.

"Goddamn it," he mutters, jaw clenched as he looks me over. "Guess that's that." That's all he says, but it's enough to understand.

I was their hope.

"Stun gun," comes another voice, and I swing my eyes around to find Tristian slouching against the wall. He doesn't look much better than Rath and

Ms. Crane. His T-shirt and neck are streaked in an alarming amount of blood, but I can't find a source for it. That means there's only one of us left. My eyes hold Tristian's, but his are droopy and glazed. Years of football have taught me the early signs of a concussion. I'm hoping like hell he understands the panic that must roll off me in waves, anyway. I dart my eyes up to the ceiling, and then back.

Story.

She's up there alone, completely unaware. Even if she has her gun, these odds are absolute *shit*.

The man paces back and forth between us, looking out the door twice like he's waiting for something—or someone. He's got this antsy, jittering buzz about him. Bouncing on his toes. Fists clenching and unclenching. I've seen Avenue tweakers more relaxed than this shithead. It brings me a little pleasure to see the limp in his gait. He's favoring his right arm, and every now and then, he'll reach up to push his palm into his side.

My boys fought back.

I stare at his shoes as he passes. They're clean. New. Expensive boots. I try to make my brain work, to get the gears moving. Whoever this is, he's too boujee to be South Side, and not nearly tough enough to be a Royal. This is someone else.

Tristian gives me a single, slow nod, and I know we've come to the same conclusion.

Rath, however, has no issue voicing this aloud. "So, am I wrong, or is this the Ted fucker we've been waiting for?" He looks unimpressed as his eyes rise, taking him in. "I was expecting someone taller. Scarier." His shoulders shift, and it doesn't matter that he looks half naked and sort of above what's going down here. Ten bucks says he's working his wrists out of the zip ties. He mastered that shit back in middle school. "This guy's a total bitch. Did he sucker punch you, too?" Shaking his head, Rath declares, "You're never going to get her like this, dude. She likes her men tall, competent, and vaguely sane.

You aren't hitting any of her checklist—"

"Shut up," he snaps, slamming the toe of his fancy boot into Rath's jaw.

Rath's head jerks back at the force of it, but when his chin comes back down, heavy against his bare chest, his shoulders give another twist.

Ms. Crane cries out, "For Pete's sake, Dimitri!" and watches on as he spits out a glob of bright red blood. "Grow a goddamn brain cell and keep your mouth shut for once!" Below the sharpness of the words is a flash of alarm I didn't think Ms. Crane was even capable of.

Tristian and I share a grim look.

"That's for the little mark you left me!" the man barks, hitching his shirt up to reveal a small gash. The guy spends a moment inspecting the blood sluggishly bubbling from the wound, which is when I realize Rath *fucking stabbed* him. I don't know how deep it is, but I know from the brief flash of his sweaty, pale torso that he's probably lost a good amount of blood. If he weren't tweaking so hard, it might even do us some good.

Instead, the man drops in front of me, those dilated pupils drilling into mine. "It must drive you crazy, Killer. Incapacitated and out of the game. Bested by someone half your size. You're a heavy guy, I'll give you that. I had to use the highest voltage to make sure it took you down." He lets out a rabid laugh, nudging my knee with his foot. "Look at you now! You're like a big, dumb rag doll." He presses his palm to his wound as he turns, asking Ms. Crane, "Not much different from how he usually is, am I right?"

I take a breath through gritted teeth, forcing the words from my chest like a growl. "At least I'm not hiding my face like a pussy." Every muscle in my jaw fights to lock me down, but I struggle through it. "At least I fight like a fucking man."

"Oh, I'm man enough," he says, jerking his chin at the others. "I took down all the Lords in," he rucks up his sleeve, darting a glance at a sleek luxury watch, "Jesus, under an hour. Pathetic."

Even though he looks a little out of it from that kick, Rath's shoulders are squirming more deliberately now. I get a surge of adrenaline when the guy's eyes zero in on him.

"Yeah, we're the pathetic ones." Tristian gives a low laugh, getting his attention. "While you were slinking around down here, trying to figure out how to avoid an evenly matched fight? The three of us were upstairs giving your woman a gold-star dicking-down." His blue eyes narrow, making his smirk look chilling. "But hey, if that's the kind of work it takes for you to get some tail…"

The man lunges forward, taking a thick fistful of Tristian's blond hair. "You know nothing," he snarls, "about my woman."

Tristian's throat strains at the angle, head bent back to stare up at him. "I know what it's like to have her want you back. Something you'll never know."

The guy pulls out a knife, brandishing it high. From the gleam of the blade in the low light, I can see that it's already bloodied. This is the knife Rath probably used. Maybe even one of his own. But even though the guy's back flexes, arm raised, he doesn't bring it down. He shoves Tristian away. "She'd be mad if I killed you," he mutters, thrumming with that manic energy as he stomps back. "But she never said anything about this one."

All three of us snap to attention as he reaches down to snatch Ms. Crane to her feet. But despite the lava running through my veins at the pained sound she makes, my limbs still won't work.

Rath's body doesn't look much better, still out of it from that kick, but he tries—*frantically,* he tries. "No, no, wait!" He struggles clumsily to his knees, then feet, face slack with horror as the man clutches her to his chest, wrenching her head back. "Wait!"

But the guy already has the point of his blade to Ms. Crane's neck, snarling, "Watch me cut your sweet little grandwhore from ear to ear."

All three of us get tangled in the panic, poised halfway between rushing him and knowing that, if we do, she's sure to die. It's only when Delores meets my gaze that I freeze, understanding the quiet in her eyes. This was never meant to be her life—cleaning our dishes by day, hiding out in our basement by night. It's not her life, and it's sure as fuck not her death. She's hated it, but she's done it, because just as much as I understand her, she understands me. This last year she's spent with us was borrowed time. After a childhood spent under her guiding hand, it was the only gift I had the power to give her, and there for a while, she let me.

But her gaze is telling me, in no uncertain terms, that she's done being our duty.

That millisecond of stone-cold serenity in her eyes is gone in a blink.

31

A TWISTED PATH

"I'll keep being like this, so long as you keep being like *that*."

I look up at him, leaning into his solid body. "Like what?"

He tips forward to answer, voice deep and low in my ear. "Mine." It sends a spatter of goosebumps down my neck and arms, prickling my damp skin.

I laugh at myself, because it takes almost nothing from these guys to electrify my blood. "Okay," I agree, fighting back a shiver as I strain up to brush my lips against his. "Can I be yours while I'm wearing underwear?" *And possibly a sweater…*

His chest expands with an inhale and then caves with a long sigh. "Can I take them off later?"

"If Dimitri doesn't get to them first." I bury a laugh into my hand as I cross his bedroom, and then the hall. I can't help but wonder if this is what every night will be like from now on. Not the worst way to live, getting constantly fucked by the three incredible men in my life. But, if that's the case, I'm going to need a tutor, because staying up all night is going to destroy my grades. A couple weeks ago, I probably wouldn't have cared about that. But now?

I love these men, and I fully plan on being part of what they're building in South Side. Part of that is knowing that I can't rely on men alone. I've seen it with my mom, Ms. Crane, and even the other Royal women. It's going to be important—essential—to have something of my own. Something useful.

When I first came to Forsyth, studying for a career in social work was little more than an indistinct ambition. It made sense to me, but I'd be lying to myself if I claimed to have felt any genuine passion for it. Ever since I enrolled, I've had trouble finding any excitement or drive about it.

Until this week.

Now social work is something I can see myself doing—down in South Side, with kids like me and Dimitri. It's how I fit, I've come to realize. It's what I'm going to bring to Killian's rule. If the four of us are going to change this tiny part of the world, then this is how I'm going to contribute.

Suddenly, I can't wait to really sink my teeth in. I'm engrossed in my lectures. I'm hungrily soaking up every word and meeting my professors to go over my notes. I'm signing up for study groups, just like the one Marcus drove me home from earlier in the day. It's this strange, fresh energy that's had me buzzing ever since Daniel died.

I've never felt a purpose before.

I step into my bedroom, opening my dresser. I snag a pair of panties from the top drawer and slip them on before grabbing a plain white tee from the bottom drawer. It's halfway over my head when I hear the soft *snick* of my door closing.

My mouth curves into a grin. "Tell me you found the pasta." I pull the shirt down before turning to Killian. "If we keep this up, I'm going to need *so many* calories to—"

But my words get lodged in my throat, caught in a tangle of fear, because I might turn to face someone, but it's not Killian.

The person standing in front of my door is motionless, masked, and dressed head-to-toe in black. My heart stampedes in my chest as I jerk back, noticing the gun. Not just any gun. *My* gun. I'd know the shape of it, the silver glint against the moonlight coming in through the window, anywhere. The hand wrapped around it is small—as small as my own—and the silhouette of the body has curves. Womanly.

"Sutton?" My voice emerges in a sandpaper-rough whisper. "This isn't cool."

The woman doesn't move, just standing there in the dark, watching me blindly flail for something to use as a weapon. My hand fumbles over perfume bottles and a picture frame, a Forsyth teddy bear, and then the round top of the sparkly LDZ skull. There's nothing that'll help against a gun.

"What do you want?" I try to make my voice strong, but I feel anything but, standing here in a T-shirt and panties with an intruder in the house. I know firsthand just how dangerous these Royal women can be. I pitch my voice low and threatening. "They'll kill you this time. Killian's not a Lord anymore. He's a King now. He'll kill you, and no one will blink an eye."

The intruder tucks the gun in her waistband and holds up her hands in a non-threatening manner. My heart pounds as she reaches for the bottom edge of the mask and pushes it up. I take a minute to process what I'm seeing—*who* I'm seeing.

When I do, the tension drains out of my body with a swiftness that takes my breath away. "What are you doing here?! You scared the crap out of me, Mom!"

She thrusts her finger against her lips, giving me a warning look, which is when my door knob rattles. Both of our gazes dart to the movement, but she holds out her hand, giving me a sharp look.

There's a soft, hesitant knock, and then Killian's muffled voice. "Come on. Seriously?" The doorknob gives another rattle. "Story? We're doing this shit again?" His voice is pitched in that flat, harsh way that makes me imagine his nostrils are flaring in annoyance.

I open my mouth to answer him, but the look in my mom's eyes stops me short, and by the time I realize something is seriously wrong here, his heavy footsteps are already retreating. "What the hell is going on?!" I try to keep my shout to a whisper, because none of this looks good. My mother, hiding in my room, holding my gun.

The Lords would get the wrong idea.

"We need to have a talk," she says, holding her palms out in a placating gesture. "Just have a—"

There's a crashing bang, the thud so powerful that the walls rattle with the force of it. I jump violently, every nerve ending in my body coiled tight and frantic at the sound of an angry, pained roar muffled through the thickness of the walls.

"Killian," I breathe, lunging for the door.

But my mom gets there first, blocking me. "Wait!" she insists, grabbing my shoulders. From this vantage, I get a good look at her eyes—wide, filled with a strange mania. "Just wait, my little storybook." She looks to the side, as if she's waiting to hear something.

But there's nothing.

No angry noises.

No sound of struggle.

The ensuing silence might be the loudest thing I've ever heard.

"There it is." It makes her face split into a slow, relieved grin. "I'm here to fix everything." She reaches for the gun again, sliding her finger over the curve of the trigger.

I stumble back, horror rising thick in my chest. "What are you doing?"

She gives me a patient look, following me further into the room. "Baby, I'm not going to hurt you. I'm here to *save* you." Her eyes hold mine, swimming with some unfathomable intensity. "That happy ending we've been looking for? It's finally here."

"Oh my god," I breathe, clutching my stomach. She's losing it. "Mom, I know you've had a hard week. Losing Daniel was devastating, but—"

She darts toward me, eyes wild. "It wasn't devastating. It went off without a hitch!" Her sharp laugh sends a chill up my spine. "I wasn't even expecting that fire. Can you believe the luck?"

My face falls as I stumble back, claves bumping into the chair at my vanity. "Mom. *Mom.* What are you saying?"

She dips her chin, staring at me. "You know what I'm saying, Story."

Of course I know what she's saying. I just wish I didn't. "You killed him." I whisper the words, as if I'm afraid to put form to them.

She sets the gun on the edge of my dresser, removing a black glove. "It was supposed to land on Killian, you know. But then the two of you went to that goddamn awards show." Her mouth curves into an irritated slant. "Don't worry, I don't blame you for that. That's why it's always important to have a plan B."

"This is plan B?" I exclaim, making a wide, expansive gesture. "Breaking into the Lords' house in the middle of the night? Mom, this is crazy! The guys will be here soon." But even as I say it, I know it's not true. It's been too long. Dimitri leaving the room and not coming back. Tristian vanishing when I need something. And Killian...I know that was his yell out in the hall. "I need you to *stop* and explain what's going on. Now."

"I've been wanting to," she says, eyes pleading as she removes her other glove. "Every day, I'd have to talk myself down from spilling it all. It's been killing me to keep so many secrets from you." Her eyes roam over my dresser, hand reaching out to straighten the objects I'd knocked over a few minutes before. Her fingers linger over the glittery skull, a darkness crossing her features. "But you know all about secrets, don't you?"

Swallowing, I look toward the window, wondering if I'm really doing this. Am I really looking for a way to escape my own mother? "What do you mean?"

"I know about everything, Story." Her voice is ominously one-note, and when she lifts her gaze to mine, I find an awareness there that chills me. It'd be so much easier if she were truly losing it, crazed and broken, but she's completely lucid. This is a woman who knows exactly what she's *done.* "I know what Daniel wanted with you. I know what you did on the internet when you were younger. I even know about all the things your brother's done to you." Her voice drops. "And his friends."

A tightness clutches my lungs, making it painful to breathe through. "How?"

She flicks the glitter off her fingertips. "A mother always knows, but it makes it easier when your husband has the entire house fitted with security cameras." A weariness crosses her face as she edges closer, propping her hip against the dresser. "It's like I told you before. I blame myself. I put you into that home, with those…" Her mouth contorts, but she doesn't finish—doesn't put a word to what the Paynes are. There's a strange appeal in the way she looks at me. "I had to stay, though. Daniel was our way out, but he was also a part of this…*sickness*. I had to find a way to protect you while still being his wife, so that's what I tried to do. You understand, don't you?"

I shake my head, at a complete loss. "I don't."

Frustration sparks in her eyes, but she visibly bats it down. "You wanted to go away, so we sent you to the boarding school. That might have worked, but Daniel…" Her jaw goes tight and she looks away. "He knew where you were, and he never stopped. Not once. He was still talking to those *monsters* about you. The *Kings*." She spits the word like it's bitter. "He said he was keeping you whole for them. That you could still belong to them. That he could call you back whenever they wanted, their little Royal virgin whore." She raises her eyes, pinning me with a fierce stare. "So I sent you some letters and made you run."

Every cell in my body turns to ice, and I fall back into the chair without really experiencing it. "You?" It's as though I've left my body and I'm nothing more than what Killian had described that day out back. *Meat*. Flesh and bone, and nothing more. "It was you?"

She reaches for the hairbrush on the vanity, raising her chin. "The Executive Daddy. Not very inspired, was it? Daniel rarely was." I don't move as she gathers my hair into her hand, her knuckles cold as they brush against the back of my neck. "I knew what it was like at that age, having creepy old men lusting after you. I knew the fears. The panic. The constant worry that they might find you, corner you." She runs the brush through my hair, bristles tickling my scalp.

"I also knew the power that attention could wield, how it sucked you in. I just needed you to be hidden—just for a while. Just until I found my opportunity."

"You're Ted." It feels like there's a cost in saying it aloud. I pay it with the shattered pieces of my heart as I struggle to grasp the magnitude of this knowledge. "You killed Jack."

The brush snags in a knot, and she carefully frees the bristles. "Not me. Not directly." Sighing, she parts my hair down the middle, just like she always used to do when I was small. "I found you before Daniel did, but then I saw how you were living. With those…criminals." I can hear the displeased moue of her mouth. "When you were smaller, I used to think to myself…this child is going to be easy. Oh, you were so polite and well-mannered. All the other mothers I knew used to tell me how lucky I was to have a good one. And that's what you were. You were honest and open. You were *so good*." This time, when the brush snags a knot, she yanks. "Then all these men came along, hell bent on turning you into something twisted and *wrong*."

"You killed him," I repeat, stuck in the memory of his blood. His blank, vacant eyes. "You murdered him."

"Ugly Nick killed him," she snaps, giving my hair a rough tug. "And I wouldn't have had to if you'd just stayed on a straight path, Story. Honestly! Burglars and degenerates?" She emits a hard huff of breath, separating my hair. "He was just another in the long line of men who were using you. Can't you see that now? I know you're young, but you must see that." Flippantly, she adds, "It doesn't matter. By the time I realized how you were living, Daniel had already tracked you down again, so that degenerate served a purpose. I needed just a little more time."

The tickle of the tear tracking down my cheek barely penetrates. "You tormented me."

She pauses at this, fingers stilling in my hair. Softly, she says, "That's not fair."

"Not fair?" I try to turn to look at her, but the grip on my hair, already half braided, snaps me back. "Not *fair*?!"

"Enough," she begins, voice full of indignation, "I knew the second you stepped foot back in this town that you were too much like me. Did you ever stop to wonder why you never went to the police? Oh, it'd be useless to do it here, but in California? In Colorado? You had multiple chances to get away from this, Story, and what did you do?" She roots around my vanity for a hair tie, sounding more and more angry. "You came right back to their fucking doorstep because you can't stay away. A part of you craves it—the pain and humiliation you feel when they defile you like a little pet, even when I try so hard to—"

"Ah!" I cry out when she pulls my hair, snapping my head back.

Suddenly, she's in front of me, taking my hands in hers. "Listen to me, my little storybook." Her eyes bore beseechingly into me. They're eyes just like mine. The same color. The same shape. Probably even the same vibrant edge of desperation. "I've been down this road, and I know where it leads. You'll spend a few years being the scum on the bottom of their shoes. They'll pull you out when they want some excitement. They'll use you. Debase you. Soil you. One of them will eventually put a baby into you." At this, she smiles, but it's a broken, jagged thing. "You'll give birth to her after seven hours of excruciating labor. You'll hold her in your arms for the first time, and she'll be so beautiful and lovely and *good*. You'll be amazed that something so perfect could come from such an ugly person." She reaches up to thumb my tear away. "You'll look into the eyes of this marvelous thing you've made, and it'll change you. You'll make a promise to her that it'll be different. That she'll never have to know a life on her knees. That you'll do whatever it takes. You'll beg, borrow, steal— and yes, if it means keeping that promise, you'll kill, too."

A sad, mangled laugh claws its way from my throat at the idea of it—this dream of hers. As if she's sacrificed and worked so hard to save me from the very fate I've been subjected to for years. "Like Vivienne?" I ask, stomach roiling at the magnitude of her sins. "Was that for me, too? How did slitting her throat and leaving me her finger help me in any fucking way."

Her mouth presses into a tense line. "Vivienne was getting in the way of my plans for you."

"Vivienne was getting in the way of your *marriage*," I correct, snatching my hands from her grip.

My mother sits back on her heels, eyes hardening. "You're right. She was servicing my husband. *Regularly.* You know why that was a problem, don't you?" She snorts at my blank expression, rising to her feet. "Jealousy is above me, Story. Otherwise the Velvet Hideaway's payroll would be a hell of a lot smaller." She walks to my dresser and begins going through the drawers. "She knew too much. Had too much access. She was beginning to notice the money missing." Glancing at me over her shoulder, she explains, "Money that I used to pay Ugly Nick to take Killian out." She pauses, pulling out a pair of my old jeans. "Or try, at least. He's a slippery one, isn't he?"

"You were wrong before," I say, my voice just as perfectly controlled as Tristian's taught me. "I didn't come back here because I craved humiliation. I came back to get revenge."

She drops the jeans in my lap and lingers, hands on her hips. "By spreading your legs over and over again?"

My brain spins, my heart aches, and the rage in the pit of my belly—all that fire I thought I'd buried from all the years of abuse—flickers back to life. "I did what I had to do. Don't tell me you don't understand that." I look up and hold her eye. "And I won. I beat them. They don't own me."

"That bracelet." She jerks her chin at my wrist, sneering. "Those scars on your chest. The tracker in your neck. They're the mark of a *pet*."

My back straightens, eyes flashing. "Right now, they're the mark of a Queen."

My mother's face pinches at the word, like she's tasted something bitter. "Have you been listening to anything I've said?" She takes the jeans from me, crouching down to slip the legs over my feet, motions jerky and stiff. "I was married to Daniel for years. I was his confidante. I single-handedly formed the foundation for one of his most successful businesses. I advised him, elevated him, fucked him, and even *I* wasn't a Queen. Women like us?" She shakes her head, letting out a resentful laugh. "We'll never be Queens." When I tear my jeans from her hands, working them up over my thighs and hips myself, she raises her eyes to mine. "Not unless we take it."

"So that's what this is about," I stall, seeing the gleam of the gun in my periphery. If I lunged for it, I could turn it on her. But could I use it? Could I kill her? If I bluffed, would she believe me? "You just want the power. The control."

Her expression softens as she stands. "Not me. *Us*." She curls a wisp of hair over my ear, eyes wistful. "We'll rule this place together. The right way. And we'll never have to get on our knees again." Her smooth hand cups my cheek. "You're my world. My sweet little fairytale. I made you a promise, and I'm going to kill them for what they've done to you." Her lips curve. "I'll start with Tristian Mercer, for shoving his cock in your mouth all those years ago. Then that little street urchin for thinking he can carve you up like a piece of meat." Sighing, she lifts my wrist, thumbing at the bronze skull. "And then I'm going to kill your brother, because he's the one that let them do it to you."

I see the lie for what it is now. Killian is the heir. He's the King. She'll kill him because he's what's standing between her and the life she wants. None of this is really about me. It's about her desire for power.

"No, you won't." I pull my wrist away easily, remembering how Dimitri sounded in the parlor earlier when I walked in on the meeting with the Kings. So blasé and cold and vicious. It's as embedded into my flesh as his knife once was, because that's what they are to me now. A part of me. "I came here for a reason. They're not yours to kill."

She watches me, eyes searching my face. For a long stretch, there's nothing but silence. And then she grabs the gun, tucking it into her waistband. "You don't need to bloody your hands with this. You're not capable of such a thing.

It's what makes you so special, Story."

"Show me where they are," is my bland reply, "and I'll show you exactly what a Lady is capable of."

3 2

BLADES & BULLETS

THAT MILLISECOND OF stone-cold serenity in her eyes is gone in a blink.

I see it for what it is. Delores is sick of hiding. She's done with a life of laying low, watching the clock tick toward her end years. She's finished with being the defenseless old lady who lives behind our pantry, and *oh*, most of all…

She's done being a victim to stupid, cruel men.

Even with his hands bound and kicked off-kilter, Rath almost gets there before it happens.

Almost.

Ms. Crane moves so fast that I doubt even Tweaker Ted sees it coming. A lot of people don't know this about Delores Crane, but she's actually a pretty proficient fighter when it comes to self-defense. They think because she got her teeth kicked in by her old man all the time that she's just some frail little doormat with a bad attitude.

They're wrong.

She snatches his wrist and twists, jamming the blade right into his gut. "Eat shit, you motherfucker!"

"Ah!" he howls, lurching forward to grab for her, but the sound of a metal click stops everyone where they stand.

We'd know the sound of a hammer being cocked anywhere.

"What in the heavens is going on in here?" a voice rings out, footsteps thumping into the room. I have to blink through the rush of receding panic to make out a face. When I do, I don't feel relieved. I don't feel afraid.

Mostly, I just feel really fucking confused.

"Posey!" Tristian works his way to his knees, nodding at the guy, still hunched over and panting. "Shoot him! Quick!" He tosses me a glance, and I see the same hope in his eyes. Story is still safe upstairs behind that locked door.

Posey's face sets into a deep frown as she approaches the intruder, and it clicks for me before she even rests her palm on his back. She's wearing black, from head to toe, hair mussed—probably from the mask.

She gives the guy an affectionate little pet.

"Son of a bitch." I watch, stunned and off balance, as she raises the gun— not to the guy, but at me. "You're together."

Tristian and Rath catch on next, both collapsing in disbelief against the wall. "What the fuck," Rath breathes.

"Put the knife down, Delores," she says serenely.

Ms. Crane stares at my stepmother for a long beat, then throws the knife to the ground with a defeated clatter. "Well, this just turned into a different fight."

"She fucking stabbed me!" the masked man exclaims through gnashed teeth.

Posey carefully lifts his shirt, cooing, "Let's have a look." This wound is a hell of a lot gushier than the first one, and from the way Posey pauses at the sight of it, she's probably not expecting something this severe. Sighing, she slips off one of his gloves and presses it into the wound. "You know better than to let Delores Crane near a knife, sweetie."

He grunts, pressing his bloody hand over hers. "Can we kill them now?"

Posey looks at him. Throughout the whole exchange, she's kept the barrel of that gun fixed on me, but now she lowers it, saying, "In a moment. First, you should be thanked for a job so well done."

I scoff, because this guy's one good stiff breeze away from collapsing.

But then she works her fingers beneath his mask, slowly lifting it. When his mouth appears, she tilts her head to kiss it. It's during that disgusting moment that the three of us look for a new angle. She's distracted. The gun is down. We could probably rush her, get it away, and then—

And then she rips the rest of the mask off.

It's not the shock that it should be, but maybe I'm reeling from both being tased and my stepmother holding a gun at me.

When his face connects to the voice, the shoes, the luxury watch, the build, it makes perfect sense. He's such a fixture around here, as invisible to me as the grandfather clock in the hallway upstairs. As unassuming as the empty vase on the mantel. As innocuous as the rug below our feet.

Martin.

"You've got to be fucking with me," Tristian says, sneering as Posey breaks away. "How the hell did you even get in here?!"

"Oh, I never left," Martin says, tossing his mask aside. He leans back on the desk—the same desk he was standing in front of eight hours ago as I rattled off a list of duties—and grunts as he inspects his shiny new stab wound. Breathlessly, he adds, "You really had this place locked down tight, Mercer. I waited weeks to finally get an in after I left that finger upstairs. Must have really shaken you up."

I frantically think back to the meeting, leading out Tristian's dad, Lionel Lucia, and the mayor. That's the problem with Martin. He's fucking wallpaper— there, but not. In the company of Kings, he's so easy to overlook. I invited him in and never escorted him out.

Goddamn it.

But there's one thing I'm almost sure of. "You're not Ted," I say, giving him a derisive look. Martin was still a little law school peon when Story began getting his letters.

"No, he isn't," a voice rings out.

Tristian, Rath, and I have known each other for a long time, and we've done a lot things together. There's almost nothing we haven't been through. We've even been inside of the same girl, at the same time, and still.

I don't think we've ever been as connected as we are at this moment, hearing her voice.

The heart pounding relief flows between us like an avalanche, like marionettes having their strings cut, and even before we look to the door to set our eyes on her, the rhythm of our exhales is its own language, and it's saying *she's okay*.

It's begging, *run.*

She coolly enters the parlor, dressed in a plain t-shirt and jeans, her feet bare. Her gaze passes over us, one by one, taking us in. Her hair is still wet from our shower, but it's hanging in a smooth braid over her shoulder, and when she extends her arm, lifting a finger toward her mother, she doesn't even look surprised at the scene in front of her. "She is."

Tristian's jaw works around the same panic I'm feeling. "She's *what?*"

"Ted," Story clarifies, watching her mother dab at a cut on Martin's forehead. "It was her all along. She was just trying to protect me. I see that now." She pauses, eyes growing tight at the corners. "Although, I wasn't expecting Martin to be here."

Ms. Crane snorts, propping herself in the far corner. "Any port in a storm, right, Posey?"

Posey straightens, swinging the barrel of the gun to her, but Story steps in front of it, batting the gun down. "No. We're not going to hurt her."

The back of my teeth ache from how hard I'm grinding them. "Bit late for that, little sister."

She tilts her head just-so—just enough for me to make out the curve of her cheek. "Killian, please."

A sick realization builds in my gut, and I glare at Posey. "This fucking bitch tried to kill me. She killed Viv." Rage wracks though me. "She killed my dad."

"And then she tried to frame us for it," Rath adds, edging toward Ms. Crane.

Posey lowers the gun, narrowing her eyes as she skirts around her daughter. "This should have gone a lot smoother, you know. I wanted you out of the picture before I got rid of Daniel. I didn't particularly care how." She flings a hand out, which is when I notice the gun. Silver. Small. If the light were better—if I were closer—I bet I could make out the engraving. *Lady's Choice.* "If Ugly Nick had aimed a little higher. If Daniel had blamed you for Vivienne and he'd had the balls to do something about it. If he'd connected your threat on that video from Thanksgiving and the severed finger…" She lifts the gun again, pointing it right at my head. Her face hardens, eyes surging with bright fury. "If you hadn't gone to that goddamn awards banquet!"

"Mom!" Story barks, pulling her back. "We had a deal."

In my periphery, I see Rath's shoulders moving again. I see Tristian looking back and forth between me and Posey. I see Ms. Crane cross her arms, as if she's waiting. But we all notice the same thing.

Story isn't taking the gun from her.

Posey backs off, and I look at Martin, bloody and pale, so sweaty that it's dripping down his temples. He's shaking, but it's hard to know if it's from the injuries, or if he's just coming down from whatever drugs she probably pumped him full of.

"You're such an idiot," I tell him, distantly tracking Rath's movements in the corner of my eye. "You realize she's using you, right? Just like she used my dad. She's a gold digging whore who'll fuck anything for a taste of power, even a sorry-ass simp like you."

He reacts with incredible speed, flying off the desk and dropping before me to shove the tip of the knife under my chin. "Don't you fucking talk about her like that! This woman," He points at her, even though his crazed eyes stay on me, "is a goddess. Your father never appreciated her. Never understood how smart she is, how fucking *genius*! He never deserved her, and neither did you!"

I don't give away that a tingling sensation is traveling through my limbs, like they're finally awakening. I keep myself carefully still, unflinching at the blade beneath my chin. "And you do, because you're a nice little lapdog, huh?"

"You'd know all about having a lapdog," Posey snaps, yanking Martin away. She takes the knife away from him and slides it into the cargo pocket of her pants. "You think I'd overlook the way you treat my daughter?" She turns to Story, her eyes swimming with anguish. "You took my sweet, precious baby, and you abused her. Humiliated her. Defiled her!"

I look at Story, waiting for her to set the record straight, because—well, yeah. We did all of that. We hurt her and debased her. But we also saved her. We cherished her. Loved her.

Story meets my gaze, but she doesn't hold it.

She looks away, silent.

"I'm here to give her the one thing I know she wants most," Posey continues, pulling Story to her side. "Justice."

"Bullshit," Tristian says, staring at the two of them—mother and daughter—with a tight, outraged expression. "Story, tell her that's *bullshit*!"

"She won't." My voice is low but certain, because I can see it in her eyes. Less than an hour ago, those eyes were staring back into mine as the water beat down on our heads, and it was warm—even when the shower ran cold. I want to believe it was real. That Story couldn't kiss me like that, touch me like that, look at me like that, and then turn around and be a part of our demise. I want to believe I know her better.

But I also know myself.

I know the shit I've done to her. I remember every cruel word and bruising touch. I remember the stroke of my pen as I bound her to us in this house. I remember her tears that night. I found her upstairs with a shard of glass pressed to her wrist. I remember *breaking her*.

"If she wants justice," I offer in a bland tone, "then it's hers to take. I won't stop her."

Posey raises an eyebrow, mouth caught halfway into a smile. "Is that supposed to sway her or something?"

"It's just the way it is." I shift my gaze to Story, making sure she hears every word. "If she wants me dead, then there's no point in living, anyway."

When Story first came back, she was scared and angry, so nervous that it fell off of her in waves. I don't know how it was for the others, but for me, being around her was damn near over-stimulating, like standing next to a superconductor. But as time went on, she grew into someone new, and this person—this woman who finally came to love me back—wasn't so easy to read.

Right now, she's giving nothing away. Not blinking. Not frowning. Not smiling.

This must be what other people feel like when they're talking to Tristian.

Tristian's blue eyes peer up to search hers, and when he says, "Sweetheart?" It's painful to hear. Too tender, too exposed to these intruders. I know that tone—that word. It's only ever been meant for her.

Martin lets out a loud, harsh laugh. "This is the best part of all of this. Watching her bury the knife into your backs."

"The best part will be the police report," Rath says. He's in fine form, chin lowered to glare at Martin through his lashes. "Male suspect, two stab wounds to the torso. Multiple contusions. Victims found with defensive wounds, tied and executed. It still hasn't hit you yet." His lip rings catch the light with a tepid, cruel smirk. "You're the fall guy, Martin."

Martin's smile falls. "You don't know what you're talking about."

Scoffing, I tear my gaze from Story to look at him. "Why do you think she didn't bring her own gun? Who else do you think she's going to pin this on? Her own daughter? For a lawyer, you're pretty fucking thick. This is textbook Daniel Payne." I lift my chin to my stepmother. "You paid attention."

Posey isn't like her daughter. She reacts instantly, lifting the gun and bolting forward to press it right to my forehead. It's how Rath and I know we've hit the bullseye. "I'm going to enjoy snuffing you out, Killian," she grits out, fingering the trigger. "Just like I did your hapless, insipid mother." I feel the blood draining from my face, because she must be lying. My mother left, but she didn't die. Posey gives a wide, manic grin. "Oh, you didn't think the great Daniel Payne would marry just anyone, did you?" She looks at Story over her shoulder, eyes flashing proudly. "It's how kingdoms are won, you know. The blood price isn't just about exterminating the competition. It's a test of will and commitment. It's also mutually assured destruction. Daniel had to know my crimes before I could be privy to his." She rattles this off like it's a lesson, and from the slack part of Story's mouth, she's almost as shocked as I am.

I look up at this woman who's orphaned me, beyond the barrel of the gun, past the features that she passed onto the girl I love, and all I feel is a sick, black hatred. "I knew from the start you were trash. Nothing but a saggy pair of tits desperate for a crumb of relevance in a world that never wanted you." I flick my eyes at Story. "If that's the kind of person you made, then put the bullet in me and get it over with."

Posey fingers the trigger, eyes tightening.

Story shouts, "No!" and lurches between us, knocking the gun away. She looks at her mother with eyes of steel, shoulders rising and falling with short, hard breaths. "It has to be me. You said it yourself. Kingdoms are won with blood. You've passed your test." Story nods at me, gently prying the gun from her mother's grip. "This is mine."

Posey searches her eyes for a long moment, but ultimately gives a slow, meaningful nod. "You're right." She lets Story take the gun, reaching out to cup her cheek. "Earn this, so you'll know it's yours." With that, Posey steps back, her eyes pinging from the gun to the three of us. "Go on."

Story takes a visibly deep breath before turning to us. She looks at Tristian first. He's managed to get on his knees beside me, but he's leaning against the wall now, and from the way he's gazing up at her, so still and blank, I'm guessing he's come to the same conclusion as I have.

What happens here, happens.

"Over here," she whispers, waving her gun between Rath and the space on my other side. He complies limply, crossing the distance to crouch beside me. I can't help but notice his shoulders have stopped their deliberate wriggling from the zip ties. Either he's gotten his hands free, or he's given up, and Rath's a lot of things, but he's no quitter.

Until now.

"Look at me, baby." Rath's voice is gentle, placating as Story meets his gaze. His right eye is even worse now, puffy and purpling. "Just be quick. Don't blink." He gives her a slow, encouraging nod, but it's Posey who steps up to help her raise the gun.

Story squares her shoulders, and even after all this time, she still has flawless trigger discipline—just like I taught her—finger resting over the guard.

"First rule of gun safety: Never point a gun at something you aren't looking to kill..."

"It's easier than you think," Posey says, eyes alight with excitement as they pass over the three of us, all lined up for our execution.

An image flashes in my head of the girl who tied me up and enacted her revenge. My memory is still fuzzy from the drugs that night, but I recall the tremor in her hand when she pressed the gun to my head. When she forced herself onto my cock. When she destroyed my secret, sacred things.

Not tonight.

This Story Austin keeps her chin up and her eyes hard. Confident. Unfaltering.

We made this girl—through tenderness and blood, ecstasy and tears—and when she lowers the barrel to my forehead, pressing the cool steel against my skin, I know I deserve it.

"Just take a deep breath," Posey says, coaching her, "and count to five." Story's chest expands, and then slowly contracts, eyes falling closed. Posey counts for her, "One…"

When she parts her lips, Story breathes, "Two…" She slips her finger onto the trigger. "Three…" And then she opens her eyes, voice smooth and sure. "Seven."

My eyes jolt up.

237.

Mayhem.

Rath springs forward, but I barely notice it beyond the blur of the gun swinging to Posey. The shot is close—too close—and I cringe at the ear-splitting crack of it going off just as much as the shriek from Posey that follows. I don't give myself time to process the aftermath of it, because I'm too busy struggling to my feet. Ms. Crane is already lunging for the knife in Posey's pants, so even though Rath is gunning for Martin, he doesn't get there first. Martin scrambles for Delores, one hand clutching his side, but Tristian swipes out a leg, sending him crashing to the floor. Ms. Crane jumps on his back while Tristian hurdles toward the gun. It's how I realize he's broken from his zip ties, too, his hands grabbing the gun from Story's grip in a quick, skilled motion.

Ms. Crane won the race for the knife and is shoving it into Martin's throat, snarling, "I guess I *can* keep stabbing men to death."

I'm sucking on the hind tit here, but I stumble toward Story, shoving her back to place myself between her and the mayhem.

Perfect word for it.

Rath is yelling and Story is gasping, Tristian barking at Martin to, "Get down, motherfucker!" and Posey's on the floor making these wet, agonized noises, clutching at her thigh as she screams through clenched teeth.

But even though Delores Crane is proficient with a blade, she's small and old and no match for a tweaker who's fighting for his life. He snatches her hair and flips, slamming her hard onto the floor. It's a blur of a scuffle, too fast for me to get to, but the second Martin gets the knife, all three of us are kicking into gear. It's the flash of fear in her eyes more than anything that makes me fly toward her.

I don't get there.

Not before a second shot rings out.

Tristian pulls the trigger mid-march, catching Martin square in the middle of his back. Even when it hits, bowling Martin over, Tristian bears down on them with a fury in his eyes that no one would want to be on the other side of. I stop short, surprised he's not just emptying the entire fucking clip into Martin's ass. Instead, he grabs him by the collar of his black sweater, wrenching him away from Ms. Crane.

He hauls him up, snarling into his face, "That's the last fucking time you touch her!" But Martin is barely conscious now, head flopping back with a sickening gurgle, so he throws him aside like the discarded meat he is, huffing.

Ms. Crane stares up at him, wide-eyed and breathless. "My big dumb goddamn hero," she gasps, accepting his hand when he gingerly lifts her to her feet.

"I'm sorry." Story's voice draws our attention to where she's standing, staring down at her mother with a lost expression. She wrings her fists, eyes wide with distress. "I'm sorry, mom. I had to."

Posey tries to sit up, but she slips in the blood pooling beneath her. "You stupid girl!" she cries, writhing around, eyes clenched shut. "You stupid, stupid—I'm your mother! What are they?! They're nothing!"

Story's eyes swim with tears, but they don't fall.

Not when she raises her gaze to us.

There we stand, three Lords and their cranky housekeeper—bloody, beaten, and exhausted, but too full of adrenaline to think of dropping our guard. I know we don't look like much. Certainly not Kings.

But when Story speaks, her voice is even and sure.

"They're mine," she answers.

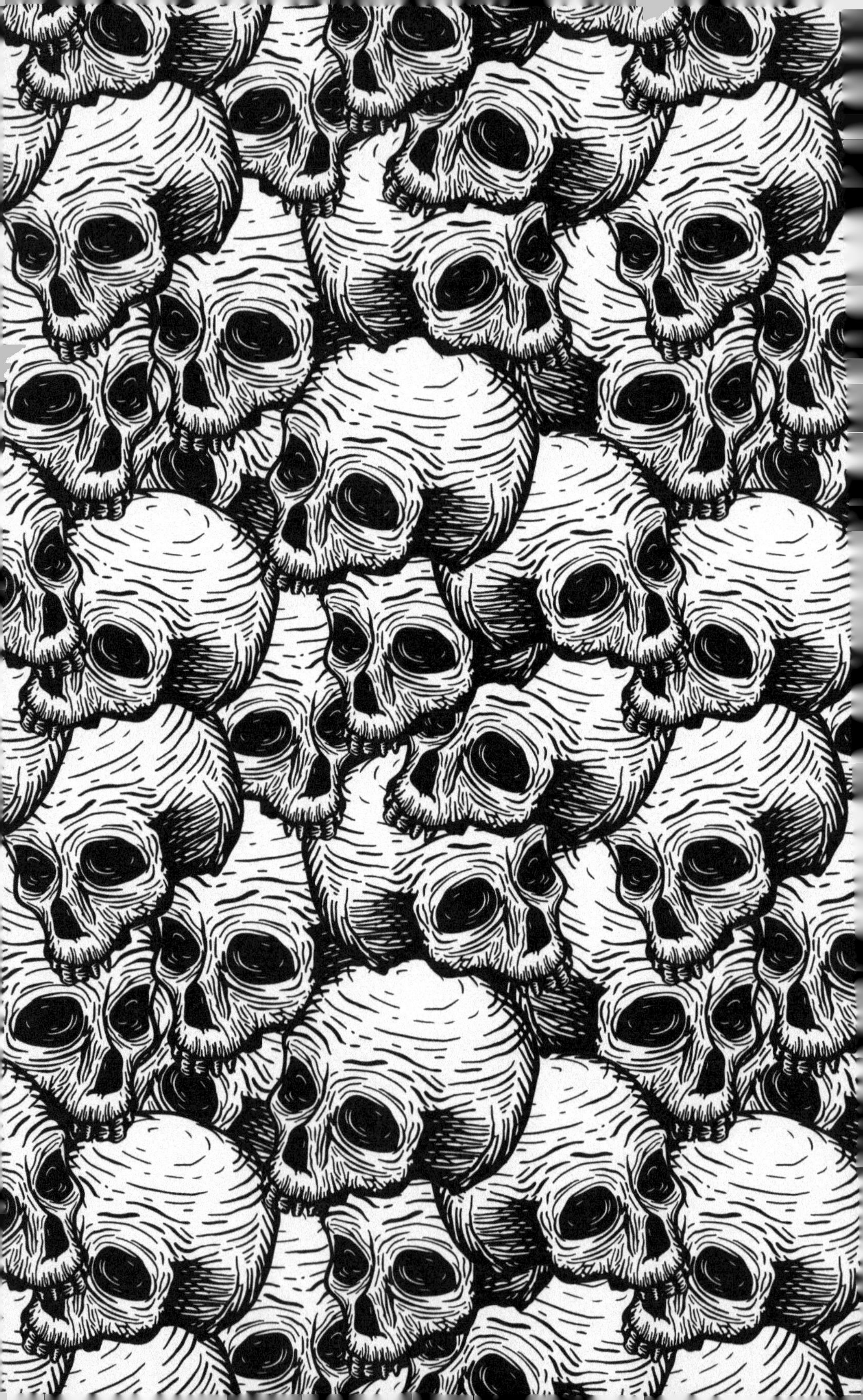

33

MERCY

I DON'T WANT to wake up.

Not completely.

It's warm here in Dimitri's bed. Everything, from the smell in the air, to the low hum of music coming from the speakers, to the plush give of the mattress, is comfortably familiar. There's an arm around my middle, and one beneath my neck, and I can feel their breaths—safe, close, whole—as if they were my own. I don't want to open my eyes and see the damage that's been wrought. Facing my mother last night was bad enough, watching the ambulance cart her away, cuffed to the gurney. I think Killian wanted to kill her, and he has every right. She took his father, and if she's to be believed, his mother, too.

"*It's up to you*," he said last night, right before we called the police. Gun in hand, he kissed my mouth and stroked my jaw, and I knew he was asking for permission.

But I just couldn't bring myself to give it.

"You're awake." Dimitri's rough murmur comes from behind me—a caress of his breath on the nape of my neck. "You always breathe different when you're awake."

I sigh as his hand moves down to the hem of my shirt, wiggling beneath it to rest against my ribs. "It feels late."

He hums into my skin, fingertips skating over my belly. "Almost dark out. We were fucking beat."

The police were crawling all over the brownstone for hours after the incident. Dimitri and Tristian had followed Ms. Crane to get checked out at the triage, while Killian dealt with the local authorities. I suspect it was his first flex as King, because when they told him we'd need to find somewhere else to stay for a couple days, he'd flashed them a card and a stiff smile, and then casually ushered me back inside.

'Beat' doesn't even begin to encompass the exhaustion.

"What do you think will happen to her?" I ask, dreading the pause that comes after. I know I shouldn't care. My mom tormented me for years. She murdered Jack. She wove me into a plot to steal South Side from the men I love, and she hurt them—Killian most of all, but Dimitri and Tristian, too. If things were black and white, I could have let Killian put that bullet into her head.

But they aren't.

She's a murderer, but she's also the woman who used to brush my hair and call me her little storybook. She terrorized me over and over again, but she also sacrificed for me—for my health and safety. Nothing about this is simple or easy.

"I sent the detective the video." *Tristian.* He's on the other side of Killian, reaching over him to feather the tips of his fingers down my closed eyelids. They're puffy and sore from crying last night, shut up in the downstairs bathroom until I saw the faint shadow of feet beneath the crack of the door.

Killian didn't ask to be let in. But I did anyway.

Tristian sighs, adding, "That was really smart, you know. Turning on the camera on your dresser?"

I hadn't known it was my mom at the time. I figured it'd be a Royal woman, or someone from the Hideaway, like Augustine or Lavinia. "It'll put her away for a long time," I note, cracking my eyes enough to see Dimitri's hand moving beneath the fabric of my shirt. After a suspended moment, I bring myself to ask the question that's filling my head like a rain cloud. "Are you mad that I couldn't—"

"*No.*" Killian's voice rumbles beneath the ear I have pressed to his chest, ringing with finality. "I know how complicated it can be, Story. I could have killed my dad a hundred times, but I didn't."

I exhale, finally letting myself look up at them.

Tristian is the first one I see. Even after so many hours of sleep, he still looks sapped, a bruise blooming on his temple. I extend a hand to push my fingers through his hair, straightening it up, but it doesn't calm this agitated need buzzing in the pit of my chest. This is why I push up, meeting him over Killian's chest to press a slow, grateful kiss to the bruise. It's better then, feeling him against me, so warm and alive.

When I turn to look at Killian, I'm relieved to find him mostly uninjured. He has some bruises on his neck, his chest, but his face is perfectly whole, making it easy for me to lean down to brush our mouths together. Killian takes it greedier than Tristian had, tangling his fingers in the back of my hair to hitch me closer, chest vibrating with a ragged, hungry sound.

He doesn't hold me, though, letting me get an arm beneath me to turn to Dimitri.

My heart twists painfully at the sight of him. His eye is a swollen mass of hurt, and the edge of his jaw has every shade of purple covering it. He took out his piercings last night due to the swelling, so he looks strangely bare, vulnerable. I reach out to touch him, but wince and pull back.

Dimitri stares at me. "That bad, huh?"

Killian glances around my shoulder to say, "You look like you got hit in the face with a dick-shaped hammer."

"Fuck off." Dimitri grabs my hip, pulling me flush. "I've had worse, baby. Don't sweat it."

"It looks painful," I argue, carefully kissing his jaw.

"Pssh." He turns to catch my lips with his. "I woke up three hours ago and raided Ms. Crane's pill stash. I feel like a million bucks."

I pull back, searching his eyes, and—yeah, now that he mentions it, he is absolutely sporting that lazy, glazed look. Ms. Crane isn't even here. She's staying overnight at the hospital for tests, because the hit she took over the head was worrying for someone her age. "She's probably going to need those, Dimitri." The chide is half-hearted, but it springs me into action.

All three of them groan in varying degrees of protest when I climb out of the bed. "We're going to need supplies." I explain, pointing to Dimitri. "Ice pack," and then Tristian, "Ice pack and Motrin," and then Killian, "Caffeine and whatever Dimitri's stoned off of." Ms. Crane will understand, and I'm sure the doctor probably already has her high as a kite, too. "All of us are going to need food, hydration, sleep—"

"Blow jobs," Dimitri coolly adds.

"And beer." Tristian throws me a wink.

Rolling my eyes, I snatch Killian's hoodie from the floor. "The only action the three of you are going to be getting is *rest*. Look at you." I zip up the hoodie and do exactly that, hands on my hips as I survey the scene in front of me. Dimitri's still on his side, but he's propped on an elbow, peering down the bed at me with his one good eye. Tristian is reclined back against the headboard, prodding at the bruise on his temple. Killian is sprawled out on his back between them, looking like he doesn't know what to do with his arms now that I'm gone. "You look like a defeated group of horny apocalypse survivors," I note.

Killian finds out what to do with his arm.

He flips me off.

Downstairs, I discover the bottle of pain pills Dimitri had left by the sink, but I pause at the refrigerator. Feeding these guys is never anything but a harrowing task. Between Tristian's anal retentive culinary preferences, the sheer volume of food Killian can consume, and Dimitri's total lack of nutrition,

I take my time putting something suitable together.

I'm just about to assemble the sandwiches when the phone in my hoodie pocket goes off. I guess Killian must have left his phone in it. When I fish it out, it's locked. The texts still pop up, though.

Lord Tristian: *no mayo, extra tomatoes, and use the whole wheat bread*

Lord Tristian: *please*

My chin drops and I spin, scanning the kitchen. The camera is up in the corner beside the pantry. I don't even know why I'm surprised. If I could, I'd be watching a screen to make sure they're okay, too. The text alone is enough to make some of the tightness in my chest ease.

I don't know if it can capture audio, but I still yell anyway, thrusting my finger toward the lens. "You'll eat what I make, and you'll fucking like it!"

I'm rooting through the lettuce when the phone dings again.

Lord Tristian: *Ms. Crane has been a terrible influence on you :(*

Ten minutes later, I'm planning to haul everything up the two flights of stairs to Dimitri's room, but I discover I don't have to. Tristian is waiting for me at the bottom of the stairs, shirtless and distracted. For the split second before he sees me, I catch the look on his face as he stares at the blood stain on the floor. He swears that the stun blast he took didn't have a lasting effect, but the curve of his shoulders has an odd slackness that I'm not used to seeing. That, plus the caustically somber cast of his eyes, makes my chest clench.

"Hey," I say, trying not to startle him.

His head snaps up anyway, blue eyes blinking as if he didn't expect to find me here. It's gone just as quickly, and he smoothly steps forward, taking the tray out of my hands. "You didn't really have to go out of your way," he says, gazing at the sandwiches. "I was just…"

When he trails off, throwing me a wretched look, I strain up to kiss the tension from his mouth. Everyone jokes and complains about Tristian's fussy food demands, but I think we all know deep down that it's not always something he can help. "It's okay," I assure.

He nods at the stairs. "After you."

Together we take everything up to the third floor, entering Dimitri's room to a greeting that's more enthused than I'm expecting. Dimitri holds out his hands in a 'gimme' gesture, deftly catching the ice pack I throw a little off center. Killian goes for the bottled water, downing half of it in three gulps. Between us, we straighten out the bed to hunch around the tray in the middle, picking through everything I'd brought.

"Jesus Christ," Killian mutters, reading the pill bottle. "Since when is Ms. Crane hoarding Percocet?"

As he's picking the lettuce out of his sandwich, Dimitri nonchalantly explains, "Oh, I asked her to get some to keep on hand in case Story had those cramps again."

Tristian snorts. "Those old bridge club bitches sling more weight than the Counts."

"Pure shit, too. Not even generic." Dimitri glances up to catch my eye, winking. "Only the best for you, baby."

"Stop," I stress, pushing the lettuce back his way, "trying to give me narcotics."

"Fuck." Killian's low, alarmed curse makes all of us go rigid, swinging our gaze to him. He's looking at the laptop Tristian must have had opened earlier, tracking me through the house on the cameras. Killian stands, grabbing the gun from the bedside table. "Sy and Pretty Nick are coming up to the front door."

Before I can parse that, he's already plucking his jeans from the floor and pulling them on, marching out into the hall with the gun gripped in his fist.

Tristian and Dimitri are right behind, wincing and grimacing as they hastily pull on pants. "Stay here," Dimitri orders, giving me a look that would be a lot more commanding without the swollen eye and pained expression.

Nervously, I watch them file out, and then scramble to the laptop, pulse kicking up as I see Killian appear in one of the little boxes labeled '*05 - Foyer*'. The doorbell sounds through the muffled distance of the house, but interestingly,

Killian pauses at the front door. I wonder why at first, but then Tristian and Dimitri appear, standing tall behind him, and I realize he was waiting. For his backup. For his court. For his brothers.

When he swings the door open, I get a partial image of Nick on the foyer camera, but a full HD image of both him and his brother on the feed right beside it. I can't hear what they're saying, but from the looks of everyone's posture, things are tense. Nick goes to put his hands in his pockets—casual, like an afterthought—but seems to think better of it, letting them hang at his sides instead. It's an oddly apprehensive gesture from someone who looks and acts like Nick. He knows he's outgunned here, even with his brother beside him. He's trying to look non-threatening.

Killian stands with one hand on the doorknob and the other grasping the jamb, gun visible in the waistband of his pants. His posture, the ink over his muscled upper body rippling with tension, is a clear signal that they're not welcome in, but perfectly free to try.

I take a few moments to locate the keystroke that cycles through the different audio feeds, but finally, I do, catching Nick in the middle of speaking.

"...and you know I didn't have anything to do with that," he's saying, voice tinny through the speakers.

Sy's voice rings out next. "He can't keep hiding out just because your old man stuck his dick into some crazy."

Nick agrees, "Let's just hash this shit out."

Killian seems to think about it, eyes narrowing as he observes him. He glances over his shoulder, and from the foyer camera, I can see him making eye contact with Dimitri, and then Tristian.

Each of them gives a nod.

Killian looks back at Nick and slowly lets his arm drop. "Ten minutes."

I track them entering the house, through the foyer, and then into the den. But there's a dead spot in the footage, and all I can make out is Tristian sitting in the armchair closest to the entryway, Dimitri on the sofa beside him. The others must be up by the fireplace.

Nervous yet determined, I leave the room just as I am, clad in nothing but my panties and Killian's oversized hoodie as I bound down the staircase. I don't really give it much thought—none of them are wearing much, either— until I get close enough to the den to hear their voices.

"Rath," Killian's voice rumbles. "Go upstairs and get her."

"I'm here," I say, tugging the sweater closer to my knees before stepping forward into the room.

From the first glance, I see I was right. Sy is standing in front of the fireplace with his arms crossed, his perfectly defined eyebrows furled in annoyance. Nick is stiff at his side, both their eyes instantly jumping to mine. Their similarities are more striking than ever with the two of them side by side, but so are their differences. Sy is well-dressed and just as immaculately groomed as I remember. But Nick is wearing a wife beater, grimy jeans, and his hair is a mess. Their eyes—their features—might be similar, but it stops there.

There's a pause, and then Sy lets out a begrudging greeting. "Lady."

Killian, Tristian, and Dimitri are all looking at my state of dress, gazes dropping to my thighs. I don't miss the possessive flash in Killian's eyes when he grabs the throw blanket from the couch, nor Tristian's hand on my wrist, dragging me into his lap. I settle there, flushing as Killian drapes the blanket over my legs.

"What's going on?" I ask, hoping to divert everyone's attention.

Thankfully, Killian's quick to accept it. "Nick wants to make a deal to clear his name."

"Clear his name?" I adjust the blanket as Tristian pulls me close, arms closing around my middle. "But he had nothing to do with it." After talking to my mom, I realize that. The fire happening right after Daniel's murder was just a lucky coincidence. Clearly, everyone was just scheduling around Killian's award banquet.

Nick thrusts out a palm, exclaiming, "See! She knows that whole shitshow was set up."

Dimitri ignores him, looking at me. "Baby, your mom could have gotten to him."

"Who knows who all she had working for her," Tristian agrees, body solid and warm beneath me. He dips his thumb beneath the sweater to caress my thigh. "If she got to Ugly Nick and Martin, there could be more. We have to start from scratch with this, Killer." The last part is said to the man looking stony and troubled in the middle of the room.

Killian gives a heavy nod. "I need to know who I can trust. It doesn't help that another King has it out for me." He tosses Sy a dark glance, and the man scoffs.

"It's not my fault you beat the shit out of him over a case of mistaken identity. Go and apologize like a man."

"Apologize?" Killian's jaw goes rigid, eyes filling with fire. "Over my dead fucking body."

"Saul Cartwright forced himself on me." I glare at Sy, making sure he understands. "He cornered me, attacked me, and tried to rape me. We're not sorry for any of it." Beneath me, I can feel Tristian getting hard, which is making it difficult to inject the necessary acid into my voice.

"Whatever." Sy shrugs, looking unconcerned. "I'm not a Duke yet. I don't have any loyalty to Saul, and I sure as fuck don't have any pull with him."

"It's not his, anyway," Dimitri adds, looking up at Nick. "Why are we ignoring the obvious here? The Dukes' Kingdom belongs to a Bruin."

Nick makes a short, dismissive sound. "Possession is nine-tenths of the law."

"Wait. What does that mean?" I ask, looking between them. "It belongs to a Bruin?"

Killian's the one who explains. "Remember what I told you before, about Kingdoms being won by blood?" At my nod, he gestures to Nick. "Well, his dad was King, but he left. Walked away from it all."

"Saul Cartwright took it over," Tristian goes on. The low tenor of his voice combined with his fingers shoots straight to my center. "But he didn't win it. Nick still has a legitimate claim."

"I don't want it," Nick says, lifting a shoulder in a loose shrug. "I don't give a fuck about your dumb frat drama. I just want to take what's mine and fuck off."

"What's *yours*?" Dimitri's chest bounces with an ominous laugh. "Even if we helped you get Lavinia, you couldn't keep her. She doesn't want anything to do with you."

"That's my problem to solve," Nick says, eyes hard when he turns to Killian. "Our deal's still good, Killer. I got your boys into the office."

Too tired to keep up with their bickering, I let myself get distracted by what Tristian's fingers are doing. They started out doing these idle little sweeps against my thigh, but they're growing more deliberate now. When I lean back, letting my legs relax, I feel it.

His cock gives a strong, eager twitch.

I'm only half expecting it when he wedges a hand between us. I know Tristian well enough to understand that we're recovering from a tense situation and he'd absolutely want something like this—exposed yet private. It's not all fun and games for him. Sometimes I suspect he just needs a connection.

But I'm not expecting the boldness. I feel him take his cock from his boxers, the head dragging against the small of my back, and then reach for the crotch of my panties.

But before he tugs them aside, he stops.

His breath is even and controlled, and I know without glancing over my shoulder that he's watching them with a perfectly normal expression—concerned when Killian gets too energized with his gestures, annoyed when Nick reacts with amusement, threatening when Sy looks like he might jump in. He's playing the part, but his attention is fixed to me. I can feel it.

He's waiting for a signal, I realize.

He's waiting for me to tell him I want it.

He's waiting for my answer to his request.

I give it by adjusting, and I try to do him proud, acting like I'm just squirming my way out of a minor discomfort. Swiftly, he tilts his hips and positions his cock, allowing me to slip right onto it.

It's hardest right here, as his cock is stretching and filling me, to remain impassive and tuned in. But I do, sinking onto his cock in one smooth motion. He holds me there, his forearm locked immovably around my hips, as we secretly revel in it.

Killian's just made Nick a proposal that's completely flown by me. "I'm a King now, I can get you in," he says. Whatever he's asking for, neither looks particularly happy about it. Killian crosses his arms, bearing down on him with his stare alone. "Come on, Nick, what are you going to do now? My dad's dead. Are you going to find another King to run the streets for? Because that's not something I want or need from you."

Sy looks between them, and even though the irritated crease in his forehead never disappears, I can see a hint of agreement in his eyes. "He has a point, Nick."

"Shut the fuck up," Nick snaps, flicking his brother a quick scowl. Lower, to Killian, he says, "I don't have enough credits to be a senior. I barely have enough to be a sophomore."

"So?" Killian shrugs, looking over at Tristian. "We made Lords as Juniors. It's not set in stone."

"Plus." Tristian's cock swells when everyone turns to look at him. They have no idea that he's buried inside of me right now. "You're legacy. Exceptions are always made for legacies."

When everyone looks back at Nick, I rock my hips, unable to curb the impulse. Tristian's arm tightens, almost painful with the pressure of keeping me still.

"Jesus Christ," Nick mutters, running his fingers through his hair. "I'll think about it."

Dimitri kicks a foot up on the coffee table. "Good choice."

"It's late," Killian agrees, even though the sun only just set. He reaches up to rub his temple, wincing. "We're still getting our bearings here, dude, could you…?" He gestures to the door.

Sy rolls his eyes, grabbing his brother's arm. "We'll be in touch." Tristian and I watch as Killian follows them out of the room doggedly. Instinctively, I know he won't return until he's sure they've both gone.

Dimitri remains on the couch, arm slung over his head, all slouched down like he's halfway to calling it a bed. "I thought none of us were getting any action tonight," he says, lolling his head to level us with a dark, heavy stare.

I freeze, clenching around Tristian's cock. "How did you…?"

Tristian puffs a laugh into my neck. "Never could get one over on him. He's fucking annoyingly perceptive."

Dimitri's mouth tugs up into half a smirk. "The tips of your ears get glowing-ass red when you're fucking, Tris. Not that I'd need it." His hand goes lazily to his crotch, squeezing. "Story's got a pretty good poker face these days, but she gnaws on her lip like a bone when she's trying not to make slutty sex noises."

My brows crouch down into a glare. "I do *not*."

"You really do." Killian appears from out of nowhere, snatching out to yank the blanket away. He raises an eyebrow at our lap, my panties all twisted and askew. He lifts a palm, saying, "Seriously, Tris? While we're conducting business?" The words are as stern as his glare, but the tent in his pants and the tick in his jaw as he watches Tristian buck into me are pure sex. "Never fucking make me pop wood in front of Nick again." I startle when he drops to his knees in front of us, edging close to part my thighs. He looks up at me through thick, dark lashes. "Promise us it'll always be like this." He extends his tongue, brushing it over my clit so feather light that I pull away from Tristian to chase it.

"Yes," I gasp, so laser focused on the wet point of his tongue that I don't even notice Dimitri appearing beside the chair until he reaches out to tangle his fingers into my hair.

"Promise," he gently demands, pushing his palms up my sides, "that you'll always be ours."

"As much as we are yours," Dimitri adds in a ragged octave, freeing his cock from his boxers.

I thread my fingers into Killian's hair, and it's easy to give him this answer. "I promise."

Still, I wait until he lowers his mouth to me—until I have the flushed head of Dimitri's cock on my lips—until Tristian begins sucking a bruise into the junction of my neck—to make the real vow.

"Always."

34

THE THREE THORNS

"Shit, here she comes," Dimitri says, shoving his phone into his pocket and pushing to his feet.

We've been in the waiting room for half an hour, and Ms. Crane finally comes hobbling through the double doors—even though an orderly is pushing a wheelchair behind her. She looks over her shoulder to shoot him a nasty look. "Bean-shaped looking motherfucker."

"Christ, Ms. Crane," Killian mutters in a disapproving tone.

Dimitri curls an arm around her protectively. "Give the guy a break. He's just doing his job, you dusty old cunt." The orderly's jaw drops in outrage on her behalf, as if he hasn't been subjected to her mood for however long now.

"Find me a bat. I'll give him a couple of breaks." Ms. Crane flaps a hand, shooing him off, and then turns to us. Her gaze takes us in, seeming apathetic at the reception. "So this is my welcome party? I see you spared me the balloons." Tristian's eyebrow arches, and then he whips out the bouquet of wildflowers he purchased in the gift shop twenty minutes ago. The oddest thing happens. I'm not sure at first what I'm seeing, but Ms. Crane stares at the bouquet, her mouth clenching up into a tight purse. Her shoulders curl inward, and it doesn't even matter that she mutters, "Fucking limp-dick wasting money on glorified weeds that grow for free," I could swear she's *blushing*.

Dimitri notices, too, head snapping back as he scrutinizes her through his dark sunglasses. "*Delores. Are you flattered?*"

"No," she snaps, seizing the bouquet. "You three are about as flattering as the selfish love pump your daddies made you with."

"Guess I'm not your favorite anymore, you fickle hag." Dimitri smirks, covertly pulling a brand new pack of cigarettes from the pocket of his leather jacket. "I know how to win you back, though."

Ms. Crane's eyes actually *twinkle* as she grabs for it. "Hallelujah. Now move out of the way so I can get out of here and smoke one of these."

But before they do, each of them press a kiss to her cheek, causing more of that grimace-shoulder-curl-blushing, and by the time I get to her, she's stiff, uncomfortable, and—I don't care what she says—flattered.

I hug her gingerly, whispering a soft, "I'm sorry," near her ear.

"What the hell for?" she asks, shifting restlessly until I step back. "You didn't hit me over the head and hold a knife to my throat." I don't tell her what I feel in my heart, which is that I'm indirectly the cause of all of this. Jack, Vivienne, Daniel, the home invasion. She sees it on my face anyway, mouth flattening into a grim line. "You're going to have a lot of fuck-ups in life, girl. No point in taking on someone else's."

With that, she gestures to the door, leading us through. There's a moment outside, as Killian goes to get the car and pulls it around, where she tips her face up to the sun, soaking up the warmth. It lasts for as long as it takes Dimitri to find his lighter.

"So," I say, pointing to the doors. "I'll just be a few minutes."

A shadow passes over Tristian's and Dimitri's faces, but Tristian is the one to step up to me, palms framing my face. "You don't have to," he says, blue eyes moving between mine. "If there's anyone left, we'll find them."

I wonder if my smile looks as artificial as it feels. "It's not just about the intel."

"Then one of us can go with you." He tips his head to the side in that way that makes my stomach flip. Tristian is a lot to take when he's being cool and unflappable, but when he's like this—soft eyes boring right through the façade I've built—it's nearly too much.

I place my hand on his broad chest. "It's just something I have to do."

He searches my face for a moment, giving me a solemn nod. "I trust you."

I turn to Dimitri, who lifts his sunglasses, revealing his battered eye. To Ms. Crane, I plead, "Would you see that he gets that checked out by someone? He'll listen to you."

She sucks another drag from her cigarette, eyes pinging between us. "You're going to see the thundercunt."

"Killian made some calls before we came," I explain, nodding up at the building. "She's still here."

I don't miss the ring of disappointment in Ms. Crane's tone, but she does me the favor of not showing it, giving me a nod instead. "I'll take care of your little fuckface, Lady. Don't you worry." I think I do a good job of hiding my surprise. It's the first time she's ever used that word with something other than mockery or derision. *Lady*. She points her fingers at me, cigarette wobbling between them. "I'll tell you what I've told all these fuckers at one point or another. Just because someone brought you into this world doesn't mean they made you."

I reach out to take the hand hanging at her side, giving it a squeeze. "Thank you."

When I walk through the double doors, back into the hospital, I can feel the weight of their eyes on me. I take it into myself, fortifying these bones that hold my shoulders straight, because Ms. Crane is right.

My mother didn't make me.

She didn't break me, either.

LOOKING BACK, I see a lot of things how they actually were. The way my mom was with Daniel, her letting me leave, not trying to find me, being surprised when I returned, but not happy. Not sad. Not angry. I think back to that Thanksgiving where she left me in the diner, disappearing into a truck for a quick holiday trick. *"They pay extra on days like these,"* is what she said after, mussed and unaffected. I realize now that my mom's always been exceptionally good at bartering with people's loneliness. And that's exactly what she gave me, with long nights spent alone in hotel bathrooms. Holidays at truck stops, watching happy families on fuzzy TVs. Mornings spent fending for myself while she slept off another rough John. My mother, through years of carefully balanced affection and neglect, created such a loneliness inside me.

And then she exploited it.

I see that now, as I stand in the door to her hospital room. Her hair is ratty and limp, skin sallow, lips dry and tense—a far cry from the sleek, elegant woman I'm used to being awed by. She's cuffed to the bed, which has a uniformed officer parked in the chair beside it. The room is meant for two patients, but the other side is vacant. A television in the corner is running an old soap opera that the officer is paying more attention to than my mom.

I gather up the steel in my bones and clear my throat, getting their attention. "Officer Maddox?" I ask, clutching my bag close. "I'm Story. Story Austin. Killian spoke to you earlier?"

His shrewd eyes sweep over me, losing some of the glazed boredom as he stands. "Five minutes," he says, adjusting his belt. I step inside as he leaves, relieved that Killian has this sort of pull now. All it took was one phone call to secure me an unsupervised visit with my mother.

Her laugh makes my gaze whip to hers. "You're hot shit now, aren't you? The King's little concubine." The smile she gives me is bitter enough to choke me. "I never knew you were so easily bought."

I place my bag on the chair the officer just vacated, remaining standing. "Why not?" I ask, holding her stare. "You were." I spent all morning anxious about this, worried this would be difficult. Looking her in the eye. Facing her down. Reconciling my sweet, misguided mother with the ruthless cruelty of Ted. The reality is a lot more simple than I'm expecting.

She looks frayed and tattered, her glare as toxic as her heart. "So this is how you repay your mother?" She yanks at the cuff binding her to the bed, metal rattling. "After all, I've done for you?"

I look at her bound wrist, fighting the urge to touch the cuff covering my own. "You forced me into a family with a man who wanted to sell me. You terrorized me for years. You watched me cower and subject myself to cruelty, all because of a fear you caused." I meet her gaze, voice hardening. "I'd say you got off light."

She looks up at me, her expression filling with an acrid-edged wonder. "What have they done to you?"

I shrug, walking nonchalantly to the end of the bed. "Nothing you didn't know about and willingly let happen." Her leg is elevated, and all wrapped up. Curious about the damage, I pick up her chart and start flipping through. "I suppose I see now how you knew so much. Access to Daniel's security gave you access to ours. I'd be disappointed in myself for not seeing it sooner, except you were such a non-factor to me." I slide her a look. "It must have been so easy."

She erupts with an indignant, "Easy?!"

"Well, it's just that I had this idea of Ted." My eyes skim over the writing, but it's all gibberish to me. Vitals, medical history, pain medication, all signed off by a doctor who bears the sloppy initials 'RM'. I put the clipboard back on the hook. "Like he was some unbeatable, omnipotent mastermind. That's how it felt, you know. Like I was truly helpless." I turn to her, feigning casualness. "But it turns out everything just fell into your lap."

I didn't get into trouble much as a child. There was the usual stuff, of course. Being too messy. Being too loud. I stole a candy bar once, which up until high school had been my greatest crime. But whenever she was angry at me, she threw it around, unable or unwilling to hold in her frustration, even for the sake of a confused little girl.

That's what I see now—the flare of outrage in her expression. "You have *no idea*," she seethes, lips pulling back into a snarl, "the things I had to do to get you where you are today. The pieces I had to move. The people I had to pay. The men I had to *fuck*." She spits the word like its venom, which is smart. A few days ago, having that thrown in my face would have cut me somewhere deep. Now, I don't even blink.

"Daniel and Martin must not have been too bad," I hedge, picking at my fingernail. "Ugly Nick, I'll give you. But that's just one lousy lay, and he *did* kill for you. That seems like a bargain."

She barks a low, biting laugh. "Oh, if you want to know the truth, Ugly Nick was the best of the four."

Four.

"Yeah?" I ask, letting my disgust bleed through. "And who was the worst? Daniel always struck me as particularly sleazy."

"Daniel was nothing." There's a glaze to her eyes that I'm glad to see. Her chart had made it clear to me that the IV bag to her right has some nice drugs in it, but it isn't until she babbles on that I realize how beneficial they are. "Daniel, Nick, Martin…all so easy. Nothing like *him*." Her head drops back, eyes rolling sluggishly to the ceiling. "But I needed to get into that tracker he put in your neck…"

My blood turns to ice.

I dive for my bag, pulling out my phone and pressing it to my ear. "Did you hear that?" I ask, ignoring my mom's baffled expression.

"Ray." Dimitri's voice is quiet, but no less severe. The Lord's 'medic' has been busy with more things than patching up injured soldiers and tagging their women.

"That's not all," I rush out. "The doctor on her chart? The initials are RM."

There's some energetic chatter in the background, Tristian's voice mingling with Killian's, and then Dimitri responds. "That's him. We're on our way to take care of it now."

"Ms. Crane," I protest, but Dimitri makes a sharp, dismissive sound.

"We just dropped her off at home. Go there and wait for us, okay?" His next words are low and dangerous. "This won't take long."

The phone cuts out, leaving me alone with the slack, betrayed expression on my mother's face. "You played me," she breathes.

Learned from the best, I think. This was the easiest way of finding out who else had her loyalty. Certainly better than standing around waiting for them to make themselves known. We've had quite enough of that, thanks.

I ignore the angry, wounded thing swimming in her eyes as I collect my bag. Keeping my voice even and sure, I say, "If you try to contact me again— letters, phone calls, messengers, *anything*—Killian will kill you." I hold her stare, making sure she hears the steel in my voice. "This time, I'll let him." A gentle rap sounds out against the door, but I don't flinch. It's just the officer letting me know my time is up. I take in my mother's shocked face, the eyes I used to think of as home, the hair I used to press my nose to for comfort. "And if you try to harm them again? I'll do it myself."

"No, you won't." I know she's high when she shakes her head, eyelids heavy as they fall. "You're my little storybook."

"I might be…" I get close. Close enough to say goodbye to the woman I loved. Close enough to finally overlay the concept of Ted against the crease in her brow. Close enough to let her go. "But I'm not your fairytale, mom." When her eyelids flutter, I lean down to sweetly whisper, "I'm a motherfucking horror novel."

FREEDOM FEELS NICE.

That's what I'm thinking of when I get home from classes, pulling up in my Dodge. There's no more Ted. No Daniel. No Martin or Ugly Nick. The final three are all dead. Ted? Well, he never even existed.

After that hospital visit three days ago, there's no Ray, either.

"Clean kill," is what Killian had said to me afterward. I didn't ask for details, and they didn't offer any. I've had enough murder for the year, and it's barely March.

I bound up the steps toward the brownstone, taking in the crisp air and hints of a slowly budding spring. I still remember the first day I came here, standing in front of this door and feeling sick with dread. Now, the sight of the skull on the door knocker unwinds the tension from my shoulders.

Home.

I'm glad we'll be here again next year, since Killian's decided to play out his tenure as Lord and graduate before ceding it to the next bunch of degenerates. I'm proud that he's focused on getting his diploma and not just control of South Side. Hopefully, a second academic year of being a Lady is a lot less fraught than my first has been.

Walking inside, I'm greeted with the muffled, distant sound of an argument. Rolling my eyes, I follow the source to the den, dropping my bag in the foyer.

"I just want to be sure," Tristian is saying as I approach. "Not all inks are vegan. I read it online."

Oh, right. Tristian is vegan this month. I'm getting better at seeing his cycles. The vegan thing comes and goes. He must have a meeting with his dad coming up, or a test or something.

"What's going on?" I ask, entering the room. They all turn to look at me, and my brows hike all the way up at the scene. Tristian and Killian are shirtless—*nice view*—while Dimitri lazes back on the couch, looking on with amusement. There's a strange guy doing something to Killian's back. He's tall, with messy, platinum blond hair, and almost as full of tattoos as Killian, and green eyes that somehow still feel dark.

"This here is Remy," Dimitri explains, noticing my discomfort. "Remington

Maddox. Don't worry, he's Sy's friend. Another Delta Kappa." Oh, I know the name Maddox. It's as well-known around here as Mercer. Tristian and Dimitri had used Maddox towers as their alibi.

Remy plants those piercing green eyes on me, making me squirm. "I think you met my uncle recently."

I nod, remembering the call Killian had made. "He was the officer guarding my mom in the hospital."

"Real stand-up guy." The smile Remy gives me is cold and embittered, but doesn't feel directed at me.

I suspect we're all still a little twitchy about having people in the house, but they know as well I do that we have to work past it. A King can't do business in isolation. Dimitri explains, "Remy's the best artist on campus. He's giving Killer some new ink."

"Really?" I take off my jacket and get closer. "Can I see?"

Remy backs off so Killian can twist, showing me the design. I've seen it before, tattooed on Pretty Nick Bruin, tagged up and down the Avenue, even in bathroom stalls sometimes. It's two 'S's in an old-fashioned, spiky style. South Side.

I reach up to touch his arm, getting a better look. It's been slathered with something shiny and thick, and the edges are red, a bit raised. "Does it hurt?"

Killian's intense eyes are staring back at me when I raise my gaze to his. "Not anymore."

Before my hand can fall away, he catches it in his own, pulling me into his chest to brush our lips together. "How was the study group?" he asks, as Remy bandages the area.

"Fine," I assure, giving the 'S' scar on his chest a little caress. "No problems." There's a Baron in my group, but aside from an initial nasty comment—"*Lord's trash.*"—he hasn't paid me much mind.

Dimitri's still smarting from the original comment, though. "Jackoff's just salty the Barons are losing The Game."

Tristian wryly points out, "*We're* losing The Game."

"First of all, we're doing fuckloads better than the Barons, and second…" Dimitri thrusts a hand toward Killian. "He's a King now. That's the ultimate win. Points don't matter."

"Tell that to the LDZ guys," Killian grumbles, gently pulling a shirt over his head. I give him a hand, easing it over the bandaged portion of his shoulder. "They really want to kick it up these next few months. Try to get the lead." His tone clarifies that he's ready to facilitate this, and I understand why. We've been so shut up and isolated from the frat since the holidays. It's easy to forget we're leading something here, other than ourselves.

Tristian clears his throat, nodding at Remy. "Come on, guys. We're hosting the opposition here." It's not said super seriously. It's almost like after all the drama with the Kings, the frats' big 'Game' seems laughably low-stakes.

That's when I notice Remy is pulling out more plastic-sealed, sterile supplies. Tristian is sitting on the stool in the middle of the room. The one Killian had been occupying. And he's still suspiciously shirtless.

"Uh, Tris?" I mosey over to him, eyes glued to his deliciously toned abs.

"Yes, sweetheart?" He gives me a cocky grin, like he knows just how hard it is to tear my eyes away from his perfect body. He's *definitely* flexing his pecs.

Somehow, I manage to lift my eyes to his face. "Correct me if I'm wrong, but it kind of looks like you're about to get a tattoo."

Remy's gaze passes dubiously between us. "You haven't told your Lady you're getting ink?"

"She doesn't mind," he insists with an easy confidence. He grabs one of my belt loops and drags me between his knees. "She likes her guys a little trashed up."

I bury a half-hearted punch into his shoulder before winding my arms around his neck. "I like my guys as they are." The last thing Tristian needs is to be any sexier, anyway. His ego is already too big to fit through standard-sized doorways. "What are you getting?" I ask, unsurprised when he dips forward to steal a kiss.

He answers against my mouth, "You'll see."

"Okay, we're ready," Remy says, shooting a pointed look at the way I'm wrapped around my Lord.

I reluctantly peel myself away, walking to the couch to unceremoniously flop into Dimitri's lap. He catches me easily, as if I weigh nothing, and adjusts me so I'm twisted, legs folded beneath me. When I lean in to press a gentle kiss to his healing eye, they slide closed. "It's getting better," I notice, running a ginger fingertip around it. It'd looked so gruesome those first couple days, but the swelling's almost completely gone now.

He hums, chest vibrating beneath my palm. "Ms. Crane has a worrying amount of traumatic injury lifehacks."

I peck a lingering kiss to his bottom lip, indulging in the feel of his lip rings against my skin. "When is he going to ask her?"

"About the Velvet Hideaway?" Dimitri shifts his gaze To Killian, who's perching on the edge of his leather chair, eyes fixed to his phone. "Killer, when you gonna ask Ms. Crane?"

Killian only spares us a brief glance. "Tonight, probably. I wanted Augustine to be there." He pauses at this, locking eyes with me. "If that's okay."

Satisfied, I nod. These last few days, we had a lot of conversations. None of us are particularly down with working in the flesh business. I wasn't really expecting Killian to completely let it go—it is a significant part of the Payne empire, after all. But while he owns the property, he doesn't have to own the business that occurs within it. It'd make sense to pass it to Ms. Crane. She knows the business, and at least half of the girls there were hers first.

"She'll say yes," Dimitri comments, sweeping my hair from my face. "Let's face it. She's bored stiff here."

"You're probably right." I look down at where his shirt meets his neck, thinking of Auggie coming to dinner. Sitting at our table. Looking across at Dimitri. Wanting him. Not being able to have him.

I'm already halfway into sucking a large, obnoxious bruise into his neck when he snorts. "And you say we're territorial."

I pop off, admiring the dark bloom of blood beneath his skin. "You *are* territorial. And you only have one person to be territorial over. Imagine how I feel with *three*."

His dark gaze holds mine, jumping back and forth between my eyes. "Then you're going to enjoy what's about to happen." Before I can do more than raise a questioning eyebrow, he touches my chin, slowly guiding my gaze to Tristian.

Remy's doing something to his chest, hunched over and laser-focused. It isn't until he pulls back that I realize he's applying a stencil. He gives it a few pats before peeling away the edge, revealing the design.

It's an 'S'.

In the same spot Dimitri and Killian have their 'S'.

In the same spot I have his 'T'.

Tristian catches my gaze, shrugging. "I love you, but I'm not slicing some bacteria-infested, toxin-laden knife blade into my chest. Remy keeps his shit exceptionally sterile."

"Thank you for noticing," Remy says, looking genuinely pleased.

"This is going to be fantastic," Dimitri mutters into my ear. "He's been 'researching' all day about the various ways tattoos can go wrong. Look at that. You see the eye twitch? He's dying to tell this guy how to do his job."

Tristian's glare burns into us. "I can hear you, dickface."

Well, I suppose this explains the situational veganism.

I lay my head on Dimitri's shoulder, giving Tristian a soft smile. "It's not really necessary, you know." But the thought makes a happy little zing rush through my chest. I suppose Dimitri is right. Apparently I *am* territorial.

Tristian carefully inspects the design, giving Remy a thumbs up before the tattoo gun buzzes to life. I worry at first it'll hurt, which is stupid. Tristian carved his initial into my chest in a far more painful way. But even though we're bound by the blood of pain and the scars of wrath, we're also bound by the grace of mercy.

I don't want him to hurt.

Luckily, the needle touches his skin, and he doesn't look bothered. It's not a very large design. I imagine it won't take long at all. I look into Tristian's placid blue eyes for the duration, hoping he sees the truth in mine.

These initials we bear are forever.

Dimitri and Killian are just as quiet as they watch, and it's almost as if this is a sacred moment. I have no idea what the future holds, but I know it won't be easy. It'll be a thorny path, because we don't know any other road to take than the one that keeps us together. None of us are built for it—least of all me.

This strange, sacred ritual only takes fifteen minutes. Remy's tattoo gun ceases its shrill buzz, and he swipes over the new ink, cleaning it diligently. "How's that?" he asks, waiting for his approval.

Tristian never breaks my gaze. "Perfect."

Remy does this half-nod, half-shrug, and begins treating it the same way he must have Killian's. Ointment slathered over the skin. A bandage ready to go. Idly, he inquires, "What about you, Rathbone? You're still a virgin. Ready to finally get some ink?"

Dimitri shakes his head, arms looped loosely around my waist. "I like my needles to go all the way through and leave some metal behind. Sorry."

I chew on my lip for a moment before making the decision. "Could I get something?" One by one, they look at me. Killian's face is carefully blank, but Dimitri's eyebrows are disappearing behind his messy hair, and Tristian… well, he looks like he's trying very hard to push down that disapproving thing pinching the corners of his eyes. "I still have some money from the wrestling match," I add, gaze passing between them. "I can pay."

"No," Killian bursts, tongue sweeping out to wet his lips. "Remy's here to pay a debt. Get what you want."

Remy finishes applying the bandage on Tristian and gestures to the stool. "You're up."

Dimitri lets me go, fingers dragging against my hips as I make my way to the center of the room. The stool is still warm from Tristian, who stands off to the side, not bothering to put his shirt on.

Remy shucks off his gloves and pulls out a sketch pad. "What do you want, and where do you want it?"

"I want it here," I say, showing him my wrist. There's a thin scar, barely noticeable unless you know what you're looking for. It was made upstairs in the ruins of my bathroom, a shard of glass pressed against my wrist. This isn't like the letters on my chest. It's the only scar on my body that hasn't been touched by the beauty of something worthwhile. That's why I decide, "I want a daisy."

Remy glances at me, perking up as he puts his pencil to paper. "Yeah, that's easy."

Before he can get too into it, I add, "With three thorns."

"Daisies don't have thorns." He says it matter-of-factly, but still begins outlining them down the crudely sketched stem.

I look at my men—my lovers, my fighters, my Lords—and grin. "They do if they're lucky."

3 5

OURS

14 months later

THE FIRST THING I notice are the pillars. They draw the eye to the front porch, which must have been elaborately constructed, even back in its heyday. It's a stately colonial, with a stone façade and strong, classical details. But the vines creeping up the north-facing side of the house, and the willow tree framing the west, do a lot to soften its presence. I'm immediately enchanted.

I step out of the car, having driven here with Tristian, and meet the others around the front.

Killian's eyes find me and he pauses, staring intently. He recovers just as quickly, touching my back to usher me forward. Leaning down, he murmurs, "Nice dress," which would be a sweet compliment if it weren't followed by, "Trying to get fucked?"

I purposely remain silent, letting my sundress sway around my knees. I'm far from the days of these three picking my outfits, but I still know what riles them up, and I use the information accordingly. Clearing my throat, I say, "So, this one looks interesting."

We all stare up at the house with matching, pensive expressions.

"Check it out." Killian jerks his chin to the side of the property. "Three-car garage."

"And two acres of pure charm!" Harried, Linda comes stumbling up the drive, struggling to adjust one of her tan pumps. "This home is truly a showcase to detail, gentlemen." She pauses, addressing me. "And Lady."

Tristian's cheek puckers up into a half-grimace. "It looks old, Linda."

"Oh, but it's been modernized!" the real estate agent says, fumbling with her briefcase and phone. "This home has been here since the town of Forsyth's incorporation. But don't let its age fool you, Mr. Mercer. The previous owners updated it in every fashion." She gestures to the front door. "Well, I'll let her speak for herself. Shall we?"

Tristian shoots me a look, but I just shrug back. The last house we'd seen had felt much too new. Sterile. Cold. Walking through it gave me nothing. No feelings. No comfort. No joy. Linda had apparently taken my malcontent to heart, because now she shoots me a wink, swinging the door open.

"You are going to love it," she whispers. The foyer is just as impressive as the outside had been, with high ceilings and a bold pendant light that descends to a point. "The first lady of this house had that commissioned from a local blacksmith," Linda explains, pointing to the heavy metal and glass design. "Her husband was a general in the army. She wanted a light to be seen from all the way across the world, so he'd always be able to find his way back home. It was originally gas-lit, but it's been very carefully restored."

I feel a bit of awe imagining something so antique above our heads. What was the first lady of the house like? Did she worry when her husband left, waiting impatiently for him to return home safe? Because lately, I've been finding myself doing the same.

None of the guys look like they could care less.

"I'm going to check out the kitchen," Tristian says, throwing us a lazy salute as he wanders away.

"Living room?" Dimitri gestures to the entryway, letting Linda lead.

Despite my feelings, I fall behind, letting Killian and Dimitri walk ahead. It doesn't feel like I belong here, even though I know they'd all tell me differently. The huge picture window above the eaves casts the large room in a bright patch of golden warmth, and despite my reservations, I can't help but imagine what it'd be like to stand beneath it during sunrise. I do a little turn in the rays, my sundress swooshing.

"There are six bedrooms, including one main with a bath and sitting room," she says, not even needing to read from her phone, "along with a large space in the basement that can be turned into an in-law-suite or an entertainment room."

"Entertainment room," Killian and I say at the same time, sharing a look. When your parents are dead, absent, fuck-you rich, or in prison, there's no need for a guest room. Killian looks over his shoulder at me, realizing I'm hanging back, and instantly grabs for me, folding me under an arm. He's wearing a crisp, well-tailored suit that hugs his muscles in ways I'm still unprepared to see, but he's removed his tie and undone his top two buttons. These are the trappings of a King: luxury clothing and a nice home to hang them in. "Maybe a pool table?" he adds, peering around the space.

I grab the hand he has slung over my shoulder, reluctantly suggesting, "And a big screen?" Killian may not play football anymore, but he definitely watches it. "We might be too old to go to LDZ parties, but we could still invite people over."

"Who's too old for a frat party?" Tristian asks, walking back from the kitchen. Much like Killian, he's dressed to impress, having just come from a meeting with his father's investors. "Alumni come back all the time. We're welcome and revered."

"You were Lords for a year longer than you were supposed to be." I remind him, eyes rolling. "You've had your glory days."

Once again, I get a swell of emotion at the reminder they've all graduated now. That means no more walks with them across campus. No more lunches with them in the student center. No more library make-out sessions with

Tristian. No more sneaking into the music department's studio rooms to listen to Dimitri's newest piece. No more sneaking off with Killian in the middle of the day for target practice and some hasty backseat fucking.

No more brownstone.

"This place gets fiber, and it already has a great sound system," Dimitri says, shutting a closet door. He came here straight from some sort of Avenue dealings, and he looks the part, gun peeking from the holster hiding beneath his worn leather jacket. He jerks his chin at Killian. "Good security, but we'll definitely have to upgrade."

"Oh, hey," Tristian says, eyes lighting up. "Maybe we can get a dog. Izzy and Lizzy have been dying for a puppy, but you know my mom and her 'allergies'." He makes finger quotes around the word and rolls his eyes.

"That just sounds a lot like *I'll* be taking care of a puppy. Hard pass." I shake my head, undeterred by the very convincing plea in his eyes when he takes my hand, pressing a kiss to the knuckles.

He whispers, "Lady's choice." What a load of horseshit, and Tristian knows it, mouth curling against my hand.

Linda, the real estate agent, watches our banter, and I immediately recognize the questions in her eyes. Which one is my partner? Are the four of us going to live together? How does this work? What's the dynamic, and who should she be appealing to? Even after all this time, she still doesn't take the risk of actually asking. One thing she knows for certain is that Killian is King of South Side, which means discretion is important. "I'll, um, let you all look around a little by yourselves. I'll be outside if you have any questions."

Once she's out of the room, Dimitri emits this little wicked laugh. "Man, she's confused as fuck."

"She's freaked out," Tristian elaborates, crouching down to inspect the floor. "The last real estate agent for the King of South Side ended up with a bullet in her skull."

Killian lets his arm fall away from my shoulder, walking to the French doors. "And the one before that still hasn't been found." A darkness crosses his expression as he stares outside, something wistful in his eyes.

For the millionth time, I carefully suggest, "Then maybe we should look for something a little less elaborate."

They groan in an eerily perfect unison, each man turning to throw me an exasperated glance. "This again?" Tristian laments, gesturing to Dimitri. "Even Rath stopped pushing back on this."

Dimitri urges, "We need a place to *live*, Story."

"I know." I shift from foot to foot, worrying, "But we don't need a mansion."

Tristian unapologetically disagrees, "I do."

"I don't *not* need one," Killian mutters.

Dimitri and I share a look, but he's long since stopped trying to talk any sense into these two. Instead, he approaches me, pulling me close. "Come on, baby. You know the deal." Six months ago, Dimitri got an eyebrow piercing to go with the rest, and it makes every movement of his brow look impossibly expressive. Right now, as his dark eyes bore into mine, they're crouched all low and intense. "It's the family fund. What else are we going to do?"

The deal was that each of us contributes a percentage of our income to the family fund. For me, that's a paltry amount. For Dimitri, it's a little more substantial, since he still works South Side. For Killian, it's an unspeakable amount, and for Tristian?

Well, for him, it's utterly ridiculous.

But Dimitri is right. What else are we going to do? It'd be frankly hilarious to watch Tristian and Killian survive in a small starter home, but it wouldn't be fair to them. They have money. They should be able to live within their means, even if it's so far outside of mine, it might as well be Jupiter.

"Yeah," I sigh, straining up to brush my lips against his. "I'll keep looking around."

"Let's check out this entertainment room," Killian says, waving the guys over.

While they do that, I walk through the living room and up the stairs, peeking into each of the bedrooms. Even though I know some of it is due to my hesitation, the clock is ticking. This is the seventh house we've looked at in two days, and we need to leave the brownstone soon. The guys graduated two days ago, and the new Lords are ready to start rolling into the place. In a few months, they'll pick a new Lady and fill the house with their own parties and insanity. We're not old, but we're moving to a new place in life. A good place. Apparently, a very expensive place.

I walk to a small room with a door that opens into the main bedroom. It's a bright room with a large window that overlooks the backyard, and I spend a long time staring out of it, not entirely sure why. Something about the space is just so calming, like I could see myself standing here again. A part of it is the view of the yard below. There's a pool and a hot tub, plus space for the guys to put in a basketball court, or—

"A swing set would be good there," Tristian says, wrapping his arms around my waist.

I touch his solid forearms, leaning back into his chest. "For the girls?"

"Or…" His hand ghosts over my flat belly. "…other kids."

I twist my neck, arching an eyebrow. "You have plans I don't know about?" It's not the first time babies and the future of our little family have been brought up. The way they pump me full of their cum, it's probably a miracle I haven't had a slip-up. But I'm diligent with my birth control. I had to be. I've made a lot of mistakes in my life and getting knocked up in a frat house wasn't going to be one of them. I'm not a goddamn princess.

"I have a lot of plans," he says, kissing me on the neck. "Most involve defiling you in every room in the house once we buy it." He looks around, fingers tapping against my belly. "Well, maybe not this one."

Snorting, I ask, "Why not?" and he gives me a slow, crooked grin.

"Even I draw the line at fucking in the baby's room."

I shake my head, partly because there's no possible way that's true. Tristian will literally have sex anywhere, anytime, anyplace. But I'm also shaking my head because he can't be for real. I know part of buying a house like this instead of a simple starter home is planning for the future. Knowing how you want to fill it. Understanding that you'll have room to grow. I just haven't quite let myself look that far into the future yet.

Tristian slips away, leaving me to my thoughts as he enters the bedroom. But I follow, enticed by the comforting feeling of the room and alternately intimidated by it. Dimitri and Killian are already in the room when we wander in.

"What do you think?" Killian asks, stuffing his hands in his pants pockets. "Pretty nice."

"The kitchen is great," Tristian says, even though he looks begrudging about it. "I've really been honing my skills lately, don't you think?"

"Anything is an improvement to the slop Ms. Crane cooked," Dimitri says. "No wonder the girls at the Hideaway are so skinny. People think it's drugs."

Dimitri and Tristian both turn to look at me. "Well?" Killian asks.

Feeling put on the spot—*god*, they always do this—I take a quick peek in the en suite bathroom, trying to imagine all of us crammed in here. It's rare that any of us take showers alone anymore. Luckily, the shower is huge, fitted with three different heads and plenty of arm room. There's also an expansive tub— perfect for Dmitri's and my late night soaks. Satisfied, I prop a shoulder against the jamb, surveying the largeness of the bedroom. "It's close enough to campus for me to get to my last two years of classes." See? I can think of the future.

"But not too close to South Side," Killian notes, peering out the window.

Dimitri agrees. "The grounds are nice and tight. Plenty of space."

Tristian stresses, "Yeah, it checks the boxes, but guys," He raises his hands, spinning. "Do we like it?"

I know what he's asking. Is this the place we can see ourselves living—not just for the next couple of years, but for good. Can we see ourselves in this room, waking up every day, coming back to it at night, piling onto the bed, making love? Can we see ourselves downstairs entertaining Marcus and the other LDZ guys? Can we see ourselves in the backyard, swimming and having cookouts? Is this a house with the potential of being more than wood and stone?

Is this home?

I look around the big room, big enough for a bed to fit all of us, and think of the nursery next door. I imagine standing in front of that window a few years from now, holding a little Killian or Tristian or Dimitri in my arms. Maybe, soon, once I finish school and the guys get settled… maybe?

The big secret I've been holding inside is that it doesn't really matter. Home is wherever they are.

"I think we should make an offer," I say, firm and decisive.

Killian's eyebrows shoot up his forehead, but he looks pleased, giving me a nod. "I agree."

Tristian brings his hand together in a clap. "Are we doing this?"

Dimitri answers, "Looks like it," and whips out his phone. "I'll give Linda the all clear."

The guys exit the bedroom, all caught up in the negotiations of purchasing the house. I let them go ahead, placing my hands on either side of the hallway wall, feeling the sturdiness of it, the stability. This will be the first real home I'll ever have. Mom and I never owned anything—just bounced around from shitty motel to crappy apartment, then to Daniel's house, boarding school, and the little hovel in Colorado. The LDZ house is the closest thing, but even that wasn't really mine—it wasn't even the Lords', because it belongs to the frat. But this?

This would actually be ours.

I stand at the top of the staircase, looking out over the foyer, and imagine that pendant light beckoning my generals home.

12 months later

I'm ALWAYS THE last one down to breakfast.

Usually, it's because I have to scrub the sweat and semen off my body, and forcing them out of the bathroom as I do is the only way to ensure it doesn't start all over again. Sleeping with three horny men who have been instructed to save their cum just for me may have been a misstep. I think about reneging on it, telling them to go back to jerking off in the shower or into my panties or whatever, but then they pump me full, and like a greedy bitch, I just want it all.

That's the problem *usually*.

Today, I spend thirty minutes trying to find something to wear. Finally, I give up and pull on a Forsyth shirt with Killian's number on the back. I stole it a couple years ago, from some blond sorority girl in my stats class who kept wearing it around campus. I suspect she knew it irritated me. All it took was following her into the showers one day and snatching it up. He may not be with me on campus anymore, but people still need to know he's mine.

"I can take Tris up there with me," Dimitri says when I walk in. His eyes are fixed to his phone, even though his hand is shoveling a fork full of sausage to his mouth. "But you'll probably get an earful from Ms. Crane about it later."

"About what?" I ask, stopping to pour myself a mug of coffee.

Dimitri looks up to answer, but freezes, eyes lingering on my chest. "Uh. You know, she complains when she goes more than a couple weeks without verbally abusing one of us in person."

"Well, I can't miss this drop," Killian complains, tapping distractedly at his laptop. "Tristian's dad is already pissy enough we've corrupted his firstborn into a life of…" His words fade off when he looks up, eyes zeroing in on my chest. "What are you *wearing*?"

Grimacing, I try to stretch my top. "All my shirts shrunk in the dryer," I say, tugging at the front. "I think it's running too hot or something."

Dimitri makes a saluting motion with his fork. "Hey, I'm not complaining.

I think you look great."

"I look like I'm wearing a shirt designed for a twelve-year-old," I grumble, taking my seat. "Did I hear that right before? You're going to the Hideaway?"

"Some dickbrained John is causing problems," Dimitri explains, slathering some butter over his toast. "Augustine requested some muscle to scare him off the premises. For good, this time."

"Someone's causing problems?" A knot of worry tangles in my gut. "Is Ms. Crane okay?"

Killian gives me a puzzled look. "Of course she's okay. You know Delores. She'd handle it herself, except she's on doctor's orders to relax."

Ms. Crane's blood pressure was too high at her last doctor appointment, which is something that's been nagging at my mind. "She needs to be careful," I fret, and even though I know it's futile and not what she'd want, a part of me still wishes she'd move in downstairs. "You should take this John out once and for all. She needs people who can watch over her." Unbidden, my eyes begin swelling with unshed tears, imagining her alone and in distress. Ms. Crane doesn't deserve such a fate. I don't know who this John is, but I hope they kill him. Slowly.

"The fuck are you talking about?" Dimitri gawks at me. "She's got twenty hookers up her ass twenty-four-seven. She probably couldn't take a piss without the whole whorehouse knowing."

"Seriously," Killian argues, adjusting his shirt cuff. "Why do you think Auggy asked us to come?"

"Oh, I know why she asked you to come," I darkly mutter, narrowing my eyes at Dimitri. It's such a sudden turn of emotion from heart clenching worry to blood boiling jealousy that it makes my head spin, but I just can't help it. "I'm sure she'll be waiting to welcome Dimitri through the doors with an erotic dance parade."

There's a long stretch of tense silence, but I have a difficult time letting it penetrate. My thoughts are just so full of Ms. Crane getting hurt again. And then Augustine with her slender waist and glamorous makeup and shirts that *actually fucking fit.* I want to hit something, and then double over and have a really good cry about it.

This must be PMS from hell.

"I'm confused." Dimitri's fork clatters to the plate and he sits back, dark eyes boring into me. "Do you want us to ride in like big fucking heroes, or let them fend for themselves?"

A lump forms in my throat at his tone, and I have to clench my jaw to stop my chin from wibbling. "You don't have to snap at me."

His jaw drops, and he looks at Killian. "I'm not snapping! I'm just completely fucking lost!"

Killian at least notices the tears shining unshed in my eyes. He leans forward to touch my wrist, thumb stroking over my daisy tattoo, and asks, "What's going on, little sister?"

"What's going on," I grind out, both wanting to take his hand in mine and fling it away, "is that I'm tired, and sore, and all of my shirts are ruined, and I wish you didn't have to waltz into a brothel to save Ms. Crane, but you do, and that's just something I'm allowed to be irked about." The first tear falls, even though I've moved past the unexpected grief and into overwhelming frustration. I angrily swipe at my cheek. "Just forget it."

Now they're both staring at me like I'm an actual alien, and the thing is, I understand why. I'm not being rational this morning. These are the ramblings of a crazy woman.

Just like your mother, says a nasty voice in my head. *Augustine would never…*

God, where did that come from? I bolt out of the chair and storm from the room, tears hot at the corner of my eyes. Just before I get out of earshot, I hear Tristian come in from the kitchen to bark, "What the fuck did you Neanderthals do?"

I go up to the bedroom and yank open a dresser drawer, looking for a shirt that actually fits, but it takes a while, since my vision is completely distorted from the tears. It looks like I'm doing this—crying at eight in the morning, for no good reason—so I accept defeat. I go ahead and free the clench of sobs in my chest. It feels good. Cathartic. Like an emotional bloodletting. When the pressure has released, I pull in a noisy sniffle and find one of Tristian's workout shirts in my drawer. That's sure to fit. His laundry never gets ruined.

I'm just pulling the tight shirt off when Tristian appears in the doorway, face etched into a frown. "I don't know what those assholes said to you, but don't let it ruin breakfast. I made these *incredible* pancakes—they taste like real wheat."

My stomach lurches and I freeze, swallowing down bile in the back of my throat. "No, thanks."

"Sweetheart," he says, approaching me much like Jack Hanna approaches a pack of hyenas. Slow and cautious. "What's going on? You've been crying."

I shake my head as another tear tracks down my cheek. "I'm just having a shitty day. My shirts have all shrunk, and Ms. Crane is out there all alone, and Augustine wants to fuck my boyfriend, and—" *And gluten-free pancakes that taste like wheat are disgusting.*

Tristian places his hands on my shoulders. "Story, look at me. We can buy you new shirts. Ms. Crane is never alone. And Augustine has her own boyfriend now. Her run at Rath is ancient history. Not like she'd ever make a move on a Queen's man, anyway." His eyes drop to my tits, and I try not to hold it against him. I know better than to attempt a serious conversation in this house while I'm shirtless. "Hey, wait," he says, taking in my half-bare torso. "It's the sixteenth, isn't it?"

I groan, knowing he was going to bring this up. "Yes, okay? I'm obviously PMSing! Sorry if that throws a wrench in your weekend plans, but..."

My words cut off when he abruptly grabs my breasts.

It's not really a grab, since it's gentle and testing, but he cups his palms around them, engulfing them, weighing them. His face is pulled into a calculating expression.

I squirm away. "Tristian, I don't have time for your kinky shit today."

"Just… wait. Hold on." He keeps touching them, and when Killian and Dimitri appear in the doorway, he throws them a quick look. "Come feel these."

I bat his hands away, wrestling my shirt up my arms. "You've lost your mind!"

"I have not," he demands, gesturing to the tits I'm stuffing into his workout shirt. "I know your tits, Story. I know the size, shape, circumference, weight. They're absolute perfection. Your shirts didn't shrink. Your tits are bigger."

I give him a wry look. "Yeah, right."

"Seriously!" he insists, grabbing my shoulders and spinning me toward the mirror on the dresser. "Look at them! They're bigger." At my skeptical expression, he raises an eyebrow. "If one of our dicks grew an inch, would you notice?"

Huh.

Well, when he puts it like that…

"Why would my tits grow?" I argue, pulling at my top. "I'm twenty three. I think I'm done outgrowing bras."

He makes a sharp sound, like he's willing me to catch onto something only he can see. "It's the sixteenth." He punctuates this with a thump on the dresser. "Your period is over a week late."

Everything slows down. Murky. Thick. Indistinct. I struggle to wade through it, to find my way to reason, because there's no way.

There is *no goddamn way.*

Dimitri rolls his eyes. "This is dumb."

"It's not dumb," Tristian bites back. "You're just in denial."

"You can't tell she's pregnant just by feeling her up, Tris. Jesus, look at her." Dimitri lifts a hand, indicating my general demeanor. "You're freaking her out."

I cup my own breasts, demanding, "I'm still on birth control."

"Then you better throw it out, because you're pregnant." Tristian says it with such utter conviction that it shoots through me like a cattle prod.

"Bullshit." Dimitri drops down onto the bed, eyes looking me over. "She looks completely normal. You're full of it."

He says the words with certainty, but there's something in his eye that makes me nervous. A detachment. More like he doesn't want it to be true.

Killian is just standing there, all rigid as he stares at my stomach, and his face eerily expressionless. He looks like he's doing long division in his head, trying to count the days. "What if he's right?" he says, tearing his eyes from me to look at Dimitri.

"He's not," Dimitri says, but he leans forward, elbows propped on his knees, and makes a suggestion. "Let's go get her some tests. Twenty bucks says we just need a new dryer."

"Fine," Tristian says, snapping straight. "I'll go pull the car around."

* * *

Thirty minutes later, I have the tests all laid out on the edge of the tub like some kind of science experiment. Tristian had bought one of every brand and type, and some of them are unnecessarily complicated, digital things that make me want to pitch them right into his face.

But armed with a cup of pee, I go through the motions of dipping every test. It's not the first time I've had to take a pregnancy test. There was an incident a year ago between my implant coming out and going on a new pill that I thought I might have gotten knocked up. Turns out, I just had some light food poisoning.

This feels different, though, and as I wait for the tests to give my results, I try to ignore the sound of pacing feet on the other side of the bathroom door.

"What does it say?" Tristian asks, his anxious voice muffled through the wood.

Rolling my eyes, I shout, "It says to wait!"

It's sooner than I wanted to have a baby. I'm still a year out from receiving my degree. We're just now getting settled into our new home. The guys have only just entered into the professional world, no matter its illegal elements. Are we ready to have a child? Am I ready to be someone's mother?

Beyond the nagging self-doubt is a seed of a thought. It's the nursery next door, and that first day I stepped foot inside of it, imagining holding one of their babies. I wonder what they'd be like. A wily, curious, somber son, like Killian? A bright, golden-haired charmer like Tristian? Or a raven-haired, soulful, creative daughter, like Dimitri?

Mostly I think of a child that's a part of them all. Killian's seriousness, Tristian's easy nature, and Dimitri's gifted talents. That's what I'd want to create, more than anything; a child that represents everything good and pure about them.

That's what I'm thinking of when I step out of the bathroom, laying eyes on them. They're all lined up on the side of the Alaskan bed, heads jolting up at the sound of the door opening. In their eyes, I see nervousness, fear, and an inkling of dread. But I also see hope, wonder, and the unmistakable presence of love.

I tap the pregnancy test against my palm. "They're all positive."

There's a long stretch of stunned silence—even from Tristian, who was so confident before. "All of them?" he asks.

I nod, twisting to glance back at the neat little row of tests. "All twelve."

"Holy shit," Dimitri breathes, pushing his hair back from his forehead. "Holy fucking… oh, shit."

"So you're…" Killian gestures to my belly, face slack. "There's a baby in there. Right now."

"Yes." I give them a moment to work through this, watching as it hits them in waves. Dimitri keeps shoving his hair back, and Killian keeps staring, and Tristian—

He jumps up and grabs me, spinning me around. "Fuck me, I'm going to be a dad!" He takes my face in his hands, and through the spark of excitement in his eyes is a reservation I'm surprised to see. "Is this okay? I know you wanted to wait until you got your degree, but—"

I grin, grabbing his wrists. "It's okay. Honestly, I'm kind of relieved."

"Relieved?" Killian asks, finally tearing his eyes away from my stomach.

"I've just been feeling so off," I explain, knowing that my cheeks are glowing red. "Sometimes it's like I was going crazy. But this makes sense." I look over at Dimitri who looks shell-shocked. "Are you okay with this?"

"Yeah, I just…" Slowly, a little bit of clarity spreads through his dark eyes and he crosses over to me, touching my stomach. "I never let myself think this far ahead. I'm not sure I ever thought I'd live long enough to do something like this. Jesus. We made a baby."

Tristian dips down to kiss me, so hard and deep that I almost miss Killian's words.

"Whose do you think…?"

I tear away from Tristian's lips to blurt, "It's *ours*." I tackle my step brother right there on the bed, pressing a kiss to his mouth. "It's all of ours, no matter what." He gazes at me with this dumbfounded expression, which I suppose is fair. We might have been talking about this, but it was such a hypothetical. "That's the one thing I want," I tell him, holding his face in my hands. "I want it to be all the best parts of all of you." Looking back and forth between all of them, I plead, "Promise me we'll never need to know. Promise me if it comes out looking more like one of you than the others, you won't love it any less."

The tears come again, springing them all into action. They huddle around me with soft words and gentle touches, but I don't have the chance to explain that I'm not sad or frightened.

I just already see the promise in their eyes.

3 6

TRIUMPHS

"SHE TAKES HER prenatal vitamins and I cook all her food—all natural, nothing packaged or processed, organic when possible. We follow the diet given by the doctor." I say all of this while the nurse fusses with the machine, flipping switches and adjusting knobs. I really wish she'd give me something here. "The birthing classes start next month, but Story is already taking pregnancy yoga. Twice a week. Her last blood tests were—" I pause to flip through the folder, trying to find her latest lab results, but they're all mixed up in insurance papers and legal forms. "They looked… fine," I lamely finish.

"Sounds like you're doing everything right." The smile she gives me is a little pandering, and that only causes my blood pressure to rise. *Higher*. Here we are, being the model almost-parents, and we can't even get a little validation? She turns to Story, giving her a warm look. "The technician will be here in a few minutes."

"Thank you." Story winces and shifts on the bed. "I'm just eager to get it done so I can finally pee."

The nurse laughs, acting breezy and annoyingly carefree. Story had to drink an entire bottle of sugary juice beforehand to both fill her bladder and provide a marker for the insulin test. "I'll tell her to hurry."

The instant the door closes, I pounce. "Are you comfortable? That table looks like something they picked up off the side of the fucking road. Do you need a pillow? We really should have done this at home. My mother's doctor makes home visits. I'm sure—" I lean over Story, trying to adjust the exam table, but she swats me away.

"Tris, *Jesus Christ*, I'm fine."

"You seriously need to chill," Rath says, frowning at a chart on the wall. It's a graphic showing the stages of a pregnancy, and the four of us have already isolated Story's position in the timeline. Our baby is the size of a lemon. He tilts his head, squinting at the fetus drawing. "It's just a sonogram of a lemon-sized clump of cells."

"Just a—" I snap, fighting back the wave of anxiety. It's new and difficult to control. Story is only fourteen weeks pregnant and I'm already about to go insane. I don't know how these other two can seem so casual about it all. "It's a test, dickhead. That means you can pass, and it means you can *fail*."

I rest my hand on Story's belly, but there's not really a bump there yet. If the doctors in this town were a little more prone to bribery, then maybe we could have gotten this sonogram earlier. But they kept insisting it was useless before ten weeks, and then pushing me off until this afternoon. Ever since we got the news, I've suffered through a string of emotions. Usually, I keep it a little closer to the vest, but now that we're here, I can't help but feel nervous about what the sonogram will show.

"Bro, we got her the best doctor, vetted by you personally." Killian is kicked back comfortably on the stool by Story's other side, fiddling with the end of her braid. "The practice has a dietician, midwife, doula—the whole deal. They provide home visits, give Story excellent care, and didn't even blink at the fact this kid has three dads. There's no reason to micromanage this. It's out of our hands."

"Out of our hands?" I gape at him, flinging a hand out toward her stomach. "Easy for you to say. You're not the one measuring her macros, controlling her dairy intake, ordering her lab tests, making sure she eats enough iron and—"

"That's why we have the dietician," Killian says, shooting me a glare. "We hired him specifically so you *wouldn't* do any of that."

Rath wanders over to kiss her forehead. "You ever think all your stress is stressing her out?" He raises an eyebrow. "That's not good for her or the baby."

"I'm not stressing," I lie, pulling at my hair. "I'm just being realistic." I don't list the possibilities that could happen today. Spina bifida. Heart problems. Brain malformations. Story's eyes meet mine and I see a flicker of worry cross her face. *Shit.* Maybe Rath has a point. I suck back my concerns and take her hand. "But it's going to be fine."

"Hey, guys?" She squeezes my fingers, tossing the others a look. "Can Tristian and I have a minute alone?" The three of them share a look that I know well enough by now. It's the '*Tristian is being crazy*' eye-roll, so they leave without argument. Sometimes it feels like I'm the only one taking this seriously.

When the door shuts behind them, I say, "Look, I'm sorry. I'm not trying to—"

"Hey," she says, looking up at me from the table. "I know you can be a little neurotic. I love that about you, because sometimes when I'm feeling down or out of sorts, you'll do something completely bonkers like steal all of my sodas and replace them with vitamin water, and I'll remember that you love me." She slowly amends, "But, Tris, this is getting out of hand, even for you. Talk to me. What's going on?"

"What's going on?" I look around the room, incredulous. "Do you have any idea how many atoms there are in the observable universe? I can't even say the number, because it's too big. But somehow, while one of us was railing you with a premium creampie, a few of those atoms hooked up and began creating *life*." This will never stop blowing my mind, and when I collapse onto the stool Killer just vacated, I wonder how anyone *isn't* terrified by that. "It's a blip, Story. Two little things went right, against all odds, and then a baby happened.

It'd take nothing," I bring my fingers together in a snap, "to snuff it out. I don't know how we aren't having panic attacks on the reg."

She stares at me, eyebrows slanted miserably. "Because you're the only one trying to fight the universe, Tristian." She reaches out to take my hand, dragging it over her stomach. "You can't keep looking at it like that. It'll drive you insane."

I fold her hand in mine. It's warm and soft. Smooth knuckles. Creamy skin. When I look her in the eye, I hope like hell she'll forgive me. "I know we promised not to wonder who the father is," I begin, voice quiet like a sordid confession. "But what if it's mine?"

The flash of hurt in her eyes—hurt I caused by breaking the promise—is extinguished just as quickly as it arrives. It probably has something to do with the bald terror in my eyes. "Would that be so bad?"

It seems like this fear has been swelling within me for weeks now. Haunting me at night while I try to sleep. Nipping at my heels in the mornings when I wake. Ever present throughout my day. I stare at our interlocked hands, feeling weary but too determined to give in to the exhaustion. "My genes are defective, Story. It's why my mom had to stop with Izzy and Lizzy, even though she wanted more." Reluctantly, I meet her gaze, finally putting my fears to words. "What if it's twins, and the problem my mom had passes through me?"

Her face crumples. "That's what you've been freaking out about? You think it could be twins?"

"It could be," I stress, darting a glance at her belly. "Do you have any idea the complications that come with a multiple birth labor?"

Her grip on my hand tightens, drawing my eyes to hers. The small, sad smile that greets me is enough to make my chest clench painfully. "You told me once that losing your brother didn't have any effect on you. But you lied." Before the protest on my face can form into words, she hastily adds, "Not intentionally. I just know you well enough now to understand. It's a big part of the reason you take such good care of yourself. You feel..." Her eyes search mine as she chooses her words carefully. "You feel grateful, Tristian. You see life as this precious, fragile thing, because you think it could have just as easily been you."

I've been naked in front of this woman more times than I can count, but I've never felt so exposed before. It makes my shoulders shift uncomfortably, but I don't slide away. "It's a problem we need to consider," I say.

"I've considered it." She nods, holding my gaze. "But Tristian, we also need to consider that I'm healthy. That you've found me excellent care. That I have three partners to help me through this." She lifts our fists, pressing a gentle kiss to the back of my hand. "I have faith in us," she says, giving me a watery smile, "and I want this to be good, Tris. I want this to be happy. I want to bring this child into a world where we can enjoy our triumphs. Okay?"

I push the hair off her forehead, overcome by a wave of emotion.

God, I love this woman so much.

I just want to bask in that forever, pick her up and carry her out of here to live in ignorant bliss with my two best friends. But there's a hard tap on the door, and a moment later, the technician is sweeping into the room with the guys right on her heels.

"Everything okay in here?" she asks, lowering the lights.

I take a step back, needing a little air. "We're good." Still, when Killian grabs my shoulder, giving me a firm, supportive shake, I let him take a little bit of the weight.

The technician circles the exam table and takes her place on the stool, giving Story an encouraging grin. "Just lift up your shirt when you're ready."

Story grabs the hem of her sweater and reveals her belly, shimmying her waistband low. Even though there's no bump yet, it's clearly not as flat as it once was, a soft roundness beginning to appear below her bellybutton. Rath takes one of her hands and Killian the other, but I pace at the end of the bed, unable to stand still.

I watch as the technician puts on her gloves and pours a heaping glob of gel on the highest point of Story's stomach. I glance down as she places the wand in the gel, spreading it around, but the sound of the sonogram, the wishy-washy amplification draws my attention.

Freezing, I ask, "Is that…?" and the technician sends me a grin.

"The heartbeat," she confirms, adjusting the wand. I wish I had something a little more sentimental or glamorous to compare it to, but the truth is, the rhythm and sound is almost exactly like our washing machine back home—just with a little more echo.

Story tears her eyes away from the monitor to look at me, a gentle awe filling her gaze. "It sounds strong!"

Killian is similarly transfixed, leaning closer to the image on the screen. "I think I see it."

The technician hums. "Actually, that's her pancreas. But if we move over a few inches…" The wand presses into her belly, making an indent. "Ah, there it is…" Our gazes all lurch to the screen, but try as I might, I can't make out anything. The technician does us the favor of pointing out, "Right here, see? That's the head."

It takes me a minute to make it out—everything looks so fuzzy and undefined—but when I finally spot it, I nudge in beside Rath and gawk at the image. "There's only one?"

Story's hand finds mine, and we knit our fingers together. "Twins run in Tristian's family," she explains.

The tech flashes me a look, nodding. "Well, let's see. Here's the womb. Here's the fetus. And…I don't see another embryo." She flashes me a gentle grin. "Looks like just one baby for you."

My shoulders sink in relief.

In a quiet, deep voice, Rath asks, "Is it okay? Is it growing like it's supposed to?"

The technician hits some buttons, and the screen freezes, like maybe she's taking still images. "At this stage of development, your baby is beginning to sense light and form taste buds," she explains, the little blob on the screen coming in and out of focus. "From what I can see here, I'd say everything looks perfectly normal so far." She raises an eyebrow at Story. "I'm pretty sure I even see the sex." Looking between the four of us, she asks, "Do you want to know, or would you rather be surprised?"

We haven't talked about this yet, and my back goes rigid at the possibilities. Rath and Killer look equally as paralyzed at the choice.

Story is the one to snort, saying, "I think we've had enough surprises for a lifetime. Go ahead and tell us, doc."

The technician laughs, nodding. "Then allow me to introduce you all to," she tilts to monitor, showcasing our little lemon, "your healthy baby girl."

"JUST SNEAK ME in through the back," Killian says, reaching for the door handle.

I grab his arm, stopping him—not that it's a difficult thing to do. He's cradling his ribs like he's personally holding them together. "Oh, hell no. I'm not lying to the mother of our child because you're too much of a pussy to take the heat on this."

He falls back against the seat, sending me an exhausted glare. It's accentuated by the blood running down his temple and the split in his lip. "She's going to freak out."

"Yes, she is." I undo my seatbelt and step out of the car, walking around the front to get to Killer's side. The look he gives me when I wrench his door open says magnitudes already. "The longer you stall, the more she's going to worry." I point up to the house, lights glowing through the windows. "She's been waiting up all night."

Rath's up there with her, which is… something. But it's just after midnight and neither Killer nor I came home this evening, all tangled up in a little misunderstanding with a few of Lionel's boys that ended with some gunfire, so yeah.

She's going to freak out.

"Come on." I haul him out of the passenger seat, largely ignoring the pained grunt he makes as he lets me take his weight. Then it's *my* turn to make a pained grunt, because I came out of that scuffle a lot less bloody and battered, but Killer weighs roughly the size of a tractor trailer.

Rath meets us at the door, wearing nothing but a pair of boxers and a hard glower. "Those motherfuckers," he growls, springing forward to catch Killian's other side. "Please tell me someone died for this," he says, voice strained as we lumber over the threshold.

"One," Killer answers, hissing as we lower him to the ottoman. He wrestles with his jacket, saying, "Help me get this off before she—"

But Story is already there, watching us from the entryway. She looks soft and delicate, her hair pulled up into a messy knot. She's wearing a simple pair of panties and a tight tank top, and I know it wasn't intentional—this is how she dresses comfortably—but she looks like an erotic slumber party caricature.

Her hand flutters over her mouth. "Oh, my god…"

"This isn't my blood," he rushes out, struggling to pull the sleeve off. "Some is, but not… uh, most. It's not as bad as it looks." He shoots me a hard look, jerking his chin.

I give it to her straight. "He's got a cut on his scalp from a bullet graze, and his ribs are probably bruised. Other than the split lip and the crooked nose, he's good as new." I give him a firm pat on the back.

"Nothing happened to my nose," he argues, yanking his jacket from my grip.

"Oh." I shrug, trying to keep my voice light. "It's just like that, then."

He holds up his hands, as if Story is some wild animal. "I've already been stitched and had x-rays. That's what took me so long. I'm fine."

Despite those assurances, her lip is still wobbling even as she does her best to put on a brave face. "Dimitri, could you bring me some towels and some warm water?" To me, she says, "Pull out the big bed?"

It's not often we sleep downstairs, but sometimes we'll do a movie marathon, or get too drunk to bother with the stairs, and we'll pull out the big bed. It's a mattress that rolls away into the bookcase, and I immediately begin hunting down a set of sheets for it. I get a crystal clear memory of that night at the cabin—Christ, Killer was shot then, too—as we all rushed about and tried to come down off the adrenaline high of almost dying. Much like then, my dick is hard and my head is pounding, and the only thing I want to do is crawl into bed and press up against something naked and wet.

When I return, she has his shirt off, fingertips skating over his left side. They hover over the old gunshot wound, the one he got from Ugly Nick, and then across to the letter brand on his chest. The tattoos and scars and self-inflicted damage tell a story—his story, our story—and I remember that not so long ago, we were all at odds. Now we're a family.

Rath walks into the room, already dressed again and shrugging on his leather jacket. The handle of his pistol hangs out of the waistband of his jeans. "I'm heading out to go make sure everything is under control."

"Alone?" Story asks, eyes wide.

"No. One of the boys is picking me up." His phone vibrates. "That should be him."

"Be careful," she pleads, hauling him in by the lapel of his jacket.

"I will." He bends and kisses her cheek. "Love you."

"Love you, too."

He nods at me and Killian before heading out the back door. Story refocuses on her brother, eyeing the stitches.

"I'm fine," he tells her, taking her hand and weaving their fingers together.

"Someone shot at you," she says. She lowers their entwined hands to her belly. "I know this is your job. I understand the risks, but you have soldiers for a reason, Killian."

Her eyes flick over to me and I see the accusation there. I shouldn't have let this happen. She's right. "Sweetheart, you know how it is. Everyone's measuring dicks and they're jealous that Killian's is so big." I give her a wink. "As you're aware."

She rolls her eyes at me. "Seems to me it's time for a regime change with the Counts. Lionel Lucia has been a problem for too long."

"Working on it, babe," Killian says, cupping her cheek. He leans in and brushes his lips over hers tentatively, like he's assessing exactly how mad she is. When her lips part, his tongue sweeps in, claiming her fully.

His hand dips between her legs, rubbing the crotch of her panties. Looks like I'm not the only one with an adrenaline boner. He groans against her mouth. "You're still damp. Rath fucked you good?"

"So good," she says, hips rocking against him. Her nipples tighten, peaking beneath the thin tank, and I abandon the sheets to get me a piece of the action.

My palm presses into the middle of her back, sweeping down as I duck in to whisper into her ear. "You and the baby too tired for another round?"

She tilts her head for my mouth, arching her back into Killer. "Nope. Wide awake."

Killian frowns at that, but it's not enough to stop him. We're both too pumped up on the action. The fight to survive, the need to fuck. It's all connected in some fundamental lizard-brain way. He cups her tits, massaging them gently, and she lets out this soft little moan. "Keep that up and I'll come right here."

I never knew I was a tit guy until she got pregnant. Now I can't get enough of them. None of us can. They're sensitive as fuck, and sometimes, when she just needs to get off, a little sucking and pinching is all it takes to make her come.

"No shame in that," Killian says, taking one into his mouth. He sucks and laves until she pushes him off.

"Not tonight." She looks between us. "I want to feel you inside."

I sweep aside the strands of hair on her neck and plant a kiss on the warm skin. "Big bed?" I prompt, wanting her splayed out in front of me.

Killian stands and lifts her with him, muscles rippling under his ink with the last of his energy. Shirts, shoes, pants are discarded from one room to the other, until we're at the end of the bed with Story sandwiched between us. Killian pushes at the hem of her shirt while I lower her panties, cupping her ass in my palms. "How do you want it?" I ask her, because god, at this point, we've come inside her a million different ways. On a night like tonight, she may need something comforting or something raw. Whatever she wants is what she'll get.

Killian's fingers tug and toy with the nipple of her swollen tit as he strokes himself, waiting like a dog who's been promised a treat.

She looks over her shoulder at me. "I want to taste your cock," she says, licking against my lips. "I want you to fuck my mouth."

"Yes, mama." I thumb her bottom lip, balls clenching at the easy way she takes me in. "I won't be gentle. Promise."

She grins at the name, then looks back at Killian. "And I want you buried inside." She grabs his cock and rubs it between her ass cheeks. "Deep."

Killian's eyes glaze, but he snaps out of it. "Are you sure. Can that hurt the baby?"

Her expression melts. "I keep telling you. The baby is fine. Protected inside by fluids and cushion. At most, she'll feel like she's getting a little massage."

I help her on the bed and Killian gets behind her, both on their knees. I stand by the edge, working my cock, getting it nice and hard. I cup her tit in my hand while guiding the tip of my cock to her lips. Killian positions himself behind her, doggy style, slotting his cock between her legs. She hums from the sensation, and opens her pink, puffy lips, tongue darting out to taste me. I grab the back of her neck and say, "That's right. Taste how much I want you."

My days as sex referee are mostly over, but I do give Killian a nod to let him know she's ready. He's been the most hesitant about sex since she got pregnant—worried about the size of his cock or being too rough. Now, I'm more like an OBGYN, telling him it's okay to rail his little sister even with a bun in her oven. "Fuck her, daddy," I tell him. "Give mama exactly what she needs."

These two have always gotten off the hot and taboo of their relationship. Fuck, I get off on it, too, but our roles are changing rapidly. One mama and three devoted daddies. Killian's hips draw back and then plunge inside. The action forces her forward, and she takes me in, her hot mouth surrounding my shaft. I swallow hard and rock into her, grabbing the base of my shaft and fingering my balls.

"Can you feel Rath in there?" I ask him, knowing it turns him on.

"God, yes," his neck strains as he pauses, stretching her around his cock. He's holding back.

Story looks up at me with wide eyes, her mouth full of me and I ask, "You want him deeper don't you, mama?"

She nods, a muffled, "... yes," around my cock.

"Give her what she wants, daddy."

The battle visibly wages within him. The urge to pound into her fighting with the need to treat her as delicately as he believes she needs. Story releases me, a long sticky string of spit connecting us, and looks over her shoulder. "Killian, I can take it. Fuck me. Please, big brother?"

The begging always gets to him, but it's the endearment that flips the switch in his eyes. He clenches her hip with one hand, fingers pressing into the soft flesh. His other hand vanishes between her legs and she moans. "Always so goddamn wet," he says, leaning over and kissing her side of her neck.

He rears back with powerful force, pulling almost all the way out, and then plunges back in. She yelps, then gives me a twisted, thankful grin, and unhinges her jaw. I guide myself back in and fall into rhythm, mesmerized by the three of us together. It's a goddamn beautiful sight that makes my balls clench and my cock swell. There is nothing in this universe better than watching my woman get fucked. Nothing.

Once I'm close, I reach out to lay a hand on Story's back. Killian's hand falls on top of it, fingers twining with mine. The action draws us closer, all three of us, and my balls tighten and twitch, caught up in the heat and movement. How did I get so lucky to be a part of something so intense?

Story cries out around my cock, her nose wrinkling as her breath comes out in short, choked bursts. I still for a moment to let her breathe, but I reach for her tits, massaging them between my hands, drawing her closer and closer to pleasure. She cries out again, hips bucking against Killian's hand until she groans in a mixture of pain and pleasure, latching back onto my cock and lazily sucking through her orgasm.

Killian grabs onto her hips, her muscles now loose, and lifts her back onto his cock. Any worries of needing to be gentle go right out the window. He fucks into her hard, hips pounding erratically as he buries himself deep inside, cock pressed to the hilt. My eyes slide down his body, over the tattoos, to the tight muscles that anchor him to her backside. When these two fuck, it's always a sort of art. She moans against my dick, breath hot and slippery.

"Can you take both of us?" I ask her, forcing her eyes up. They're glazed from her orgasm, but she knows what I mean. Not our cocks. *That*, she's already handling. I mean our cum. Our Lady loves cum and doesn't want to miss a drop.

She nods, her mouth too full of me to verbalize it, and I squeeze Killian's hand. "Fill her up," I tell him, painfully holding my load until the right moment. I sense the roar before it rips through his throat, a rumble deep in his chest as his orgasm begins. I grab the base of my cock and the back of her neck and say, "Hold on, mama." Giving her a warning.

The cum shoots through us and I'm lost in the sensation, barely aware of Killian other than his loud groans as he pumps into Story. Slick heat rushes through me, starting at my balls and pulsing through my length. Story flattens her tongue to catch it all, letting it accumulate where I can see it. "Good girl," I tell her and she swallows it down, throat bobbing with the motion. When she's done—when she's drained us dry and taken every drop we have to give—I lean down to kiss her, pushing my tongue in her mouth to steal a taste of my own bitterness. "I love you."

"I love you, too," she says, looking over her shoulder. "And you, too, big brother." Smirking, she breathlessly adds, "*Daddy*."

He gives an exhausted laugh, but when he hunches over her to push a kiss to her temple, his voice is nothing but serious. "Always."

None of us are going to sleep well until Rath is home, safe and whole. But we collapse onto the mattress anyway, naked and slick with sweat and old blood. Killian runs a finger up her inner thigh to push his cum back into her, and I know instinctively that he'll go again. After she's limp and sleeping, warm in my arms, he'll rock back inside of her as I watch. Rath will come in and take her again, hard and fast, until they're both too fucked out to do anything but lose consciousness. And then tomorrow, we'll wake up and do it all over again.

A lot has changed between these past few years.

But the way we love never will.

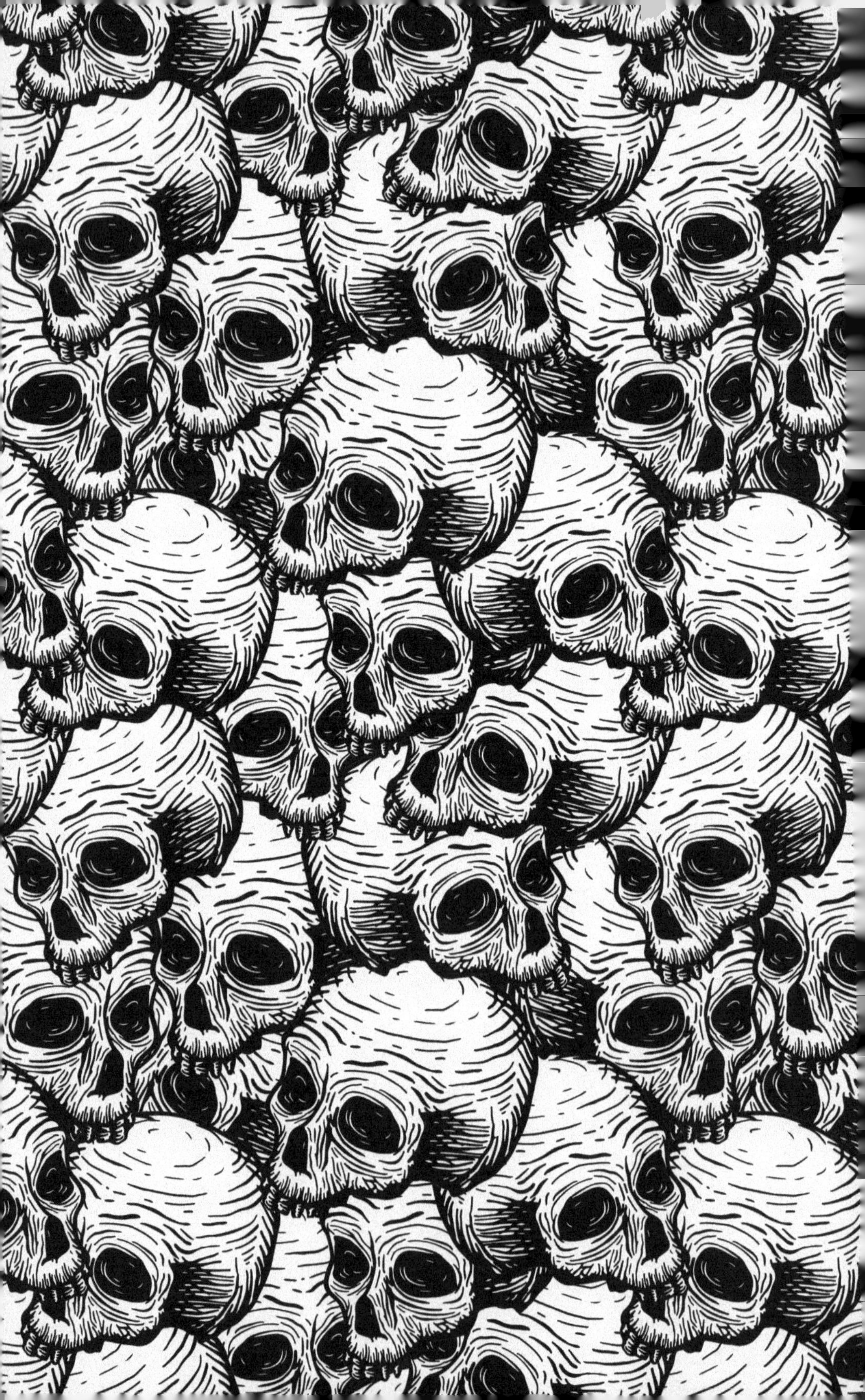

3 7

B R A M B L E S

"YOU OKAY?" EVEN though there's only the faint flicker of a candle to light the room, I can still make out the frown etched on Story's face.

I hastily squash the ember of my blunt, clearing my throat. "Yeah, just a headache."

She lingers by the door, shoulders heavy. "You don't have to stop on account of me," she says, gesturing to my makeshift ashtray; one of Killian's discarded Red Bull cans.

Shrugging, I sink deeper into the water, letting the heat unwind my muscles. "I do if I want you to get in here with me." This tub is one of the best parts of the house. Long enough for my legs, wide enough to accommodate a pretty, naked brunette.

She ducks her head, but I can still make out the edge of her grin. "I don't want to intrude."

I grab the sides of the tub to heave myself into a sitting position. It helps me level her with a dark, threatening look. "If you don't take off your clothes and get into this tub, then I'll come over there and do it for you."

There's a beat of tense silence, but it's broken by her snorted laugh. "Don't threaten me with a good time," she says, lifting her shirt over her head.

Smirking, I lean back to watch as she uncovers herself, inch by inch. Her tits are truly something else already, full and heavy and begging to be licked and fondled and sucked. Her baby bump is more obvious now than it was even a couple weeks ago, slightly stretching the elastic of her panties. Unthinkingly, I take her hand to help her into the water, spreading my legs to give her room to settle between them.

It's a new view for me, looking over her shoulder at the swell of belly that rises out of the water. I press her against my chest and melt back against the tub, letting the sensations of warmth and skin and Story soothe me. I'm just coming off the afternoon shift at the community center, so I'm already tired. It was seven hours of scaring the living daylights out of fucked up teenagers and the even more fucked up adults who think it's somehow cool to deal to them on our goddamn turf. I don't think any of us are dumb enough to think we can clean up South Side, but we can at least try to keep the kids sheltered from the reality of it. For a little while, anyway.

In any case, South Side might be my obligation, but I'm doing what I can to make sure I have a career. That means auditions, studio time, and late night performances that pay something adjacent to jack shit. But I never got into music for the glory. Glory is something I'll earn at my brothers' sides, with a gun in one hand, and a knife in the other.

Still, the late nights are beginning to make my head throb.

"It's okay, you know." The words emerge in a soft breath of air I can feel against my chest.

"What's okay?"

Her fingertips glide lazily through the water, and I watch them, hypnotized. "That you're not sure about this yet," she answers, rubbing her stomach. "I can tell you're not quite on board. Not like Tris and Killian. But it's okay." She twists to meet my gaze, blinking those big, soulful eyes at me. "I just wanted you to know I can wait."

Brows pulling together, I touch the curve of her jaw, rubbing my thumb into the skin. "You've got it all wrong." She raises a shrewd eyebrow, as if she's expecting me to deny being a little distant lately. I don't do her that disservice. "I'm on board for this," I assure, reaching down to place my palm over the swell of stomach. "I guess I'm just finding out what that looks like. For someone like me."

She puts her hand over mine, lacing our fingers together. "What do you mean?"

Sighing, I observe our hands on her stomach. It's so fucking weird to think that there's a baby in there. A baby I possibly made. "Tristian and Killer would be good dads on their own. I'm not bringing anything to the table for them, you know? But take them away, and what am I? Just a South Side reject with a fine arts degree who wouldn't even be able to afford rent with it."

There's a stretch of stillness, the water settling around us, and then Story is spinning to face me, features hard and sure. "Bullshit."

I shield my nuts, yelping, "Careful!" but she steamrolls over me.

"First of all, there's a difference between being a good provider and being a good father." She tucks her knees up, but I pry them apart, threading her feet around my hips. "Second of all, Killian and Tristian don't shoulder our financial burdens because you wouldn't be able to. They do it so you won't have to. So you can chase your dream and do something you love." There's an unbearable sadness in her eyes when she looks at me, cupping her hands around my elbows. "I don't believe for a minute you couldn't provide for us if you absolutely had to. What was it you told me?" Her lips quirk up into a shadowed grin. "People like us find a way, because there's no other option."

Those are nice words, but they don't really cut to the center of this roiling doubt in my chest. It's been a long time since I could look into this girl's eyes and make her cower away, and it doesn't work now. Instead, it just pulls the words out of me like a decaying tooth. "Baby, I don't know what my place is here." I soften it by touching her belly again, fanning my fingers out as if I could hold the future inside.

"You still don't get it," she says, head tilted as she regards me. "That *is* your place, Dimitri. Killian and Tristian… they're practical men. And that's useful and good, and it suits them. But you," she holds my hands to her belly, giving me a wistful smile, "you're going to be the dad that teaches her to follow her heart. You're going to show her music, and who knows—dance, art, whatever makes her heart sing. You're going to teach her that it's worth something, and she's going to be such a happier person for it, because I don't care what you say. You could earn money hand over fist by making commercial music."

My head snaps back in outrage. "*Commercial* music? I'd rather be poor."

"Exactly," she says, laughing. When it dies down, she gives me this long look—soft and assured. "You're going to be a fantastic dad. You'll see."

Still, I frown, eyes falling to her stomach. "And what am I going to tell her the first time she comes home crying because some jackass at school was a dick to her?" Quieter, I wonder, "What am I going to tell her when she asks why boys are so mean?"

"You tell her the truth," she says, reaching out to cup my cheek. "That you're all sentient manifestations of Satan's ballsack."

I swat her wrist away, glaring halfheartedly. "You've been spending too much time with Ms. Crane." When she's done laughing, I add, "I'm serious. Being a girl must be shit. All the guys want to fuck you, hurt you, or some combination of both, and the girls all want to compete with you for the privilege. One day, she's going to ask us how we met. What the fuck am I supposed to say?"

She lifts a shoulder, all casual. "We'll tell her we met through Killian."

Blandly, I correct, "We'll lie."

"It's not a lie," she argues, scooting closer. "It's just a little stripped down."

I pitch forward, my forehead landing on her shoulder, and it feels like the flutter of her fingers in my damp hair is the only thing anchoring me down. "Can I tell you a secret?" I whisper, eyes falling closed. At her hum, I confess, "I've been looking into this music academy nearby…"

She pauses. "You want to go back to school?"

I roll my forehead against her shoulder. "Not for me. For *her*."

"Oh," she breathes.

When her fingers resume their soft massage against my scalp, I explain, "I could teach her piano. Or guitar. Drums. Violin. Anything that calls to her." I rub my thumb against her belly, imagining it. "We could play music together."

There's a smile in her voice when she says, "You could."

Nodding, I conclude, "So I don't want you to think I'm not in this. The problem is that I might be into it *too much*. Sometimes I think of some little fuckface doing to her what we did to you, and it makes me fucking crazy. Because I know what I'd do." I glide my hand up her ribs, watching as it cups her breast. "I'd fucking murder him."

"Mmm." She arches her back, pressing her tits into my palms. "So would I."

It's been a while since we were like this, and not entirely because I've been so distant. Story's been so busy with school, trying to speed up her credits to give herself some downtime farther along in the pregnancy. I've been all tangled up in the dregs of South Side, struggling to balance it with all those dreams she seems to think are worth half a shit.

My cock's been hard since she took off her shirt, but it surges at the sight of her tits in my hands, and when I dip down to press my lips to one, the sound she makes in response is enough to make every muscle in my body flex in anticipation.

Grunting, I push her back against the other side of the tub. The water sloshes messily over the edge, but I'm too busy licking into her mouth to notice it. She makes a plaintive sound and wraps her legs around my waist, a hand fisted tightly in the back of my hair.

"Please," she mewls into my mouth, reaching down to wrap her fingers around the hard length of me. But I know what she wants—what she *needs*. Tris and Killer have been treating her like spun glass. Even when they're fucking her, it's usually planned and slow and painstakingly *normal.*

But she's right. I'm not like them.

I am *not* a practical man.

With a twist of my hips, I enter her in a hard thrust, hands clamped onto each side of the tub for leverage. Her eyes fly wide as she grasps for me, fingertips slipping against my wet shoulders. I give her a moment to send me a signal that it's too much—too rough—too fast.

She traps her lip between her teeth and bucks up into me.

Alright then.

I pull my hips back and slam forward. The sound of her sharp cry mingles with the slap of water against the tiles, but I don't stop. Not this time. I fuck my girl the same way I always have. Ruthless, seeking, desperate for her desperation. My muscles strain and flex as I hold myself up, surging into her like waves battering a coastline. The dim glow of my candle throws the cut of her jaw in sharp relief when she throws her head back, gasping. She digs her fingernails into my shoulders, a nice slice of pain to go with my pleasure.

I like making love to Story. At night, when all of us are in bed, moving together or waiting our turn, the way she looks at us as we fill her up is so potent that my knees still feel weak the day after.

But goddamn, I love doing this too.

Steady, hard fucking.

I shift my weight to one hand so the other can palm her tit, thumb toying at her nipple. It makes her cries bite off into something high-pitched and full of agony.

"Tell me, baby," I grit out, slamming my hips into hers. "Tell me what you want."

Her throat swells with a moan, but she lifts her head long enough to look me in the eye for her answer. "I want your cum."

My balls tighten, jaw clenching. "You gonna come with me?"

She's nodding before the words even leave my mouth. "So close, Dimitri…

please…" Her ankles lock around my waist, and beyond the sloppy, wet sounds of bathwater splashing between us, her voice trails off into sharp, indistinct fricatives.

I take them into my mouth with a deep kiss, feeding her my grunts as we move together. The tub is hard and unforgiving against my knees, but I soldier on, driving my hips faster and deeper into her hot cunt.

She comes first, heels digging into the small of my back to grind me closer. She rips her mouth away from mine, pulling in these deep, strained gulps of breath as it shudders viciously through her body. I have a split second to think that Tristian would kick my ass if he saw how thoroughly I was fucking her before my brain whites out.

After, when we're both a breathless mess of wet skin and shivering muscles, I pull her back up into my lap, crushing her to my chest in a borderline animalistic embrace.

"You don't need to wait for me," I say, pressing a kiss to her neck. "I'm here. Forever."

ONE DOWNSIDE TO having a house the size of a fucking cruise ship is that it takes like a week to actually find someone in it. I shoot off another text.

D: *its 3, where r u?*

Usually, the use of text speech would at least grant me a disapproving emoji, but today, nothing. Sighing, I keep searching, looking in the entertainment room downstairs, checking the garage to make sure her car's still here, even popping my head into the bathrooms. Her bladder *has* been a demanding bitch lately.

I find Tristian and Killer before I catch sight of her, both of them out back bickering.

"It should be three feet," Tristian says, spreading his arms between the pool and the grass. "That way we're not losing real estate."

Killian marches about twenty feet out from the pool, raising his palms in a '*see?*' gesture. "This will give us room for some deck chairs and some tables."

Tristian storms over and snatches the measuring tape from his hand. "Those can go outside of the fence!"

"Why the fuck,'" Killian asks belligerently, "would they go outside of the fence?! Who wants to walk around to a gate after checking their phone or having a sip of beer? That's asinine!"

"Rath," Tristian says, waving me over when he notices me. "Give us your opinion. We need a fence around the pool to keep the baby out, but—"

"This idiot thinks it should be right up on the edges." Killer demonstrates this by pointing to a little orange flag that's been buried into the grass. "Tell him that's stupid."

I look at the grass, then the pool, then at both guys. "Yeah, I'm just gonna level with you here. I couldn't possibly give less of a fuck. This is some shit-tier rich-people problems, guys. Where's Story?"

They both looked annoyed at my lack of investment, but Tristian tosses the measuring tape aside, saying, "I think she's upstairs napping."

"Oh." Well, that works out nicely. "Carry on, then."

But before I can walk away, Killer mentions, "Maybe I should go up and see if her back still hurts."

Tristian adds, "I should take her a smoothie, too. The ones I've been making have been helping her with morning sickness."

"I think fucking *not*," I snap, thrusting a finger at them. "Three to four is our time. Tristian gets her at the ass crack of dawn and Killer gets her all night. But the afternoons are *mine*."

Tristian raises his hands defensively. "Geez, fine. Bite our fucking heads off about it."

But Killian's eyes narrow. "What exactly is it you do from three to four?"

Catching on, Tristian adds, "Yeah, you're so touchy about it. Are you painting her toenails or something?"

Killian slides him a look, muttering, "Fuck off, I painted her toenails last week."

"What we do from three to four," I stress, giving them both a threatening look, "is none of your business. Enjoy your urgent fence crisis, you lame-asses."

I trudge back inside and then up the stairs, stopping on the way to grab the paper bag I'd stashed in the nursery a few days ago. When I carefully push the door open, the sight of her on the bed greets me. She's above the covers, fully dressed, like maybe she just collapsed there. I'm quiet as I enter, closing the door softly behind me. After a second of thought, I lock it, too. She's on her back, right in the middle of the mattress, pillows stacked up around her. Her belly rises up, so fucking cutely round that we have a hard time keeping our hands and faces off it. She's at the end of her second trimester, which is why we've set up these little afternoon dates.

Around week 25, your baby may begin responding to voices and other noises.

I unpack all the supplies, laying them out on the bed as I kick off my shoes. I'm careful not to jostle her too much as I settle in at her side, my head beside her belly. Propped up on an elbow, I take a moment to observe the bump. It's kind of fucking freaky to think there's a human being in there. It's kind of fucking freaky to think I *made* the human being in there. Slowly, I ease the hem of her shirt up, tipping down to press a kiss to the highest point. My hand still seems large in comparison when I press my palm to it in a gentle hello.

Like Story, I never knew my dad. Maybe he would have been awesome, or maybe he would have been utter shit at fatherhood. Either way, I don't exactly have anyone to look to for advice. The closest thing to a role model I ever had was Daniel Payne, and the thought makes me scowl.

I don't know what makes a man a good father.

But I know the kind of father I would have wanted.

With a deep breath, I pick up the book. "The Light Behind Your Eyes, by Jan Clare," I read, giving the belly a peek of the cover. Keeping my voice quiet,

I turn to the first page. "Once upon a time, a brave girl was on her way to see her Mommy." I turn the book so the illustrations are visible; a girl in a cape skipping through an autumn forest. "This girl was so brave, she de—" I take a second to sound the word out in my head. "—decided to take a shortcut through the…" *Hm.* This is a harder word. I glare at the letters, annoyed this isn't one I've memorized yet. "The Bramble Woods," I finally figure out, flipping to the next page. Annoyed, I mutter, "I'm better at this than it seems—trust me."

I'd chosen this book because the art was really nice, and I thought the girl with shining eyes on the cover vaguely resembled the woman currently dozing beside me.

"The woods were very dark," I say to her belly, keeping a close eye for any movement. "But she wasn't any normal girl, for whenever she got scared or lost, her eyes would light up." I flip the page, and it doesn't matter that I'm talking to my girlfriend's stomach. I still show it the page. "All the other kids would make fun of her strangely glowing eyes, but her Mommy said it was her… uh, co—*courage.*"

I'm just getting the word out when I feel the flutter of fingers in my hair. My eyes jolt up, finding Story's staring back at me. Her gaze is still heavy with sleep, but the small, gentle smile she gives me feels more alive than anything I've ever known.

Her fingers skate down to touch my mouth. "I love hearing you read."

I look away, shifting uncomfortably. "Is she moving?"

Story hums, stretching her legs. "A little bit. It's like I have butterflies dancing around in there or something." I put my palm on her stomach, hoping to feel it. I've only been doing this for a few days, but a secret part of me hoped she'd begin reacting a little more boisterously to my voice. Tristian and Killian have both felt the kick. I've gotten fuck-all. Story's belly bounces with a laugh. "You look so grumpy. She's just a fetus, Dimitri. She probably sleeps when I do." Quieter, she asks, "Read us some more?"

I don't think I'll ever be great at reading, but after a couple years of literacy coaching and practice, I've gotten good enough to bumble my way through books harder than the ones I bought for our little girl. It makes something hot and embarrassed rise up inside me at the knowledge she'll surpass me one day. She'll come home from school with a worksheet or assignment that I won't be able to make heads or tails out of, and then I'll have to send her to Tristian or Killer, and it'll fucking kill me. But I'm going to make damn sure that she never has to feel this. I'm going to make sure we teach her all there is to know, even if some of us have less to teach than others. I'm going to make sure people look at my girl and see someone who's just as smart as she is beautiful and strong.

Clearing my throat, I turn the page. "Even though she had her eyes to light the path, the little girl was still frightened, because she knew some things were drawn to her light, and not all of them were good." In the story, the little girl's shining eyes attract a group of woodland friends; a moth, a fawn, and a wily raccoon. Together, they take her to shine a light in the deepest, darkest parts of the Bramble Woods. "Seems a little exploitative to me, but alright," I mutter, raising an eyebrow as I flip the page. They run across an evil spirit who wants to take the little girl's light, which, as I tell the belly in front of me, "is probably a metaphor for capitalism. More on that when you're twelve…"

Story laughs, resting her hand on mine against her stomach.

At the end of the book, the girl finds her Mommy, who'd been searching for her daughter all along. She tells her, "The special thing about the light behind your eyes is that it isn't special at all. Everyone has a ray of courage in their soul, eager to brighten their way." I raise my eyes to Story's and make an exaggerated gagging sound.

"It's sweet!" She gently whacks me upside the head. Catching her hand in mine, I laugh, lacing our fingers together. "You know what it reminds me of?" she asks, raising an eyebrow. "Remember that first year, when I was reading your Lit assignments, and Robert Frost—"

I recite it without even needing to think, "Whose woods these are I think I know…" I've long since memorized the whole poem—not that it's very long. The truth is, I kind of wish I could go back to those three idiots and that gorgeous girl who did us the honor of calling herself our Lady. If I could, I'd tell them to pull their heads out of their asses and treat her right. I'd tell her it gets better. I'd ask her to hold on, just a little longer, until we found that cheesy fucking ray of courage in our souls. I finish, "The woods are lovely, dark and deep. But I have promises to keep. And miles to go before I—"

She gasps, eyes flying wide, and before I can even scramble upright, she has my palm pressed to her stomach, face splitting into a grin. "Do you feel it?!"

It's a kick.

It's such a little thump of movement that it takes me by surprise. I'd been expecting something bigger, stronger, but this is somehow even more significant. This little human being only has so much strength and energy, and she's using it right now to press against my hand.

"Holy shit," I breathe, fanning my fingers out.

Story lets out this excited little laugh. "Think she just prefers poetry?" she asks.

I'm still gob smacked by the movement under my hand, but I tear my eyes away long enough to shoot Story a grin. "Poetry? Wait until she hears music."

38

WANTED

"I DON'T SEE why I can't just wear leggings and Killian's jersey." I slouch through the store, doing my best to look invisible. "I'm pregnant. No one gives a fuck how I look." Tristian and I stare at one another over a stack of high-end maternity clothes. We're at a fancy place that has hippie music flowing out of the speakers and flickering candles in soothing scents all over the place.

I think I want to stab something.

Tristian isn't having it. He raises a hand, beckoning a salesperson from across the store. "Because you're getting honored for the incredible work you've been doing down at the community center, and although I have no problem with you wearing," his eyebrow quirks up, "or *not* wearing whatever you want, you're going to have to dress up."

I cross my arms, feeling out of sorts among the sleek, designer clothing. For the past month, I've been hard pressed to make much more effort than some light makeup and curled hair. Part of that is the fact I'm the size of a planet, but another factor is the end of term. Even with the help of three distinguished alumni, I still struggled my way through finals.

"What can I do for you today?" the saleswoman asks, but even before I turn to peer over my shoulder at her, I realize I recognize the voice. *Autumn.*

The second she notices me, her face pinches into a scowl. "Oh, it's you."

Placing my hand on my belly, I turn, fully enjoying the flash of shock in her eyes when they fall to my very pregnant form. "The one and only." I give her a sharp, barbed smile.

She blinks at my stomach before her gaze jerks up to Tristian. "You're still…?"

He rests his elbow on the rack, giving her a chilly stare down. "You were the Princess, weren't you?"

"For, like, a blink," I clarify. There was a time I might have made a show of rubbing this in her face, but now the thought seems vaguely exhausting. I won. I settled down with my Royals, became Queen of South Side, and now I'm building a family.

Now, I just feel sorry for her.

"I need a dress," I say, rubbing my whale-like baby bump. "Something I can cram all of this awesomeness into."

Okay.

Maybe a *little* face-rubbing.

Tristian tosses me a little smirk, like he knows. "She looks great in green."

I spin to argue, "I'll look like a bipedal watermelon!"

"Gold, then." He fingers something shiny, holding up a finger. "No, you will not look like a foil-covered candy truffle."

"I'll just go pull a few options," Autumn says, talking through her teeth as she smiles. Minutes later, we're headed to the back, where she hangs various dresses onto a rack. I can't help but notice all of them are black. She doesn't miss the question in my eyes, nor the opportunity to throw me a nasty look. "Black is *slimming*," she sneers before flouncing away.

"Rude," Tristian mutters, glaring daggers at her back, but she's not wrong. It's going to take a lot more than a hundred yards of black fabric to slim down my figure.

Frowning, I pick through them. The dressing room is lush, with a comfortable seating area and soft lights that attempt to wash away the puffiness and exhaustion. I pick up a dress and look at the tag, my jaw dropping. "Almost six-hundred-dollars for a dress that will only fit me for three more months? Tristian, this is stupid!"

"Sweetheart," he says, taking the hanger from my grip, "you know money isn't an object, and you deserve some nice clothes for a special event."

I know I'm being irrational. The reception for my work at the community center is a big deal, something I worked hard for. I just wish I didn't look like a beached whale for it. I tried talking Clara, the director, into pushing it back a couple months, but no dice.

"Fine," I say, grabbing the dress and stepping behind the curtain to the smaller stall. It's fancy, too, with a soft armchair and carpeted floor. I listen to the other women going in and out of the other stalls as I peel off my clothes, trying to avoid the mirror, but it's one of those three-sided monstrosities, so it's impossible not to get a big, ugly view of my massive tits and protruding belly. My hips are bigger, curvier, and there are purplish stretch marks streaking up the sides. Blinking back tears, I struggle into the dress. It's black—'slimming', my ass—with a low-plunging V that barely contains my cleavage. Suddenly, I want to go literally anywhere else. She probably picked these out intentionally to make me feel like a fucking cow.

And the depressing thing is, it's working.

"How does it look?" Tristian asks.

I avert my gaze from the mirror. "Like I swallowed a beach ball."

His sigh is audible and a moment later, I see his head peeking around the edge of the curtain. He makes a frustrated sound, gesturing to me. "What are you talking about? You look gorgeous."

"You don't need to lie," I insist, blinking back a hot wave of tears. "I'm not blind, Tristian. You fell in love with this young, sexy girl who could get on her knees anytime you snapped your fingers. Now I'd need help to get up and down." I glance at the foreign woman in the mirror, wondering what happened to the hot college co-ed who brought three Lords to their knees. "I know you don't think this is sexy. No one could."

He steps into the room, letting the curtain fall behind him, and slides his hand behind my neck. "You seriously think I'm not into this?"

"I know you're into the baby," I say, eyes rolling. God, do I know. With the way he fusses over me so obsessively, sometimes it seems like the only thing I'm good for. "I know you'll support us. We're solid," I say, even through the prick of anxiety in my chest. My mom's voice still rings in my memory, unbidden and unwelcome.

"A man like that wants a woman who looks good on his arm and better in his bed... He won't want you if he thinks you're cheap and all used up..."

"But I know I'm gross, Tristian. My ankles are swollen, and I can't wear my rings on my fingers. I fall asleep in the middle of the day, and the food... I know my diet repulses you." A hot tear rolls down my cheek as I wonder what he could possibly see in me anymore. "I wouldn't blame you if you found some side-piece down at the Hideaway. It would hurt, but I wouldn't blame you. This is not what you agreed to." That's exactly what he should do. Find some sexy woman he doesn't have to dote over all the time. A woman who isn't a job. A woman who can ride him without fearing for the integrity of his pelvic bone.

He stares at me for a long moment, the clink and clatter of hangers sounding from the rooms around us. It's not the right place to make this kind of insecure confession, but that's who I am right now. A hot fucking mess.

Autumn looked so annoyingly fucking slender.

Tristian's fingers twist in the hair at the nape of my neck. "Are you done?"

"I'm uh…" The question throws me off, but my lack of answer seems to satisfy him.

"Good." He directs me to the chair. "Sit."

"I'll wrinkle the dress," I whine, not wanting to pay half a grand for a dress that doesn't even look good on me.

"Fuck the dress." He pushes my shoulders, guiding me down, and then he crouches there, fixing me with a long, meaningful look. "I'm not going to discount your feelings here, or lie and say your body hasn't changed, or that your tits aren't the size of cantaloupes and don't taste as sweet." His hands spread over my belly. "I won't pretend this little one doesn't sometimes get in the way when Rath and I want to bury our cocks in you at the same time. But, sweetheart…" He reaches up to stroke the tear from my cheek, eyes blazing. "None of that would ever, *ever* send me or the guys to someone else. Ever." His eyes search mine, pinging back and forth. "I don't need you on your knees, Story. That's not where a Queen belongs."

Bracing himself on the arms of the chair, he kisses my jaw first, seeming to savor the little gasp I make in response. Then his lips travel down my neck to my chest. My heart pounds, basking in his attention, the diligent way he sucks and licks my skin. Running my hands through his hair, I force his eyes to mine. "Thank you, for always making me feel wanted."

"You're welcome," he says, lowering to his knees, "but I'm not done yet."

My eyes dart to the curtain behind him, realizing he's got me right where he wants me, that cheeky grin spreading as he pulls aside the cups of the dress and my bra. My tits fall out—they were halfway there anyway—and he thumbs my nipple. "God, these are driving me wild. All I think about is kissing them, licking them, fucking them." His motions follow his words, tongue toying with the hard pebble of my nipple, face buried between them. He's gentle, and thank god for that, because they're sensitive as fuck. Knowing Tristian, he's done his homework, researching how to make a pregnant woman fall apart.

"Oh god," I moan softly, hips rising on the chair. I try to stifle the sound, hyper-aware of the women in the dressing room around me. "We can't do this here," I hiss, even though I arch into his mouth.

He looks up at me, lips shiny from sucking on my breast. "You know that's not true. I can and will do this anywhere." His hands push up the hem of the dress, smooth palms dragging up my thighs. He holds my eyes as he spreads me open, but then lowers them to get a good look at my center. "Black lace," he mutters, licking his lips.

I think about arguing as he slides them down my thighs. Really, I do. We're in a public place. Anyone could hear us. Hell, anyone could *see* us. There's nothing but a curtain shielding me from the other shoppers.

But it's just so hard when he's looking up at me with that obnoxiously cocky expression, leaning in to lick a hot, wet path up my pussy. I gasp, but try to shove my fist into my mouth to stifle it. Tristian can do things with his tongue that should frankly be illegal—not that it would stop him. This is made all the more obvious by his complete tenacity, hooking my legs over his shoulders as he settles in. I think I do a pretty good job of hiding my moans and too-loud breaths, but then he makes this sound—this low, deep rumble that I can feel all the way to the tips of my toes, and I just can't help it.

I whimper, "Tristian," and all the movement in the adjacent stall conspicuously ceases. I bite down hard on my lip to stave off another outburst, but this is Tristian between my legs. He's not having any of that.

His fingers join in on the action, two thick digits thrusting into my pussy as his tongue makes fast work of my clit. I pant like a dog, hands swinging out to find something—anything—to anchor me. I fist one into his hair while the palm of the other slides noisily against the mirror.

I shatter apart into jagged pieces against his tongue, convulsing around his fingers as a small, tortured cry escapes my mouth. My thighs tremble around his ears, and past the curtain, footsteps falter, but I just can't bring myself to feel any shame, so caught up in the explosion of it all.

I barely register Tristian jolting to his feet, fingers quick and nimble as they undo his belt buckle. The sound must be unmistakable—the jangle of metal on metal, the zip of his pants being undone, the low, rough sound he makes as he frees his cock.

I'm too exhausted and strained to do much more than lick out with my tongue, slicking the way for his sure fist. He reaches down to cup my chin, tugging my face up so his eyes can lock with mine. "Almost three years now," he says, voice ragged as he strokes his cock. "I never broke my promise, Story. Not once." Thumbing my mouth open, he thrusts forward, rubbing the head of his cock on my bottom lip. "I only ever come when I can give it to you."

With that, his cock surges, warm cum shooting onto my tongue. I scoot forward to make sure I catch it—all of it—pleased by the spark of satisfaction in his eyes as he feeds it to me. It's messy and raw, just the way we like it, and when some of it dribbles out the corner of my mouth, he uses the head of his cock to catch it, pushing it back inside.

The look Autumn gives us when we step out of the dressing room can only be described as outraged. I don't intentionally make a show of rubbing the corners of my mouth, checking for any remnants of his cum, but her eyes zero in on the motion, anyway. There was a time that might have embarrassed me, made my face glow hot with the words I've heard thrown at me from her and her ilk.

Whore. Trash. Slut.

But the roundness of my belly and the way he's looking at me are evidence enough that I'm more than just a fucktoy now.

"We'll take this one," Tristian says, lifting my hand high in the air to give me a little spin. I indulge him, laughing, because I'm remembering how fun it is to dance with him.

"You were right," I tell her, batting my lashes obnoxiously. "It is quite slimming. Thank you for all your help."

We leave five minutes later, hand in hand. The dress might not have been worth six-hundred-dollars, but making Autumn witness me living the life she so desperately craved?

That was worth every cent.

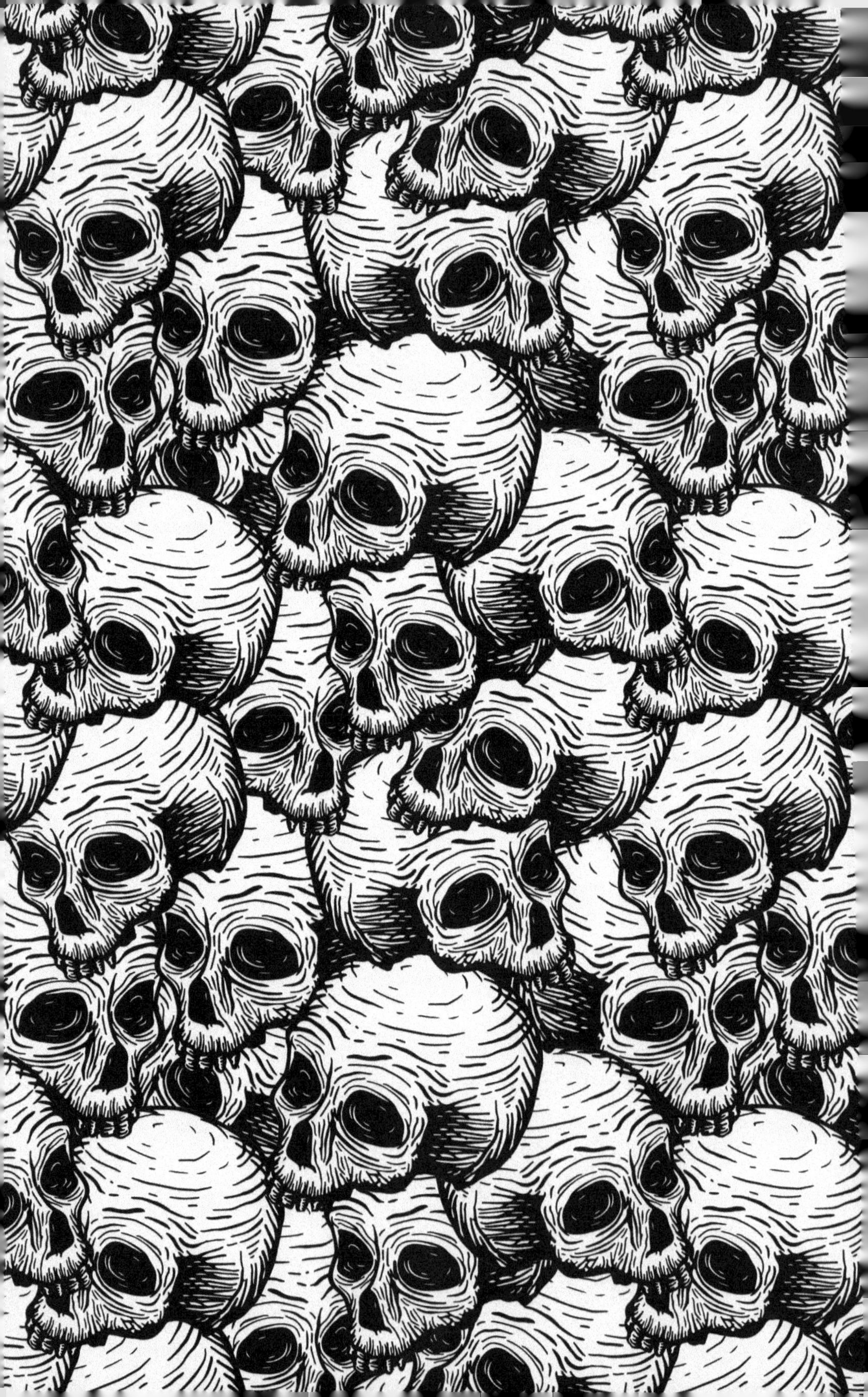

3 9

MELODY

I PINCH THE bridge of my nose as our 'guest' drones about past slights. As a show of good faith, I didn't call my right and left hands to be present for this meeting, but if I thought the lack of Rath's dead-eyed glare and Tristian's chilly smirk would make our old arms dealer swayed to peace, then I'm sorely fucking mistaken.

"We know those feds were in your pocket," Yolanda is saying, eyes narrowed as she sits across from me. "They took three of our shipments, which we'd personally delivered all the way from across the shore."

We're in the old refinery just over territory lines. It's supposed to be neutral territory, but right now, it's anything but. She has two guys behind each shoulder, each wielding a ridiculously massive rifle. Complete overkill. It's how I know she doesn't plan on killing me.

Yolanda isn't someone I've ever done business with personally. She's part of the criminal old guard I've been trying so desperately to dismantle. People like her, my dad, Lionel, Cartwright…they're yesterday's news. They don't understand the world today.

"I didn't have anything to do with that." I tap my heel against the ground, lounged back in my rickety chair. Being King, I've discovered, is about twenty percent violence and eighty percent posturing. "I don't have the feds in my pocket. I only deal local."

She barks a humorless laugh. "Then why did your men ambush mine at the border?"

I give her lackeys a look. In my head, I've been referring to them as Thing One and Thing Two. They're big and dumb and pretty. Actually, come to think of it, they kind of remind me of Nick.

I almost consider texting him about it, but a part of the negotiation to meet was that we turned off our phones. "You were selling guns to our rivals," I reason.

Yolanda gives me a long, hard look. "I wouldn't have had to if you hadn't reneged on our previous deal."

"That," I snap, nearly at my limit, "was a deal you made with my father. Not me. Daniel Payne might have been fine with seeing pieces all over the streets, but it's not a good look for South Side. Look at this shit." I gesture to the ridiculous rifles. "I'm not building a goddamn infantry. I just want to keep things moving smoothly. You know what makes things *not* run smoothly? Someone walking around with enough firepower to take down a fucking armada."

Yolanda inspects her nails, looking bored. "That's one opinion."

Nostrils flaring, I lean forward, elbows propped on my knees. "Let's cut the shit, Yolanda. You don't like me. I don't like you. I say the best course of action here is to steer clear of our respective paths, which is going to be a lot easier when you realize where mine is." I lift my arm, pointing to our right. "South Side is mine. The guns that enter South Side are mine. The guns that leave South Side are mine. The fucking ammo is mine. If I see another one of your pieces in the hands of some low-level, shit-for-brains drug dealer, I'm going to make sure to send it back." My voice drops to a low, deadly finality. "And you'd better trust that I'll have someone behind it to pull the trigger."

Thing One steps forward, tightening his grip on his rifle. "No one threatens

Yolanda, boy."

"Oh, you don't need to worry," I tell him, showing him my teeth. "I'll make sure the two of you get it first."

"Enough!" she snaps, and with a flick of her hand, Thing One falls back. "Once the guns are sold, I don't control where they go. What do you expect me to do, follow them around?"

"You don't need to follow them around," I answer, trying to tamp down my temper. "Choose a better caliber of clientele and all of our problems are solved."

She looks almost as irked as I feel, eyeing me up and down. "And just who do you expect me to sell them to?"

"I'm glad you asked." Without missing a beat, I reach into my pocket, not even flinching when The Things jump to attention. I flash the paper I'd brought, blandly offering, "I brought a list."

We go over it for what feels like forever. Yolanda has beef with half of my suggestions, and I have beef with half of hers. The entire time, I'm building this suspicion, though. She's far too quick to make a negotiation. Who the fuck am I to tell her who to do business with? The Southern empire is formidable, but it's not like my arm has much reach. Outside of the bounds of this territory, I'm jack shit, and that's just the way I like it.

Yolanda wants something from me.

It's really bristling her hedges, too, because I wasn't lying before. I know she can't stand me. She holds me to my father's word, but she also holds me to his crimes. It's not the first time I've had to answer for them, and I'm not stupid enough to think it'll be the last. The Payne name hanging over my head can, at any point, be a crown or a storm cloud.

I decide to play it out, because she wouldn't expect it of me. "Then we have a deal," I say, ready to wrap this shitshow up.

"For now," she says ominously. No doubt, a little realignment in the future will provide her a nice opportunity to bring up whatever favor is brewing in her eyes.

I'll burn that bridge when we get to it.

The first thing I do when I stand up is retrieve my pistol, holstering it beneath my jacket. The second thing I do is turn on my phone.

52 unread messages.

15 new voicemails.

"Shit," I hiss, already knowing something is wrong. I thumb open Tristian's name first, watching his messages ping through, but all the words are a murky blur. Mostly, I just see the number.

T: 237 237 237 237 237 237 237 237 237 237 237 237 237 237 237

"Mayhem…" I bolt out of the warehouse so fast that Things One and Two assume a defensive position, like they're expecting an all out assault. Guess I can't blame them. It makes it really inconvenient when I get to the dilapidated, sorry excuse for a garage and find they've blocked me in.

"Motherfucker!" I growl, kicking the tire of their big, dumb, completely fucking predictable black SUV. I can hear them hoofing it behind me, probably confused and on high alert, but I don't take this into question when I double back, belligerently demanding, "Move your five-door fucking cliché! I have to get out of here!"

"What is wrong with you?" Yolanda's face screws up in baffled fury. "You said this was neutral territory, that no one would—"

"My…" *Lady. Queen. Basically, wife…* "Story! She's at the hospital having the baby. I'm missing it!" I bark, fully prepared to push that SUV out of the way myself. God, please let her be having the baby and not something else.

But Yolanda's face goes blank, eyes flying wide, and suddenly she's the one stepping into action, grabbing my arm and directing me toward the cars. "Get in," she says, wrenching the passenger side open. To The Things, she snaps, "Hurry up! And stow those rifles." I'm panic-rushing so fucking hard that I obey instinctually. Someone's telling me to sit so I can get to where I need to be—I fucking do it. Yolanda has us tearing out of there before I come to my senses. "You'd be a menace to the roads," she explains, shooting me a quick look as she speeds toward my territory. "Tell me where to go and let me do the work."

I rattle off the name of the birthing center, which means functionally nothing to someone who's not native—and probably less to someone who is. Luckily one of the Things is ready, shoving up from the back seat to slam his phone into the dash holder. A GPS map comes up, guiding Yolanda to the place.

Meanwhile, I'm trying to reach Tristian or Rath, and having zero luck. "Fucking fuck of a motherfuck!"

Yolanda shushes me. "It's just a few more minutes. I'm sure everything is fine."

My voice is strained as I explain, "Story isn't due for another week, at least." I'd made plans to pull back with work starting tomorrow in preparation, staggering responsibilities with the Kings I don't totally fucking hate. That means Tristian is probably freaking the hell out, Rath is likely lost without someone calm to direct him, and Story…

God, she must be losing her shit.

"Yolanda, I mean this with all due respect." I turn to her, completely aware of what my face is doing. "If you don't drive faster, then I'm going to shoot someone."

She slams her foot down on the gas, sending Thing Two lurching back into his seat. "This is your first?" she asks.

"Yes," I say distractedly, thumbing through the texts.

She makes a pensive sound. "Is it true what they say? You share your woman with two other men?"

My face screws up, because it sounds *dirty* when it's said like that. "She's not a goddamn gaming console. We don't pass her around like an object. We're family."

She doesn't seem offended by my tone, which doesn't bode well for me. She must really want something big. She also seems to notice my skepticism.

"I respect a man who knows the value of family, Payne. And I mean the real value of family. Not this pompous legacy nonsense all you Kings have such a hard-on for." She glances back at the Things, snorting, "Kings. Can you believe it? Bunch of arrogant, privileged pricks who need to fantasize about leading a monarchy to feel important. Where I come from, we just call them politicians."

"Turn left!" I bark, seeing the road up ahead.

The rest of the drive is lost to my mounting panic, because what the fuck? Is my first act as a father going to be my own goddamn absence? Probably for the best, anyway. I don't know anything about being a father. I couldn't even handle being the son to one.

I've spent months pushing aside this paranoia, allowing Tristian to be the one who worries and frets. I've thrown myself into my role—King—but I'm not scared of leading South Side. That's easy. I can face down guns and politicians, pay off agencies and execute my enemies. But being a father? That's the only thing I've found terrifying in a long time. What if it's genetic? What if I'm like Daniel?

Finally, we arrive at the birthing center, and once again, I shove aside those negative thoughts. Tristian tied himself in fucking knots finding the right practice, but this one has been with us throughout the whole pregnancy. All the nurses, OBGYNs, doulas, birthing coaches, and technicians know me on sight, which is probably why when I roll through the doors like a lunatic with the biggest arms dealer in the region right on my heels, all the receptionist does is point to the doors on her left.

I fly through them, only vaguely noting that Yolanda and her Things have hung back. Hardly ten feet into my sprint down the hall, I hear it.

Story's deep, agonized sob.

I jolt toward the sound, heartbeat thundering in my ears, vision narrowing down to a single point. Everyone violently jumps when I crash through the door, panting and terrified, but there they are.

Tristian and Rath are on either side of the bed, holding her hands, and I know I'm late—fucking unforgivably, insanely late—but there isn't a baby. Not yet.

Story breaks down the second she lays eyes on me, chest hitching with a sob. "Where were you?!"

"I'm sorry," I say, rushing to her side. I press a kiss to her forehead, her cheeks, her chin, chanting, "Sorry, sorry, sorry. Is she okay?"

Story nods. "Other than deciding today is the day she's evacuating my body." She seizes and yowls, gripping Tristian's hand so hard he grimaces in pain. "I'm peachy."

The birthing coach is between her legs, saying, "It's time to push again, okay? You think you can be stronger now that all the daddies are here?" It's not said unkindly, but still makes my chest clench angrily. Not at the coach. Not at Story. Not even at Yolanda.

At myself.

She gives a tired nod, face red and damp with sweat, and Tristian puts her hand in mine, moving up to the head of the bed. No one blinks when he slips in behind her, taking her weight against his chest as Rath and I bolster her hands.

"You've got this, sweetheart," he says into her ear, and she nods, seeming to steel herself.

"I'm ready," she says, determination flashing in her eyes.

What happens next is something too magical to put into words. I don't mean magic in the cutesy, Disney sense. I'm talking deep, dark sorcery. Something ancient and primal. It's in the tenor of her screams and the snarl on her face. It's the sheen of sweat on her forehead, glistening. It's the cut of her teeth as her lips pull back with the ferocity of her pushes. It's the way her hand trembles in mine—not out of weakness, but out of the pure magnitude of her strength. It's life, but it's also death. The death of something I might think to grieve later on.

That sweet, innocent, doe-eyed girl I fell into a fatal obsession with is gone.

But in her place is a woman.

A warrior.

A Queen.

Our daughter arrives thirty minutes later, screaming into this world in a rush of angry cries. She's the only thing I can bring myself to look at, but I can still feel Rath and Tristian's awe as the doctor places the baby on Story's chest.

Story folds her into her arms without question or concern, giving an exhausted, breathless laugh as she lays eyes on our tiny, writhing, furious daughter. "Hello there," she greets, eyes heavy and wet. She runs a gentle knuckle over her wrinkled cheek, and before she looks at us—before she even registers anyone else is in the room—she presses a kiss to her head and whispers, "I have so many promises to make."

THE FIRST TIME Tristian holds her, he looks like someone just asked him to solve all of the world's problems in the next seven hours. He looks overwhelmed and a little crazy, but there's a warmth in his eyes I'm not used to seeing—not even with his little sisters.

"She's perfect." He says this with a hint of shock, as if she's been in this world for mere minutes and she's already done something incredible. Quieter, he tells the baby, "You're perfect," and gently brushes his lips over her forehead.

The first time Rath holds her, he looks all shifty and nervous, as though he's done some indescribable criminal act. It makes Story give a slow, tired laugh, which seems to ease some of the tension in his shoulders. "So you're what all the fuss is about, huh?" Rath asks the baby, carefully cradling her head. Her little fists, which had been squirming around, stiffen before going still. Rath's head snaps back as he observes her. "You recognize my voice?" She responds by essentially going limp in his hands, and Rath is a pretty stoic guy most of the time, but right now, there are too many emotions on his face to quantify. He presses a kiss to her forehead, whispering something that's almost too low to hear.

Almost.

He tells her, "I'd definitely go commercial for you."

I don't know what that means, but it makes Story's lip wobble, like maybe she wants to start crying again.

When it's my turn, I shove my hands into my pockets and back away. "Uh, maybe later."

Rath gives me a long, dark look. "Later."

I shrug, avoiding his gaze. "I'm all dirty and my nerves are shot. What if I drop her or something?"

There's a quick beat of silence before Rath replies, "Shut the fuck up and hold your daughter, you gigantic pussy. Jesus Christ, you're a quarterback. You won't drop her." He thrusts her at me, but in this really slow, tender way that makes my stomach seize with anxiety, because he's right.

I've never been so terrified in my fucking life.

Sweating bullets, I pull my fists from my pockets and reluctantly put a palm beneath her back. Luckily, Tristian is there to coach me. "Support her head," he says, moving close to guide me. He keeps a palm beneath her, too, even when I finally have her in my hands—seven pounds of absolute terror. When Tristian goes to pull away, I blurt, "Wait!"

He rolls his eyes, but stays close, which is a slight comfort.

She's so tiny, but so inexplicably *huge.*

The size of my hands dwarfs her, and for a long second, all I can think is that these are dirty hands. Hands that have killed people. Hands that have beat men to a gruesome pulp. Hands that have pressed bruises into her mother's flesh. It feels like all it'd take is a twitch for me to ruin everything.

Then her little mouth opens in a wide yawn, and she burrows deep in the blanket, toward the protection of my palms. Just watching her, feeling her after all these months, causes my heart to flip-flop in my chest and I just snap the fuck out of it.

I look up at Story, and she gives me an exhausted grin. I lift an eyebrow,

"We still good on the name?"

"Yes," she says. "I think it's perfect."

"She's going to flip," Rath says, running a hand over his worn, exhausted face.

"She'll love it," Story says.

Tristian smoothes the blanket over Story's legs. "We may never hear the end of it."

Story lifts her arms, asking for the baby, and carefully I hand her back over, making sure to support her head. Although I won't admit it, Rath's not wrong. It kind of is like holding a football.

Story peers down at the baby's pink, pinched face and says, "Melody Delores."

We all agreed on giving the baby the middle name Delores. Without her, we never would have survived that night of the home invasion. Story picked the name Melody, though. She said stories are better when they're set to a tempo, a voice, an expression, and a melody to bring them together.

It's how I know I could never be my father. We were a lot of things, but never this. Never family. It took blood, sweat, and tears to build my own. Over the years, we've weaved together the pain of love, the wrath of loss, and the mercy of forgiveness. This is what it means to love something more than yourself, and this is what we've created with it.

Our own little Kingdom.

A THANK YOU
FROM ANGEL

As MANY OF you know, Lords of Mercy released at #1 in the Amazon Kindle store. You may not know that Sam and I had no idea what to do about this. We were shocked, but mostly just excited that people were reading and loving our terrible monsters. That we didn't run everyone off after the Fun House Scene. We knew if you could handle that and The Pit, we were all going to be best friends forever.

After the release of Lords of Mercy, we realized we had to do something about the request for book plates. People seem confused when they ask why we did a Kickstarter and I tell them, "Well, mostly to get book plates to the readers." Because that seems like a pretty elaborate system for sending out stickers! But you guys were also asking for bookmarks and a few other swag items, as well as discrete covers.

Oh, boy.

For the record, there's no such thing as asking Sam to whip up a discrete cover. (Trust me, I tried) So then… well, have you ever read the book *If You Give a Mouse a Cookie*? That is basically what happened here. If you give Sam the opportunity to make a special edition, she'll want it to have gold foil. And if she gets the gold foil, she's going to want sprayed edges. And if you give her the sprayed edges, she's going to want the interior illustrations… you see where this is going. If you don't, go read the book and replace a cookie with super exclusive, insane, special Royals of Forsyth Hardback Editions.

So anyway, that is basically what happened, and you guys CAME FOR

IT and made my bookplate dreams and Sam's cookie dreams come true.

Thank you all for supporting this crazy project. We hope it meets all of your expectations and we can't wait to see pictures of them on your bookshelves (we're also excited to be able to put these front and center in our own homes without having to explain to everyone in our lives about manchest.)

Until next time (aka: The Dukes)

Angel

A THANK YOU
FROM SAMANTHA

LOOK, YOU CAN'T eat just one cookie. I really hope you all love the three we've whipped up for you, and hopefully the twelve still left to come. Maybe you'll even catch the few Easter eggs Angel and I have sprinkled around in here, hmm?

Our eternal thanks to the Kickstarter backers. The silent readers. The loud readers. The shakers. The hand-holders. The die-hards. The ones who followed us from the Preston Prep era. The ones who made playlists. The Queens. The rogues.

You are in our hearts and epilogues.